The Portable Russian Reader

The Viking Portable Library

Each Portable Library volume is made up of
representative works of a favorite modern or
classic author, or is a comprehensive anthology
on a special subject. The format is designed
for compactness and for pleasurable reading.
The books average about 700 pages in length.
Each is intended to fill a need not hitherto
met by any single book. Each is edited by
an authority distinguished in his field, who
adds a thoroughgoing introductory essay and
other helpful material. Most "Portables" are
available both in durable cloth and
in stiff paper covers.

KING: How, madam! Russians!
PRINCESS: Ay, in truth, my lord;
trim gallants, full of courtship and
of state.

Love's Labour's Lost

THE PORTABLE

Russian Reader

A Collection Newly Translated from Classical and Present-Day Authors

Chosen and Done into English, with a Foreword

and Biographical and Other Notes, by

Bernard Guilbert Guerney

New York

The Viking Press

To

CLIFTON FADIMAN

ON THE RUSSIAN TONGUE

Carolus V, Emperor of Rome, was wont to say that the Hispanic tongue was seemly for converse with God, the French with friends, the German with enemies, the Italian with the feminine sex. Had he been versed in the Russian tongue, however, he would of a certainty have added to this that it is appropriate in converse with all of the above, inasmuch as he would have found in it the magnificence of the Hispanic tongue, the sprightliness of the French, the sturdiness of the German, the *tendresse* of the Italian and, over and above all that, the richness and the conciseness of powerful imagery, of the Greek and Latin tongues.

MIKHAIL VASSILIEVICH LOMONOSSOV

The language of Turgenev, of Tolstoy, of Dobroliubov, of Chernyshevsky, is great and mighty.

VLADIMIR ILICH ULIANOV (NIKOLAI LENIN)

CONTENTS

ix

POST-REVOLUTIONARY

A BUDGET OF LETTERS

A NEW HANDFUL OF OLD PROVERBS

Editor's Foreword

WERE all the sky parchment (so, we are told, that grand old Rabbi, Jochanaan ben Zakkai, was fond of saying)—were all the sky parchment, and all the seas ink, and were all the reeds by all the rivers sharpened into writing implements, and all men turned into scribes, and were they to write unceasingly through all eternity, they nonetheless would never record the wisdom he had learned from his master, the gentle Hillel. And yet what the son of Zakkai had imbibed from his master was no more than a gnat imbibes from the ocean when it dips therein. . . .

Without pretending to have imbibed any more of Russian literature than some lesser insect might imbibe from the veins of a gnat, the present anthologist has nevertheless often felt very much the same way about that literature as the old sage did about his master. Given years enough, one could turn out scores of collections, all diverse, from each of the fields of Russian literature (these are very many), and from each of its recorded centuries (known to be ten). But even if an opaque paper thinner than india were ever made, and faces still more condensed than the present ones were ever to be cast, the anthologist from the Russian would still have to be an unwilling Procrustes, and an exhaustive compendium of Russian writings will have to remain a fata morgana.

Probably no other literature (as the Editor has tried to show elsewhere) would afford so great a field day for

1

Mr. Robert Ripley as the Russian. For one thing this amazing literature, as it is now generally known in English (and it has been thus known for less than seventy years) is really only Modern Russian literature and, as such, is not yet two hundred years old; its language was first used as a literary instrument only ninety years before the formal beginning,[1] while its very alphabet preceded that beginning only by something like sixty years.[2] But there is also an Intermediate Russian literature, of about a century, and an Ancient Russian literature, of six centuries and a half, the latter containing a few productions whose very authors are unknown yet who are as titanic as the giants of the nineteenth century (*The Lay of the Host of Igor; The Tale of Misery-Misfortune*); there is even an oral literature, which the Russians did not begin to formulate much before the seventeenth century—and even in that they had been anticipated by an Englishman. All these three precedent literatures are, save to the specialist, *terrae incognitae* in English. And, within the last quarter of a century, we are confronted with two factors in Russian literature for which it would be hard to find analogies in any other: there is a Russian literature-in-exile, an aerophyte that occasionally assumes French, German, English and other linguistic forms, yet is not to be passed over without a note, and a Soviet literature, now in its lusty twenties. And even here we are faced with a unique phenomenon: if one wants to be precious about it, the Soviets contain

---

[1] 1762, the year of the Russian publication (in a corrected form) of *The Satires* of Prince Antioch Kantemir (1708–1744). These were first published not in Russia but in England (London, 1749 and 1750), not in Russian but in French, not in the original verse but in prose, and the author was not a native Russian.

[2] The modern Russian alphabet came into being during the reign of Peter the Great, which lasted from 1682 to 1725. Wilhelm Mons, his Empress's lover, wrote genuinely Russian love lyrics—in German characters.

seven score or so different peoples, whose literatures, written in almost as many languages, dialects and alphabets, all constitute Soviet Literature. . . .[1]

This Reader, then, does not lay the least claim to exhaustiveness. It is, however, comprehensive insofar as the prose of the nineteenth century classics is concerned, generously representative of Russian Soviet literature, and even includes some material from pre-Modern Russian literature. The chief aim has been a simple one: to present a considerable number of good but unhackneyed things by comparatively many authors, old and new; should the reader gain some conceptions of Russia, Russians, and Russian life and letters somewhat nearer the mark than those which unfortunately still persist, a secondary end will have been achieved.

The selections range from a group of sketches, to short stories of practically novelette length and miscellaneous brief pieces. About half the book has never, to the best of the Editor's knowledge and belief, appeared in English before. The rest of the material has hardly been tapped by the anthologists. All the translations are new, both by choice and through necessity, and only one selection has been taken from a previously published collection of the Editor's.

A wary attitude toward High Lights (or Elegant Extracts) from Novels is, on the whole, a wholesome thing; excerpts have their place, but that place is in a chrestomathy rather than an anthology. The reader, it is felt, generally prefers to form a personal, ever-varying selection of such things by the extremely simple expedient of taking down the books he or she likes and re-reading the

---

[1] Having no overwhelming love for formalism, the Editor has cut all these Gordian knots by dividing this Reader into four sections: Pre-Revolutionary, Post-Revolutionary, and a Budget of Letters and a Handful of Proverbs, both containing certain timeless things.

favorite pages as the mood prompts. Also, quite often, the inclusion of extracts offers appealing fare only to lovers of steak-tatar, while not infrequently it is actually a disservice not only to the authors but to the readers as well. But where extracts are perfect (or almost perfect) integers, there is little sense in being fanatical about the thing. Only two extracted chapters are given here, but both are entities in their own right. Abridgment, a device always to be used sparingly and circumspectly, was also but little resorted to.

Treasuries of the Familiar have, no doubt, their appeal; yet the matter of familiarity, at least in non-English literatures, is always a ticklish one, for while it may not breed contempt it may create an unjustified impression that most Russian writers tend to be men of but one story. It is therefore hoped that the favorites the reader finds here are those he first met outside of anthologies. If the present Editor has not included *The Queen of Spades, Mumu, The Death of Ivan Ilyich, Twenty-Six Men and One Girl, The Darling, Lazarus,* and *The Insult* it was simply because Pushkin, Gogol, Turgenev, Leo Tolstoy, Gorky, Chekhov, Andreyev and Kuprin have, after all, written other things every whit as good—if not better. One exception, however, proved inescapable. There is apparently an unwritten law compelling every anthology from the Russian to present the ineluctable "The Overcoat"; thus the pleasure of proving that Gogol, as storyteller, had more strings than one to his bow had to be put off till some other (and happier) occasion.

Re-readability is another moot point; it is doubtful if any anthology has ever had its *every* page dogeared by any one reader. Most of the inclusions are lifelong favorites of the Editor's (and almost every Russian's); other items met the very severe test of a re-reading after being remembered for decades; each final selection had to undergo at least five readings during the brute tasks of translation and editing—and still was not found boring at any time. It is hoped, then, that a not inconsequential number of things herein will be re-read by the purchaser, and that a few may become perennial favorites.

To be quite candid, the usual (and almost lethal) scrapiana of sleazy mysticism and metaphysical frumpery, the obvious, the ersatz, the over-emphasized, the pseudo-profound and, above all, that which is commonly (but fallaciously) regarded as ever so delectably typical of the Slav Soul, have all been shunned as earnestly as the ragweed, the polecat and the Arizona rock-rattler, since, basically, the Slav Soul is not a jot better or worse than, or even different from, the American Soul or the Patagonian Soul. The mysterious Slav Soul and Melancholy double-talk is the favorite butt and target of the better writing Slavs themselves. Including Dostoevsky, who surely knew his Souls.[1] On the other hand, bearing in mind Heine's dictum that it is more difficult to create something short and droll than something long and dour, a genuine welcome was given to humor, satire and folk-material, all of which abound in Russian but which are not usually presented in English or, if they are, are muffed in the presentation.

There seems to be a tendency in reading foreign literatures (especially the Russian!) to expect certain things from them that just aren't characteristic, and not to expect others that definitely are. Thus, certain sub-

---

[1] Whenever Ilf had a loafing spell, Petrov used to ask when the Mysterious Jewish Soul would feel like working, and when Petrov had an idle streak, Ilf wanted to know when the Mysterious Slav Soul would buckle down to the typewriter. And it was Chekhov who said that Melancholy was to the Russian writer what the potato was to the skilled French chef: it could be dished up in two hundred tasty ways.

jects may strike the reader as strange, yet they are hardly strange to the Russian. Russian authors are intensely interested (as much so as are Americans or Englishmen) in the phenomenon of Thought, for instance; yet if a cold-blooded survey were to be made of Russian literature (a task which the present writer would much rather leave to others) it would be found that it is certainly not Morbidity and Mysticism which are among the predominant Russian themes, but that, odd as it may sound, the Steppe and the Horse are. Or, at least, as dominant as the sea and ships are in English literature.

Then, too, the Russians seem as taken up with love as are Americans or Italians, as intrigued by the Devil as are Americans or Afghans, as interested in the supernatural as are Americans or Spaniards, and as proud of their Revolution as Americans and Frenchmen are of their respective Revolutions.

Yet although there are but thirty-odd miles at one point separating Russia and United States territory, in the understanding each forms from reading the literature of the other the Russian and the American still are, regrettably, far as the poles apart. The Russians realized, ever so many years ago, that Edgar Allan Poe is neither the only American voice nor the last American word, but one hesitates to think for how many otherwise wide-awake Americans Russian literature has, apparently, never emerged from under Dostoevsky's sombre cape. (This may sound blasphemous, but there are moments when one wishes that Dostoevsky had not been among the very first Russian authors to be introduced into English.)

However, the only answer a symptom deserves is the suggestion of a remedy. The cultured non-Russian knows that the diapaison of Russian music is from the ribald *chastoushka* to Shostakovich's *Seventh,* that Russian pictorial art ranges from the Soudeikin backdrops for the *Chauve Souris* to Repin's *Ioann the Awesome Mourning His Son;* he has also seen Russian films and the Russian ballet. But Russian literature has to vault the barrier of language (not infrequently breaking its neck in doing so), and it isn't the English reader's fault if he receives a one-sided, monotonous and blurred impression of Russian writing and can't quite make up his mind as to what Russia and Russians are all about.

The remedy is simple and effective—and, for those very reasons, has been and will probably continue to be disregarded: it consists of exercising greater catholicity and eclecticism, a little more good taste, in the choice of the material to be presented in English, somewhat less bad taste in such presentation, and an insistence upon versions that should be at least adequately Englished.

One disclaimer seems inevitable in every book of this nature, a disclaimer usually brought forward by the harshest critics themselves. Exclusions are not always due to sheer ignorance nor inclusions to the editor's own poor taste, but, overwhelmingly, to the inexorability of space. Why on earth did So-and-so find place, and why in heaven is Such-and-such out in the cold? The only answers are: An anthology is like a madhouse—some of those in it ought to be out; an anthology is also like Congress—many a good man out of it ought to be in. And—it's an ill-wind that has no silver lining: perhaps it's just as well, unless one wishes to be as unoccupied as Othello, that all the golden eggs cannot be put in any one basket.

There is an ancient adage (probably from the Burmese), to the effect that if the host does his best his guests feast with zest; it is hoped that it applies here.

Reader, you are cordially bidden welcome. Or (since this book derives from the Russian): *Meelosti prossim— naslazhdaitess!*

BERNARD GUILBERT GUERNEY

New York, February, 1947.

A Note on Russian Names

There is really no more sense in spelling Chichikov as Tschitschikowff or Cziczikow than there is in spelling Churchill as Tschioeowrtschiouill or Czërczel, and still less reason for thirty-two different English spellings (an actual tabulation) of so simple a name as Turgenev; but the *oweoueffsky, owitsch* and *itch* school of translators is still, unfortunately, not dead. All such horrors are due to the heinous practice of re-translating or re-transliterating from the French, German and Polish, rather than working directly from the Russian, or to clinging to pseudo-scholarly precedents that were none too bright to begin with. However, radio comedians (those sensitive barometers of the public's reaction) have long ceased trying for laughs by sprinkling their scripts with *sky's* and *ovich's,* and there are other hopeful signs.

Russian names can be just as meaningful as American names, say, even though it is not always possible to translate them. Russians don't regard "Longfellow" as weird; there is really no reason for regarding Tolstoy (Stout Fellow) as outlandish. The *sky* ending is generally and concisely descriptive: Alexander Nevsky is Alexander of the Neva—or, more particularly, Alexander, Victor of the Great Battle of the Neva River. The

Russians also (along with other folk) cling to the charming courtesy of the patronymic; the masculine suffixes *ovich, ievich* (or *ich,* or even *ych*) are tantamount to such prefixes as *Mac* or *O'*. Peter Petrovich Petrov is Peter McPeter Peters; *ovna, ievna* (or even *ishna*) are feminine: Olga Andreievna is Olga, daughter of Andrew. The *a* ending is generally feminine (even though Garnett quaintly calls Anna's husband Karenina instead of Karenin). Many masculine nicknames, however, end in *a*: Sasha (Aleck), or even in the extremely familiar *ka*: Sashka.

As to pronunciation: diacritical marks, in the Editor's not unshared opinion, accomplish little save irritating the compositor, wearying the eye of the reader, and pockmarking the fair printed page. Two minutes with any Russian will avail more than a ton of such flyspecks. Therefore, save for a few unavoidable umlauts, they have been shunned. There is no language fraught with more *Gemütlichkeit* than the Russian, there is no better language to make love in, and Russians can be genuinely charming even when they are cursing one another out— therefore, you'll generally fare best by avoiding harshness in pronouncing a Russian word or name.

Accent marks are just another nuisance. But one suggestion may be extended—utterly empirical and unorthodox, but you'll find it works, ninety times out of a hundred: stress a Russian name exactly contrary to the way you may feel like accenting it. You will probably want to say Dunya*sha*; try Du*nya*sha, and you'll do better than the best American, British and French stars of the stage, screen and radio. Oh, yes—Ivan is not *Eye*van but Ee*van*.

The Editor's heartiest thanks are hereby extended to Irina Aleksander for her exceptional knowledge (among many other things) of Moscow (Pushkin's as well as today's) and of Petersburg, under all its three names; to Miss Ida Judge for the loan of a rare text; to Miss Marjory Langer for her familiarity with the Orient; to Mr. Morris Orans for access to his highly specialized Russian collections, to Mr. Charles J. Phelan, champion weight-lifter, for help with certain first-hand, non-dictionary sporting and other terms. And thanks, too, to those who helped in the non-glamorous tasks of preparing the script, and who offered suggestions, but who preferred to remain unnamed.

B. G. G.

Pre-Revolutionary

FOLK SATIRE

EDITOR'S NOTE

UNIVERSAL folklore appears to have but few judges who are both just and ingenious (King Solomon and solomonics are prominent in the Russian Apocrypha); occasionally folk wit presents a judge whose judgments are so madly ingenious as to be considered poetic justice, akin to that of the folk-fools—Dracula [Devil], the Wallachian Leader-in-Battle, who had a historical prototype about the middle of the XVth century, and later became identified with Czar Ioann the Awesome, is a case in point; it is the judge who is as unjust as he is ingenious who predominates in folk satire, probably going even further back than the Judges of Sodom (who also figure in the Russian pseudepigrapha).

Such a judge is Shemyaka, identified with **Dmitri** Shemyaka, Prince of Galicia (d. 1453), who put out the eyes of his brother, Vassili II, Prince of Muscovy. So notorious was Shemyaka that, according to one chronicler, "from his time, throughout Great Russia, *Shemyaka's judgment* was used as a term of reproach against all judges and takers of bribes."

Not the least curious aspect of Russian literature is the derivative mania of Russian literary scholars. Thus, while they rummage for Scandinavian and Icelandic origins of the indigenously Russian *byliny* (lays-of-things-that-have-been), non-Russian scholars establish incontrovertibly that German minstrelsy and Norse Edda borrowed Ilya of Murom, one of the chief giant-heroes

13

of those same *byliny*. Similarly, one hypersensitive Slav actually tried to saddle *The Judgments of Shemyaka* with a Polish origin, but even Russian scholars could not stomach this, and have definitely proven this theory to be utterly baseless. The story is now generally considered a typically Russian folk satire against judges. "Fear not the law but the judge," says a Russian proverb (one of very many similar ones), while another runs: "The law is like an axle—you can turn it as you please, if you give it plenty of grease."

The manuscript versions are of the seventeenth century, but the story itself is, naturally, much older. In the eighteenth century it became very popular in chapbooks and, since then, has served as a basis for poetic and dramatic treatments.

Three texts have been followed for the translations, with an eye mainly to the story as a story.

The Judgments of Shemyaka
(XVIIth Century)

ONCE upon a time, in a certain land and region, there lived two brothers, tillers of the soil both. One was well off, the other poor as poor can be; the one that was well off used to help out the poor one for many years and long, yet could not abide him because of his poverty.

So one day the poor brother came to the one that was well off and begged for the loan of a horse, to haul a load of firewood to keep him warm through the winter, but the brother that was well off was loath to lend his horse to the one that was poor, saying: Thou hast borrowed much, brother, yet couldst never repay.—

Yet when the poor brother did get the horse at last, what does he do but ask for the loan of a horse-collar as well! Whereupon the brother that was well off waxed wroth at him and fell to railing at his poverty, saying: What, thou hast not even a horse-collar?—But give him one he would not.

So the poor brother left the one that was well off, got out his sledge, hitched the horse thereto by its tail, drove to the forest, chopped a lot of wood and loaded the sledge with it, as much as the horse could draw. When he got home he opened the gates and gave the horse the whip, but he had forgotten to remove the bottom bar on the gates, so that the horse ran the sledge full tilt against it and tore its tail right out.

And when the poor brother brought back the horse, the brother that was well off, seeing that his horse now lacked a tail, fell to upbraiding his poor brother, because he had maimed his horse all for nothing and, refusing to take the animal back, started off for town to lodge a complaint against his poor brother before Shemyaka the Judge. As for the poor brother, when he saw the brother that was well off setting out to lodge a complaint against him, he decided to go along, knowing that otherwise a summons would come for him, and he would have to pay the expenses of the sumner on top of everything else.

With the darkness coming on and the town still far off, when they reached a certain hamlet the well-off brother decided to lodge with the priest, whom he knew; as for the poor brother, he also went to the same priest's house, but climbed up on a sort of unrailed balcony and laid him down there. And the well-off brother started telling the priest of the mishap that had befallen his horse, and why he was on his way to town, after which he and the priest fell to their supper; however, they never called the poor brother to join them. But the poor brother became so taken up in watching what his brother and the priest were eating that he tumbled off the balcony and, falling upon a cradle, crushed the priest's little boy to death.

So the priest, too, started off to town to lodge a complaint against the poor brother for having been the cause of his little son's death, and the poor brother tagged right along.

As they were crossing a bridge that led into the town, a certain citizen thereof happened to be passing through the moat below, bringing his sick father to the public baths. In the meanwhile the poor brother, pondering on the utter ruin that would be brought upon him by his brother and the priest, and deciding to put an end to himself, cast himself headlong off the bridge, thinking he would be smashed to death in the moat below. But it was the sick old man he landed on, causing him to die before the eyes of his son, who laid hold of the poor brother and dragged him off before the judge.

Now the poor brother, mulling over how he might get out of his scrape, and what he could give the judge, yet having nought upon him, struck on the idea of picking up a stone and, wrapping it in a kerchief, he placed it in his cap as he took his place before the judge.

So then his well-off brother laid a complaint against him before Judge Shemyaka, seeking damages for his horse. And, having heard the complaint to the end, Shemyaka spake to the poor brother, saying: Make answer.—But the poor brother, knowing not what answer to make, took the wrapped stone out of his cap and, showing the bundle to the judge, bowed low before him. Whereupon the judge, thinking the defendant was offering him a reward if the decision went his way, spake unto the rich brother: Since he has plucked out thy horse's tail, thou art not to take thy horse back from him until such time as it hath grown a new tail; but when the said horse shall have grown a new tail, then wilt thou take the said horse back from him.—

And thereafter the second suit began: the priest sought to have the poor brother executed for having crushed his son to death; but the poor brother, even as before, took the same stone wrapped in a kerchief and showed the bundle to the judge. The judge saw this, and again thinking that the defendant was promising him another bag of gold for a second favorable decision, spake unto the priest: Since he hath crushed thy son to death, thou shalt even let him have thy wife, until such time as he shall have begotten a son upon her, when thou shalt take from him thy wife and the child.—

And thereupon the third suit began, concerning the poor brother's having cast himself off the bridge and, by falling on the sick old man, having killed the townsman's father. But the poor man, once more taking out of his cap the stone wrapped in a kerchief, showed it to the judge for the third time. And the judge, looking forward to a third bag of gold for a third decision favorable to the defendant, spake unto the man whose father had been killed: Go thou up on the bridge, while the slayer of thy father shall take his place below it, and do thou cast thyself down upon him in thy turn, slaying him even as he hath slain thy father.—

The trials over, the plaintiffs left the courtroom together with the defendant.

Now when the well-off brother approached the poor one and asked him for the return of the horse, the latter answered him, saying: According to the decision, as soon as that horse will have grown back its tail, I shall surely give it back to thee.—Whereupon the rich brother offered him five rubles, and seventeen bushels and a little over of grain, and a milch goat, and the poor brother promised to give him back the horse, even without a tail, and the two brothers made up their differences and lived in amity to the end of their days, even as all brethren should.

And when the poor brother approached the priest, asking him to turn his wife over to him, according to Shemyaka's decision, that he might beget a child upon her and, having begotten the same, give both wife and child back to him, the priest fell to pleading with him not to take his wife from him, and the poor man at last agreed to accept fifty rubles from the priest, and twenty-three bushels and a little over of grain, and a cow with a calf, and a mare with a foal, and they made up their difference and lived in amity to the end of their days.

And in the same way the poor brother spake unto the third plaintiff: In accordance with the decision, I shall take my place under the bridge; see that thou go up on the bridge and cast thyself down upon me, even as I did upon thy father.—But the other bethought himself: I may cast myself down, right enough, but what if I not only miss him but kill myself into the bargain?—And he began making peace with the other, and gave him two hundred rubles, and all but a little short of twenty-nine bushels of grain, and a bull, and they made up their difference and lived in amity to the end of their days.

And thus did the poor brother collect payment from all three.

As for Judge Shemyaka, he sent one of his men out to the defendant, and bade him bring back the three bags the poor brother had shown him; but when the judge's man began asking for these three bags: Give me that which thou didst show to the judge, which is in those three bags thou hadst in thy cap; he told me to take it

from thee,—the poor brother did take out of his cap
the stone in the kerchief and, unwrapping the kerchief,
showed him the stone, whereupon the judge's man asked
him: Wherefore showest thou me a stone?—Whereupon
the defendant told him: That was for the judge. I
showed him the stone that he might not decide against
me, for had he done so I would have let him have it over
his head.—

And the messenger went back and told this to the
judge. And Judge Shemyaka, having heard his messenger
out, spake, saying: I thank and praise my God that I
decided in his favor, for had I not done so he would
have brained me.—

And the poor man went thence, and home, rejoicing
and praising God.

FROM *The Russian Truth* or *Justice*

(XIth Century)

EDITOR'S NOTE

The following is from the oldest Slavic codex extant,
promulgated by the Russian Solon, Prince Yaroslav the
Wise (978–1054), son of Vladimir. Legal minds will
easily perceive its indebtednesses to early Scandinavian
laws and certain parallels to the English law of the same
period.

IF ONE man of gentle birth slay another, let the slain
man be avenged by his father, or brother, or son, or
nephew. If there be none to take blood-vengeance, let
a wergild [blood-fine] of seventy *grivny*[1] be levied upon

---

[1] A grivna was a unit of value; as a weight, it is thought to have
approximated a pound, troy, eventually decreasing to half a pound

the slayer, if the slain man were a Prince's thane, or a
Prince's thane's retainer. If the slain man was a Russ [a
Scandinavian bearing no arms], or a henchman, or a
trader, or a noble's vassal, or a sword-fighter, or a churl,
or a Slovene [man of Novgorod], let the wergild be
forty *grivny.—After Yaroslav his sons Isyaslav, Svyato-
slav, Vsevolod, and their adherents Kuznyachko, Pechen-
yeg and Nikiphor did convene and did abrogate blood-
vengeance, making wergild the sole penalty; but in all
else the sons of Yaroslav left his decrees untouched.*

If one man smite another with naked sword, or the
hilt thereof, the werwite [fine paid into the Prince's
treasury] shall be twelve *grivny*. If one smite another
with staff, or goblet, or horn, or the back of a sword,
the werwite is likewise twelve *grivny;* should such be
done in warding off a stroke of the sword, however,
there is to be no werwite. If one man smite the hand
of another, so that it be lopped off, or shall wither,
or if he gouge out an eye, or sever a foot, or cut off the
nose, the werwite shall be twenty *grivny* and, to the
maimed man, ten *grivny* also, in compensation. If one
man lop off the finger of another, the werwite shall be
three *grivny* and, to the maimed man, in compensation,
a *grivna* also, of seven marten skins.

If the plaintiff [in a case of assault] come bloodied or
bruised, he need not bring witnesses; however, if he be
unmarked, let him bring witnesses. If it be a counter-
suit, let him that began [the fight] pay six marten skins.
If the bloodied man be the one that began, let him keep
his bruises for his pains. . . .

If a man ride another's horse, without having first
asked the owner's permission therefor, the werwite is

---

or less. Three monetary values were recognized for the *grivna:* in
marten skins, in silver, and in gold.—*Trans.-Ed.*

three *grivny*. If a man lose his steed, or his battle-gear, or his raiment, and have his loss cried in the market-place, and later recognizes his property . . . he may repossess it, and a fine of three *grivny* shall be paid over to him. But if he recognize his property, whether lost or stolen . . . he is not to claim it merely by saying: This is mine—but shall come before a judge, who shall question [the accused]: How camest thou by this?— And he that is guilty shall pay the fine, and thereupon the plaintiff shall take that which is his, and the fine also. If the offender be a horse-thief, let him be turned over to the Prince, to be banished; if the offender be one who thieves from the stalls of the merchants, he shall be fined three *grivny*. . . .

If a hired hand runs away from his master, he becomes a slave; but if he leave to collect moneys due him, and does so openly, or if he flees to the Prince, or to the judges, because of a wrong done him by his master, he shall not be enslaved but receive his just dues. . . .

If any steal a boat, the werwite is six marten skins, and the boat is to be given back; if it be a sea-craft, the werwite is three *grivny*, and for a war-galley, two *grivny*, and for a fishing-smack, eight marten skins, and for a scow, a *grivna*. . . .

If one poach upon preserves, and take a falcon or a hawk, the werwite is three *grivny*, and to the owner a *grivna* besides; for a dove, nine marten skins; for a hen, nine marten skins; for a duck, twenty marten skins; for a goose, twenty marten skins; for a swan, twenty marten skins, and for a crane, twenty marten skins. And if it be hay that is stolen, or timber, the werwite is nine marten skins, and the owner is to be compensated also, two *nogati* for each cartload stolen.[1]

---

[1] There were twenty *nogati* to a *grivna*.—*Trans.-Ed.*

If a man set another's barn on fire, the offender, after first making good the damage, is to be banished by the Prince. The same applies if it be a house that is burned down. And whosoever doth injure horse or livestock in malice, the werwite shall be twelve *grivny,* and a *grivna* compensation for the injury done.

DENIS IVANOVICH FONVIZIN

(1745–1792)

EDITOR'S NOTE

FONVIZIN was of the nobility. He began his career with translations (from the French), publishing his first one in 1761; in 1762 he joined the staff of translators in the Department of Foreign Affairs. His first play, a rhymed comedy adapted from the French, was staged in 1764; in 1769 he became secretary to N. I. Papin, which liberal statesman's dreams of reforming the government and serfdom he shared to the end. His *Hobbledehoy,* a caustic and witty attack on slavocracy, a comedy which is now a world masterpiece, was produced in 1782; with it he became an innovator of realism on the Russian stage and broke with the classicism of Soumarokov. In the same year he engaged in polemics with Catherine the Great, with the usual results: he had to apologize in print and, in 1783 (the year of the publication of *Hobbledehoy*) went into retirement and had to give up literature; the only thing he published thereafter was a necrologue of Papin (1784, in French and anonymously). He began his memoirs in 1789, but these were left unfinished.

The following was written about 1783.

Universal Courtiers' Grammar

DENIS IVANOVICH FONVIZIN

ADVERTISEMENT

This *Grammar* is not intended for any one Court in particular; it is Universal, or Philosophical. The manuscript original thereof was found in Asia where, so it is said, the first Czar and the first Court came into being. The antiquity of this work is of the profoundest, for on its first leaf, even though no year is designated, the following words are precisely set forth: *Shortly after the Universal Deluge.*

CHAPTER THE FIRST. INDUCTION

QUESTION: What is Courtiers' Grammar? *Answer:* Courtiers' Grammar is the Art, or Science, of flattering cunningly, with tongue and pen. *Q:* What is meant by "flattering cunningly"? *A:* It means uttering and writing such untruth as may prove pleasing to those of high station and, at the same time, of benefit to the flatterer. *Q:* What is Courtly Untruth? *A:* It is the expression of a soul inglorious before the soul vainglorious. It consists of shameless praises heaped upon a Great Man for those services which he never performed and those virtues which he never had. *Q:* Into how many Categories are the mean-spirited souls divided? *A:* Six. *Q:* What mean-spirited souls constitute the first Category? *A:* Those that have contracted the miserable habit of cooling their heels in the anterooms of Great Gentlemen all day and every day, without the least need there-for. *Q:* What mean-spirited souls constitute the second Category? *A:* Those that, standing in reverent awe in the presence of a Great Man, gaze into his orbs in servility and thirst to anticipate his thoughts, so that they may gratify him by base yea-saying. *Q:* What truly mean-spirited souls constitute the third Category? *A:* Those that, before the face of a Great Man, rejoice, out of sheer pusillanimity, in falsely imputing to themselves all sorts of unheard-of things and in disavowing all things. *Q:* And what mean-spirited souls constitute the fourth Category? *A:* Those that exalt with great praises even such things in Great Gentlemen as honest men ought to despise. *Q:* What truly mean-spirited souls con-stitute the fifth Category? *A:* Those that, for their servil-ity to the Great, are shameless enough to accept re-wards appertaining to meritorious services alone. *Q:* What truly mean-spirited souls, then, constitute the sixth Category? *A:* Those that, through the most con-temptible dissembling, deceive the Public: Outside the palace they seem the veriest Catos, they clamor against flatterers, they revile without the least mercy all those before whose mere gaze they tremble, they preach in-trepidity and, from their reports, one would gather that they alone, through their firmness, are standing guard over the integrity of the fatherland and warding off ruin from the unfortunate; but, once they set foot within the chambers of the Sovereign, they undergo utter transformation: the tongue that had reviled flatterers prompts them, of itself, to the ignoblest flattery; he is a voiceless slave before the one whom he had reviled but half an hour ago; the preacher of intrepidity is afraid of looking up inopportunely, of inopportunely approach-ing; the guardian of the integrity of the fatherland will be the first, if he find the chance, to stretch out his hand to plunder the fatherland; the intercessor for the unfortunate rejoices, for the sake of the smallest benefit accruing to him, in sending an innocent man to his ruin.

Question: What Division of Words is to be noted at Court? *Answer:* The Words ordinarily occurring are: Monosyllabic, bisyllabic, trisyllabic and polysyllabic.— Monosyllabic: *yea, Prince, slave;* bisyllabic: *potent, event, fallen;* trisyllabic: *gracious, humoring, favoring;* and, lastly, polysyllabic: Yourmostexaltedexcellency.

CHAPTER THE SECOND. OF VOWELS AND THE PARTS OF
SPEECH

Question: What people usually make up a Court? *Answer:* Those who sound off, or Vowels, and Mutes. *Q:* What does the Grammarian mean by Vowels? *A:* By Vowels are meant those powerful Grandees who, for the most part through the simplest of sounds, by the mere opening of their mouths, already bring about the desired action on the part of the Mutes. Example: Should a Great Man, while a report is being read to him, frown and utter *O!*—no one, ever, will venture to carry that matter out; unless, perchance, someone explains the same to the Great Man in a different manner and he, having gotten different ideas on the subject, will, in a tone that proclaims his error, utter *A!*—in which case, usually, the matter is settled right then and there. *Q:* How many Vowels are there at Court? *A:* No overwhelming number, usually; three or four—rarely five. *Q:* But is there not some Intermediate Classification? *A:* There is: semi-Vowels, or demi-Lords. *Q:* What is a demi-Lord? *A:* A demi-Lord is one who has come up from the Mutes but has not yet wormed his way in among the Vowels. Or, to put it another way: One who, while he is still a Mute before the Vowels, is already a

Vowel before the Mutes. *Q:* What does the Grammarian mean by Mutes at Court? *A:* They are at Court what the sign denoting the hard ending is in the Russian alphabet: of themselves, without the help of others, they make never a sound.

Question: What things should be noted in connection with Words? *Answer:* Gender, Number, and Declension. *Q:* What is Gender at Court? *A:* There is a distinction between the Masculine soul and the Feminine. This distinction, however, does not depend upon sex, for, at Court, a woman may at times be of greater worth than any man, while many a man is worse than any female creature. *Q:* What is Number? *A:* Number at Court means Calculation: How many favors can one obtain for how many base deeds? Sometimes the Calculation will be: How many semi-Vowels and Mutes will it require to bring one Vowel down with a crash? Or else, at times: How many semi-Vowels and Mutes must one Vowel topple over to survive as a Vowel? *Q:* What is Declension at Court? *A:* Declension at Court consists mostly of the Mood of brazenness on the part of those in power, and of baseness on the part of those without. However, Nobles for the most part regard all others as compared with themselves as being in the Accusative; the condescension and patronage of these Nobles, on the other hand, is usually sought through the Dative [L., *dativus,* of giving]. *Q:* How many kinds of Verbs are there at Court? *A: Three:* Active, Passive [L., pp. of *patior,* to suffer], and, most frequently of all, Deponent [L., *deponere,* laid aside]. What Moods are in use at Court? *A:* Imperative and Infinitive. *Q:* What Tense, generally, is used at Court by persons who have done meritorious services but are now helpless, in conversing with Great Gentlemen? *A:* The Past: I *have borne* wounds, I *have served,* and the like. *Q:* In what Tense,

as a rule, is the answer such unfortunates receive? *A:*
The Future. Example: I *will see,* I *will file* a report—
and so on.

CHAPTER THE THIRD. OF VERBS

Question: What Verb is conjugated most frequently
of all at Court, and in what Tense? *Answer:* Even as at
Court, so in the Capital, no one lives out of debt; therefore, the Verb conjugated most frequently of all is: *to
be in debt.* (The appended Exemplary Conjugation is
in the Present, since that is the Tense used most frequently of all.)

> I am in debt
> Thou art in debt
> He, She or It is in debt
>
> We are in debt
> You, Ye are in debt
> They are in debt

Question: Is this Verb ever conjugated in the Past
Tense? *Answer:* Ever so rarely—inasmuch as no he or
she pays his or her debts. *Q:* And in the Future Tense?
A: The conjugation of this Verb in the Future Tense is
in good usage, for it goes without saying that if one be
not in debt yet, he or she inevitably *will be.*

IVAN ANDREIEVICH KRYLOV

(1768 or '69–1844)

> Krylov spent more than three hours
> sitting without a move . . . and did
> not as much as turn his colossal, pon-
> derous and majestic head. . . .
>
> —*Turgenev*

EDITOR'S NOTE

AN ARMY captain's son, brought up in poverty, without
formal schooling, forced to be a minor government clerk
almost from childhood, Krylov became Russia's greatest
fabulist. His fables were (and are) immensely popular
and have immortalized him—but they have also obscured his other work. Some of his comedies, for instance, were unqualified hits.

By fifteen he had written a comic opera (a satire on
serfdom); in 1789 he was publishing a satirical periodical, *The Ghostly Post Office,* attacking the nobility, officialdom, the *mores* of serfdom; in 1792 he issued *The
Spectator.*[1] Czardom was prompt with its usual recognition; on orders of a rival satirist, Catherine II, the print-
ing plant of which he was part owner was raided and
he was placed under police surveillance. Like Dostoevsky after him, he found out that a new name will not
revive a suppressed periodical and, in 1794, was forced
to abandon both Petersburg and literature. Years of
misery in the provinces followed.

---

[1] *Káib,* a salty satire on autocracy, appeared in this periodical.
Space permits only the portrait of this amusing potentate.

From 1801 to 1804 he again worked for the government; in 1802 he staged *The Pie*, a comedy (curiously, his first comic opera was called *The Coffee-Can*); in 1806 he settled in Petersburg permanently; during this year and the next he wrote two more comedies and an opera about Ilya of Murom. It was also in 1806 that, encouraged by Dmitriev, himself a fabulist, he went back to writing fables, a form with which he had first experimented in the 1780's. He wrote at least three hundred twenty-four, of which only thirty-eight are borrowed—and even these are improvements.

He was one of the true and great eccentrics. On seeing a Hindu juggler, he remarked: "A Hindu is the same sort of human creature as I; why, then, shouldn't a Russian be able to do what a Hindu does?" Procuring similar objects for juggling and a rug, he secluded himself—and weeks later, to prove that "there is nothing impossible for mortals," displayed all of the Hindu's feats before the children of a friend's family—and then abandoned the whole business.

In 1818 (at fifty) he made a wager with Gnedich, who had spent half his life mastering Greek and had translated Homer into Russian. Gnedich maintained that no man could learn a new language at Krylov's age. Two years later, at another gathering of the same people, Krylov won the trifling stake, passing brilliantly the examination in Greek syntax and literature through which Gnedich himself put him.

He knew French and Italian excellently, was a virtuoso on the violin—and a confirmed feeder of the pigeons that haunted his living quarters at the St. Petersburg Public Library, where he held a sinecure; he was utterly indifferent to his surroundings, despised dress, and was a legend as a glutton.

"He never attempted to be a counterfeit of anything,

and in his way of life was original to oddity," wrote
Belinski. "Yet his oddities were no mask, nor calculated
—on the contrary, they constituted an inseparable part
of his self, they were his nature."

Kaïb

IVAN ANDREIEVICH KRYLOV

KAÏB was one of the Oriental potentates; his name
filled all Creation. "Thy fame," one of his versifiers
was wont to say to him, "thy fame might be likened unto
the sun—were it not that the sun goeth down." Kaïb was
fond of apt similes, and therefore, after having graciously
made the versifier a eunuch, he put him in charge over
his seraglio.

The riches of Kaïb were inexhaustible; his palace,
one historian informs us, was girt about with a thousand
pillars of jasper, the capitals thereof being of solid emerald, and of the Corinthian order, while their bases were
of refined gold; the palace itself was builded of black
marble, and its walls were so smoothly polished that the
daintiest damsels regarded themselves therein as if in a
mirror. The proportions of the windows were those of
the latest Italian architecture—constructed only just a
trifle bigger than the gates of a city—and each window
was set with but a single pane, yet so strong was the
glass that the most brazen-browed yea-saying men of our
time would have found it beyond them to break a hole
therein with their foreheads. The roof was of sheet silver,
but so trimly worked that often, on clear days, the whole
city would come running to the palace thinking it on
fire, whereas all the alarum had been created solely by

the glitter of the roof. Mark you, amiable reader, all this is told us by an historian of Kaïb's.

The magnificence within the palace overwhelmed whosoever set foot therein: the common folk were dazzled by the gold, pearls and precious stones, of all of which there was a greater profusion than there is of misspellings in the works of our new writers; the cognoscenti were attracted by the refulgence of the art that shone in all the adornments of the palace: one came upon swaying draperies of opaque stuff thicker than all the four parts of the *Conversing Citizen* [1] bound together, and beheld glittering carved work, done with such neatness that no author could wish to see a greater on the bindings of his works; many of the chambers were adorned with paintings that deceived the eye and, to render full justice to Kaïb, it must be said that, though he would not admit men of learning into his palace, their portraits constituted not the least ornament of his walls. True, his versifiers were poor, yet his immeasurable liberality compensated for this great failing of theirs: Kaïb commanded that they be depicted in rich raiment, and that their portraits be hung in the best chambers, inasmuch as he sought to encourage learning in every way. And, truly, there was not in the domain of Kaïb a single versifier who did not envy his portrait.

Elsewhere in the palace (our historian continues) one could see small stuffed birds of precious plumage, mounted with such taste that, no matter how the ladies of the court strove to imitate them in the motley hues of their tirings, they nonetheless often perceived with vexation that the splendidly beautiful stuffed birds were more

---

[1] A magazine published in 1789, with the participation of A. N. Radishchev, whose case is an almost perfect antecedent of Dostoevsky's. Catherine II condemned him to death for his *Journey from St. Petersburg to Moscow* (privately printed in 25 copies), then "graciously" commuted the sentence to ten years in Siberia.—*Trans.-Ed.*

admired than they. In some places amusing marmosets frolicked upon slender chains of gold, grimacing so pleasantly that the most adroit courtiers held it an honor to ape them, and not infrequently (such is human frailty) put forth the conceits of the monkeys as their own, because of which there was at that time great enmity between the marmosets and the courtiers, concerning which an history in six and thirty elephant folios was issued by the Academy of that realm.

There, upon magnificent pedestals, glittered the busts of Kaïb's ancestors, the artistry of which busts was in no way unworthy of their exalted originals. His inner chambers were adorned with rugs of such rare beauty and value that the greatest kings, the contemporaries of Kaïb, came from far and wide to take part in the pastime of racing upon them on all fours, and then bade their historiographers to inscribe this among the number of their greatest deeds. His mirrors, although each was twelve yards in height and of the purest steel, were considered rare not so much because of their size as for a virtue which had been bestowed upon them by a certain sorceress: these mirrors had the property of showing things a thousandfold more beautiful than they really were; the dotard saw himself in them as a beautiful springald, a decrepit coquette saw herself as a maid of fifteen, a monster of homeliness as a paragon of comeliness, and a lout as an adroit fellow. For all that Kaïb never contemplated himself therein but kept them solely for his courtiers, and then only for the amusement he derived from seeing how those with the most repulsive faces disputed about their beauty before these mirrors and became embroiled in quarrels which Kaïb loved to watch.

Thousands of parrots in his cages uttered extempore verses; many of these parrots were more eloquent than

the academicians of that day, even though the Academy
of Kaïb was considered the first in the world, inasmuch
as no other academy whatsoever had so rich a collection
of baldpates as Kaïb's, and not a one among them but
could easily read by syllables and, on occasion, even
write quite legible letters to friends. For all that, many
of them had to yield first place to the parrots, many of
whom Kaïb, who cherished learning, made members of
the Academy merely because they could utter in tolerably clear accents that which some other may have
thought of.

As for plenty, that of Kaïb's court surpassed all the
courts of the Orient, and Kaïb's least scullion had more
savory fare than the kings of Homer. The calendar of
Kaïb's court was made up wholly of holidays, and week-
days were scarcer therein than are the birthdays of those
who are born on the twenty-ninth of February.

His seraglio was filled with the first beauties of the
world, and not a one of them was over seventeen. No
matter how hard the factories strive nowadays to attain
perfection in the compounding of rouges, their best ones
would nevertheless seem savagely crude by comparison
with the natural blush of the least of his sultanas. His
maidens did not spoil their charms with uncalled-for af-
fectations of daintiness; they did not swoon away at the
sight of spiders and roaches, merely to fall into disarray
pleasing to the eye. . . .

His magnificent stables were filled with horses of the
rarest blood, which were of better build than our popin-
jays and more submissive than his prime viziers. His
icehouses were crammed to bulging with wines of the
most exquisite bouquets. The very gods (we are told)
were delighted to drink themselves into unconsciousness in his wine-cellars and preferred his wines to nectar,
which they had grown heartily weary of ever since the

versifiers had taken to pouring it out to their heroes just as off-handedly as countrywives pour out slops to the pigs.

The whole world, as it contemplated Kaïb, considered him happy; the printers waxed rich publishing the thickest of books concerning his state of bliss. Whenever the versifiers of that day wanted to describe the triumphs of the gods and paradisaical merrymakings they would never buckle down to their task unless they contrived an opportunity, through some eunuch, of worming their way in among the musicians of Kaïb for a peep of the magnificence at court and the festal days in the seraglio; however, despite all that, their descriptions of the feasts of the gods not infrequently reeked of the fusty straw amid which they had been composed.

The whole world clamored that Kaïb was happy, and Kaïb was the only one who knew that this was not the case, but he told this to none, fearing lest he be considered ungrateful for the favors of fortune, something which he was always on his guard against. He frequently read, in the works of his versifiers, descriptions of his happiness and laughed at the vacuous imagination of the poetasters or, at times, felt envy because he was not even as blind as they, so that he might perceive himself only from his happy side.

At any rate, Kaïb was not as happy as popular clamor proclaimed him; within his heart there persisted a certain emptiness which the objects surrounding him could not fill. The princelings at court, the women, the marmosets, the parrots—nothing gladdened him; he regarded all these from his lofty throne with a yawn; occasionally he smiled at the cavortings of the marmosets or at the grimacing and posturing of his courtiers, but in these smiles was to be seen more of regret than of pleasure. . . .

ALEXANDER SERGHEIEVICH PUSHKIN
(1799–1837)

EDITOR'S NOTE

FRANCE's greatest historical novelist was of Negro descent; Russia's Pushkin was proud of his maternal great-grandfather, Ibrahim Hannibal (described as an Abyssinian princeling), and immortalized him in *The Blackamoor of Peter the Great*. The poet's more or less lackadaisical father came from a clan whose names (together with those of the Turgenevs and the Tolstoys) are of the warp and woof of the bizarre fabric of Russia's past. When Pushkin makes another of his ancestors a leading character in *Boris Godunov* he is not being a squireen genealogist but a true historian.

No one in the world can pervert the Russian language as a Teuton can—and a German was appointed to instruct the young Pushkin in Russian; his other preceptors were certain Frenchmen vomited forth by the French Revolution. At eight he was spending whole nights reading—but his books were French; he started writing at nine—in French. He was saved for Russia by his nurse, Arina Rodionovna, just as Turgenev was by an old serf who used to read to him in Russian, on the sly.

At twelve Pushkin entered the recently founded (and aristocratic) Lyceum; his first poem in print appeared when he was about fifteen; at eighteen he graduated.

During the next three years (1817-20) he had a taste of government service; he lived the life of the Petersburg wit and beau; and wrote *Russlan and Liudmilla,* his first, longest and greatest folk-poem, the publication of which novelty in 1820 won him a place in the front ranks as an author. However, the circulation (in manuscript), during the same year, of his "Ode to Liberty" and other poems gained him nothing but his first set-to with the powers that were, and banishment to Ekaterinoslav and Kishenev, in the depths of southern Russia. In 1823 he was transferred to Odessa, in Russia proper; but here, too, an intercepted letter of his, filled with atheistic sentiments, led to his dismissal and to enforced residence at Mikhailovskoe, a family estate in Pskov, where he was spied upon by police, priests (naturally), and even his father. Yet *Eugene Oneghin* and *Boris Godunov* were produced during this period.

The regrettably abortive uprising of December 14 (Old Style), 1825, marking the accession of the hardly mentionable Nicholas I, involved Pushkin as well. The Emperor not merely pardoned but almost smothered him by his monarchic protection, appointing himself the poet's censor and putting him under the unremitting surveillance of the unspeakable Section III, a secret *Polizei* within the Czar's general gestapo. There were two other occasions when Pushkin was in jeopardy again: over *André Chenier,* and when he had to deny his authorship of the exceedingly racy and anything but Orthodox *Gabrieliad.*

In 1831 (a year after the publication of his *Tales of Belkin*) Pushkin married Natalie Goncharova, scarcely half his age, whose beauty was as great as her wit was small. A court intrigue, involving an anonymous letter that called Pushkin a cuckold and accused him of having in his turn cuckolded the Czar, brought about a duel with one George Heckeren, Baron d'Anthès, fop, mohock, and brother-in-law to Pushkin's wife. On February

8th (New Style), 1837, the poet received a pistol wound, which caused his death two days later.

Master poet, dramatist, storyteller, historian, critic, Pushkin gave to Russian literature both form and new content, and has done more than any other to make Russian the superb literary instrument it is, far superior even to French, and second only to English.

The best and most complete collection of his poetry and prose in English is Avrahm Yarmolinsky's *The Works of Alexander Pushkin,* with an able biographical sketch of the great Russian.

The Shot

ALEXANDER SERGHEIEVICH PUSHKIN

> We fought with pistols.
> —*Baratynski*

> I vowed to shoot him, in accordance with the code of dueling (he still had to face my shot).
> —*Evening at a Bivouack*

WE WERE stationed in the small town of ——. Everybody knows what the life of an army officer is like. In the morning, drilling and the riding-school; then dinner with the commander of the regiment, or at a Jewish tavern; in the evening, punch and cards. There was not one open house at ——, nor even one marriageable young lady; we used to gather in one another's rooms, where we never saw anything save our own uniforms.

There was only one man who, while he was not of the military, nevertheless belonged in our society. He was about five and thirty, and for that reason we considered him an ancient. His store of experience gave him many advantages over us; besides that, his habitual moroseness, stern nature, and sharp tongue had a strong influence on our youthful minds. A certain mysteriousness surrounded his destiny; he appeared to be Russian, yet bore a foreign name. At one time he had served in the Hussars, and that brilliantly; no one knew the reason that had induced him to resign from the service and settle down in a miserable little hole, where he lived both poorly and extravagantly: he always went about on foot, in a badly worn frockcoat of black, yet kept a table at which all the officers of our regiment were ever welcome. True, the dinner he offered consisted of but two or three courses, prepared by a superannuated soldier, but the champagne flowed like water. No one knew anything about either his circumstances or his income—and none ventured to ask him about either.

You could find books at his place, military treatises and novels, for the most part; he lent them willingly enough, never demanding their return, but then he never gave back to its owner any book he had borrowed. His chief exercise consisted of pistol-shooting. The walls of his room were all bullet-riddled, all honey-combed with chinks. An expensive collection of pistols was the sole luxury in the lowly clay-daubed hut where he lived. The skill he had attained was past all belief, and had he undertaken to knock a pear off anyone's cap with a bullet, not a man in our regiment would have had any qualms about presenting his head to him as part of the target. Our talk often turned upon duels; Sylvio (I will give him that name) never took part therein. To the question whether he had ever had occasion to duel, he would answer drily that he had, but did not go into any details, and it was evident that he found such questions disagreeable. We supposed that his conscience was burdened by the memories of some unfortunate victim of his dreadful skill. However, it never even entered our heads to suspect him of anything in the least like timorousness. There are men whose mere appearance removes such suspicions. It was an unexpected incident which astonished us all.

On one occasion there were ten of us, all officers, dining at Sylvio's. We drank as we usually did—which is to say, a very great deal; after dinner we fell to persuading our host to be our banker at faro. For a long while he refused, inasmuch as he practically never played; at last he ordered cards to be brought, put out fifty gold pieces or thereabouts on the table, and sat down to deal. We gathered around him and the play caught on. Sylvio had a way of preserving perfect silence while playing; he never argued and never made any explanations. If the punter miscalculated, Sylvio immediately either paid him the difference or marked down the extra sum. We were already familiar with this procedure and did not interfere with his running things his own way; however, we had among us an officer who had been only recently transferred to our regiment. Joining in our game, he absent-mindedly turned down an extra corner on a card. Sylvio picked up the chalk and, after his wont, made the necessary correction. The officer, thinking that Sylvio was in error, launched into explanations. Sylvio kept on dealing in silence. The officer, losing patience, took the eraser and rubbed out that which to him seemed an incorrect entry. Sylvio took the chalk and re-wrote the score. The officer, heated by wine, the game, and the laughter of his messmates, deemed himself grossly affronted and, enraged, seized a brass candlestick off the table and let it fly at Sylvio, who barely managed to duck the missile. We were thrown into consternation. Sylvio stood up, turning pale from wrath and said, his eyes flashing:

"My dear sir, be good enough to leave, and you may thank God that this has occurred under my roof."

We had no doubt as to the outcome and considered our new messmate as good as slain already. The officer left, saying that he was prepared to give satisfaction for the offence in any manner suitable to the gentleman keeping the bank. The play went on for a few minutes more but, sensing that our host was anything but inclined to further play, we fell out one after the other and dispersed to our respective quarters, discussing the impending vacancy in our regiment.

The next day, at the riding-school, we were already asking if the poor lieutenant was still among the living, when he himself appeared in our midst. We put the same question to him; he answered that so far he had had no word whatsoever from Sylvio. This astounded us. We set out to see Sylvio, and came upon him in his courtyard, sending bullet upon bullet into an ace stuck against the gates. He received us as usual, without a word in reference to last night's incident. Three days went by; the lieutenant was still among the living. "Can it be that Sylvio isn't going to fight a duel?" we asked in amazement.

Sylvio did not fight. He was content with a very off-handed explanation and became reconciled with the lieutenant.

This, at first, did exceeding damage to the reputation he had enjoyed among the younger men. A lack of courage is least of all excused among the youth, who usually see in bravery the height of all human virtues and the excuse for all possible vices. However, little by little everything was forgotten, and Sylvio regained all his former influence.

I alone could not be on close terms with him again. Being by nature endowed with a romantic imagination, I had been more strongly than all the others attached to this man whose life was an enigma, and who seemed to me to be the hero of some mysterious romance. He had loved me; or, at least, I was the only one before whom he dropped his usual caustic and malicious manner of speech and spoke on various matters with simple-heartedness and unusual pleasantness. But after that unfortunate evening the thought that his honor had been besmirched and that, through his own volition, the stain had not been removed—that thought never forsook me and stood in the way of my resuming our former footing; it embarrassed me to look at him. Sylvio was far too intelligent and worldly not to perceive this and surmise the reason for it. This apparently grieved him; at least I noticed, once or twice, a desire on his part to explain things to me, but I avoided such opportunities and Sylvio drew back from me. Thenceforth I saw him only in the presence of my fellow-officers, and our former frank conversations ceased.

Those who live amid the distractions of a metropolis have no conception of many experiences which are so familiar to those who live in villages and small towns— such as waiting for the day when the mail comes. On Tuesdays and Fridays the office of our regiment was thronged with officers, some expecting money, others letters, still others newspapers. The packets were usually unsealed on the spot, there was an interchange of news, and the office presented a very animated picture. Sylvio had his letters addressed to the regiment, and was usually to be found at the office on mail days. One day he was handed a letter the seal of which he tore off with an air of the greatest impatience. His eyes, as they ran through the letter, were sparkling. The officers, each one taken up with his own letters, did not notice anything.

"Gentlemen," Sylvio addressed them, "circumstances demand my immediate departure; I am setting out to-night—I hope you will not refuse to dine with me for the last time. I expect you also," he went on, turning to me. "I expect you, without fail."

With that he hastened away, while we, after we had agreed to get together at Sylvio's, went our respective ways.

I arrived at Sylvio's place at the appointed time and found almost all our regimental staff there. All his possessions were already packed; he was leaving behind only the bare, bullet-riddled walls. We took our places at the table; our host was in exceptionally fine humor, and shortly his gaiety became general; corks were popping every minute, the glasses foamed and seethed incessantly, and most earnestly did we wish our departing friend *bon voyage* and every blessing. When we got up from the table the evening was already far gone. As we were picking out our caps and Sylvio was bidding farewell to all, he took me by the arm and detained me just as I was about to leave.

"I must have a talk with you," said he in a low voice. I remained.

The guests had gone; left alone, we two sat down face to face and silently lit our pipes. Sylvio seemed preoccupied; by now not even a trace remained of his former strained gaiety. His sombre pallor, his sparkling eyes and the dense smoke issuing from his mouth made him look like a veritable devil. Several minutes passed, and then Sylvio broke the silence.

"Perhaps we shall never see each other again," said he. "I would like, before our parting, to explain things to you. As you may have noticed, I care but little for the opinion of outsiders; but I am fond of you, and I feel it would be hard for me to have an unjust impression remaining in your mind."

He stopped; his pipe had burned out, and he began to refill it; I kept silent, with my eyes fixed on the ground.

"You found it strange," he went on, "when I did not demand satisfaction from that tipsy and harebrained fellow R———. You will agree that, since the privilege of choosing the weapons was mine, his life was in my hands, whereas mine was practically in no danger; I might ascribe my forbearance to magnanimity, but I do not want to lie. Were I in a position to chastise R——— without subjecting my life to any risk whatsoever, I would not have forgiven him under any circumstances."

I was looking at Sylvio with amazement. Such a confession threw me into utter confusion.

"That's just it—I haven't the right to expose myself to death," Sylvio went on. "Six years ago I received a slap in the face—and my enemy is still among the living."

My curiosity was greatly aroused:

"You did not fight him?" I asked. "Certain circumstances probably prevented your meeting—"

"I did fight him," replied Sylvio, "and here is a memento of our duel."

He got up and took out of a cardboard box a red cap, trimmed with a gold tassel and galloon (what the French call a *bonnet de police*) and put it on—it had been riddled with a bullet about an inch above his forehead.

"As you know," Sylvio went on, "I served in the —th Regiment of Hussars. You are aware what my character is like—I am used to being the first in all things, but when I was young this was a mania with me. In our day wildness was all the fashion; I was the wildest fellow in the army. We used to boast of our drinking ability;

Burtzov, whom Denis Davidov has hymned, was in his glory then—and I drank him under the table. Hardly a moment passed in our regiment without a duel; I was either a second or a principal in all of them. My messmates deified me, while the regimental commanders—there seemed to be a different one every few minutes!—regarded me as a necessary evil.

"I was enjoying my fame at my ease (or rather with unease), when a certain young man from a rich and distinguished family—I would rather not name him—joined our regiment. Never, since the day I was born, have I met so illustrious a favorite of fortune! Picture him in your imagination: youth, brains, good looks, the maddest gaiety, the most reckless bravery, a resounding name, money which he could not keep track of and of which he never ran short—and then imagine what an effect he was bound to produce among us. My supremacy was shaken. Captivated by my reputation he at first sought my friendship, but I received him coldly and, without the least regret, he became aloof to me. I grew to hate him. His successes in the regiment and in feminine society threw me into utter despair. I took to seeking quarrels with him; he responded to my epigrams with epigrams which always seemed to me more spontaneous and pointed than mine, and which, of course, were incomparably more mirth-provoking; he was jesting, whereas I was being malicious. Finally—the occasion was a ball at the house of a Polish landowner—seeing him the cynosure of all the ladies, and especially of the hostess herself, with whom I had a liaison, I whispered some vulgar insult or other in his ear. He flared up and gave me a slap in the face. We dashed for our sabres; the ladies swooned away; we were dragged apart, and that same night we set out to fight a duel.

"This was at dawn. I was standing at the designated spot with my three seconds. With inexplicable impatience did I await my opponent. The spring sun had risen, and it was already growing hot. I saw him from afar. He was on foot, the coat of his uniform slung on a sabre over his shoulder, and was accompanied by but one second. We went toward him. He approached, holding his cap, which was filled with cherries. Our seconds measured off twelve paces for us. I had to fire first, but my resentment made me so agitated that I could not rely upon the steadiness of my hand and, to give myself time to cool down, I conceded the first shot to him; to this my opponent would not agree. It was decided to cast lots; the first number fell to him, the constant favorite of fortune. He took aim, and his bullet riddled my cap. It was my turn. His life, at last, was in my hands; I eyed him avidly, trying to detect even a single shadow of uneasiness. He stood before my pistol, picking out the ripe cherries and spitting out the stones, which flew to where I was standing. His equanimity maddened me. 'What would be the use,' it occurred to me, 'to deprive him of life when he does not treasure it in the least?' A malicious thought flashed through my mind. I lowered my pistol.

" 'You apparently have other things on your mind outside of death,' I said to him. 'It pleases you to be breaking your fast; I have no wish to interfere with you.'

" 'You are not interfering with me in the least,' he retorted. 'You may shoot, if you like; however, please yourself; you may keep back the shot—I am always at your service.'

"I turned to the seconds, informing them that I had no intention of shooting just then, and with that the duel was over.

"I resigned from the army and withdrew to this little town. Since then not a day has passed without my thinking of revenge. Now my hour has come—"

Sylvio took out of his pocket the letter he had received that morning, and handed it to me to read. Someone (apparently his business agent) wrote him from Moscow that a *certain person* was soon going to marry a young and beautiful girl.

"You can surmise," said Sylvio, "who that *certain person* is. I am off to Moscow. We shall see if he will meet death now, when he is about to marry, with the same equanimity as he faced it then, over his cherries!"

With these words Sylvio stood up, dashed his cap against the floor, and took to pacing up and down the room, like a tiger in his cage. I had listened to him and never stirred; strange, contradictory feelings agitated me.

The servant entered and announced that the horses were waiting. Sylvio squeezed my hand hard; we kissed each other. He seated himself in the small cart, lying in which were two valises, one containing his pistols, the other his belongings. We bade each other farewell once more, and the horses started off at a gallop.

II

Several years passed, and domestic circumstances forced me to settle in a poor little village in the N——district. Busying myself with husbandry, I did not cease from sighing in secret about my former noisy and carefree life. The hardest thing of all for me was to become accustomed to passing the spring and winter evenings in utter solitude. I did manage to get through the time before dinner somehow or other, discussing things with the overseer, riding about to see how this work or that was coming along, or inspecting new undertakings;

but no sooner did it begin to get dark than I absolutely did not know what to do with myself. The few books I had found under cupboards and in the store-room I had read till I knew them by heart; all the fairy-tales which Kirilovna, my housekeeper, could recall had been told me over and over; the songs of the peasant women brought on a mood of depression. For a while I took to drinking unsweetened fruit liqueurs, but they made my head ache; besides, I confess, I felt afraid of becoming a "drunkard from misery," that is to say, the most "bitter" drunkard, of which kind I had seen a multitude of examples in our district.

I had no close neighbors, save for two or three "bitter" drinkers, whose conversation consisted for the most part of hiccupping and deep sighs. Solitude was easier to bear. Finally I decided to go to bed as early as possible and to dine as late as possible; in this manner I shortened the evening and added length to the days, and gained thereby, since *it is good for a man so to be.*

A little less than three miles from my place was a rich estate belonging to Countess B——; but there was nobody living there save the steward; as for the Countess herself, she had visited her estate only once, during the first year of her married life, and then she had stayed there for no more than a month. However, during the second spring of my life as a recluse, a rumor spread that the Countess with her husband would come to her country estate for the summer. And, at the beginning of June, they actually came.

The arrival of a rich neighbor marks a great epoch for those who live in the country. The landowners and their house serfs discuss the matter for two months before the arrival and for three years afterward. As for me, I confess that the tidings of the coming of a young and beautiful neighbor affected me greatly; I burned with impatience to see her, and consequently on the first Sunday after her arrival set out after dinner for the settlement of ——, to introduce myself to their Excellencies as their nearest neighbor and most obedient servant.

A flunky showed me into the Count's study and then went off to announce me. The spacious study was furnished with every possible luxury; along the walls were bookcases, and each one was surmounted by a bronze bust; hanging over the marble fireplace was a large mirror; the floor was covered with a green carpet, with rugs over it. Having become unused to luxury in my poor nook, and not having seen the wealth of others for a long time by now, I became timid and awaited the Count with a certain trepidation, as a petitioner from the provinces awaits the appearance of a prime minister.

The doors opened and an exceptionally handsome man of thirty-two entered. The Count approached me with a frank and cordial air; I tried to perk up and began to introduce myself, but he forestalled me. His conversation, free and amiable, soon dispelled my backwoods shyness; I was already beginning to feel at my ordinary ease when the Countess suddenly entered, and embarrassment overcame me worse than ever. Truly, she was a beauty. The Count presented me. I wished to appear at ease, but the more I strove to assume an air of unconstraint the more awkward did I feel. In order to give me time to recover my self-possession and become accustomed to this new acquaintance, they began conversing with each other, treating me as a good neighbor and without standing on ceremony. In the meanwhile I began walking about, looking over the books and pictures. I am no connoisseur of pictures, but one of them attracted my attention. It represented some view or other in Switzerland, but it was not the way it was painted which struck me, but the fact that two bullets, one driven into the other, were imbedded in the picture.

"There's a good shot," I said, turning to the Count.

"Yes," he replied, "a most remarkable shot. Do you shoot well?" he went on.

"Tolerably well," I responded, rejoicing that the conversation had at last touched upon a subject I was familiar with. "I won't miss hitting a card at thirty paces—using pistols that I am used to, of course."

"Really?" spoke up the Countess, with an appearance of great interest. "And you, my dear—could you hit a card at thirty paces?"

"We shall have a try at it some day," answered the Count. "In my time I did not shoot at all badly, but it's four years by now since I have handled a pistol."

"Oh, in that case," I remarked, "I am ready to wager that Your Excellency will not hit a card at twenty paces; the pistol demands daily practice. That I know from experience. I was considered one of the best marksmen in our regiment; once a whole month happened to pass by without my touching a pistol—all of my weapons were being overhauled; well, what do you think was the result, Your Excellency? On the first occasion I began to shoot again I missed four times in a row, shooting at a bottle at twenty paces. Our captain, a wit and a wag, happened to be there: 'I can see you can't raise your hand against a bottle,' said he to me. No, Your Excellency, you mustn't neglect practice, or you'll lose the knack, sure as shooting. The best shot I ever came across used to shoot at least three times every day, before dinner. This was as much of a habit with him as a glass of vodka."

The Count and Countess were happy to see me so talkative.

"And what sort of a shot was he?" the Count asked me.

"Why, here's the sort he was, Your Excellency: if he happened to see a fly settle on a wall—are you laughing, Countess? By God, it's the truth! If he happened to see a fly, he'd call out: 'Kuzka, my pistol!'—and Kuzka would bring him a loaded pistol. He'd go *bang!*—and plug the fly into the wall!"

"Amazing!" declared the Count. "And what was his name?"

"Sylvio, Your Excellency."

"Sylvio!" cried out the Count, leaping up from his seat. "You knew Sylvio?"

"How else, Your Excellency? He and I were close friends; he was treated as a messmate and brother in our regiment, but it's five years by now since I've had any word of him. Your Excellency knew him as well, then?"

"I did know him, and that very well. Didn't he tell you about a certain very strange incident?"

"Was it about a slap in the face, Your Excellency, which he received at a ball from some rake or other?"

"And did he happen to mention to you the name of this rake?"

"No, Your Excellency, he didn't. . . . Ah, Your Excellency!" I continued, surmising the truth. "Pardon me, I didn't know . . . could it have been you, by any chance?"

"I, and none other," replied the Count, looking extremely upset. "As for that bullet-riddled picture—it is a memento of our last encounter."

"Ah, dearest," interposed the Countess, "for God's sake don't speak of it; it would frighten me to hear that story."

"No," retorted the Count, "I am going to relate the whole thing; he knows how I offended his friend—let him learn, then, how Sylvio had his revenge upon me."

The Count moved an armchair up for me, and I

listened, with the liveliest interest, to the following story:

"Five years ago I married. The first month—*the honeymoon*—I spent here, in this village. To this house I am indebted for the best moments of my life—and for one of my most painful recollections.

"One evening we were out for a horseback ride together; my wife's horse became stubborn for some reason —she became frightened, handed the reins over to me and set out for home on foot. I rode on. In the courtyard I saw a traveling cart; I was told there was a man sitting in my study, waiting for me—he had not wanted to give his name but merely said that he had business with me. I entered this room and saw a man in the dusk, covered with dust and unshaven; he was standing right here, by the fireplace. I approached him, trying to recall his features.

" 'You haven't recognized me, Count?' he asked in a quavering voice.

" 'Sylvio!' I cried out—and, I confess, I felt that my hair had suddenly stood up on end.

" 'Precisely,' he went on. 'There is a shot coming to me; I have come to discharge my pistol—are you ready?'

"He had a pistol sticking out of a side pocket. I measured off twelve paces and took my stand there, in that corner, begging him to fire as quickly as possible, before my wife came back. He dallied—he asked for a light. Candles were brought in. I locked the doors, gave orders that no one was to come in, and begged him anew to fire. He drew out his pistol and took aim. I counted the seconds . . . I was thinking of her. A terrible minute passed! Sylvio lowered his arm.

" 'What a pity,' said he, 'that the pistol is not loaded with cherry stones . . . a bullet is heavy. The notion persists that we are not engaged in a duel but a murder: I am not accustomed to taking aim at an unarmed man.

Let's start it over anew; we will cast lots as to who is to fire first.'

"My head was swimming. I believe I refused to agree to this. . . . Finally we loaded another pistol, rolled up two slips of paper—he put the latter in a cap, the one I had on a time riddled with a bullet; I again drew the first number.

" 'You have the devil's own luck, Count,' said he with a sneer which I shall never forget.

"I can't understand what came over me, and in what way he compelled me to do such a thing . . . but I fired—and hit that picture."

The Count pointed a finger at the bullet-damaged picture. His face seemed to be on fire; the Countess was whiter than the handkerchief she was holding; I could not restrain an exclamation.

"I fired," the Count resumed, "and, God be praised, shot wide of the mark, whereupon Sylvio—at that moment he was really terrible—Sylvio began taking aim at me. Suddenly the doors flew open, Mary ran in, and with a piercing shriek threw herself upon my neck. Her presence restored to me all my alertness.

" 'My dear,' I told her, 'can't you see that we're indulging in a practical joke? How thoroughly frightened you were! Go, drink a glass of water and then come to us; I will present to you an old friend and comrade.'

Mary was still doubtful.

" 'Tell me, is my husband telling the truth?' she asked, turning to Sylvio, who was awesome. 'Is it true that you are both having a joke?'

" 'He is always having his joke, Countess,' Sylvio answered her. 'Once, by way of a joke, he gave me a slap in the face; by way of a joke, he shot this cap through for me; by way of a joke he missed when he shot at me just now; now I, too, have gotten into the mood for a joke—'

"With that he wanted to take aim at me—in her presence! Mary cast herself down at his feet.

" 'Get up, Mary—this is disgraceful!' I cried out in a frenzy. 'As for you, sir—will you cease torturing and humiliating a poor woman? Are you going to fire or no?'

" 'I am not going to,' answered Sylvio. 'I am satisfied. I have seen your confusion, your timorousness; I have compelled you to fire at me; that is enough for me. You will remember me. I give you over to your conscience.'

"He was about to go out then, but he paused in the doorway, looked back at the picture my bullet had hit and, firing at it almost without taking aim, disappeared.

"My wife was lying in a swoon; the servants dared not stop him and were gazing at him in horror; he went out upon the steps, called his driver and rode off before I could regain my presence of mind."

The Count fell silent. It was thus that I came to know the conclusion of the story whose beginning had on a time made such an impression upon me. The hero thereof I never met again. They say that, during the uprising of Alexander Ypsilanti, Sylvio commanded a detachment of hetaerists, or Greek patriots, and that he was killed in the battle of Skulyani.

NIKOLAI VASSILIEVICH GOGOL

(1809–1852)

EDITOR'S NOTE

GOGOL-YANOVSKI (he did not use the latter name; *gogol* is a species of wild duck, and the Russian for "strutting" is "to walk like a *gogol*") was born in a family of landed gentry in the Ukraine. His father was a passionate theatromane, and wrote two comedies which hold high rank in Ukrainian literature. But, although a superb amateur actor and reader, Gogol failed in his one tryout for the professional stage, his style proving too natural for the stilted histrionics of the time.

He took up law but never practiced it; civil service he quit in a short while, unable to stomach bureaucracy and its ways. He had very hard sledding in St. Petersburg; his first book and his second (poetry, published pseudonymously) failed so dismally that he burned all the copies he could draw back from the booksellers. (This tendency for *burning* his unsuccessful works, or those he thought failures, led to the burnings of several drafts of the second part of *Dead Souls* and the final holocaust of Part Two and, probably, the outline of Part Three.) His first success came to him with the publication of *Evenings on a Croft Near Dikanaka, Published by Rood Panco the Beekeeper*—a fresh, fantastic work which gained him the friendship of Zhukovsky, Pushkin and others.

Gogol's ultimate debacle was due to the influence of his evil demon, an ignorant lout of a country priest, who had turned the writer's latent mysticism into downright religious mania. And his death, although he did not die actually raving but merely quoting a Slavic version of Jeremiah, was one of the most harrowing scenes in the history of literature.[1]

The Overcoat

NIKOLAI VASSILIEVICH GOGOL[2]

IN THE Bureau of . . . but it might be better not to mention the Bureau by its precise name. There is nothing more touchy than all these Bureaus, Regiments, Chancelleries of every sort and, in a word, every sort of person belonging to the administrative classes. Nowadays every civilian, even, considers all of society insulted in his own person. Quite recently, so they say, a petition came through from a certain Captain of Rural Police in some town or other (I can't recall its name), in which he explained clearly that the whole social structure was headed for ruin and that his sacred name was actually being taken entirely in vain, and, in proof, he documented his petition with the enormous tome of some romantic work or other wherein, every ten pages or so, a Captain of Rural Police appeared—in some passages even in an out-and-out drunken state. And so, to

---

[1] The best (and only readable) book on this writer in English is, despite certain quirks, Vladimir Nabokov's *Gogol* (New Directions), which treats him as a supreme fantast.—And the reader should, by all means, read Belinski's famous *Letter to Gogol*, now available in English.

[2] From *A Treasury of Russian Literature*, copyright, 1943, by the Vanguard Press, Inc., and republished by arrangement.

avoid any and all unpleasantnesses, we'd better call the Bureau in question *a certain Bureau.* And so, in *a certain Bureau* there served a *certain clerk*—a clerk whom one could hardly style very remarkable: quite low of stature, somewhat pockmarked, somewhat rusty-hued of hair, even somewhat purblind, at first glance; rather bald at the temples, with wrinkles along both cheeks, and his face of that complexion which is usually called hemorrhoidal. Well, what would you? It's the Petersburg climate that's to blame. As far as his rank is concerned (for among us the rank must be made known first of all), why, he was what they call a Perpetual Titular Councilor—a rank which, as everybody knows, various writers who have a praiseworthy wont of throwing their weight about among those who are in no position to hit back, have twitted and exercised their keen wits against often and long. This clerk's family name was Bashmachkin. It's quite evident, by the very name, that it sprang from *bashmak* or shoe, but at what time, just when and how it sprang from a shoe—of that nothing is known. For not only this clerk's father but his grandfather and even his brother-in-law, and absolutely all the Bashmachkins, walked about in boots, merely resoling them three times a year.

His name and patronymic were Akakii Akakiievich. It may, perhaps, strike the reader as somewhat odd and out of the way, but the reader may rest assured that the author has not gone out of his way at all to find it, but that certain circumstances had come about of themselves in such fashion that there was absolutely no way of giving him any other name. And the precise way this came about was as follows. Akakii Akakiievich was born —unless my memory plays me false—on the night of the twenty-third of March. His late mother, a government clerk's wife, and a very good woman, was all set to christen her child, all fit and proper. She was still lying in bed, facing the door, while on her right stood the godfather, a most excellent man by the name of Ivan Ivanovich Eroshkin, who had charge of some Department or other in a certain Administrative Office, and the godmother, the wife of the precinct police officer, a woman of rare virtues, by the name of Arina Semenovna Byelobrushkina. The mother was offered the choice of any one of three names: Mokii, Sossii—or the child could even be given the name of that great martyr, Hozdavat. "No," the late lamented had reflected, "what sort of names are these?" In order to please her they opened the calendar at another place—and the result was again three names: Triphilii, Dula, and Varahasii. "What a visitation!" said the elderly woman. "What names all these be! To tell you the truth, I've never even heard the likes of them. If it were at least Baradat or Baruch, but why do Triphilii and Varahasii have to crop up?" They turned over another page—and came up with Pavsikahii and Vahtissii. "Well, I can see now," said the mother, "that such is evidently his fate. In that case it would be better if he were called after his father. His father was an Akakii—let the son be an Akakii also." And that's how Akakii Akakiievich came to be Akakii Akakiievich.

The child was baptized, during which rite he began to bawl and made terrible faces as if anticipating that it would be his lot to become a Perpetual Titular Councilor. And so that's the way it had all come about. We have brought the matter up so that the reader might see for himself that all this had come about through sheer inevitability and it had been utterly impossible to bestow any other name upon Akakii Akakiievich.

When, at precisely what time, he entered the Bureau, and who gave him the berth, were things which no one could recall. No matter how many Directors and his superiors of one sort or another came and went, he was always to be seen in the one and the same spot, in the same posture, in the very same post, always the same Clerk of Correspondence, so that subsequently people became convinced that he evidently had come into the world just the way he was, all done and set, in a uniform frock and bald at the temples. No respect whatsoever was shown him in the Bureau. The porters not only didn't jump up from their places whenever he happened to pass by, but didn't even as much as glance at him, as if nothing more than a common housefly had passed through the reception hall. His superiors treated him with a certain chill despotism. Some assistant or other of some Head of a Department would simply shove papers under his nose, without as much as saying "Transcribe these," or "Here's a rather pretty, interesting little case," or any of those small pleasantries that are current in well-conducted administrative institutions. And he would take the work, merely glancing at the paper, without looking up to see who had put it down before him and whether that person had the right to do so; he took it and right then and there went to work on it. The young clerks made fun of him and sharpened their wits at his expense, to whatever extent their quill-driving wittiness sufficed, retailing in his very presence the various stories made up about him; they said of his landlady, a crone of seventy, that she beat him, and asked him when their wedding would take place; they scattered torn paper over his head, maintaining it was snow.

But not a word did Akakii Akakiievich say in answer to all this, as if there were actually nobody before him. It did not even affect his work: in the midst of all these annoyances he did not make a single clerical error. Only when the jest was past all bearing, when they jostled his arm, hindering him from doing his work, would he say: "Leave me alone! Why do you pick on me?" And there was something odd about his words and in the voice with which he uttered them. In that voice could be heard something that moved one to pity—so much so that one young man, a recent entrant, who, following the example of the others, had permitted himself to make fun of Akakii Akakiievich, stopped suddenly, as if pierced to the quick, and from that time on everything seemed to change in his eyes and appeared in a different light. Some sort of preternatural force seemed to repel him from the companions he had made, having taken them for decent, sociable people. And for a long time afterward, in the very midst of his most cheerful moments, the little squat clerk would appear before him, with the small bald patches on each side of his forehead, and he would hear his heart-piercing words "Leave me alone! Why do you pick on me?" And in these heart-piercing words he caught the ringing sound of others: "I am your brother." And the poor young man would cover his eyes with his hand, and many a time in his life thereafter did he shudder, seeing how much inhumanity there is in man, how much hidden ferocious coarseness lurks in refined, cultured worldliness and, O God! even in that very man whom the world holds to be noble and honorable. . . .

It is doubtful if you could find anywhere a man whose life lay so much in his work. It would hardly do to say that he worked with zeal; no, it was a labor of love. Thus, in this transcription of his, he visioned some sort of diversified and pleasant world all its own. His face expressed delight; certain letters were favorites of his and, whenever he came across them he would be beside himself with rapture: he'd chuckle, and wink, and help things along by working his lips, so that it seemed as if one could read on his face every letter his quill was outlining. If rewards had been meted out to him commensurately with his zeal, he might have, to his astonishment, actually found himself among the State Councilors; but, as none other than those wits, his own co-workers, expressed it, all he'd worked himself up to was a button in a buttonhole too wide, and piles in his backside.

However, it would not be quite correct to say that absolutely no attention was paid him. One Director, being a kindly man and wishing to reward him for his long service, gave orders that some work of a more important nature than the usual transcription be assigned to him; to be precise, he was told to make a certain referral to another Administrative Department out of a docket already prepared; the matter consisted, all in all, of changing the main title as well as some pronouns here and there from the first person singular to the third person singular. This made so much work for him that he was all of a sweat, kept mopping his forehead, and finally said: "No, better let me transcribe something." Thenceforth they left him to his transcription for all time. Outside of this transcription, it seemed, nothing existed for him.

He gave no thought whatsoever to his dress; the uniform frock coat on him wasn't the prescribed green at all, but rather of some rusty-flour hue. His collar was very tight and very low, so that his neck, even though it wasn't a long one, seemed extraordinarily long emerging therefrom, like those gypsum kittens with nodding heads which certain outlanders balance by the dozen atop their heads and peddle throughout Russia. And, always, something was bound to stick to his coat: a wisp of hay or some bit of thread; in addition to that, he had a peculiar knack whenever he walked through the streets of getting under some window at the precise moment when garbage of every sort was being thrown out of it, and for that reason always bore off on his hat watermelon and cantaloupe rinds and other such trifles. Not once in all his life had he ever turned his attention to the everyday things and doings out in the street—something, as everybody knows, that is always watched with eager interest by Akakii Akakiievich's confrère, the young government clerk, the penetration of whose lively gaze is so extensive that he will even take in somebody on the opposite sidewalk who has ripped loose his trouser strap—a thing that never fails to evoke a sly smile on the young clerk's face. But even if Akakii Akakiievich did look at anything, he saw thereon nothing but his own neatly, evenly penned lines of script, and only when some horse's nose, bobbing up from no one knew where, would be placed on his shoulder and let a whole gust of wind in his face through its nostrils, would he notice that he was not in the middle of a line of script but, rather, in the middle of the roadway.

On coming home he would immediately sit down at the table, gulp down his cabbage soup and bolt a piece of veal with onions, without noticing in the least the taste of either, eating everything together with the flies and whatever else God may have sent at that particular time of the year. On perceiving that his belly was beginning to bulge, he'd get up from the table, take out a small bottle of ink, and transcribe the papers he had brought home. If there were no homework, he would deliberately, for his own edification, make a copy of some paper for himself, especially if the document were remarkable not for its beauty of style but merely addressed to some new or important person.

Even at those hours when the gray sky of Petersburg

becomes entirely extinguished and all the pettifogging tribe has eaten its fill and finished dinner, each as best he could, in accordance with the salary he receives and his own bent, when everybody has already rested up after the scraping of quills in various departments, the running around, the unavoidable cares about their own affairs and the affairs of others, and all that which restless man sets himself as a task voluntarily and to an even greater extent than necessary—at a time when the petty bureaucrats hasten to devote whatever time remained to enjoyment: he who was of the more lively sort hastening to the theater, another for a saunter through the streets, devoting the time to an inspection of certain pretty little hats; still another to some evening party, to spend that time in paying compliments to some comely young lady, the star of a small bureaucratic circle; a fourth (and this happened most frequently of all) simply going to call on a confrère in a flat up three or four flights of stairs, consisting of two small rooms with an entry and a kitchen and one or two attempts at the latest improvements—a kerosene lamp instead of candles, or some other elegant little thing that had cost many sacrifices, such as going without dinners or good times—in short, even at the time when all the petty bureaucrats scatter through the small apartments of their friends for a session of dummy whist, sipping tea out of tumblers and nibbling at cheap zwieback, drawing deep at their pipes, the stems thereof as long as walking sticks, retailing, during the shuffling and dealing, some bit of gossip or other from high society that had reached them at long last (something which no Russian, under any circumstances, and of whatever estate he be, can ever deny himself), or even, when there was nothing whatsoever to talk about, retelling the eternal chestnut of the commandant to whom peo-

ple came to say that the tail of the horse on the Fal-
conetti monument had been docked—in short, even at
the time when every soul yearns to be diverted, Akakii
Akakiievich did not give himself up to any diversion.
No man could claim having ever seen him at any evening gathering. Having had his sweet fill of quill-driving, he would lie down to sleep, smiling at the thought
of the next day: just what would God send him on the
morrow?

Such was the peaceful course of life of a man who,
with a yearly salary of four hundred, knew how to be
content with his lot, and that course might even have
continued to a ripe old age had it not been for sundry
calamities, such as are strewn along the path of life, not
only of Titular, but even Privy, Actual, Court, and all
other sorts of Councilors, even those who never give
any counsel to anybody nor ever accept any counsel
from others for themselves.

There is, in Petersburg, a formidable foe of all those
whose salary runs to four hundred a year or thereabouts. This foe is none other than our Northern frost
—even though, by the bye, they do say that it's the
most healthful thing for you. At nine in the morning,
precisely at that hour when the streets are thronged
with those on their way to sundry Bureaus, it begins
dealing out such powerful and penetrating fillips to all
noses, without any discrimination, that the poor bureaucrats absolutely do not know how to hide them. At this
time, when even those who fill the higher posts feel
their foreheads aching because of the frost and the
tears come to their eyes, the poor Titular Councilors are
sometimes utterly defenseless. The sole salvation, if
one's overcoat is of the thinnest, lies in dashing, as
quickly as possible, through five or six blocks and then
stamping one's feet for a long time in the porter's room,

until the faculties and gifts for administrative duties, which have been frozen on the way, are thus thawed out at last.

For some time Akakii Akakiievich had begun to notice that the cold was somehow penetrating his back and shoulders with especial ferocity, despite the fact that he tried to run the required distance as quickly as possible. It occurred to him, at last, that there might be some defects about his overcoat. After looking it over rather thoroughly at home he discovered that in two or three places—in the back and at the shoulders, to be exact—it had become no better than the coarsest of sacking; the cloth was rubbed to such an extent that one could see through it, and the lining had crept apart. The reader must be informed that Akakii Akakiievich's overcoat, too, was a butt for the jokes of the petty bureaucrats; it had been deprived of the honorable name of an overcoat, even, and dubbed a *negligee*. And, really, it was of a rather queer cut; its collar grew smaller with every year, inasmuch as it was utilized to supplement the other parts of the garment. This supplementing was not at all a compliment to the skill of the tailor, and the effect really was baggy and unsightly.

Perceiving what the matter was, Akakii Akakiievich decided that the overcoat would have to go to Petrovich the tailor, who lived somewhere up four flights of backstairs and who, despite a squint-eye and pockmarks all over his face, did quite well at repairing bureaucratic as well as all other trousers and coats—of course, be it understood, when he was in a sober state and not hatching some nonsartorial scheme in his head. One shouldn't, really, mention this tailor at great length, but since there is already a precedent for each character in a tale being clearly defined, there's no help for it, and so let's trot out Petrovich as well. In the beginning he had been called simply Gregory and had been the serf of some squire or other; he had begun calling himself Petrovich only after obtaining his freedom papers and taking to drinking rather hard on any and every holiday —at first on the red-letter ones and then, without any discrimination, on all those designated by the church: wherever there was a little cross marking the day on the calendar. In this respect he was loyal to the customs of our grandsires and, when bickering with his wife, would call her a worldly woman and a German *frau*. And, since we've already been inadvertent enough to mention his wife, it will be necessary to say a word or two about her as well; but, regrettably, little was known about her—unless, perhaps, the fact that Petrovich had a wife, or that she even wore a house-cap and not a kerchief; but as for beauty, it appears that she could hardly boast of any; at least the soldiers in the Guards were the only ones with hardihood enough to bend down for a peep under her cap, twitching their mustachios as they did so and emitting a certain peculiar sound.

As he clambered up the staircase that led to Petrovich—the staircase, to render it its just due, was dripping all over from water and slops and thoroughly permeated with that alcoholic odor which makes the eyes smart and is, as everybody knows, unfailingly present on all the backstairs of all the houses in Petersburg—as he clambered up this staircase Akakii Akakiievich was already conjecturing how stiff Petrovich's asking-price would be and mentally determined not to give him more than two rubles. The door was open, because the mistress of the place, being busy preparing some fish, had filled the kitchen with so much smoke that one actually couldn't see the very cockroaches for it.

Akakii Akakiievich made his way through the kitchen, unperceived even by the mistress herself, and at last entered the room wherein he beheld Petrovich, sitting on a wide table of unpainted deal with his feet tucked in under him like a Turkish Pasha. His feet, as is the wont of tailors seated at their work, were bare, and the first thing that struck one's eyes was the big toe of one, very familiar to Akakii Akakiievich, with some sort of deformed nail, as thick and strong as a turtle's shell. About Petrovich's neck were loops of silk and cotton thread, while some sort of ragged garment was lying on his knees. For the last three minutes he had been trying to put a thread through the eye of a needle, couldn't hit the mark, and because of that was very wroth against the darkness of the room and even the thread itself, grumbling under his breath: "She won't go through, the heathen! You've spoiled my heart's blood, you damned good-for-nothing!"

Akakii Akakiievich felt upset because he had come at just the moment when Petrovich was very angry; he liked to give in his work when the latter was already under the influence or, as his wife put it, "He's already full of rot-gut, the one-eyed devil!" In such a state Petrovich usually gave in willingly and agreed to everything; he even bowed and was grateful every time. Afterward, true enough, his wife would come around and complain weepily that, now, her husband had been drunk and for that reason had taken on the work too cheaply; but all you had to do was to tack on another ten kopecks—and the thing was in the bag. But now, it seemed, Petrovich was in a sober state, and for that reason on his high horse, hard to win over, and bent on boosting his prices to the devil knows what heights. Akakii Akakiievich surmised this and, as the saying goes, was all set to make back tracks, but the deal had already been started. Petrovich puckered up his one good eye against him very fixedly and Akakii Akakiievich involuntarily said "Greetings, Petrovich!" "Greetings to you, sir," said Petrovich and looked askance at Akakii Akakiievich's hands, wishing to see what sort of booty the other bore.

"Well, now, I've come to see you, now, Petrovich!"

Akakii Akakiievich, the reader must be informed, explained himself for the most part in prepositions, adverbs, and such verbal oddments as had absolutely no significance. But if the matter was exceedingly difficult, he actually had a way of not finishing his phrase at all, so that, quite frequently, beginning his speech with such words as "This, really, is perfectly, you know—" he would have nothing at all to follow up with, and he himself would be likely to forget the matter, thinking that he had already said everything in full.

"Well, just what is it?" asked Petrovich, and at the same time, with his one good eye, surveyed the entire garment, beginning with the collar and going on to the sleeves, the back, the coat-skirts, and the buttonholes, for it was all very familiar to him, inasmuch as it was all his own handiwork. That's a way all tailors have; it's the first thing a tailor will do on meeting you.

"Why, what I'm after, now, Petrovich . . . the overcoat, now, the cloth . . . there, you see, in all the other places it's strong as can be . . . it's gotten a trifle dusty and only seems to be old, but it's really new, there's only one spot . . . a little sort of . . . in the back . . . and also one shoulder, a trifle rubbed through —and this shoulder, too, a trifle—do you see? Not a lot of work, really—"

Petrovich took up the *negligee*, spread it out over the table as a preliminary, examined it for a long time, shook his head, and then groped with his hand on the

window sill for a round snuffbox with the portrait of
some general or other on its lid—just which one nobody could tell, inasmuch as the place occupied by the
face had been holed through with a finger and then
pasted over with a small square of paper. After duly
taking tobacco, Petrovich held the *negligee* taut in his
hands and scrutinized it against the light, and again
shook his head; after this he turned it with the lining
up and again shook his head, again took off the lid with
the general's face pasted over with paper and, having
fully loaded both nostrils with snuff, covered the snuffbox, put it away, and, at long last, gave his verdict:

"No, there's no fixin' this thing: your wardrobe's in
a bad way!"

Akakii Akakiievich's heart skipped a beat at these
words.

"But why not, Petrovich?" he asked, almost in the
imploring voice of a child. "All that ails it, now . . .
it's rubbed through at the shoulders. Surely you must
have some small scraps of cloth or other—"

"Why, yes, one could find the scraps—the scraps will
turn up," said Petrovich. "Only there's no sewing them
on: the whole thing's all rotten: touch a needle to it—
and it just crawls apart on you."

"Well, let it crawl—and you just slap a patch right
on to it."

"Yes, but there's nothing to slap them little patches
on to; there ain't nothing for the patch to take hold on
—there's been far too much wear. It's cloth in name
only, but if a gust of wind was to blow on it, it would
scatter."

"Well, now, you just fix it up. That, really, now . . .
how can it be?"

"No," said Petrovich decisively, "there ain't a thing
to be done. The whole thing's in a bad way. You'd bet-

ter, when the cold winter spell comes, make footcloths out of it, because stockings ain't so warm. It's them Germans that invented them stockings, so's to rake in more money for themselves. [Petrovich loved to needle the Germans whenever the chance turned up.] But as for that there overcoat, it looks like you'll have to make yourself a new one."

At the word *new* a mist swam before Akakii Akakiievich's eyes and everything in the room became a jumble. All he could see clearly was the general on the lid of Petrovich's snuffbox, his face pasted over with a scrap of paper.

"A new one? But how?" he asked, still as if he were in a dream. "Why, I have no money for that."

"Yes, a new one," said Petrovich with a heathenish imperturbability.

"Well, if there's no getting out of it, how much, now—"

"You mean, how much it would cost?"

"Yes."

"Why, you'd have to cough up three fifties and a bit over," pronounced Petrovich and significantly pursed up his lips at this. He was very fond of strong effects, was fond of somehow nonplusing somebody, utterly and suddenly, and then eyeing his victim sidelong, to see what sort of wry face the nonplusee would pull after his words.

"A hundred and fifty for an overcoat!" poor Akakii Akakiievich cried out—cried out perhaps for the first time since he was born, for he was always distinguished for his low voice.

"Yes, sir!" said Petrovich. "And what an overcoat, at that! If you put a marten collar on it and add a silk-lined hood it might stand you even two hundred."

"Petrovich, please!" Akakii Akakiievich was saying in

an imploring voice, without grasping and without even trying to grasp the words uttered by Petrovich and all his effects. "Fix it somehow or other, now, so's it may do a little longer, at least—"

"Why, no, that'll be only having the work go to waste and spending your money for nothing," said Petrovich, and after these words Akakii Akakiievich walked out annihilated. But Petrovich, after his departure, remained as he was for a long time, with meaningfully pursed lips and without resuming his work, satisfied with neither having lowered himself nor having betrayed the sartorial art.

Out in the street, Akakii Akakiievich walked along like a somnambulist. "What a business, now, what a business," he kept saying to himself. "Really, I never even thought that it, now . . . would turn out like that. . . ." And then, after a pause, added: "So that's it! That's how it's turned out after all! Really, now, I couldn't even suppose that it . . . like that, now—" This was followed by another long pause, after which he uttered aloud: "So that's how it is! This, really, now, is something that's beyond all, now, expectation . . . well, I never! What a fix, now!"

Having said this, instead of heading for home, he started off in an entirely different direction without himself suspecting it. On the way a chimney sweep caught him square with his whole sooty side and covered all his shoulder with soot; enough quicklime to cover his entire hat tumbled down on him from the top of a building under construction. He noticed nothing of all this and only later, when he ran up against a policeman near his sentry box (who, having placed his halberd near him, was shaking some tobacco out of a paper cornucopia on to his calloused palm), did Akakii Akakiievich come a little to himself, and that only because the policeman said: "What's the idea of shoving your face right into mine? Ain't the sidewalk big enough for you?" This made him look about him and turn homeward.

Only here did he begin to pull his wits together; he perceived his situation in its clear and real light; he started talking to himself no longer in snatches but reasoningly and frankly, as with a judicious friend with whom one might discuss a matter most heartfelt and intimate. "Well, no," said Akakii Akakiievich, "there's no use reasoning with Petrovich now; he's, now, that way. . . . His wife had a chance to give him a drubbing, it looks like. No, it'll be better if I come to him on a Sunday morning; after Saturday night's good time he'll be squinting his eye and very sleepy, so he'll have to have a hair of the dog that bit him, but his wife won't give him any money, now, and just then I'll up with ten kopecks or so and into his hand with it—so he'll be more reasonable to talk with, like, and the overcoat will then be sort of . . ."

That was the way Akakii Akakiievich reasoned things out to himself, bolstering up his spirits. And, having bided his time till the next Sunday and spied from afar that Petrovich's wife was going off somewhere out of the house, he went straight up to him. Petrovich, sure enough, was squinting his eye hard after the Saturday night before, kept his head bowed down to the floor, and was ever so sleepy; but, for all that, as soon as he learned what was up, it was as though the Devil himself nudged him.

"Can't be done," said he. "You'll have to order a new overcoat."

Akakii Akakiievich thrust a ten-kopeck coin on him right then and there.

"I'm grateful to you, sir; I'll have a little something to

get me strength back and will drink to your health,"
said Petrovich, "but as for your overcoat, please don't
fret about it; it's of no earthly use any more. As for a
new overcoat, I'll tailor a glorious one for you; I'll see
to that."

Just the same, Akakii Akakiievich started babbling
again about fixing the old one, but Petrovich simply
would not listen to him and said: "Yes, I'll tailor a new
one for you without fail; you may rely on that, I'll try
my very best. We might even do it the way it's all the
fashion now—the collar will button with silver catches
under appliqué."

It was then that Akakii Akakiievich perceived that
there was no doing without a new overcoat, and his
spirits sank utterly. Really, now, with what means, with
what money would he make this overcoat? Of course
he could rely, in part, on the coming holiday bonus, but
this money had been apportioned and budgeted ahead
long ago. There was an imperative need of outfitting
himself with new trousers, paying the shoemaker an
old debt for a new pair of vamps to an old pair of boot-
legs, and he had to order from a sempstress three shirts
and two pair of those nethergarments which it is impolite to mention in print; in short, all the money was
bound to be expended entirely, and even if the Director
were so gracious as to decide on giving him five and
forty, or even fifty rubles as a bonus, instead of forty,
why, even then only the veriest trifle would be left over,
which, in the capital sum required for the overcoat,
would be as a drop in a bucket. Even though Akakii
Akakiievich was, of course, aware of Petrovich's maggot
of popping out with the devil knows how inordinate an
asking price, so that even his wife herself could not
restrain herself on occasion from crying out: "What, are
you going out of your mind, fool that you are! There's

times when he won't take on work for anything, but
the Foul One has egged him on to ask a bigger price
than all of him is worth"—even though he knew, of
course, that Petrovich would probably undertake the
work for eighty rubles, nevertheless and notwithstanding where was he to get those eighty rubles? Half of
that sum might, perhaps, be found; half of it could have
been found, maybe even a little more—but where was
he going to get the other half?

But first the reader must be informed where the first
half was to come from. Akakii Akakiievich had a custom
of putting away a copper or so from every ruble he
expended, into a little box under lock and key, with
a small opening cut through the lid for dropping money
therein. At the expiration of every half-year he made an
accounting of the entire sum accumulated in coppers
and changed it into small silver. He had kept this up a
long time, and in this manner, during the course of
several years, the accumulated sum turned out to be
more than forty rubles. And so he had half the sum for
the overcoat on hand; but where was he to get the other
half? Where was he to get the other forty rubles? Akakii
Akakiievich mulled the matter over and over and decided that it would be necessary to curtail his ordinary
expenses, for the duration of a year at the very least;
banish the indulgence in tea of evenings; also, of evenings, to do without lighting candles, but, if there
should be need of doing something, to go to his landlady's room and work by her candle; when walking
along the streets he would set his foot as lightly and
carefully as possible on the cobbles and flagstones,
walking almost on tiptoes, and thus avoid wearing out
his soles prematurely; his linen would have to be given
as infrequently as possible to the laundress and, in
order that it might not become too soiled, every time

he came home all of it must be taken off, the wearer having to remain only in his jean bathrobe, a most ancient garment and spared even by time itself.

It was, the truth must be told, most difficult for him in the beginning to get habituated to such limitations, but later it did turn into a matter of habit, somehow, and everything went well; he even became perfectly trained to going hungry of evenings; on the other hand, however, he had spiritual sustenance, always carrying about in his thoughts the eternal idea of the new overcoat. From this time forth it seemed as if his very existence had become somehow fuller, as though he had taken unto himself a wife, as though another person was always present with him, as though he were not alone but as if an amiable feminine helpmate had consented to traverse the path of life side by side with him—and this feminine helpmate was none other than this very same overcoat, with a thick quilting of cotton wool, with a strong lining that would never wear out.

He became more animated, somehow, even firmer of character, like a man who has already defined and set a goal for himself. Doubt, indecision—in a word, all vacillating and indeterminate traits—vanished of themselves from his face and actions. At times a sparkle appeared in his eyes; the boldest and most daring of thoughts actually flashed through his head: Shouldn't he, after all, put marten on the collar? Meditations on this subject almost caused him to make absent-minded blunders. And on one occasion, as he was transcribing a paper, he all but made an error, so that he emitted an almost audible "Ugh," and made the sign of the cross.

During the course of each month he would make at least one call on Petrovich, to discuss the overcoat: Where would it be best to buy the cloth, and of what color, and at what price—and even though somewhat preoccupied he always came home satisfied, thinking that the time would come, at last, when all the necessary things would be bought and the overcoat made.

The matter went even more quickly than he had expected. Contrary to all his anticipations, the Director designated a bonus not of forty or forty-five rubles for Akakii Akakiievich, but all of sixty. Whether he had a premonition that Akakii Akakiievich needed a new overcoat, or whether this had come about of its own self, the fact nevertheless remained: Akakii Akakiievich thus found himself the possessor of an extra twenty rubles. This circumstance hastened the course of things. Some two or three months more of slight starvation—and lo! Akakii Akakiievich had accumulated around eighty rubles. His heart, in general quite calm, began to palpitate. On the very first day possible he set out with Petrovich to the shops. The cloth they bought was very good, and no great wonder, since they had been thinking over its purchase as much as half a year before and hardly a month had gone by without their making a round of the shops to compare prices; but then, Petrovich himself said that there couldn't be better cloth than that. For lining they chose calico, but of such good quality and so closely woven that, to quote Petrovich's words, it was still better than silk and, to look at, even more showy and glossy. Marten they did not buy, for, to be sure, it was expensive, but instead they picked out the best catskin the shop boasted—catskin that could, at a great enough distance, be taken for marten.

Petrovich spent only a fortnight in fussing about with the making of the overcoat, for there was a great deal of stitching to it, and if it hadn't been for that it would have been ready considerably earlier. For his work Petrovich took twelve rubles—he couldn't have taken any less; everything was positively sewn with silk thread, with a small double stitch, and after the stitching Petrovich went over every seam with his own teeth, pressing out various figures with them.

It was on . . . it would be hard to say on precisely what day, but it was, most probably, the most triumphant day in Akakii Akakiievich's life when Petrovich, at last, brought the overcoat. He brought it in the morning, just before Akakii Akakiievich had to set out for his Bureau. Never, at any other time, would the overcoat have come in so handy, because rather hard frosts were already setting in and, apparently, were threatening to become still more severe. Petrovich's entrance with the overcoat was one befitting a good tailor. Such a portentous expression appeared on his face as Akakii Akakiievich had never yet beheld. Petrovich felt to the fullest, it seemed, that he had performed no petty labor and that he had suddenly evinced in himself that abyss which lies between those tailors who merely put in linings and alter and fix garments and those who create new ones.

He extracted the overcoat from the bandanna in which he had brought it. (The bandanna was fresh from the laundress; it was only later on that he thrust it in his pocket for practical use.) Having drawn out the overcoat, he looked at it quite proudly and, holding it in both hands, threw it deftly over the shoulders of Akakii Akakiievich, pulled it and smoothed it down the back with his hand, then draped it on Akakii Akakiievich somewhat loosely. Akakiievich, as a man along in his years, wanted to try it on with his arms through the sleeves. Petrovich helped him on with it: it turned out to be fine, even with his arms through the sleeves. In a word, the overcoat proved to be perfect and had come in the very nick of time. Petrovich did not let slip the opportunity of saying that he had done the work so cheaply only because he lived in a place without a sign, on a side street and, besides, had known Akakii Akaiievich for a long time, but on the Nevski Prospect they would have taken seventy-five rubles from him for the labor alone. Akakii Akakiievich did not feel like arguing the matter with Petrovich and, besides, he had a dread of all the fancy sums with which Petrovich liked to throw dust in people's eyes. He paid the tailor off, thanked him, and walked right out in the new overcoat on his way to the Bureau. Petrovich walked out at his heels and, staying behind on the street, for a long while kept looking after the overcoat from afar, and then deliberately went out of his way so that, after cutting across a crooked lane, he might run out again into the street and have another glance at his overcoat from a different angle—that is, full face.

In the meantime Akakii Akakiievich walked along feeling in the most festive of moods. He was conscious every second of every minute that he had a new overcoat on his shoulders, and several times even smiled slightly because of his inward pleasure. In reality he was a gainer on two points: for one, the overcoat was warm, for the other, it was a fine thing. He did not notice the walk at all and suddenly found himself at the Bureau; in the porter's room he took off his overcoat, looked it all over, and entrusted it to the particular care of the doorman. None knows in what manner everybody in the Bureau suddenly learned that Akakii Akakiievich had a new overcoat, and that the *negligee* was no longer in existence. They all immediately ran out into the vestibule to inspect Akakii Akakiievich's new overcoat. They fell to congratulating him, to saying agreeable things to him, so that at first he could merely smile, and in a short time became actually embarrassed. And when all of them, having besieged him, began telling him that the new overcoat ought to be baptized and that he ought, at the least, to get up an evening party for them, Akakii Akakiievich was utterly at a loss, not knowing what to do with himself, what answers to make, nor how to get out of inviting them. It was only a few minutes later that he began assuring them, quite simple-heartedly, that it wasn't a new overcoat at all, that it was just an ordinary overcoat, that in fact it was an old overcoat. Finally one of the bureaucrats—some sort of an Assistant to a Head of a Department, actually —probably in order to show that he was not at all a proud stick and willing to mingle even with those beneath him, said: "So be it, then; I'm giving a party this evening and ask all of you to have tea with me; today, appropriately enough, happens to be my birthday."

The clerks, naturally, at once thanked the Assistant to a Head of a Department and accepted the invitation with enthusiasm. Akakii Akakiievich attempted to excuse himself at first, but all began saying that it would show disrespect to decline, that it would be simply a shame and a disgrace, and after that there was absolutely no way for him to back out. However, when it was all over, he felt a pleasant glow as he reminded himself that this would give him a chance to take a walk in his new overcoat even in the evening. This whole day was for Akakii Akakiievich something in the nature of the greatest and most triumphant of holidays.

Akakii Akakiievich returned home in the happiest mood, took off the overcoat, and hung it carefully on the wall, once more getting his fill of admiring the cloth and the lining, and then purposely dragged out, for comparison, his former *negligee*, which by now had practically disintegrated. He glanced at it and he himself had to laugh, so great was the difference! And for a long while thereafter, as he ate dinner, he kept on smiling slightly whenever the present state of the *negligee* came to his mind. He dined gayly, and after dinner did not write a single stroke; there were no papers of any kind, for that matter; he just simply played the sybarite a little, lounging on his bed, until it became dark. Then, without putting matters off any longer, he dressed, threw the overcoat over his shoulders, and walked out into the street.

We are, to our regret, unable to say just where the official who had extended the invitation lived; our memory is beginning to play us false—very much so—and everything in Petersburg, no matter what, including all its streets and houses, has become so muddled in our mind that it's quite hard to get anything out therefrom in any sort of decent shape. But wherever it may have been, at least this much is certain: that official lived in the best part of town; consequently a very long way from Akakii Akakiievich's quarters. First of all Akakii Akakiievich had to traverse certain deserted streets with but scant illumination; however, in keeping with his progress toward the official's domicile, the streets became more animated; the pedestrians flitted by more and more often; he began meeting even ladies, handsomely dressed; the men he came upon had beaver collars on their overcoats; more and more rarely did he encounter jehus with latticed wooden sleighs, studded over with gilt nails—on the contrary, he kept coming across first-class drivers in caps of raspberry-hued velvet, their sleighs lacquered and with bearskin robes, while the carriages had decorated seats for the drivers and raced down the roadway, their wheels screeching over the snow.

Akakii Akakiievich eyed all this as a novelty—it was several years by now since he had set foot out of his house in the evening. He stopped with curiosity before the illuminated window of a shop to look at a picture, depicting some handsome woman or other, who was taking off her shoe, thus revealing her whole leg (very far from ill-formed), while behind her back some gentleman or other, sporting side whiskers and a handsome goatee, was poking his head out of the door of an adjoining room. Akakii Akakiievich shook his head and smiled, after which he went on his way. Why had he smiled? Was it because he had encountered something utterly unfamiliar, yet about which, nevertheless, everyone preserves a certain instinct? Or did he think, like so many other petty clerks: "My, the French they are a funny race! No use talking! If there's anything they get a notion of, then, sure enough, there it is!" And yet, perhaps, he did not think even that; after all, there's no way of insinuating one's self into a man's soul, of finding out all that he might be thinking about.

At last he reached the house in which the Assistant to a Head of a Department lived. The Assistant to a Head of a Department lived on a grand footing; there was a lantern on the staircase; his apartment was only one flight up. On entering the foyer of the apartment Akakii Akakiievich beheld row after row of galoshes. In their midst, in the center of the room, stood a samovar, noisy and emitting clouds of steam. The walls were covered with hanging overcoats and capes, among which were even such as had beaver collars or lapels of velvet. On the other side of the wall he could hear much noise and talk, which suddenly became distinct and resounding when the door opened and a flunky came out with a tray full of empty tumblers, a cream pitcher, and a basket of biscuits. It was evident that the bureaucrats had gathered long since and had already had their first glasses of tea.

Akakii Akakiievich, hanging up his overcoat himself,

entered the room and simultaneously all the candles, bureaucrats, tobacco-pipes and card tables flickered before him, and the continuous conversation and the scraping of moving chairs, coming from all sides, struck dully on his ears. He halted quite awkwardly in the center of the room, at a loss and trying to think what he ought to do. But he had already been noticed, was received with much shouting, and everyone immediately went to the foyer and again inspected his overcoat. Akakii Akakiievich, even though he was somewhat embarrassed, still could not but rejoice on seeing them all bestow such praises on his overcoat, since he was a man with an honest heart. Then, of course, they all dropped him and his overcoat and, as is usual, directed their attention to the whist tables.

All this—the din, the talk, and the throng of people —all this was somehow a matter of wonder to Akakii Akakiievich. He simply did not know what to do, how to dispose of his hands, his feet, and his whole body; finally he sat down near the cardplayers, watched their cards, looked now at the face of this man, now of that, and after some time began to feel bored, to yawn—all the more so since his usual bedtime had long since passed. He wanted to say good-by to his host but they wouldn't let him, saying that they absolutely must toast his new acquisition in a goblet of champagne. An hour later supper was served, consisting of mixed salad, cold veal, meat pie, patties from a pastry cook's, and champagne. They forced Akakii Akakiievich to empty two goblets, after which he felt that the room had become ever so much more cheerful. However, he absolutely could not forget that it was already twelve o'clock and that it was long since time for him to go home. So that his host might not somehow get the idea of detaining him, he crept out of the room, managed to find his

overcoat—which, not without regret, he saw lying on
the floor; then, shaking the overcoat and picking every
bit of fluff off it, he threw it over his shoulders and
made his way down the stairs and out of the house.

It was still dusk out in the street. Here and there
small general stores, those round-the-clock clubs for
domestics and all other servants, were still open; other
shops, which were closed, nevertheless showed, by a
long streak of light along the crack either at the outer
edge or the bottom, that they were not yet without
social life and that, probably, the serving wenches and
lads were still winding up their discussions and conversations, thus throwing their masters into utter bewilderment as to their whereabouts. Akakii Akakiievich walked
along in gay spirits; for reasons unknown he even made
a sudden dash after some lady or other, who had passed
by him like a flash of lightning, and every part of whose
body was filled with buoyancy. However, he stopped
right then and there and resumed his former exceedingly
gentle pace, actually wondering himself at the sprightliness that had come upon him from none knows where.

Soon he again was passing stretch after stretch of
those desolate streets which are never too gay even in
the daytime, but are even less so in the evening. Now
they had become still more deserted and lonely; he
came upon glimmering street lamps more and more infrequently—the allotment of oil was now evidently decreasing; there was a succession of wooden houses and
fences, with never another soul about; the snow alone
glittered on the street, and the squat hovels, with their
shutters closed in sleep, showed like depressing dark
blotches. He approached a spot where the street was
cut in two by an unending square, with the houses on
the other side of it barely visible—a square that loomed
ahead like an awesome desert.

Far in the distance, God knows where, a little light flickered in a policeman's sentry box that seemed to stand at the end of the world. Akakii Akakiievich's gay mood somehow diminished considerably at this point. He set foot in the square, not without a premonition of something evil. He looked back and on each side of him —it was as though he were in the midst of a sea. "No, it's better even not to look," he reflected and went on with his eyes shut. And when he did open them to see if the end of the square were near, he suddenly saw standing before him, almost at his very nose, two mustachioed strangers—just what sort of men they were was something he couldn't even make out. A mist arose before his eyes and his heart began to pound.

"Why, that there overcoat is mine!" said one of the men in a thunderous voice, grabbing him by the collar. Akakii Akakiievich was just about to yell "Police!" when the other put a fist right up to his mouth, a fist as big as any government clerk's head, adding: "There, you just let one peep out of you!"

All that Akakii Akakiievich felt was that they had taken the overcoat off him, given him a kick in the back with the knee, and that he had fallen flat on his back in the snow, after which he felt nothing more. In a few minutes he came to and got up on his feet, but there was no longer anybody around. He felt that it was cold out in that open space and that he no longer had the overcoat, and began to yell; but his voice, it seemed, had no intention whatsoever of reaching the other end of the square. Desperate, without ceasing to yell, he started off at a run across the square directly toward the sentry box near which the policeman was standing and, leaning on his halberd, was watching the running man, apparently with curiosity, as if he wished to know why the devil anybody should be running to-

ward him from afar and yelling. Akakii Akakiievich,
having run up to him, began to shout in a stifling voice
that he, the policeman, had been asleep, that he was
not watching and couldn't see that a man was being
robbed. The policeman answered that he hadn't seen
a thing; all he had seen was two men of some sort stop
him in the middle of the square, but he had thought
they were friends of Akakii Akakiievich's, and that instead of cursing him out for nothing he'd better go on
the morrow to the Inspector, and the Inspector would
find out who had taken his overcoat.

Akakii Akakiievich ran home in utter disarray; whatever little hair still lingered at his temples and the nape
of his neck was all disheveled; his side and his breast
and his trousers were all wet with snow. The old
woman, his landlady, hearing the dreadful racket at the
door, hurriedly jumped out of bed and, with only one
shoe on, ran down to open the door, modestly holding the shift at her breast with one hand; but, on opening the door and seeing Akakii Akakiievich in such a
state, she staggered back. When he had told her what
the matter was, however, she wrung her hands and said
that he ought to go directly to the Justice of the Peace;
the District Officer of Police would take him in, would
make promises to him and then lead him about by the
nose; yes, it would be best of all to go straight to the
Justice. Why, she was even acquainted with him, seeing as how Anna, the Finnish woman who had formerly
been her cook, had now gotten a place as a nurse at the
Justice's; that she, the landlady herself, saw the Justice
often when he drove past her house, and also that he
went to church every Sunday, praying, yet at the same
time looking so cheerfully at all the folks, and that consequently, as one could see by all the signs, he was a
kindhearted man. Having heard this solution of his

troubles through to the end, the saddened Akakii Akakiievich shuffled off to his room, and how he passed
the night there may be left to the discernment of him
who can in any degree imagine the situation of another.

Early in the morning he set out for the Justice's, but
was told there that he was sleeping; he came at ten
o'clock, and was told again: "He's sleeping." He came
at eleven; they told him: "Why, His Honor's not at
home." He tried at lunchtime, but the clerks in the
reception room would not let him through to the presence under any circumstances and absolutely had to
know what business he had come on and what had occurred, so that, at last, Akakii Akakiievich for once in
his life wanted to evince firmness of character and said
sharply and categorically that he had to see the Justice
personally, that they dared not keep him out, that he
had come from his own Bureau on a Government matter, and that, now, when he'd lodge a complaint against
them, why, they would see, then. The clerks dared not
say anything in answer to this and one of them went to
call out the Justice of the Peace.

The Justice's reaction to Akakii Akakiievich's story of
how he had been robbed of his overcoat was somehow
exceedingly odd. Instead of turning his attention to the
main point of the matter, he began interrogating Akakii
Akakiievich: Just why had he been coming home at so
late an hour? Had he, perhaps, looked in at, or hadn't
he actually visited, some disorderly house? Akakii Akakiievich became utterly confused and walked out of
the office without himself knowing whether the investigation about the overcoat would be instituted or not.

This whole day he stayed away from his Bureau (the
only time in his life he had done so). On the following
day he put in an appearance, all pale and in his old
negligee, which had become more woebegone than ever.

The recital of the robbery of the overcoat, despite the
fact that there proved to be certain ones among his co-
workers who did not let pass even this opportunity to
make fun of Akakii Akakiievich, nevertheless touched
many. They decided on the spot to make up a collection
for him, but they collected the utmost trifle, inasmuch
as the petty officials had spent a lot even without this,
having subscribed for a portrait of the Director and for
some book or other, at the invitation of the Chief of the
Department, who was a friend of the writer's; and so
the sum proved to be most trifling. One of them, moved
by compassion, decided to aid Akakii Akakiievich with
good advice at least, telling him that he oughtn't to go
to the precinct officer of the police, because, even
though it might come about that the precinct officer,
wishing to merit the approval of his superiors, might lo-
cate the overcoat in some way, the overcoat would in
the end remain with the police, if Akakii Akakiievich
could not present legal proofs that it belonged to him;
but that the best thing of all would be to turn to a *certain important person;* that this important person, after
conferring and corresponding with the proper people
in the proper quarters, could speed things up.

There was no help for it; Akakii Akakiievich summoned up his courage to go to the important person.
Precisely what the important person's post was and
what the work of that post consisted of, has remained
unknown up to now. It is necessary to know that the
certain important person had only recently become an
Important Person, but, up to then, had been an unimportant person. However, his post was not considered an
important one even now in comparison with more important ones. But there will always be found a circle of
people who perceive the importance of that which is unimportant in the eyes of others. However, he tried to

augment his importance by many other means, to wit:
he inaugurated the custom of having the subordinate
clerks meet him while he was still on the staircase when
he arrived at his office; another, of no one coming
directly into his presence, but having everything follow
the most rigorous precedence: a Collegiate Registrar
was to report to the Provincial Secretary, the Provincial
Secretary to a Titular one, or whomever else it was necessary to report to, and only thus was any matter to
come to him. For it is thus in our Holy Russia that
everything is infected with imitativeness; everyone apes
his superior and postures like him. They even say that
a certain Titular Councilor, when they put him at the
helm of some small individual chancellery, immediately
had a separate room for himself partitioned off, dubbing
it the Reception Centre, and had placed at the door
some doormen or other with red collars and gold braid,
who turned the doorknob and opened the door for every
visitor, even though there was hardly room in the Reception Centre to hold even an ordinary desk.

The manners and ways of the important person were
imposing and majestic, but not at all complex. The chief
basis of his system was strictness. "Strictness, strictness,
and—strictness," he was wont to say, and when uttering
the last word he usually looked very significantly into
the face of the person to whom he was speaking, even
though, by the way, there was no reason for all this,
inasmuch as the half-score of clerks constituting the
whole administrative mechanism of his chancellery was
under the proper state of fear and trembling even as it
was: catching sight of him from afar the staff would at
once drop whatever it was doing and wait, at attention,
until the Chief had passed through the room. His ordinary speech with his subordinates reeked of strictness
and consisted almost entirely of three phrases: "How

dare you? Do you know whom you're talking to? Do you realize in whose presence you are?" However, at soul he was a kindly man, treated his friends well, and was obliging; but the rank of General had knocked him completely off his base. Having received a General's rank he had somehow become muddled, had lost his sense of direction, and did not know how to act. If he happened to be with his equals he was still as human as need be, a most decent man, in many respects—even a man not at all foolish; but whenever he happened to be in a group where there were people even one rank below him, why, there was no holding him; he was taciturn, and his situation aroused pity, all the more since he himself felt that he could have passed the time infinitely more pleasantly. In his eyes one could at times see a strong desire to join in some circle and its interesting conversation, but he was stopped by the thought: Wouldn't this be too much unbending on his part, wouldn't it be a familiar action, and wouldn't he lower his importance thereby? And as a consequence of such considerations he remained forever aloof in that invariably taciturn state, only uttering some monosyllabic sounds at rare intervals, and had thus acquired the reputation of a most boring individual.

It was before such an *important person* that our Akakii Akakiievich appeared, and he appeared at a most inauspicious moment, quite inopportune for himself—although, by the bye, most opportune for the important person. The important person was seated in his private office and had gotten into very, very jolly talk with a certain recently arrived old friend and childhood companion whom he had not seen for several years. It was at this point that they announced to the important person that some Bashmachkin or other had come to see him. He asked abruptly: "Who is he?" and was told:

"Some petty clerk or other." "Ah. He can wait; this isn't the right time for him to come," said the important man.

At this point it must be said that the important man had fibbed a little: he had the time; he and his old friend had long since talked over everything and had been long eking out their conversation with protracted silences, merely patting each other lightly on the thigh from time to time and adding, "That's how it is, Ivan Abramovich!" and "That's just how it is, Stepan Varla- amovich!" But for all that he gave orders for the petty clerk to wait a while just the same, in order to show his friend, a man who had been long out of the Civil Service and rusticating in his village, how long petty clerks had to cool their heels in his anteroom.

Finally, having had his fill of talk, yet having had a still greater fill of silences, and after each had smoked a cigar to the end in a quite restful armchair with an adjustable back, he at last appeared to recall the matter and said to his secretary, who had halted in the door- way with some papers for a report, "Why, I think there's a clerk waiting out there. Tell him he may come in."

On beholding the meek appearance of Akakii Akakii- evich and his rather old, skimpy frock coat, he sud- denly turned to him and asked, "What is it you wish?" —in a voice abrupt and firm, which he had purposely rehearsed beforehand in his room at home in solitude and before a mirror, actually a week before he had re- ceived his present post and his rank of General.

Akakii Akakiievich already had plenty of time to ex- perience the requisite awe, was somewhat abashed, and, as best he could, in so far as his poor freedom of tongue would allow him, explained, adding even more *now*'s than he would have at another time, that his over- coat had been perfectly new, and that, now, he had been robbed of it in a perfectly inhuman fashion, and that he was turning to him, now, so that he might interest himself through his . . . now . . . might correspond with the Head of Police or somebody else, and find his overcoat, now. . . . Such conduct, for some unknown reason, appeared familiar to the General.

"What are you up to, my dear sir?" he resumed abruptly. "Don't you know the proper procedure? Where have you come to? Don't you know how matters ought to be conducted? As far as this is concerned, you should have first of all submitted a petition to the Chancellery; it would have gone from there to the head of the proper Division, then would have been transferred to the Secretary, and the Secretary would in due time have brought it to my attention—"

"But, Your Excellency," said Akakii Akakiievich, trying to collect whatever little pinch of presence of mind he had, yet feeling at the same time that he was in a dreadful sweat, "I ventured to trouble you, Your Excellency, because secretaries, now . . . aren't any too much to be relied upon—"

"What? What? What?" said the important person. "Where did you get such a tone from? Where did you get such notions? What sort of rebellious feeling has spread among the young people against the administrators and their superiors?" The important person had, it seems, failed to notice that Akakii Akakiievich would never see fifty again, consequently, even if he could have been called a young man it could be applied only relatively, that is, to someone who was already seventy. "Do you know whom you're saying this to? Do you realize in whose presence you are? Do you realize? Do you realize, I'm asking you!" Here he stamped his foot, bringing his voice to such an overwhelming note that even another than an Akakii Akakiievich would have been frightened. Akakii Akakiievich was simply bereft of his senses, swayed, shook all over, and actually could not stand on his feet. If a couple of doormen had not run up right then and there to support him he would have slumped to the floor; they carried him out in a practically cataleptic state. But the important person, satisfied because the effect had surpassed even anything he had expected, and inebriated by the idea that a word from him could actually deprive a man of his senses, looked out of the corner of his eye to learn how his friend was taking this and noticed, not without satisfaction, that his friend was in a most indeterminate state and was even beginning to experience fear on his own account.

How he went down the stairs, how he came out into the street—that was something Akakii Akakiievich was no longer conscious of. He felt neither his hands nor his feet; never in all his life had he been dragged over such hot coals by a General—and a General outside his Bureau, at that! With his mouth gaping, stumbling off the sidewalk, he breasted the blizzard that was whistling and howling through the streets; the wind, as is its wont in Petersburg, blew upon him from all the four quarters, from every cross lane. In a second it had blown a quinsy down his throat, and he crawled home without the strength to utter a word; he became all swollen and took to his bed. That's how effective a proper hauling over the coals can be at times!

On the next day he was running a high fever. Thanks to the magnanimous all-round help of the Petersburg climate, the disease progressed more rapidly than could have been expected, and when the doctor appeared he, after having felt the patient's pulse, could not strike on anything to do save prescribing hot compresses, and that solely so that the sick man might not be left without the beneficial help of medical science; but, on the whole, he announced on the spot that in another day and a half it would be curtains for Akakii Akakiievich, after which he turned to the landlady and said: "As for you, Mother, don't you be losing any time for nothing; order a pine coffin for him right now, because a coffin of oak will be beyond his means."

Whether Akakii Akakiievich heard the doctor utter these words, so fateful for him, and, even if he did hear them, whether they had a staggering effect on him, whether he felt regrets over his life of hard sledding— about that nothing is known, inasmuch as he was all the time running a temperature and was in delirium. Visions, each one stranger than the one before, appeared before him ceaselessly: now he saw Petrovich and was ordering him to make an overcoat with some sort of traps to catch thieves, whom he ceaselessly imagined to be under his bed, at every minute calling his landlady to pull out from under his blanket one of them who had actually crawled in there; then he would ask why his old *negligee* was hanging in front of him, for he had a new overcoat; then once more he had a hallucination that he was standing before the General, getting a proper raking over the coals, and saying: "Forgive me, Your Excellency!"; then, finally, he actually took to swearing foully, uttering such dreadful words that his old landlady could do nothing but cross herself, having never in her life heard anything of the sort from him, all the more so since these words followed immediately after "Your Excellency!"

After that he spoke utter nonsense, so that there was no understanding anything; all one could perceive was that his incoherent words and thoughts all revolved about that overcoat and nothing else.

Finally poor Akakii Akakiievich gave up the ghost.

Neither his room nor his things were put under seal; in the first place because he had no heirs, and in the second because there was very little left for anybody to inherit, to wit: a bundle of goose quills, a quire of white governmental paper, three pairs of socks, two or three buttons that had come off his trousers, and the *negligee* which the reader is already familiar with. Who fell heir to all this treasure-trove, God knows; I confess that even the narrator of this tale was not much interested in the matter. They bore Akakii Akakiievich off and buried him. And Petersburg was left without Akakii Akakiievich, as if he had never been therein. There vanished and disappeared a being protected by none, endeared to no one, of no interest to anyone, a being that actually had failed to attract to itself the attention of even a naturalist who wouldn't let a chance slip of sticking an ordinary housefly on a pin and of examining it through a microscope; a being that had submissively endured the jests of the whole chancellery and that had gone to its grave without any extraordinary fuss, but before which, nevertheless, even before the very end of its life, there had flitted a radiant visitor in the guise of an overcoat, which had animated for an instant a poor life, and upon which being calamity had come crashing down just as unbearably as it comes crashing down upon the heads of the mighty ones of this earth!

A few days after his death a doorman was sent to his house from the Bureau with an injunction for Akakii Akakiievich to appear immediately; the Chief, now, was asking for him; but the doorman had to return empty-handed, reporting back that "he weren't able to come no more," and, to the question: "Why not?" expressed himself in the words, "Why, just so; he up and died; they buried him four days back." Thus did they learn at the Bureau about the death of Akakii Akakiievich, and the very next day a new pettifogger, considerably taller than Akakii Akakiievich, was already sitting in his place and putting down the letters no longer in such a straight hand, but considerably more on the slant and downhill.

But whoever could imagine that this wouldn't be all about Akakii Akakiievich, that he was fated to live for several noisy days after his death, as though in reward for a life that had gone by utterly unnoticed? Yet that is how things fell out, and our poor history is taking on a fantastic ending.

Rumors suddenly spread through Petersburg that near the Kalinkin Bridge, and much farther out still, a dead man had started haunting of nights, in the guise of a petty government clerk, seeking for some overcoat or other that had been purloined from him and, because of that stolen overcoat, snatching from all and sundry shoulders, without differentiating among the various ranks and titles, all sorts of overcoats: whether they had collars of catskin or beaver, whether they were quilted with cotton wool, whether they were lined with raccoon, with fox, with bear—in a word, every sort of fur and skin that man has ever thought of for covering his own hide. One of the clerks in the Bureau had seen the dead man with his own eyes and had immediately recognized in him Akakii Akakiievich. This had inspired him with such horror, however, that he started running for all his legs were worth and for that reason could not make him out very well but had merely seen the other shake his finger at him from afar. From all sides came an uninterrupted flow of complaints that backs and shoulders—it wouldn't matter so much if they were merely those of Titular Councilors, but even those of Privy Councilors were affected—were exposed to the danger of catching thorough colds, because of this oft-repeated snatching-off of overcoats.

An order was put through to the police to capture the dead man, at any cost, dead or alive, and to punish him in the severest manner as an example to others—and they all but succeeded in this. To be precise, a policeman at a sentry box on a certain block of the Kirushkin Lane had already gotten a perfect grip on the dead man by his coat collar, at the very scene of his malefaction, while attempting to snatch off the frieze overcoat of some retired musician, who in his time had tootled a flute. Seizing the dead man by the collar, the policeman had summoned two of his colleagues by shouting and had entrusted the ghost to them to hold him, the while he himself took just a moment to reach down in his bootleg for his snuffbox, to relieve temporarily a nose that had been frostbitten six times in his life; but the snuff, probably, was of such a nature as even a dead man could not stand. Hardly had the policeman, after stopping his right nostril with a finger, succeeded in drawing half a handful of rapee up his left, than the dead man sneezed so heartily that he completely bespattered the eyes of all the three myrmidons. While they were bringing their fists up to rub their eyes, the dead man vanished without leaving as much as a trace, so that they actually did not know whether he had really been in their hands or not.

From then on the policemen developed such a phobia of dead men that they were afraid to lay hands even on living ones and merely shouted from a distance: "Hey, there, get going!" and the dead government clerk began to do his haunting even beyond the Kalinkin Bridge, inspiring not a little fear in all timid folk.

However, we have dropped entirely a certain *im-*

portant person who, in reality, had been all but the cause of the fantastic trend taken by what is, by the bye, a perfectly true story. First of all, a sense of justice compels us to say that the *certain important person,* soon after the departure of poor Akakii Akakiievich, done to a turn in the raking over the hot coals, had felt something in the nature of compunction. He was no stranger to compassion; many kind impulses found access to his heart, despite the fact that his rank often stood in the way of their revealing themselves. As soon as the visiting friend had left his private office, he actually fell into a brown study over Akakii Akakiievich. And from that time on, almost every day, there appeared before him the pale Akakii Akakiievich, who had not been able to stand up under an administrative hauling over the coals. The thought concerning him disquieted the certain important person to such a degree that, a week later, he even decided to send a clerk to him to find out what the man had wanted, and how he was, and whether it were really possible to help him in some way. And when he was informed that Akakii Akakiievich had died suddenly in a fever he was left actually stunned, hearkening to the reproaches of conscience, and was out of sorts the whole day.

Wishing to distract himself to some extent and to forget the unpleasant impression this news had made upon him, he set out for an evening party given by one of his friends, where he found a suitable social gathering and, what was best of all, all the men there were of almost the same rank, so that he absolutely could not feel constrained in any way. This had an astonishing effect on the state of his spirits. He relaxed, became amiable and pleasant to converse with—in a word, he passed the time very agreeably. At supper he drank off a goblet or two of champagne—a remedy which, as everybody knows, has not at all an ill effect upon one's gaiety. The champagne predisposed him to certain extracurricular considerations; to be precise, he decided not to go home yet but to drop in on a certain lady of his acquaintance, a Caroline Ivanovna—a lady of German extraction, apparently, toward whom his feelings and relations were friendly. It must be pointed out the important person was no longer a young man, that he was a good spouse, a respected paterfamilias. He had two sons, one of whom was already serving in a chancellery, and a pretty daughter of sixteen, with a somewhat humped yet very charming little nose, who came to kiss his hand every day, adding, *"Bonjour,* papa," as she did so. His wife, a woman who still had not lost her freshness and was not even in the least hard to look at, would allow him to kiss her hand first, then, turning her own over, kissed the hand that was holding hers.

Yet the important person, who, by the bye, was perfectly contented with domestic tendernesses, found it respectable to have a lady friend in another part of the city. This lady friend was not in the least fresher or younger than his wife, but such are the enigmas that exist in this world, and to sit in judgment upon them is none of our affair. And so the important person came down the steps, climbed into his sleigh, and told his driver: "To Carolina Ivanovna's!"—while he himself, after muffling up rather luxuriously in his warm overcoat, remained in that pleasant state than which no better could even be thought of for a Russian—that is, when one isn't even thinking of his own volition, but the thoughts in the meanwhile troop into one's head by themselves, each more pleasant than the other, without giving one even the trouble of pursuing them and seeking them. Filled with agreeable feelings, he lightly recalled all the gay episodes of the evening he had spent, all his *mots* that had made the select circle go off into peals of laughter; many of them he even repeated in a low voice and found that they were still just as amusing as before, and for that reason it is not to be wondered at that even he chuckled at them heartily.

Occasionally, however, he became annoyed with the gusty wind which, suddenly escaping from God knows where and no one knows for what reason, simply cut the face, tossing tatters of snow thereat, making the collar of his overcoat belly out like a sail, or suddenly, with unnatural force, throwing it over his head and in this manner giving him ceaseless trouble in extricating himself from it.

Suddenly the important person felt that someone had seized him rather hard by his collar. Turning around, he noticed a man of no great height, in an old, much worn frock coat and, not without horror, recognized in him Akakii Akakiievich. The petty clerk's face was wan as snow and looked utterly like the face of a dead man. But the horror of the important person passed all bounds when he saw that the mouth of the man became twisted and, horribly wafting upon him the odor of the grave, uttered the following speech: "Ah, so there you are, now, at last! At last I have collared you, now! Your overcoat is just the one I need! You didn't put yourself out any about mine, and on top of that hauled me over the coals—so now let me have yours!"

The poor important person almost passed away. No matter how firm of character he was in his chancellery and before his inferiors in general, and although after but one look merely at his manly appearance and his figure everyone said: "My, what character he has!"—in this instance, nevertheless, like quite a number of men who have the appearance of doughty knights, he experienced such terror that, not without reason, he even began to fear an attack of some physical disorder. He even hastened to throw his overcoat off his shoulders himself and cried out to the driver in a voice that was not his own, "Go home—fast as you can!"

The driver, on hearing the voice that the important person used only at critical moments and which he often accompanied by something of a far more physical nature, drew his head in between his shoulders just to be on the safe side, swung his whip, and flew off like an arrow. In just a little over six minutes the important person was already at the entrance to his own house. Pale, frightened out of his wits, and minus his overcoat, he had come home instead of to Caroline Ivanovna's, somehow made his way stumblingly to his room, and spent the night in quite considerable distress, so that the next day, during the morning tea, his daughter told him outright: "You're all pale today, papa." But papa kept silent and said not a word to anybody of what had befallen him, and where he had been, and where he had intended to go.

This adventure made a strong impression on him. He even badgered his subordinates at rarer intervals with his, "How dare you? Do you realize in whose presence you are?"—and even if he did utter these phrases he did not do so before he had first heard through to the end just what was what. But still more remarkable is the fact that from that time forth the apparition of the dead clerk ceased its visitations utterly; evidently the General's overcoat fitted him to a *t;* at least, no cases of overcoats being snatched off anybody were heard of any more, anywhere. However, many energetic and solicitous people simply would not calm down and kept on saying from time to time that the dead government clerk was still haunting the remoter parts of the city.

And, sure enough, one policeman at a sentry box in

Colomna had with his own eyes seen the apparition coming out of a house; but, being by nature somewhat puny, so that on one occasion an ordinary well-grown shoat, darting out of a private yard, had knocked him off his feet, to the profound amusement of the cab drivers who were standing around, from whom he had exacted a copper each for humiliating him so greatly, to buy snuff with—well, being puny, he had not dared to halt him but simply followed him in the dark until such time as the apparition suddenly looked over its shoulder and, halting, asking him: "What are you after?" and shook a fist at him whose like for size was not to be found among the living. The policeman said: "Nothing," and at once turned back. The apparition, however, was considerably taller by now and was sporting enormous mustachios; setting its steps apparently in the direction of the Obuhov Bridge it disappeared, utterly, in the darkness of night.

IVAN SERGHEIEVICH TURGENEV

(1818–1882)

> Great fellows, the Russians, for the telling of a story; the best storytellers are the Russians, and the best amongst them was Turgenev.
>
> —*George Moore*

EDITOR'S NOTE

SPASKOYE-LUTOVINOVO, the family estate of the great writer's mother, was a more fantastic circus than even the one at Mikhailovskoye, the estate of Pushkin's father. And, even as Saltykov and Nekrassov, Turgenev grew up to hate serfdom.

Influenced by his life abroad, while finishing his studies and afterwards, he became a Westernizer (anti-isolationist), for which he was naturally attacked by the hundred-percent professional Slavs. In 1842 he entered government service but, just as Pushkin and Gogol before him, found it but little to his liking and resigned the next year. It was also in 1843 that he took his first serious literary step, with the publication of an anonymous long poem. By 1846 he realized that poetry was not his strong point (he has wistfully and whimsically voiced this realization several times, in *Senilia* and elsewhere) and seriously considered abandoning literature. But the publication in 1847, by Nekrassov, of *Hor and Kalinich,* followed by a succession of similar pieces, proved Turgenev's great talent as a prosateur. These formed that unique work (his best and most significant one), *Hunting Sketches,* published in 1852 (the year of Gogol's death and the appearance of the truncated Part II of *Dead Souls*), and played an exceedingly important and effective part in the emancipation of the "white Negroes." The immediate result, however, of this publication, and, in the same year, of his essay on the death of Gogol, was to win him the recognition which Czarism extended to almost all Russians of talent or genius. Turgenev had to sit a month in the precinct jail and was sentenced to two years of enforced residence on his country estate.

In 1856 he published *Rudin;* in 1858, *A Nest of Gentlefolk;* in 1860, *On the Eve* and in 1862, *Fathers and Sons,* which created a furore, led to a misunderstanding on the part of Young Russia, which he loved so well and thought he knew, and brought about what amounted to a self-imposed exile and embitterment on his part. (See, in *Senilia*, "Thou Shalt Hear the Judgment of a Fool," written sixteen years after the publication of *Fathers and Sons*, and only four years before his death.)

He wrote and published comparatively little after that. *Smoke* appeared in 1867;*Virgin Soil*, his last novel, ten years later and, in 1882, the year of his death, *Senilia: Poems in Prose*, surely the most characteristic, Turgenevian work, the most lovable, and one of his best things. A second cycle of these short, exquisite pieces was discovered and published, in Russian and French, in 1933; but, despite the first cycle's having something very like a cult in Great Britain and over here, this new Turgenev item has not yet been honored by book publication in English.

His last years were literally agonizing. He died at Bougeval, near Paris; autopsy showed cancer of the spine, with three vertebrae destroyed.

At least two of Turgenev's critical articles seem to have been written directly in English; one of his last stories he did in French and had translated into Russian by another hand, although he himself had not deemed it beneath him to render Flaubert's "Herodias" into Russian; another story he dictated on his deathbed in French, German and Italian.

Turgenev is Russia's greatest poet-in-prose. No other can work quite the same gentle, misty magic in Aeolian Russian. Yet for all the velvetiness, the steel is underneath, as in the *Hunting Sketches*, wherein he attacks serfdom with a deceptive objectivity. How effective Turgenev's disguise of mere hunting adventures was can be judged by the fact that the cumulative anti-serfdom tone and the full impact of these superb sketches were apparently not perceived by officialdom until their publication in collected form.

Those who do not know Russian, or French, or German, or Italian will fare best if they hunt down the individual English versions of the '80's, made not directly from the Russian but from French translations. This advice is not as wild as it may sound, for Turgenev himself kept an eye on a number of the French (and perhaps even the German) translations. The Italian *Slavia* versions are, the Editor is assured on good authority, excellent. The writer has in his possession a heavily insured *Senilia*, Englished from a Danish adaptation of a German version from a French translation of the Russian— and even that evinces more love for the author and respect for his intent, as well as greater probity, than English translations.

Specters

A FANTASY

IVAN SERGHEIEVICH TURGENEV

One moment only—and gone the magic tale,
And with the commonplace again the soul is teeming.
                                                  A. Fet

I HAD been unable to fall asleep for a long time and had kept incessantly tossing from side to side. "The devil take all this table-turning foolishness!" I reflected. "All it does is upset your nerves." At last I felt drowsiness coming over me.

Suddenly I thought I heard a sound, as if a harp string had twanged faintly and plaintively in the room.

I raised my head. The moon hung low in the heavens, and was peering right into my eyes. Its glow, white as chalk, fell upon the floor. The strange twang was plainly repeated.

I leaned upon my elbow, a slight fear plucking at my heart. A minute passed; then another. Somewhere far off a rooster crowed; still farther off another answered it. I let my head fall back on the pillow. "There, that's the state you can get into," I again reflected. "First thing you know your ears will start ringing."

A little later I fell asleep—or so it seemed to me. And I had an extraordinary dream. I thought I was lying in my bedroom, on my bed—and I was not asleep; I could not even close my eyes. There, that twang came again. I turned around. The moonglow on the floor began, ever so gently, to rise; it straightened out, became slightly rounded at the top. A woman in white, transparent as mist, stood motionless before me.

"Who are you?" I asked with an effort.

The answering voice sounded like the rustle of leaves:

"It is I—I—I. . . . I have come for you—"

"For me? But who are you?"

"Come tomorrow night to the edge of the forest, where the old oak stands. I shall be there."

I wanted to peer more closely into the features of the mysterious woman—and suddenly shuddered involuntarily. A wave of cold air was blowing upon me. And then I was no longer lying down but sitting up in bed —and at the spot where the specter had apparently been standing the moonlight whitened the floor in a long streak.

The day passed somehow. I remember I attempted to read, to work—but could not get on with anything. Night came. My heart was pounding, as though anticipating something. I lay down and turned my face to the wall.

"Why didn't you come?" a clear whisper sounded through the room.

I quickly looked over my shoulder.

It was she again. Again that mysterious specter. Unmoving eyes in an unmoving face—and their gaze was filled with pensiveness.

"Come!" I heard the whisper again.

"I shall," I answered with involuntary terror. The specter swayed gently forward, became all blurred, lightly swirling, like smoke—and the moon again rested whitely upon the smooth floor.

I passed the day restlessly. At supper I drank off almost a full bottle of wine; I went out on the veranda but left it soon and threw myself on my bed. My blood was surging heavily.

Again that sound. . . . I shuddered, but did not turn around to look. Suddenly I felt someone clasp me tightly from behind, at the same time babbling in my very ear: "Come, come, come—"

Startled and trembling, I got out in a moan: "I shall!" —and sat up straight.

The woman was bending over as she stood close to the head of my bed. She smiled faintly and vanished. I, however, managed to get a good look at her face. It seemed to me that I had seen her before. But when? Where?

I rose late and all day long roamed through the fields; several times I walked up to the old oak at the edge of the forest and looked about me closely.

Before evening I sat down at the open window in my study. The old woman who was my housekeeper placed a cup of tea before me, but I left it untouched. I was constantly wondering, and asking myself if I were not going out of my mind. The sun had just set, and it was not the sky alone that mantled red: all the air had suddenly filled with some almost unnatural purple tint; the leaves and grasses, looking as if they had been freshly lacquered, did not stir; in their petrified immobility, in the sharp vividness of their outlines, in this coupling of overpowering glitter and dead silence there was something strange, enigmatic. A rather large bird suddenly, without the least noise, flew up and perched on the very edge of my windowsill. I looked at it—and it looked at me askance with its round, dark eye.

"Haven't you, by some chance, been sent to remind me?" I mused.

The bird at once flipped its soft wings and flew off, as noiselessly as it had come. For a long while yet did I sit by the window, but I no longer gave myself up to perplexed conjecturing. It was as though I had gotten into an enchanted circle—and an insuperable yet gentle force was drawing me along, even as, long before coming to a waterfall, the rushing of the current draws along a boat. Finally I pulled myself together. The purple tinge in the air had long since vanished, its pigments had darkened, and the enchanted stillness had ended. A fluttering breeze sprang up; the moon was emerging ever more clearly against a sky that was now turning to indigo, and shortly, under its chill rays, the leaves of the trees were glinting with the sheen of silver and black. My old housekeeper entered the study carrying a lit candle, but a puff of air blew upon it through the window and its flame went out. I could not keep myself back any longer; getting up hastily I drew a cap low over my forehead and set out for the edge of the forest, for the old oak.

Lightning had struck this oak many years ago; its crest had split in two and withered, yet there was enough life left in the tree for several centuries more. As I was drawing near it a small cloud scudded toward the moon and hid it; it was very dark under the spreading branches of the oak. At first I did not notice anything out of the way; but then I happened to look to one side —and my heart simply sank: a white figure was standing motionlessly near a large bush between the oak and the forest. My hair began to stir slightly, as if it were about to stand up on end, but I pulled myself together and walked toward the forest.

Yes, it was she—my nocturnal visitant. As I came near her the moon began to shine anew. She seemed to be all woven out of semi-transparent, milky mist; I could see, through her face, a twig gently swaying in the wind; her hair alone, and her eyes, were ever so faintly dark, while upon one of the fingers of her clasped hands gleamed a narrow ring of white gold. I stopped before her and was about to speak, but my voice died away in my breast, even though by now I really felt no fear. Her eyes turned upon me: their gaze expressed neither sorrow nor joy, but a certain lifeless attentiveness. I waited for her to utter some word, but she remained motionless and speechless, still regarding me with her lifelessly fixed gaze. I again fell into an eldritch mood.

"I have come!" I said at last, loudly and with an effort. My voice had a stifled and odd sound.

"I love you," came her whisper.

"You love me?" I repeated in astonishment.

"Give yourself to me," the soughing came anew in answer.

"Give myself to you? But you are a specter—you haven't even a body." A strange animation took possession of me. "What are you—smoke, air, vapor? Give myself to you! Answer me first—who are you? Have you ever lived upon earth? Whence have you come?"

"Give yourself to me. I will do you no harm. Say but two words: 'Take me.'"

I looked at her. "What is she saying?" I mused. "What does all this mean? And how would she take me? Or should I try it?"

"Very well, then," I uttered aloud, and with unexpected loudness, as though someone had nudged me from behind. "Take me!"

Hardly had I said these words when the mysterious figure, with an inward laughter which made her face quiver for an instant, swayed forward, with arms outflung. I was about to leap away, but I was already in her power. She embraced me; my body rose half a yard above the ground—and we both soared off, smoothly and not too fast, over the unstirring wet grass.

At first my head swam, and I involuntarily closed my eyes. A moment or two later I opened them anew. We were soaring along as before, but the forest was no longer to be seen: a plain spread out below us, with dark blotches strewn over it. I became convinced, to my horror, that we had ascended to a frightful height.

"I am lost; I am in the power of Satan!" the thought flashed through me like lightning. Up to that instant the idea of possession by the Foul One, of the possibility of perdition, had not entered my head. We were still rushing along and, it seemed, going higher and higher.

"Where are you carrying me?" I got out in a moan at last.

"Wherever you like," answered my companion. She

was clinging to me, all of her; her face was almost touching mine. However, I hardly felt her touch.

"Let me down to the ground; I feel bad at this height."

"Very well; all you have to do is close your eyes and hold your breath."

I obeyed—and at once felt myself falling, like a hurled stone. The wind whistled through my hair. When I came to, we were again soaring smoothly over the very ground, so that the tops of the tallest grass-blades clung to us.

"Put me on my feet," I began. "What pleasure is there in flying? I am no bird!"

"I thought you would find it pleasant. We have no other occupation."

" 'We?' But who are all of you?"

There was no answer.

"You dare not tell me that?"

A plaintive sound, like that which had awakened me that first night, quavered in my ears. In the meanwhile we kept on moving at a barely perceptible rate through the damp night air.

"Do let me go!" I spoke up. My companion gently leaned over, away from me—and I found myself on my feet. She stopped before me and clasped her hands anew. I calmed down and looked her in the face: as hitherto, it bore an expression of submissive sorrow.

"Where are we?" I asked. I could not recognize the vicinity.

"Far from your home—but you can be there in an instant."

"In what way? By entrusting myself to you again?"

"I have done you no harm, nor will. You and I will fly about until the dawn-glow—and that is all. I can carry you off to any place you may think of—to all the ends of the earth. Give yourself to me! Say once more: 'Take me!' "

"Well then—take me!"

Again she drew close to me; my feet again left the ground—and we flew off.

"Where to?" she asked me.

"Straight ahead—straight ahead, all the time."

"But the forest is in our way."

"Rise over the forest—but as gently as you can."

We whirled upward, like a snipe that had collided with a birch—and again soared off in a straight line. Treetops, instead of grassblades, were now flitting by under our feet. It was wondrously odd to see the forest from above, to see its bristling back in the light of the moon. It looked like some enormous beast that had fallen asleep, and it sped us on our way with a sweeping, ceaseless rustling that sounded like indistinct, low growling. Here and there we would come upon a small glade, a serrated strip of shadow lying in a beautiful black silhouette to one side of it. Now and then we heard the piteous squeal of a rabbit below; up above an owl hooted, and its hoot also sounded piteously; there was a smell of mushrooms in the air, and of buds, of lovage; the moonlight was fairly flooding the earth in all directions, chillily and austerely; heat-lightnings flashed over our very heads.

Now the forest, too, had been left behind; a streak of mist stretched across the open field: that streak was a flowing river. We sped along one of its banks, over bushes weighed down and motionless from the night-damp. The river waves now shone with an indigo sheen, now rolled on, darkly, as if they were wrathy. In places thin vapor hovered in an odd fashion over the waves, and the cups of the water-lilies virginally and sumptuously flaunted the whiteness of their fully opened petals, as though aware that it was impossible to get at them. The idea came to me of plucking one of them— and lo, I found myself over the smooth surface of the water. The damp struck me in the face inimically as soon as I had severed the tough stalk of a large flower.

We began to flit from bank to bank, like sandpipers, whom we kept constantly awaking and whom we pursued. More than once we happened to fly full tilt against a small family of wild ducks, disposed in a small circle in some small clear space among clumps of reeds—but the birds would not stir, save that one of them might hastily take its head from under its wing, look about it, and fussily thrust its beak again into the downy feathers, while some other might quack faintly, at which a slight tremor would run through all its body. We frightened one heron: it rose up out of some willow bushes, its legs dangling, and beating its wings with a clumsy effort; that was when it struck me as actually looking like a German. Not a fish splashed anywhere; the fish, too, were asleep.

I was beginning to grow accustomed to the sensation of flight, and even found pleasure therein: everyone who has ever happened to fly in a dream will understand me. I began to scrutinize with greater attentiveness the strange being through whose favor such improbable events were befalling me.

This woman's face was small, not at all a Russian one. Grayish-whitish, semi-transparent, with barely defined shadows, it reminded one of the figures upon an alabaster vase lighted from within—and again it seemed familiar to me.

"May I speak with you?"

"You may."

"I see a ring on your finger; you have, therefore, lived upon earth once—you were married?"

I paused. There was no response.

"What is your name—or, at any rate, what was it?"

"Call me Ellis."

"Ellis—that's an English name. Are you an English-woman? Did you know me before?"

"No, I never did."

"Why, then, did you appear to me and not to some other?"

"I love you."

"And are you content?"

"Yes; you and I are soaring, circling through the pure air—"

"Ellis!" said I suddenly. "Are you, perchance, a soul that has transgressed, that is condemned?"

My companion bowed her head:

"I do not understand you," said she in a whisper.

"I adjure you in the name of God—" I began.

"What are you saying?" she uttered uncomprehendingly. "I do not understand." It seemed to me that the arm that lay about my waist like a chill girdle stirred gently. "Be not afraid," Ellis uttered. "Be not afraid, my dearest one!" She turned her face and drew it near to mine. I felt some strange sensation upon my lips, as if of the touch of a slender and pliant sting. . . . Sluggish leeches take hold in that fashion.

I glanced downward. We had again had time to ascend to a rather considerable height. We were flying over some provincial town unfamiliar to me, situated on the slope of a spreading knoll. Churches towered amid the dark mass of wooden houses, of orchards; a long bridge showed darkly at the bend of a river; everything was in silence, weighed down by slumber. The very cupolas and crosses, it seemed, gleamed with a mute gleaming; the tall poles of water wells stuck up mutely near the rounded caps of willows; the whitish, paved highroad was plunging mutely like a slim arrow in at one end of the town and emerging mutely at the other end into the murky spaciousness of monotonous fields.

"What town is that?" I asked.

"——sov."

"In the province of——?"

"Yes."

"I surely am at a great distance from home!"

"Distance does not exist for us."

"Really?" A sudden venturesomeness flared up within me. "In that case carry me to South America!"

"Not to America. It is day there now."

"And you and I are birds of the night. Well, bring me to some place where you can go—only as far off as possible."

"Close your eyes and hold your breath," answered Ellis, and we darted off with the speed of a whirlwind. The air rushed into my ears with a stunning din.

We stopped, but the noise did not cease. On the contrary, it had turned into some awesome roar, into the rumbling of thunder.

"You may open your eyes now," said Ellis.

I obeyed. My God, where was I?

Heavy, smoky clouds overhead; they huddled, they ran, like a herd of malevolent monsters—and there, below, was another monster: an infuriated—yes, an infuriated—sea. White foam flickered convulsively and seethed upon it in hillocks, and the sea, tossing its shaggy billows, pounded with a harsh rumbling against an enormous cliff as black as pitch. The howling of the storm, the icy breath of the heaving abyss, the heavy surge of the incoming tide, in which at times one imagined something like screams, like far off cannonading, like the ringing of church bells, the ear-splitting screech and grinding of pebbles along the shore, the sudden cry of an unseen gull, the shaky skeleton of a wrecked ship against the turbid horizon—all these told of death, death everywhere, death and horror. My head began to reel, and I shut my eyes again, on the verge of swooning.

"What is this? Where are we?"

"On the south shore of the Isle of Wight, before the Blackgang Chine, against which so many ships shatter," said Ellis, this time with especial distinctness and, as it seemed to me, not without evil joy.

"Carry me away—away from here . . . home! Home!"

I shrank into myself, hiding my face in my hands. I felt that we were speeding still more rapidly than before; the wind no longer howled, no longer whistled—it whined through my hair, through my clothing. I could not catch my breath.

"*Do* stand up on your feet!" I heard the voice of Ellis.

I strained to get possession of myself, of my consciousness. I felt the ground underfoot, but could not hear anything, as though everything about me were in a swoon—save that the blood was pounding unevenly at my temples, and my head still swam, with an inward faint ringing. I straightened up and opened my eyes.

We were on the dam of my mill-pond. Straight before me, through the pointed leaves of the willows, I could see its broad, smooth expanse, with here and there filaments of downy mist clinging to it. To the right was the dull glint of a field of rye; to the left, in the garden, the trees rose up, elongated, motionless; they seemed damp: morning had already breathed upon them. Two or three small, slanting clouds, like streamers of smoke, were straggling across the clear gray sky; they looked yellowish—the first faint reflection of the dawn-glow was falling upon them, God knows whence: the eye still could not discern upon the now wan horizon the spot where that glow would begin. The stars were vanishing; nothing stirred as yet, although all things were awakening amid the bewitched stillness of the early half-light.

"Morning! Morning is here!" Ellis cried out at my very ear. "Farewell. Until tomorrow!"

I turned around. Lightly detaching herself from the earth, she was floating past me—and suddenly raised both her hands; her shoulders glowed instantaneously with a fleshy, warm color; living sparks quivered in the dark eyes; a sly smile of secret languor stirred her blushing lips. A woman of splendid beauty suddenly arose before me. But, as if falling into a swoon, she immediately fell backward, and dissolved like vapor.

I remained motionless.

When I came to and looked about me, it seemed to me that the flesh-tinted, palely roseate hue that had flitted across the figure of my specter still had not vanished and, diffused through the air, was pouring upon me from all around. It was the dawn flaring up.

I suddenly felt extreme fatigue and set out for home. As I was going past the poultry yard I heard the first morning babble of the goslings (there is no bird that awakens before them); along the roof, at the end of every beam, perched a jackdaw, and all of them were fussily and silently preening themselves, clearly drawn against the milky sky. At rare intervals they would all take wing and, after a short flight, again perch next to one another, without giving their call. From the near-by forest came floating, twice, the vigorous snuffling of a blackcock that had just flown down into the dewy grass thick with berries.

With a light shiver running through my body, I got to my bed and shortly fell into a dead sleep.

The next night, as I began to approach the old oak, Ellis darted forth to meet me as if I were an old friend. I did not fear her, as I had done yesterday; I was almost glad to see her, nor did I even try to understand what was happening to me: all I wanted was to fly a while, as far as possible, over interesting places.

Ellis' arm again entwined me—and again we sped away.

"Let us go to Italy," I whispered in her ear.

"Wherever you will, my dearest one," she answered solemnly and gently, and gently and solemnly turned her face to me. It struck me as less transparent than it had been the night before, and more muliebrile and imposing; it reminded me of that splendidly beautiful being that had flitted before me in the morning glow before our parting.

"This night is a great night," Ellis continued. "It comes but rarely: when seven times thirteen—" here I failed to catch several words. "Now one can see that which is kept hidden at other times."

"Ellis," I implored her, "come, who are you? Tell me, at last!"

She silently raised her slender, white hand.

In the dark sky, there where her finger pointed, amid the lesser stars, a comet shone in a reddish streak.

"How am I to understand that?" I began. "Or, even as that comet wanders between the planets and the sun, are you wandering between mortals and—what?"

But the hand of Ellis unexpectedly fell over my eyes.

It was as if the white mist of a damp valley had blown upon me.

"To Italy! To Italy!" came her whisper. "This night is a great night!"

The mist before my eyes dissipated, and I saw an endless plain below me. But through the mere touch of the warm and soft air against my cheeks I could grasp that I was not in Russia; and besides, that plain bore no resemblance to our Russian plains. This was an enormous, dim expanse, a grassless wasteland; here and there, along its entire stretch, stagnant waters glittered like mirror-splinters; in the distance one could catch vague glimpses of an inaudible, immobile sea. Great stars shone in the interstices of big, beautiful clouds; a thousand-voiced, never silenced and yet low trill rose from everywhere—and wondrous was this piercing and drowsy hum, this nocturnal voice of the wilderness.

"The Pontine Marshes," Ellis uttered. "Do you hear the frogs? Do you feel the smell of sulphur?"

"The Pontine Marshes—" I repeated, and a sensation of grandiose despondence came over me. "But why have you brought me hither, into this sad, godforsaken region? Let us fly to Rome, rather."

"Rome is near," answered Ellis. "Prepare yourself!"

We descended and sped along an ancient Latin road. A water buffalo slowly raised out of clinging slime his shaggy, monstrous head with short tufts of bristles between back-slanting horns. He rolled the whites of his senselessly malevolent eyes askance and snorted hard through his dripping nostrils, as if he had scented us.

"Rome—Rome is near," Ellis was whispering. "Look —look ahead."

I raised my eyes.

What was that, darkling against the rim of the night

sky? The high arches of an enormous bridge? What
river did it span? Why were there gaps in it here and
there? No, this was no bridge; it was an ancient aqueduct. All around us was the sacred soil of the Campagna,
while there, in the distance, were the Alban Hills, and
their summits, and the hoary back of the old aqueduct,
gleamed faintly in the rays of the newly risen moon.

We suddenly spiraled upward and hovered in the
air above an isolated ruin. None could have said what
it had once been—mausoleum, palace, tower. Black ivy
entwined it with all of that growth's lethal force, while
below, a half-fallen arch gaped like a maw. An oppressive odor like that of a cellar was wafted in my face
from this pile of small, closely set stones, from which
the granite facing of the wall had long since fallen.

"This is the spot," said Ellis, and raised her hand.
"This is the spot! Utter aloud, thrice in succession, the
name of some great Roman."

"And what will happen?"

"You will see."

I pondered.

"Divus Gaius Julius Caesar!" I called out sharply.
"Divus Gaius Julius Caesar!" I repeated, dwelling on
each syllable. *"Caesar!"*

The last reverberations of my voice had not yet had
time to die away when I thought I heard . . . it is
hard for me to say exactly what. At first I thought I
heard an indistinct outburst of sounding trumpets and
of plaudits, barely caught by the ear yet endlessly repeated. It sounded as if somewhere, fearfully far off, at
some bottomless depth, a countless horde had suddenly
begun to stir, and was rising up—rising up, turbulent
and calling to one another barely audibly, as if in slumber, as if in the crushing slumber of many ages. Then
the air streamed and darkened over the ruin. I began

to imagine I was seeing shadows, myriads of shadows, millions of outlines, now rounded like helmets, now extended like spears; the rays of the moon shattered into momentary bluish sparks against these spears and helmets—and all this host, this horde, was coming nearer and nearer, growing, swaying at an increasing tempo. An indescribable tension, a tension that would suffice to lift the whole world, could be sensed about it, yet not a single visage stood out clearly. And suddenly it seemed to me that a tremor ran through all things around me, as though some enormous waves had ebbed and parted. *"Caesar, Caesar venit!* Caesar is coming!" rose the murmur of voices, as of forest trees under the sudden onslaught of a storm. The muffled thunderclap rumbled by, and a head—pale, austere, in a wreath of laurel, with eyelids lowered—the head of the Emperor began to emerge slowly out of the ruin. . . .

There are no words in the speech of man to express the terror that gripped my heart. It seemed to me that, were this head to open its eyes, to unseal its lips, I would die on the instant.

"Ellis!" I got out in a moan. "I do not want this, I cannot endure it; I have no need of Rome—of harsh, awesome Rome. Away, away from here!"

"Faint-heart!" she whispered—and we sped away. I still had time to hear behind me the clangorous, by now thunderous, cry of the legions. Then all grew dark.

"Look about you," said Ellis, "and compose yourself."

I obeyed: and, I remember, my first impression was delectable to such a degree that I could merely sigh. Something smokily cerulean, silvery soft that was either light or mist was beating down upon me from all sides. At first I distinguished nothing—this azure glitter

blinded me; but then the outlines of splendidly beautiful mountains, of forests, began to emerge; a lake
spread out under me, with stars quivering in its depths,
with the caressing murmur of waves plashing shore-
ward. The fragrance of oranges billowed upon me and,
together with it, and also as if in a billow, there were
borne to me the powerful, clear sounds of a young
feminine voice. This fragrance, these sounds fairly drew
me downward, and I began to descend—to descend
toward a magnificent marble palace, hospitably white
in the midst of a cypress grove. The sounds were flowing out of its wide open windows; the waves of the
lake, strewn with the pollen of flowers, plashed against
its walls and, directly facing it, all clad in the dark
greenery of orange trees and laurels, all inundated in a
radiant vapor, with statues, stately pillars, and porticoes
of temples scattered all over it, there rose from the
bosom of the waters a steep, round island.

"Isola Bella!" spake Ellis. "Lago Maggiore—"

All I could utter was a gasp of admiration, and I kept
on descending. The feminine voice sounded ever more
loudly, ever more clearly within the palace; I was
drawn to it irresistibly. I wanted to look upon the face
of the fair singer, making such a night resound with
such strains. We paused before one of the windows.

In the center of a chamber in the Pompeiian style,
and bearing greater resemblance to a pagan temple
rather than the newest of newly built palatial rooms,
surrounded by Greek sculptures, Etruscan vases, rare
plants, precious weaves, illuminated from above by the
soft beams of two lamps enclosed in crystal globes, a
young woman was seated at a pianoforte. With her
head slightly tilted back and her eyes half closed she
was singing an Italian aria; she was singing and smiling
and, at the same time, her features expressed dignity,

even austerity: a sign of full enjoyment. She was smiling
—and the Faun of Praxiteles, as languid, as young as
she, pampered, voluptuous, seemed to be smiling to her
from around a corner, from behind the branches of an
oleander, through the tenuous smoke rising from a
bronze thurible upon an antique tripod. The beauty
was alone. Enchanted by the sounds, the splendor, glitter and fragrance of the night, moved to the depths of
my heart by the sight of this youthful, radiant happiness, I forgot utterly about my companion, forgot in
what a strange manner I had come to be a witness to
such a life, so remote, so alien to me, and I was just
about to set foot on the window ledge, about to
speak. . . .

All my body shuddered from a powerful jolt, as
though I had touched a Leyden jar. I looked over my
shoulder. Ellis' face (for all its transparency) was somber and sinister; malice was dully glowing in her eyes,
which had instantly opened wide.

"Away!" she whispered in a rage—and again the
whirlwind, and murk, and vertigo. Only this time it was
not the shouting of the legions but the voice of the fair
singer, broken off on a high note, which lingered in my
ears.

We stopped. A high note, the same note, still rang
on, and would not cease from its ringing, although I
now sensed an altogether different air, a different odor.
An invigorating freshness was wafted upon me, as if
from some great river, and there was an odor of hay,
of smoke, of hemp. The long-drawn note was followed
by another, then by a third, but with such an indubita-
ble shading, with such a familiar, native trill, that I at
once said to myself: "This is a Russian man, singing a
Russian song"—and that same instant all my surroundings became clear to me.

We were above a flat river-bank. On the left, losing themselves in infinity, stretched mown meadows, with enormous hay-ricks standing all over them; to the right, to the same infinity, receded the level expanse of a great river of many waters. Not far from the bank great, dark barges were ever so gently rocking at anchor, slightly dipping the tips of their masts, like so many index fingers. From one of these barges there came floating up to me the sound of a voice in the full tide of song; burning upon this barge was a small fire, its elongated red reflection quivering and swaying on the water. Here and there, both upon the river and in the fields (the eye could not grasp whether near or far) other small fires were twinkling, now seeming to pucker up like eyes, then suddenly moving forward like large, rayey dots; countless grasshoppers were chirking without cease, yielding in no way to the frogs of the Pontine Marshes, and under the cloudless but low-hanging dark sky unknown birds called at infrequent intervals.

"Are we in Russia?" I asked Ellis.

"This is the Volga," answered she.

We sped off along the bank.

"Why did you tear me away from there, from that beautiful region?" I began. "Were you envious, by any chance? Or is it possible that jealousy has awakened within you?"

Ellis' lips twitched ever so faintly, and menace again flashed in her eyes. But her face immediately became stony again.

"I want to go home," said I.

"Wait, wait!" answered Ellis. "This night is a great night. It will not recur soon. You may be an eyewitness of . . . wait!"

And we darted across the Volga in an oblique direction over the very water, flying low and fitfully, as swal-

lows fly before a storm. The broad waves gurgled
heavily below us; a cutting river wind beat upon us
with its chill, powerful wing. The high right bank soon
began to rear before us in the half-murk. Steep hills
with big clefts appeared; we drew near to them.

"Call out: *Saryn na kichku!*" [1] Ellis whispered to me.

I recalled the terror I had experienced at the apparition of the Roman phantoms; I felt fatigue and a
certain strange depression, just as if the heart within me
were melting away; I did not want to utter the fateful
words; I knew beforehand that in answer to them there
would appear something monstrous, as in the Wolf
Dale of *Der Freischutz*—but my lips opened against
my will and, also against my will, I cried out in a faint,
strained voice: "*Saryn na kichku!*"

At first all remained silent, even as had been the case
when we were hovering over the Roman ruin; but suddenly, near my very ear, there resounded the raucous
laughter of barge-haulers—and with a heavy plash
something struck the water and, after a moan, began to
gurgle there. I looked about me: not a soul was to be
seen anywhere, but an echo rebounded from the bank,
and instantaneously and from all quarters there arose
a deafening clamor. What couldn't one hear in that
chaos of sounds! Cries and squeals, furious curses and
laughter—laughter above all!—the plashing of oars and
the blows of axes; a splitting sound, as of doors and
chests being broken open; the creaking of rigging and
of wheels, and the galloping of horses; the tocsin peal-
ing and the clangor of chains; the rumbling and roar of
a conflagration; drunken songs and grating, quick
speech; inconsolable weeping; supplication piteous and

---

[1] Every soul aboard—face down on the foredeck!"—the traditional
warning of the Volga pirates when boarding an attacked vessel.
—Trans.-Ed.

despairing—and imperious outcries; death-rattle and shrill, audacious whistling; whooping, and the stamping of a wild dance. . . . "Kill! Hang! Drown! Slash away! Fine, fine! That's it! No quarter!" One could hear these shouts plainly, could hear even the gasping breath of winded men—and yet, all around, as far as the eye could reach, nothing showed, nothing changed; the river rolled by, mysteriously, almost sullenly; the bank itself seemed more deserted and wilder than ever, and that was all.

I turned to speak to Ellis, but she laid a finger upon her lips.

"Stepan Timotheich! Stepan Timotheich is coming!" the noise arose all around us. "Our father, our hetman, our provider is coming!" [1]

As before, I saw nothing, but suddenly it appeared to me as if some enormous body were coming straight at me.

"Frolka, where are you, you hound!" thundered a frightful voice. "Put the place to the torch from every quarter—and let 'em have the edge of the axe, the lily-handed drones!"

The heat of a blaze close by struck me in a blast—and at the same instant something warm, that felt just like blood, spattered my face and hands. A thunder-clap of savage laughter shook the air around me.

---

[1] Stepan Timotheievich Razin was the celebrated Stenka Razin, Don Cossack, Russian Robin Hood—as well as the Russian John Brown, the Russian Henry Morgan, and the Russian William Tell. The Razin Uprising had great historical significance as a protest against the hardships of the peasants and the persecutions of schismatics; it endangered even Moscow, and was quelled only after fearful conflagrations and wholesale executions of over 100,000. Razin began his career as a brigand in 1667; among his exploits were the destruction of the Persian navy and the capture (or sacking) of Tsaritsin, Astrakhan, Saratov, Samara. Defeated in 1670; drawn on the wheel, in Moscow, in 1671. Frolka, his younger brother, was his Little John. —Trans.-Ed.

I lost consciousness—and when I came to Ellis and I were gently gliding along the familiar outskirt of my forest, right toward the old oak.

"Do you see that path?" Ellis asked me. "There, where the moon shines dully, and two small birches lean toward each other? Would you care to go there?"

But I felt myself so broken and exhausted that all I could say in answer was:

"Home . . . home—"

"You are home," Ellis answered.

I actually was standing before the very door of my house—alone. Ellis had vanished. A yard-dog walked up to me, looked me over suspiciously—and fled from me, howling.

I found it difficult to drag myself to bed, and fell asleep without undressing.

All that morning my head ached, and I could barely move my feet, but I paid no attention to my bodily indisposition; remorse was gnawing at me, vexation was stifling me. I was extremely dissatisfied with myself. "'Faint-heart!'" I kept constantly repeating. "Yes, Ellis is right. What did I become frightened at? How could one have missed such an opportunity? I might have beheld Caesar himself—and I swooned away from fear, I squeaked, I turned away, as a child would at the sight of birchrods. When it comes to Razin—well, that's another matter. As one of the gentry and a landowner. . . . However, in this instance also: just what did I become frightened at? 'Faint-heart! Faint-heart!' But come, am I not seeing all this in a dream?" I finally asked myself. I summoned my housekeeper.

"Martha, at what hour did I go to bed last night—do you remember?"

"Why, who knows what you do, my provider? Late,

I guess. You left the house as dusk was coming on; and when you were stomping around in the bedroom with your big heels it was 'way past midnight. Right close to morning it was—yes. And two nights ago it was the same way. Some worriment must have gotten hold of you, I figure."

"Oho, ho!" I reflected. "My flying is beyond all doubt, then. Well, and how does my face look today?" I added aloud.

"Your face? Here, let me have a look at you. Your cheeks are a little sunken. And, my provider—there, as I live, you haven't as much as a drop of blood in your face!"

That ruffled me a little. I dismissed Martha.

"If you go on like that you'll die, likely as not, or go out of your mind," I reasoned, sitting pensively before the window. "You'll have to abandon all this. It's dangerous. There, your heart is pounding so peculiarly. And when I'm flying, it seems as if someone were sucking at it, or as though something were oozing out of it —yes, the way sap oozes out of a birch in the spring, if you drive an ax into it. And yet . . . it would be a pity to stop. Then there's Ellis, too. She's playing with me, like a cat with a mouse. But still, it's hardly likely that she wishes me ill. I'll give myself up to her for the last time; I will have my fill of sight-seeing, and after that . . . But what if she's drinking my blood? That is horrible. Also, such rapid locomotion cannot but be harmful. They say that in England the railroads are forbidden to go more than eighty miles an hour—"

Thus did I reason with my own self. But at ten that night I was already standing before the old oak.

The night was chill, dim, gray; one could smell rain in the air. To my astonishment I found no one under the oak; I circled it several times, went as far as the edge of the forest and peered intently into its darkness. Everything was deserted. I waited a little, then repeated Ellis' name several times in succession, each time more loudly, but she did not appear. Sadness—almost pain—overcame me; my former apprehensions vanished: I could not reconcile myself to the idea that my companion would return to me no more.

"Ellis! Do come! Is it possible that you won't come?" I called out for the last time.

A crow, awakened by my voice, suddenly began to fuss on the summit of a tree near by and, becoming entangled among the twigs, began to flap its wings. But Ellis did not appear.

With head downcast I set out for home. The willows along the mill-pond were already darkling ahead, and the light in the window of my room gleamed between the apple trees in the garden—gleamed and disappeared, like the eye of a man who might be lying in wait for me—when suddenly I heard a high-pitched hum in the air, as if something were hurtling through it, and I felt myself suddenly embraced and caught from behind, then being borne upward: thus does a merlin snatch up a quail with its talons, *striking* it. It was Ellis who had swooped upon me. I felt her cheek against mine, her arms in a ring about my body, and, like a piercing little chill, her whisper plunged into my ear: "Here I am!" I became frightened and overjoyed at the same time. We were soaring along a little above the ground.

"You did not wish to come today?" I asked.

"Why, have you longed for me? You do love me? Oh, you are mine!" Her last words abashed me. I did not know what to say. "They detained me," she continued. "They were watching me."

"Who could detain you?"

"Where do you want to go?" asked Ellis, as usual without answering my question.

"Bear me off to Italy, to that lake—do you remember?"

Ellis drew away a little and shook her head. It was then I first noticed that she had ceased to be transparent. And her face had taken on color, somehow: a ruby tinge was mantling its misty whiteness. I glanced into her eyes—and an eldritch feeling came over me: something was stirring in those eyes with the slow, ceaseless and sinister motion of a coiled and poised snake whom the sun is beginning to warm.

"Ellis!" I cried out. "Who are you? Do tell me: Who are you?"

Ellis merely shrugged a shoulder.

I felt irked. I wanted to revenge myself upon her— and suddenly the idea came to me of ordering her to transport both of us to Paris. "There, that's where you'll have occasion for jealousy," I mused. "Ellis," said I aloud, "you're not afraid of large cities? Of Paris, for instance?"

"No."

"No? Not even those places which are lit up as brightly as the Boulevards?"

"That is not the light of day."

"Splendid; in that case bear me off at once to the Boulevard des Italiens."

Ellis threw over my head the end of her long, hanging sleeve. I was immediately swathed in some sort of a white murk, permeated with the soporific fragrance of poppies. Everything vanished on the instant: all light, all sound—and almost consciousness itself. The sensation of life alone remained, and this state was not unpleasant.

Suddenly the murk vanished: Ellis had taken her sleeve off my head, and I beheld below me an enormous mass of buildings huddling together, a mass filled with glitter, movement, rumbling.

I beheld Paris.

I had been to Paris before, and therefore immediately recognized the place toward which Ellis was heading. It was the Garden of the Tuilleries, with its old chestnut trees, its iron gratings, fortress moat and bestial-looking Zouaves on guard. Passing by the palace, passing by the Church of St. Roch, on the steps of which the first Napoleon had spilt the first French blood, we halted high above the Boulevard des Italiens, where the third Napoleon had done much the same thing, and with much the same success. Crowds of people, dandies young and old, workers in smocks, women in resplendent clothes, were jostling upon the sidewalks; gilded restaurants and cafés blazed with lights; omnibuses, carriages of every sort and description darted along the Boulevard; everything simply seethed, simply glowed— everything, no matter where one's gaze fell. But, a strange thing! I felt no desire to forsake my pure, dark, nocturnal height, felt no desire to draw near to this human ant-hill. A hot, oppressive, rubescent vapor was, it seemed, rising thence, but one could not decide whether it was fragrant or malodorous, for far too many lives had herded together there in a single heap.

I wavered. But at that point the voice of a street *lorette*, grating as the clangor of iron bars, suddenly came floating up to me: like an impudent tongue it thrust itself forth, did this voice; it stung me, like the sting of a reptile. I at once pictured to myself a stony, greedy, flat Parisian face with high cheek-bones, the eyes of a usurer, and whitening, rouge, frizzled hair, and a bouquet of artificial flowers under a conical hat,

nails manicured into talons, a hideous crinoline. . . .
I also pictured to myself my brother squires, fresh from
their steppes, running at an obscene trot after this
meretricious poppet. I pictured to myself how such a
one, so embarrassed that he became rude and forced
himself to lisp, tried to ape the manners of the *garçons*
at Vefour's, squeaking, fawning, wheedling—and a feeling of revulsion swept over me. "No," I mused, "Ellis
will have no occasion to be jealous here!"

In the meanwhile I noticed that we had begun to
descend. Paris was swirling up toward us with all its
din and fumy hurly-burly.

"Stop!" I turned to Ellis. "Is it possible you don't feel
stifled here, that you don't feel oppressed?"

"You yourself asked me to bring you here."

"My fault; I take back what I said. Take me away,
Ellis, I beg of you. There, it's just as I thought: there
goes Le Grand Duc Koulmametioff, hobbling along the
boulevard, and his crony, Serge Waraxine, is waving his
hand to him daintily and shouting: 'Ivan Stepanitch,
allons souper, but quick—*j'ai engagé* Rigolbosch itself!'
Bear me away from these *mabilles* and Maisons d'Or,
from these *gandins* and *biches*, from Le Jockey Club
and *Figaro*, from the soldiers with their foreheads
cropped as a brand of their conscription and from their
spick-and-span barracks, from the *sergents de ville* with
their goatees, and from the glasses of turbid absinthe,
from the domino players in the cafés and those who
gamble on the Bourse, from bits of red ribbon in the
buttonholes of coats and the buttonholes of overcoats,
from M'sieu' de Fois, inventor of 'Specializing in Mar-
riages,' and from the free consultations of Doctor
Charles Albert, from free lectures and the brochures
put out by the government, from Parisian comedies and

Parisian operas, from Parisian *bons mots* and Parisian boorishness. . . . Away! Away! Away!"

"Look down," Ellis answered me. "You are no longer over Paris."

I lowered my eyes. She was right. A dark plain, with the whitish streaks of roads traversing it here and there, was running swiftly into the distance below us, and only behind us, on the horizon, like the glow of an enormous conflagration, did the spreading reflection of the countless lights of the world capital beat upward.

Again the veil descended over my eyes. Again I fell into a coma. Finally that veil dissipated.

But what was that, below? What park, with paths of trimmed lindens, with isolated firs clipped into the shape of open parasols, with porticoes and temples *à la* Pompadour, with statues of satyrs and nymphs of the Bernini school, with rococo tritons in the center of curving ponds bordered with low balustrades of time-blackened marble? Was this Versailles, perchance? A small palace, also rococo, peeped out from behind a copse of curly-leafed oaks. The moon, enveloped in vapor, shone dimly, and the thinnest of smoke seemed to have carpeted the earth; the eye could not make out what it was: moonlight or mist. There, on one of the ponds, floated a sleeping swan; its long back gleamed as white as the frost-chilled snow of the steppes; while over yonder glowworms flashed like adamants in the bluish shadows at the feet of the statues.

"We are near Mannheim," Ellis remarked. "This is the park of Schwetzingen."

"So we are in Germany," I reflected, and cocked my ears. All was silent, save that somewhere a small rill of falling water plashed and babbled, lonelily and invisibly. It seemed to be repeating the unvarying words: "Aye, aye, aye—forever aye!" And suddenly I imagined I saw, in the very middle of one of the paths, between the walls of clipped verdure, a gallant stepping out on red heels, in long, gold-embroidered coat and lace cuffs, with a light damascus sword on his hip, daintily offering his arm to a *Fräulein* in a powdered coiffure and a bright *robe ronde*. . . . Strange, wan, their faces. I wanted to peer into them more closely—but everything had already vanished, and only the water was babbling as before.

"Those are dreams, wandering," Ellis whispered to me. "Yesterday one might have seen a great deal—a great deal! Tonight even dreams flee from the eye of man. Onward! Onward!"

We ascended and flew on. So smooth and level was our flight that it seemed as if we were not moving, but that on the contrary everything was moving toward us. Mountains appeared, dark, undulating, clothed with forests; they grew higher and floated toward us. There, they were already flowing past below us, with all their windings, ravines, narrow dells, with dots of light in the slumber-held hamlets along rapidly running streams in the bottomlands, while ahead other mountains were in their turn looming and floating toward us. We were in the depths of the Black Forest.

Mountains, mountains everywhere. And forest: splendidly beautiful, old, mighty forest. The night sky was clear; I could recognize every species of tree. Especially magnificent were the silver-firs, with their white, straight trunks. Here and there, on the borders of the forest, one could see wild goats; graceful and alert they stood upon their slim legs and hearkened, with their heads beautifully turned to one side, and their big, trumpet-shaped ears cocked. A ruined tower sadly and

blindly thrust forth from the summit of a naked cliff its
half-fallen battlements; a small golden star glowed
warmly and peacefully over these old, forgotten stones.
From a small, almost black tarn rose, like a mysterious
plaint, the moaning croaks of small toads. I imagined I
heard other sounds: prolonged, languishing, like to the
sounds of an Aeolian harp. There it was, the land of
legend! The same tenuous, lunar smoke which had
aroused my wonder at Schwetzingen inundated everything here, and the further apart the mountains, the
denser this smoke. I counted five, six, ten different tones
in the different layers of shadow along the faces of the
mountains, and above all this silent diversity reigned
the pensive moon. The air streamed past softly and
buoyantly; I myself felt buoyant and somehow exaltedly
serene and melancholy.

"Ellis, you must love this region!"

"I do not love anything."

"How is that? And what about me?"

"Yes . . . I love you," she answered apathetically.

It seemed to me that her arm embraced me more
tightly than before.

"Onward! Onward!" said Ellis with a certain chill enthusiasm.

"Onward!" I repeated.

A powerful, trilling, sonorous cry suddenly resounded
over us, and was at once repeated, but this time a little
ahead of us.

"Those are belated cranes flying to your country, to
the north," said Ellis. "Would you like to join them?"

"Yes, yes! Bring me up to them."

We spiraled upward, and in an instant found ourselves alongside of the migrating flock.

The large, beautiful birds (there were but thirteen

of them in all) were flying in a triangle, beating their convex wings sharply and at long intervals. With head and legs stretched out taut, their breasts sharply outthrust, they went ahead unrestrainably and with such speed that the air whistled about them. It was wondrously odd to see, at this height, at such a distance from all things living, such warm, strong life, such undeviating will. Without ceasing to cleave triumphantly through space, the cranes called from time to time to the companion at their head, their leader, and he would answer, and there was something proud, dignified, something insuperably self-assured in these loud calls, in this communion under the clouds. "We will fly to our goal, never fear, even though it be hard," they seemed to be saying, encouraging one another. And here it occurred to me that there were but few men in Russia (and not in Russia alone, but in the whole world) who were like to these birds.

"We are now flying to Russia," announced Ellis. This was not the first time I had been able to notice that she almost always knew what I was thinking about. "Do you want to turn back?"

"Should we turn back or no? I have been to Paris; carry me to Peterburg."

"Now?"

"This minute. Only cover my head with your pall, for otherwise I feel ill."

Ellis lifted up her arm. But before the fog enveloped me, I had time to feel upon my lips the touch of that soft, dull sting.

"Ha-a-a-a-ark!" a long-drawn call sounded in my ears. "Ha-a-a-a-ark!" came the answering echo in the distance, as if in despair. "Ha-a-a-a-a-ark!" the call died away, somewhere at the end of the world. I became alert. A towering golden spire obtruded on my sight: I recognized the Fortress of SS. Peter and Paul.

The wan night of the North! Yes, but was it really night? Was it not a wan, an ailing day? I had never been fond of Petersburg nights, but this time I actually grew frightened: the countenance of Ellis was vanishing utterly, melting away like morning mist under the July sun, and I clearly saw my whole body as it hung ponderously and solitarily at the level of the Alexander Column. So this was Petersburg! Yes, this was it, of a certainty. These empty, broad, gray streets; these gray-whitish, yellow-gray, gray-lilac houses, stuccoed or with their plastering peeling off, with their windows sunken in, with lurid shop-signs, with metal marquees over their front entrances and wretched little vegetable shops: all these frontals, inscriptions, sentry-booths, barriers, the gold cap of the Cathedral of St. Isaac; the superfluous, gaudy Stock Exchange; the granite walls of a fortress and the roadway of broken boards; these barges of hay and firewood; this odor of dust, cabbage, matting and stable; these petrified janitors in sheep-lined short coats at the gateways; these cabbies writhingly hunched up in the sleep of the dead, perched upon their ramshackle droshkies. . . . Yes, this was it: our Palmyra of the North. Everything around us was visible, everything was clear, distinct and clear, to the verge of eeriness, and all was sadly slumbering, strangely piled up and outlined in the dully transparent air. The blush of the evening glow—a phthisic blush!—had not gone yet, and would not go until morning, off the wan, starless sky; it was spreading over the silky evenness of the Neva, while that river did but barely gurgle and barely heave, hurrying its chill, indigo waters onward.

"Let us fly away," Ellis implored.

And, without waiting for my answer, she bore me off across the Neva, across Palace Square, toward Liteinaya Street. I heard steps and voices below: a knot of young people with drink-ravaged faces was walking along the streets and discussing dancing classes. "Second Lieutenant Stolpakov the Seventh!" a soldier standing on guard over a small pyramid of rusty cannon-balls called out suddenly through his half-doze and, a little farther on, near the open window of a tall building, I saw a miss in a rumpled silk dress, without cuffs, with a pearl-net on her hair and with a cigarette dangling in her mouth. She was reverently reading a book: it was a volume of one of our latest Juvenals.

"Let us fly away!" said I to Ellis.

A moment—and already flitting before us were the wretched, rotting woods of fir and mossy bogs surrounding Petersburg. We were headed due south; sky and earth and all things were, little by little, becoming darker and darker. The ailing night, the ailing day, the ailing city—all had been left behind.

We were flying more slowly than usual and I had an opportunity of watching a vast expanse of my native land as it gradually unrolled before my eyes like an endless panorama. Forests, bushes, fields, ravines, rivers; at rare intervals villages, churches—and again fields, and forests, and bushes, and ravines. . . . I grew sad, and somehow apathetically weary, because I had flown precisely over Russia. But no! The earth itself, this flat surface which spread out below me, all the terrestrial globe with its population, living for the moment, frail, crushed by need, grief, diseases, shackled to a clod of contemned dust; this brittle, rough-surfaced crust; this excrescence upon the fiery dust-particle that is our planet, which excrescence had broken out with a mold that we glorify as the organic vegetable kingdom; these men-flies, a thousand times more insignificant than flies; their dwellings, molded out of mud; the microscopic traces of their petty, monotonous fossicking, of their diverting struggle against the immutable and the inevitable: how loathsome all this had suddenly become to me! The heart within me heaved slowly, and I felt no further desire to gaze upon these insignificant pictures, upon this vulgar exhibition. Yes, I became bored—and worse than bored. Not even pity did I feel for my cobrethren; all the feelings within me had been drowned in but one, which I hardly dare to name: in a feeling of revulsion. And strongest of all and above all within me was the revulsion toward my own self.

"Cease," whispered Ellis. "Cease, or I shall not be able to bear you up. You are becoming heavy."

"Home!" I told her in the same voice I used to give this command to my coachman whenever, at four in the morning, I would leave the house of my Moscow friends with whom, ever since finishing dinner, I had been discussing the future of Russia and the meaning of the common good. "Home!" I repeated, and shut my eyes.

But I opened them shortly. Ellis was pressing against me somehow strangely; she was almost nudging me along. I looked at her—and my blood froze. Whoever has happened to see upon the face of another a sudden expression of profound terror, the reason for which the spectator does not suspect—such a spectator will understand me. Terror, excruciating terror, was distorting, disfiguring the wan, almost vanished features of Ellis. I had never seen anything like it even upon a living human face. A lifeless, misty specter, a shade—and this swooning horror. . . .

"Ellis, what is wrong with you?" I got out at last.

"It is she—she—" Ellis answered with an effort. "It is she!"

"She? Who is she?"

"Do not name her—do not name her!" she gibbered. "We must save ourselves, otherwise there will be an end to everything—and for all time. . . . Look—over there!"

I turned my head in the direction her quivering hand was pointing out to me, and beheld something—something truly dreadful.

It was all the more dreadful because it had no definite image. Something ponderous, somber, yellowishly black, mottled, like the belly of a lizard; something that was neither cloud nor smoke was slowly, with the motion of a snake, slithering over the earth. A measured, sweeping sway up and down and down and up, a sway reminiscent of the sinister sweep of the wings of a bird of prey when it is seeking its victim; from time to time an inexplicably repulsive clinging to the earth, the way a spider clings to the captured fly. . . . Who art thou, what art thou, thou sinister mass? Under its influence—I saw this, I felt this—everything was turned to naught, everything grew mute. A putrid, noxious chill emanated from it—and because of this chill one's heart was nauseated and all grew dark before the eyes, and the hair stood up on end. This was Force coming; that Force against which there is no resistance, to which everything is subject, which without sight, without image, without sentience sees all things, knows all things, and like a bird of prey chooses its victims, like a snake crushes them and licks them with its frigid sting. . . .

"Ellis! Ellis!" I began to scream like one in a frenzy. "This is death. Death itself!"

A piteous sound I had heard before escaped the lips of Ellis—this time it resembled a human wail of despair more than anything else—and we sped away. But our flight was strangely and fearfully uneven; Ellis tumbled in the air, she fell, she darted from side to side, like a partridge mortally wounded or intent on drawing a dog away from her brood. Yet in the meanwhile, separating from the inexplicably horrible mass, certain long, undulating tendrils, just like extended hands, just like talons, darted after us. . . . The enormous image of a muffled figure on a white horse momently arose and reared up to the very sky. . . . Still more distractedly, still more despairingly did Ellis flutter and dart about.

"She has seen me! All is ended! I am lost!" I heard her broken whispering. "Oh, unhappy I! I might have availed myself of life, might have accumulated life—but now . . . Non-being! Non-being!"

This was past all bearing. I lost consciousness.

When I came to I was lying flat on my back in the grass, feeling a dull ache throughout my body, as if from a powerful blow. Morning was breaking in the sky: I could distinguish objects plainly. Not far off, along a small birch of groves, ran a road lined with willows; the locality seemed familiar to me. I began to recall what had happened to me, and shuddered all over when that last hideous apparition came to mind.

"But why did Ellis become frightened?" I mused. "Can she, too, be subject to *Its* sway? For is she not deathless? Or is she, too, subject to non-being, to destruction? But how can that be?"

A low moan sounded close to me. I turned my head. A young woman in a white garment, with her thick hair scattered and one shoulder bared, was lying outstretched two paces away from me. One arm was flung over her head; the other had fallen upon her breast. Her eyes were closed, and a slight scarlet froth had come out upon her compressed lips. Could this possibly be Ellis? But Ellis was a specter, whereas it was a living woman I saw before me. I crept up to her, bent over—

"Ellis! Is it you?" I cried out. Suddenly, after a slow flutter, the wide eyelids lifted; dark, piercing eyes fixed me with their gaze—and at that same instant her lips as well, warm, moist, with the odor of blood, fixed themselves to mine. Soft arms entwined my neck; her warm, full bosom pressed convulsively to mine.

"Farewell! Farewell forever!" her dying voice uttered clearly—and everything vanished.

I stood up, swaying on my legs as if I were intoxicated and, after passing my hand several times over my face, looked about me attentively. I was near the ——oya Road, a little over a mile from my estate.

The sun was already up when I managed to reach home.

All the following nights I awaited—and, I confess, not without fear—the appearance of my specter; but it never visited me more. Once, at dusk, I actually set out for the old oak, but even there nothing out of the ordinary occurred. However, I did not regret overmuch the termination of so strange a friendship. Much and long have I pondered over this incomprehensible, almost preposterous adventure, and I have become convinced that not only does science fail to explain it, but that even in fairy tales, in legends, one does not come across anything like it. Really, what does Ellis represent? An apparition, a vagrom soul, an evil spirit, a sylphide—a vampire, finally? Again, it occasionally seemed to me that Ellis was a woman whom I had known upon a time, and I made frightful efforts to recall where I might have seen her. There, there, it seemed to me at times, right now, this very moment, I would recall everything. In vain! Everything would dissipate again, like a dream. Yes, I thought a great deal and, as usually happens, did not think of any solution. I could not bring myself to ask the counsel or opinion of others, since I was afraid of becoming known as a madman.

I finally abandoned all my reflections; to tell the truth, I had other things to think of. On the one hand the Emancipation turned up, with the repartition of land, and so on; and, on the other, my own health went all to pieces: my chest has begun to pain me, I have insomnia, I cough. All my body is wasting away. My face is as yellow as that of a dead man. The doctor assures me that I haven't enough blood, calls my ailment by a Greek name—*anemia*—and is for packing me off to Gastein. But the arbitrator calls God to witness that there'll be no *contriving* anything with the peasants if I go away.

There, go ahead and contrive anything!

Yet . . . what is the meaning of those piercingly clear and high-pitched sounds, the sounds as of a harmonica, which I hear as soon as people start talking about someone's death in my presence? They are becoming ever more loud, these sounds, ever more piercing. And why do I shudder so excruciatingly at the mere thought of non-being? . . .

IVAN SERGEIEVICH TURGENEV   141

FEDOR MIKHAILOVICH DOSTOEVSKY

(1821–1881)

EDITOR'S NOTE

DOSTOEVSKY is the culminating point in that indictment of Czarist Russia which led to the sentence and execution of October, 1917.

Read this slowly: 1): *All* of Dostoevsky's master-pieces came within a few seconds (thirty, at his own estimate) of never being written. 2): His imprisonment before he was sentenced to be shot, plus the nine years in Siberia to which this sentence was commuted, short-ened his creative life by a third—and that the best third. "Most certainly he wrote only one tenth of the stories which for years he had planned," says Strakhov.—"A monstrous and uncalled-for affront," Dostoevsky called this reprieve, granted "through the great mercy of His Imperial Majesty, Nicholas I. A period of burial alive. I was put in a coffin. The torture was unutterable and unbearable." And his latent epilepsy was intensified to such an extent that the fits came "every few days." 3): This, the ghastliest in the long, unbroken succession of Czarism's crimes against Russian genius, was based upon accusations of the author's having conducted a private press, or having read, or having listened to the reading of, tracts on Utopian Socialism, and of having circulated a "letter [to Gogol] of one Belinski, a journal-ist. . . ." 4): We are told (amazingly enough, in a book brought out by a reputable New York publisher) that "Dostoevsky's incarceration was a most paradoxical affair which should be looked upon as a classic in the voluminous history of police blunders both within and without Russia." Eight months in the notorious oubliette of SS. Peter and Paul, plus five years of inhuman penal labor, plus four years of military servitude in the ranks (Dostoevsky had graduated as a second lieutenant from the School of Military Engineers) amount, jesuitically, to no more than an "incarceration." 5): Siberia had the same effect on Dostoevsky that religious mania had on Gogol: Fedor came back to spout the most appalling rubbish and mystic twaddle about the Divine Spark, the Christian Morality-of-the-Slave, the infallibility of Orthodoxy—because it was Russian. No wonder so much drivel has been written about the Slavic Soul!

Every effort has been made to claim the Great Plebeian for the *aristoi*, although in fact he came from a poverty-haunted, Puritanical family that ran mostly to priests, just as it has been attempted, repeatedly, to canonize his father, a minor medico who was killed by his quondam serfs. Dostoevsky pursued one friar's-lantern after another in his search of fame and security; he gained the first when his *Poor Folk* was published by Nekrassov in 1846, and Belinski hailed him as a new literary luminary. But he was soon made to feel (by Turgenev and others) that his was to be the "word of the burgher"; page after page in his novels is devoted to parodying the "nobleman's prose," the "land-owning style."

He did not return to St. Petersburg until 1860; by 1862, with *The House of the Dead* and *The Humiliated and Wronged* he had re-won his position, but in 1863 all his struggles were again nullified by the government's suppression of his magazine; he ran into debt to the tune of $11,000—a considerable sum in the '60's. 1865 was the nadir of his fortunes. His wife, his child, his brother Michael (a sincere writer, naturally obscured by his illustrious brother), and his friend Grigoriev, all died; he was forced to sell to an overshrewd publisher not only the copyrights of all his published works, but also the yet unwritten *The Gambler,* for a sum amounting to about $1,500, and to seek escape in a second trip abroad. There he wrote what is indubitably his supreme novel, *Crime and Punishment,* and was able to return to Russia and stave off his creditors. In 1867 he married again and once more went abroad. The four years there were far from happy ones. A nomadic life, nostalgia, chronic poverty, shameful exploitation amounting to peonage, all took their toll. *The Idiot, The Eternal Husband, The Possessed* were among the things written during this period, but even this extraordinary productivity could not improve his circumstances. He risked debtors' prison and came home.

But this time he returned to St. Petersburg as a world-famous author, and by 1873 he was a success even financially. By 1880 he had become prophet, apostle, preceptor; with the publication of *The Brothers Karamazov* in that year he reached his apogee; his speech on Pushkin was his swan song. He had been (literally) living on his nerves for years; he died of pulmonary emphysema on February 9th (New Style), 1881.

The Grand Inquisitor is a unique. Had Dostoevsky written never another word before or after it, or if all his works were to perish cataclysmically, and nothing were to remain save this one chapter from his last novel, it would be enough to mark him as an Alpimalyan mind and a supreme master of the word. Whether its recognition as one of the world's comparatively few superlative short stories is very general is, however, something that one is not at all certain about. At any rate, it is believed that the present attempt is the first (at least in

English) to present *The Grand Inquisitor* (through reverent editing) as a perfect short story in its own right, rather than merely an extract from *The Brothers Karamazov*.

Most of Dostoevsky is available in English but, with no exceptions hitherto known to the Editor, only in the feeblest parodies on the elemental force of the original, while the only English version of *The Brothers Karamazov* (unfortunately in the public domain) is, beyond all doubt, one of the wretchedest translations ever made from any language into any other. The same advice as that given in the case of Turgenev is, therefore, reluctantly offered for Dostoevsky as well.

The Grand Inquisitor[1]

FEDOR MIKHAILOVICH DOSTOEVSKY

"YOU have written a poem?"

"Oh, no—I didn't *write* it, nor have I put together even two lines of verse in all my life. But I did make up the poem and have retained it in my memory. And I was at fever heat when I made it up. You'll be my first reader —or listener, rather. Really, why should an author forego even a single listener?" Ivan smiled slyly. "Should I tell the story or no?"

"I'm all ears," said Alësha.

"This prose-poem of mine is called *The Grand Inquisitor*—an incongruous thing, but I feel like imparting it to you. . . ."

---

[1] All notes for this selection are on page 175.

Fifteen centuries had already passed since He had given His promise to come into His kingdom, fifteen centuries since His prophet had written: *Behold, I come quickly.*[1]—*But of that day and that hour knoweth no man, no, not the angels which are in heaven, neither the Son, but the Father,*[2] even as He Himself hath uttered in His days upon earth. Yet mankind awaits Him with the same faith and the same fervor as it has always done. Oh, with even greater faith, inasmuch as fifteen centuries had already passed since the heavens have ceased issuing pledges to man:

> Have thou faith in what the heart says,
> For the heavens send no pledges.

And there was nothing save this faith in what the heart said! True, there were many miracles even then. There were saints who wrought miraculous cures; to certain men of righteousness (if we are to believe their hagiographies), the Queen of Heaven used to come down Herself. But the Devil slumbers not, and doubt as to the authenticity of these miracles had already sprung up among mankind. And it was precisely then that, in the North, in Germany, a fearful new heresy appeared. "An enormous star, like to a church-lanthorn (*quasi dicat,* like to a church), fell upon the well-springs of waters, and they turned bitter." These heresies began blasphemously to deny miracles. But those who had clung to their faith believed all the more vehemently. The tears of mankind welled up to Him as before; men awaited Him, loved Him, placed their trust in Him, thirsted to suffer and to die for Him, going through all this even as they had always done.

And lo, for so many centuries had mankind prayed in faith and fervor: *O Lord, our God, come unto us!*—so

many ages had it called unto Him, that He, in His immeasurable compassion, yearned to come down to His
supplicants. He had come down to, He had visited certain of the men of righteousness, certain of the martyrs
and sainted anchorites, even before this, in His days
upon earth, even as it is recorded in the Lives of the
Saints. . . .

And so He yearned to appear, if but for a moment,
before the people—the racked, all-suffering people,
stinking in their sins yet like little children loving Him.

My action takes place in Spain, at Seville, during the
most ghastly period of the Inquisition when, to the
greater glory of God, bonfires blazed day in and day
out all over the land, and

> In resplendent *autos da fé*
> The evil heretics were burned.

Oh, of course, this was not that Coming in which He
will appear, according to His promise, at the end of
time, in all His glory, and which will befall suddenly, *as
the lightning cometh out of the East and shineth even
unto the West*[2]. . . . (I do bring Him on; though, true
enough, He does not speak even a single line in my
poem, but merely comes on and crosses the stage. . . .)
No, He yearned to visit, if but for a moment, His
children, and nowhere else save where the bonfires to
roast the heretics had begun to crackle. Because of His
immeasurable compassion He passes once more among
men in that very same image of man in which He walked
among men for three years, fifteen centuries before.

He descends upon the *heated flagstones* of that very
Southern town wherein only the evening before, in a
resplendent *auto da fé*, in the presence of King, court,
hidalgos, Cardinals, and ladies of honor of the most
bewitching beauty, before the multitudinous population

of all Seville, almost an hundred heretics had been burned at the stake, and at one clip, *ad majorem gloriam Dei,* by the Cardinal who was Grand Inquisitor.

He had appeared quietly, unperceived, and yet all (and this is odd!)—all recognize Him. (This might be one of the best parts in the poem—that is, the statement of the precise reasons for their recognition of Him.) The people, through some invincible force, are drawn to Him, surround Him, grow in numbers about Him, follow in His steps. He passes among them in silence, with a gentle smile of infinite commiseration. The sun of love glows in His heart; rays of Light, Enlightenment and Strength stream from His eyes and, pouring forth upon the people, move their hearts with a responsive love. He stretches out His hands to them, He blesses them, and from His mere touch—or even the touch of His garments—there issues a healing power.

Over there, from out of the throng, an old man who has been blind from childhood cries out:

"Heal me, O Lord, that I may behold Thee!" And it is as if scales were falling off his eyes, and the blind man sees Him.

The people weep and kiss the ground He walks upon. Children strew flowers before Him, chanting and lifting up their voices to Him: *Hosanna!*

"This is none other than He Himself," all repeat. "This must be He—this is none other than He!"

He halts on the parvis of the Cathedral of Seville, at the very moment when a child's coffin, small, white and unlidded, is being borne amid weeping into the temple; in the coffin is a girl of seven, the only daughter of a certain illustrious citizen. The dead child is lying amid a profusion of flowers.

"He will bring thy daughter back from the dead!" voices in the crowd call out to the weeping mother.

The Cathedral padre who had come out to meet the coffin looks on in perplexity and knits his eyebrows. But at this moment the cry of the dead child's mother resounds; she casts herself down at His feet:

"If it be Thou, then bring my child back from the dead!" she cries out, stretching out her hands to Him. The cortège halts, the little coffin is lowered to the floor at His feet. He regards it with compassion, and His lips softly, and once again, utter:

"Talitha cumi,"—which is, being interpreted, Damsel, I say unto thee, arise.[4]

The little girl rises in her coffin, sits up and looks about her, her little eyes, wide open in wonder, smiling the while; the bouquet of white roses wherewith she had lain in the coffin still in her hand. There is confusion among the people, and outcries, and sobs—and lo, at that very moment, that very Cardinal who is Grand Inquisitor comes through the square, passing by the Cathedral.

He is an ancient of almost ninety, tall and erect, emaciated of face, with eyes sunken yet still agleam and aglitter with a glow like that of a coruscating spark. Oh, he is not clad now in his magnificent vestments of a Cardinal, those vestments in which he displayed himself in all his glory the evening before, in front of all the people, when they were burning the foes of the Faith of Rome—no, at the moment he is wearing only his monk's robe, coarse and old. He is followed—at a certain distance—by his sombre assistants, and his servitors, and his "holy" guards.

He halts before the crowd and watches everything from afar. He has seen all; he has seen how the coffin had been set down at His feet; he has seen the damsel arise from the dead. And his face has become clouded over. He knits his gray, bushy eyebrows, and his gaze flashes with a sinister fire. He holds up a finger and bids his guards to seize Him. And lo, such is his power, and to such an extent were the people trained, cowed and tremblingly submissive to him, that the throng immediately parts before the guards and the latter, amid the suddenly fallen silence, a silence as of the grave, lay their hands upon Him and lead Him away.

The throng instantly, as one man, bow their heads to the ground before that ancient, the Inquisitor; the latter silently blesses the people and strides past.

The guards bring their Captive into the cramped and gloomy vaulted prison in the ancient edifice of the Holy Office, and lock Him therein.

The day passes; night comes, the dark, sultry and "breathless" night of Seville. The air is "fragrant with laurel and with citron." Amid the profound murk the iron door of the dungeon opens abruptly and the ancient, the Grand Inquisitor himself, enters slowly with a lanthorn in his hand. He is alone; the door is immediately locked after him. He pauses near the entrance and protractedly, for a minute or two, scrutinizes His face. At last he approaches softly, puts his lanthorn on the table, and speaks to Him:

"Is it Thou? Thou?" But, receiving no answer, he quickly adds: "Answer not; be silent. And, to boot, what couldst Thou say? I know all too well what Thou wouldst say. Furthermore, Thou hast no right to add aught to that which Thou hast already said. Wherefore, then, hast Thou come to hinder us? For it is to hinder us Thou hast come, and Thou knowest that Thyself. Yet dost Thou know what will befall on the morrow? I know not who Thou art, nor do I want to know whether it is Thou or but a similitude of Him, but on the very morrow I shall condemn Thee and burn Thee at the stake as the most pernicious of heretics, and those very people who this very day were kissing Thy feet will, no later than on the morrow, at the merest wave of my hand, race to rake up the embers of Thy bonfire—dost Thou know that? Ay, it may be Thou dost know that," he added with thoughtful discernment, not taking his eyes off the Captive for even an instant.

"I don't quite understand, Ivan. What's all this?" smiled Alësha, who had been listening in silence throughout. "Is it out-and-out shoreless fantasy, or some sort of error on the old man's part, some sort of impossible *quid pro quo?*"

"You might take it as the last," Ivan broke into laughter, "if contemporary realism has pampered you to such an extent that you can't stand up under anything fantastic; if you hanker after a *quid pro quo,* so be it. True enough," he again broke into laughter, "the old man is ninety, and he may well have gone out of his mind over this idea of his. Then, too, he may have been overcome by the looks of his Captive. It might, finally, be simply delirium, the ante mortem vision of a nonagenarian ancient who, on top of everything, had been fired by yesterday's *auto da fé* with its cast of a hundred heretics burned to a crisp. But isn't it all one to us whether it's *quid pro quo* or shoreless fantasy? The whole point here lies merely in that the old man wants to have his full say, that at last after all of his ninety years he is having his say and is uttering aloud that about which he has been keeping mum for all of his ninety years."

"But what about the Captive—is He keeping silent too? Just gazes at the other and utters never a word?"

"Why, that's just how it must be, under any and all circumstances," Ivan once more began to laugh. "The old man himself remarks to Him that He actually has no right to add anything to that which He has already said, long ago. That, if you like, constitutes precisely the most fundamental feature of Roman Catholicism—at least in my opinion: 'There, now, everything has been handed over by Thee to the Pope and, therefore, everything is now in the Pope's hands, and as for Thee, there's no need now of Thy coming at all; the least Thou couldst do would be not to bother us ahead of time.' They not only talk but even write to that effect—at least the Jesuits do. I've read that myself in the works of their theologians."

"Hast Thou the right to declare to us even a single one of the mysteries of that world whence Thou hast come? [my ancient asks Him—and himself makes answer for Him:] Nay, Thou hast not, for Thou mayest add naught to that which has already been said of old, and Thou mayest not take away from men that freedom for which Thou didst contend so in Thy days upon earth. All that Thou wilt declare anew will be an attempt against men's freedom of faith, inasmuch as it will come as a miracle, and yet their freedom of faith was dear to Thee above all things even then, fifteen hundred years ago. Was it not Thou who didst say so often in those days: *I would make you free?* [5] But just now Thou didst see these *free* men," the old man adds with a pensively mocking smile. "Ay, all this business has cost us dear," he goes on, regarding Him sternly, "but we have accomplished it, in Thy name. For fifteen centuries have we striven agonizingly against this freedom, but now it is all over and done with—and done with for good. Thou dost not believe it is done with for good? Thou gazest upon me meekly and dost not deign to honor me even by becoming indignant? Know, then, that now, and precisely today, these men feel more certain than they ever did that they are utterly free, yet at the same time they themselves have brought their freedom to us and have submissively laid it at our feet. But it is we who have brought this about. However, was that what Thou didst desire—was it freedom such as that?"

"Again I don't understand," Alësha interrupted. "Is he indulging in irony? Is he sneering?"

"Not in the least. He is in all seriousness claiming as a meritorious service on the part of himself and his kind their having at last won the contest against freedom, and having done so in order to make men happy."

"For it is only now [of course he is talking of the Inquisition at this point] that it has become possible to give any thought to the happiness of men. Man is constituted as a rebel; come, can a rebel be happy? Thou wast forewarned [says the ancient to Him]; Thou hadst no lack of forewarnings and directives; but Thou didst not heed the forewarnings, Thou didst reject the only way to bring about happiness for men—fortunately, however, at Thy departure Thou didst hand over the task to us. Thou didst promise, Thou didst confirm with Thy word, Thou didst give us the authority *to bind and to loose*,[6] and quite naturally Thou couldst not now even contemplate taking this authority back from us. Wherefore, then, hast Thou come to hinder us?"

"But what do you mean by 'No lack of forewarnings and directives'?" asked Alësha.

"Why, that's just the main thing the old man wants to have his full say about."

"The dread and intelligent Spirit, the Spirit of self-annihilation and non-being [the old man goes on], the great Spirit spake with Thee in the wilderness, and it has been transmitted to us in books that he allegedly *tempted* Thee. Was it so? And could anything have been said more truthful than that which he annunciated to Thee in the form of three questions, and which Thou didst reject —that which is called *temptations*[7] in the books? And yet, if ever there was an utterly authentic, thunderous miracle on this earth it took place that day, the day of these three temptations. And it was precisely in the advent of these three questions that this miracle lay. Were it possible to suppose—merely tentatively and for argument's sake—that these three questions of the dread Spirit had vanished without a trace from the books and that it was necessary to re-establish them, to invent and create them anew, so as to insert them in the books again, and that to do so it were necessary to convene all the sages of the world—rulers, high priests, scholars, philosophers, poets—and then put the problem up to them: Invent, create three questions—but such questions as should not only be in keeping with the magnitude of the event (that would not be enough) but, over and above that, voice in three words, in but three human phrases, all the future history of the universe and of mankind—well, dost Thou think that all the combined great wisdom on earth could invent anything at all approaching the force and profundity of those three questions which were actually put to Thee at that time in the wilderness by the mighty and sage Spirit? By these questions alone, merely through the miracle of their advent, one can grasp that one is dealing not with the transient mind of man but with a mind sempiternal and absolute. For in these three questions all the subsequent history of man is, as it were, combined into one whole and foretold, and they present three images wherein all the unsolvable historical contradictions of the nature of man the world over will come together. At that time this could not be so clearly perceived, since the future was unknown; but now, with the passing of fifteen centuries, we perceive that everything in these three questions has been divined and foretold to such an extent, and to such an extent has come true, that it is no longer possible to add anything to them or to take anything away from them.

"Decide Thou Thyself, then, who was right: Thou, or he who put these questions to Thee at that time? Recall the first question—I may not be quoting it literally, yet its purport was this: 'Thou wouldst go forth into the world, and Thou art going forth with hands bare and empty, with some promise or other concerning freedom, a promise which men in their simplicity and inborn licentiousness cannot even take in with their minds, which they dread and shy away from—inasmuch as nothing, at any time, has been more insupportable to man and man's social structure than freedom! But dost Thou see those stones in that barren, incandescent wilderness? Turn them into loaves of bread, and mankind will run after Thee like to a herd, grateful and submissive, even though forever trembling lest Thou take away Thy hand and Thy loaves of bread will fail them.'

"But Thou wouldst not deprive man of freedom and didst spurn the suggestion—for, Thou didst reason, what kind of freedom can there be when submission is bought with bread? Thou didst retort: *Man doth not live by bread alone*[8]—yet dost Thou know that in the name of this same earthly bread the spirit of the earth will rise up against Thee and do battle with Thee and overcome Thee, and all will follow after the spirit of the earth, huzzaing: *Who is like unto the beast?* . . . *He maketh fire come down from heaven on the earth in the sight of men.*[9] Dost Thou know that ages will pass, and mankind will proclaim through the lips of its super-wisdom and science that there is no such thing as transgression and, therefore, no such thing as sin either, but that there are only the hungry. 'Feed them, and then go ahead and ask virtue of them!'—that is what they will inscribe upon the banner they will raise against Thee and through which Thy temple will be destroyed. On the site of Thy temple a new edifice will rise, there will rise anew the dread Tower of Babel, and even though this one, too, will never be builded to the end, even as its predecessor, Thou couldst nevertheless obviate this new tower and shorten the sufferings of men by a thousand years— inasmuch as it is to us, and us only, that they will come after having striven a thousand agonizing years over this tower of theirs! They will then seek us out once more underground, in the catacombs where we shall be in hid- ing (inasmuch as we will be persecuted and martyred anew), will find us, and cry out unto us: 'Feed us, for they who have promised us fire from heaven have not made it come down on earth in our sight.' And only then will we finish building their tower for them, for the only ones who can finish building it are those who will give them their fill of food—and it will be we alone who will give them that in Thy name, and we will lie that it *is* in Thy name. Oh, never, never will they feed them- selves without us! No science whatsoever will yield them bread as long as they remain free, but it will all wind up by their bringing their freedom to our feet and saying unto us: 'Better make slaves of us, but give us our fill to eat.' They will come to understand at last, by themselves, that freedom and earthly bread enough for everyone are inconceivable together, inasmuch as they will never, never be able to share among themselves!

"They will also become convinced that they can never be free, either, inasmuch as they are of but little strength, depraved, insignificant and rebels all. Thou didst promise them heavenly bread, but I again repeat: Can it com- pare with the earthly in the eyes of the weak, eternally depraved and eternally ignoble tribe of men? And even if thousands and tens of thousands should follow after Thee for the sake of heavenly bread, what is to become of the millions and tens of thousands of millions of those beings who will find it beyond their strength to contemn earthly bread for the heavenly? Or are only the tens of thousands of the great and strong dear to Thee, while the millions of others, numerous as the sands of the sea, who are weak yet love Thee, are merely to serve as material for the great and the strong? Nay, to us even the weak are precious. They are depraved and they are rebels, but in the end it is just they who will become submissive as well. They will be wonderstruck by us and will consider us gods because we, having taken our place at their head, have consented to endure freedom and to lord it over them—so dreadful will they at last find it to be free! We, for our part, will say that we are in submission to Thee and are lording it over them in Thy name. Once more will we deceive them, inasmuch as we will no longer let Thee come to us. And in that very deception will lie our suffering, inasmuch as we will have to lie. There, that is what the first question in the wilderness signified, and that is what Thou didst reject in the name of that freedom which Thou hast put above all things else.

"Yet at the same time this question held the great mystery of this world. Hadst Thou accepted the *loaves of bread,* Thou wouldst have supplied an answer to the universal and sempiternal yearning not only of man as a unipersonal being but of mankind as one whole: 'Before whom are we to bend the knee?' Man, on finding himself free, hath no care more unremitting and excruciating than to seek out, as speedily as may be, someone or something before whom or which he might bend his knee. But man seeks to bend his knee before that which is already indisputable, so very indisputable that all men might simultaneously agree to do their knee-bending before it in common. For the care of these pitiful creatures does not consist solely of seeking out something before which I or another may bend the knee, but to seek out something or other in which even all might come to believe and bend the knee before—and all this must absolutely be done by *everybody in common*. And it is precisely this need of a *communality* of genuflection which constitutes the chiefest martyrdom of man individually as well as of mankind as a whole, since the start of time. Because of universal genuflection they have been extirpating one another with the sword. They have reared up gods and called to one another: 'Forsake your gods and come to bend your knee before ours—otherwise, death unto you and your gods!' And thus will it be to the end of the world; even when the very gods vanish from the world men will fall on their faces before idols just the same. Thou didst know, Thou couldst not but have known, this basic mystery of the nature of man, yet Thou didst reject the sole absolute banner—the banner of earthly bread—which was being offered Thee in order to compel all to bend their knees incontrovertibly before Thee—and it was in the name of freedom and heavenly bread Thou didst reject it.

"Now look upon that which Thou didst thereafter. And, again, still in the name of freedom. I tell Thee, man has no care more excruciating than to find as speedily as possible someone to whom to hand over the gift of freedom which this miserable creature is born with. But only he who will lull men's conscience can gain mastery over their freedom. Together with the bread an incontestable banner was being proffered to Thee: Give him bread and man will bend his knee, inasmuch as there is naught more incontestable than bread; yet if at the same time anyone outside of Thyself should gain mastery over man's conscience—O, man will then abandon even Thy bread and follow after him who will seduce his conscience. In this instance Thou wert right. Inasmuch as the mystery of man's being lies not in merely living but in what one is to live for. Without a definite notion of what he is to live for man will not consent to live, and would rather destroy himself than remain upon earth even if he were to have nothing but loaves of bread all around him. Yea, verily. Yet what was the upshot? Instead of gaining mastery over men's freedom, Thou didst make it still greater for them! Or hast Thou forgot that tranquility—and even death—is dearer to man than freedom of choice in the knowledge of good and of evil?

"There is naught more seductive to man than freedom of his conscience, but there is also naught more excruciating. And lo, instead of accepting firm grounds for the lulling of man's conscience once and for all, Thou didst prefer everything that is extraordinary, enigmatic and vague, everything that is beyond the strength of men—and therefore Thou didst act as if there were no love in Thee for them at all. And just see Who did this: He who had come to give His life for them! Instead of gaining mastery over the freedom of man, Thou didst increase it and burden for all time with its torments man's spiritual kingdom. Thy desire was to have man love Thee freely, to have him freely follow after Thee, enticed and captivated by Thee. Instead of resorting to the unyielding ancient law, man was henceforth to decide for himself with a free heart what is good and what is evil, having only Thy image before him for guidance—yet can it be possible it never occurred to Thee that he would at last spurn and impugn even Thy image and Thy truth if he were to be crushed down by such a frightful burden

as freedom of choice? Men will cry out in the end that
the truth is not in Thee, for none could have left them in
greater confusion and torment than Thou hast done,
leaving them so many cares and unsolvable problems.
Thus it was that Thou Thyself hast furnished the basis
for the destruction of Thy very kingdom, and Thou
needst no longer blame any other therefor.

"And yet, was it that which was being proffered to
Thee? There be three forces, the only three forces upon
earth, capable of overcoming and capturing forever the
conscience of these debile mutineers—for their own
happiness; these powers are Miracle, Mystery, Authority.
Thou hast rejected the one, and the other, and the third,
and hast Thyself set the example for such rejection.
When the awesome and super-wise Spirit set Thee on a
pinnacle of the temple, and said unto Thee: *If Thou
wouldst know if Thou be the Son of God, cast Thyself
down from hence: for it is said concerning the same, that
the angels shall bear Him up and carry Him in their
hands, and He will not fall and will not bruise Himself;
and Thou wilt learn then if Thou be the Son of God, and
wilt prove then what Thy faith in Thy Father is like*—[10]
Thou, having heard him out, didst spurn the suggestion,
and submitted not, and cast not Thyself down. Oh, of
course, in this instance Thou didst act as proudly and
magnificently as a god! But the people, now, that weak,
mutinous tribe—come, are *they* gods? O, Thou didst
comprehend then that hadst Thou taken but one step,
hadst Thou made but a move to cast Thyself down, Thou
wouldst have tempted even the Lord and lost all faith in
Him, and dashed Thyself against the earth Thou hadst
come to save, and the intelligent spirit tempting Thee
would have rejoiced. But, I repeat: Are there many like
to Thee? And canst Thou possibly admit for even a moment that such temptation could be borne by men as

well? Is the nature of man so fashioned that he is able to reject a miracle and, at such fearful moments of life, moments of the most basic, dread and excruciating spiritual questionings, can be left only to the free decision of the heart? Oh, Thou wert aware that Thy great exploit would be chronicled in books, would come down to the remotest reaches of time and the uttermost limits of the earth, and Thy hope was that, following after Thee, man also would retain God, without having need of any miracle. But Thou didst not know that no sooner would man reject miracle than he would on the instant reject God as well, for it is not so much God as miracles that man seeks. And since it is beyond man's strength to remain without miracles, he is bound to create for himself a mess of new miracles, this time all his own, and will bend his knee this time to the miracle of the witch-doctor, to the black magic of the witch-woman, though he may be a rebel, a heretic and an atheist a hundred times over.

"Thou didst not come down from the cross when they screamed at Thee, reviling and mocking Thee: *Descend now from the cross, that we may see and believe.*[11] Thou didst not come down because, this time as well, Thou wouldst not enslave man through miracle and didst thirst after a free faith and not a miraculous one. Thou didst thirst after a love in freedom, and not the slavish raptures of a thrall before a might that had stunned him with horror once and for all. But in this instance, too, Thou hadst too high an opinion of men since they are, as a matter of course, so many thralls, even though they had been created rebels. Gaze about Thee and judge: Lo, fifteen centuries have passed, yet go Thou and look upon them—whom hast Thou raised to Thy level? I swear to Thee, man is created weaker and lower than Thou didst think him! Can he—*can* he—fulfill that which Thou

canst? In esteeming him so greatly Thou hast acted as if
Thou hadst ceased to commiserate with him, for Thou
didst actually ask too much of him. And who did this?
The very same One Who had come to love man even
above Himself! Hadst Thou esteemed him less, Thou
wouldst even have demanded less of him, and that would
have proven nearer love, in that his burden would have
been lighter. Man is weak and vile. What is there to
his present mutinying everywhere against our power,
and to his pride in that he is mutinying? It is the pride
of an infant and a schoolboy. Little children, who have
mutinied in class and driven out their instructor. But an
end will come to the jubilation of the urchins; they will
have to pay for it dearly. They will overthrow temples
and inundate the earth with blood. But the foolish
children will at last surmise that, even though they are
rebels, they are rebels of but little strength, unable to
endure their own rebellion. Bathed in their foolish tears,
they will confess at last that He Who had created them
rebels had doubtlessly done so for a laugh at their
expense. They will utter this in despair, and their utterance will be a blasphemy because of which they will
become still more miserable, since the nature of man
cannot bear blasphemy and at the very last it will avenge
that blasphemy upon none other than its own self.

"And so uneasiness, consternation and misery form the
present portion of men after Thou hast endured so much
for their freedom! A great prophet of Thine tells in a
vision and an allegory that he had beheld all the participants in the first Resurrection, and that there were
twelve thousand of them in each tribe. But even if there
were so many of them, they too were not like unto men,
but gods, as it were. They had borne up under Thy
cross, they had borne up under decades in the famished
and naked desert, feeding upon locusts and roots—and,

of course, Thou mayest well point proudly to these children of freedom, children of love in freedom, children of a free and splendid sacrifice in Thy name. Yet recall that there were but a few thousand of them in all, and that they were gods, at that—but what of the rest? And wherein are the remaining weak ones at fault because they had not been able to endure that which the mighty ones could? Wherein is a weak soul at fault because it finds it beyond its strength to contain such awesome gifts? Come, didst Thou come only to the chosen and for the chosen? But if that be so, then there is a mystery here, and it is not for us to understand it. Yet if a mystery there be, then we, too, were in the right in promulgating a mystery, and in teaching men that it is not the free decision of their hearts that matters, and not love, but a mystery to which they must submit blindly, even outside their conscience. And that is just what we did. We emended Thy great exploit and based it upon *Miracle, Mystery and Authority*. And the people were overcome with joy, because they were led off once more like a herd, and because so awesome a gift, which had brought them so many torments, was at last lifted from off their hearts. Speak—were we right, teaching and acting thus? For can it be that we did not love mankind, having with such resignation realized its impotency, having with such love eased its burden, and having granted dispensation to its frail nature for even sin, let us say, but sin by our sanction?

"Wherefore, then, hast Thou now come to hinder us? And wherefore art Thou gazing at me, silently and penetratingly, with Thy meek eyes? Wax angry—I want not Thy love, since I myself have no love for Thee. And what have I to conceal from Thee? For am I not aware Whom I am talking to? All that I am impelled to tell Thee—I read this in Thy eyes—is already known to Thee. And

am I the one to conceal our mystery, our secret from
Thee? Mayhap it is Thy wish to hear it only from my
lips—hearken, then: We are not with Thee but with *him*
—for eight centuries by now. It is exactly eight centuries
since we have taken from him that which Thou didst reject with scorn, that last gift which he did offer Thee,
shewing Thee all the kingdoms of the world; we have
accepted Rome and the sword of Caesar at his hands,
and have proclaimed only ourselves the kings of the
world, the sole kings, even though to this very day we
have not succeeded in bringing our enterprise to full
completion. Yet who is to blame for that?

"Oh, that enterprise is to this very time still at its
beginning—but at least it has been begun. There is a
long wait yet to its consummation, and the earth will yet
undergo many sufferings, but we shall attain our ends
and be Caesars, and only then will we give thought to
the universal happiness of men. And yet, Thou couldst
even at that time have taken the sword of Caesar. Wherefore didst Thou reject this last gift? Hadst Thou accepted
this third counsel of the mighty spirit, Thou wouldst
have rounded out the sum of everything that man seeks
upon earth; that is: before whom to bend his knee, to
whom to hand over his conscience, and in what manner
all are to become united at last into a single, incontro-
vertible, common and harmonious ant-heap, for the
third and ultimate agony of man is his necessity for
universal unification. Mankind, as a whole, has always
striven to settle, infallibly, in one universal mould. Many
have been the great nations, each with its great history,
but the greater their height has been, the greater was
their misery also, inasmuch as their realization of the
need of universality in the unification of mankind was
greater than that of other nations. The great conquerors,
the Tamerlanes and Genghis-Khans, swept like tor-

nadoes over the earth, striving to conquer Creation, yet even they expressed, though unconsciously, the very same great need of mankind for universal and general unity.

"Hadst Thou accepted the world and Caesar's purple, Thou wouldst have founded a universal kingdom and brought universal peace. For who is to have dominion over man if not they who have dominion over man's conscience and hold man's loaves of bread in their hands? And so we did take the sword of Caesar and, having taken it, we have as a matter of course rejected Thee and followed after *him*. Oh, more ages of their free mind, of their science and anthropophagy will yet pass—for, having started to rear their Tower of Babel without us, they will wind up with anthropophagy. But it is then, then! that the beast will come crawling to us on its belly and will fall to licking our feet and asperging them with the tears of blood spurting out of its eyes. And we shall mount the beast, and shall raise up the cup, and MYSTERY will be inscribed thereon. And then, and then only, will the kingdom of peace and happiness arrive for men.

"Proud art Thou of Thy chosen ones, yet all Thou hast are Thy chosen, whereas we shall set all men at peace. Yet come—how many of these chosen ones, of the mighty men who could have become chosen ones, have wearied at last of biding for Thee and have borne (and will still bear) the forces of their spirit, and the fervor of their hearts, to another fallow field, and will end up by raising their *free* banner against none other than Thee! However, Thou Thyself hast raised that banner. Whereas under us all will be happy, and will no longer rebel, nor extirpate one another, as they will go on doing the world over under Thy freedom. Oh, we will convince them that they can become really free only

when they renounce their freedom in our favor and submit to us.

"Well, now, shall we prove right, or shall we be lying?
They themselves will become convinced that we are in
the right, for they will recall to what horrors of bondage
and of consternation Thy freedom brought them. Freedom, the free mind and science, will lead them into such
thick woods and confront them with such miracles and
unsolvable mysteries that certain of them, the unsubmissive and ferocious ones, will destroy their own selves;
others, unsubmissive yet having but little strength, will
destroy one another; while others still, those who are
left, impotent and miserable, will come crawling at our
feet and raise their voices, wailing: 'Ye alone were possessed of His mystery, and we are returning to you—
save us from our own selves!'

"Receiving loaves of bread from us they will, of
course, perceive that we are taking from them none other
than their own loaves of bread, gotten by none other
than their own hands, so that we might distribute those
loaves to none other than themselves, without any miracle whatsoever about the transaction. They will perceive
that we have not turned stones into loaves of bread—
yet truly, more than over the bread itself, will they rejoice over receiving it from our hands! For they will
remember only too well that hitherto, without us, the
very loaves of bread obtained by them turned in their
hands into mere stones, whereas when they came back
to us the very stones in their hands turned into loaves
of bread. Only too, too well will they come to appreciate
what it means to submit once and for all! And as long
as men do not understand that they will be unhappy.

"Who above all others helped this incomprehension
along—tell me that! Who scattered the herd and dispersed it over paths unknown? But the herd will gather

anew, and anew will yield—and this time it will be once and for all. Then will we give them a gentle, resigned happiness, the happiness of the impotent, of creatures created as they have been. Oh, we will convince them at last not to be proud, for Thou hast raised them on high and taught them to be proud; we will prove to them that they are impotent, that they are no more than pitiful children, yet that childish happiness is the sweetest of all. They will wax timorous and take to looking up to us, and huddle close to us, even as chicks to a brood-hen. They will *wonder at us with great admiration*,[12] and be awestruck by us, and feel proud because we are so mighty and so intelligent that we were able to subdue so mutinous a herd of thousands of millions. Enfeebled, they will tremble before our wrath, their minds will grow timorous, their eyes as easily moved to tears as those of babes and women, yet they will just as easily, at the merest wave of our hands, shift to gaiety and to laughter, to radiant joy and the happy little song of children.

"Yea, we will compel them to labor, but in the hours free from labor we will arrange their life like a children's game, with childish songs, choir-singing, and innocent dances also. O, we shall grant them dispensation even to sin—they are weak and impotent, and they will love us with the love of children because we shall allow them to sin. We shall tell them that every sin will be redeemed if it be committed with our sanction, and as for our granting them dispensation to sin—well, we are doing it out of love for them; in the matter of chastisement for that sinning—well, so be it: we take it upon ourselves. And take it upon ourselves we will, and they will deify us as benefactors, who have taken on the load of their sins before God. And they will have no secrets from us whatsoever. We shall permit or forbid them to live with their wives and mistresses, to have or not to have children—depending entirely upon their obedience—and they will submit to us with blitheness and joy. The most excruciating secrets of their conscience—everything, everything!—will they bring to us, and we will decide everything for them, and they will believe our every decision with rejoicing inasmuch as that will deliver them from great care and their present torments of personal and free decision.

"And all will be happy, all these millions of beings, all save the hundred thousand or so governing them, that is. For we alone, we who guard the mystery, we alone will be unhappy. There will be thousands of millions of happy infants, and a hundred thousand scapegoats who took upon themselves the curse of the knowledge of good and of evil. Gently will these beings die, they will go out as little tapers in Thy name, and beyond the grave they will attain naught but death. Yet we will keep the secret and, for no other end save their own happiness, we will keep on luring them with a reward heavenly and eternal. For, even if there were anything in the other world, then, of a certainty, it would not be for the likes of them.

"They say and they prophesy that Thou wilt come and conquer anew, that Thou wilt come with Thy chosen, with Thy proud and mighty ones. But we shall say that these have saved themselves alone, whereas we save all men. They say that the whore sitting upon the scarlet-colored beast and having in her hands the *mystery* will be made desolate, that those of little strength will mutiny again, that they will rend the purple upon her and make naked her *loathsome* flesh. But when that time comes I shall rise up and point out to Thee thousands of millions of happy infants who knew no sin. And we, who have for the sake of their happiness taken their sins upon ourselves, we will stand up before Thee and say: 'Judge us, if Thou canst—and darest.'

"Know, that I fear Thee not. Know, that I, too, have been in the wilderness—that I, too, fed upon locusts and roots; that I, too, once blessed that freedom wherewith Thou hast blessed men; I, too, was preparing to take my place among the number of Thy chosen ones, among the number of the mighty and the strong thirsting to *make up the number.* But I came to my senses and did not want to be in the service of madness. I turned back and adhered to the host of those who have *emended Thy great exploit.* I went from the proud and turned back to the meek, for the happiness of the meek. That which I am telling Thee will come to pass, and our Kingdom will be built up. I repeat to Thee, that no later than on the morrow Thou wilt see this submissive herd rush forward, at the first wave of my hand, to rake up the hot embers upon Thy bonfire, that bonfire upon which I shall burn Thee because Thou hast come to hinder us. For if ever there was anyone deserving one of our bonfires most of all, Thou art surely the one. On the morrow I will burn Thee. *Dixi.*"

Ivan stopped. He had warmed up while speaking, carried away by his story; when he had done, however, he suddenly smiled. Alësha, however, who had been listening to him in silence throughout, but had toward the end made many extremely agitated attempts to interrupt his brother's speech, although he had managed to restrain himself, now began speaking with a rush:

"But . . . that's an absurdity!" he cried out, flushing. "Your poem is praise to Jesus, and not blasphemy—as you wanted it to be. And whoever is going to believe the things you say about freedom? Is that—is *that* to be our understanding of it! Have we any such understanding of it in the Orthodox Church? That's Rome—and not all of Rome, either; that's a falsehood; those are the worst ones in Catholicism—inquisitors, Jesuits! And besides, such a fantastic personage as your Inquisitor is utterly out of the question. What sins of mankind are you talking about, which the others have taken upon themselves? What bearers of mystery be these, who have taken upon themselves some sort of curse for the happiness of men? Who has ever beheld them? We know the Jesuits—they are in ill repute; are they by any chance the way you have drawn them? They aren't at all—not at all. They are simply a Romish army for the future universal kingdom on earth, with an Emperor—the Pontiff of Rome—at its head. There you have their ideal, but without any mysteries and exalted melancholy about it. The commonest sort of lust after power, after filthy earthly benefits, after the enslavement of others—something in the nature of a system of serfdom for the future—with the stipulation that they be the landowners—and that's all they're after. It may well be that they don't even believe in God. Your agonizing Inquisitor is sheer fantasy—"

"Come, hold on, hold on!" Ivan laughed. "How hot under the collar you've gotten! Fantasy, you say—let it go at that. It's fantasy, of course. However, let me ask you this: Can it be that you really think all this Catholic movement of the latter ages is in reality nothing but a lust for power, solely for the sake of filthy benefits, and nothing else? Can it be that that is what Father Paissy is teaching you?"

"No, no; on the contrary, Father Paissy on one occasion said something of the same sort as you did, actually. But, of course, not that—not that at all," Alësha suddenly brought himself up short.

"That's a precious bit of information just the same, despite your 'not that at all.' What I am asking you, specifically, is why your Jesuits and inquisitors have banded together solely for material, vile benefits, and nothing else? Why can't a single agonizing soul spring up in their midst, a soul tormented by a great sorrow and filled with love for mankind? Look: suppose there has been found even one among all those desiring only material and filthy blessings—just one, let's say, such as this ancient, this Inquisitor of mine, who has himself eaten roots in the wilderness, who has raged as he subdued his flesh, so that he might make himself free and perfect, yet who nevertheless had loved mankind all his life, and then had his eyes suddenly opened, and perceived that it is no great moral bliss to attain perfection of will only to become convinced at the same time that the millions of other beings of God have remained set up only as a mockery, that they would never have the strength to get the hang of their freedom, that from among those sorry mutinous creatures there would never emerge any Titans for the completion of the Tower, that it is not for such geese that the Great Idealist dreamt of His harmony. . . . Having grasped all this, he turned back and attached himself to—the clever ones. Really, mightn't that have happened?"

"To whom did he attach himself—to what clever ones?" Alësha cried out, all but losing his temper. "There is no intelligence of that sort among them, nor any such mysteries and secrets. Godlessness alone, if you like—and there's their whole secret. This Inquisitor of yours has no faith in God—and there's the whole of *his* secret!

"Even so! You've caught on at last. And that is actually so, and it is actually of this that their whole secret consists—but then, isn't that suffering, even though it be suffering only to such a man as he, who has immolated his whole life in an exploit in the wilderness and yet hasn't cured himself of his love for mankind? At the sunset of that life he becomes clearly convinced that only the counsels of the great, awesome Spirit may put into any sort of tolerable order those mutinous creatures of little strength, 'the unfinished trial beings, created as a mockery.' And so, having become convinced of this, he perceives that it is necessary to follow the directive given by the intelligent Spirit, the awesome Spirit of death and destruction, and that to do so it is necessary to accept falsehood and deception and, with full awareness this time, to guide men to death and destruction, and on top of that to hoodwink them throughout the journey, so that they might not somehow notice whither they are being led, so that during this journey, at least, these pitiful blind men might deem themselves happy. And mark you this: the hoodwinking is in the name of Him in Whose ideal the old man had had such passionate faith all his life long! Come, is that not misery? And should even one such come to be at the head of all this army 'thirsting after power for the sake of filthy benefits alone—' then, truly, doesn't even one such suffice to create a tragedy? And not only that: it is enough to have but one such, standing at the head, for the finding at last of a genuinely guiding idea for the whole Roman business with all its armies and Jesuits— the supreme idea of that business.

"I tell you plainly that I firmly believe there has never been a paucity of such unique men among those standing at the head of the movement. Who knows, perhaps these unique ones may have occurred by chance, now and then, even among the Roman pontiffs. Who knows, perhaps this accursed old man, loving mankind so stubbornly and in a way so very much his own, may exist even now in the guise of a whole host of such unique old men, and that not at all by chance but as a concord, as a secret league, formed long since for the preservation of the mystery, for its preservation from men unhappy and of but little strength, for the purpose of assuring their happiness. That must be the case, absolutely—and, besides, that's how it should be.

"I have a glimmering notion that even the Masons have something in the nature of this very mystery as their cornerstone, and that the very reason why Catholics hate the Masons so is because they regard them as business rivals, splitting up the unity of the idea, whereas there should be but *one fold and one shepherd.*[13] However, this defence of my idea must make me look like a literary man who can't stand your criticism. Enough of this."

"Perhaps you're a Freemason yourself!" suddenly escaped from Alësha. "You don't believe in God," he added, but by now with exceeding sorrow. Besides that, it had struck him that his brother was looking at him with a mocking smile. "Well, and how does your poem end?" he asked abruptly, looking at the ground. "Or was that the end?"

"Here's how I wanted to end it—"

When the Inquisitor falls silent, he waits for some time for whatever answer his Captive may make. He finds His silence hard to bear. He had seen how the Captive had been listening to him all the while in absorption, gently gazing straight into his eyes and evidently without wishing to argue with him. The ancient wants Him to say something, even though it be something bitter, something dreadful.

Instead, He suddenly approaches the ancient and gently kisses him upon his bloodless, nonagenarian lips.

And therein is all His answer. The old man shudders.

Something stirs at the corners of his lips. He goes toward
the door, opens it, and says to Him:

"Go, and come no more—do not come at all. Never,
never!"

And the Grand Inquisitor releases Him, lets Him out
upon the "dark flagstones of the city."

The Captive departs.

"But what of the old man?"

The kiss blazes upon the Grand Inquisitor's heart—
but does not change his idea by a jot.

"And you are with him—you too?" Alësha exclaimed
sorrowfully.

Ivan laughed.

"Why, all this is nonsense, Alësha. For it's only the
muddled poem of a muddled student, who has never
written even two lines of verse. Why do you take it so
seriously? Are you thinking, perhaps, that I'm heading
straight there, to the Jesuits, to take my place in the host
of those who are rectifying His exploit? O, Lord—
what's it to me? For I've told you: all I'm after is to drag
along until I'm thirty, and after that—dash the goblet to
the ground! . . ."

Alësha was looking at him in silence.

"I was thinking, brother, since I am going away, that
I have you, at least, in all this world," Ivan uttered suddenly with unexpected emotion. "But now I see that in
your heart as well I have no place, my beloved anchorite.
I will not disown the 'all is permissible' formula; well,
what then—will you disown me for that? Will you? Will
you?"

Alësha got up, walked up to him and silently, gently,
kissed him upon the lips.

"Literary theft!" Ivan cried out, in some transport of delight. "You lifted that out of my poem! Thanks, just the same. Come on, Alësha, let's go; time for both of us to be leaving. . . ."

NOTES

[1] Rev. XXII: 7; 12; 20.

[2] Mark XIII:32.

[3] Matt. XXIV:27.

[4] Mark V:41.

[5] Thus in the Russian. Apparently based on John VIII:36—*If the Son therefore shall make you free, ye shall be free indeed.*

[6] Derived from Matt. XVI:19; XVIII:18.

[7] Luke IV:13 reads: *all the temptation.*

[8] Matt. IV:4 and Luke IV:4 read: *It is written, Man shall not live by bread alone;* Deut. VIII:3 reads: *Man doth not live by bread only.*

[9] Rev. XIII:4; 13.

[10] *Cf.* Matt. IV:5,6; Luke IV:9-11.

[11] Mark XV:32.

[12] Based on Rev. XVII:6. *Admiration* is here used in its archaic sense of wonder, surprise or astonishment.

[13] John X:16.

NIKOLAI SEMËNOVICH LESKOV

(1831–1895)

> *Leo Tolstoy:* But Leskov, now . . . there's a real writer—have you read him?
> *Gorki:* Yes. I like him very much; especially his language.
> *Tolstoy:* He knew the language wonderfully—so much so that he could perform feats of magic with it.
>
> *Gorki*

EDITOR'S NOTE

AFTER a youth of hardships Leskov, at 29, became a provincial journalist and, two years later, a St. Petersburg one. Here, through a misinterpretation of one of

his articles, he ran into much the same difficulty with
the younger radical element as Turgenev did; Leskov,
however, carried on the feud for years and, despite the
boycott of the radicals and the animosity of the critics,
won popular approval. Subsequently he wrote for liberal periodicals, and one of his anti-clerical stories deprived him of a government sinecure. Toward the end
of his life he became badly, but not hopelessly, infected
with Tolstoyanism.

His novel, *Cathedral Folk,* is by now accepted as a
classic, but it is as a story teller that he is among the
greatest, not only in Russia but in the world. No other
Russian has told such odd, racy, droll tales as Leskov
and, next to Chekhov, he is the most loved of Russian
humorists. Some of his stories were such *naturals,* that
he could not convince the critics that they were pure
creations of his, and not mere retellings of folk or other
material. There were three wizards of the word (in
Gorki's phrase) each of whom fashioned Russian into
an instrument peculiarly his own: Saltykov, Leskov, and
Zoshchenko; of these Leskov is, in this respect, the
greatest and, also in this respect, as well as in "the
breadth of his grasp of life" and "the depth of his understanding of its folk-enigmas," he not infrequently
"towers," in Gorki's opinion, above Leo Tolstoy, Gogol,
Turgenev, Goncharov.

After his death interest in him waned considerably,
but his popularity since the Revolution can be described
only as immense. And that popularity extends to drama-
tizations of his works. *Lady Macbeth of Mtsensk* was a
success not only as a play but as a grand opera (with
music by Shostakovich), and Zamiatin's dramatic version of *The Flea* was also a hit. The story here given
was likewise dramatized, within the last ten years.

Ivan Yakovlevich Koreisha (of whom Leskov wrote

more than once) was an actual figure, an innocent who
spent half his life (1780–1861) in a madhouse and, as
a miracle man, had a vast following among the Moscow
merchants. *A Slight Error* is an exquisite vignette of the
mores of that ignorant and quite depressing class.

A Slight Error

(A Certain Moscow Family's Skeleton-in-the-Closet)

NIKOLAI SEMËNOVICH LESKOV

ONE evening during the Christmas holidays, at a
gathering of sensible people, a great deal was
said about belief and lack of belief. The talk did not,
however, deal with the higher questions of deism or
materialism, but with belief in people gifted with the
special powers of foresight and prediction and, if you
like, the power, *sui generis,* of working miracles. And
as it happened there was a certain person there, a
sedate citizen of Moscow, who spoke up as follows:

"It is no easy matter, ladies and gentlemen, to judge
who is living according to belief and who isn't, for in
this life there are all sorts of circumstances for believing
or not believing; sometimes our very reason may fall
into error in such cases."

And, after this prologue, he told us a curious tale,
which I shall try to give in his own words.

My uncle and my aunt were alike adherents of the
late miracle worker, Ivan Yakovlevich Koreisha. Especially my aunt: she would never begin any undertaking without consulting him beforehand. She would visit

him in the madhouse, first thing, and get his advice, and then beg him to pray for her undertaking. Uncle had a mind of his own and placed less reliance on Ivan Yakovlevich; however, he too had faith in him, now and then, and did not object to gifts and offerings being brought to this miracle worker. They weren't rich people, yet they were very well off, carrying on a trade in sugar from a shop in their own house. They had no sons, but they did have three daughters: Kapitolina Nikitishna, Katerina Nikitishna, and Olga Nikitishna. All of the three were very far from being hard on the eyes, and they all knew well how to do different things and how to run a house. Kapitolina Nikitishna was married, only her husband wasn't a merchant but a painter; however, he was a most kindhearted man and doing rather well; he was getting well-paying commissions right along for painting church murals and so on. There was one thing about him, though, which the whole clan found disagreeable; he was painting divine subjects all the time, yet was familiar with certain free-thinking ideas from Kourganov's *Epistolary Guide*. He loved to talk about Chaos, about Ovid, about Prometheus, and was fond of comparing fables with historical writings. If it weren't for that everything would have been just fine. And another thing was that he and his wife had no children, and this grieved my uncle and aunt ever so much. So far they had married off only their first daughter, and to their surprise she had been childless for all of three years. Because of that the suitors had taken to giving the other sisters the go-by.

My aunt kept asking Ivan Yakovlevich, the miracle worker, the reason her daughter wasn't having a child. "They're young and handsome, the both of them," she said, "how come, then, there are no children?"

"There is therefore a heaven of heavens; and then

there is a heaven of heavens," Ivan Yakovlevich began
to mutter.

The nuns, his Sibyls, interpreted the thing for my
aunt:

"The Holy Father bids your son-in-law to pray to
God—but, probably, he must be the one of little faith
amongst you."

My aunt, she just oh'd:

"Everything," said she, "is revealed unto him!"

And she took to pestering the painter to go to confes-
sional, but the other just didn't care a straw! He had a
free and easy attitude toward everything; why, he even
ate meat on fast-days—and not only that, but they'd
heard in a roundabout way that, apparently, he ate
both snails and oysters. And they were all living in the
one house, now, and often felt downhearted that there
was such a fellow, with no faith in him at all, amongst
their merchant clan.

II

And so my aunt went to Ivan Yakovlevich, to ask him
for a double-barreled prayer: That the womb of Kapitolina, the handmaiden of God, might be opened, and
that Larii (as they called the painter), the servant of
God, might see the light of faith.

Both my aunt and my uncle joined in asking the
miracle worker to pray thus.

Ivan Yakovlevich began babbling something or other
which you just couldn't understand, while the holy
women who were in his service and attended on him,
made the thing clear:

"Just now," said they, "there's no making him out,
but you tell us what you're asking for, and we'll give
him a note about it tomorrow."

So my aunt started telling them, and they wrote it

down: "That the womb of Kapitolina, handmaiden of God, might be opened, and that Larii, the slave of God, might be strengthened in faith."

So the old couple left this note with their request and went home with light steps.

At home they didn't tell a thing to anybody, save to Kapochka, and only then on the condition that she would not pass it on to her husband, the unbelieving painter, but would only live with him as lovingly and amicably as possible, and keep an eye on him: whether he wouldn't be drawing any closer to believing in Ivan Yakovlevich. And this painter, now, used to curse in the devil's name something awful, and always had some funny saying while he did so, just like a merry-andrew at a country fair. All he had in mind was having his joke and his bit of fun. He'd come at twilight to his father-in-law: "Come on," he'd say, "let's read the prayer-book with fifty-two pages"—meaning, that is, a game of cards. Or, as he would be sitting down, he'd say: "With the condition that we play until the first man keels over."

My aunt, now, she just couldn't stand hearing things like that. So my uncle he up and told him:

"Don't upset her like that; she loves you, and she has taken on a vow for you."

But the other burst out laughing, and said to his mother-in-law:

"Why do you make rash vows? Or don't you know that it was because of such a vow that John the Precursor had his head chopped off? Watch out; there may be some unforeseen misfortune in your home."

That threw still more of a scare into his mother-in-law, and every day she would dash over to the madhouse in alarm. There they would reassure her, telling her the matter was going well; the Holy Father was reading the note every day, and that what was written on it would now be soon fulfilled.

And fulfilled it was, most suddenly—and it was of such a nature that one doesn't feel like telling it, even.

III

Her second daughter, the unmarried Katechka, came to my aunt, and right off fell on her knees before her, and sobbed, and wept bitterly:

"What's up with you?" asked my aunt. "Who has wronged you?"

And the other answered, through her sobs:

"Mamma, dearest, I myself don't know what it is, and what from—it's the first time and the last such a thing has happened to me. . . . Only do you hide my sin from daddy."

My aunt gave her one look, jabbed a finger at her belly, and asked:

"This the spot?"

"Yes, mamma dear," answered Katechka. "How did you ever guess it? I myself don't know what it's from—"

My aunt just oh'd and wrung her hands.

"My child," said she, "don't even try to get to the bottom of it; I myself may be to blame for this mistake; I'm going right now to find out—" and she flew off at once in a cab to Ivan Yakovlevich.

"Show me," said she, "the note in which we request the Holy Father to pray about the fruit of the womb for a handmaiden of God—how is it written?"

The attending holy women searched on the window sill and handed her the note.

My aunt looked at it and all but lost her mind. What do you think? Why, sure enough, all this business had come about on account of an error in praying, because

instead of the handmaiden of God Kapitolina, who was
a married woman, they had written down the handmaiden of God Katerina, a still unmarried girl.

Said the holy women:

"There, what a come-uppance! The names are so
much alike . . . howsomever, it don't matter: *it can
be fixed.*"

But my aunt thought to herself: "No, you're lying;
it's past your fixing now; Kate has already had her
bellyful of prayer—" and she tore the bit of paper into
tiny scraps.

IV

The main thing they dreaded was, how break the
thing to my uncle? For he was the sort of a man that,
once he let himself go, it was the devil and all to check
him. Besides that, he liked Kate least of all, for his
favorite daughter was Olenka, the youngest, and it was
her he had promised to leave the most to.

So my aunt thought and thought, and she saw that
with her one head there was no thinking a way out of
this trouble; she called in her painter son-in-law for a
council, and revealed everything to him, with all the
particulars, and then she begged him:

"You," she told him, "even though you have no faith,
you may have some feelings in you—please, take pity
on Kate; help me hide her maidenly sin."

But a sudden frown came to the painter's forehead,
and he told her sternly:

"Excuse me, please, but even if you are my wife's
mother I have neither liking nor patience for being considered an unbeliever, for one thing, and, for another, I
can't understand: what sort of sin you are imputing to
Kate, since it was Ivan Yakovlevich who all the time was
doing all that imploring for her? I have all the feelings

of a brother for Katechka, and I will intercede for her because she is not at all at fault in this matter."

My aunt was biting her fingers and crying, but still she said:

"Well, now . . . how can she be not at all at fault?"

"Naturally she isn't, not at all. It's your miracle worker who balled everything up, and it's him you ought to ask for satisfaction."

"Come, how can one ask him for satisfaction! He's a saint of righteousness!"

"Well, now, if he's a saint of righteousness, just don't say anything. Send Kate to me with three bottles of champagne wine."

My aunt asked him, to find out if she had heard him aright:

"What was that?"

But he told her again:

"Three bottles of champagne; one right now, to my rooms, and two later on, wherever I tell you to bring them to, only they must be on hand in the house, and be kept on ice."

My aunt looked at him and only nodded her head:

"God be with you," said she. "I was thinking you were only without faith; but you paint the images of saints, yet you yourself turn out to have no feelings of any sort. That's why I can't bow down before your icons."

But he answered her:

"No, forget all about my faith—it's you, apparently, who are doubting and keep on thinking of physical nature, as though this thing were due to Kate's own fault, whereas I firmly believe that it's all the fault of none other than Ivan Yakovlevich; as for my feelings, you will perceive them when you send Kate to my studio with the champagne."

V

My aunt mulled over it some more, and in the end sent the wine to the painter, with Katechka herself. She went there with the wine on a tray, and she herself all in tears, but he sprang up, seized both of her little hands, and started crying himself.

"I feel sorrow, my little darling," said he, "over what has befallen you; but just the same you can't be napping with this business—come right out with all your secrets without wasting any time."

The girl confessed to him how she had happened to make this slip, and he up and put her under lock and key in his studio.

My aunt met her son-in-law with her eyes red from tears and didn't say anything. But he took her around, kissed her and said:

"There, now, don't be afraid; stop crying. Maybe God will help us."

"But tell me," my aunt whispered, "who's the guilty one in all this?"

But the painter shook his finger at her kindlily and said:

"There, now, that's already bad—you yourself were reproaching me all the time with lacking faith, but now, when your own faith has been put to a test, I see that you yourself haven't the least faith. Really, don't you see clearly that there are no guilty ones, but that the miracle man has simply made a slight error?"

"But where is my poor Katechka?"

"I spellbound her with an artist's frightful spell—and she scattered into dust, like magic treasure after an Amen!"

And at the same time he showed the studio key to his mother-in-law.

My aunt surmised that he had hidden the girl from her father's first wrath, and she took him around.

"Forgive me," she whispered, "you do have feelings of tenderness in you."

VI

My uncle came home, had his fill of tea as usual, and said:

"Well, shall we read the prayer-book of fifty-two leaves?"

They sat down to cards. And all those in the house shut all the doors on the two and walked about on tiptoes. As for my aunt, she kept walking away from the doors and walking up to them again: eavesdropping all the time and all the time crossing herself.

At last there was a sound of something smashing in the room. . . . She ran off and hid herself.

"He has revealed it," said she. "He has revealed the secret! Now there will be hell to pay!"

And sure enough: the doors flew open at once and my uncle shouted:

"Bring me my fur coat—and my big stick!"

The painter drew him back by his arm and said:

"What are you up to? Where are you bound?"

"I am going to the madhouse," said my uncle, "to beat up that miracle worker!"

My aunt, behind another door, started moaning:

"Run fast as you can to the madhouse and tell them to hide the Holy Father, Ivan Yakovlevich!"

And, true enough, uncle would have beaten him without fail, within an inch of his life, but his painter son-in-law restrained even him, awing him with the old man's own faith.

VII

The son-in-law started reminding his father-in-law that he had still another daughter.

"It don't matter," said the other. "She'll get her share of the inheritance, but I want to beat up this Ivan Yakovlevich Koreisha fellow! Let them law me after that."

"Why, I'm not trying to scare you with the law, but you just judge for yourself: think of the harm Ivan Yakovlevich can work to Olga. Why, it's horrible, the thing you are risking!"

My uncle stopped and became thoughtful.

"What sort of harm, now," he asked, "can he work?"

"Why, precisely the same sort of harm he worked to Katechka."

Uncle gave him a look and answered:

"Stop spouting bosh! Why, can he do anything like that?"

But the painter came right back at him:

"Well, if you have no faith, as I can see, then you can do as you know best; only don't be lamenting later and blaming the poor girls."

And that brought uncle up short. But his son-in-law dragged him back into the room and fell to convincing him.

"It would be best, the way I see it," said he, "to shove the miracle worker off to one side, but to tackle this business and mend it with domestic remedies."

The old man agreed, only he himself had no notion of what remedies to mend it with. But the painter came to his aid even in that.

"You've got to look for good ideas not when you're in wrath but when you're joyful."

"What sort of merrymaking can there be now, little brother," countered the other, "in a fix like this?"

"Why, this sort: I've got two flasks of the bubbly stuff, and until you drink them out with me I'm not going to tell you a word. You'd better agree. You know how mulish I am."

The old man looked at him and said:

"Keep on with your shenanigans—keep right on! What will come after that?"

But, in the end, he agreed.

VIII

The painter issued his orders, right lively, and came back—and his helper, also a master painter, came right behind him, carrying a tray, with two bottles and goblets.

No sooner had they come in than the painter locked the door after himself and put the key in his pocket. My uncle gave one look and grasped everything; as for his son-in-law, he nodded to the artist: the latter launched at once into humble supplication:

"I am the guilty one—forgive me and give us your blessing—"

My uncle asked:

"Is it all right to beat him up?"

His son-in-law said:

"It's all right, only there's really no need of it."

"Well, in that case, let him at least get down on his knees before me."

The son-in-law whispered to the other:

"There, for the sake of the girl you love, get down on your knees before her dad."

The other got down on his knees.

And what did the old man do but burst into tears.

"Do you," he asked the young painter, "love her very much?"

"I do."

"Well, kiss me."

And that's how they glossed over Ivan Yakovlevich's slight error. And all this remained in blessed secrecy, and the suitors began flocking to the youngest sister too, for they saw that these girls could be relied upon.

N. SHCHEDRIN
(MIKHAIL EUGRAPHOVICH SALTYKOV)
(1826–1889)

EDITOR'S NOTE

SALTYKOV is the direct inheritor of Gogol's mantle, and his undisputed classic, *The Golovlev Family*, is considered as great as *Dead Souls;* but he is also the creator of an original, castigatory genre, of a gallery of unforgettable scenes and portraits which, in addition to their artistic merits, furnish rich material for the social historian of Russia during serfdom and the period of emancipation; as a "master of the laughter which makes men wise" he surpasses even Gogol.

His mother, as a tyrant, seems to have been more than a match to Turgenev's. Saltykov's portrait of her is one of the most sardonic in all literature. But just as Pushkin was saved for Russia and humanity by his fabulous nurse, and Turgenev by an old serf, Saltykov found himself when, as a child, he came upon the Bible. This is not to imply Gogolian smugness in religion or Dostoevskian mysticism; there was no fighter against hypocrisy and bigotry more valiant than he.

He wrote his first poem at fifteen; since the days of Pushkin, each graduating class of the Alexandrovsky Lyceum had voted for a future Pushkin: in 1844 Saltykov was the choice. His first story, *A Muddled Affair*, was published in 1847; for his second, *Contradictions*, published in the sinister year of 1848 (he was involved in the same affair with Dostoevsky), he was banished for eight years to the hell-hole of Viatka. Saltykov had begun in the War Ministry after graduation, eventually attaining to a Lieutenant-Governorship; in 1868 he resigned to devote himself entirely to writing.

He made his reputation in 1856 with *Provincial Sketches; Innocent Stories, Prose Satires, Life's Trifles* and, above all, *Fairy Tales* (the selection here given is one of these), are works of satirical genius. Saltykov's sworn enemy was the hydra of Czarism, and he himself has enumerated some of its heads: "The law of the club, double-dealing, lying, rapaciousness, perfidy, emptyheadedness."

Saltykov, like so many other Russian writers, was forced to form a peculiar style as a "mask of naïve humor" to foil the censors; it was, by his own description, Aesopic. The homeliest colloquialisms will be found in it, and allusions, slang, half-utterances, coinages. Next to Leskov he is just about the hardest Russian to put over in English, even without the usual deadly insistence, on the part of others beside translators, upon *niceness* in translations, no matter how sprightly the originals may be. These factors may explain why so little of Saltykov has been Englished. *Fairy Tales* is available in a thoroughly feminine version, under the title of *Fables;* of

The Golovlev Family, however, there are no less than three English translations; of these, *A Family of Noblemen,* by Avrahm Yarmolinsky, is definitely to be preferred.

A Tale of How One Muzhik Kept Two Brass-Hats Well Fed

N. SHCHEDRIN

ONCE upon a time there were two Brass-Hats, and since both of them were feather-brained, they found themselves one fine day, through some magic spell, upon an uninhabited island.

They had served all their lives in some Registry or other, had these two Brass-Hats; there they had been born, and brought up, and grown old, and consequently hadn't a single notion of what was what. They even knew no other words save: With assurances of my highest esteem, I beg to remain, Your Most Humble Servant—

That Registry had been found superfluous and abolished, and the two Brass-Hats had been released. Upon retirement they settled in St. Petersburg, on Podyachevskaya Street, but each kept his own apartment; each had a woman to cook for him, and each had his own pension.

Well, then, they found themselves on an uninhabited island; they woke up and there they were, both of them under the same blanket. Naturally, at first they didn't realize anything, and began talking just as though nothing at all had happened to them.

"That was an odd dream I had just a little while ago,

Your Excellency," said one of the Brass-Hats. "Seems I was living on an uninhabited island—"

No sooner had he said this than up he leapt! And so did the other Brass-Hat.

"Oh, Lord! What's all this, now? Where are we?" they cried out in voices that they themselves wouldn't have been able to recognize. And then they started in feeling each other: Maybe it was in a dream, after all, and not in reality that such a mishap had befallen them? However, no matter how they tried to assure themselves that all this was no more than a dream, a conviction of the sad reality was forced upon them.

Stretching away before them was the sea on the one hand, and, on the other, there lay a mere clod of earth, beyond which spread the same illimitable sea. That was when the Brass-Hats burst into tears, for the first time since the shutting down of their Registry. They started eying each other, and saw that they were in their nighties, and that each had his order hung about his neck.

"A cup of coffee would be just the thing now!" spoke up one of the Brass-Hats, but then he recalled what an unheard-of thing had befallen them and burst into tears all over again. "Come to think of it, what are we to do now?" he went on through his tears. "Suppose we *did* draw up a report right now, whatever good would that do?"

"Tell you what," the other Brass-Hat responded, "you go east, Your Excellency, and I'll go west; then, toward evening, we'll come together here again; who knows, maybe we'll discover something or other."

So they began trying to find out which was east and which was west. They remembered that their Chief had once said: If you want to find where the east is, face north, and the east will be on your right hand. So they started trying to find out which was north; they stood this way and that way and made a stab at every quarter of the globe, but since they had worked all their lives in the Registry they got just nowhere at all.

"Tell you what, Your Excellency—you go to the right and I'll go to the left; that'll be best of all!" said one of the Brass-Hats—the one who, beside working in the Registry, had at one time taught penmanship in a government military school, and was consequently a little brighter than the other.

No sooner said than done. One Brass-Hat started off to the right—and what should he see but trees growing, with all sorts of fruit upon them. The Brass-Hat would have been glad to pluck just one apple, but all the fruit hung so high that one had to climb the trees. He did make a try at climbing, but nothing came of it save that he tore his nightie all to shreds. A brook was the next thing he came to; it was just teeming with fish, like a tank in a restaurant window.

"My, what I wouldn't give to have some of those fish and to be on Podyachevskaya Street!" yearned the Brass-Hat, and his face actually changed, what with the appetite he had worked up.

Then he wandered into a forest—there the grouse were whistling away, and heathcocks drumming, and rabbits scurrying hither and yon, all over the place.

"Lordy, Lordy! Look at all that food, now!" said the poor man, feeling himself getting queasy, he was that hungry by now.

But there was no help for it; he had to return to the rendezvous empty-handed. And when he got there, there was the other Brass-Hat, waiting for him.

"Well, now, Your Excellency, have you bagged anything?"

"Why, I came on this old copy of the *Moscow News*[1]—and that's all!"

So they laid them down to sleep again, but it's not so easy to sleep on an empty stomach. Now they would be upset by thinking of who would be drawing their pensions, now by the recollection of the fruits, fish, grouse, heathcocks and rabbits glimpsed during the day.

"Who could have thought, Your Excellency, that the food of man, in its original form, either flies, or swims, or grows on trees?" spoke up one of the Brass-Hats.

"Yes," responded the other, "I must confess that up to now I, too, used to think that rolls come into the world in the very shape they are served in with the morning coffee."

"It follows, then, that if one would partake of a partridge, for instance, he must first catch it, kill it, pluck and dress it, and broil it. . . . The only thing is, how is all that to be done?"

"How *is* all that to be done?" repeated the other Brass-Hat, like an echo.

They lapsed into silence and did their darnedest to fall asleep, but hunger drove sleep away. Grouse, turkey-hens, suckling pigs kept flitting before their eyes, each bird or porker succulent, done to a turn, garnished with salted cucumbers, piccalilli and other such fixings.

"Seems like I could eat up one of my own boots right now!" remarked one of the Brass-Hats.

"Gloves aren't so bad, either, provided they have seen long wear," sighed the other.

Each Brass-Hat suddenly eyed the other: there was a sinister light gleaming in their eyes, their teeth were snapping, low growling issued from their breasts. They

---

[1] Not the least reactionary member of old Russia's Newspaper Axis.—*Trans.-Ed.*

began stalking, creeping up on each other—and in an instant both became ravening wolves. The air was filled with handfuls of hair torn out by the roots and was rent by squeals and much oh'ing; the Brass-Hat who had once taught penmanship bit off his colleague's order and wolfed it on the spot. But the sight of flowing blood seemed to bring them to their senses.

"The Power of the Cross be with us!" they cried out in chorus. "Why, if things go on like this we'll wind up by devouring each other!"

"And how did we ever come to be here? What villain has played such a trick upon us?"

"The thing to do, Your Excellency, is to divert ourselves by talking about something or other—for otherwise there will be murder done here!" one of the Brass-Hats let drop.

"Begin, then!" responded the other.

"Well, to start the ball rolling—why, in your opinion, does the sun rise first and then set, and not the other way 'round?"

"What an odd fellow you are, Your Excellency! Why, you, too, rise first, go to your Bureau, do your paperwork, and only then lie down to sleep!"

"Yes, but why not assume a different sequence? First I lie down to sleep, see all sorts of things in my dreams, and only after all that do I rise—"

"Hmm . . . yes. And yet, I confess, when I was still serving in my Bureau, I always thought of things this way: There, it's morning, then it'll be day, afterwards they'll serve supper—and it's time for sleep!"

The mention of supper, however, threw both speakers into despond, and cut their conversation short at the very start.

"A certain doctor was once telling me that a human

being can find nourishment in his own juices for a long time," one of the Brass-Hats resumed after a while.

"How come?"

"Why, just so. One's own juices, it would seem, produce other juices; these, in their turn, produce still others, and so on, until all the juices come to an end at last."

"And what happens then?"

"Then one has to stoke up with some food—"

Whereupon the other had to spit in vexation and disgust.

In short, no matter what the two began to talk about, the conversation kept coming around to something that reminded them of food, and this whetted their appetite still more. So they decided to put an end to all talk and, happening to think of the back-number of the *Moscow News* one of them had found, they fell to reading it avidly.

"'Yesterday,'" one of the Brass-Hats read out in a moved voice, "'was signalized by the formal banquet tendered by His Honor, the Mayor of our ancient capital. The table was set for a hundred persons, with a magnificence that was truly overwhelming. The tributes of all lands seemed to have made this enchanted gala occasion a rendezvous, as it were. Here one found what our great poet Derzhavin has called "the Sheksna sterlet, golden-hued," and that offspring of the forest, the Caucasian pheasant, and strawberries, which are so rare in our Northern latitudes in the month of February—'"

"Good Lord! Can't Your Excellency really find anything else to read about?" the second Brass-Hat cried out in despair, and spat again; then, taking the paper from the other, he began to read aloud in his turn: "'From our Correspondent in Tula. The local Chamber

of Commerce had a festal occasion yesterday, to mark
the taking of a sturgeon in the Upa river—something
which even the oldest inhabitants cannot recall, and all
the more remarkable since the said sturgeon bore a most
recognizable resemblance to the Commissioner of Police.
The prime mover of the celebration was brought in on a
large wooden platter, garnished with salted gherkins and
with a sprig of parsley stuck in its mouth. Dr. P——,
who acted as the master of ceremonies on this great day,
saw to it that everyone present received his share of the
pièce de résistance. The sauces were almost infinite in
variety, and even *recherché*—' "

"If Your Excellency will permit me to say so, you
also do not seem to exercise over-much care in choosing
what to read!" the first Brass-Hat interrupted him and,
taking the paper in his turn, read out: " 'From our Correspondent in Viatka. One of the oldest inhabitants here
has evolved the following original recipe for fish-
chowder: Take a live burbot and, first of all, give it a
sound flogging; when, because of its hurt feelings, its
liver has become enlarged—' "

Both Brass-Hats let their heads droop. It did not matter what their gaze fell upon: everything testified to the
phenomenon of food. Even their thought conspired to
work malicious mischief against them, for no matter how
they strove to drive all notions of beefsteaks from them,
those notions nevertheless forced their way irresistibly
into their consciousness.

And it was at this darkest hour that the Brass-Hat
who had once taught penmanship was suddenly illuminated by an inspiration!

"But how would it be, Your Excellency," he began
joyously, "if we were to find ourselves a muzhik?"

"A muzhik? Why, just what do you mean?"

"Yes, yes! Just an ordinary, everyday sort of muzhik,

like all muzhiks! He would serve us with rolls on the spot, and snare grouse for us, and catch fish!"

"Hmm . . . a muzhik. But where are we to get this muzhik, when there isn't a one around?"

"Come, whatever are you saying! There's always a muzhik around wherever you are—all you have to do is look for him! There's bound to be one hiding somewhere, trying to dodge work!"

This thought put so much heart into the Brass-Hats that they leapt up as if they had been stung and rushed off headlong in search of a muzhik.

Long did they wander the whole island over without the least success but, at last, the pungent odor of bran-bread and a musty sheepskin jacket put them on the right trail. Under a tree, belly up and with head pillowed on his fists, a mountain of a muzhik was sleeping his head off and dodging work in the most brazen manner. The indignation of the two Brass-Hats knew no bounds.

"So you're sleeping, are you, you lazybones!" they pounced on him. "It looks as if you didn't care a straw that there are two Generals dying of hunger for the second day in a row! Off with you, this minute—get to work!"

The mountain of a muzhik heaved himself up—and saw that these two Brass-Hats wouldn't stand any nonsense. He did think of showing them a clean pair of heels, but the others just froze on to him, and hung on tight.

And so, with their eyes up on him, he buckled down to work.

First off, he shinned up a tree and plucked ten ripe apples for each Brass-Hat, but took only one for himself, and that one sour. Then he dug about in the ground for a while and brought up some potatoes. Then he took two pieces of wood, rubbed them against each other, and got fire that way. Then, out of his own hair, he made a snare and caught a grouse. Finally he got the fire going really well, and prepared so much cooked provender of all sorts for them that the Brass-Hats actually got to flirting with the idea of, perhaps, giving some small portion to this drone.

They watched the muzhik exerting himself, and their hearts leapt for joy within them. By now they had already forgotten that the day before they had all but died from hunger, but instead were thinking: "My, what a good thing it is to be Generals! No General ever came to grief, no matter where!"

"Are you satisfied with me, my masters?" that mountain of a muzhik, that lazybones, kept asking them in the meanwhile.

"We are, dear friend—we can see how hard you try!" the Brass-Hats assured him.

"Would you allow me to take a rest, then?"

"Do, our friend—only twist a little rope first."

So the man-mountain gathered some wild hemp, and soaked it in water, and pounded it, and mauled it till it was all in strands and, come evening, there was a lovely little rope, all twisted. And the Brass-Hats, they took that lovely little rope, and tied the mountain of a muzhik to a tree, so's he wouldn't run off, while they themselves laid them down to sleep.

A day went by, then another; the man-mountain had become so clever that he actually took to cooking soup for the Brass-Hats in his cupped hands. How happy our Brass-Hats were then, how plump, well-fed, and what a lovely color they had! They began pointing out to each other that they were living on the fat of the land here, with everything found, and yet back home, in Petersburg, their pensions kept piling up and piling up.

"What do you think, Your Excellency," one Brass-Hat

would say to the other, after they had fortified themselves with breakfast, "did the building of the Tower of
Babel ever really take place, or is that just an allegory,
so to speak?"

"I think, Your Excellency, that it really did take place,
for otherwise how would you explain there being all
those different languages in the world?"

"Therefore, the Flood also must have taken place?"

"Yes, the Flood too, for if it hadn't how would you
explain the existence of antediluvian animals? All the
more so, since the *Moscow News* informs us—"

"What do you say we look over the *Moscow News?*"

They would find the back-number, seat themselves
comfortably in the shade and read the whole thing from
the front page to the last, about what things people were
eating in Moscow, eating in Tula, eating in Penza, eating
in Ryazan—and it all went down with them; they didn't
even gag!

However, that which was bound to happen sooner or
later did happen: the Brass-Hats grew homesick. More
and more often they would get to thinking about the
cooks they had left behind them in St. Petersburg and,
now and then, when nobody was looking, would even
have a good cry.

"I wonder what's doing on Podyachevskaya Street
now, Your Excellency?" one Brass-Hat would ask the
other.

"Oh, don't even talk of it, Your Excellency!" the other
Brass-Hat would answer. "All my heart has wasted away
with pining."

"Everything is just fine and dandy here—there's no
gainsaying it. But still, don't you know, a ram feels
somehow uneasy without his yearling ewe. Then, too,
one misses one's uniform!"

"I should say so! Especially when it's a uniform of the

Fourth Class—why, just one look at all the gold braid on it is enough to make your head swim!"

And so they started nagging away at the muzhik to get them back, to get them back to Podyachevskaya Street! And, would you believe it, it turned out that that muzhik actually knew about the street; just as the fairy-tales have it: he'd been there indeed, and drunk ale and mead; only instead of going down his throat the drinks had spilt all over his coat!

"Why," the Brass-Hats rejoiced, "we're both Podya-chevskaya Street Generals!"

"Well, now, you may have chanced on me there too," the muzhik assured them. "Ever see a fellow in a sort of cradle on a rope slung over the walls and slapping paint on to 'em, or clambering over a roof, like he were a fly or something? Well, that same fellow was me!"

So then that muzhik started working the old bean, figuring and planning how he might pleasure his two Brass-Hats, seeing how gracious they had been to a drone like him and hadn't turned up their noses at his lowly efforts. And so he built a ship—well, no, not a ship exactly, but a vessel of sorts that you could cross the ocean-sea in, right up to Podyachevskaya Street itself.

"You just watch out, though, you canaille—don't you drown us!" the Brass-Hats told him when they laid eyes on the queer craft bobbing on the waves.

"You can rest easy on that score, my masters; this ain't my first try!" the muzhik assured them, and started getting ready for departure.

He gathered a lot of swansdown, ever so soft, did that muzhik, and lined the bottom of the cockleshell with it; after that he made his two Brass-Hats all nice and cumfy and, making the sign of the cross over himself, shoved off from shore.

What a lot of horrors the two Brass-Hats went through

on that journey because of storms and all sorts of gales, how they upbraided that coarse muzhik for the drone he was—that's something no pen could write, no tongue could tell. But the muzhik, he just kept on rowing and rowing, and never stopped feeding his two Brass-Hats on herring.

And then, one fine day, Mother Neva hove into view, and next the glorious Ekaterininski Canal, and at last that grand street, Great Podyachevskaya itself!

The cooks, they were *that* surprised when they saw how well-fed their Generals were, what fine color they had, and how cheerful they felt! So then the two Brass-Hats drank their fill of coffee, filled themselves up with rolls, and put on their full uniforms. After that they drove to the Treasury—and the money they raked in there, why, that too is something no pen can write, no tongue can tell!

However, they didn't forget the muzhik, either. They sent out a noggin of vodka to him, and five kopecks in silver on top of that:

There, stout fellow—have yourself a time!

LEO NIKOLAIEVICH TOLSTOY [1]

(1828–1910)

EDITOR'S NOTE

TOLSTOY the Artist is Mt. Everest; Tolstoy the Man, Tolstoy-Ecclesiastes, is Mt. Godwin-Austen.[2] But while Tolstoy the Artist is credited (by English critics, at least) with three of the world's greatest novels, Tolstoy-Ecclesiastes has merely proven, for the nth time, that a pink plaster will never work when the surgeon's knife is imperative. Tolstoyanism, today, is as vastly unimpor-

---

[1] Selected Data: Born at Yasnaya Polyana (Serene—[or Radiant]—Meadow), in the Province of Tula; orphaned at nine; 1843: entered University of Kazan, to study languages; 1844: began study of law; 1847: left University; 1851: entered the Army, saw action in Caucasus against mountaineers (re-reading of The Foray, The Cossacks suggested for this period); 1852: began literary career (Childhood); 1854: Boyhood; 1855: Youth; 1854-55: took part in Crimean Campaign (Sebastopol Sketches); 1857: resigned commission; traveled in Germany, France, Italy, England; 1859: second trip abroad, to study schools, do-good institutions—and jails; 1860: began War and Peace; 1861: most serious quarrel with Turgenev; 1862: marriage, at 34, to 18-year-old daughter of a Teutonic medico; 1864-69: publication of War and Peace; 1870: learned Greek; 1873-76: publication of Anna Karenina; 1876: Styx-crossing year for Tolstoy the literary titan; 1876-86: umbilicular contemplation; 1881: publication (in Geneva) of A Criticism of Dogmatic Theology; 1886: Tolstoy-Ecclesiastes born; publication of The Death of Ivan Ilyich—a green shoot from a dead oak; 1894: Guy de Maupassant and the Art of Fiction (an article—another green shoot); 1898: What is Art?—which soars to the depths of Nordau's Degeneration; 1901: excommunicated by Orthodox Church; 1910: night-escape from Serene Meadow; death at way-station of Astapovo, now named after him; followed by unbelievable persecution of Tolstoyans by Russian Church and State.

[2] Everest: 29,141 feet high; Godwin-Austen: 28,250.

tant as Couéism, and toward the end of his life Tolstoy himself used the substantive *Tolstoyan* as a term of opprobrium.

It is therefore a mistake, as lamentable as it is prevalent, to regard every writing of Tolstoy's as literature, merely because it bears his titanic name. Only one story after 1876 is good Tolstoy; *A Criticism of Dogmatic Theology* and *The Devil* are the only other works of importance after that date—but hardly as literature. Sunday School tracts, rehashings of the Bible and the Talmud, translations of minor Frenchmen, pleas for vegetarianism and thunderbolts against the Demon Rum and the Filthy Weed, even when all of them are by a Tolstoy, simply aren't literature, and Tolstoy-Stylites just isn't Tolstoy-the-green-oak-on-a-magic-strand. Ironically enough, Tolstoy's two greatest preachments, *War and Peace* and *Anna Karenina*, were uttered by Tolstoy the Artist.

"It never occurred to me to compare myself with him —never," Tolstoy wrote of Dostoevsky (the two giants had never met). Yet, as one critic has put it, not unmaliciously, Tolstoy came into the world apparently for the sole purpose of juxtaposition with Dostoevsky. Neither giant, precisely because he was a giant, was free from spiritual inconsistencies, and even contradictions. But the supreme difference between them, as literary artists, lay in that Dostoevsky embodied the spirit, while Tolstoy spiritualized the body.

Three Deaths is thoroughly typical both of Tolstoy the Artist coming into the flood of his power, and of the still nascent Tolstoy the Moralist.

There are innumerable translations of Tolstoy in English. No others (with the exception of two or three iso-

lated instances) merit consideration or even mention
save those of Louise and Aylmer Maude, far and away
the best available, done with honesty and, above all, with
love.

Three Deaths

LEO NIKOLAIEVICH TOLSTOY

IT WAS autumn. Two carriages were rolling at a fast
trot along the highway. There were two women in
the first. One was the mistress, thin and pale; the other
her maid, plump and with glossily red cheeks. Her short,
crinkly hair escaped from under a faded, small hat; she
kept tucking the loose strands in impulsively with a red-
dened hand in a glove out at the tips. Her high bosom
under a paisley shawl exuded health; her quick-darting
dark eyes now watched the fields rushing past the window, then glanced timidly at her mistress, or restlessly
examined the corners of the carriage. Her mistress's hat,
hanging from a rack, dangled before the maid's very
nose; a puppy was resting in her lap; her feet were elevated by the boxes on the floor, tapping out a barely
audible tattoo upon them to the sound of the bouncing
springs and the jarring of the panes.

With her hands folded on her lap and her eyes shut,
the mistress swayed feebly on the cushions piled up behind her and, with a slight frown, was stifling her in-
termittent coughs. She had on a white nightcap; a
baby-blue kerchief was bound about her delicate, bloodless neck. A straight parting, retreating under the cap,
divided her fair hair, pomaded and lying very flat, and
there was something desiccated, deathlike about the

whiteness of the scalp revealed by this wide parting. The flabby, rather yellowish skin was drawn loosely over the fine and beautiful features, with flushed cheeks and cheekbones. The lips were dry and restless, the lashes were scanty and straight, and her cloth traveling cloak formed straight folds upon her sunken bosom. Despite her eyes being closed, the face of the mistress expressed fatigue, irritation and suffering that had become a habit.

A footman, with one elbow on an arm-rest, was dozing up on the box; the coachman, shouting now and then, was briskly urging on four big, sweating horses, from time to time looking over his shoulder at the coachman of the other carriage, who was also shouting now and then. Quickly, evenly, the tires left their broad, parallel impressions upon the limy mud of the road. The sky was gray and chill; a raw mist was coming down upon the fields and the road. The carriage was stuffy and smelled of eau de cologne and dust. The sick woman drew her head back and slowly opened her eyes; great, splendidly dark, they were aglitter.

"Again!" said she, nervously putting aside with a beautiful, gaunt hand a tip of the maid's cloak, which was barely touching her leg, and her mouth twisted sensitively. Matrësha picked up the hem of her cloak with both hands, raised herself up on her sturdy legs, and resumed her seat a little farther off. Her fresh face mantled a bright red. The sick woman's splendid dark eyes avidly followed the maid's every motion. The mistress propped both her hands against the seat and in her turn wanted to raise herself, so as to sit up higher, but could not find the strength to do so. Her mouth became twisted, and her whole face was distorted by an expression of impotent, malicious sarcasm.

"You might help me, at least! Ah, no need! I can manage it myself—only, as a favor to me, don't put those bags and things of yours behind me! Come, you'd better not touch me if you don't know what to do!"

The mistress shut her eyes; then, quickly lifting her eyelids again, glanced at the maid. A heavy sigh escaped the sick woman's breast, but that sigh, stopping short, turned into coughing. She turned away, wrinkled up her face, and clutched at her breast with both hands. When the coughing was over she closed her eyes anew and resumed her motionless pose. The carriage and barouche entered a village. Matrësha thrust a stout arm from under her shawl and made the sign of the cross over herself.

"What place is this?" asked the mistress.

"A posting-station, Madam."

"Why are you crossing yourself, then, may I ask?"

"There's a church, Madam."

The sick woman turned to the window and began crossing herself slowly, her great eyes opened to their fullest as she looked at the big village church, which her carriage was now skirting.

The carriage and the barouche halted at the same time before the posting-station. The sick woman's husband and a doctor got out of the barouche and walked up to the carriage.

"How do you feel?" asked the doctor, feeling her pulse.

"Well, my dear, how are you—tired?" the husband asked, in French. "Wouldn't you like to come out?"

Matrësha, having gathered up her bundles, was squeezing herself into a corner so as not to interfere with their conversation.

"It doesn't matter; my condition is the same," answered the sick woman. "I won't come out."

The husband, after staying near her a little while, went inside the building. Matrësha, jumping out of the carriage, ran off on tiptoe through the mud into the gate.

"Just because I do not feel well is no reason for you to go without your breakfast," the sick woman said with a slight smile to the doctor standing by the window of the carriage.

"Not a one of them is concerned about me now," she added to herself as soon as the doctor, having walked away from her at a sedate pace, ran up the steps of the posting-station at a round trot. "They feel fine, so nothing matters to them. Oh, my God!"

"Well, now, Edward Ivanovich," said the husband, in greeting to the doctor, at the same time rubbing his hands with a cheery smile, "I've ordered the cellarette to be brought in—what do you think of the idea?"

"Quite acceptable," answered the doctor.

"Well, how is she?" asked the husband with a sigh, lowering his voice and arching his eyebrows.

"I told you, she can never reach Italy—God grant she may get as far as Moscow. Especially in this weather."

"What's to be done, then! Ah, my God, my God!" the husband put a hand over his eyes. "Put it here," he added, turning to the man who was bringing in the cellarette.

"You should have remained at home," answered the doctor, with a shrug.

"But tell me, what could I do?" retorted the husband. "Why, I did everything in my power to keep her from going; I told her of our resources, I mentioned the children, whom we would have to leave behind, and my affairs—she won't listen to anything. She is making plans for living abroad just as though she were well. Yet to tell her about her condition—why, that would mean her death."

"Well, death has laid hold of her already—you ought to know that, Vassily Dmitrich. No one can live when he or she has no lungs, and there's no growing a new set of lungs. It's sad, it's distressing, but what's to be done? Your concern—and mine—consists solely of seeing that her end should be as easy as possible. The situation calls for a spiritual adviser."

"Ah, my God! Why, just enter into my situation, having to remind her of the last rites. Come what may, but I won't tell her that. Surely, you know how kind-hearted she is—"

"Just the same, try to persuade her to wait till the roads are frozen," said the doctor, shaking his head significantly. "Otherwise something very bad may happen on the way—"

"Axiusha—hey, Axiusha!" the station-master's daughter was screeching as she threw a sleeveless jacket over her head and stamped about on the dirty backstairs. "Let's go and have a look at the lady from Shirkin; they say she's being taken abroad because she's got trouble with her chest. I never yet saw what people with consumption look like!"

Axiusha darted out on the threshold and, seizing each other by the hand, the two ran out of the gates. Slowing down their pace, they walked past the carriage and peered in at its lowered window. The sick woman turned her head in their direction but, noticing their curiosity, she frowned and turned away.

"My good-*ness!*" remarked the station-master's daughter, turning her head away quickly. "What a stunning beauty she must have been—and what's become of her now? It's frightening, actually. Did you see her, Axiusha —did you see her?"

"Yes; how thin she is!" Axiusha seconded the other. "Let's go and have another look—make believe we're going to the well. See how she turned away, but I got a look at her just the same. What a pity, Masha!"

"And it's so muddy, too!" answered Masha, and both started running back to the gates.

"Apparently I have become a fright," the sick woman was thinking. "Oh, to get abroad as soon as possible— as soon as possible! There it won't take long for me to get better."

"Well, how are you, my dear?" asked the husband, coming up to the carriage and still munching a mouthful.

"Always the same invariable question," reflected the sick woman, "but that doesn't keep him from eating!"— "There's nothing out of the way," she let drop through clenched teeth.

"Do you know, my dear, I'm afraid you will feel worse, traveling in this weather, and Edward Ivanovich says the same thing. Hadn't we better turn back?"

She maintained an angry silence.

"The weather may improve, the roads will be fit for traveling; you would get better, too, and then all of us could go together."

"Pardon me—if I had stopped listening to you long ago I would be in Berlin now and would be entirely well."

"What could one do, my angel—that was impossible, as you know. But now, if you would remain for a month, you would improve gloriously, I would wind up my affairs, and we would take the children with us—"

"The children are in good health, but I'm not."

"But do understand, my dear, that with the weather the way it is, if you should get worse while traveling . . . at least you'd be better off at home, under those circumstances."

"Well, suppose I were at home? What am I to do— die at home?" the sick woman retorted, flaring up. But the word *die* apparently had terrified her; she looked at her husband imploringly and questioningly. He lowered his eyes and kept silent. The sick woman's mouth suddenly twisted, like a child's, and tears flowed from her eyes. Her husband covered his face with a handkerchief and walked away from the carriage in silence.

"No, I'm going," said the sick woman, lifting her eyes up to heaven; she folded her hands and fell to whispering disjointed words. "My God! What is this punishment for?" she was saying, and her tears flowed still more copiously. Long and fervently did she pray, but her chest felt just as painful and constricted, the sky, the fields and the road were just as gray and overcast, and the autumnal mist, neither denser nor lighter but still the same, fell in the same way upon the mire of the road, upon the roofs, upon the carriage and on the sheepskin jackets of the coachmen who, talking to each other in vigorous, cheerful voices, were greasing the axles of the carriage and harnessing fresh horses to it.

II

The carriage was harnessed, but the coachman still tarried. He had gone into the driver's hut. It was hot in this hut, stuffy, dark and depressing; it reeked of living quarters, baking bread, cabbage soup and sheepskins. There were several drivers in the main room; the cook was fussing near the oven; on a ledge atop the oven lay a sick man wrapped in sheepskins.

"Uncle Hvedor—hey, Uncle Hvedor!" said a driver, a young country fellow in a sheepskin jacket and with a whip stuck in his belt, entering the room and hailing the sick man.

"What do you want with Fedka, you lunkhead?" one of the others spoke up. "Can't you see the people in your carriage are waiting for you?"

"I'm after asking him for his boots—mine is all wore out," answered the country fellow, tossing his hair back and adjusting the gauntlets stuck in his belt. "Or is he asleep? Hey, Uncle Hvedor?" he repeated, approaching the oven.

"What is it?" came a weak voice, and a gaunt face covered with red hair bent over from the ledge. A broad, wasted, bloodless hand, all hairy, was pulling a drab overcoat over a bony shoulder in a dirty shirt. "Give us a sip of water, brother; what is it you want?"

The young fellow handed him a dipper of water.

"Well, now, Fedka," said he, shifting from foot to foot, "I guess you won't be needing your new boots now; give 'em to me—you won't be doing any walking, I guess."

The sick man, with his weary head close to the gleaming dipper and his scanty, drooping mustache soaking in the turbid water, was drinking weakly and avidly. His tangled beard was unclean; he had difficulty in raising his sunken, dimmed eyes to look at the young fellow's face. Done with the water, he wanted to raise his hand to wipe his dripping mouth, but could not, and wiped it against the sleeve of the coat. In silence and breathing hard through his nose, he was looking straight into the young fellow's eyes, trying to get his strength together.

"Maybe you've already promised them to somebody?" asked the young fellow. "In that case, let it go. Main thing is, it's sopping wet out, and I got me a job, driving; so I thought to myself—let's ask Fedka for his boots; guess he won't be needing 'em any more. In case you need 'em yourself, you just say so—"

Something began to gurgle and rumble within the sick man's chest; he bent over, strangling from a throaty, unceasing coughing.

"He's just the one to need 'em!" the cook unexpectedly

began to rattle away, angrily, her voice filling the whole hut. "It's the second month he hasn't set foot off that oven. Look at the way he's straining himself; why, it makes your own inwards ache, just to hear him. Where does he come to be needing boots? They're not going to bury him in any new boots. And yet it's time they did, long since—Lord forgive me the sinful thought! Look at the way he's straining himself. If they'd only shift him into another hut or somewhere else, now! There's hospitals for that in the city, I've heard tell; for that's no way—he's taken up the whole corner, and that's that. There's not enough room to turn around in. And yet they demand that the place be kept clean."

"Hey there, Serëga! Go on, get up on the box—the gentry are waiting for you!" the supervisor of the drivers called out, looking in at the door.

Serëga was about to leave without waiting for an answer, but the sick man, in the midst of his coughing, signalled to him with his eyes that he wanted to reply.

"You take them boots, Serëga," said he, having suppressed his cough and rested a little. "Only buy me a stone when I die—you hear?" he added, wheezing.

"Thanks, Uncle; I'll take 'em, then; as for the stone, I'll buy you one—by God, I will!"

"There, fellows, you've heard him," the sick man managed to get out, before he bent over in a new fit of strangling coughing.

"All right, we heard him," said one of the drivers. "Go on, Serëga, for there's that supervisor coming on the run again. The lady from Sharkin is sick, see."

Serëga briskly threw off his torn, inordinately large boots and tossed them under a bench. Uncle Fedor's new boots fitted him just right and, eying them, Serëga went out to the carriage.

"Eh, but those are grand boots! Here, let me grease

'em for you," said a driver who was holding a pot of axle-grease, just as Serëga, climbing up on the box, was picking up the reins. "Did he give 'em to you for nothing?"

"Why, are you envious?" retorted Serëga, rising up a little and tucking the skirts of his drab coat about his legs. "Never mind! Hey there, my darlings!" he called out to the horses, brandished his short whip, and the carriage and the barouche with their occupants, suitcases and boxes, disappearing in the gray autumnal fog, rolled off at a lively pace over the wet road.

The sick driver remained atop the oven in the stuffy hut and, having cut his coughing short, turned over on the other side with a superhuman effort and quieted down.

Until evening people kept coming and going and having their meals in the hut—there was never a sound from the sick man. Just before nightfall the cook clambered up on the ledge and reached over his legs for a sheepskin jacket.

"Don't you bear any hard feelings against me, Nastasia," the sick man got out, "I'll leave your corner free soon."

"That's all right, that's all right—it don't matter none, after all," muttered Nastasia. "But what's hurting you Uncle, eh? You go ahead and tell me."

"All my insides is just wore out with pain. God knows what it is."

"Guess even your throat hurts when you cough?"

"It hurts me all over. My death has come—that's what. Oh, oh, oh!" the sick man let out a moan.

"You cover your feet, now—there, like that," said Nastasia, pulling a drab coat over him as she clambered down off the oven.

A small lamp burned dimly in the hut all night.

Nastasia and half a score drivers were sleeping and snoring loudly on the floor and on the benches. The sick man alone kept groaning feebly, coughing and tossing on his ledge atop the oven. Toward morning he quieted down altogether.

"That was a queer dream I had last night, somehow," the cook was saying the next morning, stretching herself in the half-light. "I saw Uncle Hvedor get down off the oven, like, and go to chop wood. 'Here, Nastya,' says he, 'let me give you a hand.' But I says to him: 'Come, how can *you* chop wood?' But he just grabs the ax and starts chopping away, so fast, ever so fast; all you could see was the chips flying. 'How come,' I says, 'you was sick, wasn't you?' 'No,' says he, 'I'm all well,' and with that he swings back the ax so that a fright come over me. Then I let out a scream and awoke. Has he died, by any chance? Uncle Hvedor! Hey, Uncle!"

Fedor did not answer to her call.

"Maybe he has died, at that? Let's go and have a look," said one of the awakened drivers.

From the top of the oven a hand was dangling; gaunt, covered with red hair, it was cold and bloodlessly white.

"Let's go and tell the station-master—he has died, it looks like," said the driver.

Fedor had no known kin—he had come from distant parts. Next day they buried him in the new graveyard beyond the grove, and for several days Nastasia kept telling everybody of the dream she had seen, and how she had been the first to guess that Uncle Fedor had died.

III

Spring came. Over the wet streets of the city bustling streams murmured, meandering between small floes of frozen manure; the colors of the clothing on the people moving about, and the sounds of their talk, were lively. In the little fenced-in gardens the buds on the trees were swelling, and their branches made a barely audible rustling as they swayed in the fresh wind. Transparent water-drops were trickling or falling one by one everywhere. . . . The sparrows were chirping shrill nonsense and fluttering up now and then to no great height on their tiny wings. On the sunny side of fences, houses and trees all was movement and glitter. There was a feeling of joy, of youthfulness in the sky, and upon earth, and in the heart of man.

On one of the principal streets straw had been spread before a seigniorial house; within the house the same sick woman who had been hastening abroad was now dying.

Standing near the closed doors of the sick woman's room were her husband and an elderly woman. Sitting on a divan was a priest; his eyes were lowered, and he was holding something wrapped up in his stole. A little crone—the mother of the sick woman—was reclining in an easy chair and weeping bitterly. A maid was standing near her, with a fresh handkerchief thrown over her arm in readiness for the little crone, whenever she should ask for it; another was massaging the little crone's temples with something and, lifting up the cap, was blowing upon her gray head.

"Well, Christ be with you, my dear," the husband was saying to the elderly woman (a cousin) who was standing with him by the door. "She has such trust in you, you know so well how to talk to her—persuade her for the best, darling. Come, now!" He was just about to open the door for her, but the cousin restrained him; she applied the handkerchief several times to her eyes and then tossed up her head.

"There, I think now I don't look as if I had been crying," said she and, having opened the door herself, went through it.

The husband was greatly agitated and seemed utterly at a loss. He started going toward the little crone but, having stopped a few paces from her, wheeled around, took a turn about the room, and approached the priest. The priest glanced at him, his eyebrows went up, heavenward, and he heaved a sigh. His small beard, thick and grizzled, also went up and then sank back.

"My God! My God!" said the husband.

"What can one do?" said the priest, heaving another sigh, and his small beard went up anew and then sank back.

"And her mother is here, too!" said the husband, almost in desperation. "She will never be able to go through this. For, when you love anyone as much as she loves her . . . I don't know. If you could but try to calm her down, Father, and persuade her to leave this room—"

The priest got up and walked over to the little crone.

"Verily, none can appreciate a mother's heart," said he, "however, God is merciful."

The little crone's whole face suddenly began to twitch, and she had an attack of hysterical hiccupping.

"God is merciful," the priest went on, when she had calmed down a little. "There was a sick man in my parish, I must tell you, who was much worse than Maria Dmitrievna, and yet a simple townsman cured him with herbs in a short time. And this same man that cured him is in Moscow right now. I was telling Vassily Dmitrievich —we might give him a trial. It might be a comfort to the sick woman, at the least. All things are possible for God."

"No, she isn't fated to live on," uttered the little crone. "Instead of taking me, God is taking her." And her hysterical hiccupping increased to such an extent that she lost consciousness.

The sick woman's husband buried his face in his hands and dashed out of the room.

The first one he met in the hallway was a six-year-old boy, running with all his might after a younger girl.

"Well, what are your orders—shouldn't the children be brought to their mother?" asked their nurse.

"No, she doesn't wish to see them. It would upset her."

The boy halted for a moment, eying his father's face intently, then suddenly kicked back with one foot and ran on with a merry shout.

"She's making believe she's our black horse, daddy!" he shouted, pointing to his sister.

Meanwhile, in another room, the cousin was sitting by the sick woman's side and, by leading the conversation skillfully, was trying to prepare her for the idea of death. The doctor, standing at one of the windows, was compounding a draught.

The sick woman, in a white robe, propped up on all sides with pillows, was sitting up in bed and looking at the cousin in silence.

"Ah, my friend," said she, unexpectedly interrupting her, "there is no need for you to prepare me. Don't regard me as a child. I am a Christian woman. I know everything. I know I haven't long to live; I know that if my husband would have listened to me sooner I would be in Italy and probably, or even certainly, would be well by now. Everybody told him that. However, what's to be done? Evidently God willed things thus. All of us bear many sins, that I know, but I trust in God's mercy; all men and women will be forgiven—probably all men and women will be forgiven. I am trying to understand myself. There have been many sins upon me also, my friend. But then, how much suffering I have gone

through! I have tried to bear my sufferings in patience—"

"Shall we call in the priest, then, my friend? You will
feel still better after taking the sacrament," said the
cousin.

The sick woman bowed her head as a sign of assent.

"God! Forgive me, who am a sinner," she got out in a
whisper.

The cousin walked out and made a sign to the priest
with her eyes.

"She is an angel!" she said to the husband, with tears
in her eyes. The husband began to weep; the priest went
through the door; the little crone was still unconscious,
and utter silence fell in the outer room. After five
minutes the priest walked out of the door and, having
taken off his stole, put his hair to rights.

"Glory be to God, she is calmer now," said he. "She
wishes to see you."

The cousin and the husband went in. The sick woman
was softly weeping, gazing at a holy image.

"I congratulate you, my dear," said the husband.

"Thank you! How fine I feel now, what incomprehensible delectation I am experiencing!" the sick
woman was saying, and a slight smile played upon her
thin lips. "How merciful God is! Isn't that so? Merciful
He is, and almighty!" And anew, in avid imploring, she
gazed with tear-filled eyes at the holy image.

Then, suddenly, she seemed to recall something. She
signed to her husband to come near.

"You never want to do anything I ask of you," said
she in a weak and discontented voice.

The husband, craning his neck, was listening to her
submissively.

"What is it, my dear?"

"How many times have I told you that those doctors don't know anything; there are healers, just ordinary peasant women—they're the ones who work cures. . . . There, the priest was telling me . . . about a simple townsman . . . send for him."

"Send for whom, my dear?"

"My God, he doesn't want to understand anything!" And the sick woman wrinkled up her face and closed her eyes.

The doctor, walking up to her, took her hand. The pulse was perceptibly beating more and more feebly. He made a sign to the husband with his eyes. The sick woman noticed this pantomime and looked about her in fright. The cousin turned away and began to weep.

"Don't cry; don't torture both yourself and me," the sick woman was saying. "It deprives me of whatever peace of mind is left me."

"You're an angel!" said the cousin, kissing the other's hand.

"No, kiss me just so—it's only the dead whose hands are kissed. My God! My God!"

That same evening the sick woman was already a corpse, and the corpse was laid out in a coffin standing in the drawing-room of the great house. Sitting all by himself in the big room, with its doors closed, was a minor deacon, reading the Psalms of David in a measured voice and through his nose. The vivid light of wax candles in their tall sticks of silver fell upon the pallid brow of her who had fallen into the long sleep, upon her heavy, wax-like hands, and the stonelike folds of the pall, sinisterly rising at the knees and toes. The minor deacon, without grasping the meaning of the words he was uttering, kept on with his measured reading, and his words sounded and died away strangely in the quiet room. From time to time the sounds of childish voices and of their romping came floating in from a distant room.

Thou hidest Thy face, they are troubled: Thou takest away their breath, they die, and return to their dust.

Thou sendest forth Thy spirit, they are created: and Thou renewest the face of the earth.[1]

The glory of the Lord shall endure for ever.

The face of her who had fallen into the long sleep was austere and majestic. Naught stirred upon the pure, cold brow, nor upon the firmly set lips. She was all heed. Yet did she grasp even now the meaning of these grandiose words?

IV

A month later a stone chapel had been raised over the grave of her who had gone to her long sleep. Over the grave of the driver there still was no stone, and only light-green grass was springing up over the small mound that served as the only sign of a man's existence in the past.

"It will be a sin on your part, Serëga," the cook at the posting-station remarked one day, "if you don't buy a stone for Hvedor. You kept on saying 'It's winter, it's winter,'—but why don't you keep your word now? Remember, I was there when you promised. He came back once already to ask you for it; if you won't buy that stone he'll come back once again, and strangle you."

"Well, now, am I going back on my word?" Serëga retorted. "I'll buy him a stone, like I said; I'll buy it— even if it costs me a ruble and a half in silver, I'll buy it. I haven't forgotten, but then it's got to be carted here. First chance I get to go to the city, why, I'll buy it."

"Tell you what—you ought to put up a cross at least,"

---

[1] In the Russian: *. . . and they renew the face of the earth.* Psalm CIV: 29-31.—*Trans.-Ed.*

commented an old driver, "for the way things are it's a downright shame. You're wearing the boots, all right."

"Where's one to get a cross, now? Hew it out of a log of firewood, or something?"

"What are you talking about? Sure you won't hew it out of a log of firewood; you take an ax, now, and go to the grove early in the day as you can—that's how you'll hew out the cross. Chop down a small ash, or something. And there's the monument, even though it's of wood. Otherwise you'll have to treat the forester to vodka. There ain't money enough to treat all the riff-raff. There, just the other day I broke a swingle-tree; so I cut me down a grand new one—nobody said a word to me about it."

Early in the morning, when the dawn-glow was just breaking, Serëga took his ax and set out for the grove.

A chill, dull-colored pall of still falling dew, not yet made sparkling by the sun, lay over everything. The east was imperceptibly growing lighter, its faint light reflected on the vault of the sky, overcast with tenuous clouds. Not the least blade of grass below, not a leaf on any branch above, was stirring. Wings fluttering in a thicket, or some rustle along the ground, were the only sounds that occasionally broke the stillness of the forest. Suddenly a strange sound, alien in nature, spread and died away on the edge of the forest. But the sound was heard anew, began to be repeated at measured intervals at the base of one of the motionless trees. One of the treetops broke into an unusual tremor; its sap-filled leaves began to whisper something, and a redbreast perched on one of its branches fluttered from twig to twig a couple of times, whistling, and then, its small tail twitching, perched on another tree.

The ax sounded more and more dully at the root, the sap-filled, white chips flew upon the dewy grass, and a light crackling was heard through the ax-strokes. A shudder ran through all the body of the tree, it bent and quickly straightened up, swaying at its roots in dismay. For an instant everything grew still, but the tree bent anew, the crackling of its trunk was heard and, breaking off its deadwood and lowering its branches, its top crashed against the dank earth.

The sounds of ax and footsteps became stilled. The redbreast whistled and fluttered upward. The branch its wings had caught against swayed for some time and then, even as all the others, became deadly still, down to its last leaf. Still more joyously did the trees flaunt the beauty of their motionless branches in the newly found space.

The first rays of the sun, having forced their way through a diaphonous cloud, flashed in the sky and darted over both earth and sky. The fog, billowing in the dales, began to play with the colors of the rainbow; the dew, glittering, became gemlike against the greenery; transparent little clouds, grown white, were scattering in haste over the vault of the sky, now taking on an azure hue. The birds were fussing in the thicket and, as if utterly carried away, were jargoning some song of happiness; the sap-filled leaves were joyously and calmly whispering upon the summits, and the branches of the living trees began to stir slowly, majestically over the dead, felled tree.

VSEVOLOD MIKHAILOVICH GARSHIN

(1855–1888)

His father was an officer in the Cuirassiers, his mother's father was a naval officer. When he was five his mother went off with a revolutionary, the tutor of the future writer's two elder brothers, whom she took with her; when he was nine she took him away from his father as well. And Vsevolod grew up to be a fighter against an intolerable autocracy.

It is of record that certain underground periodicals were literally his ABC's; at eight he was reading *What's To Be Done?* Other books which left their impress upon his early childhood were *Uncle Tom's Cabin* and *Notre Dame de Paris*. Social problems were not his sole interest; even as a boy he became fascinated by natural history; later on he studied physiology and psychiatry.

Garshin was so taken in by the Slavophile propaganda (which had no nobler purpose than the acquisition of markets in the Orient) that he tried, in 1876, to enlist in the Serbian army; in 1877 he was a rank-and-file soldier in the Russian infantry, and served in the Russo-Turkish War (1877–78), the only abiding good derived therefrom by Russia being *Four Days*, which laid the foundation of his literary reputation and, as a war story, surpasses even *The Red Badge of Courage*. He also wrote several other stories showing the senselessness of war and the stultifying effects of army life, stories that found an exceedingly wide and appreciative public.

There was a psychopathic taint in the Garshin family; both of the elder brothers committed suicide, one before Vsevolod's self-inflicted death, the other after it. Vsevolod, although of a cheerful disposition and physically strong, had had his first attack at seventeen; in 1880, after an unsuccessful personal appeal (at midnight, weeping and on his knees) to a nobly born satrap for the life of his would-be assassin, Garshin became seriously deranged and did not fully recover for months, and only after being in two psychiatric institutions. It was during this period that he went on a pilgrimage to Tolstoy at Serene Meadow and, unfortunately, came under the influence of the Master of the Pink Plaster— which influence had a far more serious effect upon him than his medically recognized derangement and resulted, among other things, in a maudlin novel that is now hardly readable.

However, all of Garshin's Russia was one vast madhouse that could unbalance even the soundest man. Garshin, in a final mood of depression, committed suicide by leaping down a stairwell.

Poet, short story writer, initiator of the socio-psychological novelette which Chekhov subsequently brought to such perfection, allegorist, art-critic, translator— Garshin made his impress upon Russian literature and ranks high therein. In less than a decade of creative life he has left a comparatively small yet a most significant body at work, fraught with altruism and passionate humanity.

In English Garshin (like so many other important Russian writers) has fared none too well. His exquisite allegory, *Attalea Princeps*, his unbelievably sensitive *The Red Flower*, and his truly wonderful *The Bears* are available in English, but that English is neither exquisite, nor very sensitive, nor at all wonderful.

Four Days

VSEVOLOD MIKHAILOVICH GARSHIN

I REMEMBER how we ran through the forest, how the bullets hummed, how the twigs they tore off came showering down, how we smashed our way through the bushes of hawthorn. The shots became more frequent. Something red, flickering, appeared here and there through the trees at the edge of the forest. Sidorov, a private of the first company, ever so young and small ("How did he ever get into our detachment?" flashed through my head), suddenly squatted on the ground and looked around at me with big, frightened eyes, without a word. A jet of blood was flowing out of his mouth. Yes, I remember that well. I remember also how, when I was almost at the edge of the forest, among the thick bushes, I caught sight of . . . *him.* He was an enormous, stout Turk, but I ran straight at him, even though I am puny and thin. Something banged; something enormous (so it seemed to me) flew past; my ears began to ring.

"That was his doing—he fired at me," the thought came to me.

But he, with a scream of horror, pressed his back against a thick bush of hawthorn. He could have gone around the bush but he was out of his senses from fear and kept clambering against the prickly branches. With one blow I knocked the gun out of his hands, with another I stuck my bayonet in, somewhere. Something began either to growl or to moan—one couldn't tell which it was. Then I ran on. Our men were hurrahing, falling, shooting. I remember I, too, fired a few shots out on a meadow, after I had already emerged from the forest. Suddenly the hurrahing rang out louder, and we instantly started to advance. That is, not *we* but our men, because I remained behind. This struck me as odd. What was still more odd was that everything suddenly vanished; all shouts and shots had become stilled. I heard nothing, but merely saw a blue something—it must have been the sky, in all likelihood. Then it, too, vanished.

Never before did I find myself in such an odd situation. I seem to be lying on my belly, and all I see before me is a tiny patch of ground. A few small grass-blades, an ant, head down, crawling off one of them, certain bits of litter from last year's grass—there is my whole universe. I see it with but one eye, inasmuch as the other is pressed down by something hard, probably by the branch against which my head is propped. I feel dreadfully cramped and I want to move, but utterly fail to grasp why I cannot. Thus does time pass. I hear the chirr of grasshoppers, the buzzing of a bee. Nothing more. At last I make an effort, free my right hand from under me and, propping both hands against the ground, want to get up on my knees.

Something keen and abrupt, like lightning, transpierces all my body from the knees to the chest and head, and I fall down anew. Again murk; again there is nothing.

I awoke.

Why do I see stars, which glow so vividly in the indigo sky of Bulgaria? Come, am I not in a tent? Why have I crawled out of it? I make a move—and feel excruciating pain in my legs.

Yes, I have been wounded in battle. Dangerously or not? I clutch at my legs—there, where the pain is. The right leg has become covered with encrusted blood, and so has the left. When I put my hands to them the pain becomes still greater. The pain is like a toothache: steady, nagging at the soul. There is ringing in my ears; my head has grown heavy. I grasp, dimly, that I am wounded in both legs. What's all this, then? Why haven't I been picked up? Can it be that the Turks have put us to rout? I begin to recall what had happened to me, at first dimly, then more clearly, and I arrive at the conclusion that we hadn't been put to rout at all. For I had fallen (this, however, I do not remember, but I do remember how all had started running forward, whereas I had been unable to run, and only a blue something had remained before my eyes)—I had fallen on a small meadow at the top of a knoll. It had been to this small meadow that the diminutive leader of our battalion had been pointing. "We'll make it, lads!" he had called out to us in his ringing voice. And we had made it, which meant that we had not been put to rout. Why, then, hadn't I been picked up? For here, on the meadow, the spot was all out in the open; everything was in plain sight. Why, I was probably not the only one lying here. Their fire had been so rapid. I must turn my head to take a look. I can do this with less discomfort now, for at the time when, having come to, I had seen the short grass and the ant crawling head down, I had, in attempting to get up, fallen not into my previous position but turned over on my back. That's the real reason why those stars are visible to me.

I raise myself a little and sit up. This is a thing hard to do when both legs have been smashed. You are forced to despair, time after time; finally, with tears in my eyes, I sit up.

Over me is a tatter of indigo sky, blazing on which are a great star and several small ones; around me is something dark, high. It's the bushes. I'm in the bushes—they have failed to find me!

I feel the hair on my head stirring at its roots.

But, how did I ever come to be in the bushes, when it was out on the little meadow that they had shot me down? Wounded, out of my senses from pain, I must have crawled over here. The only odd thing is that now I can't stir yet at that time I had been able to drag myself all the way to these bushes. Yet it may be that at that time I had had but one wound, and another bullet had caught up with me when I was already here.

Wan, roseate blotches began moving around me. The great star paled; the several small ones vanished. It was the moon, rising. How fine it must be now at home!

Odd sounds of some sort reach me. As if someone were moaning. Yes, it is a moan. Is there someone lying near me, just as forgotten as I, with legs smashed or a bullet in his belly? No, the moans are so near and yet, it seems, there is no one else near me. . . . My God—why, it is I, my own self, moaning! Low, plaintive moans; can it really be that my pain is as great as that? It must be. The only thing is that I do not grasp this pain, inasmuch as my head is filled with fog, with lead. Better lie down again and fall asleep—sleep, sleep. . . . The only thing is, will I ever awaken again? No matter.

At that moment, as I am getting ready to lie down, a broad, wan streak of moonlight brightens the spot and I see something dark and big lying five paces away from me. Here and there one can see glints of moonlight on it. Those are buttons or ammunition. It's a corpse or a wounded man.

No matter; I'm going to lie down.

No, it's impossible—our men haven't gone off. They're here, they've dislodged the Turks and have remained holding this position. Why, then, is there neither the hum of talk nor the crackling of bivouac fires? Come, it is because of my weakness that I can't hear a thing. They must be here, certainly.

"Help! Help!"

Wild, insane, hoarse screams escape my breast, and there is no answer to them. Loudly do they spread through the night air. All else is silent. Only the crickets keep chirring as indefatigably as before. The moon's round face is gazing upon me with pity.

Were *he* merely wounded, he would have come to from such an outcry. It's a corpse. One of our men or a Turk? Ah, my God! As though that mattered in the least.

And sleep falls upon my inflamed eyes.

I am lying with my eyes closed, although I have awakened long since. I do not feel like opening my eyes, for I can feel the sunlight through my closed eyelids: if I open my eyes, the sunlight will cut them. And besides, it's better not to stir. Yesterday (it was yesterday, wasn't it?) they had wounded me; a day and a night have passed; other days and nights will pass; I will die. No matter. It's better not to stir. Let the body stay motionless. How fine it would be to stop the working of the brain as well! But there is no way of holding it back. Thoughts, recollections throng my head. However, all this isn't for long; the end will come soon. All that will remain will be a few lines in the newspapers, to the effect that our losses, now, are insignificant: wounded, so many; killed, one Ivanov, a private in the ranks, one of the volunteers. No, they won't write down the name, even; they'll simply say: killed, one. One private in the ranks—just like that puppydog.

A whole picture flares up in my imagination. It had all happened long ago; however, all things, all my life, that *other* life, before I came to be lying here with my legs smashed, had been so long ago. . . . I was walking down a street; a knot of people blocked my way. The crowd was standing in silence and looking at something small and white, all in blood, piteously whimpering. It was a bitch, pretty and little; a street horsecar had run her over. She was dying—there, just the way I was doing now. Some janitor or other elbowed his way through the crowd, took the little bitch by the scruff of her neck and carried her away. The crowd dispersed.

Would anyone carry me away? No; lie there and die. And yet how fine life is! On that day (when this misfortune had befallen the little bitch) I had been happy. I had been walking along in some sort of intoxication— yes, and there had been reason for it. You, my recollections—do not torture me, let me be! Happiness that was; torments that are . . . if but the torments alone would be left, if but the recollections, which willy-nilly force one to make comparisons, would not torment me. Ah, yearning, yearning! Thou art worse than wounds.

However, it is getting hot. The sun is burning. I open my eyes, see the same bushes, the same sky—only in the light of day. And, right over there, is my neighbor. Yes, it's a Turk, a corpse. How enormous he is! I recognize him, it's that same one—

Lying before me is a man killed by me. Why did I kill him?

He lies there dead, all in blood. Why had fate driven him here? Who is he? Perhaps he, too, has an old mother, even as I have? For long will she sit of evenings at the door of her lowly clay-daubed hut and keep glancing toward the distant north to see if her son, whom she could never sate her eyes with, her toiler and her bread-winner, isn't coming.

But what about me? Why, the same holds true in my

case as well. I would even exchange places with him. How happy he is—he hears nothing, he feels neither the pain of wounds, nor a deathly yearning, nor thirst. The bayonet had gone straight to his heart. See, there's a great black hole in the coat of his uniform; that hole is ringed with blood. *It was I who did that.*

I hadn't wished this. I hadn't wished evil to anyone when I had been setting out to do battle. The thought that I, too, would be compelled to kill people had somehow eluded me. I had pictured to myself only how *I* would be offering *my* breast to the bullets. And I had gone, and had offered up my breast.

Well, and what had come of it? Foolish man, foolish man! And this unfortunate *fellah* (he has on an Egyptian uniform)—he is still less to blame. Up to the time he and his fellows had been packed on a steamer, like herrings in a barrel, and transported to Constantinople, he had not as much as heard either of Russia or Bulgaria. He had been ordered to go, and he had gone. If he hadn't gone they would have bastinadoed him, or else, like as not, some pasha or other would have sent a pistol-bullet through him. He had gone by a long, hard march from Stamboul to Roushchouk. We had attacked; he had defended himself. But, seeing that we were frightful men who, unafraid of his patented English rifle (a Peabody and Martini), were constantly pushing on and on, he had been overcome with terror. When he had wanted to get away some manikin or other, ever so small, whom he could have killed with one blow of his black fist, had leapt close to him and stuck a bayonet into his heart.

Wherein, then, is he at fault?

And wherein am I at fault, even though I did kill him? Wherefor is thirst torturing me? Thirst! Who knows the meaning of that word? Even when we had been going through Rumania, by marches of thirty-five miles during dreadful hot spells with the thermometer at 110 degrees —even then I had not felt what I was feeling now. Ah, if someone would but come!

My God! Why, in that enormous canteen of his he surely must have water. Yet one has to get to it, somehow. At what a cost that will be! No matter; get to it I shall, somehow.

I crawl along. My legs drag; my arms, grown weak, barely move the inert body. There are only fifteen feet or so to the corpse, but for me that is greater—no, not greater, but worse—than scores of miles. Nevertheless, crawl one must. My throat is burning, searing, as if on fire. Besides, death will come quicker without water. But still, perhaps. . . .

And I crawl along. My legs catch on the ground, and every move evokes unbearable pain. I cry out; I cry out and my cries are screams, yet I crawl along just the same. And, at last, there he is. There's the canteen . . . there's water in it—and what a lot of it! The canteen is more than half-full, apparently. Oh, the water will last me a long time . . . to my very death!

Thou wilt save me, my victim! . . . I began to unfasten the canteen, leaning on my elbow, and suddenly, losing my balance, fell face down on the breast of my savior. One could already sense a strong charnel odor coming from him.

I drank my fill. The water was warm but had not gone bad, and in addition there was a lot of it. I will live through several days more. If I remember rightly, it says in the *Physiology of Everyday Life* that man can live without food for a week, as long as there is water. Yes, and the same book tells the case of a suicide, who starved himself to death. He kept on living for a very long time, because he drank water.

Well, and what of that? Even if I should live on for another five or six days, what will come of it? Our men were gone; the Bulgarians had run off in all directions. There was no road near-by. One would have to die any-way. All it amounted to was that instead of a three days' agony I had created for myself one that would last a week. Wouldn't it be better to put an end to myself? Lying near my neighbor was his gun, an excellent piece of English workmanship. All one had to do was to stretch out one's hand; then—an instant, and the end. The cartridges were lying here too, in a heap. He hadn't had time to expend them all.

Should I end everything thus—or wait? Wait for what? Deliverance? Death? Wait until the Turks come and start flaying the skin off my wounded legs? It would be best, after all, to get the thing over with by one's self. . . .

No, you mustn't let your spirits sink; I'll struggle on to the end, to the last of my strength. For, should I be found, I would be saved. Perhaps the bones hadn't been touched; I would be made sound again. I shall see my native land, my mother, Mary—

Lord, let them not learn the whole truth! Let them think that I had been killed outright. What will happen to them when they learn that I had suffered for two, three, four days!

My head is going 'round; the tortured journey toward my neighbor had worn me out completely. And there was that horrible odor, to top everything off. How black he had turned—what would he be like on the morrow or the day after? And the only reason I'm lying here now is because I haven't the strength to crawl off. I'll rest up and then crawl off to my old spot; by the way, the wind is blowing from that direction, and will be carrying the evil stench away from me.

I lie there in utter exhaustion. The sun is burning my face and hands. There's nothing I could put over myself. If but the night would come more quickly; this night, I think, will be the second one.

My thoughts become tangled, and I fall into a coma.

I slept a long while, because when I awoke it was already night. Everything was as it had been: the wounds were paining; my neighbor was lying there, just as enormous and motionless as ever.

I cannot avoid thinking of him. Can it really be that I had abandoned all that was endearing and dear, had come here by a march of nearly seven hundred miles, had hungered, endured cold, suffered from the heat; can it really be that I am now lying at last amid such torments—only to the end that this unfortunate should have ceased to live? For, after all, had I done anything of use for the military objectives save this murder?

Murder, murderer. . . . And who was that, now? I!

When I'd gotten the notion of going off to fight, my mother and Mary had not dissuaded me, even though they did weep over me. Blinded by an idea, I had not seen those tears. I had not understood (that understanding had come now) what I was doing to the beings so close to me.

But why recall things? There's no bringing back the past.

And what an odd attitude many of my acquaintances evinced toward my action! "What a holy innocent! Pushing himself forward without knowing a thing!" How could they say a thing like that? How do such words tie in with *their* conception of heroism, of love for one's native land, and the like? For in *their* eyes I represented all the heroic virtues. Yet, nonetheless, I was a "holy innocent."

And there I am, on my way to Kishenev; they load me down with a knapsack and all sorts of military equipment. And I slog along with thousands of others, among whom you could hardly gather a handful of those who, like me, had gone willingly. The others would have stayed at home, had they been allowed to do so. However, they slog along just as we, "those who are aware," are doing; they cover thousands of miles and fight just as we do—or even better. They fulfill their duties, regardless of the fact that they would drop everything and go off in a minute—were they allowed to do so.

A slight, keen morning breeze sprang up; the bushes stirred; some small bird, half-asleep, fluttered upward. The stars dimmed. The indigo sky turned grayish, became flecked with tender, feathery little clouds; a gray half-murk was rising from the earth. It was the coming of the third day of my . . . what am I to call it? Life? Agony?

The third. How many more of them were left? Not many, in any event. I have become very weak and, it seems, won't be able even to move away from the corpse. Soon he and I will be on the same footing, and will cease to be disagreeable to each other.

I must have a good drink. I am going to drink three times a day: at morning, at noon, and in the evening.

The sun has risen. Its enormous disc, all criss-crossed and segmented by the black branches of the bushes, is red as blood. Looks as if it's going to be hot today. My neighbor, what will become of you? You're horrible enough, even as it is.

Yes, he was horrible. His hair had begun to fall out.

His skin, naturally black, had paled and yellowed; his bloated face had stretched to such an extent that it had split behind one ear. Maggots were busily stirring there. His legs, with boots drawn over them, had become bloated, and enormous blisters had forced their way between the hooks fastening these boots. And all of him had become mountainously bloated. What would the sun make of him this day?

To be lying so close to him is unbearable. I must crawl away, at any cost. But will I be able to do so? I'm still able to raise my arm, to open the canteen, to take a good swig; but—to shift my heavy, immobile body? Nevertheless, shift it I shall, even though a little, even though half a pace an hour.

My whole morning passes in this transit. The pain is strong, but what is it to me now? I no longer remember, I cannot picture to myself, the sensations of a hale man. I have, apparently, actually become accustomed to the pain. On this morning I did, after all, crawl fifteen feet away, and found myself on the spot where I had been before. But I do not have the benefit of fresh air for long —if there can be such a thing as fresh air six paces from a putrefying corpse. The wind shifts and again brings down upon me the evil stench, now so powerful that I am nauseated. My empty stomach contracts excruciatingly and convulsively; all my inwards turn. But the malodorous, infected air simply keeps floating toward me.

I fall into despair and weep.

Altogether crushed, stupefied as if with a narcotic, I am lying almost unconscious. Suddenly . . . was it my disordered imagination deceiving me? It seems to me that such is not the case. Yes, it's the sound of voices.

The beat of horse hoofs; the sound of human voices. I almost sent up a shout, but restrained myself. For what if they should prove to be Turks? What then? To these present torments would be added others, still more terrible, which make one's hair stand on end when one reads about them in the newspapers. They will flay off my skin, will broil my wounded legs. It would be well if it were no more than that; but then, they're so ingenious. Can it really be better to get done with life at their hands than to die here? But what if these are our men? Oh, these accursed bushes! Why have you grown up about me in so thick a fence? I don't see a thing through them; only in one spot does something like a little window open up a view for me into the distance, into a hollow. There seems to be a little stream there, the one out of which we had drunk before the battle. Yes, and there's that enormous slab of sandstone, laid across the little stream to bridge it. They'll ride across it, most probably. The sound of voices dies down. I can't hear clearly the language they're talking in—my hearing, too, has become weakened. Lord! If these are our men. . . . I'm going to shout to them; they'll hear me even as far away as that little stream. That's better than to risk falling into the paws of the *bashi-bazouks*. But how is it they're so long in coming? Impatience wearies me; I do not notice even the odor of the corpse, although it has not abated in the least.

And suddenly on the crossing over the stream Cossacks appear! Blue coats, red stripes down the sides of their trousers, lances. There's all of half a hundred of them. With a black-bearded officer on a magnificent horse at their head. No sooner had the half-a-hundred made its way across the stream than he turned his whole body around in the saddle and called out:

"At a trot, forward!"

"Hold on, hold on, for God's sake! Help me, help me, brothers!" I shout; but the trampling of the great chargers, the clatter of the sabres and the noisy Cossack speech are louder than my hoarse wheezing—and they do not hear me!

Oh, damnation! I fall in exhaustion with my face to the earth and begin to sob. Out of the canteen I had overturned the water—my life, my salvation, my reprieve from death—is flowing. But I notice this only when there is no more than half a tumblerful left, while the rest has gone into the avid, dry earth.

Can I ever recall that lethargy which took possession of me after this terrible incident? I lay motionless, with eyes half closed. The wind was forever shifting, and was by turns blowing fresh, pure air at me, or wafting the evil stench toward me. My neighbor had on this day become frightful past all description. Once, when I opened my eyes to have a look at him, I was horrified. He no longer had a face. It had crept off the bones. The frightful bony smile, an eternal smile, seemed to me as repulsive, as horrible as never before, even though I have had occasion more than once to hold skulls in my hands and to dissect whole heads. This skeleton in a uniform threw me into shudders.

"That's war," I reflected. "There is its image."

But the sun is burning and baking as before. My face and hands have long since become scorched. I had drunk all the water that had remained. Thirst was torturing me so much that, having decided to take but a small sip, I had gulped everything down at one draught. Ah, why hadn't I yelled out to the Cossacks when they had been so close to me! Even if it had been the Turks, I would still have been better off. Well, so they would have tortured me for an hour, for two hours, but as it is I still don't know how much longer I will have to sprawl here and suffer. Mother of mine, my dear one! You will pluck out your gray braids, will strike your head against the wall, will curse the day when you gave me birth, will curse the whole world for that it has conceived such a thing as war to make men suffer!

However, you and Mary will probably never even hear of my torments. Farewell, mother; farewell, my bride, my love! Ah, how hard this is, how bitter! Something is creeping up on my heart. . . .

That little white bitch, again! The janitor had taken no pity upon her, had smashed her head against a wall and thrown her into a pit into which garbage was thrown and slops were poured. But she had been still alive. And had been in torment through all of another day. Yet I am more unfortunate than she, because I have been in torment for all of three days. Tomorrow it will be the fourth day, then it will be the fifth, then the sixth. . . . Death, where art thou? Come, come! Take me!

But death comes not, nor does it take me. And I lie under that fearful sun, and have not as much as a swallow of water to refresh my inflamed throat, and the corpse is infecting me. It has oozed apart altogether. Myriads of maggots are tumbling off it. How squirmingly busy they are! When he will have been eaten up and all that will be left of him will be bones and uniform, my turn will come. And I will be even as he is.

The day passes; the night passes. Everything is still the same. One more day passes. . . .

The bushes are stirring and soughing, as though in quiet converse. "For you will die, will die, will die!" they whisper—"You will never see them, never see them, never see them!" the bushes on the other side respond.

"Why, they're where you'll never see them!" someone says loudly close to me.

I shudder and at once come to myself. The kindly blue eyes of Yakovlev, our corporal, are looking at me out of the bushes.

"Bring the spades!" he shouts. "There's two more on 'em here, one of our men and one of theirs."

"No need of spades, no need of burying me—I'm alive!" I want to shout, but only a feeble moan issues from my parched lips.

"Lord! Why, can it be that he's alive? Master Ivanov! Hey there, lads! Hurry over here—our master is alive! And call the doctor!"

Half a minute later they are pouring water into my mouth, and vodka, and something else. Then everything vanishes.

The stretcher moves along, swaying evenly. This even motion lulls me. I awaken and become oblivious again, by turns. My bound wounds are no longer painful; some sort of inexpressibly joyous feeling has suffused itself through all my body.

"Ha-a-alt! Let 'er do-o-o-own! Orderlies of the fourth squad, march! Grab hold of the stretcher! Lift 'er up!"

It's Peter Ivanich, our medical officer, a tall, gaunt and very kindly man, who is issuing these commands. He is so tall that, on turning my head in his direction, I never lose sight of his head, his long, scanty beard, and his shoulders, even though my stretcher is being carried on the shoulders of four well-grown soldiers.

"Peter Ivanich!" I whisper.

"What is it, dear man?" Peter Ivanich bends over me.

"What did the doctor tell you, Peter Ivanich? Am I going to die soon?"

"Whatever are you saying, Ivanov—that'll do you!

You're not going to die. Why, all your bones are whole. What a lucky fellow! Neither the bones nor the arteries were touched. But how did you ever live through those three days and a half? What did you eat?"

"Nothing."

"And what did you drink?"

"I took the canteen from the Turk. I can't talk now, Peter Ivanich. Later on—"

"Well, the Lord be with you, dear man; sleep in peace."

Again sleep, oblivion.

I come to in the divisional lazaret. There are doctors standing over me, and Sisters of Mercy and, besides these, I also see a familiar face, that of a famous professor from Petersburg, who is bending over my legs. His hands are covered with blood. He does not fuss with my legs overlong, and turns to me:

"Well, young man, you're in luck and God has been good to you. We did take off one of your legs; but then, that's just a trifle. Can you talk?"

I can, and I tell them everything that is written here.

ANTON PAVLOVICH CHEKHOV

(1860–1904)

> Chekhov is inexhaustible, because, despite the everyday life which he is supposed to be always depicting, he speaks, always, in his basic, spiritual leitmotif, not of the casual, not of the personal, but of that which is Human —with a capital H. . . .
>
> I have had occasion to play the one and the same rôle in the plays of Chekhov several hundred times, yet I do not remember a single performance during which there were not revealed in my soul new sensations and, in the piece itself, new depths or refinements which I had not remarked before!
>
> —*Stanislavsky*

EDITOR'S NOTE

OF ALL the acts of vandalism wrought by Germans upon the shrines of Russian genius and culture, the most symbolic is the destruction of the house at Taganrok in which Chekhov was born. There was no gentler soul, no heart warmer than Chekhov's, no spirit more opposed to the Germanic.

Chekhov, the son of an ex-serf, graduated as a physician in 1884; although he did not practice very long, he was prouder of his medical knowledge than of his literary talent. To help his family and pay for his tuition he became an unabashed funnyman, selling everything from squibs to short stories to newspapers and comic sheets—and even his most ephemeral things retain their humor to this day. His first story appeared in 1880 (the rate was 2½ cents a line); however, as early as 1877, he had been sending skits and jokes to be placed by his brother Alexander, another contributor to the humorous publications; still another brother, Nicholas, used to draw for them. Chekhov's first book, *The Stories of Melpomene*, was brought out at his own expense in 1884; his second, *Motley Stories*, appeared in 1886, by which time he was breaking into the "thick-paper" field.

As supreme master of the short story, Chekhov not merely perfected it in Russia and gained recognition for it as a literary form in Russian; his influence upon the short story throughout the world has been vast—in the case of certain British lady-writers it may be said to have been nothing short of disastrous. This despite the fact that, as noted as late as 1903, "in English has appeared but *Philosophy at Home*, in *Short Stories*, October, 1891," and that, up to now, only two hundred or so of the thousand and more stories he has written have been done into English which hardly conveys his full charm and power.

Chekhov, as playwright, is the creator of a theatre wherein lyricity and atmosphere predominate over plot and incident and character is almost action—the untheatrical theatre. Naturally, Chekhov fared as did other innovators: *Ivanov*, his first full-length play, scored success only three years after its first production in 1886, when it was met with both applause and hisses; *The Sea Gull* became a furore only in Stanislavsky's hands, two years after it was booed off the stage in 1896. And, in English, we find such comments as: "A pessimistic vein runs through all his productions, and all his characters seem to be fit subjects for the psychiatrist; this is especially the case in two of his dramas, *The Mew* and

Three Sisters, in which there is not one redeeming person, and where the very language of the dramatis personae is nothing but a series of semi-articulated hysterical ejaculations." That was written (in a scholarly anthology from the Russian) in 1903—one year before Chekhov's death, and when he had been writing for a quarter of a century.

Since then, English (or at least British) criticism has pronounced *The Cherry Orchard* the greatest play since Shakespeare, and *The Three Sisters* the supreme play of all time and all tongues. (First produced in 1901, the year of Chekhov's marriage to Olga Knipper, the great actress.)

There may be among the world's outstanding stories a few which approach *Ward No. 6* in poignancy. The Editor knows of none which surpasses this short novel in that respect. It was written over fifty years ago, yet it is as timely as the next recurrent exposé of our bedlams and lazar houses. And it is curious to what an extent Chekhov's negativist doctor anticipated the most recent of our philosophical fads: Existentialism.

Chekhov died, not unironically, in Germany, at Badenweiler, in the Black Forest.

Ward No. 6

ANTON PAVLOVICH CHEKHOV

THE small wing, surrounded by a whole forest of nettles, burdocks, and marijuana, is out in the courtyard of the hospital. The roof of this wing is rusted, its chimney half-fallen, its front steps are rotted and grown over with grass; as for the whitewash, there are only traces of it left. Its façade is toward the hospital, its rear looks out upon a field, from which it is divided by the gray hospital fence with its coping of nails. These nails, their sharp points up, and the fence, and the wing itself, all have that peculiar, dismal, hopelessly accursed air which is to be found only in our hospital and prison buildings.

If you are not afraid of being stung by the nettles, let us take the narrow little path leading to the wing and have a peek at what is going on within. The front door admits us into the entry. Here, along the walls and near the stove, are piled up whole mountains of hospital odds and ends. Mattresses, old tattered robes, trousers, shirts with narrow stripes of blue, utterly useless worn out footgear—all this rag-fair has been dumped in piles, has become rumpled, tangled; it is rotting and giving off a stifling odor.

Nikita the keeper, an old retired soldier whose service stripes have turned rusty from time, is lolling upon these odds and ends, his eternal pipe clenched between his teeth. His face is morose, drink-ravaged; his eyebrows are beetling, bestowing on his face the look of a steppe sheepdog, and his nose is red; he is not tall, rather spare to look at, and sinewy, but his bearing is impressive and his fists are huge, hard. He belongs to the number of those simple-hearted, positive, reliable, and stolid persons who love order above all things on earth, and are therefore convinced that people must be beaten. When he beats somebody he beats him about the face, the chest, the back—wherever his blows may fall—and is convinced that without this there would be no order in this place.

Next you enter a large, spacious room which takes up the whole wing—that is, if the entry is not taken into consideration. The walls here are daubed over with a dirty light-blue paint; the ceiling is covered with soot, as in a smoke-house: it is evident that the furnaces here smoke in winter and give off asphyxiating fumes. The windows are made hideous by iron bars on the inside. The floor is gray and splintery. There is a stench of sauerkraut, of charred lamp-wicks, of bedbugs and ammonia, and from the very first this stench gives you the impression that you are entering a menagerie.

Beds, screwed down to the floor, are placed about this room. Men in blue hospital bathrobes and in anti-quated nightcaps are sitting or lying on them. These are the madmen.

There are altogether five of them here. Only one of them is of high birth; all the others are mere burghers. The man nearest the door, a tall, gaunt burgher with a red, shiny mustache and tearstained eyes, is sitting with his head propped up and his eyes fixed on one point. Day and night does he grieve, shaking his head, sighing and smiling a bitter smile; rarely does he take any part in the conversations and usually does not answer when questions are put to him. He eats and drinks mechanically, if food and drink are given him. Judging by his excruciating, hacking cough, his thinness and the flush on his cheeks, he has incipient consumption.

The next is a small, lively, exceedingly spry old man, with a little pointed beard, and black, kinky hair, like a Negro's. In the daytime he strolls about the ward, from window to window, or sits on his bed with his legs tucked in under him, Turkish fashion, and with never a let-up, like a bullfinch, whistles, hums, and snickers. He evinces his childish and lively character at night as well, when he gets up to pray to God—that is, to thump his breast and scrape at a doorpost with his finger.[1] This

---

[1] Under the impression that nailed up on the doorpost is a mezuzah: a tiny scroll, usually of parchment, whereon is inscribed

is the Jew Moisseika, an innocent, who lost his mind twenty years ago, when his hat factory burned down.

Of all the inmates of Ward No. 6 he is the only one who is allowed to go out of the wing—and even out of the hospital, into the street. He has enjoyed this privilege for a long, long time, probably because he is one of the time-honored hospital inmates and a quiet, harmless innocent, the butt of the town, whom the people have long since grown used to seeing upon the streets, surrounded by urchins and dogs. In his miserable little bathrobe, his funny nightcap, and in slippers (at times barefooted and even without his trousers) he goes about the streets, stopping at gateways and shops and begging for coppers. In one place they may give him some bread-cider, in another bread, in a third a copper, so that he usually returns to the wing sated and rich. All that he may bring back with him Nikita takes away from him for his own benefit. The soldier does this roughly, with great heat, turning out the idiot's pockets and calling upon God to be his witness that he's never going to let the sheeny go out into the street again, and that such irregularities are to him the most hateful things in the world.

Moisseika loves to make himself useful. He brings water to his fellows, tucks them in when they are asleep, promises each one to bring him back a copper from his street expeditions, and to sew a new hat for him; it is he, too, who feeds with a spoon his neighbor to the left,

---

the krishma, the most important and frequent prayer of the Jews. It admonishes that "these words" shall be spoken "when thou liest down, and when thou risest up"; also: "And thou shalt write them upon the doorposts of thy house, and upon thy gates." The case is almost invariably of some metal, with an opening through which can be read the three Hebrew letters signifying HADASHEM (one of the sacred names of the Lord) written on the outside of the scroll.—Trans.-Ed.

a paralytic. He acts thus not out of any commiseration, or because of any considerations of a humane nature, but in imitation of and involuntary submission to his neighbor on the right, one Gromov.

Ivan Dmitrich Gromov, a man of thirty-three, nobly born, at one time a court clerk and the secretary of the district, suffers from a persecution mania. He spends his time either lying in bed, curled up in a ball, or else paces from corner to corner, as if he were taking his constitutional; as for sitting, he indulges in that only very rarely. He is always agitated, excited, and tense because of some vague, undefined expectation. The least rustle in the entry, or a shout in the yard, will suffice to make him raise his head and prick up his ears: Are they coming to fetch him, perhaps? Is it him, by any chance, they are looking for? And his face at such a time bears an expression of extreme disquiet and revulsion.

I like his broad face with its high cheekbones, a face always pale and unhappy which reflects in itself, as in a mirror, his soul, tortured almost to death by struggling and long continued fear. His grimaces are queer and sickly, but the fine lineaments put on his face by profound, sincere suffering are discerning and intelligent, and his eyes have a warm, wholesome gleam. I like him for himself: polite, accommodating, and unusually delicate in his treatment of all save Nikita. When anyone happens to drop a button or a spoon he is quick to jump off his bed and pick up the fallen object. Every morning he greets his companions with a good morning; when he lies down to sleep he wishes them good night.

Besides his constant state of tension and his grimacing, his madness is also evinced by the following. At times, of evenings, he will muffle himself up in his miserable bathrobe and, with his whole body shaking, his teeth chattering, will take to striding rapidly from corner to corner and between the beds. It looks as if he were in the throes of a severe fit of the ague. One can see by the way he stops abruptly and glances at his fellows that he wants to say something of the utmost importance but, evidently surmising that no one will listen to him or understand him, he impatiently tosses his head and resumes his pacing. But the desire to speak shortly gets the upper hand over all and any considerations and, letting himself go, he speaks warmly and passionately. His speech is disorderly, feverish, like delirium, impulsive and not always intelligible, yet at the same time one can hear in it (both in the words and the voice) something exceedingly fine. When he speaks, you recognize in him a madman—and a human being. It is difficult to convey his insane speech on paper. He speaks of human baseness, of oppression trampling upon truth, of a splendid life which will in time prevail upon earth, of the window bars which at every moment remind him of the stupidity and cruelty of the oppressors. The result is a disordered, inchoate potpourri of songs that are old yet which thus far have never been sung to the end.

II

Some twelve or fifteen years ago a civil servant by the name of Gromov used to live in this town, in his own house, situated on the most important street. He had two sons, Serghei and Ivan. Serghei, when he was already a student in his fourth semester, contracted galloping consumption and died, and this death seemed to serve as the beginning of a whole series of misfortunes which suddenly fell upon the Gromov family. A week after Serghei's funeral the patriarchal head of the family was brought to trial for forgeries and embezzlements, and died shortly from typhus in the prison hospital. The house and all his personal property were sold under the hammer, and Ivan Dmitrich and his mother were left without any means.

Formerly, when his father had been alive, Ivan Dmitrich, who was living in St. Petersburg, where he was studying at the University, had been getting from sixty to seventy rubles a month and had had no conception of what need was, but now he had to change his life abruptly. He had to tutor from morning to night for coppers, to work at transcribing, yet go hungry just the same, since he sent all his earnings to his mother for her support. Ivan Dmitrich had not been able to stand such a life; his spirits sank, he began to ail and, leaving the University, he came back home. Here, in this little town, he obtained through influential friends a teaching position in the district school; however, he did not find his fellow-teachers congenial, was not liked by the pupils, and soon left the post. His mother died. For half a year or so he went without a position, living on nothing but bread and water; then he became a court clerk. This post he filled until he was dismissed because of his derangement.

Never, even during the years of his youth as a student, did he give the impression of a healthy man. He had always been pale, thin and subject to colds; he ate but little and slept poorly. One glass of wine sufficed to make his head swim and to bring on hysterics. He had always been drawn to people but, thanks to his irritable temper and his self-consciousness, he had never gotten on an intimate footing with anybody and had no friends. Of the people in the town he always spoke with contempt, saying that their boorish ignorance and drowsy, animal life seemed to him abominable and revolting. He spoke in a tenor, loudly, heatedly, and never otherwise than indignantly and wrathfully, or else with rapture and wonder, and always sincerely. No matter what one might begin a conversation with him about, he always brought it around to one thing: life in this town was stifling and tedious; its society had none of the higher interests; it was leading a drab, senseless life, diversifying it with oppression, coarse depravity, and hypocrisy; the scoundrels went well-fed and well-clad, while honest men subsisted on crumbs; there was need for schools, for a local newspaper with an honest policy, a theater, public readings, a consolidation of intellectual forces; there was need for society to recognize itself, and to be horrified by that recognition. In his judgments of people he laid the colors on thick, using only black and white, without admitting any shadings; he divided mankind into honest men and scoundrels—as for any middle ground, there was none. Of women and love he always spoke passionately, with rapture, yet he had not been in love even once.

In the town, despite the harshness of his judgments, he was liked and, behind his back, they called him Vanya. His innate delicacy, his obliging nature, decency, moral purity, and his threadbare, wretched little frock-coat, his ailing appearance and his family misfortunes, inspired people with a fine, warm and melancholy feeling; besides that, he was well educated and widely read; in the opinion of the townsmen he knew everything and, in this town, constituted something in the nature of a walking encyclopedic dictionary.

He read a very great deal. He was forever sitting in the club, nervously tugging at his little beard and turning the leaves of periodicals and books, and one could see by his face that he was not so much reading as swallowing everything, having barely masticated it. It must be supposed that reading was one of his unwhole-

some habits, since he fell with equal avidity upon everything that came to hand, even newspapers and almanacs
years old.

III

One autumn morning, his coat-collar turned up and
his feet squelching in the mud, Ivan Dmitrich was making his way through lanes and backlots to the house of
a certain burgher, to collect on a writ of execution. His
mood was a somber one, the usual thing with him of
mornings. In one of the lanes he came upon two convicts in leg-irons, convoyed by four soldiers with guns.
Ivan Dmitrich had very often come upon convicts
before, and every time they had aroused within him
feelings of commiseration and ill-ease, but now this
encounter made some sort of a peculiar, strange impression. For some reason or other it suddenly struck him
that he, too, could be put in leg-irons and, in the same
way, be led off through the mud to prison. On his way
home after calling on the burgher he met, near the post
office, a police inspector whom he knew, who greeted
him and went a few steps with him along the street—
and for some reason this struck him as suspicious.

At home, all that day, he could not get those convicts
and the soldiers with their guns out of his head, and an
incomprehensible psychic disquiet hindered him from
reading and concentrating. When evening came he did
not light the lamp, while at night he could not sleep and
kept on thinking incessantly of the possibility of his being arrested, put in irons and planted in prison. He
knew himself to be utterly innocent of anything culpa-
ble and could vouch that in the future as well he would
not commit murder, or arson, or theft; but then, is it
hard to commit a crime accidentally, involuntarily?
And being slandered—was that an impossibility? And,

finally, what about a miscarriage of justice? It is not in vain that age-old folk-experience teaches that no man is certain of escaping the beggar's sack or prison. As for a miscarriage of justice: that, under present-day judicial procedure was very possible—nothing out of the way about that. Men whose duties, whose business had to do with the sufferings of others—for instance judges, policemen, physicians—became, in the course of time and through the force of habit, inured to such a degree that they could not, even if they wanted to, regard their clients otherwise than formally; in this respect they are in no way different from the muzhik who butchers sheep and calves in his backlot and does not even notice the blood. And where the attitude to the individual is formal, soulless the judge needs, in order to deprive a man of all his property rights and to condemn him to penal servitude, only one thing: time. Only time, for the observance of certain formalities—which is just what the judge receives his salary for—and then it's all over! After that, go and seek justice and protection in this miserable, filthy little town, a hundred and twenty-five miles away from any railroad! Yes, and wasn't it amusing even to think of justice, when every oppression was hailed by society as a sane and salutary necessity, whereas every act of mercy, such as an acquittal, for instance, evoked nothing less than an explosion of unsatisfied, vindictive passion?

In the morning Ivan Dmitrich got up in a state of terror, with sweat beading his forehead, by now altogether convinced that he might be arrested at any minute. Since the oppressive thoughts of yesterday would not leave him in all that time (he reflected), it meant that there must be a modicum of truth in them. Really, they could not have come into his head for no reason at all.

A policeman leisurely passed by under his window; it was not for nothing. There, two men had stopped near the house, and just stood there, in silence. Why were they keeping silent?

And tormenting days and nights set in for Ivan Dmitrich. All the people who passed by his windows and all who entered the courtyard seemed to him spies and detectives. The captain of police usually drove a two-horse carriage through the street about noon; he was merely on his way from his suburban estate to the police station, yet every time it struck Ivan Dmitrich that he was driving much too fast and that his expression was somehow peculiar: evidently he was in a hurry to make known the appearance in the town of a very important criminal. Ivan Dmitrich started at every ring and at every knock on the gate; he was on tenterhooks whenever he encountered a new face at his landlady's; each time he came across policemen and gendarmes he smiled and whistled, so as to appear nonchalant. He stayed awake whole nights through in expectation of an arrest, but snored loudly and breathed deeply, like one sleeping, to make his landlady think he was asleep—for, if he was not sleeping, it would mean he was tormented by the pangs of his conscience: what a piece of circumstantial evidence! Facts and sane logic strove to convince him that all these fears were nonsense and psychopathy; that, if one were to take a broad view of the matter, there was really nothing frightful about arrest and prison—provided one's conscience were clear; however, the more intelligently and logically he reasoned, the more powerful and tormenting did his psychic disquiet become. His was something like the case of a certain anchorite in a wilderness, who wanted to make a tiny clearing for himself in a virgin forest; but, the more assiduously he wielded his ax, the thicker and greater did the forest grow. At the very last Ivan Dmitrich, seeing how useless it was, abandoned reasoning and gave himself up wholly to despair and fear.

He began to isolate himself and to avoid people. Even before this he had found his work repellent, but now it became unbearable to him. He was afraid somebody would trip him up somehow or other, that someone would slip a bribe in his pocket unperceived and then expose him, or that he himself would inadvertently make some error in his official papers, tantamount to a forgery, or that he would lose money in his keeping for others. Strangely enough, at no other time had his mind been as flexible and inventive as now, when every day he was thinking up thousands of reasons for being seriously apprehensive about his liberty and honor. But then his interest in the external world grew markedly weaker, as was also the case, to some extent, with his interest in books, and his memory became very treacherous.

In the spring, when the snow was gone, two half-putrefied corpses were found in a ditch near the graveyard—those of an old woman and a boy, with indications of their having met a violent death. Nothing else was talked of in the town save these two corpses and their unknown slayers. Ivan Dmitrich, in order that people might not think that it was he who had killed these two, went about the streets with a smile; but whenever he met any acquaintances he paled, then turned red, and asserted that there was no crime more vile than the killing of the weak and the defenseless. However, this lie soon wearied him and, after some reflection, he decided that the best thing to do in his position would be to hide in his landlady's cellar. He sat there for a whole day, then through the night and another day, caught a great chill and, after waiting until it was growing dark, made his way to his room stealthily, as if he were a thief. Until the day broke he stood in the middle of his room without stirring and on the alert for every sound.

Early in the morning, before the sun was up, some bricklayers came to his landlady. Ivan Dmitrich knew well enough that they had come to make over the oven, but his fear prompted him that these were policemen disguised as bricklayers. Even so he left his room, ever so quietly and, gripped by terror, without his hat and coat, started running down the street. Dogs, barking, ran after him; somewhere behind him a muzhik was shouting; the wind whistled in his ears, and it seemed to Ivan Dmitrich that all the oppression throughout the world had gathered behind his back and was pursuing him.

They caught him, led him home, and sent his landlady for a doctor. Andrew Ephimich, the doctor (of whom more will be said further on) prescribed cold packs for his head and bay-rum drops, shook his head sadly and took his departure, after telling the landlady that he would not call again, because it was not right to hinder people from going out of their minds. Since Ivan Dmitrich had no means to live on at home and to take treatment, he was shortly sent off to the hospital, and there they placed him in the ward for venereal patients. He did not sleep of nights, was capricious and disturbed the patients, and in a short while by orders of Andrew Ephimich, he was transferred to Ward No. 6.

In a year the town had already completely forgotten Ivan Dmitrich, and his books, which his landlady had dumped in a sleigh out in the shed, were dragged off by little boys.

IV

The patient to the left of Ivan Dmitrich's bed is, as
I have already said, the Jew Moisseika, while the patient
on his right is a muzhik with a dull, utterly imbecilic
face; he is bloated with fat and is almost globular. This
is a motionless, gluttonous, and uncleanly animal that
has long since lost the ability to think and feel. There
is constantly a pungent, stifling odor coming from him.

Nikita, who cleans up after him, beats him frightfully, swinging back with all his might, without sparing
his fists—and the frightful thing is not that he is beaten
(one can get used to that): what is frightful is that this
stupefied animal does not respond to these beatings by
either sound, or any move, or the expression of his
eyes, but merely keeps teetering slightly, like a heavy
cask.

The fifth and last inmate of Ward No. 6 is a townsman who had at one time sorted letters in the post office
—a small, rather spare blond fellow with a kindly but
somewhat sly face. To judge by his intelligent, calm
eyes, with their clear and cheerful look, he is out for
Number One, and is harboring some exceedingly important and pleasant secret. He keeps under his pillow
and his mattress something or other which he will not
show to anybody—not out of any fear that it may be
taken away or stolen, however, but out of bashfulness.
Occasionally he will walk up to a window and, turning
his back on his companions, pin something on his breast
and, bending his head, contemplate it; if one approaches
him at such a time he becomes confused and plucks that
something off his breast. But it is not hard to fathom his
secret.

"Congratulate me!" he often says to Ivan Dmitrich. "I have been presented with the Order of Stanislaus, of the Second Class—with a star. The Second Class—with a star—is given only to foreigners but, for some reason, they want to make an exception in my case." He smiles, shrugging his shoulders in a puzzled way. "There, now, I must confess I never expected that!"

"I don't understand anything about such things," Ivan Dmitrich declares glumly.

"But do you know what I'm going to win, sooner or later?" the one-time sorter continues, puckering up his eyes slyly. "I am absolutely bound to receive the Swedish Polar Star. Now *that* is a decoration which is really worth going to a lot of trouble for. A white cross and a black ribbon. Ever so beautiful."

Probably nowhere else is life as monotonous as in this wing. In the morning the patients (with the exception of the paralytic and the blubbery muzhik) wash themselves in the entry at a big tub, using the skirts of their robes for towels; after this they drink tea out of pewter mugs; the tea is brought to them from the main building by Nikita. Each one is supposed to get just one mug. At noon they eat soup made with sauerkraut and, with it, buckwheat grits; in the evening they sup on the grits left over from dinner. In between they lie on their beds, sleep, look out of the windows, and pace from corner to corner. And thus every day. Even the one-time sorter speaks always of the very same decorations.

Fresh faces are rarely seen in Ward No. 6. The doctor has long ago stopped admitting new mental cases, and there are but few people in this world who like to visit madhouses. Once every two months Semën Lazarich, the barber, calls at the wing. Of how he clips the insane, and how Nikita assists him, and into what confusion the patients are thrown at every appearance of the intoxicated, smiling barber—of that we will not speak.

Save for the barber no one looks in at the wing. The patients are condemned to see no one but Nikita, day in and day out.

However, a rather strange rumor has recently spread through the hospital building.

Someone has started a rumor that, apparently, the doctor has taken to visiting Ward No. 6.

v

A strange rumor!

Doctor Andrew Ephimich Raghin is, after his own fashion, a remarkable man. They say that in his early youth he was exceedingly pious and had been preparing himself for a career in the church, and that, after he had finished studying in the gymnasium in 1863, he had intended to enter a seminary; but his father, a doctor of medicine and a surgeon, had apparently jeered at him caustically and had declared categorically that he would not consider him his son if he joined the psalm-snufflers. How true that is I do not know, but Andrew Ephimich has confessed more than once that he had never felt any call for medicine and, in general, for the applied sciences.

Be that as it may, after finishing his medical courses he did not become a long-haired priest. He did not evince any piety, and at the beginning of his healing career resembled a person of the spiritual calling as little as he did now.

In outward looks he is ponderous, coarse, like a muzhik; his face, his beard, his flat hair and his strong, unwieldy physique make one think of someone who keeps a tavern along some main road, who has overindulged himself in food, is intemperate and hard-headed. His face is stern and criss-crossed with small blue veins, his eyes are small, his nose is red. In keeping with his great height and broad shoulders he has enormous feet and hands—it seems that, were he to swing his fist at you, you would be done for. Yet his step is soft and his walk cautious, stealthy; when you meet him in a narrow corridor he is always the first to stop and give you the right of way, and says "Excuse me!"—not in the bass you expect, however, but in a high, soft little tenor. He has a small swelling on his neck which keeps him from wearing hard, starched collars, and so he always walks about in a soft shirt of linen or calico; in general, he does not dress the way doctors do. He wears the self-same old suit for ten years at a stretch, while his new clothes (which he usually buys at some cheap place) look just as worn and wrinkled on him as his old ones; he will wear the very same coat when receiving patients, or dining, or paying social calls—this is not out of stinginess, however, but from a complete disregard for his appearance.

When Andrew Ephimich came to this town to take his post, the "eleemosynary institution" was in a dreadful state. It was hard to breathe in the wards, the corridors, and the hospital courtyard because of the stench. The hospital orderlies, the nurses, and their children, all used to sleep in the same wards with the sick. Everybody complained there was no living on account of the cockroaches, the bedbugs, and mice. There was never a shortage of erysipelas in the surgical division. For the whole hospital there were but two scalpels and not a single thermometer; the bathtubs were used as storage bins for potatoes. The superintendent, the woman who had full charge of the linen and so forth, and the assistant doctor—they all robbed the sick; while it was told of the old doctor, Andrew Ephimich's predecessor, that he bootlegged the hospital alcohol and had set up for himself a whole harem of nurses and female patients.

The people in the town were very familiar with these irregularities and even exaggerated them, yet regarded
them with equanimity; some justified them by the fact
that the only ones who filled the hospital beds were
burghers and muzhiks, who could not possibly be dissatisfied, since they lived far worse at home than they
did at the hospital: no use pampering them with deli-
cacies, you know! Others said, in justification, that the
town found it beyond its means to maintain a good
hospital without any aid from the county: thank God
there was even a bad one. As for the county, it would
not open a hospital either in the city or near it, giving
the excuse that the town already had a hospital of its
own.

After an inspection of the hospital Andrew Ephimich
came to the conclusion that this institution was immoral
and in the highest degree harmful to the health of the
inhabitants. The most intelligent thing to do, in his
opinion, would be to turn the patients loose and close
the hospital. But he reasoned that his will alone was not
enough for this, and that it would be useless: were the
physical and moral uncleanliness driven from one place
it would pass on to some other; one had to wait until
the thing had thoroughly aired itself. In addition to
that, if the people opened a hospital and tolerated it in
their midst, it meant that they found it necessary; the
prejudices and all those everyday vilenesses and abominations were necessary, since in the course of time they
become worked over into something useful, even as
manure is worked over into black loam. There is nothing on this earth so good that it had not some vileness at
its prime source.

After accepting the post Andrew Ephimich evidently
took a rather indifferent attitude toward the irregularities. He merely requested the orderlies and the nurses

not to pass their nights in the wards, and put in two wall-cases of surgical instruments; as for the superintendent, the woman in charge of linen, the assistant doctor, and the surgical erysipelas, they all stayed put.

Andrew Ephimich is exceedingly fond of intelligence and honesty, yet he has not sufficient character and belief in his rights to establish an intelligent and honest life about him. To order, to forbid, to insist—these things he is utterly unable to do. It seems as if he had taken a vow never to raise his voice and never to use the imperative mood. To say "Let me have this," or "Bring me that," is for him a difficult matter; when he wants to eat he coughs irresolutely and says to the cook: "What about some tea, now?"—or: "What about dinner?" As for telling the superintendent to stop stealing, or driving him out, or doing away altogether with this needless, parasitical post—that is something altogether beyond his strength. Whenever Andrew Ephimich is being taken in or flattered, or a palpably and vilely doctored account is submitted for his signature, he turns as red as a boiled lobster and feels himself guilty, yet he signs the account just the same; whenever the patients complain to him about being starved or about the boorish nurses he becomes confused and mumbles guiltily: "Very well, very well—I'll look into that later. . . . Probably there's some misunderstanding here—"

At first Andrew Ephimich had worked very assiduously. He received patients from morning until dinnertime, performed operations, and even practiced obstetrics. The ladies said of him that he was conscientious and diagnosed complaints excellently—especially those of women and children. But as time went on the work markedly bored him with its monotonousness and obvious futility. Today you received thirty patients; on the morrow, before you knew it, they ran up to thirty-five;

the day after there would be forty, and so on from day to day, from year to year, yet the death-rate in the town did not decrease and the sick never ceased coming. It was a physical impossibility, in the time between morning and noon, to extend any real aid to the forty patients who came; therefore, willy-nilly, the result was plain humbug. During the fiscal year twelve thousand out-patients had been received; therefore, it simply stood to reason that twelve thousand people had been humbugged. As for placing those seriously ill into the wards, and treating them in accordance with all the rules of science, that also was impossible—for although there were rules there was no science; on the other hand, were one to abandon philosophy and follow the rules pedantically, as other physicians did, you would need for that, first and foremost, cleanliness and ventilation instead of filth, wholesome food instead of soup cooked out of stinking sauerkraut, and decent assistants instead of thieves.

And besides, why hinder people from dying, since death is the normal and ordained end of every being? What did it matter if some haggling shopkeeper or petty government clerk did live five or ten years extra? But if one saw the aim of medicine as the alleviation of suffering through drugs then, involuntarily, the question bobbed up: Wherefore should sufferings be alleviated? In the first place, they say that sufferings lead man to perfection and, in the second, should mankind really learn to alleviate its sufferings through pills and drops, it would abandon altogether religion and philosophy, in which it has found up to now not only a defense against all tribulations but even happiness. Pushkin, just before death, experienced dreadful tortures; that poor fellow Heine, lay for several years stricken by paralysis —why, then, shouldn't some Andrew Ephimich or

Matrëna Savishna ail for a bit, since their lives are devoid of all content and would be altogether vacuous and like the life of an amoeba, were it not for their sufferings?

Crushed by such reflections Andrew Ephimich let his spirits sink and became irregular in his attendance at the hospital.

VI

Here is the way his life goes on. Usually he gets up about eight in the morning, dresses, and has his tea. Then he sits down in his study to read, or goes to the hospital. Here, in the hospital, in a narrow, dark little corridor, sit the ambulatory patients, waiting to be received. Orderlies, their boots clattering on the brick floor, and nurses hurry past them; gaunt patients walk by in their robes; dead bodies and filled bed-pans are carried by; the children are crying; there is a windy draft. Andrew Ephimich knows that for the ague-stricken, for the consumptives, and, in general, for all the susceptible patients such a setting is excruciating, but what can one do?

In the reception room he is met by Serghei Sergheich, the assistant doctor, a small, stout man with a clean-shaven, well-groomed puffy face, with soft, stately manners and wearing a new, roomy suit: he looks more like a senator than an assistant doctor. He has an enormous practice in town, wears a white cravat and considers himself better informed than the doctor, who has no practice whatsoever. Placed in one corner of the reception room is an icon, in a case, with a ponderous lampad glowing before it; standing near it is a lectern in a white slip-cover; hanging upon the walls are portraits of arch-priests, a view of Holy Mount Monastery and wreaths of dried corn-flowers. Serghei Sergheich is religious and loves churchly pomp. The holy image has been placed here at his expense; of Sundays, in this reception room, one patient or another reads an acathistus at his orders, at which all stand, while after the reading Serghei Sergheich makes the round of all the wards with a censer and thurifies them with frankincense.

The patients are many but the time is short, and therefore the whole business is limited to putting a few brief questions and issuing some medicine or other, such as volatile ointment or castor oil. Andrew Ephimich sits with cheek propped up on his fist, in deep thought, and puts his questions mechanically. Serghei Sergheich is also sitting, rubbing his little hands from time to time and putting in his oar every now and then.

"We ail and endure need," he will say, "because we pray but poorly to the merciful Lord. Yea, verily!"

At these clinical sessions Andrew Ephimich does not perform any operations whatsoever; he has long since grown disused to them and the sight of blood agitates him unpleasantly. When he has to open a baby's mouth to look down its throat, and the baby squalls and defends itself with its tiny hands, his head swims from the noise in his ears and tears appear in his eyes. He hastens to prescribe some medicine and waves his hands at the peasant woman to take the baby away in a hurry.

During such a session he soon becomes bored with the timidity of the patients and their lack of sense, with the proximity of the pompous Serghei Sergheich, with the portraits on the walls and with his own questions, which he has been putting, without ever varying them, for more than twenty years by now. And, after having received five or six patients, he leaves. The assistant doctor receives the rest without him.

With the pleasant reflection that, thank God, he has

had no private practice for a long, long time now, and that no one will interrupt him, Andrew Ephimich upon getting home immediately sits down at the desk in his study and falls to reading. He reads a very great deal, and always with great pleasure. Half his salary goes for the purchase of books, and out of the six rooms in his quarters three are piled up with books and old periodicals. Most of all he loves works on history and philosophy; in medicine, however, he subscribes only to *The Physician,* which he always begins reading from the end. Each time his reading goes on for several hours without a break and never tires him. He does not read as rapidly and fitfully as Ivan Dmitrich used to do at one time, but slowly, with penetration, frequently pausing at passages which are to his liking or which he cannot grasp. Always standing near his book is a small decanter of vodka, while lying right on the cloth, without any plate, is a pickled cucumber or a pickled apple. Every half hour, without taking his eyes off the book, he pours out a pony of vodka and drinks it down, then, without looking, he gropes for the cucumber and takes a small bite.

At three o'clock he cautiously approaches the kitchen door, coughs and says:

"Dariushka, what about some dinner?"

After dinner, rather badly cooked and sloppily served, Andrew Ephimich paces through his rooms, with his arms crossed on his breast, and meditates. Four o'clock chimes, then five, but he is still pacing and meditating. At rare intervals the kitchen door creaks and Dariushka's red, sleepy face peeks out:

"Isn't it time for your beer, Andrew Ephimich?" she asks solicitously.

"No, not yet," he answers. "I'll wait . . . I'll wait a while—"

In the evening Michael Averianich, the postmaster, usually drops in—the only man in town whose society does not oppress Andrew Ephimich. At one time Michael Averianich had been an exceedingly rich landed proprietor and had served in the cavalry, but he had become ruined and, out of necessity, had in his old age entered the post-office department. He has a wide-awake, hale appearance, luxurious gray side-whiskers, manners that show his fine upbringing, and a booming, pleasant voice. He is kind and responsive but quick-tempered. When, at the post office, any patron protests, disagrees, or simply starts an argument, Michael Averianich turns purple, quivers all over and shouts "Quiet, you!" in a thunderous voice, so that the post office has long since gotten a deep-rooted reputation of an institution a call at which is a frightening experience. Michael Averianich respects and loves Andrew Ephimich for his culture and the nobility of his soul; all the other inhabitants of the town he looks down upon, however, as if they were his subordinates.

"Well, here I am!" he says as he enters Andrew Ephimich's place. "How are you, my dear fellow! Guess you must be tired of me by now—eh?"

"On the contrary, I am very glad," the doctor answers him. "I am always glad to see you."

The friends seat themselves on the divan in the study and for some time smoke in silence.

"If we could only have some beer now, Dariushka!" says Andrew Ephimich.

The first bottle they drink in the same silence: the doctor in a pensive mood, and Michael Averianich with a gay, animated air, like a man who has something interesting to tell. It is the doctor who always begins the conversation.

"What a pity it is," he says slowly and softly, without

looking into the eyes of his companion (he never looks anyone in the eye), "what a profound pity it is, my dear Michael Averianich, that there are absolutely no people in our town who can, and like to, carry on an intelligent and interesting conversation. That is an enormous deprivation for us. Even the intelligents aren't above vulgarity; the level of their development, I assure you, is not in the least above that of the lower masses."

"You're absolutely correct. I agree with you."

"You yourself know," the doctor continues softly, and with frequent pauses, "that everything in this world is insignificant and uninteresting except the higher spiritual manifestations of the human mind. The mind draws a sharp dividing line between animal and man, hints at the divinity of the latter and, to a certain degree, even replaces for him immortality, which is nonexistent. Hence it follows that the mind serves as the sole possible source of enjoyment. True, we have books, but that's not at all the same as animated conversation and sociability. If you will allow me to make a not altogether apt analogy, books are notes, while conversation is singing."

"Absolutely correct!"

A silence ensues. Dariushka emerges from the kitchen and, with an air of stolid sorrow, propping up her chin on her fist, stops in the doorway to listen.

"Eh!" sighs Michael Averianich. "The very idea of expecting anybody nowadays to have a mind!"

And he tells how full of zest, and gaiety, and interest life used to be; what clever intelligents there had been in Russia, and how highly they held the concepts of honor and friendship. Money was loaned without any promissory notes, and it was considered a disgrace not to extend a helping hand to a comrade in need. And what campaigns there had been, what adventures and

set-tos—what comrades, what women! Take the Caucasus—what an astonishing region! Then there was the
wife of a certain battalion commander—a strange
woman, who used to put on the uniform of an officer
and go off into the mountains of evenings, all by herself, without any guide. They said she had a romantic
affair in one of the eyrie-settlements with some native
princeling or other.

"Queen of Heaven, Our Mother—" Dariushka would
sigh.

"And how we drank! How we ate! And what reckless
liberals there were!"

Andrew Ephimich listens and does not hear; he is
meditating upon something and from time to time sips
his beer.

"I frequently dream of clever people and of conversations with them," he says unexpectedly, interrupting Michael Averianich. "My father gave me a splendid
education but, under the influence of the ideas of the
'sixties, compelled me to become a physician. It seems
to me that if I had not heeded him then I would now be
in the very center of the intellectual movement. Most
probably I would be a member of some faculty or other.
Of course, the mind is also not eternal but transitory;
however, you already know why I cherish an inclination
to it. Life is merely an irritating snare. When a thinking
man attains the prime of his manhood and arrives at a
mature consciousness of life, he involuntarily feels as
if he were in a snare from which there is no escape.
Really, now, against his own will, through certain ac-
cidental circumstances, he has been summoned from
non-being into life. Wherefore? Should he desire to
learn the significance and purpose of his existence he is
either told nothing or he is told absurdities—he knocks,
but it will not be opened unto him; then death comes

to him—likewise against his will. And so, even as people in prison, bound by a common misfortune, feel themselves more at ease when they get together, even so in life one does not feel the snare one is in when people inclined to analysis and generalizations get together and pass the time in exchanging lofty, free ideas. In that sense the mind is a delight for which there is no substitute."

"Absolutely correct!"

Without looking into his companion's eyes, softly and with pauses, Andrew Ephimich goes on speaking of clever people and of conversations with them, while Michael Averianich listens to him attentively and concurs:

"Absolutely correct!"

"But don't you believe in the immortality of the soul?" the postmaster suddenly asks.

"No, my esteemed Michael Averianich, I do not believe in it, nor have I any basis for believing."

"I must confess that I, too, have my doubts. But then, I have a feeling as if I'll never die. Come, I think, you old curmudgeon, it's time for you to die. But in my soul there is some sort of a tiny voice: 'Don't you believe it—you won't die!' "

Just a little after ten Michael Averianich leaves. As he is putting on his fur-lined coat out in the entry he says with a sigh:

"But what a wilderness fate has cast us into! And the most vexing thing of all is that we'll even have to die here. Eh!"

VII

After seeing his friend off Andrew Ephimich sits down at his desk and starts reading again. The quietness of the evening, and then of the night, is not disturbed by a single sound, and time seems to stand still and to be rooted to the spot together with the doctor poring over his book, and it seems that nothing exists save this book and the lamp with its green shade. The doctor's coarse, peasant face becomes little by little illuminated by a smile of touched delight and rapture before the courses of the human mind. "O, why is not man immortal?" he thinks. Why has he been given cerebral centers and convolutions, why his sight, speech, consciousness of self, genius, if all these things are fated to go back into the soil and, in the very end, turn cold together with the earth's core and then go careering with the earth for millions of years around the sun, senselessly and aimlessly? Just to have him turn cold and then go off careering there is altogether no need to draw man with his lofty, almost divine mind out of non-being and then, as if in mockery, to turn him into clay.

Transubstantiation! But what cowardice it is to console one's self with this surrogate of immortality! The inanimate processes taking place in nature are beneath even human stupidity, inasmuch as in stupidity there are present, after all, consciousness and will, whereas in these processes there is just nothing at all. Only a coward who has more of the fear of death in him than of dignity is capable of consoling himself with the idea that his body will, in time, live again as grass, as stone, as toad. . . . To see one's immortality in transubstantiation is just as queer as to prophesy a brilliant future to a violin case after the priceless Stradivarius it once held has been shattered and become useless.

Whenever the clock strikes Andrew Ephimich throws himself back in his armchair and closes his eyes for a little thought. And unintentionally, under the influence of the fine thoughts he had read out of his books, he casts a glance over his past and his present. The past is execrable: better not recall it. As for the present, it is filled with the same sort of thing as the past. He knows that even as his thoughts go careering with the cooled earth around the sun, in the great barrack-like structure of the hospital, alongside of the quarters he occupies, people are languishing amid diseases and physical uncleanliness; someone is perhaps not sleeping but warring with insects; someone is being infected with erysipelas or moaning because of a bandage too tightly applied; the patients are, perhaps, playing cards with the nurses and drinking vodka. During the fiscal year twelve thousand people had been humbugged; this whole hospital business, just as the case was twenty years ago, is built upon thievery, squabbles, slanders, nepotism, and upon crass charlatanry, and the hospital, just as hitherto, represents an institution immoral and in the highest degree harmful to the inhabitants. He knows that behind the barred windows of Ward No. 6 Nikita is beating the patients, and that Moisseika goes through the town every day and collects alms.

On the other hand, he knows exceedingly well that a fairy-tale change has taken place in medicine during the last twenty-five years. When he had been studying at the university it had seemed to him that medicine would shortly be overtaken by the same fate as alchemy and metaphysics; but now, when he reads of nights, medicine amazes him and arouses wonder and even rapture in him. And really, what unexpected brilliancy there is here, and what a revolution! Thanks to antiseptics, surgeons perform such operations as the great Pirogov had deemed impossible even *in spe*. Ordinary country doctors have the courage to perform resections of the knee-joint; out of a hundred Caesarian sections one case only ends in mortality; as for gallstones, they are considered such a trifle that no one even writes about them. Syphilis can be radically cured. And what about the theory of heredity, and hypnotism, the discoveries of Pasteur and Koch, hygiene and its statistics? What about the county medical centers in Russia? Psychiatry, with its present classification of derangements, its methods of investigation and treatment—why, by comparison with what used to be, it towers nothing short of the Elbruz. The heads of the insane are no longer doused with cold water, nor are they strapped into straitjackets; they are maintained humanely and, actually (so the newspapers write), theatrical entertainments and balls are arranged for them. Andrew Ephimich knows that, judged by present-day views and tastes, such an abomination as Ward No. 6 is possible only a hundred and twenty-five miles from any railroad, in a miserable little town where the mayor and all the councilmen are semiliterate burghers who regard a physician as a high priest who must be believed without any criticism, even though he were to pour molten lead into your mouth; in any other place the public and the newspapers would long since have left not one stone of this little Bastille standing upon another.

"But what of it?" Andrew Ephimich asks himself, opening his eyes. "What of all this? There are antiseptics, and Koch, and Pasteur, yet in substance the business hasn't changed in the least. Ill-health and mortality are still the same. Balls and theatrical entertainments are arranged for the insane—but, just the same, they're not allowed to go free. Therefore, everything is bosh and pother and, substantially, there's no difference between the best clinic in Vienna and my lazar-house."

However, sorrow and a feeling resembling envy hinder him from being indifferent. This, probably, is due to fatigue. His ponderous head droops toward the book;

he places his hands under his face, to make it more comfortable, and reflects:

"I am serving an evil cause, and receive my salary from people whom I dupe: I am not honest. But then I, by myself, am nothing; I am but a particle of a necessary social evil: all the district bureaucrats are harmful and receive their salaries for nothing. Therefore, it is not I who am to blame for my dishonesty but the times. . . . Were I to be born two hundred or so years from now, I would be an honest man."

When three o'clock strikes he puts out the lamp and goes to his bedroom. He does not feel sleepy.

VIII

Two years before the county administration had had a fit of generosity and had voted a yearly appropriation of three hundred rubles as a subsidy for the enlargement of the medical personnel in the town hospital, until such time as the county hospital would be opened, and so the district doctor, Eugene Fedorich Hobotov, was invited to the town to assist Andrew Ephimich. Eugene Fedorich is still a young man, not even thirty yet; he is tall, dark-haired, with broad cheekbones and tiny eyes: probably his ancestors were aliens. He arrived in town without a copper, with a wretched little handbag and a young, homely woman, whom he calls his cook. This woman has a breast baby. Eugene Fedorich walks about in high boots and a round cap with a stiff brim and, in winter, in a short fur-lined coat. He has become very chummy with Serghei Sergheich, the assistant doctor, and with the treasurer; but as for the other officials, he for some reason or other calls them aristocrats and steers clear of them. In his entire flat he has exactly one book: *The Latest Prescriptions of the*

Vienna Clinic for 1881. Whenever he goes to call on a patient he infallibly takes this book along with the rest of his equipment. Of evenings, at the club, he plays billiards, but he does not like cards. He is very fond of interlarding his conversation with such phrases as "Long drawn out mess," "Poppycock oil," "That'll do you, trying to pull the wool over my eyes," and so forth.

He visits the hospital twice a week, makes the round of the wards and receives the patients. The complete absence of antiseptics and the presence of cupping-glasses arouse his indignation, but he does not introduce any new ways, being afraid of offending Andrew Ephimich thereby. He considers his colleague Andrew Ephimich an old knave, suspects him of having large means and, in secret, envies him. He would be willing enough to step into his place.

IX

On a certain evening in spring, when there was no longer any snow on the ground and the starlings were singing in the hospital garden, the doctor stepped out to see his friend the postmaster to the gate. Precisely at that moment the Jew Moisseika was entering the yard, returning from his foraging. He was hatless and had shallow galoshes on his bare feet, and was holding a small sack with the alms.

"Gimme a copper!" He turned to the doctor; he was shivering from the cold and smiling.

Andrew Ephimich, who never refused anybody, gave him a ten-kopeck silver coin.

"How bad that is," he thought, glancing at the bare legs, with red, bony ankles. "Why, it's wet out."

And, moved by a feeling which resembled both pity and squeamishness, he set out for the hospital wing after the Jew, glancing now at his bald spot, now at his ankles. At the doctor's entrance Nikita jumped up from his mound of rubbish and drew himself up at attention.

"How do, Nikita," Andrew Ephimich said softly. "What about issuing a pair of boots to this Jew, or something of that sort—for he's likely to catch cold."

"Right, Your Honor. I'll report it to the superintendent."

"Please do. Ask him in my name. Say I asked him to do it."

The entry door was open into the ward. Ivan Dmitrich, lying on his bed and propped up on an elbow, was listening uneasily to the unfamiliar voice, and suddenly recognized the doctor. His whole body began to quiver with wrath; he sprang up and, with a red, angry face, his eyes bulging, ran out into the middle of the ward.

"The doctor has come!" he cried out, and burst into laughter. "At last! Gentlemen, I felicitate you—the doctor is honoring you by his visit! You damned vermin!" he screeched, and stamped his foot in such fury as no one in the ward had ever seen before. "This vermin ought to be killed! No, killing him is not enough! He ought to be drowned in the privy!"

Andrew Ephimich, who had heard this, peeped out into the ward from the entry and asked gently:

"For what?"

"For what?" cried out Ivan Dmitrich, walking up to him with a threatening air and convulsively drawing his robe about him. "For what? You thief!" he uttered with revulsion and shaping his lips as if he wanted to spit. "Quack! Hangman!"

"Calm yourself," said Andrew Ephimich with a guilty smile. "I assure you I have never stolen anything; as for the rest, you probably exaggerate greatly. I can see that you are angry at me. Calm down if you can, I beg of you, and tell me without any heat what you are angry at me for."

"Well, why do you keep me here?"

"Because you are unwell."

"Yes—unwell. But then scores, hundreds of madmen are going about in full freedom, because your ignorance is incapable of distinguishing them from normal people. Why then must I, and all these unfortunates sit here, like so many scapegoats for everybody? You, your assistant doctor, the superintendent, and all your hospital riff-raff are, as far as morals are concerned, immeasurably beneath each one of us: why, then, are we sitting here and not the whole lot of you? Where's the logic in that?"

"A moral attitude and logic have nothing to do with all this. Everything depends on chance. He who has been placed in here stays here, while he who hasn't been placed here goes about in full freedom: that's all there is to it. In the fact that I am a doctor and you are a psychopathic case there is neither morality nor logic, but only trivial chance."

Moisseika, whom Nikita had been too bashful to search in the doctor's presence, had spread out on his bed pieces of bread, scraps of paper and little bones and, still shivering from the cold, began saying something in Hebrew, rapidly and in sing-song. Probably he had gotten the idea that he had opened a shop.

"Let me out," said Ivan Dmitrich, and his voice quavered.

"I can't."

"But why? Why?"

"Because that isn't in my power. Judge for yourself: what good would it do you if I were to let you out? Go ahead. The people in town and the police will detain you and send you back."

"Yes, yes, that's true enough," Ivan Dmitrich managed to say, and rubbed his forehead. "This is horrible! But what am I to do? What?"

The voice of Ivan Dmitrich, and his youthful, clever face with its grimaces proved to the doctor's liking. He felt an impulse to be kind to him and to calm him. He sat down next to him on the bed, thought a while, and said:

"You ask, what's to be done? The best thing to do in your situation is to escape from here. But, regrettably, that is useless. You would be detained. When society fences itself off from criminals, psychopaths, and people who are generally embarrassing, it is insuperable. There is but one thing left for you: to find reassurance in the thought that your staying here is necessary."

"It isn't necessary to anybody."

"Since prisons and madhouses exist, why, somebody is bound to sit in them. If not you, then I; if not I, then some third person. Bide your time; when in the distant future prisons and madhouses will have gone out of existence, there will be no more bars on windows, nor hospital robes. Of course, sooner or later, such a time will come."

Ivan Dmitrich smiled mockingly.

"You jest," said he, puckering his eyes. "Such gentry as you and your helper, Nikita, have nothing to do with the future; but you may rest assured, my dear sir, that better times will come! I may be expressing myself in a banal way—laugh, if you like—but the dawn of a new life will shine forth, truth will rise triumphant—and then it will be our turn to rejoice. I will not live to see the day, I will have perished even as animals perish— but then somebody's grandchildren will live to see it. I hail them with all my soul, and I rejoice—I rejoice for them! Onward! May God be with us and help us, my friends!"

Ivan Dmitrich, his eyes shining, stood up and, stretching his arms out toward a window, continued with excitement in his voice:

"From behind these window-bars I bless you! May truth prevail! I rejoice!"

"I can't find any particular cause for rejoicing," said Andrew Ephimich, whom Ivan Dmitrich's gesture had struck as theatrical while, at the same time, it had been very much to his liking. "There will be a time when jails and madhouses will no longer exist and truth, as you were pleased to put it, will rise triumphant; but then, the substance of things will not have changed; the laws of nature will still remain the same. Men will ail, will grow old, and die, even as they do now. No matter how magnificent a dawn may be illuminating your life, after all is said and done you will be nailed up in a coffin just the same and then pitched into a hole in the ground."

"But what of immortality?"

"Oh, come, now!"

"You do not believe; but then I do. Dostoevsky or Voltaire makes somebody say that if there were no God, men would have to invent Him. And I believe profoundly that if there is no immortality, some great human mind will, sooner or later, invent it."

"Well put," Andrew Ephimich let drop, with a smile of pleasure. "It's a good thing, your having faith. With such a faith one can live as snug as a bug in a rug even bricked up in a wall. Did you receive your education anywhere in particular?"

"Yes; I attended a university, but did not graduate."

"You are a thinking and meditative person. You are capable of finding tranquility within your own self, in any environment. Free and profound reasoning, which strives toward a rationalization of life, and a complete contempt for the foolish vanities of this world: there you have two blessings, higher than which no man has known. And you can possess them, even though you live behind triple bars. Diogenes lived in a tun—yet he was happier than all the princes of this earth."

"Your Diogenes was a blockhead," Ivan Dmitrich said morosely. "Why do you talk to me of Diogenes and of some rationalization or other?" he suddenly became angry and sprang up. "I love life—love it passionately! I have a persecution mania, a constant, excruciating fear; yet there are moments when I am overwhelmed by a thirst for life, and then I am afraid of going out of my mind. I want to live—I want to terribly, terribly!"

In his agitation he took a turn about the ward and then said, lowering his voice:

"When I am in a reverie, I am visited by phantoms. Some people or other come to me; I hear voices, music, and it seems to me that I am strolling through some sort of woods, or along the shore of a sea, and I feel such a passionate yearning for worldly vanity, for striving. . . . Tell me, now, what's new there?" asked Ivan Dmitrich. "What's going on there?"

"Do you want to know about the town, or about things in general?"

"Well, tell me about the town first, and then about things in general."

"What can I tell you, then? It is oppressively dreary in the town. There's nobody to exchange a word with, nobody one can listen to. There are no new faces. However, a young physician arrived recently—a certain Hobotov."

"He arrived even in my time. What sort of a fellow is he—a lout?"

"Yes, he is not a man of culture. It's odd, don't you

know . . . judging by all things, there is no mental stagnation in our capital cities, everything is in motion there; consequently, there also must be real people there—but for some reason or other they always send to us such men as one would rather not even look at. What an unfortunate town!"

"Yes, what an unfortunate town!" Ivan Dmitrich sighed, and began to laugh. "But how are things in general? What do they write in the newspapers and magazines?"

It was dark by now in the ward. The doctor got up and, standing, began telling the madman what was being written abroad and in Russia, and what trend of thought was to be noticed now. Ivan Dmitrich listened attentively and put questions, but suddenly, as though having recalled something horrible, clutched his head and lay down on his bed, with his back to the doctor.

"What is the matter with you?" asked Andrew Ephimich.

"You won't hear another word out of me!" Ivan Dmitrich said rudely. "Leave me alone!"

"But why?"

"Leave me, I tell you! What the devil!"

Andrew Ephimich shrugged his shoulders, sighed, and walked out. On his way through the entry he said:

"What about cleaning up a bit, Nikita? There's a terribly oppressive odor here."

"Right, Your Honor."

"What an agreeable young man!" reflected Andrew Ephimich, as he was going to his quarters. "All the time I've been living here this would seem to be the first man with whom one could chat. He knows how to talk about things, and is interested in precisely the right ones."

While he was reading and later, as he was going to bed, he kept thinking all the time of Ivan Dmitrich, and

on awaking the next morning he recalled that he had
made the acquaintance of an intelligent and interesting
man yesterday, and decided to drop in on him once
more at the first opportunity.

x

Ivan Dmitrich was lying in the same pose as yesterday, his hands clutching his head and with his legs
tucked up. One could not see his face.

"Good day, my friend," said Andrew Ephimich. "You
aren't sleeping?"

"In the first place I am not your friend," Ivan Dmitrich spoke into his pillow, "and, in the second, you
are putting yourself out for nothing: you won't get a
single word out of me."

"How odd—" Andrew Ephimich muttered in embarrassment. "Yesterday we were conversing so peacefully,
but suddenly you took offense for some reason and at
once cut our conversation short. Probably I must have
expressed myself clumsily, somehow, or perhaps have
come out with some idea incompatible with your con-
victions—"

"Oh, yes—catch me believing you, just like that!"
said Ivan Dmitrich, raising himself and regarding the
doctor mockingly and in disquiet; his eyes were red.
"You can go and do your spying and interrogating
somewhere else, but there's nothing for you to do here.
I understood even yesterday what you had come here
for."

"What a strange fancy!" smiled the doctor. "That
means you take me for a spy?"

"Yes, I do. Either a spy or a doctor assigned to testing
me—it's all one."

"Oh, come, you must excuse me for saying so, but really—what an odd fellow you are!"

The doctor seated himself on a tabouret next to the madman's bed and shook his head reproachfully.

"Well, let's suppose you are right," he said. "Let's suppose that I am treacherously trying to trip you up on something you say, so as to betray you to the police. You are arrested and then brought to trial. But then, will you be any worse off in the courtroom and in prison than you are here? And even if they send you away to live in some remote part of Siberia, or to penal servitude—would that be worse than sitting here, in this hospital wing? I don't think it would be. What, then, is there to fear?"

Evidently these words had an effect on Ivan Dmitrich. He sat up, reassured.

It was five in the afternoon—the time when Andrew Ephimich, as a rule, was pacing through his rooms, and Dariushka was asking him if it weren't time for his beer. It was calm, clear out of doors.

"I happened to go out for a walk after dinner, and just dropped in on you, as you see," said the doctor. "It's actually spring out."

"What month is it now? March?" asked Ivan Dmitrich.

"Yes—the end of March."

"Is it muddy out?"

"No, it's not so bad. You can see the paths in the garden."

"It would be fine to drive a carriage now, somewhere outside the town," said Ivan Dmitrich, rubbing his red eyes, just as though he were coming out of his sleep, "then to come home to a warm, cozy study and . . . to take treatments for headaches from a decent doctor.

. . . It's a long while since I have lived like a human being. But everything here is abominable! Unbearably abominable!"

After the excitement of yesterday he was fatigued and listless, and spoke unwillingly. His fingers were shaky, and one could see by his face that his head ached badly.

"Between a warm, cozy study and this ward there is no difference whatsoever," said Andrew Ephimich. "A man's tranquility and contentment lie not outside of him but within his own self."

"Just how do you mean that?"

"The ordinary man expects that which is good or bad from without—from a carriage and a study, that is; whereas a thinking man expects it from his own self."

"Go and preach that philosophy in Greece, where it is warm and the air is filled with the fragrance of oranges, but here it is not in keeping with the climate. Whom was I speaking with about Diogenes? Was it you, by any chance?"

"Yes, it was with me—yesterday."

"Diogenes had no need of a study and of warm quarters—it's hot enough there as it is. Just lie in your tub and eat oranges and olives. But had he chanced to live in Russia he would be begging his head off for a room not only in December but even in May. Never fear, he would be perishing from the cold."

"No. It is possible not to feel the cold, as well as every pain in general. Marcus Aurelius has said: 'Pain is a living conception of pain; exert thy will, in order to change this conception; put it away from thee, cease complaining, and the pain shall vanish,' [1] which is true

---

[1] The references to pain in Marcus Aurelius (Book VII, 33, 64 and VIII, 28) have nothing quite corresponding to this, in either the Jeremy Collier or the George Long version.—*Trans.-Ed.*

enough. A sage, or simply a thinking, meditative man, is distinguished precisely by his holding suffering in contempt; likewise, he is always content, and is not astonished by anything."

"That means I am an idiot, since I suffer, feel discontent, and am astonished at human baseness."

"You are wrong in saying so. If you will think deeply and often, you will comprehend how insignificant are all these matters which perturb you. One must strive toward a rationalization of life; therein lies the true good."

"Rationalization—" Ivan Dmitrich made a wry face. "The inward, the outward. . . . Pardon me, I don't understand it. All I know," he said, getting up and regarding the doctor angrily, "is that God created me out of warm blood and nerves—yes! And organic tissue, if it be imbued with life, must react to every irritant. And I do react! To pain I respond by screaming and tears; to baseness, by indignation; to vileness, by revulsion. According to me that, precisely, is what they call life. The lower the organism the less sensitive it is, and the more weakly does it respond to irritation, and the higher it is the more receptively and energetically does it react to reality. How can one be ignorant of that? You are a doctor—and yet you don't know such trifles! In order to despise sufferings, to be always content and never astonished at anything, one must reach such a state as this—" and Ivan Dmitrich indicated the obese muzhik, bloated with fat—"or else one must harden one's self through sufferings to such a degree as to lose all sensitivity to them: that is, in other words, cease to live. Pardon me, I am no sage and no philosopher," Ivan Dmitrich went on with irritation, "and I understand nothing of all this. I am in no condition to reason."

"On the contrary, you reason splendidly."

"The Stoics, whom you parody, were remarkable men; but their teaching had congealed even two thousand years ago and hasn't advanced by a jot, nor will it advance, since it is not practical and does not pertain to life. It succeeded only with a minority, with those who spend their time in dabbling in and smacking their lips over all sorts of teachings; as for the majority, it never did understand it. A teaching which preaches indifference to riches, to the comforts of life, a contempt for sufferings and death, is altogether incomprehensible to the vast majority, since this majority has never known either riches or the comforts of life; and as for despising sufferings, that would mean for it to despise life itself, since all of man's nature consists of sensations of hunger, cold, affronts, losses and a Hamletian trepidation in the face of death. All life consists of these sensations: one may find it burdensome, may hate it, but never despise it. Yes. And so I repeat: the teaching of the Stoics can never have a future; but, as you can see, the things that have been progressing from the start of time to this day are struggle, a keen sensitivity to pain, the ability to respond to irritation—"

Ivan Dmitrich suddenly lost the thread of his thought, stopped, and rubbed his forehead in vexation.

"I wanted to say something important but got off the track," he said. "What was I talking about? Oh, yes! And so I say: one of the Stoics had sold himself into bondage in order to redeem a fellow-man. There, you see: it means that even a Stoic reacted to an irritant, since for such a magnanimous act as self-abnegation for a fellow-man one must have a soul that has been aroused to indignation, that is compassionate. Here, in this prison, I have forgotten everything I learned, or else I would have recalled a thing or two besides. And what about Christ? Christ responded to reality by weeping, smiling, grieving, raging—even yearning; He went to meet sufferings with a smile and did not despise death, but prayed in the Garden of Gethsemane that *this cup* might pass from Him!"

Ivan Dmitrich laughed and sat down.

"Let us suppose that man's tranquility and contentment are not outside of him but within his own self," he said. "Let us suppose that one ought to despise sufferings and be astonished at nothing. However, on what basis do *you* preach that? Are you a sage? A philosopher?"

"No, I am not a philosopher; but every man should preach this, because it is reasonable."

"No—what I want to know is why, in these matters of rationalization, contempt for pain, and so forth, you deem yourself competent? Why, have you ever suffered? Have you any conception of sufferings? Pardon me—but were you ever whipped as a child?"

"No; my parents had a deep aversion for corporal punishment."

"Well, my father beat me cruelly. My father was a willful, hemorrhoidal bureaucrat, with a long nose and a yellow neck. However, let's speak about yourself. In all your life no one has ever laid a finger on you, no one frightened you or repressed you with beatings; you are as healthy as a bull. You grew up sheltered under your father's wing and studied at his expense and then, right off, grabbed this sinecure. You have, for more than twenty years, been living in free quarters, with heat and light and servants thrown in, having at the same time the right of working as you liked and only as much as you liked—even to the extent of not working at all. You are, by nature, a lazy, flabby fellow, and therefore you tried to arrange your life so that nothing might perturb you or dislodge you from your place. Your work you

turned over to the assistant doctor and the other riff-
raff, while you yourself sat in warmth and in quiet, saving up money, reading your books, finding delectation
in reflections concerning all sorts of elevated twaddle
and [here Ivan Dmitrich glanced at the doctor's rubi-
cund nose] tippling. In a word, you haven't seen life,
don't know it perfectly, and when it comes to reality
you have only a theoretical acquaintance with it. And
as for your contempt of sufferings and your being astonished at nothing, that's all due to a very simple
cause: vanity of vanities, internality and externality,
contempt for life and death, rationalization, the true
good—all these form the most suitable philosophy for
the Russian sluggard.

"You may, for example, see a muzhik beating his
wife. Why intervene? Let him beat her: both are bound
to die anyway, sooner or later, and besides, he who is
doing the beating is wronging by his beatings not the
one whom he is beating but himself. To be a drunkard
is stupid, indecent—yet if one drinks one dies and if
one does not drink one dies. A countrywoman comes to
you—her teeth are aching. . . . Well, what of it? Pain
is but a concept of pain and, on top of that, in this world
one can't go through life without illnesses, we've all got
to die, and so get you gone, woman, don't interfere with
my cogitating and drinking vodka. A young man comes
seeking advice as to what he is to do, how he is to live;
before answering him another man would go off into
deep thought, but you already have an answer all pat:
Strive toward rationalization, or toward the true good.
But just what is this fantastic *true good?* There is no
answer, of course. We are kept here behind iron bars;
we are forced to rot, we are mocked and tortured—but
that is all splendid and reasonable, inasmuch as, between
this ward and a warm, cozy study, there is no difference

whatsoever. A handy philosophy: there's not a thing to be done, and one's conscience is clear, and one feels he is a sage. No, my dear sir, this is not philosophy, not reflection, not breadth of view but laziness, fakirism, a somnolent daze. . . . Yes!" Ivan Dmitrich again became angry, "You despise sufferings—but if someone happened to pinch your finger in a door you would yell your head off!"

"And then, again, perhaps I wouldn't yell," said Andrew Ephimich, smiling meekly.

"Oh, yes, to be sure! But, were you to be struck all of a heap by paralysis or, let's say, if some brazen fool, taking advantage of his position and rank, were to insult you publicly, and you knew that he would get away with it—why, you would understand then what it means to refer others to rationalization and the true good."

"That is original," said Andrew Ephimich, laughing from pleasure and rubbing his hands. "I am agreeably struck by your inclination toward generalizations, while the character sketch of me which you were kind enough to make just now is simply brilliant. I must confess that conversing with you affords me enormous pleasure. Well, I have heard you out to the end; I hope you will now be inclined to hear me out—"

XI

This conversation went on for about an hour more and, evidently, made a profound impression on Andrew Ephimich. He took to dropping in at the hospital wing every day. He went there of mornings and after dinner, and often the dusk of evening would find him still conversing with Ivan Dmitrich. At first Ivan Dmitrich had fought shy of him; he suspected him of some evil design and frankly expressed his hostility; later on, however, he became used to him and changed his harsh attitude to a condescendingly ironical one.

It was not long before a rumor spread all through the hospital that Doctor Andrew Ephimich had taken to frequenting Ward No. 6. Nobody—neither the assistant doctor, nor Nikita, nor the nurses—could understand why he went there, why he sat there for hours on end, what he spoke about, and why he did not write out any prescriptions. His actions seemed queer. Many times Michael Averianich failed to find him at home, something that had never happened before, and Dariushka was very much put out because the doctor drank his beer no longer at the designated time, and occasionally was actually late for dinner.

Once (this was already toward the end of June) Doctor Hobotov dropped in at Andrew Ephimich's about something; not finding him at home, he set out to look for him in the courtyard; there he was told that the old doctor had gone to see the psychopathic cases. As he entered the wing and paused in the entry, Hobotov heard the following conversation:

"We shall never sing the same tune, and you won't succeed in converting me to your belief," Ivan Dmitrich was saying in irritation. "You are absolutely unfamiliar with reality and you have never suffered but, like a leech, have merely found your food in the proximity of the sufferings of others, whereas I have suffered ceaselessly from my birth to this very day. Therefore I say frankly: I consider myself superior to you and more competent in all respects. It isn't up to you to teach me."

"I do not at all presume to convert you to my belief," Andrew Ephimich let drop quietly and with regret because the other did not want to understand him. "And that's not where the gist of the matter lies, my friend. It does not lie in that you have suffered, whereas I have not. Sufferings and joys are transitory; let's drop them—God be with them. But the gist of the matter does lie in that you and I do reason; we see in each other someone who can think and reason, and this makes for unity between us, no matter how divergent our views may be. If you only knew how fed up I have become with the general insanity, mediocrity, stolidity, and what a joy it is each time I converse with you! You are an intelligent man, and I find you delightful."

Hobotov opened the door an inch or so and peered into the ward: Ivan Dmitrich in his nightcap and Doctor Andrew Ephimich were sitting side by side on the bed. The madman was grimacing, shuddering and convulsively muffling himself in his bathrobe, while the doctor sat motionless, with his head sunk on his chest, and his face was red, helpless and sad. Hobotov shrugged his shoulders, smiled sneeringly and exchanged glances with Nikita. Nikita, too, shrugged his shoulders.

The next day Hobotov came to the wing with the assistant doctor. Both stood in the entry and eavesdropped.

"Why, it looks as if our grandpa has gone off his nut completely!" Hobotov remarked as they were leaving the wing.

"The Lord have mercy upon us sinners!" sighed the benign-visaged Serghei Sergheich, painstakingly skirting the small puddles so as not to soil his brightly polished shoes. "I must confess, my dear Eugene Fedorovich, I have been long anticipating this!"

XII

After this Andrew Ephimich began to notice a certain atmosphere of mysteriousness all around him. The orderlies, the nurses, and the patients, whenever they came across him, glanced at him questioningly and then fell to whispering among themselves. Masha, the super-intendent's little daughter, whom he liked to come upon in the garden, whenever he approached her now with a smile to pat her little head, would run away from him for some reason or other. Michael Averianich, the post-master, whenever he was listening to the doctor no longer said "Absolutely correct!" but kept mumbling "Yes, yes, yes . . ." in incomprehensible confusion and regarded him thoughtfully and sadly; for some reason he took to advising his friend to leave vodka and beer alone, but in doing so did not speak directly, since he was a man of delicacy, but in hints, telling him now about a certain battalion commander, a splendid per-son, now about a regimental chaplain, a fine fellow, both of whom had been hard drinkers and had fallen ill; after leaving off drink, however, they had gotten per-fectly well. Andrew Ephimich's colleague, Hobotov, dropped in on him two or three times; he, too, advised him to leave spirituous drinks alone and, without any apparent reason, recommended him to take potassium bromid.

In August Andrew Ephimich received a letter from the mayor, requesting the doctor to call on him concern-ing a very important matter. On arriving at the ap-pointed time in the city offices Andrew Ephimich found there the head of the military, the civilian inspector of the county school, a member of the city council, Hobo-tov, and also some gentleman or other, stout and flaxen-fair, who was introduced to him as a doctor. This doc-tor, with a Polish name very hard to pronounce, lived some twenty miles out of town, on a stud-farm, and hap-pened to be passing through the town just then.

"There's a little report here, dealing with your depart-ment," said the member of the city council to Andrew Ephimich, after they had all exchanged greetings and seated themselves around a table. "Eugene Fedorovich here tells us the pharmacy is in rather cramped quarters in the main building, and that it ought to be transferred into one of the wings. Of course, that's nothing—one can transfer it, right enough; but the main thing is, the wing will require alterations."

"Yes, it can't be done without alterations," said Andrew Ephimich, after a little thought. "If the corner wing, for instance, were to be fitted out as a pharmacy, it would, I suppose, require five hundred rubles, at a minimum. An unproductive expenditure."

They were all silent for a little while.

"I have already had the honor of submitting a report ten years ago," Andrew Ephimich went on in a quiet voice, "that this hospital, in its present state, appears to be a luxury for this town beyond its resources. It was built in the forties—but at that time the resources were different from what they are now. The town is spending too much on unnecessary buildings and superfluous posts. I think that, under different conditions, two model hospitals could be maintained for the same money."

"There, you just try and set up different conditions!" the member of the city council said with animation.

"I have already had the honor of submitting a report: transfer the medical department to the supervision of the county."

"Yes: transfer the money to the county—and the county will steal it," the flaxen-fair doctor broke into laughter.

"Which is the way of things," concurred the member of the city council, and laughed in his turn.

Andrew Ephimich threw a listless and dull glance at the flaxen-fair doctor and said:

"We must be just."

They were again silent for a little while. Tea was

served. The head of the military, who for some reason was very much embarrassed, touched Andrew Ephimich's hand across the table and said:

"You have forgotten us altogether, Doctor. However, you are a monk; you don't play cards, you don't like women. You must feel bored with us fellows."

They all began speaking of how boresome life was for a decent person in this town. No theater, no music, while at the last evening dance given at the club there had been about twenty ladies and only two gentlemen. The young people did not dance but were clustered around the buffet all the time or playing cards. Andrew Ephimich slowly and quietly, without looking at anybody, began saying what a pity, what a profound pity it was that the people in town were expanding their life energy, their hearts and their minds, on cards and gossiping, but neither could nor would pass their time in interesting conversation and in reading, they would not avail themselves of the pleasures which the mind affords. The mind alone is interesting and remarkable; as for everything else, it is petty and base. Hobotov was listening attentively to his colleague and suddenly asked:

"Andrew Ephimich, what's today's date?"

Having received his answer he and the flaxen-fair doctor proceeded, in the tone of examiners conscious of their lack of skill, to ask Andrew Ephimich what day it was, how many days there were in the year, and whether it was true that there was a remarkable prophet living in Ward No. 6.

In answering the last question Andrew Ephimich turned red and said:

"Yes, he is ill, but he is an interesting young man."

No further questions were put to him.

As the doctor was putting on his overcoat in the

foyer, the head of the military put his hand on his shoulder and said with a sigh:

"It's time we old fellows were given our rest!"

When he had come out of the city offices Andrew Ephimich grasped that this had been a commission appointed to examine his mental faculties. He recalled the questions that had been put to him, turned red and for some reason felt, for the first time now, bitterly sorry for medicine.

"My God!" he reflected, recalling how the physicians had been putting him through a test just now. "Why, they were attending lectures on psychiatry not so long ago, they had to pass examinations—whence, then, comes this all-around ignorance? They haven't the least conception of psychiatry!"

And, for the first time in his life, he felt himself insulted and angered.

That same day, in the evening, Michael Averianich dropped in on him. Without exchanging greetings, the postmaster walked up to him, took both of his hands, and said in an agitated voice:

"My dear friend, prove to me that you believe in my good intentions and consider me your friend. . . . My friend!" And, preventing Andrew Ephimich from saying anything, he went on, still agitated: "I love you because of your culture and the nobility of your soul. Do listen to me, my dear fellow. The ethics of science obligate doctors to conceal the truth from you but, military fashion, I tell the truth and shame the devil—you are not well! Excuse me, my dear fellow, but that's the truth: all those around you have noticed it long ago. Just now Doctor Eugene Fedorovich was telling me that for the sake of your health you absolutely must take a rest and have some diversion. Absolutely correct! Excellent! In a few days I'll take a leave of absence and go away for a change of air. Prove to me that you are my friend—let's go somewhere together! Let's go—and recall the good old days!"

"I feel myself perfectly well," Andrew Ephimich said, after thinking a while. "But as for going somewhere, that's something I can't do. Do let me prove my friendship for you in some other way."

To be going off somewhere, for some unknown reason, without books, without Dariushka, without beer, breaking off sharply the order of life established through twenty years—the very idea struck him, at the first moment, as wild and fantastic. But he recalled the conversation that had taken place in the city offices and the oppressive mood which he had experienced on his way home from there, and the thought of going away for a short time from the town where stupid people considered him mad appealed to him.

"But where, in particular, do you intend going?" he asked.

"To Moscow, to Peterburg, to Warsaw! I spent five of the happiest years of my life in Warsaw. What an amazing city! Let's go, my dear fellow!"

XIII

A week later it was suggested to Andrew Ephimich that he take a rest—that is, that he hand in his resignation, something which he regarded apathetically—and after another week he and Michael Averianich were already seated in a posting tarantass, bound for the nearest railroad station. The days were cool, clear, with blue skies and a transparent vista. The one hundred and twenty-five miles to the station they covered in two days, and on the way stopped over twice for the night. When, at the posting stations, their tea was served in badly washed tumblers, or too much time was spent in harnessing the horses, Michael Averianich turned purple, his whole body shook, and he shouted "Quiet, you! Don't you dare to argue!" And when he was seated in the tarantass he kept talking without a minute's rest about his journeys through the Caucasus and the Kingdom of Poland. How many adventures there had been, and what encounters! He spoke loudly and, as he spoke, such an astonished look came into his eyes that one might have thought he was lying. To top it off, in the heat of his story-telling he breathed right in Andrew Ephimich's face and laughed in his very ear. This embarrassed the doctor and hindered him from thinking and concentrating.

For reasons of economy they went by third class on the train, in a car where smoking was not permitted. The passengers were halfway decent. Michael Averianich in a short while became well acquainted with all of them and, passing from seat to seat, declared loudly that such exasperating roads ought not to be patronized. All-around knavery! Riding horseback, now, was an altogether different matter: you could cover sixty-five miles in a single day and still feel yourself hale and hearty. As for the poor crops we've been having, that was due to the Pinsk swamps having been drained. As a general thing, everything was at sixes and at sevens—frightfully so. He grew heated, spoke loudly, and gave no chance to the others to say anything. This endless chatter, alternating with loud laughter and expressive gestures, wearied Andrew Ephimich.

"Which one of us two is the madman?" he reflected with vexation. "Is it I, who am trying not to disturb the passengers in any way, or is it this egoist, who thinks he is more intelligent and interesting than all those here, and therefore will not give anybody any rest?"

In Moscow Michael Averianich donned a military frockcoat without any shoulder-straps and trousers with red piping. He went through the streets in a military cap and a uniform overcoat, and the soldiers saluted him. To Andrew Ephimich he now seemed a man who out of all the seigniorial ways that had been his had squandered all that was good and had retained only that which was bad. He loved to be waited on, even when it was unnecessary. Matches might be lying on the table right in front of him, and he saw them, yet he would shout to a waiter to bring him some; he was not at all embarrassed about walking around in nothing but his underwear before a chambermaid; he addressed all waiters indiscriminately—even the old men—as patent inferiors and, if angered, called them blockheads and fools. This, as it seemed to Andrew Ephimich, was seigniorial, yet vile.

First of all Michael Averianich led his friend off to the Iverskaya Church. He prayed ardently, bowing to the very ground and shedding tears and, having done, sighed profoundly and said:

"Even though you may not believe, yet you feel more at peace, somehow, after praying. Kiss the image, my dear friend."

Andrew Ephimich became embarrassed and kissed the holy image, while Michael Averianich puckered up his lips and, shaking his head, offered up a whispered prayer, and tears again welled up in his eyes.

Next they went to the Kremlin and had a look at the Czar-Cannon and the Czar-Bell and even touched them; they admired the view of Moscow-beyond-the-River, visited the Temple of the Saviour and the Rumyantzev Museum.

They dined at Testov's. Michael Averianich studied

the menu for a long spell, and said to the waiter in the tone of a gourmet used to feeling himself at home in restaurants:

"Let's see what you will feed us with today, my angel!"

XIV

The doctor went about, saw the sights, ate and drank, yet he had but one feeling: that of vexation at Michael Averianich. He longed for a rest from his friend, to get away from him, to hide himself, whereas his friend considered it his duty not to let the doctor go a step from his side and to provide him with as many diversions as possible. When there were no sights to see he diverted him with conversations. Andrew Ephimich stood this for two days, but on the third he informed his friend that he was ill and wanted to stay in all day. His friend said that in that case he, too, would stay. Really, one had to rest up, otherwise you would run your legs off. Andrew Ephimich lay down on the divan, with his face toward its back and, with clenched teeth, listened to his friend, who assured him ardently that France was inevitably bound to smash Germany, sooner or later, that there were ever so many swindlers in Moscow, and that you can't judge the good points of a horse just by its looks. The doctor's ears began to buzz and his heart to pound but, out of delicacy, he could not find the resolution to ask his friend to go away or to keep still. Fortunately, Michael Averianich grew bored with being cooped up in the hotel room and, after dinner, he went out for a stroll.

Left alone, Andrew Ephimich gave himself up to a feeling of repose. How pleasant to lie motionless on a divan and realize that you were alone in the room! True happiness is impossible without solitude. The Fallen Angel must have betrayed God probably because he had felt a desire for solitude, which the angels know naught of. Andrew Ephimich wanted to think over that which he had seen and heard during the last few days, yet he could not get Michael Averianich out of his head.

"And yet he took a leave of absence and went on this trip with me out of friendship, out of magnanimity," the doctor reflected with vexation. "There's nothing worse than this friendly guardianship. There, now, it would seem he is kindhearted and magnanimous and a merry fellow, and yet he's a bore. An unbearable bore. In precisely the same way there are people whose words are always intelligent and meritorious, yet one feels that they are dull people."

During the days that followed Andrew Ephimich claimed he was ill and did not leave the hotel room. He lay with his face toward the back of the divan and was on tenter-hooks whenever his friend was diverting him with conversations, or rested when his friend was absent. He was vexed with himself for having gone on this trip, and he was vexed with his friend, who was becoming more garrulous and familiar with every day. No matter how hard the doctor tried he could not succeed in attuning his thoughts to a serious, exalted vein.

"This is that reality Ivan Dmitrich spoke of, which is getting me down so," he mused, angry at his own pettiness. "However, that's nonsense. I'll come home, and then things will go on in their old way again."

In St. Petersburg as well he acted the same way; he did not leave the room for days at a time, lying on the divan and getting up only to drink his beer.

Michael Averianich was rushing him all the time to go to Warsaw.

"My dear fellow, why should I go there?" Andrew Ephimich said time and again in an imploring voice. "Go alone, and do let me go home! I beg you!"

"Under no circumstances!" Michael Averianich protested. "It's an amazing city. I spent five of the happiest years of my life there!"

Andrew Ephimich had not enough firmness of character to insist on having his way and, with what heart he could, went to Warsaw. Here he did not leave his room, lay on the divan, and fumed at himself, at his friend, and at the waiters, who stubbornly refused to understand anything but Polish; Michael Averianich, on the other hand, as hale, sprightly and gay as usual, gallivanted all over the city from morning till night, seeking out his old acquaintances. Several times he passed the night away from the hotel. After one such night he came back early in the morning, in a state of great excitement, red and unkempt. For a long while he kept pacing from corner to corner, muttering something to himself; then he halted and said:

"Honor above all!"

After pacing a little longer, he clutched his head and uttered in a tragic voice:

"Yes—honor above all! May that moment be accursed when it first entered my head to come to this Babylon! My dear friend," he turned to the doctor, "despise me! I have lost—gambling! Let me have five hundred rubles!"

Andrew Ephimich counted off five hundred rubles and handed them without a word to his friend. The latter, still purple from shame and wrath, incoherently uttered some uncalled-for vow, put on his cap and went out. Returning some two hours later, he slumped in an armchair, sighed loudly, and said:

"My honor has been saved! Let us go, my friend! I do not wish to remain another minute in this accursed city. Swindlers! Austrian spies!"

When the friends got back to their town it was already November and its streets were deep in snow. Andrew Ephimich's place had been taken by Hobotov, who was still living in his old rooms while waiting for Andrew Ephimich to come and clear out of the hospital quarters. The homely woman whom he called his cook was already living in one of the hospital wings.

New gossip concerning the hospital was floating through the town. It was said that the homely woman had quarreled with the superintendent and that the latter, it would seem, had crawled on his knees before her, begging forgiveness.

On the very first day of his arrival Andrew Ephimich had to look for rooms for himself.

"My friend," the postmaster said to him timidly, "pardon my indiscreet question: what means have you at your disposal?"

Andrew Ephimich counted his money in silence, and said:

"Eighty-six rubles."

"That's not what I am asking you about," Michael Averianich got out in confusion, without having understood the doctor. "I am asking you, what means you have in general?"

"Why, that's just what I'm telling you: eighty-six rubles. Outside of that I have nothing."

Michael Averianich considered the doctor an honest and noble man, but just the same suspected him of having a capital of twenty thousand at the least. But now, having learned that Andrew Ephimich was a pauper, that he had nothing to live on, he for some reason burst into tears and embraced his friend.

XV

Andrew Ephimich was living in a small house with only three windows, belonging to Belova, a burgher's widow. There were just three rooms in this little house, without counting the kitchen. Two of them, with the windows facing the street, were occupied by the doctor, while Dariushka and the burgher's widow with her three children lived in the third room and the kitchen. Occasionally the landlady's lover, a hard-drinking muzhik, would come to pass the night with her; he was tempestuous of nights and inspired the children and Dariushka with terror. Whenever he came and, planting himself on a chair in the kitchen, started demanding vodka, they would all feel very cramped and, out of pity, the doctor would take the crying children to his rooms, making their beds for them on the floor, and this gave him great satisfaction.

He got up at eight, as before, and after tea would sit down to read his old books and periodicals. By now he had no money for new ones. Either because the books were old, or perhaps because of the change in his environment, reading no longer had as profound a hold on him and tired him out. In order not to spend his time in idleness he was compiling a catalogue *raisonné* of his books and pasting small labels on their backs, and this mechanical, finicky work seemed to him more interesting than reading. The monotonous, finicky work in some incomprehensible fashion lulled his thoughts; he did not think of anything, and the time passed rapidly. Even sitting in the kitchen and cleaning potatoes with Dariushka, or picking the buckwheat grits clean, seemed interesting to him. On Saturdays and Sundays he went to church. Standing close to the wall, with his eyes almost shut, he listened to the chanting and thought of his father, of his mother, of his university, of different religions; he felt at ease and pensive and later, as he left the church, he regretted that the service had ended so soon.

He went twice to the hospital to call on Ivan Dmitrich, to have a chat with him. But on both occasions Ivan Dmitrich had been unusually excited and bad-tempered; he begged to be left in peace, since he had long since wearied of empty chatter, and said that he begged from accursed, vile men but one reward for all his sufferings: solitary confinement. Was it possible that he was being denied even that? On both occasions as Andrew Ephimich was wishing him good night in parting, the madman had snarled back and said:

"Go to the devil!"

And now Andrew Ephimich did not know whether to go to him a third time or not. And yet the wish to go was there.

Formerly, in the interval after dinner, Andrew Ephimich used to pace his rooms and ponder; but now, from dinner until evening tea, he lay on the divan with his face turned to its back, and gave himself up to trivial thoughts, which he could not in any way overcome. He felt aggrieved because he had been given neither a pension nor temporary financial assistance for his service of twenty years. True, he had not served honestly, but then all civil servants receive a pension without any distinction, whether they are honest or not. For contemporary justice consisted precisely in that ranks, decorations and pensions were awarded not for moral qualities or for abilities but for service in general, of whatever sort. Why, then, should he constitute the lone exception? He had no money whatsoever. He felt

ashamed whenever he had to pass the general store and
see the woman who kept it. By now there were thirty-two
rubles owing for the beer. He also owed Belova, the
burgher's widow. Dariushka was selling his old clothes
and books on the quiet and lying to the landlady that
the doctor would be coming into very big money soon.

He was very angry at himself for having spent on the
trip the thousand rubles he had hoarded. How handy
that thousand would come in now! He felt vexed because people would not leave him in peace. Hobotov
considered it his duty to visit his ailing colleague at
infrequent intervals. Everything about him aroused aversion in Andrew Ephimich: his well-fed face, and his
vile, condescending tone, and the word "colleague,"
and his high boots; but the most repulsive thing was
that he considered himself obliged to treat Andrew
Ephimich, and thought that he really was giving him
treatment. At his every visit he brought a vial of potassium bromid and some rhubarb pills.

And Michael Averianich, too, considered it his duty
to drop in on his friend and divert him. On each occasion he came into Andrew Ephimich's place with an assumed insouciance, laughed boisterously but constrain-
edly, and fell to assuring him that he looked splendid
today and that matters, thanks be to God, were on the
mend, and from this one could have concluded that he
considered his friend's situation hopeless. He had not
yet paid back the debt he had contracted in Warsaw
and was crushed by profound shame, on edge, and
consequently strove to laugh more loudly and to tell
things as amusingly as he could. His anecdotes and
stories now seemed endless and were torture both to
Andrew Ephimich and to himself.

When he was present Andrew Ephimich would usually lie down on the divan, with his face to the wall, and listen with his teeth clenched; he felt the slag gathering over his soul, layer upon layer, and after his friend's every visit he felt that this slag was rising ever higher and seemed to be reaching his very throat.

In order to drown out these trivial emotions he made haste to reflect that he himself, and Hobotov, and Michael Averianich were bound to perish sooner or later, without leaving as much as an impress upon nature. If one were to imagine some spirit flying through space past the earth a million years hence, that spirit would behold only clay and bare crags. Everything— culture as well as moral law—would perish, and there would not be even a burdock growing over the spot where they had perished. What, then, did shame before the shopkeepers matter, or the insignificant Hobotov, or the oppressive friendship of a Michael Averianich? It was all stuff and nonsense.

But such reflections were no longer of any help. He would no sooner imagine the terrestrial globe a million years hence when, from behind a bare crag, Hobotov would appear in his high boots, or Michael Averianich, guffawing with constraint, and one could even catch his shamefaced whisper: "As for that Warsaw debt, my dear fellow—I'll pay you back one of these days. . . . Without fail!"

XVI

One day Michael Averianich came after dinner, when Andrew Ephimich was lying on the divan. It so happened that Hobotov with his potassium bromid put in his appearance at the same time. Andrew Ephimich rose heavily, sat up, and propped both his hands against the divan.

"Why, my dear fellow," Michael Averianich began,

"your complexion is much better than it was yesterday. Yes, you're looking fine! Fine, by God!"

"It's high time you were getting better, colleague— high time," said Hobotov, yawning. "No doubt you yourself must be fed up with this long drawn out mess."

"And get better we will!" Michael Averianich said gaily. "We'll live for another hundred years! We will that!"

"Well, not a hundred, maybe, but he's still good for another twenty," Hobotov remarked consolingly. "Never mind, never mind, colleague, don't despond. That'll do you, trying to pull the wool over my eyes."

"We'll show them what stuff we're made of!" Michael Averianich broke into loud laughter, and patted his friend's knee. "We'll show them yet! Next summer, God willing, we'll dash off to the Caucasus and ride all through it on horseback—*hup, hup, hup!* And when we get back from the Caucasus first thing you know, like as not, we'll be celebrating a wedding." Here Michael Averianich winked slyly. "We'll marry you off, my dear friend . . . we'll marry you off—"

Andrew Ephimich suddenly felt the slag reaching his throat; his heart began to pound frightfully.

"That's vulgar!" he said, getting up quickly and going toward the window. "Is it possible you don't understand that you're saying vulgar things?"

He wanted to go on suavely and politely but, against his will, suddenly clenched his fists and raised them above his head.

"Leave me alone!" he cried out in a voice that was not his own, turning purple and with his whole body quivering. "Get out! Get out, both of you! Both of you!"

Michael Averianich and Hobotov got up and stared at him, in perplexity at first, and then in fear.

"Get out, both of you!" Andrew Ephimich kept shouting. "You dolts! You nincompoops! I don't need either friendship—or your drugs, you dolts! What vulgarity! What vileness!"

Hobotov and Michael Averianich, exchanging bewildered looks, backed toward the door and stepped out into the entry. Andrew Ephimich seized the vial with the potassium bromid and hurled it after them; tinkling, the vial smashed against the threshold.

"Take yourselves off to the devil!" he cried out in a tearful voice, running out into the entry. "To the devil!"

When his visitors had left Andrew Ephimich, shivering as if in fever, lay down on the divan and for a long time thereafter kept repeating:

"Dolts! Nincompoops!"

When he had quieted down, the first thought that came to him was how frightfully ashamed Michael Averianich must feel now and how heavy at heart, and that all this was horrible. Nothing of the sort had ever happened before. What, then, had become of the mind and of tact? What had become of rationalization and philosophic equanimity?

The doctor could not fall asleep all night from shame and vexation at himself and in the morning, about ten, he went to the post office and apologized to the postmaster.

"Let's not recall what has happened," said the touched Michael Averianich with a sigh, squeezing the doctor's hand hard. "Let bygones be bygones. Liubavkin!" he suddenly shouted, so loudly that all the clerks and patrons were startled. "Fetch a chair. And you wait!" he shouted at the countrywoman who was shoving a letter at him through the grilled window for registration. "Can't you see I'm busy? Let's not recall bygones," he went on tenderly, turning to Andrew Ephimich. "Sit down, I entreat you, my dear fellow."

For a minute or so he stroked his knees in silence, and then said:

"It didn't even occur to me to be offended at you. Illness is no sweet bedmate, I understand that. Your fit frightened the doctor and myself yesterday, and we spoke about you for a long time afterwards. My dear fellow, why don't you tackle your illness in earnest? How can one act like that? Pardon my friendly candor," Michael Averianich sank his voice to a whisper, "but you are living in a most unfavorable environment: there isn't room enough, the place isn't clean enough, there's no one to look after you, you have no money for treatment. . . . My dear friend, the doctor and I implore you with all our hearts: heed our advice, go to the hospital! There the food is wholesome, and you'll be looked after, and will receive treatment. Even though Eugene Fedorovich—speaking just between you and me—has atrocious manners, he is nevertheless competent; he can be fully relied on. He gave me his word that he would take you under his care."

Andrew Ephimich was touched by this sincere interest and by the tears which suddenly began to glitter on the postmaster's cheeks.

"My worthiest friend, don't you believe them!" the doctor began whispering, placing his hand on his heart. "Don't you believe them! My illness consists solely of my having found, in twenty years, only one intelligent person in this whole town—and even that one a madman. There's no illness of any sort—but I have simply fallen into a bewitched circle, from which there is no way out. Nothing matters to me; I am ready for everything."

"Go to the hospital, my dear friend."

"Nothing matters to me—I'd even go into a hole in the ground."

"Give me your word, old fellow, that you will obey Eugene Fedorovich in everything."

"If you like: I give you my word. But I repeat, my worthiest friend, that I have fallen into a bewitched circle. Everything, even the sincere concern of my friends, now tends toward one thing: my perdition. I am perishing, and I have the fortitude to realize it."

"You will get well, old fellow."

"Why should you say that?" Andrew Ephimich asked with irritation. "There are few men who, toward the close of their lives, do not go through the same experience as mine right now. When you're told that you've got something in the nature of bad kidneys and an enlarged heart, and you start taking treatments, or you're told that you are a madman or a criminal—that is, in short, when people suddenly turn their attention upon you—know, then, that you have fallen into a bewitched circle out of which you will nevermore escape. You will strive to escape—and will go still further astray. Yield, for no human exertions will any longer save you. That's how it looks to me."

In the meanwhile people were crowding around the grilled window. So as not to be in the way, Andrew Ephimich got up and started to say good-by. Michael Averianich again secured his word of honor and saw him to the outer door.

That same day, before evening, Hobotov in his short fur-lined coat and his high boots appeared unexpectedly at Andrew Ephimich's and said, in such a tone as if nothing at all had happened yesterday:

"Well, I have come to you on a professional matter, colleague. I have come to invite you: would you care to go to a consultation with me? Eh?"

Thinking that Hobotov wanted to divert him by a stroll, or that he really wanted to give him an opportunity of earning a fee, Andrew Ephimich put on his things and went out with him into the street. He was glad to have this chance to smooth things over after having been at fault yesterday and of effecting a reconciliation, and at heart was thankful to Hobotov, who had not even hinted at yesterday's incident and, evidently, was sparing him. It was difficult to expect such delicacy from this uncultured man.

"But where is your patient?" asked Andrew Ephimich.

"In my hospital. I have been wanting to show him to you for a long while. . . . A most interesting case."

They entered the hospital yard and, skirting the main building, headed for the wing where the demented patients were housed. And all this, for some reason, in silence. When they entered the wing Nikita, as usual, sprang up and stood at attention.

"One of the patients here had a sudden pulmonary complication," Hobotov said in a low voice, entering the ward with Andrew Ephimich. "You wait here a little; I'll be right back. I'm going after my stethoscope."

And he walked out.

XVII

It was already twilight. Ivan Dmitrich was lying on his bed, his face thrust into the pillow; the paralytic was sitting motionlessly, softly crying and moving his lips. The obese muzhik and the one-time mail sorter were sleeping. Everything was quiet.

Andrew Ephimich sat on Ivan Dmitrich's bed and waited. But half an hour passed, and instead of Hobotov it was Nikita who entered the ward, holding in his arms a bathrobe, somebody's underwear, and slippers.

"Please dress yourself, Your Honor," said he quietly. "Here's your little bed—please to come over here," he added, indicating a vacant bed, evidently brought in recently. "Never mind; you'll get well, God willing."

Andrew Ephimich grasped everything. Without uttering a word he went over to the bed Nikita had indicated and sat down; perceiving that Nikita was standing and waiting, he stripped to the skin, and a feeling of shame came over him. Then he put on the hospital underwear; the drawers were very short, the shirt was long, while the bathrobe smelt of smoked fish.

"You'll get well, God willing," Nikita repeated.

He picked up Andrew Ephimich's clothes in his arms, went out, and shut the door after him.

"It doesn't matter. . . ." Andrew Ephimich reflected, shamefacedly drawing the bathrobe closely about him, and feeling that in his new outfit he looked like a convict. "It doesn't matter. . . . It doesn't matter whether it's a frockcoat, or a uniform, or this hospital bathrobe—"

But what about his watch? And the notebook in his side-pocket? And his cigarettes? Where had Nikita carried off his clothes to? Now, likely as not, he would have no occasion until his very death to put on trousers, vest, and boots. All this was odd, somehow, and even incomprehensible, at first. Andrew Ephimich was convinced, even now, that between the widow Belova's house and Ward No. 6 there was no difference whatsoever; that everything in this world was nonsense and vanity of vanities, yet at the same time his hands were trembling, his feet were turning cold, and he felt eerie at the thought that Ivan Dmitrich would awake soon and see him in a hospital bathrobe. He stood up, took a turn about the room, and sat down again.

There, he had sat through half an hour, an hour, by now, and he had become deadly wearied. Could one possibly live through a day here, through a week, and even years, like these people? There, now, he had been sitting, had taken a turn about the room, and had sat down again; one could go and take a look out of the window, and again traverse the room from one corner to the other. But, after that, what? Sit just like that, all the time, like an image carved of wood, and meditate? No, that was hardly possible.

Andrew Ephimich lay down, but immediately got up, mopped the cold sweat off his forehead with the sleeve of his bathrobe—and felt that his whole face had begun to reek of smoked fish. He took another turn about the room.

"This must be some sort of misunderstanding—" he let drop, spreading his hands in perplexity. "I must have an explanation—there's some misunderstanding here—"

At this point Ivan Dmitrich awoke. He sat up and propped his cheeks on his fists. He spat. Then he glanced lazily at the doctor and, evidently, did not grasp anything at the first moment; shortly, however, his sleepy face became rancorous and mocking.

"Aha—so they've planted you here as well, my fine fellow!" he got out in a voice still hoarse from sleep, puckering up one eye. "Very glad of it! There was a time when you drank men's blood, but now they'll drink yours. Splendid!"

"This must be some sort of misunderstanding—" Andrew Ephimich got out, frightened at Ivan Dmitrich's words; he shrugged his shoulders and repeated: "Some sort of misunderstanding—"

Ivan Dmitrich spat again and lay down.

"An accursed life!" he grumbled out. "And the thing that's so bitter about it and that hurts so, is that this life will end neither in a reward for one's sufferings, nor any apotheosis, as in an opera, but in death; the muzhik orderlies will come and haul the dead man off by his hands and feet into the basement. Brrr. . . . Well, no matter. But then, in the other world, it will be our turn to celebrate. I'll appear here from the other world as a shade and will frighten all these vermin. I'll make them sit here a while."

Moisseika came back and, catching sight of the doctor, held out his cupped hand:

"Give us one little copper!" said he.

XVIII

Andrew Ephimich walked away to the window and looked out at the field. It was getting dark by now and on the horizon, to the right, a chill, purple moon was rising. Not far from the hospital fence, seven hundred feet away at the most, stood a tall white building surrounded by a stone wall. This was the prison.

"Reality—there it is!" Andrew Ephimich reflected, and he became frightened.

Frightening was the moon, too, and the prison, and the nails, points up, on the fence, and the distant flare of a bone-burning yard. He heard a sigh behind him. He looked over his shoulder and saw a man with glittering stars and decorations on his breast, who was smiling and slyly winking. And this, too, seemed frightening.

Andrew Ephimich was assuring himself that there was nothing peculiar about the moon and the prison, that even those people who were psychically sound wore decorations, and that everything would rot in time and turn into clay, but despair suddenly took possession of him: he seized the window-bars with both hands and shook them with all his strength. The sturdy bars did not yield.

Then, so that things might not be so frightening, he went to Ivan Dmitrich's bed and sat down.

"I've fallen in spirits, my dear fellow," he muttered, trembling and wiping his cold sweat. "I've fallen in spirits."

"Why, just go ahead and philosophize a bit," Ivan Dmitrich remarked mockingly.

"My God, my God. . . . Yes, yes. . . . You were pleased to say some time ago that there is no philosophy in Russia but that everybody philosophizes—even the small fry. But then, no harm can befall anybody from the philosophizing of the small fry," said Andrew Ephimich, in such a tone as if he wanted to break into tears and stir the other's pity. "Why, then, my dear fellow, this spiteful laughter? And how can the small fry help but philosophize since it is not satisfied? An intelligent, educated, proud, freedom-loving man, in the image of God, has no other way out save to go as a medico into a filthy, stupid, miserable hole of a town—and all his life consists of cupping glasses, leeches, mustard-plasters! Quackery, bigotry, vulgarity! Oh, my God!"

"You're spouting bosh. If you detested being a medico, you should have become a prime minister."

"One can't get anywhere, anywhere. We are weak, my dear fellow. I was equanimous, my reasoning was wide-awake and filled with common sense—yet it sufficed for life merely to touch me roughly to have me fall in spirits. Prostration. . . . We are weak, we are made of shoddy. And you too, my dear fellow. You are intelligent, noble, you have imbibed noble impulses with your mother's milk; yet you had hardly entered upon life when you became wearied and fell ill. We are weak, weak!"

Some other thing, which he was unable to shake off,

outside of fear and a sense of having been wronged, had been constantly tormenting Andrew Ephimich ever since nightfall. Finally he realized that he wanted to drink some beer and have a smoke.

"I'm going out of here, my dear fellow," he said. "I'll tell them to let us have some light. I can't stand it this way—I'm in no condition—"

Andrew Ephimich went to the door and opened it, but Nikita immediately sprang up and blocked his way.

"Where you going? You mustn't, you mustn't!" he said. "Time to go to sleep!"

"But I want to go for just a minute, to take a walk in the yard!" Andrew Ephimich was taken aback.

"Mustn't, mustn't—those are orders. You know that yourself."

Nikita slammed the door shut and put his back against it.

"But suppose I were to go out of here, what harm would that do anybody?" asked Andrew Ephimich, shrugging his shoulders. "I can't understand this! Nikita, I must go out!"—and there was a catch in his voice. "I've got to!"

"Don't start any disorders—it's not right!" Nikita admonished him.

"This is the devil and all!" Ivan Dmitrich suddenly cried out and sprang up. "What right has he got not to let us out? How dare they keep us here? The law, it seems, says plainly that no man may be deprived of liberty without a trial! This is oppression! Tyranny!"

"Of course it's tyranny!" said Andrew Ephimich, heartened by Ivan Dmitrich's outcry. "I've got to, I must go out! He has no right to do this! Let me out, I tell you!"

"Do you hear, you stupid brute?" Ivan Dmitrich

shouted, and pounded on the door with his fist. "Open up, or else I'll break the door down! You butcher!"

"Open up!" Andrew Ephimich shouted, his whole body quivering. "I demand it!"

"Just keep on talking a little more!" Nikita answered from the other side of the door. "Keep it up!"

"At least go and ask Eugene Fedorovich to come here! Tell him I beg of him to be so kind as to come—for just a minute—"

"He'll come of his own self tomorrow."

"They'll never let us out!" Ivan Dmitrich went on in the meantime. "They'll make us rot here! Oh Lord, is there really no hell in the other world, and these scoundrels will be forgiven? Where is justice, then? Open up, you scoundrel—I'm suffocating!" he cried out in a hoarse voice and threw his weight against the door. "I'll smash my head! You murderers!"

Nikita flung the door open, shoved Andrew Ephimich aside roughly, using both his hands and one knee, then swung back and smashed his fist into the doctor's face. It seemed to Andrew Ephimich that an enormous salty wave had gone over his head and dragged him off toward his bed; there really was a salty taste in his mouth: probably his teeth had begun to bleed. He began to thresh his arms, just as if he were trying to come to the surface, and grabbed at somebody's bed, and at that point felt Nikita strike him twice in the back.

Ivan Dmitrich let out a yell. Probably he, too, was being beaten.

After that everything quieted down. The tenuous moonlight streamed in through the barred windows, and lying on the floor was a shadow that looked like a net. Everything was frightening. Andrew Ephimich lay down and held his breath; he anticipated with horror that he would be struck again. Just as though someone had taken a sickle, had driven it into him and then twisted it several times in his breast and guts. From pain he bit his pillow and clenched his teeth and suddenly, amid all the chaos, a fearful, unbearable thought flashed clearly in his head: that exactly the same pain must have been experienced throughout the years, day in and day out, by these people who now, in the light of the moon, seemed to be black shadows. How could it have come about, during the course of twenty years, that he had not known, and had not wanted to know, all this? He did not know pain, he had had no conception of it—therefore he was not to blame, yet conscience, just as intractable and harsh as Nikita, made him turn cold from the nape of his neck to his heels. He sprang up, wanted to cry out with all his might and to run as fast as he could to kill Nikita, then Hobotov, and the superintendent, and the assistant doctor, and then himself; but never a sound escaped from his breast and his legs would not obey him; suffocating, he yanked at the breast of his bathrobe and shirt, tore them and crashed down unconscious on his bed.

XIX

On the morning of the next day his head ached, his ears hummed, and his whole body felt broken up. He did not blush at the recollection of his weakness of yesterday. Yesterday he had been pusillanimous, had been afraid even of the moon, had given sincere utterance to feelings and thoughts which he had not formerly even suspected of having within him. The thought, for instance, about the dissatisfaction of the small fry. But now nothing mattered to him.

He did not eat, did not drink; he lay without moving and kept silent.

"Nothing matters to me," he thought when questions were put to him. "I'm not going to bother answering. . . . Nothing matters to me."

Michael Averianich came after dinner and brought him a quarter-pound packet of tea and a pound of marmalade candy. Dariushka also came and stood for a whole hour by his bed with an expression of stolid sorrow on her face. Doctor Hobotov, too, paid him a visit. He brought a vial of potassium bromid and ordered Nikita to fumigate the place with something.

Toward evening Andrew Ephimich died from an apoplectic stroke. At first he had felt a staggering ague-fit and nausea; something disgusting (so it seemed), penetrating his whole body, even into his fingers, started pulling from the stomach toward his head, and flooded his eyes and ears. Everything turned green before his eyes. Andrew Ephimich realized that his end had come, and recalled that Ivan Dmitrich, Michael Averianich and millions of men believe in immortality. And what if it should suddenly prove actual? But he felt no desire for immortality, and he thought of it only for an instant. A herd of reindeer, extraordinarily beautiful and graceful (he had read about them yesterday), ran past him; then a countrywoman stretched out her hand to him, holding a letter for registration. . . . Michael Averianich said something. Then everything vanished, and Andrew Ephimich forgot everything for all eternity.

The muzhik orderlies came, took him by his hands and feet, and carried him off into the chapel. There he lay on a table with his eyes open, and, through the night, the moon threw its light upon him. In the morning Serghei Sergheich came, piously prayed before

Christ on the Cross, and closed the eyes of his quondam chief.

The day after that they buried Andrew Ephimich. Only Michael Averianich and Dariushka attended the burial.

MAXIM GORKI

(ALEXIS MAXIMOVICH PESHKOV)

(1868–1936)

EDITOR'S NOTE

GORKI is not merely one of Russia's but one of the world's greatest self-taught men. His whole formal education consisted of five months' schooling at the age of seven when, after the death of his mother (he had lost his father, an upholsterer, at four), he became a shoemaker's apprentice. Men and books were to be his teachers from then on; as an omnivorous reader he is equalled probably only by Samuel Johnson. The shoemaker apprenticeship lasted two months when, after being fearfully scalded, Gorki was apprenticed to a draughtsman. Thereafter he followed many trades and became familiar with practically every stitch on the seamy side of life. From the hard-drinking—and exceptionally intelligent—chef of a Volga steamer he learned reading and writing and something of cookery; he tried painting and peddling icons, and selling apples; he was a railroad watchman, a baker, a pretzel-bender.

In Kazan he entered the revolutionary movement and was first arrested as a political offender; next year, at Nizhni-Novgorod (new renamed Gorki) he became clerk to A. I. Lanin, a lawyer, whom Gorki considered his greatest teacher and benefactor; in 1891 he resumed his wanderings, beginning his Volga period, when he hauled barges with another outcast and unknown—Fedor Chaliapin.

Gorki had kept a diary since ten, cherishing the dream of becoming a writer, but his first story did not appear until he was twenty-four: *Makar Chudra,* dealing with the Gypsies in as romantic a vein as Pushkin's or Borrow's. It was published in a local sheet in Tiflis, where he was working in a railroad yard as a repairman, and bore the pseudonym that was to become so famous. (*Gorki* means bitter.)

In 1894, in Nizhni-Novgorod, he began newspaper work; in the next year he formed a friendship with Korolenko, who helped him crash the "thick-paper" field with *Chelkash.* His reputation kept growing but he did not abandon newspaper work until 1898, when he scored a great success with a collection of his short stories, and became a continental celebrity. The years 1899-1901 found him very active in the revolutionary movement; his *Song of the Stormy Petrel,* a prophecy of the coming revolution, caused the suppression of a radical review he was supporting and led to his arrest and banishment from St. Petersburg.

The Stanislavsky production of *The Lowest Depths* in 1902 made him a national hero and an international figure. In January 1905, for his participation in a protest against Bloody Sunday (Jan. 9/22, the Lexington of the Revolution of 1905), he was again arrested and imprisoned in that great nursery of Russian authorship, the Fortress of SS. Peter and Paul. By now his fame was as universal as Leo Tolstoy's, and his imprisonment had world-wide repercussions. His release did not subdue him in the least; he was one of the leading spirits in the armed uprising at Moscow in the December of the same great year.

In 1906 New York City welcomed, among others, two visitors from abroad: the returning William Jennings Bryan, and Maxim Gorki, coming to the land of the free and the home of the brave after a triumphant tour of Europe. When it transpired, however, that the great writer and the equally great actress with him were man and wife without a preliminary investment of two rubles for a marriage license, the Gorkis could not find one hotel to put them up for a single night. The same newspapers whose front pages were splashed that year with a couple of especially juicy graft scandals and the piquant details of a particularly fruity murder, that of one of America's comparatively few good architects— these same newspapers became infinitely shocked. The urbane Howells and the dauntless Mark Twain, among the other gentlemen who were arranging a banquet for the great writer, scurried off, in shabby contrast to the gentle Chekhov and the impractical Korolenko, who had stood up against the Czar himself and resigned as Academicians when, in 1902, the Academy of Science at the bidding of Nicholas II had cancelled its election of Gorki. Gorki retaliated for his New York reception by writing *The City of the Yellow Devil, A King of the Republic, A High-Priest of Morals*—really effective if none too subtle satire, and superb Americana.

Gorki's weak lungs compelled him to live outside of Russia; from 1907 to 1913 he stayed in Capri. In World War I he took an antimilitaristic stand; he accepted the Revolution of 1917. Thenceforth he performed prodigies in preserving the best of old Russia's culture and bringing about a new one. In 1921 he again had to go to Capri, but did not relax his labors; he returned to live in Russia permanently in 1929; in 1932, his fortieth year as a writer, all Russia paid tribute to him; his death (or fantastic trotskyist assassination) is a matter of recent history.

Many aspects of Gorki's writing will probably remain practically unknown in English—his satire, for instance, and his poetry of protest. A considerable amount of his work has appeared in English versions—but for the most part very inadequate ones.

Birth of a Man

MAXIM GORKI

THIS happened in '92, the year of famine, between Sukhum and Ochemchiry, on the bank of the river Kodor, not far from the sea: above the merry chatter of the mountain river's clear waters one could hear the muffled plashing of the sea's waves.

It was autumn. The yellow leaves of the cherry-laurel swirled, flitted in the white foam of the Kodor; they looked just like tiny, nimble salmon. I was sitting on some rocks over the river and thinking that probably the gulls and cormorants were likewise taking these leaves for fish and were being duped: that was why they were crying in such hurt tones there, to the right, beyond the trees, where the sea was plashing.

The chestnut trees over me were arrayed in gold; lying at my feet were large drifts of leaves, looking like the palms of lopped-off hands—whose? The branches of a hornbeam on the opposite bank were already denuded and drooping in the air like a torn net; within it, just as though he had been snared, a yellow-red mountain woodpecker was hopping, tapping away with his black beak against the bark of the hornbeam's trunk, driving the insects out, while nimble tomtits and dove-gray nuthatches—guests from the far north—were pecking at them.

On my left smoky clouds, threatening rain, hung heavily along the mountain summits; shadows crawled away from them down the green slopes where the box, that dead tree, grew, while within the hollow trunks of the old beeches and lindens one could find "tipsy honey," the same which in antiquity had well nigh brought about the downfall of the soldiers of Pompey the Great with its tipsy sweetness, knocking a whole legion of iron-hard Romans off their feet; the bees make it out of laurel and azalea blossoms, while "wayfaring folk" take it out of the hollow trunks and eat it, spread on a *lavash*—a thin wafer of wheat flour.

That was precisely what I was taken up with: badly stung by the bees, I sat on the rocks under the chestnut trees and, dipping chunks of bread into a small kettle full of honey, admired, as I ate, the indolent play of the wearied sun of autumn.

The Caucasus in autumn is for all the world like a rich cathedral, builded of great sages (they also are, at all times, the great sinners)—builded to screen their past from the keen eyes of conscience; they have builded an unencompassable temple of gold, turquoise, emeralds, have hung the mountains with the finest of rugs, embroidered in silks by the Turkomans in Samarkand, in Shemaha; they have looted the whole universe and brought everything hither, before the eyes of the sun, as if they would say to it:

"This which is thine, from those who are thine, to thee."

I saw long-bearded, hoary titans, with the enormous eyes of merry children, adorning the earth as they came down from the mountains, sowing varicolored treasures everywhere with generous hand, covering the mountain summits with layers of silver and their foothills with the living weave of multiform trees—and under their hands this segment of benign earth took on a mad beauty.

It is a most excellent job, this of being a man upon earth; you see so much that is wondrous; with what an excruciatingly delectable emotion your heart is stirred in tranquil rapture before beauty!

Well, yes: now and then this comes hard; all your breast fills with searing hatred, and melancholy avidly sucks your heart's blood—but then, that is not one's perpetual portion, and besides even the sun, many a time, feels very sad as it contemplates men: it has toiled and moiled so hard for their benefit, and yet the manikins have not turned out right. . . .

Of course, there also are not a few who are good, but they stand in need of repair or—better still—of being made all over anew.

Dark heads are bobbing over the bushes to my left; amid the surge of the sea and the murmur of the river the human voices sound barely audibly: those are the "famine-stricken ones," on their way to work at Ochemchiry and coming from Sukhum, where they had been building a highway. I know them—they're from Orel; I had worked together with them and, together with them, had been discharged yesterday; I had gone off ahead of them, into the night, so as to meet the rising of the sun on the shore of the sea.

Four muzhiks and a countrywife with high cheekbones, young, pregnant, with an enormous belly blown up to her very nose, with blue-gray eyes goggling from fear. I can see above the bushes her head in its yellow kerchief; that head bobs like a full-blown sunflower in the wind. Her husband had died at Sukhum—he had overeaten himself on fruit. I had lived in a barrack amid these people: through the good old Russian habit they had discoursed so much and so loudly on their misfortunes that, probably, their jeremiads could have been heard for a couple of miles around.

Depressing people, these, crushed by their woe; it had torn them loose from their native, weary, stepmotherly soil and, as the wind bears the dead leaves of autumn, had borne them here where a magnificence of nature unknown to them had, after first amazing, dazzled them, while the harsh working conditions had finally beaten them to the ground. They regarded everything here with their faded eyes blinking in bewilderment, smiling pitifully to one another, saying softly:

"My, my—what a grand land—"

"So full it's just bursting."

"Well, yes. But, just the same, there are the stones—"

"Not an easy sort of land to work, I must say."

And they recalled Mare's Hollow, Dry Common, Little Bogs—native places, where every handful of earth was the dust of their grandsires, and everything was memorable, familiar, dear—bedewed with their sweat.

There had been another countrywife with them at Sukhum—tall, straight, flat as a board, with a horse's jaw and a lackluster look in her squinting eyes, as black as coals.

Of evenings, together with the one in the yellow kerchief, she used to go off beyond the barracks and, sitting there on a mound of rubble, her cheek resting on her palm, her head bowed to one side, would sing in a high-pitched and angry voice, dragging out almost every word:

"By the churchyard wall
        in the bushes green,
On the sand I shall
        spread a kerchief clean. . . .
For my dear to come
        I will sit and wait. . . .
When I see my dear
        I will kiss him straight. . . ."

The yellow-kerchiefed one usually kept quiet, craning her neck and contemplating her belly, but at times
suddenly and unexpectedly, indolently and in a husky
bass like a muzhik's, she would join in the song with
words that were sobs:

"Ho, there, deary-dear,
        ho, my own man. . . .
It is not my fate
        to see thee again. . . ."

In the black, sultry darkness of the southern night
these lamenting voices reminded one of the north, of
snowy wastes, the skirling of a blizzard and the far-off
howling of wolves.

Later on the squint-eyed woman was taken with a
fever and they carried her off to town on a tarpaulin
stretcher; she shook thereon and kept lowing, as though
she were still singing her song about the churchyard
and the sand.

Diving through the air, the yellow-kerchiefed head
vanished.

I finished my breakfast, covered the kettle of honey
with leaves, tied up my bundle and set off leisurely after
those who had already gone, tapping my boxthorn stick
against the hard-beaten path.

There, I too was out on the narrow, gray strip of road;
heaving on my right was the indigo sea; it looked as

if unseen carpenters were planing it with a thousand planes: the white shavings, swishing, ran toward shore, driven along by a wind that was humid, warm and fragrant as the breath of a healthy woman. A Turkish felucca, careening to larboard, was gliding toward Sukhum, its sails puffed out the way a certain pompous engineer at Sukhum, the most serious of men, used to puff out his fat cheeks. And, for some reason, he used to mispronounce certain simple words.

"Quiet, you! You may be tough, but I'll send you to the police station this instant!" And he would manage to mispronounce both *quiet* and *may be*. He loved to send people to the police station, and it is a pleasure to think that grave-maggots have probably long since gnawed his bones clean.

Walking was easy, just as though one were floating through the air. Pleasant thoughts, recollections in motley garb were going through a round dance in the memory; this round dance in one's soul was like the white crests of the waves at sea: they were on the surface but there, within the depths, everything was calm; there the radiant and pliant hopes of youth were quietly floating, like silvery fish in the sea's depths.

The road was drawn to the sea; winding snakily, it crawled nearer the strip of sand onto which the waves ran; the bushes, too, wanted to peer into the face of the wave: they bent across the ribbon of the road, as though nodding to the dark-blue, free expanse of the watery desert.

The wind had begun to blow from the mountains; there would be rain.

A low moan in the bushes—a human moan, which always stirs the soul through kinship.

Having parted the bushes, I saw the countrywoman in the yellow kerchief sitting with her back propped against the trunk of a nut tree, her head sunk on one shoulder, her mouth hideously distended, the eyes popping out and insane; she was holding her hands on her belly and breathing so unnaturally-frightfully that her whole belly was bounding convulsively, while the woman, holding it back with her hands, was lowing dully, her yellow, wolflike teeth bared.

"What—did they hit you?" I asked, bending toward her; she kept twitching her bare feet in the ashy dust like a fly and, with her heavy head jerking, she got out hoarsely:

"G-go away—you have no shame. . . . G-get away!"

I grasped what was up: I'd happened to see this sort of thing once before; of course I was frightened and leapt back; as for her, she set up a loud, prolonged howl; turbid tears spurted from her eyes, which were on the point of bursting, and ran down her blood-red face, swollen with straining.

This made me come back to her; I tossed my pack, tea-pot and kettle to the ground, turned her over on her back, and tried to make her bend her knees—she pushed me away, her hands striking my face and chest, turned around and, just like a she-bear, growling, wheezing, went on all fours farther into the bushes:

"Murderer . . . devil—"

Her arms gave way, as if broken; she fell, plunging her face in the earth, and started howling anew, convulsively, stretching out her legs.

In feverish excitement, having rapidly recalled all I knew about this business, I turned her over on her back, bending her legs—she had already obtruded the placenta.

"Lie still—you'll be giving birth right away."

I ran down to the sea, rolled up my sleeves, washed my hands, came back—and turned accoucheur.

The woman writhed like birchbark on a fire; she beat her hands on the earth around her and, plucking up the yellowed grass, was constantly trying to stuff it in her mouth; she strewed earth upon her frightful face, a face no longer human, with eyes grown wild, swollen with blood—and by now the placenta had been torn through and a tiny head was thrusting itself out: I had to restrain the spasms of her legs, to help the child, and to watch lest she shove grass into her pain-distorted, lowing mouth. . . .

We cursed each other, just a little: she through her clenched teeth, I in as low a voice as hers; she because of pain and, probably, because of shame, I because of embarrassment and excruciating pity for her.

"Lo-ordy," she wheezed; her livid lips were nipped between her teeth and in foam, while flowing out of her eyes, which seemed to have suddenly become faded from the sun, were those copious tears of the unbearable sufferings of a mother, and all her body was breaking, was being divided in two.

"G-go away, you fiend."

With weak, dislocated arms she kept pushing me away; I told her, persuasively:

"Get it over with, quick as you can, now, you big fool—"

I felt excruciatingly sorry for her, and it seemed as if her tears had spurted into my eyes; my heart contracted with anguish, I wanted to shout, and shout I did:

"Come on, hurry it up!"

And lo, there was a human creature on my hands—a red fellow. Even through tears, yet I saw: he was all red, and already dissatisfied with Creation, floundering, rioting, and bawling lustily, even though he was still bound to his mother. His eyes were light-blue; the nose was squashed in a funny way against his red, rumpled

face; the lips stirred and struck a long-drawn note: "*Ya-a
. . . ya-a—*" as if in affirmation of his *I.*

What a slippery fellow: first thing you knew he'd
glide out of your hands. Kneeling, I looked at him,
laughing: I was very glad to see him! And . . . I forgot what had to be done.

"Cut it—" the mother whispered softly; her eyes were
closed, her face had sunk in, was as earthy as that of
a dead woman, while her livid lips barely stirred:

"With a pocket-knife . . . cut it through."

My knife had been stolen in the barrack—I bit
through the umbilical cord; the baby bawled in an Orel
bass, while the mother smiled: I saw how amazingly
her bottomless eyes burst into bloom, how they burned
with a blue fire; her dark hand groped over her
skirt, seeking the pocket—and her bloodied, bitten lips
rustled:

"I . . . I haven't the strength . . . in the pocket
. . . a bit of tape to tie his little belly-button with."

I got out the bit of tape, tied the umbilical cord; she
was smiling ever more vividly, so beautifully and vividly
that I was dazzled by that smile.

"Put yourself to rights; me, I'm going to wash
him."

She mumbles uneasily:

"Watch out—go right easy . . . watch out, now—"

This red man-mountain does not in the least demand
to be handled with kid gloves; he had clenched a fist
and was bawling, bawling, as though trying to pick a
fight with me:

"*Ya-a . . . ya-a—*"

"Yes, it's you, it's you! Keep on saying *I!* Assert yourself, brother, as firmly as you know how, for otherwise
your fellowmen won't lose any time knocking your head
off."

He let out an especially earnest and loud cry when the first foaming wave of the sea swept scaldingly over him, gaily lashing out at both of us; then, when I took to patting his chest and little back, he puckered up his eyes, started threshing about and set up a piercing screech, while the waves, one after the other, kept pouring over him.

"Raise a rumpus, man of Orel! Yell with all the breath in you!"

When he and I came back to the mother she was lying, her eyes shut anew, biting her lips in the throes of ejecting the afterbirth; but, despite this, through moans and sighs, I caught her whisper as it died away:

"Let me . . . let me have him."

"He can wait."

"Come, let me have him!"

And, with trembling, uncertain hands she started to unbutton her blouse. I helped her to free a breast which nature had prepared for a score or so children, and placed against her warm body the turbulent Orel fellow; he immediately caught on to everything and grew quiet.

"Most Holy Mother, Most Immaculate Mother," the mother drew her breath in, shuddering, and kept rolling her head from side to side on her bundle.

And suddenly, after a low outcry, she fell silent; then anew those eyes, splendidly beautiful to the verge of the impossible, opened: the hallowed eyes of her who has given birth; blue, they were looking at the blue sky; a grateful, joyous smile glowed and melted within them; lifting up a heavy hand, the mother slowly made the sign of the cross over herself and the child.

"Glory to Thee, Most Immaculate Mother of God . . . oh . . . glory to Thee—"

The fire went out of her eyes and they became

sunken; for a long space she was silent, barely breathing, and then suddenly, in a businesslike tone, in a voice that had become firmer, she said:

"Untie my bundle, lad."

We untied it; she glanced at me intently, smiled ever so faintly; a flush seemed to glow—barely perceptibly—upon her sunken cheeks and sweat-beaded forehead.

"Go off a little ways, now—"

"Don't you fuss too much."

"All right, all right—go off a little ways."

I went off a little way into the bushes. My heart seemed to have tired, but within my breast some sort of glorious birds were singing softly and this, together with the never-silenced plashing of the sea, was so splendid that I could have listened to it for a whole year.

Somewhere not far off a stream was murmuring—just as though a young girl were confiding to some friend about her beloved.

A head in a yellow kerchief, by now tied in the proper way, rose over a bush.

"Hey there, sister, you're starting in to fuss much too soon!"

Holding on with one hand to a branch of a bush she sat as if she were carven, without a drop of blood in her gray face, with enormous blue lakes in lieu of eyes, and was saying in a moved whisper:

"Look at him—see how he's sleeping—"

He was making a very good job of it but, in my opinion, in no way better than other children; however, even if there were any difference, it was due to the setting: he was lying on a heap of vivid autumn leaves under one of the bushes, such as do not grow in the province of Orel.

"You ought to lie down now, mother."

"N-no," said she, shaking her head upon its disjointed neck. "I've got to put myself to rights and then go on to that there—"

"To Ochemchiry?"

"There, that's it! Our people, now, must have paced off so many versts already."

"But then, can you walk?"

"And what of the Mother of God? She'll help me."

Oh, well—if she was together with the Mother of God it behooved me to keep quiet!

She was looking under the bush at the tiny, sulkily pouting face; warm rays of a caressing light flowed from her eyes; she was licking her lips and, moving her hand slowly, stroking her breast.

I made a fire and arranged some stones to put the tea-kettle on.

"I'm going to treat you to tea right away, mother."

"Yes? Do let me have something to drink. . . . My breasts are all dried up."

"Well, now, how come your countrymen deserted you?"

"They didn't desert me—why should they? I fell behind of my own self; they'd had a drop or two, now, so . . . and everything worked out for the best, for how could I have shed my burden before them?"

With a glance at me she hid her face with her elbow; then, having spat out some blood, she smiled shamefacedly.

"This your first?"

"The very first. . . . And you—who may you be?"

"A human being—sort of—"

"Naturally, a human being! Married?"

"I haven't been found worthy of that."

"Lying, aren't you?"

"Why should I be?"

She dropped her eyes, thought a while:

"But how come you know these things about women?"

Now for the lie! And I said:

"I studied them. I'm one of those students—you've heard about them?"

"Why, how else! Our priest's oldest son is a student; he's studying to be a priest too."

"There, I'm one of those fellows. Well, guess I'll go for some water."

The woman inclined her head toward her son, listening closely: was he breathing?—then looked a while in the direction of the sea.

"I ought to wash myself, only I don't know what the water here is like. What kind of water is it? It's salty and it's bitter—"

"There, you just go and wash yourself in it—that water's good for you!"

"Honest?"

"Sure thing. And warmer than any stream—for the streams hereabouts are like ice."

"You ought to know."

Dozing, his head lolling on his breast, an Abhasian drove by at a walk; his small horse, all compact of sinews, its ears twitching, looked at us askance out of one round, dark eye and snorted; the rider warily jerked up his head in its shaggy fur cap, also gave a look in our direction, and again let his head drop.

"How outlandish the people here look, and how frightening," said the woman of Orel quietly.

I went. A stream of water, radiant and alive as quicksilver, was leaping from stone to stone, singing, the autumn leaves were gaily tumbling in it: it was wonderful! I washed my hands, my face, filled the teakettle. I started back—and saw through the bushes that the woman, looking over her shoulder uneasily, was crawling on her knees over the earth, over the rocks.

"What are you after?"

She was startled, her face turned gray, she was hiding something under her: I surmised what it was.

"Let me have it; I'll bury it."

"Oh, dear man! Bury it—but how? It ought to be buried in a bathhouse entry, by rights, under the flooring—"

"Stop and think! Will they be building a bathhouse here soon?"

"There, you're making fun of me, but I'm scared! Suppose some animal eats it up all of a sudden . . . and yet it's got to be given back to the earth."

She turned away and, handing me a damp, heavy little bundle, asked quietly, shamefacedly:

"There, now, you bury it as best you know how, deep as you can, for Christ's sake, taking pity on my little son—bury it as safe as you can."

When I came back I saw her walking swayingly and with her hand held out, coming from the sea; her skirt was wet up to the waist, while her face had taken on a slight flush and seemed to be glowing from within. I helped her to get up to the fire, reflecting in wonder: "What an animal strength!"

After that we drank tea with honey and she kept questioning me, ever so quietly:

"Did you drop studying, now?"

"I did that."

"Took to drink, or what?"

"Drank myself all the way to the bottom, mother!"

"So that's the sort you are! But I remember you; I noticed you in Sukhum, when you were scrapping with the superintendent over our grub; that's the very time I thought to myself: One can see he's a hopeless drinker, he's that fearless."

And, licking the honey on her puffy lips with gusto, she kept constantly looking out of the corners of her blue eyes under the bush where the newest-come man of Orel was peacefully sleeping.

"What will his life be like?" said she, after a sigh, letting her eyes pass over me. "You helped me out, and thanks for it . . . but whether it'll be a good thing for him I don't rightly know."

She drank her fill of tea, finished eating, crossed herself and, while I was getting my household effects together she, swaying sleepily, kept napping, thinking over something, gazing at the ground with her faded eyes. Then she started to get up.

"Are you actually going?"

"I am."

"Oh, watch out, mother!"

"Yes, but what about the Mother of God? Let me have the little one, now!"

"I'll carry him."

We argued over it, she yielded, and we started off, shoulder to shoulder.

"Hope I don't flop down," said she, smiling as if she were at fault, and placed a hand on my shoulder.

The new dweller in the land of Russia, a man of unknown destiny, was, as he lay in my arms, wheezing in a substantial-citizen sort of a way. The sea plashed and swished, all in its white lace of shavings; the bushes were whispering among themselves; the sun—it had passed its meridian—was radiant.

We went along ever so slowly, gently; now and then the mother would stop, with a deep sigh, toss her head up and look about her on all sides: upon the sea, upon the forest and the mountains, and then look into the face of her son; her eyes, laved through and through with the tears of her sufferings, were anew amazingly clear, anew blossoming and blazing with the blue fire of inexhaustible love.

Once, stopping thus, she said:

"Lord, dear God! How fine everything is—how fine! And I could simply walk on and on, to the very end of the world, now, and he, this little son of mine, would be growing, ever growing, in full freedom, next his mother's breast, my own little one, born of my flesh. . . ."

The sea was surging, surging. . . .

LEONID NIKOLAIEVICH ANDREIEV
(1871–1919)

EDITOR'S NOTE

ANDREIEV, who, after Dostoevsky, is most responsible for the erroneous impression that Russian literature is rather a gloomy affair, lived through three attempts at suicide and four epochs in Russia's history.

By 1897 (after contending with extreme poverty, hereditary alcoholism, and frustrated love) he was practicing law, and had begun his writing career—as humorist. His first story appeared in 1895; recognition came to him in 1901, when his first collection of short stories was published; his first contact with the government, in a political way, was in 1905, when he was beginning to attain his popularity. Despite the morbidity of his writings, we are told that he was cheerful and sociable. But, after 1906, his eccentricities would seem to show that he was anything but happy. He drank much, took up many fads (including painting), and alternated months of idleness with weeks of sleepless, ceaseless creativeness.

He died in Finland, when a bomb fell too near his fantastic house, and his heart, impaired by a bullet in one of his suicide attempts, was unable to bear the shock.

His *Thought* illustrates, most characteristically, his outlook on the world and life. Much greater than Artzybashev, the two nevertheless seem to agree on negation as their sole reality, in revising the Karamazovian formula of *everything is permissible* to *nothing matters.* Contemporary criticism, probably not uninfluenced by his vast popularity (at its peak in 1908, but lasting even to 1914), was exceedingly caustic to Andreiev; later critics have been far more just in appraising him as a writer of individuality.

In English, Andreiev is, on the whole, exceptionally fortunate in his translators, particularly Gregory Zilboorg, Avrahm Yarmolinsky, Archibald J. Wolfe and John Cournos. In their renditions the face of the author comes through unblurred.

Thought

LEONID NIKOLAIEVICH ANDREIEV

ON THE 11th of December, 19——, Anton Ignatievich Kerzhentsev, M.D., committed a murder. Taking into consideration all the circumstances under which the crime was committed, as well as certain particulars preceding it, there were grounds for the suspicion that Kerzhentsev was not normal mentally.

After his admission to the Elizavetinskaya Psychiatric Hospital Kerzhentsev was kept under the strict and thorough observation of several experienced psychiatrists, Professor Drzhembitsky (recently deceased) having been of their number.

Given below are some of the explanations of the occurrence, written by the Doctor himself a month after the beginning of his mental examination; together with other material procured by the legal authorities they formed the basis of the expert testimony given at the trial.

FIRST FOLIO

Up to now, *Messieurs les Experts,* I have been concealing the truth, but now circumstances force me to reveal it. And, having learned that truth, you will understand that things aren't at all as simple as they may strike the laymen: either the straitjacket or the ball-and-chain. There is a third course: neither the ball-and-chain nor the straitjacket but, if you like, something more dreadful than both of these taken together.

Alexis Constantinovich Savelov, the man I killed, had been a fellow student of mine in preparatory school and at the university, even though we chose different professions: I, as you know, am a physician, whereas he graduated in law. No one can say that I did not like the deceased; I always found him likable, and I had no friend closer than he. Yet, with all his likable traits, he was not one of those who inspire me with respect. The surprising mildness and affability of his nature, his strange instability in the domain of thought and the spirit, the harsh extremes and baselessness of his constantly changing judgments, compelled me to regard him as one would a child or a woman. The people close to him, who not infrequently suffered because of his eccentric actions yet, at the same time, owing to the illogicality of human nature, loved him greatly, sought to find justification for his shortcomings and their feeling for him, and called him an "artist." And, actually, things worked out so that this trumpery word justified him altogether and neutralized, or even turned into good, that which in the case of any normal man would have been considered bad. Such was the power of this synthetic word that even I at one time yielded to the general mood and willingly excused Alexis' petty shortcomings. Petty, since he was incapable of any great ones, just as he was of anything on a grand scale. Even his literary productions bear sufficient witness to this, for everything about them is petty and insignificant, no matter what may be said by myopic critics, who are so prone to discover new talents. His works looked good and were insignificant; good-looking and insignificant was he himself.

Alexis was thirty-one at the time of his death—my junior by a little over a year. He was married. If you have chanced to see his widow now, in mourning, you can't form any idea of how beautiful she was at one time—for she has lost so very, very much of her looks. Her cheeks are earthy, and the skin on her face is so flabby, so very, very old, like a worn-out glove. And you can see small wrinkles. They're small right now—but let another year pass and they will be deep furrows and ditches—for she loved him so much! And her eyes no longer sparkle and no longer laugh, whereas before they had always laughed, even when they should have been weeping. I saw her for but a minute, at the most, having chanced to run into her at the Prosecutor's, and I was stunned by the change in her. She could not even summon a look of indignation for me. That's how pitiful she was!

Only three people—Alexis, Tatyana Nikolaievna and

I—knew that five years ago, two years before Alexis'
marriage, I had proposed to her and had been rejected.
Of course, it is merely a supposition of mine that only
three had known of this; most probably she had fully
informed half a score of her friends, of both sexes, how
Dr. Kerzhentsev had dreamt of marriage and had been
humiliatingly rejected. I don't know if she remembers
that she had burst out laughing at the time; probably
she doesn't, having occasion to laugh so often. Remind
her, then: *On the 5th of September she burst out laughing.* Should she deny this—and deny it she will—why,
remind her how it had happened. I, a strong man who
never cried, who never feared anything—I had stood
before her and trembled. I trembled, and saw her biting
her lips, and had already put out my arm to take her
around, when she lifted up her eyes—and there was
laughter in them. My arm remained poised in midair;
she burst out laughing, and laughed for a long time. To
her heart's content. Still, she did apologize.

"Forgive me, please," she had said. But her eyes were
laughing.

And I, too, smiled, and even if I were able to forgive
her her laughter, I could never forgive her that smile of
mine. This was on the 5th of September, at six in the
evening. St. Petersburg time. St. Petersburg time, I
add, for just then we were standing on a depot platform
and, even now, I can plainly see the big, white face of
the clock and the position of its jet-black hands, straight
up and down. Alexis was killed at precisely six, too. A
strange coincidence, yet likely to reveal a great deal to
a man of acumen.

One of the grounds for placing me here was the
absence of motive for the crime. Now do you see that
a motive did exist? Of course, it wasn't jealousy. That

presupposes a hair-trigger temper and weakness of the mental faculties—that is, a temperament directly the opposite of mine, for I am a cool and calculating man. Revenge? Yes, revenge is likelier, if it be so very necessary to use an old word for the definition of a new and unfamiliar emotion. The whole thing is that Tatyana had once more made me err, and this always aroused my resentment. Knowing Alexis well, I was convinced that Tatyana would be exceedingly unhappy married to him, and would regret not having married me, and that's why I insisted so much that Alexis (at that time merely in love with her) should marry her. Only a month before his tragic death he was saying to me:

"It's you to whom I'm indebted for my happiness. Isn't that so, Tanya?"

As for her, she had looked at me and said: "That's so." And her eyes had smiled. I, too, was smiling. And after that we all broke into laughter, as he embraced her (they were not at all embarrassed by my presence) and added:

"Yes, brother, you missed out that time!"

This inappropriate and tactless jest shortened his life by all of a week: my first intention had been to kill him on the 18th of December.

Yes, their marriage turned out to be a happy one— and it was she in particular who was happy. His love for her wasn't an overwhelming one—and besides, as a general thing, he was incapable of profound love. He had his beloved work—literature—which gave him interests beyond the confines of the bedroom. Whereas she loved him alone and lived in him alone. Then, too, he was not a healthy man; he was subject to frequent headaches and to insomnia, and all this was a torture to him, naturally. But as for her, looking after him when he was ailing and fulfilling his caprices constituted her happiness. For when a woman finds love, she becomes irresponsible for her actions.

And so from day to day I saw her smiling face, her happy face—young, beautiful, carefree. And I reflected: It is I who have contrived all this. I had wanted to give her a worthless husband and to deprive her of myself, but instead I have not only given her a husband whom she loves, but have remained attached to her myself. You can grasp this odd situation: she is more intelligent than her husband and loved to converse with me; but, having had her fill of conversation, she would go off to sleep with him, and felt happy.

I don't remember when the thought of killing Alexis first came to me. It bobbed up somehow without my noticing it, but even from the first moment it became such an old idea, as though I had been born with it. I know that it was my wish to make Tatyana unhappy, and that at first I was thinking up many other plans, less disastrous for Alexis (I have always been opposed to unnecessary cruelty). Availing myself of my influence over him, I thought of making him fall in love with another woman, or of making a drunkard out of him (he had a leaning that way), but none of these quite filled the bill. The rub was that Tatyana Nikolaievna would have ingeniously contrived to remain happy, even while giving him up to another woman, or listening to his drunken maunderings and submitting to his drunken caresses. Her need was for this man to be alive, and for her to serve him, in one way or another. Slavish natures of that sort do exist. And, like slaves, they cannot understand and appraise the strength either of another or of their master. There have been clever, fine and talented women in this world, but a just woman the universe has never yet seen, nor ever will see.

I am so sincere in this confession of mine not in order to curry that favor which I consider unnecessary, but to show in what a regular, normal way my decision was coming about, that I was forced, for a rather long while, to struggle against feeling sorry for the man whom I had condemned to death. I felt sorry about his ante-mortem terror and over those seconds of suffering when his skull would be fracturing. I felt sorry (I don't know if you will understand this) about the skull itself. In a smoothly functioning, living organism there is an especial beauty, while death, even as sickness and even as senility, is, first and foremost, hideousness. I remember (this was a long time ago), when I had just finished the university, how a beautiful young bitch with graceful, strong legs had come into my hands, and what a great exertion of my will it required to strip off her skin, as the experiment demanded. And for a long while thereafter I found it unpleasant to recall the incident.

And if Alexis had not been so sickly, so puny, I don't know—perhaps I mightn't have killed him, after all. But as for that good-looking head of his—well, I feel sorry about it to this very moment. Please tell that also to Tatyana Nikolaievna. He had a good-looking head—downright good-looking. His eyes alone were his weak point: colorless, lacklustre, with nothing energetic about them.

Nor would I have killed Alexis had the critics been right, and he really had been the possessor of so great a literary gift. There is so much that is dark in life, and it does stand in such need of talents which would shed light on its path, that we ought to cherish each such talent as the most precious of gems, as that which compensates for the existence of thousands of scoundrels and vulgarians among mankind. *But Alexis was no talent.*

This is no place for a critical essay, but if you'll just read closely those works of the deceased which have created the most stir, you'll see that life stood in no need of them. A hundred or so people who had become blubbery and had to have diversion may have had need of those works, but life had no such need, nor have we, who are striving to unriddle its riddle. Whereas a writer must, through the potency of his thought and talent, create new life, Savelov merely described the old, without even attempting to unriddle its innermost, hidden meaning. The only one of his stories I like, the only one wherein he draws near to the domain of the unexplored, is *The Mystery*, but that's an exception. The most wretched thing of all, however, was that Alexis was obviously beginning to write himself out, and because his life was happy had lost the last of those teeth which one must sink into life and gnaw it with. He himself told me not infrequently about his doubts, and I saw that they were not unfounded; I had gotten out of him the exact and detailed plans of his future works—and his grieving admirers may console themselves: there wasn't a single new and big thing among them. Of the people close to Alexis his wife alone did not see the decline of his talent—nor would she ever have seen it. And do you know why? Because she did not always read her husband's writings. Yet one day, when I somehow tried to open her eyes a little, she simply considered me a scoundrel. And, having made certain that we were alone, she said:

"It's something else that you can't forgive him."

"And what may that be?"

"That he is my husband and that I love him. If it weren't for Alexis' being so partial to you—"

She stopped short, and I considerately finished her thought:

"You would show me the door?"

There was a gleam of laughter in her eyes. And, with an innocent smile, she slowly uttered:

"No. I would let you stay."

And yet I'd never shown by a single word or gesture that I was still in love with her. But at that point the thought occurred to me: So much the better, if she does surmise.

The brute fact of depriving a man of life did not deter me. I knew that it was a crime severely punished by law—but then almost everything we do is a crime, and only a blind man fails to see that. For those who believe in God the crime is before God; for others, the crime is before men; for such as I, the crime is before one's own self. It would have been a greater crime if, having found it inevitable to kill Alexis, I would have failed to carry out this resolve. And as for people dividing crimes into big ones and petty ones, and their calling murder a big one—well, that had always struck me as the usual and pitiful human lying before one's own self, an attempt to hide from responsibility behind one's own back.

Nor did I fear my own self—and that was most important of all. To a murderer, to a criminal, the most dreaded thing is not the police, not the court, but his own self, his nerves, the mighty protest of the whole body which had been brought up under certain traditions. Recall Raskolnikov, the fellow that perished so pitifully and incongruously, and the slue of others like him. And for a very long time, and very closely, I deliberated on this point, picturing to myself what I would be like after the murder. I won't say I became imbued with full assurance as to my imperturbability—such assurance was out of the question in the case of any thinking man who foresaw all the contingencies. But, having painstakingly collected all the data of my past, having taken into consideration the strength of my will, the firmness of an unexhausted nervous system, my profound and sincere contempt for current morals, I could feel comparatively assured about a favorable issue to the undertaking. At this point it might not be amiss to tell you a certain interesting fact in my life.

Once, while I was still a student in my fifth semester, I stole fifteen rubles from money entrusted to me by my fellow-students, telling them that I had been short-changed—and they all believed me. This was something more than a mere theft, as when a man in need steals from one well-to-do; in this instance there was not only a betrayal of trust, but also the abstraction of money precisely from hungry men who were also comrades *and* fellow-students and, to top it all off, a theft committed by a man of means (which was the very reason they believed me). To you this act will probably seem more revolting than even the murder of my friend which I committed—isn't that so? But as for myself, I remember I felt amused because I had been able to bring this off so well and adroitly, and I looked in the eyes (straight into the eyes!) of those to whom I was lying, boldly and freely. My eyes are dark, good-looking, straightforward—and they were believed. But what I was most proud of was that I felt absolutely no gnawings of conscience, which had been the very thing I had had to prove to myself. And up to this very day I recall with particular pleasure the menu of the needlessly luxurious dinner which I ordered for myself with the stolen money, and which dinner I consumed with gusto.

And, even now, am I experiencing any gnawings of conscience? Any repentance for that which I have committed? Not in the least.

I do feel depressed. I feel insanely depressed, as no

other man on earth, and my hair is turning gray—but that's something else. *Something else.* Something frightful, unexpected, something unbelievable in its horrible simplicity.

SECOND FOLIO

My problem was this: It was necessary that I kill Alexis; it was necessary that Tatyana should perceive that it was none other than I who had killed her husband, and with all that the lawful chastisement must pass me by. To say nothing of the fact that if I paid the penalty Tatyana would be given an extra reason for a good laugh at my expense I had, in general, absolutely no hankering for a life sentence at hard labor. I am very much in love with life.

I love to see aureate wine effervescing in a fine goblet; I love, when I am tired, to stretch myself out on snowy sheets; I am fond of breathing in deeply the clean air of spring, of watching a beautiful sunset, of reading interesting and clever books. I love myself, the strength of my sinews, the strength of my thought, so clear and exact. I love the fact of my being lonely, and that not a single curious look has penetrated into the depth of my soul with its dark depths and abysses, at the verge of which one's head begins to swim. Never have I understood or known that which men call the tedium of life. Life is interesting, and I love it for that great mystery which is comprised within it; I love it even for its cruelties, for its ferocious vengefulness and Satanically merry play with men and events.

I was the only person whom I respected—how, then, could I risk sending that person to a life sentence at hard labor, where he would be deprived of leading the varied, full and deep life which he had to have! And even from your point of view—I was right in trying to evade penal servitude. I make out very well at doctoring; not being short of means, I treat many of the poor gratis. I am useful. Surely more useful than the murdered Savelov.

And impunity was easily attainable. There are thousands of ways of killing a man without creating a fuss, and for me, a physician, it was especially easy to resort to one of them. And among the plans I conceived and rejected the following engrossed me for a long time: that of inoculating Alexis with some incurable and repulsive disease. But the inconveniences of this plan were obvious: prolonged sufferings for the subject himself, something unprepossessing about it all, something profoundly and, somehow, really . . . stupid; and, finally, that even in the disease of her husband Tatyana would have found a source of joy for herself. My problem became especially complicated by the imperative requirement that the wife must know the hand that had struck down her husband. But it is only cowards who fear obstacles; such men as I are attracted by them.

Chance, that great ally of the clever, came to my aid. And I permit myself to draw your particular attention, *Messieurs les Experts,* to this detail; it is precisely chance —*i. e.,* something external, independent of me, which served as basis and occasion for what followed. I had come across a news item (the clipping is probably around my place, or you may find it in the possession of the authorities); it had to do with a cashier—or it may have been just a clerk—who simulated an attack of the falling sickness and, allegedly during the attack, had lost a sum of money—he had really stolen it, of course. The clerk turned out to be a coward and confessed, even pointing out where he had hidden the stolen money; but the idea itself wasn't a bad one and could be put into practice. To simulate insanity, to kill Alexis in a state of suppositious madness, and then to "recover"—that was the plan which instantly sprang up in my head, but which demanded much time and work to take on a fully defined, concrete form. At that time I had only a superficial knowledge of psychiatry, like every physician who is not a specialist, and a year or so of my life went into reading all sorts of sources and into deep thought. Toward the end of that time I became convinced that my plan was fully realizable.

What the experts would direct their attention to first of all would be my hereditary influences—and my heredity, to my great joy, turned out to be quite a suitable one. My father had been a dipsomaniac; one of my uncles, his brother, had ended his days in an institution for the insane and, finally, my only sister, Anna, now dead, had been afflicted with epilepsy. True enough, all those on my mother's side were sound; but then, one drop of the poison of madness is enough to envenom a whole succession of generations. In my magnificent health I took after my mother's family, but certain inoffensive quirks did exist in my case and might prove of great service to me. My comparative unsociability (which is simply the sign of a healthy mind, a preference for passing one's time in one's own company and with one's books rather than spending it in empty, idle chatter) might pass for unwholesome misanthropy; the frigidity of my temperament, which sought no coarse, sensual enjoyments, might be considered an expression of degeneracy. My very stubbornness in the attainment of goals once set—and not a few instances of that stubbornness could be found in my rich life—would, in the language of *Messieurs les Experts,* receive the awe-inspiring name of monomania, of obsession by *idées fixes.*

Thus the soil for the simulation was exceptionally

favorable; the statics of insanity was evident; the only thing needed was the dynamics. It was necessary to draw two or three well-done strokes over the fortuitous priming-coat of nature, and the picture of insanity would be complete. And I imagined very clearly how this would come about—imagined it not in programmed thoughts but in living images: even though I'm no writer of trashy stories, I'm far from lacking in artistic sensitiveness and in fantasy.

I saw that I would be able to go through with my rôle. A bent for dissembling had always been dormant in my character, and was one of the forms my striving for inner freedom took. Even in school I had often simulated friendship, walking through the corridor with my arm around another's shoulders, the way real friends do, artfully counterfeiting the frank speech of friendship—and imperceptibly playing the inquisitor. And when my friend, ever so touched, would turn himself all inside out, I would cast his miserable little soul away from me and walk off with a proud consciousness of my power and inner freedom. At home as well, among my kin, I remained the same sort of double-dealer. Just as in the houses of the Old Faith sectarians a separate set of dishes is kept for strangers, so I, too, kept a separate set of everything for others: a separate smile, separate conversations, and a separate frankness. I saw that people do a great many things which are foolish, harmful to themselves, and unnecessary, and it seemed to me that, were I to start telling the truth about myself, I would become even as all the others, and that these foolish and unnecessary things would gain a mastery over me.

I always liked being respectful to those whom I despised, and kissing people whom I hated; this made me free and master over the others. But then, I knew no such thing as falsehood to my own self—that most widespread and lowest form of the enslavement of man by life. And the more I lied to people, the more mercilessly truthful did I become before my own self—a virtue that but few can boast of.

On the whole, I think I had the makings of an extraordinary actor in me, an actor who could combine a naturalness of acting that at times attained to a full fusion with the character being played, and an unremitting, chill control of the intellect. Even during the ordinary reading of a book I entered wholly into the psychic state of the character being depicted and—would you believe it?—when I was already an adult I shed bitter tears over *Uncle Tom's Cabin.* To be able to re-incarnate one's self: what a wondrous ability that is of the lithe mind, refined by culture! You live as though with a thousand lives, now descending into infernal darkness, now ascending to celestial, radiant heights, taking in an infinite universe at a single glance. If man is fated ever to become God, the book will be His throne. . . .

Yes. That is true. Incidentally, I want to lodge a complaint with you against the way things are run here. Either they put me to bed when I want to write, *when I must write,* or they won't shut the doors, and I am compelled to listen to the caterwauling of some madman or other. He keeps on caterwauling and caterwauling— it's downright unbearable. You can actually drive a man out of his mind that way, and then say that he was mad to begin with. And is it possible they really haven't an extra candle, and I must spoil my eyes with electric light?

Very well, then. I had entertained ideas of actually going on the stage even some time before this, but I dropped the silly notion: pretending, when everybody knows it is pretending, at once loses its value. And be-

sides, the cheap laurels of a certified play-actor on a
government stipend held but little attraction for me.
About the degree my art attained you can judge by the
fact that any number of asses to this day considers me
the sincerest and most truthful of men. And here's
something odd: it wasn't asses I always succeeded in
taking in—I said that just so, in the heat of the moment
—but none other than intelligent people; while, on the
other hand, there are two categories of beings of a lower
order whose trust I could never gain: women and dogs.

Do you know, that the most estimable Tatyana
Nikolaievna never did believe my love, and doesn't believe it, I think, even now, when I have killed her husband? Here's how the thing works out, according to her
logic: I did not love her; as for Alexis, I killed him because she loved him. And this nonsense seems to her, in
all probability, both well considered and convincing.
And yet she's a clever woman!

Putting over the rôle of a madman did not seem very
hard to me. The necessary bits of business were furnished me, in part, by books; in part I, like every good
actor given any rôle, had to round them out through my
own creativeness; as for the rest, it would be created by
the audience itself, which had long since refined its emotions through books and the theatre, where it had been
trained to create living countenances out of two or
three indistinct contours.

Of course, there were bound to be certain unavoidable lacunæ—and this was particularly dangerous in
view of the strict scientific examination to which I would
be subjected; but even here I did not foresee any serious danger. The wide domain of psychopathology is
still so little cultivated, there is in it so much that is
still dark and casual, so vast is the room left for fantasy
and subjectivism, that I boldly placed my fate in your

hands, *Messieurs les Experts.* I do hope I haven't offended you. I'm not attacking your learned authority, and feel certain that, as people trained in conscientious scientific thinking, you will agree with me.

. . . He has stopped caterwauling, at long last. It's simply unbearable. . . .

And even at the time when my plan was only in projection, a thought came to me which could hardly have come into the head of an insane man. *This was the thought of the sinister danger of my experiment.* Do you understand what I'm talking about? Insanity is a fire which it is dangerous to play with. You could start a bonfire going in the middle of an ammunition dump and feel yourself in greater safety than if even the least thought of insanity were to steal into your head. And I knew this, I knew, I knew this—but then, does danger mean anything to a brave man?

Then, too, did I not feel that my thought was firm, bright, as if it were forged of steel, and absolutely submissive to me? Just like a keenly ground rapier it wove in and out, stung, bit, parted the warp and woof of events; like a very serpent, it crept into unexplored and sombre depths, which are hidden for all eternity from the light of day; yet its hilt lay within my hand, the iron hand of a skilled and experienced fencer. How obedient it was, how faithful in execution and swift, my thought!—and how I loved it, my handmaiden, my ominous strength, my sole treasure!

. . . He is caterwauling again, and I can't go on writing. How horrible it is to hear a man howling! I've heard many frightful sounds, but this is the most frightful, the most horrible of all. It is unlike any other, this voice of a beast which passes through the gullet of a man. It is something ferocious and cowardly; something unbridled and pitiful unto baseness. The mouth writhes, all to one side; the muscles of the face become strained like ropes, the teeth bared like a dog's, and out of the dark orifice of the mouth issues this revolting, roaring, wheezing, laughing, howling sound. . . .

Yes. Yes. That's what my thought was like. Incidentally: you will turn your attention to my handwriting, of course, so I beg of you not to attach any significance to its occasional tremulousness and apparent inconsistency. It's a long time since I've done any writing; the late events and my insomnia have weakened me greatly, and so my hand jerks now and then. *This used to happen to me even before.*

THIRD FOLIO

Now you understand what sort of a fearful attack it was that overcame me on that evening at the Karganovs'. This was my first experiment, which succeeded even beyond all expectations. It was just as if everybody knew beforehand that that very thing would happen to me, just as if the sudden madness of a thoroughly healthy man seemed something natural in their eyes, the sort of thing one may always expect. No one was astonished, and all vied with one another to color my playing with the play of their own fantasy—it is a rare guest star who could have assembled as splendid a troupe as these naïve, silly, and gullible people. Have they told you how pale I was, and how frightful I looked? How a chill perspiration (yes, precisely that: a chill perspiration) covered my brow? With what an insane fire my dark eyes blazed? When they were conveying to me all these observations of theirs, I was, in appearance, sombre and crushed, but all my soul was aquiver with pride, happiness and derision.

Tatyana and her husband were not present that evening—I don't know if you have paid any attention to this fact. And this was not through mere chance: I was afraid of frightening her, or, still worse, of instilling suspicion in her. If there were any person alive who could see through my play-acting, that person was she.

And, in general, there was nothing of the fortuitous in this instance. On the contrary, every trifle, even the most insignificant, had been rigidly thought over. The moment for the fit (at supper) I had chosen because then all would be together and, to some extent, aroused by wine. I took my seat at the edge of the table farthest from the candlesticks—since I hadn't the least desire to stage a fire or to burn my nose. Alongside of me I seated Paul Petrovich Pospelov, that fat swine, upon whom I had long been wanting to inflict some unpleasantness. He's particularly revolting when he's eating. When I saw him first at this occupation, it struck me that eating is an immoral business. At this point all this came in handy. And, surely, not a soul noticed that the plate which flew into smithereens under my fist had been covered over with a napkin, so as not to cut my hand.

The trick itself was staggeringly crude, even silly, but that was precisely what I was calculating on. Any stunt of greater finesse they would have failed to understand. At first I waved my arms about and spoke "excitedly" to Paul Petrovich, until the latter's little peepers began to pop out in astonishment; then I sank into "concentrated thoughtfulness", marking time until the question from the inevitable Irina Pavlovna:

"What's the matter with you, Anton Ignatievich? Why are you so gloomy?"

And, when the eyes of all were turned upon me, I smiled a tragic smile.

"Are you unwell?"

"Yes. A little. My head is going 'round. But don't put yourself out, please. It'll pass right away."

The hostess calmed down, while Paul Petrovich gave me a sidelong look, suspicious and disapproving. And the next moment, as he brought a glass of port to his lips with a beatific air, I—one!—knocked the glass right out from under his nose and—two!—smashed my fist down on the plate. The shards flew right and left, Paul Petrovich was sprawling and *oink*'ing, the young ladies were screeching, while I, with my teeth bared, was dragging the cloth off the table with everything that was on it. Oh, that was a scene to make you split your sides laughing!

Yes. Well, at that point they all got around me, caught hold of me; some were fetching water, some were seating me in an easy-chair; I, for my part, kept growling, like a tiger in a zoo, and working my eyes for all they were worth. And all this was so incongruous, and all of them were so silly that, by God, I had more than half a mind to smash a few of their phizes, taking advantage of my privileged condition. But, of course, I refrained.

After that came the scene of slowly calming down, with the business of the breast heaving tempestuously, the eyes rolling up, the teeth gnashing, and such feeble-voiced speeches as:

"Where is it I am? What's the matter with me?"

Even that absurdly French "Where is it I am?" made a hit with this gentry, and no less than three fools informed me without any delay:

"At the Karganovs'. [In a mawkish voice:] Do you know, dear Doctor, who Irina Pavlovna Karganova is?"

They were positively too small-time to waste good acting on!

On the second day after this—I'd allowed enough time for rumors to reach the Savelovs—came my talk with Tatyana and Alexis. The latter had somehow failed to grasp what had happened and confined himself to the question:

"Well, brother, what sort of mess did you get into at the Karganovs'?"

He flipped up the tail of his little jacket and went off into his study to work. As much as to say that, were I actually to go out of my mind, he wouldn't even blink an eye. But then, the commiseration of his spouse was especially magniloquent, tempestuous and, of course, insincere. And at this point—well, I didn't exactly begin regretting what I had started, but there simply arose the question: Was it all really worth-while?

"Do you love your husband very much?" I asked Tatyana, whose eyes were following Alexis.

"Yes," she turned around quickly. "But why do you ask?"

"Oh, just so." And, after a minute's silence fraught with unuttered thoughts, I added: "Why don't you trust me?"

She glanced at me quickly, looking directly into my eyes, but made no answer. And at that moment I forgot that once, a long time ago, she had burst out laughing, and I bore her no malice, and that which I was engaged in appeared unnecessary and strange to me. That was fatigue, natural after a strong upsurge of nerves, and it lasted for but an instant.

"But could one possibly believe you?" she asked after a long silence.

"Of course not," I answered lightly, but within me the fire that had died out was blazing up anew. Strength, daring, a resolve that would stop at nothing did I come to sense within me. Proud at the success already achieved, I boldly decided to go on to the end. Struggle —therein lies the joy of life.

The second fit took place a month after the first. In this case not everything had been so well thought over, but then that was superfluous, since the general plan was there. I had no intention of staging that fit precisely on that evening but, since circumstances were arranging themselves so adventitiously, it would have been foolish not to avail oneself of them. And I remember clearly how it all came about. We were sitting in the drawing room and chatting when I became very sad. I suddenly had a vivid picture of how alien to all these people and how lonely in this world I was, forever immured in this head, in this prison, of mine. And thereupon all those there became revolting to me. And, in fury, I smashed my fist on the table and started yelling something rude, and with joy saw fright upon their paled faces.

"Scoundrels!" I kept yelling. "Vile, contented scoundrels! Liars, hypocrites, snakes in the grass! I hate you!"

And it is true that I did struggle with them, then with the waiters and the coachmen. Nevertheless, I was aware that I was struggling, aware that I was doing so deliberately. The simple truth is, it was a pleasure to beat them, to tell them straight to their faces all the truth about what they were like. Come, is every man that tells the truth a madman? I assure you, *Messieurs les Experts*, that I was conscious of everything; that as I hit out I felt under my hand living flesh that responded to the pain. But at home, left to myself, I laughed and reflected what an amazing, exquisite actor I was. Then I lay down to sleep, and I took a book to read in bed—I can even tell you what the book was: a work of Guy de Maupassant's; as always, I found him delightful, and fell asleep like an infant.

Come, do madmen read books and find them delightful? Do they sleep like infants?

Madmen do not sleep. They suffer, and everything in their heads swirls like turbid water. Yes, swirls like turbid water—and then falls. . . . And they want to howl, to lacerate themselves with their own nails. They want to get down on all fours—there, like that—and to creep along, ever so quietly, and then to jump up all of a sudden and yell out:

"Aha!"

And to burst out laughing. And to howl. To throw up their heads—so—and howl ever and ever so long, in such a long, long-drawn-out way, ever and ever so piteously.

Yes. Yes.

But I slept like an infant. Come, do madmen sleep like infants?

FOURTH FOLIO

Yesterday morning Mary (our nurse) asked me:

"Don't you ever pray to God, Anton Ignatievich?"

She was serious, and believed I would answer her sincerely and seriously. And I answered her without a smile, as she wished me to:

"No, Mary, never. But, if it will please you, you may make the sign of the cross over me."

And, still as seriously as ever, she made the sign of the cross over me, and I was very glad because I had given a moment of pleasure to this excellent woman. Like all persons highly placed and at liberty you, *Messieurs les Experts,* pay no attention to servants, but we, those under arrest and "madmen", have occasion to see them near at hand, and at times to make astonishing discoveries. So it has probably never even entered your heads that Mary, the nurse assigned by you to keep an eye on the madmen, *is mad herself?* Yet such is the case.

Take a good look at her walk, noiseless, gliding, a trifle timorous and astonishingly cautious and nimble, as though she were walking amid unseen, unsheathed swords. Look closely at her face, but do it somehow without her perceiving it, so that she might not be aware of your presence. When some one of you arrives, Mary's face becomes serious, important, yet condescendingly smiling—precisely the expression which at that moment is dominating your face. The gist of the matter is that Mary is possessed of a strange and most significant ability: that of reflecting upon her face the expression of all other faces. At times she looks at me and smiles. Such a wan, reflected smile, as if it were someone else's. And I surmise that I had been smiling when she had glanced at me. At other times Mary's face becomes a martyr's, grim, the eyebrows converging toward the bridge of the nose, the corners of the mouth drooping, the whole face aging by ten years and growing darker— probably my face is just like that at the moment. There are occasions when I frighten her by my gaze. You know how strange and a trifle frightening the face of a man in deep thought is. And Mary's eyes widen, their pupils growing darker, and, raising her hands a little, she noise-lessly goes to me and does something or other with me, something friendly and unexpected: smoothing down my hair, or adjusting my robe.

"Your belt will come undone!" says she, while her face is as frightened as ever.

I, however, have the opportunity of seeing her when she is all by herself. And when she is, all expression is, oddly, absent from her face. It is pale, comely, and enigmatic, like the face of one dead. If you call her loudly by her name, she will turn around quickly, smile her tender and timorous smile, and ask:

"Do you want me to bring you something?"

She is forever bringing something or taking something away and, if she has nothing to bring, or to take away, or tidy up, she seems perturbed. And, always, she is noiseless. I haven't even once noticed her dropping anything, or making the least clatter. I made attempts to discuss life with her, and found her strangely apathetic about everything—even about murders, fires, and every other sort of horror which has such an effect upon people of but little development.

"Do you understand—men are wounded, killed, and they leave little hungry children behind them?" I told her, speaking about war.

"Yes, I understand," she answered, and asked thoughtfully: "Oughtn't you to have a little milk? You've eaten so little today."

I laughed, and she responded with somewhat frightened laughter. She hasn't been to the theatre even once, doesn't know that Russia is a sovereign nation, and that there are other sovereign nations; she's illiterate, and knows only as much of the Bible as she may have heard read in snatches in church. And every evening she kneels and prays for a long while.

I long considered her only a limited, stolid being, born to be a slave, but a certain incident compelled me to change my opinion. You probably know—you were probably told—that I have lived through a bad moment here—which, of course, proves nothing save fatigue and a temporary physical decline. *A matter of a towel.* Of course, I am stronger than Mary and could have killed her, since there were only the two of us there, and had she cried out or seized my hand. . . . But she did nothing of the sort. She merely said:

"Don't, my dear—"

I have thought often of this "Don't" later on, and even now I can't understand the astonishing power it holds, and which I feel. That power lies not in the word itself, which is meaningless and vacuous; it lies somewhere in the depths of Mary's soul, unknown to me and inaccessible. She has a knowledge of something, but cannot or will not say what it is. Subsequently I strove to get an explanation from her of this "Don't". And she couldn't explain it.

"Do you think that suicide is a sin? That God has forbidden it?"

"No."

"Why, then, did you say 'don't'?"

"Just so. Don't." And she smiled, and asked: "Should I bring you something?"

Absolutely, she is is mad, but non-violent and useful, like many of the mad. And don't you touch her!

I have permitted myself to digress from my story, since Mary's action yesterday has impelled me toward reminiscences of childhood. My mother I don't remember, but I did have an Aunt Anphissa, who always made the sign of the cross over me to bless my night's slumber. She was a taciturn old maid with a pimply face, and used to feel very much ashamed whenever my father twitted her about marriageable young men. I was still a youngster, about eleven, at the time she strangled herself in the small shed where we used to store coal. Afterward my father kept seeing her all the time, and that jolly atheist ordered masses and requiems for her soul.

He was very clever and talented, was my father, and his courtroom speeches brought tears to the eyes not only of nervous ladies but even of serious, well-balanced people. I alone did not weep as I listened to him, inasmuch as I knew him, and knew that he himself hadn't a notion of what he was saying. He had knowledge of many things, had many thoughts and still more words; and the words, and the thoughts and funds of knowledge were often combined very successfully and beautifully, but he himself understood nothing of all this. *I even frequently doubted if he had any actual existence* —to such an extent did all of him consist of outer things, of sounds and gestures, and it frequently seemed to me that this was no man but a flickering cinema image coupled with a phonograph. He did not understand that he was a human being, that he was living at that moment but eventually would die, and therefore did not seek anything. And when he'd lie down in bed, ceasing to stir and then falling asleep, he most probably had no dreams whatsoever and did cease to exist. With his tongue (he was a lawyer) he earned thirty thousand or so a year, and not once was he struck by or think deeply about this circumstance. I remember the time he and I went to a country estate he had just bought, and I said, pointing to the trees in our park:

"Clients?"

Flattered, he smiled and answered:

"Yes, brother—talent is a grand thing."

He drank a great deal, and his inebriation showed only in an accelerated tempo in everything about him, after which it all ran down abruptly—as he fell asleep. And everybody considered him unusually gifted, while he himself was forever saying that, had he not turned out to be a famous lawyer, he would have been a famous painter or writer. Regrettably enough, it was the truth.

And least of all did he understand me. Once things so fell out that we were threatened by the loss of our fortune. And, to me, that was horrible. In our days, when only riches give freedom, I don't know what would have become of me had fate placed me in the ranks of the proletariat. Even right now I cannot picture to myself anybody daring to lay a hand on me, compelling me to do that which I don't wish to do, buying for coppers my labor, my blood, my nerves, my life. But I experienced that horror for but a moment, since in the next I understood that such people as I never turn out to be poor. But my father did not understand this. He sincerely considered me a dull young man and regarded my imagined helplessness with apprehension.

"Ah, Anton, Anton, whatever will you do!" said he.

He himself had gone all to pieces; his long, unkempt hair hung down on his forehead; his face was yellow.

"Don't be uneasy on my account, Dad," I answered him. "Since I'm not talented I'll have to kill Rothschild or rob a bank."

My father grew angry, since he had taken my answer for an ill-timed and flat jest. He saw my face, he heard my voice, yet just the same he took this for a jest. The pitiful, cardboard buffoon, who through some misunderstanding was considered a man! My soul he did not know, while all the outward, orderly arrangement of my life made him indignant, inasmuch as it did not fit into his understanding. I studied well in school, and this saddened him. Whenever we had guests—lawyers, litterateurs and painters—he would poke his finger at me and say:

"As for that son of mine—he's first rate as a scholar. Whereby have I incurred the wrath of God?"

And they all laughed at me, and I laughed at all of them. But even more than by my successes was he aggrieved by my conduct and dress. He would come into my room solely to shift the position of the books on my desk, without my noticing it, and to create some sort of disorder at least. The neat way I combed my hair deprived him of his appetite.

"We are ordered to cut our hair short by our school inspector," I would inform him, seriously and respectfully.

He'd swear roundly, and at the same time everything within me was aquiver with contemptuous laughter, and not without grounds did I at that time divide all the world into those who were inspectors pure and simple and those who were inspectors turned inside out. And all of them were straining toward my head: some to trim the hair on it, others to pull that hair out.

Worst of all for my father were my note-books. Occasionally, when he was drunk, he would look them over in despair, complete and comical:

"Did you ever happen, even once, to make a blot?" he'd ask.

"Yes, I did, Dad. Three days ago I happened to let a drop of ink fall on my trigonometry lesson."

"Did you lap it up?"

"Lap it up? Just what do you mean?"

"Just that—did you lap it up?"

"No, I applied blotting paper to it."

My father made a hopeless, drunken gesture, and growled as he stood up:

"No, you're no son of mine. No, no!"

Among these note-books which he hated so much there was one, however, which might have given him pleasure. Just like all the others, it hadn't a single crooked line, or a blot, or anything crossed out. And entered therein was, approximately, the following: "My father is a drunkard, a thief, and a coward." This was followed by certain particulars which, out of respect for the law, as well as for the memory of my father, I do not deem it necessary to give here.

At this point there comes to my memory a certain fact I had forgotten, which I now perceive will not be

devoid of great interest to you, *Messieurs les Experts*.
I'm very glad to have recalled it—very, very glad. How
could I ever have forgotten it?

We had a maid, named Kate, in our house, who was
my father's mistress and, at the same time, mine. My
father she liked because he gave her money, and me
because I was young, had beautiful dark eyes, and
didn't give her money. And, on the night when my
father's corpse was laid out in the drawing room, I made
my way to Kate's room. It wasn't far, and one could
clearly hear in it the minor cleric reading the prayers in
the drawing room.

I am of the opinion that the immortal spirit of my
father received full satisfaction!

No, this actually is an interesting fact, and I can't
understand how I could have forgotten it. To you,
Messieurs les Experts, this may seem puerility, a childish
prank void of any serious meaning, but that's not so.
This, *Messieurs les Experts*, was a cruel battle, and the
victory therein did not come to me cheaply. The stake
was my life. Had I shown cowardice, had I turned back,
had I proven incapable of making love—I would have
killed myself. *That had been decided upon, I remember.*

And that which I was doing was, for a youth of my
years, not so easy. Now I know that I was battling a
windmill, but at that time the whole business appeared
to me in a different light. Right now it is already hard
for me to bring back in my memory that which I lived
through then, but I felt, I remember, as if through a
single action I were breaking all laws, both divine and
human. And I was horribly cowardly, to the verge of the
mirth-provoking, yet just the same I got myself in hand
and, when I came into Kate's room, was as ready for
kisses as Romeo.

Yes, at that time I was still, it seems, a romantic. That

happy time, how distant it now is! I remember, gentle-men, as I was coming away from Kate, I stopped before the corpse, crossed my arms on my chest à *la* Napoleon, and looked at it with comic pride. And at that very moment I shuddered, startled by a flutter of the pall. That happy, distant time!

I hate to think so, but I'm afraid I've never ceased being a romantic. And I was all but an idealist. I believed in human thought and its unbounded might. The whole history of mankind unrolled before me as a procession consisting solely of thought triumphant—and this was still not so long ago. And it is frightful for me to think that all my life has been a deception, that all my life I have been a madman, like that mad actor whom I saw the other day in an adjoining ward. He had accumulated bits of red and blue paper every-where, and gave to each bit the denomination of a million; he importuned visitors for these bits of paper, stole and brought them back from the lavatory, and the keepers poked rough fun at him, but he sincerely and deeply despised them. I proved to his liking and, by way of a farewell gift, he gave me a million.

"It's a mere trifle, this million," said he, "but you will excuse me; just now I have such expenses—such expenses!" And, taking me aside, he explained in a whisper: "Right now I have my eye on Italy. I want to chase out the Pope and to introduce a new currency there—these very bills. And then, one Sunday, I will proclaim myself a saint. The Italians will rejoice—they always do, whenever you give 'em a new saint."

Wasn't it on that sort of a million I've been living?

It is horrible for me to think that my books, those companions and friends of mine, are still standing on their shelves as they used to and silently guard that which I considered the wisdom of the earth, its hope and its happiness. I know, gentlemen, that whether I am mad or not, I am, from your point of view, a scoundrel; well, you ought to see this scoundrel when he is stepping into his library!

Go, gentlemen, and look over my rooms; you will find the experience interesting. In the upper left-hand drawer of my desk you will find a catalogue *raisonné* of my books, paintings and bibelots; in the same place you will find the keys to the bookcases. You yourselves are men of learning, and I believe that you will treat my books with due respect and care. *I also ask you to see that the lamps should not be sooty.* There's nothing more horrible than soot; it gets in everywhere, and then a great deal of effort is required to get rid of it.

ON A SCRAP OF PAPER

Petrov, the assistant doctor, has just refused to give me chloralamid in the dose I demand. First of all, I am a physician and know what I am doing; and next, if I am refused, I intend to take decisive measures. I have not slept for two nights and have no desire whatsoever to go out of my mind. I demand that I be given chloralamid. I demand it. This is *dishonorable*—to drive anybody out of his mind.

FIFTH FOLIO

After the second attack they began to be afraid of me. In many houses all haste was made to slam the door in my face; on chancing to meet me, acquaintances would smile vilely, and ask in a tone of great significance:

"Well, how's your health, my dear fellow?"

The situation was such that I could commit whatever lawlessness I liked and yet not lose the respect of those around me. I looked at them and reflected: If I want to, I can kill this one and that one, and not a thing will happen to me because of my act. And that which I experienced at this thought was novel, agreeable and a trifle frightening. Man ceased to be something strictly protected, taboo; as though a husk of some sort had fallen away from him, he was naked, as it were, and killing him seemed an easy and a tempting matter.

Fear fenced me off from inquisitive eyes in such a close wall that the necessity of a third, preparatory fit was being obviated of itself. In that respect alone was I departing from the plan I had drawn, but that's just where the power of talent comes in: in not keeping itself within confining frames and, in accordance with changed circumstances, changing, as well, the whole course of the battle itself. But it was still necessary to receive an official remission for sins past, and dispensation for sins to come—a scientific, medical attestation of my ailment.

And here I waited until a confluence of circumstances in which my turning to a psychiatrist might seem incidental, or even somehow compulsory. This was, perhaps, actually a superfluous fine touch in the working out of my rôle. It was Tatyana and her husband who sent me to a psychiatrist.

"Please go to a doctor, my dear Anton Ignatievich," said she.

Never before had she called me dear, and it had been necessary for me to get the repute of a madman to gain this picayune endearment.

"Very well, my dear Tatyana Nikolaievna, I'll go," I answered her submissively.

The three of us—Alexis had also been present—were sitting in his study, where the murder subsequently took place.

'Yes, Anton—go, without fail," Alexis confirmed authoritatively. "Or else you'll be up to some mischief or other."

"Well, now, what could I be *up to?*" I was timidly apologetic before my stern friend.

"Who can tell? You may cave somebody's head in."

I was turning a heavy cast-iron paperweight in my hands, looking now at it, now at Alexis, and asked:

"Head? Did you say *head?*"

"Well, yes—head. You'll let go with some such thing as that, and there you are!"

This was becoming interesting. *The head, precisely, and, precisely, with this thingumbob did I intend to do the caving in, and now this very head was discoursing how it would come about.* It was discoursing and smiling insouciantly. And yet there are people who believe in premonition, that death sends out some forerunners or other—what bosh!

"Well, one could hardly do anything with this thing," said I. "It's far too light."

"Light? What are you talking about!" Alexis became indignant, snatched the paperweight out of my hands and, taking it in his slender, small hand, hefted it a few times. "Try it!"

"Yes, but I know—"

"No, you take it like this, and you'll see."

Reluctantly, smilingly, I took the heavy object. But at this point Tatyana intervened. Pale, with her lips quivering, she said—or rather cried out:

"Drop the subject, Alexis! Drop it!"

"What is it, Tanya? What's the matter with you?" he evinced his astonishment.

"Drop it! You know how I dislike such jokes."

We started laughing and the paperweight was put back on the table.

At Prof. T——'s office everything worked out just as I had expected it would. He was exceedingly circumspect, restrained in his expressions, but serious; he asked if I had any relatives to whose care I could entrust myself, advised me to stay home for a while, to rest a bit, and to calm down. Relying upon my status as a physician, I had a slight dispute with him, and even if he had had any lingering doubts at this point, after my temerity in contradicting him he irrevocably numbered me among the insane. Of course, gentlemen, you will not attach any serious significance to this inoffensive jest at the expense of one of your fraternity: as a man of science Prof. T—— is, beyond all doubt, worthy of respect and esteem.

The next few days were among the happiest of my life. I was pitied, as an admittedly sick man; I received calls, I was spoken to in some sort of broken, absurd language, and I alone knew that I was in better health than anybody else, and delighted in the clean-cut, mighty functioning of my thought. Of all the amazing, incomprehensible things in which life is so rich, the most incomprehensible and amazing one is the thought of man. Divinity is in it; in it are the pledge of immortality and a mighty force that knows no barriers. People are overcome with rapture and astonishment when they look upon the summits of mountainous masses; were they to understand themselves, they would be struck by their ability to think far more than by any mountain, far more than by all the wonders and beauties of the universe. The simple thought of a manual laborer of how most efficaciously to put one brick atop another: there you have the greatest of miracles and the profoundest of mysteries.

And so I took delight in my thought. Innocent in its beauty, it yielded itself to me with the passion of a mistress, served me like a handmaiden, and sustained me as a friend. Don't think that I spent all those days between the four walls of my home only in pondering my plan. No, everything therein was clear, everything had been thought out. I pondered over all sorts of things. My thought and I—it was just as though we were playing with life and death, and were soaring high, ever so high, above them. By the way, during those days I solved two very interesting chess problems, over which I had been working long but unsuccessfully. You know, of course, that three years ago I had participated in an international chess tournament and taken second place after Lasker. Had I not been a foe to all publicity and had I continued participating in contests, *Lasker would have had to yield the place where he had been roosting so long.*

And, from the moment when Alexis' life had been handed over to me, I came to feel particularly well-disposed toward him. I found it pleasant to think that he was living, drinking, eating and being joyous, and all this because I was permitting it. A feeling resembling that of a father for his son. And the one thing that did disturb me was his health. For all his puniness, he was unpardonably negligent; he refused to wear a sweater, and in the most dangerous, rawest weather walked out without his rubbers. Tatyana Nikolaievna reassured me. She dropped in for a visit and told me that Alexis was in perfect health and even sleeping well—a rare occurrence with him. In my joy I asked her to pass on a certain book to Alexis—a rare item that had fallen into my hands by chance and which Alexis had liked for a long time. Perhaps, as far as my plan was concerned, this gift was an error: people might have suspected therein a stacking of the cards, but I did so want to give Alexis pleasure that I decided on a slight risk. I even disregarded the circumstance that, as far as the artistry of my playing went, the gift might have been actually a hammy touch.

On this occasion I acted very charmingly and simply and made a good impression upon her. Neither she nor Alexis had witnessed either one of my attacks, and for them it was evidently difficult—even impossible—to picture me as mad.

"Do drop in on us," Tatyana begged me as she was saying good-bye.

"Mustn't," I smiled. "Doctor's orders."

"Oh, nonsense. You can come to us—it's the same as being at home. And Alësha misses you so."

I promised, *and never was a promise given with such certainty of its being fulfilled.* Doesn't it seem to you, gentlemen, when you learn of all these lucky coincidences—doesn't it seem to you that it was no longer by me alone that Alexis had been condemned to death *but by some other as well?* But, in reality, there is *no other,* and everything is so simple and logical.

The cast-iron paperweight was standing in its place when, on the 11th of December, at 5 p.m., I came into Alexis' study to see him. This time before dinner— they dine at seven—both Alexis and Tatyana spend resting. They were very glad I had come.

"Thanks for the book, old friend," said Alexis, shaking my hand. "Why, I myself was about to go to you, but Tanya told me that you'd recovered entirely. We're going to the theatre tonight—come along with us?"

We began to talk. That day I resolved not to pretend at all—that absence of pretense was an exquisite pretense of its own sort—and, being under the influence of the exaltation of thought I had lived through, I spoke much and interestingly. If the admirers of Savelov's talent did but know how many of "his" best thoughts had been engendered and gestated in the head of Dr. Kerzhentsev, whom nobody knew!

I spoke clearly, precisely, turning my phrases; at the same time I was watching the minute hand of the clock and reflecting that when it reached six I would become a murderer. And I was saying something funny, and they were laughing, while I was trying to memorize the sensation of a man who was not a murderer yet but would become one soon. No longer as an abstract notion but altogether simply I understood the process of life in Alexis, the beating of his heart, the ebb and flow of blood at his temples, the noiseless vibration of his brain—and I also understood how this process would break off, the heart cease to drive the blood, and the brain become stilled.

On what thought would it become stilled?

Never had the clarity of my consciousness attained such height and power; never had the sensation of a many-faceted, smoothly functioning *I* been so full. Just like God: without seeing I saw; without hearing I heard; without thought I was sentient.

There were seven minutes remaining when Alexis lazily got up from the divan, stretched himself, and left the room.

"I'll be back right away," said he as he was going out.

I did not want to look at Tatyana and I walked over to the window, parted the draperies, and stood there. And, without looking, I sensed how she hastened across the room and stopped by my side. I heard her breathing, knew that she was looking not through the window but at me, and I kept silent.

"How gloriously the snow glistens," said she, but I did not respond. Her breathing quickened, then broke off.

"Anton Ignatievich!" said she—and stopped.

I kept silent.

"Anton Ignatievich!" she repeated, just as hesitatingly, and thereupon I glanced at her.

She staggered, almost falling, as though thrown back by the fearful power in my glance. She staggered, and then rushed to her husband, who had entered.

"Alexis!" she babbled. "Alexis, he—"

"Well, what about him?"

Without smiling, but in a voice that shaded what I was saying into a jest, I said:

"She thinks that I want to kill you with this thing."

And, altogether calmly, without concealment, I took the paperweight, lifted it up in my hand, and calmly walked up to Alexis. He was looking at me, his faded eyes unblinking, and repeated:

"She thinks—"

"Yes, she thinks—"

Slowly, evenly, I began raising my hand, and Alexis began raising his, just as slowly, still without taking his eyes off me.

"*Hold on!*" I told him sternly.

Alexis' hand halted and, still without taking his eyes off me, he smiled mistrustfully—wanly, with his lips only. Tatyana cried out something in a frightful voice, but it was too late. I struck out with the sharp end at his temple—nearer to the sinciput than to the eye. And, when he had fallen, I bent over and struck him two times more. The coroner told me that I had struck him many times, because his head was all fractured. But that's not so. I struck him only *three times,* all in all; once while he was standing, and twice afterward, when he was on the floor.

True, these blows were very powerful, but there were *only three.* That I remember with certainty. *Three blows.*

SIXTH FOLIO

Don't attempt to make out that which is crossed out at the end of the fourth folio and, in general, don't attach any undue significance to my obliterations as putative signs of disordered thinking. In that strange situation in which I find myself I must be frightfully careful, something that I'm not concealing and that you understand very well.

The darkness of night always has a powerful effect on a tired nervous system, and that's why fearful thoughts come so often at night. And on that night, the first after the murder, my nerves were, of course, under particular tension. No matter how self-possessed I may have been, killing a man is, after all, no joke. At tea, after I had already put myself in order, having scrubbed my nails and changed my clothing, I called Maria Vasilievna to keep me company. She is my housekeeper and, to some extent, my wife. She has, it seems, a lover on the side, but she is a handsome woman, quiet and unavaricious, and I had easily become reconciled to the slight drawback, which is almost inevitable in the case of a man who obtains love through money. And so, this foolish woman was the first to deal me a blow.

"Kiss me," I told her.

She smiled foolishly and froze in her seat.

"Come, now!"

She shuddered, turned red and, having popped out her eyes in fright, stretched herself across the table to me imploringly as she said:

"Anton Ignatievich, darling, go to a doctor!"

"What next?" I became angry.

"Oh, don't yell—I'm afraid! Oh. I'm afraid of you, darling, little angel!"

And yet she knew nothing of my attacks or the murder, and I had always been kind and even-tempered with her. That meant there was something about me which was absent in other people and which was frightening— the thought flashed through me and immediately vanished, leaving a strange sensation of cold about my legs and back. I grasped that Maria had learned something on the side, from servants, or had stumbled upon the clothing I had soiled and discarded, and her fright was quite naturally to be explained by that.

"Go," I ordered her.

After that I rested on the divan in my library. I didn't want to read; I could feel fatigue throughout my body, and my mood in general was like that of an actor after a brilliant performance. I found it pleasant to look at my books, and pleasant to think that at some future time I would read them. All my rooms pleased me, and so did the divan, and Maria. Snatches of phrases from my rôle were flitting through my head, the gestures I had gone through were mentally recreated, and at rare intervals critical thoughts would creep by lazily: Well, there I might have delivered that speech, or done that bit of business, better—but with my ad-libbed "Hold on!" I was very much satisfied. Actually, this is a rare and unbelievable example of the power of suggestion even for those who have never experienced it themselves.

" 'Hold on!' " I kept repeating with my eyes shut, and smiled.

And my lids began to get heavy, and I wanted to sleep, when indolently, simply, like all my other thoughts, a new thought entered my head, possessed of all the qualities of one of *my* thoughts: clarity, exactitude, and simplicity. It entered indolently, and stopped there. Here it is, word for word and, as it happened for some reason, in the third person:

"Yet it's quite possible that Doctor Kerzhentsev

actually is mad. He thought he was pretending, yet he
actually is mad. And even right now he is mad."

Three, four times did this thought repeat itself, but I
still kept on smiling, without grasping its meaning:

"He thought he was pretending, yet he actually is
mad. And even right now he is mad."

But when I did grasp its meaning. . . . At first I
thought that Maria had uttered this phrase, because it
had sounded as if there had been a voice, and this voice
had sounded like hers. Then I thought it was Alexis'.
Yes, Alexis', the slain man's. Then I grasped that I had
thought this—and that was horror. By this time, standing for some reason in the centre of the room, I clutched
my hair and said:

"So. It's all over. That has happened which I have
been apprehensive about. I have drawn too near the
borderline, and now but one thing remains ahead of me
—madness."

When they came to arrest me I, so they say, proved to
be in horrible shape—disheveled, in torn clothing, pale
and frightful. But, oh Lord! But, doesn't living through a
night like that, yet in spite of everything not going out
of one's mind—doesn't that by itself mean that one
possesses an invulnerable brain? For all I had done was
to tear my clothes and smash a mirror. Incidentally:
permit me to give you one bit of advice. If any one of
you ever has occasion to live through what I lived
through on that night—cover over the mirrors in whatever room you will be dashing about. Cover them over,
just as you cover them over when a dead person is laid
out in the house. *Cover them over!*

It's frightful for me to write of this. I dread that which
I have to recall and tell. But it can't be put off any more
and, perhaps, through these half-hints I merely increase
the horror.

That evening—

Imagine a drunken snake—yes, yes, precisely that: a drunken snake. It hasn't lost its malevolence; its nimbleness and quickness have become intensified, if anything, while its fangs are just as keen and venomous as ever. And it's drunk, and locked in a room with a lot of people who are quivering with horror. And, in chill ferocity, it glides among them, twines about their legs, stings them right in the face, in the lips, and coils and uncoils, and plunges its fangs into its own body. And it seems as if there were not merely one snake but thousands of snakes, coiling, and stinging, and devouring themselves. Such was my thought—that same thought wherein I had placed my faith, and in the keenness and venomousness of whose fangs I had seen my salvation and my protection.

A single thought had shattered into a thousand thoughts, and each one of them was mighty, and all of them were inimical. They whirled in a wild dance, and their music was a monstrous voice, as reverberating as a trumpet, and it came streaming from some depth unknown to me. *This was runaway thought, the most fearful of serpents, inasmuch as it lurked in darkness.* Out of the head, where I had kept it fast, it had gone into the secret places of the body, into its black and unplumbed depths. And from thence it clamored, like a stranger, like a runaway slave, brazen and impudent in the consciousness of his impunity:

"You thought you were pretending, but you were really mad. You are small, you are evil, you are stupid, you are Doctor Kerzhentsev. Some Doctor Kerzhentsev or other, the mad Doctor Kerzhentsev!"

Thus did it clamor. And I knew not whence its monstrous voice issued. I do not know even what it was; I call it thought but, perhaps, it was not thought. The thoughts: they, like pigeons over a conflagration, whirled in my head—but this thing was clamoring from somewhere below, or from above, or from the flanks, where I could neither catch sight of it nor lay my hands upon it.

And the most fearful thing I experienced was the consciousness that I did not know my own self—and never had known it. As long as my *I* was to be found in my brightly illumined head, where everything moved and lived in prescribed orderliness, I understood and knew myself, I deliberated on my character and plans and was, as I thought, the lord and master. But now I perceived that I was no master but a slave, pitiful and impotent. Imagine that you had lived in a house of many rooms, that you had occupied only one of the rooms yet thought of yourself as owner of the whole house. And suddenly you learn that the other rooms are inhabited. *Yes, inhabited.* Inhabited by some enigmatic beings or other—perhaps human, perhaps of some other sort. And the house belongs to them. You want to find out who they are, but the door is locked and you can't hear either sound or voice on the other side of it. And yet you know that it is precisely there, behind that taciturn door, that your fate is being decided.

I walked up to a mirror. . . . Cover your mirrors. Cover them over!

After that I don't remember a thing, up to the time that the authorities and the police arrived. I asked the time, and was told it was nine. And for a long while I could not grasp that since my coming home only two hours had passed and, from the moment of Alexis' murder, about three.

Forgive me, gentlemen, for describing in such general and indeterminate terms this horrible state after the murder, a moment of such importance in forming your expert opinion. But that's all I remember and can convey in human speech. I cannot, for instance, convey in human speech that which I was experiencing throughout that period. Besides that, I cannot say with positive assurance that everything I have so faintly indicated had actually occurred. Perhaps it hadn't occurred, but something else had. One thing only do I remember unshakably: a thought, a voice—or it may have been something else:

"Doctor Kerzhentsev thought he was pretending he was mad, but he actually is mad."

Just now I took my pulse: 180! That's right now, at the mere recollection of it!

SEVENTH FOLIO

Last time I wrote a great deal of unnecessary and pathetic nonsense and, regrettably, you have already received and read it. I'm afraid it may give you a false conception of my personality, as well as of the actual state of my mental faculties. However, I have faith in your knowledge and in the clarity of your minds, gentlemen.

You understand that only serious considerations could compel me, Dr. Kerzhentsev, to reveal the whole truth concerning the murder of Savelov. And you will easily grasp and appreciate them when I tell you that I don't know, even now, whether I was pretending to be mad so as to kill with impunity, or whether I killed because I was mad; and, probably, I am forever deprived of the possibility of knowing this. The nightmare of that evening has vanished, but it has left a fiery mark. There are no nonsensical fears, but there is the horror of a man who has lost everything, there is the chill realization of a fall, of ruin, deception and unsolvability.

You men of science will dispute about me. Some of you will say I am mad, others will try to prove that I am

sound and will admit only certain limited factors pre-
disposing to degeneration. But, for all your learning,
you won't prove either that I am mad or that I am sound
as clearly as I shall prove the matter. My thought has
returned to me, as you will convince yourselves; neither
its potency nor keenness can be denied. Superb, energetic thought: even to one's foes should their due be
rendered.

I am mad. Would you care to hear why?

The first to condemn me is my heredity, that same
heredity over which I rejoiced so when I was pondering
my plan. The seizures I had as a child. . . . I apologize,
gentlemen. I wanted to conceal this circumstance concerning the seizures from you, and wrote that I had been
the picture of health from childhood on. This doesn't
mean that in the fact of the existence of certain trifling
seizures, which soon ended, I had seen any sort of
danger to myself. I simply did not want to clutter up
my story with unimportant details. Now this detail has
become necessary to me for a strictly logical exposition
and, as you see, I give it to you without hedging.

Very well, then. Heredity and seizures attest to my
predisposition to a psychic disorder. And it began, without my noticing it, long before I thought up the plan of
the murder. But possessed, *like all insane people,* of sub-
conscious cunning and the ability to adapt insane acts to
the norms of sane thinking, I began to deceive—not
others, however, as I thought, but myself. Drawn along
by a force alien to me, I feigned that I was going by myself. Out of the rest one can mould proofs as if out of
wax. Isn't that so?

It would not be at all hard to prove that I didn't love
Tatyana, that there was no genuine motive for the crime
but only an invented one. In the oddity of my plan, in
the coolness with which I carried it out, in the mass of

trifles, it is exceedingly easy to perceive the very same insane will. Even the very keenness and exaltation of my thought preceding the crime prove my non-normality.

> Thus, stabbed to death, I in the circus played,
> A gladiator's death portraying. . . .

Not a single trifle in my life have I left uninvestigated. I have traced my whole life. To every step of mine, to my every thought, every word have I applied the measure of madness—and it fitted every word, every thought. It turned out—and this was most amazing of all—that even before that night the thought had come to me: Am I not a madman, actually?—but somehow I managed to get rid of this thought; I would forget it.

And, having proved that I am mad, do you know what I perceived? That *I am not mad*—there you have what I perceived. Hear me out, if you please.

The gravest thing my heredity and seizures expose in me is degeneration. I am one of those who are dying out, of whom there are many, such a one as may be found, if one seek a little diligently, even among you, *Messieurs les Experts*. This furnishes a splendid key to all the rest. My moral views you can explain not by conscious reflection but by degeneration. Really, moral instincts are imbedded so deeply that only under a certain deviation from the normal type is full release from them possible. And science, still too daring in its generalizations, refers all such deviations to the domain of degeneration, even though physically a man may be built like Apollo and be as sound in health as the most abysmal idiot. However, let things stand. I have nothing against degeneration—it brings me into glorious company.

Nor am I going to stand up for my motive for the crime. I tell you with utter frankness that Tatyana Nikolaievna did insult me with her laughter, and that the offense went very deep, as it usually does with such secretive, lonely natures as mine. But let's say this isn't so. Let's even say that I actually had no love for her. But then, is it impossible to admit that through the murder of Alexis I simply wanted to try out my powers? For you do freely admit the existence of people who, at the risk of their lives, scale inaccessible mountains merely because they are inaccessible, yet do not call them mad? You wouldn't venture to call Nansen, that greatest man of the century now nearing its end, a madman? Moral life has poles of its own, and it was one of them that I was attempting to reach.

You are confused by the absence of jealousy, revenge and other preposterous motives, which you have become accustomed to consider the only genuine and sound ones. But in that case you, men of science, will be condemning Nansen, will be condemning him even as the fools and ignorami are, who consider his project, too, as madness.

My plan: It is out of the ordinary, it is original, it is daring to the verge of impudence—but then, isn't it reasonable from the point of view of my goal? And it is only my tendency to pretense, quite reasonably explained to you, that could have prompted me to this plan. My exaltation of thought: But then, is being a genius truly an aberration? My sang-froid: But then, why must a murderer inevitably tremble, turn pale and vacillate? Cowards always tremble, even when they're taking their maids around. And really, is daring insanity?

But how simple to explain my own doubts of my being sound! Like a true artist, I entered too deeply into my rôle, temporarily became one with the character I was portraying, and for a moment lost my self-accountability. Would you say that among the patent play-actors who posture day in and day out there aren't those who, when they're playing Othello, feel an actual need to kill?

Quite convincing, isn't it, *Messieurs les Savants?* Yet don't you feel a certain odd thing: When I'm proving that I am mad, it seems to you that I am sound, but when I'm proving that I am sound, you sense a madman?

Yes. That's because you don't believe me. But I, too, don't believe myself, inasmuch as *whom* within me am I to believe? Base and picayune thought, that lying varlet who is at the service of everyone? He is fit only to polish shoes, whereas I had made him my bosom friend, my god. Down from the throne, pitiful, impotent thought!

What am I then, gentlemen—a madman or no?

Mary, you dear woman, you know something I don't. Tell me, whom am I to implore for help?

I know your answer, Mary. *No, that's not it.* You're a kind and fine woman, Mary, but you know neither physics nor chemistry, you haven't been to the theatre even once, and don't even suspect that the whirligig on which you're living, taking things away, bringing them and tidying up, is revolving. Yet revolve it does, Mary—it does revolve, and we revolve along with it. You're a child, Mary, you're a stolid being, well-nigh a plant, and I envy you exceedingly, almost as much as I despise you.

No, Mary, it isn't you who'll give me an answer. And you do not know a thing; I was wrong when I said you knew something. Living in one of the dark cubbyholes in your far from cunningly builded house is somebody who is very good to you—but in my house the corresponding room is vacant. He died long ago, the one who used to live therein, and I have raised an imposing monument on his grave. *He has died, Mary; he has died, and will never rise again.*

What am I then, gentlemen—a madman or no? Forgive me for importuning you about this question with such impolite insistence, out then you are "men of science", as my father used to style you whenever he wished to flatter you; you have your books, and you are in possession of clear, exact, and infallible human thought. Of course, one half of you will keep to one opinion, the other half to the other opinion, but I will believe you, *Messieurs les Savants*—I'll believe the first group, and I'll believe the second. Do answer my question, then. . . . And, to help out your enlightened minds, I will bring forth an interesting, exceedingly interesting little fact.

On a certain quiet and peaceful evening, passed by me amid these white walls, I noted upon Mary's face, whenever my eyes fell upon it, an expression of horror, distraction, and submissiveness to something overpowering and frightful. Then she went away, while I sat down on the made-up bed and went on thinking of what I longed for. And they were strange, the things I longed for. I, Dr. Kerzhentsev, longed to howl. Not to cry out but to howl, like that other one. I longed to tear my clothing and to lacerate myself with my nails. To grab my shirt at the collar, to give it a tug (slight at first, oh, ever so slight), and then one good yank—rrrip! —to the very hem. And I, Dr. Kerzhentsev, longed to get down on all fours and creep. And it was quiet all around, and the snow was pattering against the windows, and somewhere not far off Mary was soundlessly praying. And for a long time I kept deliberating and choosing just what to do. If I howled, there'd be much noise, and then a row. If I ripped my shirt, it would be noticed on the morrow. And, quite reasonably, I chose the third course: creeping. None would hear and, should anyone see, I'd say that a button had torn loose and that I was looking for it.

And while I was choosing and deciding I felt fine, not

frightened, and even pleased, so much so that, as I remember, I dangled one of my feet. But then I happened
to think:

"But why should I creep? Am I actually mad, then?"

And I felt frightened, and immediately I wanted to do
everything together: to creep, to howl, to lacerate myself. And I became malicious.

"You want to creep, do you?" I asked.

But it kept silent. It no longer wanted to creep.

"No, but you do want to creep?" I insisted.

And it kept silent.

"Well, go ahead and creep, then!"

And, having rolled up my sleeves, I got down on all
fours and started creeping. And when I had made the
circuit of only half the room, I felt so amused by this
absurdity that I sat down comfortably, right there on the
floor, and went off into peal after peal after peal of
laughter.

With accustomed and as yet unextinguished faith that
it was possible to know something, I thought that I had
found the source of my insane desires. Evidently the
desire to creep and the other desires were the result of
auto-suggestion. The insistent thought that I was mad
called forth mad desires as well, but as soon as I had
carried them out it turned out that there actually were
no desires of any sort, and that I wasn't mad. Quite
simple reasoning, as you see, and logical. But—

*But then, I did creep, after all? I did creep? Which am
I, then—a madman justifying himself, or a sound man
driving himself out of his mind?*

Do help me then, you men of great learning! Let your
authoritative word tip the scales to this side or that, and
decide this horrible, savage question. And so, I am
waiting! . . .

In vain am I waiting. Oh, my darling little tadpoles!

Come, aren't you I? Isn't the same low-down human thought, eternally lying, perfidious, spectral, working in your bald heads as in my head? And wherein is mine inferior to any one of yours? You'll start proving that I am mad—I'll prove to you that I am sound; you'll start proving that I am sound—I'll prove to you that I am mad. You'll say that it is forbidden to steal, kill and deceive, inasmuch as doing such things constitutes immorality and crime, but I'll prove to you that it is permissible to kill and rob, and that that sort of thing is ever so moral. And you'll cogitate and speak, and I'll cogitate and speak, and all of us will be right, and none of us will be right. Where is the judge that can judge us rightly and strike upon the truth?

You have one enormous advantage, which gives the knowledge of truth to you alone: you have committed no crime, are under no indictment, and have been called in, at decent pay, to investigate the state of my psyche. And, therefore, I am mad. But had they planted you here, Prof. Drzhembitsky, and had called me in to observe you, then the madman would have been you, whereas I would have been a big shot—an expert, a liar who is distinguished from other liars only by not lying otherwise than under oath.

True enough, you have never killed, have never committed theft for the sake of theft, and whenever you hire a cabby you're bound to beat him down a few coppers, thus proving your complete psychic health. You're not mad. But then, something altogether new may happen. . . .

Suddenly, on the morrow, or right now, this very moment, a horribly silly but incautious thought will pop into your head: "Come, am I not mad?" What will you do then, M'sieu' Professor? Such a silly, nonsensical thought—for why should you ever go out of your mind?

But just try to drive it from you. You were drinking milk, and thought it was wholesome, until someone told you it was watered. And it's all over—the milk isn't wholesome any more.

You are mad. Wouldn't you like to creep a bit on all fours? Of course you wouldn't—for what man in his sound mind wants to creep? But still . . . Doesn't a sort of teeny-weeny desire—ever so teeny-weeny, ever so trifling, that makes you feel like laughing at it— come over you, a desire to slip off the chair and creep a little, oh, just a *little?* Of course it doesn't come over you —whence should it come from in the case of a man of sound mind who just now has been drinking tea and chatting with his wife. But aren't you conscious of your legs, although hitherto you weren't, and doesn't it seem to you that something odd is happening to your knees: an oppressive numbness is struggling with the desire to bend the knees and then . . . *For really, Monsieur Drzhembitsky, can anybody at all keep you back if you should want to creep about for just a teeny-weeny while?*

Nobody at all.

However, hold off from creeping. I still have need of you. My struggle isn't over yet.

EIGHTH FOLIO

One of the manifestations of the paradoxicality of my nature: I'm very fond of children, extremely little children, when they are just beginning to prattle, and bear a resemblance to all young animals: puppies, kittens, baby snakes. Even snakes can be attractive in their babyhood. And this fall, one fine sunny day, I chanced to see the following little scene. A tiny little girl in a little quilted overcoat and a sort of hood, from under which one could see nothing but pink little cheeks and the tiny nose, wanted to approach an altogether diminutive puppy upon the thinnest of little legs, with the most pointed of little muzzles, and its tail tucked timorously between its legs. And suddenly the little girl became frightened; she turned around and, like a white little ball, rolled off toward her nurse, who was standing right near by, and silently, and without tears or crying out, hid her face in the nurse's lap. As for the diminutive puppy, it kept blinking ingratiatingly and timorously keeping its tail between its legs, and the nurse's face was so kind, so simple.

"Don't be afraid," the nurse was saying, and smiled to me, and her face was so kind, so simple.

I don't know why, but this little girl often came back to my mind, even when I was free, while I was whipping the murder of Savelov into shape, as well as here. Even at that very time, at the sight of this appealing group under the serene autumnal sun, a strange feeling came over me, as though it were the solution of some puzzle, and the murder I had conceived appeared to me as a cold lie from some other, altogether strange world. And the fact that both of them, the girl and the puppy, were so small and endearing, and that they were so amusingly afraid of each other, and that the sun was shining so warmly—all this was so simple and filled with humble and profound wisdom, as though precisely here, in this group, there was contained the solution of all being. That was my feeling. And I said to myself: "This ought to be properly pondered,"—but in the end I gave it no thought.

But now I don't remember precisely what there was about this incident, and I strive excruciatingly to grasp it, but cannot. And I don't know why I told you this funny, unnecessary little incident, when there is still so much that is serious and important which I must tell you. *I must finish.*

Let us leave the dead in peace. Alexis is killed, he has long since begun to putrefy; he no longer is—the devil with him! There's something pleasant about the status of the dead.

Let us not speak of Tatyana Nikolaievna. She is unhappy, and I willingly join in the general condolences— but what does this unhappiness, what do all the unhappinesses in the world, signify by comparison with that which I, Dr. Kerzhentsev, am living through now! There are not a few wives on this earth who lose beloved husbands, and there are not a few wives who will lose theirs. Let us leave them—let them weep.

But right here, in this head—

You understand, gentlemen, how horribly all this has fallen out. Nobody in this world did I love save myself, and what I loved in myself was not this base body, something which even vulgarians love—I loved my human thought, my freedom. I knew and know nothing higher than my thought, I deified it—and truly, was it not worthy of that? Truly, did it not, like a titan, contend against all the universe and its delusions? To the summit of a high mountain did it elevate me, and I saw far below me the homunculi fossicking about, with their petty animal passions, with their eternal fear in the face of life and death, with their churches, masses and holy services.

Truly, was I not great, and free, and happy? Even as a mediaeval baron ensconced, as if an eyrie, in his inaccessible castle, looks proudly and imperiously down upon the valleys lying below—thus invincible and proud was I in my castle, behind these bones of the skull. Sovereign over myself, I was sovereign over the universe as well.

And I was betrayed. Basely, perfidiously, as women, varlets—thoughts—betray. My castle became my prison. Within my castle foes fell upon me—where, then, is salvation? In the inaccessibility of the castle, in the thickness of its walls, lay my perdition. The voice does not penetrate through those walls—and who is the mighty one that will save me? No one. Inasmuch as there is none mightier than I, while I—I am the sole foe of my *I*.

Base thought has betrayed me, who believed in it so and loved it. It has not deteriorated; it is just as clear, as keen, as springy as a rapier—but its hilt is no longer in my hand. And it is slaying me, its creator, its lord, with the same stolid indifference with which I used it to slay others.

Night is coming on, and mad, raging horror envelopes me. I was firm on the ground, and my feet stood upon it solidly—but now I am cast into the void of infinite space. It is a great and an awesome waste, for I who am living, feeling, reasoning, who am so precious and am unique—I am now so puny, infinitely insignificant and weak, and ready to go out like a candle at any instant. A sinister solitude, for I constitute but an insignificant particle of my own self, for within my own self I am surrounded and stifled by surlily silent, mysterious foes. No matter where I go, I bear them everywhere with me; solitary in the void of creation, even within my own self I have no friend. An insane solitude, when I know not who I, the solitary one, am; when with my lips, my thought, my voice *they*, the unknown ones, speak.

One cannot live thus. Yet the universe is calmly sleeping: and husbands kiss their wives, and savants deliver their lectures, and the beggar rejoices at the copper tossed to him. Mad universe, happy in your madness, horrible will be thy awakening!

What mighty one will extend the helping hand to me? No one. No one. Where will I find that which is eternal, that to which I might cling with my pitiful, impotent *I*, which is lonely unto horror? Nowhere. Nowhere. O my dear, dear little girl, why do my bloodied hands stretch out to thee now—for thou also art human and just as insignificant, and lonely, and subject to death. Whether I am pitying thee, or am desirous to have thee pity me, I nevertheless would shelter myself behind thy helpless body, as behind a shield, from the hopeless void of the ages and of space. But no, no—all this is a lie!

I would ask a great, an enormous boon of you, gentlemen, and if you feel even a little of the human within you, you will not refuse it to me. I hope we have understood one another sufficiently not to believe one another. And if I beg of you to say in court that I am of sound mind, I will believe your words least of all. For yourselves you can decide, but for me none can resolve this question:

Was I pretending to be mad in order to kill, or did I kill because I was mad?

The judges, however, will believe you, and grant me that which I want: penal servitude. I ask you not to give any false interpretation to my intentions. I do not repent having killed Savelov, I am not seeking expiation of my sins through penance, and if for the sake of proving that I am of sound mind you should deem it necessary that I kill with intent to rob, I will kill and rob someone with pleasure. But it is something else I seek in penal servitude—just what, I myself do not know as yet.

I am drawn to the people condemned to penal servitude by some dim hope or other that among them, among those who have broken your laws, the murderers, robbers, I will find sources of life unknown to me and will anew become a friend to myself. But even if this be not so, even if hope does deceive me, I nonetheless want to be with them. Oh, I know you! You are cowards and hypocrites, you love your peace above all, and you would rejoice in putting away in a madhouse every thief who sneaks a loaf of bread—you would rather acknowledge the whole universe and yourselves as mad than venture to disturb any of your beloved inventions. I know you. Crime and criminal: there is your eternal alarm, there is the awesome voice of the unexplored abyss, there is the implacable condemnation of all your rational and moral life, and no matter how tightly you plug your ears with cotton, that voice penetrates—it penetrates! And I want to go to them. I, Dr. Kerzhentsev, will take my place in the ranks of this army so fearsome to you, as an eternal reproach, as one who asks and awaits an answer.

I am not asking you in abasement, but demanding: Say that I am of sound mind. Tell a lie, if you do not believe I am. But, should you pusillanimously wash your learned hands and put me in a madhouse or set me free, I warn you as a friend: I will cause you a great deal of trouble.

For me there is no judge, no law, no thing impermissible. Everything goes. Can you picture to yourself a universe in which there is no law of gravitation, in which there is neither top nor bottom, in which all submit only to whim and chance? I, Dr. Kerzhentsev, am that new universe. Everything goes. And I, Dr. Kerzhentsev, will prove this to you. I'll pretend to be sound. I'll win to freedom. And for all the rest of my life I'll study. I'll surround myself with your books, I'll take from you all the puissance of your knowledge that you take such pride in, and will find a certain thing, the need for which has long since ripened. *This will be an ex-*

plosive. So powerful that men have never yet seen its like; more powerful than dynamite, more powerful than nitroglycerine, more powerful than the very thought of it. I am talented, persevering, and find it I shall. *And when I shall have found it I will blow up into the air your damned earth, on which there are so many gods but is no one eternal God.*

In the courtroom Dr. Kerzhentsev behaved very calmly and throughout the trial remained in the same unvarying pose which revealed nothing. He answered questions apathetically and unconcernedly, occasionally making their repetition necessary. At one point he aroused the mirth of the select public which filled the courtroom in enormous numbers. The presiding judge had addressed some order to a court attendant, and the accused, evidently having failed to catch what the judge was saying, or through absent-mindedness, arose and asked loudly:

"What? Do I have to go out?"

"Go out? Where?" the presiding judge was perplexed.

"I don't know. You said something or other."

Laughter sprang up among the spectators, and the judge explained to Kerzhentsev what had happened.

Of the psychiatric experts four were called to the stand, and their opinions were evenly divided. After the prosecuting attorney's speech the presiding judge turned to the accused, who had refused counsel:

"Prisoner at the bar—what have you to say in your defense?"

Dr. Kerzhentsev stood up. He let his dull, apparently sightless eyes pass slowly over the judges and then glanced at the spectators. And they upon whom this stolid, unseeing gaze fell experienced a strange and excruciating feeling: as though out of the empty sockets of a skull apathetic and mute death itself had looked upon them.

"Nothing," answered the accused.

And once more he let his eyes pass over the men who had come together to judge him, and repeated:

"Nothing."

ALEXANDER IVANOVICH KUPRIN

(1870–1938)

> Perhaps the greatest of living Russian novelists is Kuprin—exalted, hysterical, sentimental, Rabelaisian Kuprin.
>
> —*Stephen Graham* (1916)

EDITOR'S NOTE

ALEXANDER IVANOVICH KUPRIN[1] was born in a provincial town in Central Russia. He began his schooling at six, going on to the Second Cadet Corps in Moscow and, after graduation from a military school, entered the army. Dropping out after a few years, he was, by turns, poet, columnist, roustabout, surveyor, actor, singer, choir-singer, factory worker, medical student, hunter, and fisherman on the Black Sea. In a thinly veiled self-portrait in *Yama* he also mentions stoking on the Sea of Azov, circus-riding, tobacco-growing, typesetting and carpentering.

---

[1] The biographical sketch is from A *Treasury of Russian Literature*, copyright, 1943, by Vanguard Press, Inc., and is reprinted here through the gratefully acknowledged courtesy of the publisher.

He began writing in 1884, but did not gain recognition until 1896, with *Moloch,* a story of factory life; his first collection of stories appeared in 1903; *The Duel,* a novel exposing the bestial senselessness of army life (and clericalism), created a furore and made him famous, coming as it did in 1905, after the defeat of Russia's graft-ridden armed forces at the hands of the Japanese. His *Yama: The Pit* (1904-14-15-29) made him world-famous and, despite all censors and censorships, sold in millions of copies in practically as many languages as *Robinson Crusoe.*

Kuprin has been styled, and most aptly, the Poet of Life. Amphitheatrov called him a highly talented disciple of Chekhov and heir to Chekhov's sincerity and fine atomistic style, and compared him as an artistic storyteller with Tolstoy before the latter's conversion to religion.

Purely as a storyteller, and leaving all matters of style and literary stature out of the question, Kuprin ranks with the greatest. His range of subjects is enormous; his powers of observation and his versatility are extraordinary. Some of his picaresques, such as *The Insult,* or *Off the Street,* are sheer *tours de force.* In *The Liquid Sun* he is an innovator, with Briussov and Alexis Tolstoy, of the pseudo-scientific thriller in Russia. He writes of newspapermen, bohemians, priests, thieves, prostitutes, army men, muzhiks, Jews, Tatars, Gypsies, actors, clowns, circus people, athletes, merchants, jockeys, fishermen, hunters, sailors. And all *con amore.* There are sentimental stories and humorous stories (and parodies); animal stories and flower stories, stories for children—and for neuropaths. His popularity was fantastic: the publication of a new Kuprin story was bill-posted like a circus; his eating (and drinking) exploits were the talk of Petersburg.

When the present writer saw him in 1931, Kuprin

was editing a Russian periodical in Paris at some munificent sum in francs which amounted to $2.40 a week. He was no longer the Kuprin of the Café Vienna in Petersburg, but was still the Poet of Life.

He was at the time dreaming of returning to Russia disguised as a Tatar—he was very proud of his Tatar blood. (He had left Russia along with the staff of Yudenich, just as Bunin had left it with Denikin.) But he returned to the Soviets openly (about 1936) and was met with open arms and acclamation; special new editions of his works were brought out, and he wrote with amazement of the New Russia. He had realized his dream, and died in his native land.

The nine volumes of Kuprin available in English represent about a quarter of his work. Fortunately, only one of these translations (*Sasha*) is utterly incompetent; unfortunately, it has some of Kuprin's best stories, not translated into English elsewhere. The English translation of *Yama: The Pit* is of especial interest, containing as it does the author's final corrections and additional material especially written for it which does not appear in any other language—not even the Russian.

The Læstrygonians

ALEXANDER IVANOVICH KUPRIN

Ἑβδομάτῃ δ'ἱκόμεσθα Λάμου αἰπὺ πτολίεθρον,
Τηλέπυλον Λαιστρυγονίην...
Ἔνθ' ἐπεὶ ἐς λιμένα κλυτὸν ἦλθομεν, ὃν πέρι πέτρη
ἠλίβατος τετύχηκε διαμπερὲς ἀμφοτέρωθεν,
ἀκταὶ δὲ προβλῆτες ἐναντίαι ἀλλήλησιν
ἐν στόματι πρὔχουσιν· ἀραιὴ δ'ε"σοδός ἐστιν...
...οὐ μὲν γάρ ποτ' ἀέξετο κῦμα γ'ἐν αὐτῷ
οὔτε μέγ' οὔτ' ὀλίγον· λευκὴ δ'ἦν ἀμφὶ γαλήνη.

. . . On the seventh day we arrived at the high-
perched citadel of Lamos, even at Telypylos of
the Læstrygonians. . . .

We entered a splendid haven, around which
runs a cliff, exceedingly high and without a
break, while two lofty promontories, facing each
other, stand forth at its mouth. . . .

Never a wave, great or small, rose therein, but
all about a radiant serenity reigned.
—*The Odyssey*, x: 81, 82; 87-90; 93, 94.

I. SILENCE

TOWARD the end of October or at the beginning
of November Balaklava, that most original nook in
all of the colorful Russian Empire, begins to live a life
all its own. The days are still warm and, in an autumnal
sort of way, benign, but of nights frosts prevail, and the
ground rings reverberatingly underfoot. The last summer
guests have started migrating to Sebastopol with their
bundles, valises, hampers, trunks, scrofulous children
and arty young ladies. As a reminder of these guests

there remain only the skins of grapes (which had been strewn everywhere, on the quay and all over the narrow streets, by those who had, with an eye to their precious health, been taking the grape cure), and also that paper refuse, in the form of cigarette-butts and scraps of newspapers and letters, which is always left behind by summer residents.

And at once Balaklava becomes spacious, fresh, cozy, and businesslike in a homey way, just like an apartment after the departure of uninvited guests who had filled it with noise and smoke and quarreling. The ancient-Greek population that has been here time out of mind, and up to now has been hiding in certain crannies and small backrooms, now comes creeping out into the streets.

Fishing nets are spread out upon the quay, across the whole width of it. Against its rough cobblestones they seem delicate and fine as cobwebs, and the fishermen crawl over them on all fours, like great black spiders reweaving a torn aerial snare. Others are twisting the lines for white sturgeon and for flounder and, in the process, hasten back and forth over the cobbles with a serious and businesslike air, with the cord over their shoulders, ceaselessly winding the line into a ball before them.

Captains of fishing-smacks are sharpening sturgeon-hooks—dulled copper hooks for which, according to the time-honored tradition of the fishermen, the fish will go far more readily than for the modern English ones, of steel. On the other side of the bay they are calking, tarring, and painting dories, which have been turned with their keels up.

Near wells of stone, where the water is flowing and babbling in a never-ceasing thin stream, the gaunt, dark-faced, great-eyed, long-nosed Greek women, looking so strangely and touchingly like the depiction of the Mother of God upon ancient Byzantine icons, gossip long, for hours at a stretch, and discuss their small, domestic affairs.

And all this is consummated unhurriedly, in a homey, a neighborly way, with an age-old, habitual dexterity and seemliness, under the no longer burning sun of autumn, on the shores of a blue, cheerful bay, under the clear autumnal sky spreading calmly over the sloping, time-ruined bald mountains framing the bay.

As for the summer vacationers—out of sight, out of mind. Just as though they had never been. Two or three good rains—and the last memory of them is washed off the streets. And the whole of this senseless and bustling summer with its brassy music of evenings, and the dust raised by the ladies' skirts, and its pitiful flirtations, and disputes on political themes—all of it becomes a far-off and forgotten dream. The whole interest of the fishing settlement is now concentrated solely upon fish.

In the coffee-houses of Ivan Uryich and Ivan Adamovich, to the clicking of bone dominoes, the fishermen shape up into crews, each crew choosing its hetman, or boss. The talk is all of shares, of half-shares, of nets, of hooks, of live bait, of mackerel, sea bass, *loban, kamsa,* and surmullet, of fluke, white sturgeon and the sea-rooster. And by nine o'clock the whole town is plunged in deep slumber.

Nowhere in all Russia—and I've covered it rather thoroughly in all directions—nowhere have I heard such profound, complete, perfect stillness as in Balaklava.

You step out on the balcony—and are all swallowed up by darkness and quiet. Black sky, black water in the bay, black mountains. The water is so dense, so heavy, and so calm that the stars reflect themselves therein without refraction and without glimmer. The quiet is unbroken by a single sound of human life. Now and then, once a minute, your ears barely catch the sound of a tiny wave lapping against some rock on the shore. And this lonely, melodious sound intensifies the quiet still more, makes it still more alert. You hear the blood pounding in measured strokes in your ears. A moored boat has creaked somewhere. You feel how night and quiet have blended in a single black embrace.

I look to the left, there where the narrow neck of the bay vanishes, having narrowed between two headlands. An elongated, gently-sloping mountain lies there, crowned by old ruins. If you look closely, you can see all of it clearly, like some fabulous, gigantic monster which, pressing its breast to the bay, and with its dark muzzle thrust into the water, is drinking avidly, with one ear cocked, and cannot drink its fill.

At the spot where this monster's eye ought to be the lantern over the office of the customs patrol gleams as a minute red dot. I know that lantern; I have passed by it hundreds of times, have put my hand to it. But in the peculiar quiet and in the profound darkness of this autumnal night I see ever more clearly both the spine and the muzzle of the ancient monster, and I feel that its cunning and malevolent eye, incandescent and small, is watching me with a hidden feeling of hatred.

There flashes through my mind Homer's verse about the narrow-throated Black Sea cove in which Odysseus beheld the bloodthirsty Læstrygonians. I also think of the enterprising, lithe, good-looking Genoese who had built their colossal fortifications on the brow of this mountain. I think, likewise, of how once, on a tempestuous winter night, a whole English flotilla crashed against the breast of the old monster, together with the proud, gallant ship *Black Prince*, which is now resting at the bottom of the sea—right here, ever so near me—with its millions of gold in ingots and the lives of the hundreds that had been on it.

The old monster puckers its small, keen red eye at me as it half-dozes. That monster seems to me now an old, old, forgotten deity, which in this black stillness is dreaming its millennial dreams. And a sense of odd embarrassment overcomes me.

The lingering, lazy steps of the night watchman break the silence, and I distinguish not only every thump of his steel-shod, heavy fishing boots against the flagstones of the sidewalk, but can hear his heels scrape between one step and the next. So clear are these sounds amid the night stillness that it seems to me as if I were walking with him, even though—I know this of a certainty—he is more than two thirds of a mile away. But now he has turned aside somewhere, into a paved lane or, perhaps, has sat down on a bench: his steps are stilled. Silence. Murk.

II. MACKEREL

Autumn is coming on. The water is getting chillier. So far they are catching only small fish with dragnets, in those big vases of netting which are lowered to the bottom right off the boat. But now a rumor spreads that Ura Paratinos has rigged out his skiff and sent it off to the spot between the capes of Aia and Laspi, where he usually fishes for mackerel.

Of course, Ura Paratinos is not the German Emperor, nor a famous basso, nor a best-selling writer, nor a cantatrice specializing in Gypsy songs, but when I think of what weightiness and respect surround his name throughout the whole littoral of the Black Sea, it is with pleasure and pride that I recall his friendly attitude toward me.

Here's the sort Ura Paratinos is: he's a short, sturdy, briny and tarry Greek, of about forty. He has a bull's neck, a dark complexion, curly black hair, a mustache, a clean-shaven square chin with a brutal cleft in the middle: a chin that bespeaks a fearful will and great cruelty, thin, firm lips that go down at the corners—a sign of energy. There's not a man among the fishermen more dextrous, more cunning, stronger, and more daring than Ura Paratinos. No one yet has been able to stow away more drink than Ura—and no one has yet seen him drunk. No one can compare with Ura in derring-do— not even the famous Theodore-out-of-Oleiz himself.

In no one was that special deep-sea fisherman's indifference to the unjust blows of Fate, an indifference so highly valued by these salty folk, as strongly developed as it was in him.

When they tell Ura that the storm has torn his rigging, or that his barque, filled to the gunwales with valuable fish, was swamped by a wave and went down to the bottom, Ura will merely remark, in passing: "Eh, t'hell with it—that's where it belongs!"—and seems to have forgotten all about it right off.

Here's what the fishermen have to say about Ura:

"The mackerel may be just thinking of coming here from Kerch, but Ura already knows where to set his weir."

A weir is a trap formed of nets; it is about seventy feet long and thirty-five feet in width—the details thereof would interest hardly anybody. Suffice it to say that the fish, swimming in great schools along the shore at night, find themselves in this trap, owing to the slope at which the net is set, and can no longer get out of it save with the help of the fishermen, who lift the nets out of the water and dump the fish into their barques. The only important point is to notice in time the moment

when the water over the weir begins to seethe, like porridge in a cauldron. Let this moment slip, and the fish
will tear the net and escape.

And so, when a mysterious premonition has informed
Ura about the intentions of the fish, all of Balaklava
lives through several disquieting, excruciatingly tense
days. Boys stand guard day and night, watching the
weirs from the mountain heights; the boats are kept
in readiness. The buyers of fish have arrived from Sevastopol. The local fish cannery is preparing its storing sheds
for enormous catches.

And early one morning a rumor spreads everywhere
with the speed of lightning—through the dwellings,
through the coffee-houses, through the streets:

"They're running! They're running! There's mackerel
in Ivan Egorovich's nets, and Kota's, and Christo's, and
Spiro's, and Kapitanake's. And, of course, Ura Paratinos'!"

Every barque puts out to sea with a full crew.

All the other inhabitants, every living soul there, line
the shore: old men, women, children, and both of the
stout tavern-keepers, and Ivan Adamovich, the gray-
haired proprietor of the coffee-house, and the apothecary,
a busy man who has come on the run, puffing, for just
a moment's look-see, and Euseii Markovich, the good-
natured country doctor, and both of the local general
practitioners.

Especially important is the factor that the first boat
to come into the bay will sell its catch at the highest
price; thus self-interest, and the sporting instinct, and
ambition, and calculation, all unite to stir up those
awaiting on the shore.

At last, on the spot where the neck of the bay narrows
beyond the mountains, the first boat appears, skirting
the shore sharply.

"That's Ura."

"No, it's Kolya."

"That's Ghenali, of course."

Fishermen have a way of putting on airs all their own. When the catch is particularly rich, the thing to do is not just to come into the bay, but to come flying straight in, on oars; and so three rowers rowing as one with measured, frequent strokes, straining their backs and the muscles of their arms, bending their necks hard and then almost throwing themselves over backward, make their boat rush along the unruffled expanse of the bay with quick, short drives. Their captain, facing them, rows standing: he is steering the boat.

It's Ura Paratinos, of course!

The boat is filled to the very gunwales with white, silvery fish, so that the legs of the rowers lie stretched right out upon them and spurning them. Nonchalantly, while the boat is still on its way, while the rowers are hardly yet slackening the impetus of the boat, Ura leaps out on the wooden wharf.

The dickering with the buyers begins right then and there.

"Thirty!" says Ura and, with a full swing, smacks his palm against the long, bony hand of a tall Greek.

Which means that Ura is willing to let his fish go at thirty rubles a thousand.

"Fifteen!" yells the Greek and, in his turn, having freed his hand from under, smacks Ura's palm.

"Twenty-eight!"

"Eighteen!"

Smack, smack. . . .

"Twenty-six!"

"Twenty!"

"Twenty-five!" says Ura hoarsely: "And I've got another boatload coming along."

And at the same time another barque emerges from the neck of the bay, and a second, a third, and two more at the same time. They're trying to head one another off, inasmuch as the rates for the fish are falling, always falling. Half an hour later they are already paying 15 rubles a thousand; in an hour, 10, and toward the end 5 and even 3 rubles.

Toward evening all of Balaklava reeks unbearably of fish. Scombers are being fried or marinated in every house. The wide mouths of the ovens in the bakeries are filled with clay tiles whereon the fish are broiling in their own juice: this is called *mackerel à la shkara*—the most exquisite viand of the local gourmets. And all the coffee-houses and taverns are filled with the smoke and smell of frying fish.

As for Ura Paratinos—the most open-handed man in all Balaklava—he drops into the coffee-house where all the fishermen of Balaklava are packed in amid tobacco smoke and fishy fumes, and calls out to the proprietor in a commanding tone that drowns out the general babel:

"A cup of coffee for everyone in the house!"

There is a moment of universal silence, astonishment, and rapturous admiration.

"With sugar or without?" the enormous, swarthy Ivan Uryich, proprietor of the coffee-house, asks with deference.

Ura, for just a second, hesitates: a cup of coffee costs three kopecks, but with sugar it's five. But there's nothing small about Ura. Today the least shareholder on his smack has made not less than ten rubles.

And he lets drop, nonchalantly:

"With sugar. And let's have music!"

And the music appears: a clarinet and a tambourine. The tambourine beats and the clarinet pipes far, far into the night, playing monotonous, lugubrious Tatar songs.

New wine appears on the table—roseate wine, redolent of freshly crushed grapes; it makes one tipsy with frightful rapidity, and the next day your head aches fit to split.

And in the meantime, on the wharf, far into the night, the last smacks are being unloaded. Squatting in the boat, two or three Greeks rapidly, with accustomed deftness, seize two fish with the right hand and three with the left and toss them in a basket, keeping an exact, quick count that isn't interrupted for even a second.

And on the next day more barques come in from the sea.

All Balaklava, apparently, is overflowing with fish.

Lazy tomcats who have gorged themselves with fish, their bellies distended, are sprawled out across the sidewalks, and when you nudge them with your foot they will grudgingly open one eye a little and then go off to sleep again. And the barnyard geese, also somnolent, rock in the middle of the bay, and the tails of half-eaten fish stick out of their beaks.

The strong smell of fresh fish and the fumy smell of fish fried linger in the air for many days more. And the light, viscid fish-scales bestrew the wooden wharfs, and the cobbles of the roadway, and the hands and dresses of the happy housewives, and the blue waters of the bay, rocking lazily under the autumnal sun.

III. POACHING

It is evening. We are sitting in Ivan Uryich's coffee-house, where the light is supplied by two Lightning hanging lamps. You can cut the smoke with a knife. All the tables are taken. Some of the habitués are playing dominoes, others cards, others still sipping coffee; some are just lolling in the warmth and light, exchanging small talk and casual remarks. A protracted, lazy, pleasant evening tedium has taken over the whole coffee-house.

Little by little we embarked on a rather odd game, which all the local fishermen have found fascinating. All modesty aside, I must confess that the honor of having invented this game belongs to me. It consists of thoroughly blindfolding each one of the participants in turn, using a handkerchief which is tied with a sailor's knot; a peajacket is also put over his head, after which two others, taking the blindfolded player under his arms, lead him over every nook and corner of the coffee-house, making him turn around time after time, bringing him out of doors and back into the coffee-house, where he is again led in and out among the tables, the idea being to confuse him in every way possible. When, according to general opinion, the man being tested has been sufficiently thrown off his bearings, he is brought to a halt and asked:

"Show us where the north is!"

Each player undergoes such a test three times, and he whose sense of orientation turns out to be the worst has to treat all the others to a cup of coffee each, or to a half-bottle of new wine. It must be said that, for the most part, I was the loser. But Ura Paratinos always pointed *N* with the accuracy of a magnetic needle. What a brute!

But suddenly I turned around involuntarily and noticed that Christo Ambarzake was beckoning to me with his eyes. He was not alone; Jani, my captain and mentor, was sitting with him.

I approached. Christo called for a set of dominoes, just for the looks of the thing, and, even as we were pretending to play, said in a low voice, rattling the bone pieces:

"Take your *diphany* and come to the wharf with Jani

as quiet as you can. The bay is choked with sea-bass, as thick as black olives in a jar. The pigs have driven them in."

Diphany are very fine nets, about seven feet deep and four hundred and twenty feet long. They are in three layers; the two outside ones have wide meshes, the middle one narrow ones. Small scombers will pass through the wide mesh of the walls but become entangled in the inner meshes; on the other hand, any large and sizable sea-bass or *loban* which as much as bumped its head against the middle wall and turned back would become entangled in the wide outer meshes. I am the only one in Balaklava who owns such nets.

As quietly as possible, avoiding meeting anybody, Jani and I carry the nets to the beach. The night is so dark that we have trouble in making out Christo, who is waiting for us in a boat. We can hear some sort of snorting, *oink*'ing, heavy sighs out in the bay. These sounds are made by dolphins, or sea-pigs, as the fishermen call them. They have driven an enormous shoal, of thousands upon thousands, into the narrow cove, and are now darting all over the bay, devouring the fish on the run without any mercy.

That which we are now getting ready to do is, beyond all doubt, a crime. According to the peculiar, ancient custom it is permitted to take fish in the cove only with line and hook, or in dragnets. Only once a year, and even then for no longer than three days, is it fished by all Balaklava with communal nets. An unwritten law, this; an historical taboo of the fishermen, in its way.

But the night is so black, the sighs and *oink*'ing of the dolphins stir up the passionate curiosity of the fisherman to such an extent that, having downed an involuntary sigh of contrition, I cautiously jump into the boat and, even as Christo is soundlessly rowing, I start helping Jani to put the nets in order. He is paying out the lower edge, weighed down with big lead sinkers, while I, quickly and keeping pace with him, hand over to him the upper edge, rigged out with cork floats.

But a wondrous sight I had never seen before suddenly bewitches me. Somewhere not far off, to port, the snorting of a dolphin breaks out, and I suddenly see how, all around the boat and under the boat, a multitude of sinuous, silvery little streams darts by with frightful rapidity, looking like the tracery of expiring fireworks. These are the hundreds and thousands of fish fleeing the predatory dolphin. At this point I notice that the whole sea is ablaze with lights. Upon the crests of small, barely rippling waves blue gems shimmer. Where the oars come in contact with the water deep, gleaming furrows catch fire with a magic glow. I put my hand in the water, and when I withdraw it a handful of glowing diamonds trickles down, and exquisite, bluish, phosphorescent little flames glow on my fingers for a long time. This is one of those magic nights when the fishermen say:

"The sea is on fire!"

Another echelon of fish darts by under the boat with frightful rapidity, furrowing the water into short, silvery arrows. And now I hear the snorting of a dolphin altogether near. And, at last, there he is! He appears to one side of the boat, vanishes for a second under the keel, and immediately rushes onward. He swims far under water, and I can make out with extraordinary clearness all his powerful drive and all his mighty body, silvered by the shimmering of the infusoria, and outlined, as though in contours, by a myriad spangles, so that it resembles a glowing, speeding skeleton of glass.

Christo is rowing absolutely without a sound, and as

for Jani, he had hit the side of the boat only once with the leaden sinkers. We have already arranged the whole net, and now can begin.

We approach the opposite shore. Jani takes a firm stand at the nose of the boat, his legs far apart. A large, flat stone tied to a rope that slips gently through his hands splashes barely audibly in the water and sinks to the bottom. A big cork buoy bobs up, a hardly perceptible black mark on the surface of the bay. Now, absolutely without a sound, we describe a semicircle along the entire length of our net, and again come close to shore and throw out another buoy. We are within a closed semicircle.

If we weren't poaching, but working freely and out in the open, we would raise a shivaree—that is, by splashing our oars and making other noise we would have made all the fish within our semicircle rush into the nets spread for them, where they were bound to entangle their heads and gills in the meshes. But such work as ours demands secrecy, and therefore we merely row back and forth between the buoy twice, during which Christo churns the water with his oar noiselessly, making it boil up in light-blue, electric hillocks of splendid beauty. Then we come back to the first buoy. Jani draws up the stone that had served as an anchor just as cautiously as he had lowered it, and replaces it on the bottom of the boat without the least thud. Then, standing at the bow, his left foot forward and with his weight on it, lifting up now one arm, now the other, he hauls up the net with rhythmic motions. Bending a little over the side I see the net rushing up out of the water, and its every mesh, its least fibre, is visible to me, deep down, for all the world like an entrancing web of fire. Tiny, tremulous fires stream down Jani's fingers and fall into the water.

And by now I hear how moistly and heavily the big, live fish flop against the bottom of the boat, how plumply they quiver, their tails drumming against the boards. We gradually near the second buoy and, with the same precautions as before, draw it out of the water.

Now it is my turn to take the oars. Christo and Jani go over the whole net anew and take the sea-bass out of its meshes. Christo can't hold himself in and, with a happy, muffled chuckle throws a huge fat, silvery sea-bass at my feet over Jani's head.

"That's what I call fish!" he calls out to me in a whisper.

Jani quietly brings him up short.

When their work is done, and the dripping net is lying anew on the platform at the bow, I see that the whole bottom is carpeted with fish, alive and still quivering. However, we have to hurry. We make one more circuit, and another, and another, although prudence has been bidding us long since to go back to town. At last we approach the shore at its most forsaken spot. Jani fetches a basket and, with a savory smack, armfuls of big, meaty fish fly into it, emitting the freshest and most exciting of odors.

And ten minutes later we come back to the coffee-house, one after the other. Each one of us thinks up some pretext for his absence. But our trousers and jackets are wet, while fish-scales have caught in Jani's mustache and beard, and we still reek of sea water and fresh fish. And Christo, who can't get the upper hand of his recent piscatorial excitement, will, despite everything, throw out an occasional hint as to our venture.

"I was just walking along the quay, now—what a lot of sea-pigs have gotten into the cove! Something awful!" And he darts a sly, glowing, dark-eyed look at us.

Jani, who has carried off and hidden the haul together

with him, is sitting close to me and, in a barely audible
voice, is muttering into his cup of coffee:

"Two thousand or so, and all the biggest fellows. I
carried thirty of them over to your place."

That's my share of the booty. I nod my head, ever so
slightly. But now I feel a trifle conscience-stricken over
my recent crime. However, I catch several quick, knavish
glances among the others. Apparently we were not the
only ones who had been busy poaching that night!

IV. BELUGA

Winter is nearing. One evening there chanced to be a
snowfall, and during the night everything turned white:
the quay, the boats along shore, the house-roofs, the
trees. Only the water in the bay remains uncannily black
and plashes restlessly within this white frame of quietude.

All along the Crimean littoral—in Anap, Sudak,
Kerch, Theodosia, Yalta, Balaklava and Sebastopol—the
fishermen are getting ready for *beluga*, or white sturgeon. The fishermen are readying their boats, cleaning
their enormous boots of horse-hide that come up to the
very hips and weigh eighteen pounds each, and fixing up
their waterproof capes, daubed with yellow oil paint,
and their leather breeches; they are mending sails and
weaving seines.

That pious fisher, Theodore-out-of-Oleiz, long before
he sets out to catch white sturgeon has, in his lean-to of
branches, waxen tapers and lampads filled with the finest
olive oil glowing warmly before the image of Nicholas
the Worthy, the Thaumaturge of Myra in Lycia, and
patron saint of all those that follow the sea.[1] When he

---

[1] And not of them alone, but of all the benighted elements in
Czarist Russia. Alexis Remizov quotes two effective folk-sayings con-

puts out to sea with his crew of Tatars, the image of the
Blessed Saint of the Sea will be nailed up on the prow,
as guide and bringer of luck. All the Crimean fishermen
know about this, inasmuch as this is repeated year after
year, and also inasmuch as Theodore has the firmly
established reputation of a very daring and successful
fishing-man.

And so one morning, with the first favorable wind,
when the night is on the wane yet the darkness is still
profound, hundreds of boats cast off from the Crimean
peninsula and put out to sea under sail.

What beauty there is about such a departure! All
the five fishermen manning the boat are seated at the
prow. "God be with you! God send you luck! God be
with you!" The unfurled sail falls and, after flapping a
while hesitatingly in the air, suddenly swells out, like the
convex, pointed wing of some white bird, with its sharp
tip upward. The boat, careening all to one side, smoothly
darts out of the mouth of the cove into the open sea.
The water hisses and foams along its side and sends
spray into the boat, while on the very gunwale, at times
wetting the hem of his jacket, some young fisherman is
sitting nonchalantly and, also with a swaggering non-
chalance, lights a cigarette he has just rolled. Under the
grating at the prow there is a small store of strong vodka,
a little bread, a dozen or so smoked fish, and a cask of
fresh water.

They go out into the open sea twenty miles and more
from shore. During this long sail the captain and his
mate manage to make the fishing tackle ready. And
here's what the tackle for white sturgeon is like: just
imagine a strong rope about two thirds of a mile long,

---

cerning him: "Every countrywife has her own fairy-tale about
Nikola," and: " 'And what would happen if God were to die?'—
'Well, what do you think Saint Mikola is for?' "—*Trans.-Ed.*

lying at the bottom of the sea, about fifty fathom down; imagine, too, seven-foot leaders of stout cord tied on to it every two or three yards and, at the end of each of these leaders, a hook baited with small live fish. A flat stone at each end of the main rope serves to sink it to the bottom and anchor it there, while a buoy floating on the surface over each anchor shows its location. The buoys are round, of cork (a hundred bottle-corks wound around with a net), and each has a small red flag atop.

The mate, with a dexterity and rapidity past all understanding, baits the hooks, while the captain painstakingly coils all the tackle in a round basket, spiraling it neatly along the sides with the baited hooks within the hollow thus formed. In the darkness, almost by touch, it is not at all as easy to do this pernickety job as it may seem at first glance. When the time comes to lower the tackle into the sea, a single hook unsuccessfully baited can catch at the main rope and cruelly foul the whole business.

At dawn the fishing ground is reached. Each hetman (or captain) has his own favorite lucky spots, and he finds them out in the open sea, dozens of miles from shore, just as easily as you find a box of steel pens on your desk. All one has to do is to set the course so that the Polar Star should be just over the belfry of the Monastery of St. George, and then sail due east, without deviating from this direction, until the Phoros lighthouse is sighted. . . . Every captain has his secret guiding signs, such as lighthouses, houses, large rocks along shore, lonely pines on the mountains, or stars.

The fishing ground is decided upon. They drop the first stone of the rope, make soundings, attach the buoy and row away from it as the captain pays the tackle out of the basket with extraordinary rapidity, until they come to the end. They sink the second stone, fix the second buoy—and that's that. They row—or, if the wind permits tacking, sail—back home. Next day, or the day after, they put out to sea again and haul up the line. If God or chance so wills, the bait will have been swallowed and there will be sturgeon on the hooks—enormous, sharp-snouted fish, reaching the weight of from three hundred and fifty to over seven hundred pounds and, in rare instances, half a ton and more.

And that was just how one night Vanya Andrutsake put out of the cove in his smack. To tell the truth, no one expected any good from this venture. Old Andrutsake had died the spring before, Vanya was too young yet and, in the opinion of experienced fishermen, he should have worked as a common oarsman for a couple of years, and for a year after that as a captain's mate. Instead of that he picked out his crew from the greenest and most reckless whippersnappers, sternly raised his voice at his old mother, as if he were really the head of the house, when she began to whine; cursed out roundly, with the vilest oaths, the grumbling old fishermen who knew him, and set out to sea drunk, with a drunken crew, standing at the prow with his caracul cap devilishly shoved back on the nape of his neck, and with his hair, curly and black as a poodle's, riotously escaping from under it onto his sunburned forehead.

Out at sea a strong offshore wind was blowing, and snow was coming down hard. Some barques left the cove but came back shortly, for Greek fishermen, despite their age-old experience, are noted for their excessive prudence, not to say cowardice. "The weather ain't right," said they.

Vanya Andrutsake, however, came home about noon, with a barque filled with the biggest sturgeon, and beside that he also towed back a leviathan, a monster weighing over seven hundred pounds, which the crew had to club with mallets and oars for a long time before they killed it.

They had quite a bit of trouble with this giant. As a general thing, the fishermen say of the *beluga* that all you have to do is draw its head even with the gunwale, and after that the fish will leap into the boat of its own accord. True, in doing so it will now and then knock a careless captor over into the water with a mighty flip of its tail. But on infrequent occasions there are graver moments while catching sturgeon, threatening the fishermen with real peril. And that's just what happened to Vanya Andrutsake.

Standing at the very bow, which alternately flew up on the foaming hillocks of the broad waves or fell impetuously into smooth-sided pits of green water, Vanya had with measured motions of arms and back been hauling the tackle up out of the sea. Five sturgeon, none too large, caught at the very start, almost one after the other, were already lying motionless at the bottom of the boat, but after that the run petered out: a hundred, or a hundred and fifty hooks in a row, proved to be empty, with their live bait untouched.

The crew was rowing in silence, without taking their eyes off two points on shore that had been pointed out to them by their hetman. The mate, sitting at Vanya's feet, was getting the bait off the hooks and stowing the rope in the basket in a neat coil. Suddenly one of the fish began to flop convulsively.

"Beating its tail, waiting for its mate," remarked Paul, one of the young fishermen, repeating an old fishing omen.

And at that very second Vanya Andrutsake felt that an enormous living weight, quivering and resisting, far in the depth of the sea, was hanging on the rope that was now straining obliquely. And when, after leaning over the side, he actually saw underwater the whole of the long, silvery, agitated, shimmering body of a monster, he could not restrain himself and, turning around to the crew, whispered, with his eyes shining in rapture:

"A big fellow! Big as a bull! About fifteen hundred pounds—"

That, now, was something he should never have done, under any circumstances! God forfend, when you're out at sea, that you anticipate events or rejoice over your good fortune before you reach shore! And the old, mysterious foreboding immediately was proven true in the case of Vanya Andrutsake. He already saw, no more than a couple of feet under the surface of the water, the pointed, time-worn, bony snout and, trying to restrain the tempestuous palpitation of his heart, was all set to bring it near the side of the boat—when suddenly the mighty tail of the fish flipped out of the wave and the *beluga* started at a rush to the bottom, drawing the rope and hooks after it.

Vanya did not lose his head. "Back water!" he called out to the fishermen, ripped out a vile, intricate and very lengthy oath, and began to pay out the rope after the runaway fish. The hooks simply flashed in the air from under his hands, whipping against the water. The mate helped him, freeing the rope from the basket. The rowers bent to their oars, trying to make the boat head off the underwater progress of the fish. This was work requiring precision and frightful speed, yet not always having a happy ending. The mate fouled several hooks. "Stop paying out the rope!" he called out to Vanya, and started untangling the gear with that coolness and thoroughness which in moments of peril is to be met with only among seafaring folk. During those few seconds the rope in Vanya's hand became as taut as a musical string, while the boat leapt crazily from wave to wave, drawn along by the terrific racing of the fish and driven after it by the efforts of the rowers.

"Pay it out!" the mate called out at last. The rope started running anew through the deft hands of the captain, but suddenly the boat gave a jolt, and Vanya, with a dull moan, let out a curse: a copper hook had driven with full force into the flesh of the palm at the base of the little finger and had lodged there with its whole barb. And it was right then and there that Vanya showed himself a real briny fisherman. Looping a bight around the fingers of his injured hand, he checked the run of the rope for a second, while with the other hand he got out his knife and cut the leader. The hook was holding fast with its point, but Vanya tore it out with the flesh and threw it into the sea. And although both his hands and the rope were stained deep with his blood, and the side of the boat and the water in it turned red therefrom, he nevertheless saw the job through to the end and was himself the first to deal a stunning blow with a mallet over the noggin of the stubborn fish.

His was the first sturgeon catch that fall. His outfit sold the fish at a very high rate, so that each man's share ran to almost forty rubles. A terrific amount of new wine was drunk to celebrate the occasion, while toward evening the whole crew of *St. George the Conqueror* (as Vanya's smack was called) set out for Sevastopol in a two-horse phaeton, with musicians. There the brave Balaklava fishermen, together with some sailors from the fleet, made matchwood of the grand piano, doors, beds and chairs in one of the sporting houses and smashed all its windows to smithereens, after which they had a hearty free-for-all, and only toward daybreak did they come home, drunk and all black and blue, but with song on their lips. And no sooner did they clamber out of their carriage than they piled into a boat, hoisted sail, and put out to sea to set their line again.

From that day forth Vanya Andrutsake's reputation as a real, briny captain became firmly established.

V. THE LORD'S FISH
An Apocryphal Tale

This captivatingly beautiful, ancient legend was told me in Balaklava, by the captain of a fishing barque, one Kolya Konstande, a real briny Greek, an excellent seafarer, and a great drunkard.

He was, at that time, teaching me all the infinitely wise and strange things that go to make up the lore of the fisherman.

He showed me how to tie sailors' knots and mend torn nets, how to put live bait on *beluga* hooks, set out and clean trammel-nets, go after *kamsa,* extricate sea-bass out of the *diphany* or three-layered nets, broil the *loban* on tiles, pry the *petalide* with a knife from the rocks they had attached themselves to, and how to eat shrimps raw; how to tell what the weather would be like at night from the way the surf surged in the daytime; how to hoist and set sail; how to weigh anchor and take soundings.

He was patient in explaining to me the difference between the directions and peculiarities of the winds: the levanter, the off-levanter, the sirocco, the tramontane, the fearful bora, the propitious sea-wind and the capricious offshore one.

It is to him as well that I am indebted for the knowledge of fishing customs and superstitions to be observed while fishing: you mustn't whistle aboard the craft; you are permitted to spit over the side only; you mustn't mention the devil, although, if you're not having any luck, you may curse your faith, grave, coffin, soul, ancestors, eyes, liver, spleen, and so on. It's a good thing to leave a small fish, as though you had chanced to overlook it, in the net: that brings you luck; God save you from chucking anything edible overboard while the boat is still out at sea; but the most horrible thing of all, the most unforgivable and most malefic, is to ask a fisherman "Where are you bound for?" You can be beaten up for asking a thing like that. It was from him that I learned of the venomous little fish, the *drakos,* which looks like a small pilcher, and how to take it off the hook; of the sea-ruff's ability to inflict blisters by stinging with its fins; of the dreadful double tail of the electric skate, and of how artfully the sea-crab eats up an oyster, by first inserting a tiny pebble into its valve.

But I also heard not a few curious and mysterious stories of the sea from Kolya; I heard them during those delectable, quiet night hours in the early fall, as our yawl rocked gently, with the sea all around us, far from the unseen shores, while the two or three of us, by the yellow light of a hand-lantern, were leisurely sipping the new, roseate wine of that region, a wine redolent of freshly crushed grapes.

"There's a sea-serpent, about a mile long, living in the middle of the ocean. He is ever so lonesome. Very rarely, no more than once in ten years, he comes up from the bottom to the surface and takes a breath. He is the only one of his kind. In former days there were a lot of these sea-serpents, males and females, but they wrought such havoc among the little fish that God condemned them to die out, and now there's only one ancient, thousand-year-old male sea-serpent, living out his last years. Seamen of a former day have seen him, now here, now there, all the world over, and in all the seven seas.

"Then there's the King of all the Sea-Lobsters, living somewhere in the midst of the sea, near an uninhabited island, in his deep underwater cavern. When he strikes claw against claw, the waters above seethe in great turmoil.

"Fish talk amongst themselves—every fisherman knows that. They tell one another about the different perils and the traps set for them by man, and a green, clumsy fisherman can queer a lucky spot for a long time if he lets the fish slip out of his net."

Also did I hear from Kolya about the Flying Dutchman, about that eternal wanderer of the seas, with sails all black, and a crew entirely of dead men. However, this fearful legend is known and believed in along all the littorals of Europe.[1]

But there was one story of remote times he told me which touched me in particular by its naïve, fisherman-like simplicity.

Once toward dawn, when the sun was not yet rising but the sky was already of an orange hue and roseate mists were straying over the sea, Kolya and I were drawing up a net we had put out for scomber the evening before, at right angles to the shore. The catch was a thoroughly poor one. About a hundred scomber were tangled in the meshes of the net, five or six ruff, a few dozen golden-hued, fat little crucians and a very great deal of jellied, nacreous medusæ, looking like enormous, colorless mushroom-heads, each with a multitude of stems.

But we also came upon a very strange little fish which I had never seen up to then. It was oval and flat in form, and would have found plenty of room on a woman's palm. Its whole contour was fringed with closely set, small, transparent bristles. The head was tiny, and the eyes therein not at all those of a fish—black, rimmed

---

[1] As good a retelling of this legend as any, and decidedly one of the most curious, is Captain Marryat's The Phantom Ship.—Trans.-Ed.

with gold, and unusually lively; the body was of an even, aureate hue. But the most striking thing of all about this little fish were two blotches, one on each side, in the centre, about the size of a silver ten-kopeck piece but irregular in shape and of an exceedingly vivid, sky-blue color, such as no painter has at his disposal.

"Take a look at that," said Kolya. "That's the Lord's Fish. It's seldom you get one."

We placed it first in the boat bailer and then, on getting home, I poured some sea water into a big enameled basin and released the Lord's Fish therein. It began swimming around and around rapidly, always in the same direction. If one touched it, it would emit a barely audible, short, snoring sound, and quicken its ceaseless swimming. Its black eyes were rolling, while from the twinkling, countless little bristles the water quivered and ran swiftly in tiny streams.

I wanted to keep it alive, in order to bring it to the aquarium of the Biological Station in Sevastopol, but Kolya said, with a discouraging wave of his hand:

"It doesn't pay to bother, even. It won't live that long, anyway. That's the sort of fish it is. If you pull it out of the sea for even a second it's already done for. It's the Lord's Fish."

Toward evening it died. And at night, as we sat in the yawl, far from shore, I thought of it, and asked:

"But why is it the Lord's Fish, Kolya?"

"Well, I'll tell you why," Kolya answered with profound conviction. "The old men amongst us Greeks tell the story this way. When Jesus Christ, our Lord, rose up from the dead on the third day after his burial, why, no one wanted to believe Him. Many miracles wrought by Him had they seen while He had been alive, but this miracle they could not bring themselves to believe, and were afraid.

"His disciples denied Him, His apostles denied Him, the women who had been bringing Him myrrh denied Him. Thereupon He came to His Mother. And, just then, she happened to be standing by the hearth and frying fish in a pan, getting dinner ready for herself and those near to her. So the Lord says to her:

" 'Hail! Behold me, thy Son, risen from the dead, even as it was told in the Scriptures. Peace be unto thee!'

"But she fell to trembling, and cried out in fright:

" 'If Thou be truly my Son Jesus, work a miracle, that I may see and believe.'

"Thereupon the Lord smiled, for that she had no faith in Him, and said:

" 'Behold, I will take this fish lying on the fire, and it will come to life anew. Wilt thou have faith in me then?'

"And hardly had He put His thumb and forefinger to the fish and lifted it up in the air, than it began to quiver and came to life anew.

"Thereupon the Lord's Mother had faith in the miracle, and joyously bowed down before her Son who had risen from the dead.

"And as for that fish, ever since then the two marks, blue as the heavens, have remained upon it. They be the traces of the Lord's thumb and forefinger."

That was how the simple, far from wise fisherman told the naïve, olden tale. And a few days later I learned that the Lord's Fish bears still another appellation: the Fish of Zeus. Who can tell to what remote ages this bit of apocrypha goes back?

VI. THE BORA

Oh, the dear, simple men, manly hearts, naïve, primitive souls, stalwart bodies swept by the salt sea wind, calloused hands, keen eyes that have so many times looked into the face of death, into its very pupils! . . .

The bora is blowing for the third day. The bora[1]—otherwise the nor'-easter—is a raging, mysterious wind, which is born somewhere among the bald, denuded mountains near Novorossisk, comes crashing down upon its round cove, and spreads fearful turmoil all over the Black Sea. So great is the force of it that it blows loaded freight cars off their rails and overturns them, knocks down telegraph poles, demolishes brick walls of very recent construction, and throws solitary pedestrians to the ground. About the middle of the last century several men-o'-war, overtaken by a nor'-easter, tried to weather it out at the cove of Novorossisk: with a full head of steam, at an accelerated speed, they bucked the wind—and could not make an inch of headway; then, in the teeth of the wind, they let down double anchors—and nonetheless were torn from their anchors, dragged within the cove, and cast up, like so many pine-chips, on the rocks along the shore.

This wind is terrifying in its unexpectedness—it is impossible to foresee it; it is the most capricious of winds upon the most capricious of seas.

Old fishermen say that the only salvation from it is "to bolt into the open sea". And there are instances of the bora having carried off some square-rigged barque, or a Turkish felucca (painted sky-blue and adorned with silver stars) across all of the Black Sea, to the coast of Anatolia, more than two hundred and thirty miles away.

The bora is blowing for the third day. There's a new moon out. The new moon, as always, is coming to birth amid great throes and much travail. Experienced fishermen are not only not even thinking of putting out to sea, but have actually hauled their boats ashore, to the farthest and safest point.

---

[1] Italian; from the Greek, *Boreas.*—*Trans.-Ed.*

That reckless Theodore-out-of-Oleiz alone, who for many days before this has kept a taper glowing warmly before the image of Nicholas the Thaumaturge, has decided to put out, to haul up his white-sturgeon tackle.

Three times had he and his crew (consisting of Tatars exclusively) set out from shore, and three times did he have to row back, resorting to the utmost exertions, curses and blasphemies, yet doing no better than one-tenth of a knot an hour. In a rage that can be understood only by a seafaring man he had repeatedly torn down the image of Nicholas, Miracle-Worker of Myra in Lycia, which image he himself had fastened at the prow, throwing it to the bottom of the boat, trampling upon it and swearing abominably, while at the same time his men were bailing out with their caps and cupped hands the water that was lashing over the side.

During these days the veteran, cunning Læstrygones of Balaklava sat about in the coffee-houses, rolling their own, drinking strong tonka-bean coffee with thick grounds, playing dominoes, complaining because the weather wouldn't let up and, amid the cosy warmth, by the light of hanging lamps, recalled ancient legendary happenings, tales of which had come down to them from their sires and grandsires, of how in such and such a year the breakers had reached hundreds and hundreds of feet upward, while their spindrift had flown to the very foot of the half-ruined Genoese fortress.

One skiff, out of Phoros, manned by certain Russopeti, light flaxen-fair Ivans who had come from somewhere or other (it may have been from the Lake of Ilmen, or it may have been from the Volga) to seek their luck on the Black Sea, had been lost without any tidings. No one in the coffee-houses regretted them or bothered about them. They clicked their tongues, gave a short laugh, and decided, disdainfully and simply: *"Tsk, tsk,*

tsk! Of course they're fools—can anybody do anything in such weather? Oh, well—you know what the Russians are!" In the pre-dawn hour of a dark, roaring night they had all gone down to the bottom like so many stones, in their boots of horsehide that came up to their waists, in leathern jackets and yellow-painted waterproof capes.

It was an altogether different matter, though, when Vanya Andrutsake put out to sea just before the bora had started blowing, having spat on all forewarnings and persuasions of the old-timers. Why had he done it? God knows! In all probability out of little-boy bravado, out of riotous, youthful self-conceit, and because he was a trifle on the tipsy side. And, perhaps, because some red-lipped, dark-eyed Greek girl had been admiring him at the moment?

He hoisted sail—the wind even then was very strong—and that's the last they saw of him! With the swiftness of a purse-winning racer the craft flew out of the cove, its white sail flitting for five minutes or so against the dark-blue of the sea, and right after that you couldn't make out what that wispy whiteness in the distance was—whether a sail, or whitecaps leaping from wave to wave.

And it was only three days later that he got home.

Three days without sleep, without food and drink, day and night, and again day and night, and another day around the clock, in a tiny cockleshell in the midst of an insanely raging sea—and all around no shore, nor sail, nor beaconlight, nor steamer smoke. But no sooner did Vanya Andrutsake get back home, than he seemed to have forgotten all this, as though nothing at all had befallen him, just as though he'd merely taken a trip on the mail-wagon to Sebastopol and bought a pack of cigarettes there.

True, there were a few details, which, with difficulty,

I managed to squeeze out of Vanya's memory. For instance, something like a fit of hysterics had overcome Ura Lipiade when the second night was on the wane, and he had suddenly begun to weep and laugh loudly for no reason on earth, and was already as good as over the side if Vanya Andrutsake hadn't fetched him one with the steering oar over the head, and that none too soon. There was also one moment when the crew, frightened by the furious racing of the boat, had wanted to lower the sail, and it must have cost Vanya much effort to get a tight grip on the will of these five men and, with death breathing into their very faces, force them to submit to him. I also learned a thing or two about how the blood spurted from under the nails of the rowers because of their inordinate toil. But all this was told me in snatches, unwillingly, in passing. Yes, during these three days and nights of tense, convulsive wrestling with death much had been said and done which the crew of *St. George the Conqueror* would, of course, tell to no one, to the very end of their days, for no consideration on earth!

During these three days not a man in Balaklava had closed his eyes, save for the stout Petalide, proprietor of the Hotel Paris. And all wandered uneasily about the quay, or scaled the crags, or scrambled up to the Genoese fortress which towers over the city with its two ancient indented towers—absolutely all, old men and young, women and children. There was a flurry of telegrams to all the ends of the earth: to the Commandant of all the Black Sea ports, to the local prelate, to all the lighthouses, to the life-saving stations, to the Minister of Maritime Affairs, to the Minister of Communications, to Yalta, to Sebastopol, to Constantinople and Odessa, to the Patriarch of Greece, to the governor, and even, for some inexplicable reason, to the Russian consul at

Damascus, who chanced to be an acquaintance of a certain Greek aristocrat at Balaklava, trading in flour and cement.

The ancient bond, ages and ages old, that binds man to man stirred awake, that comradeship of the blood so little noticeable amid the petty reckonings and the rubbish of everyday life; the millennial voices of great-great-grandsires (who, long before the times of Odysseus, had stood together against the bora on just such days and nights) began to speak again in the souls of men.

No one slept. At night they built an enormous bonfire on the top of a mountain, and all walked along the shore with lights, just as if it were Easter. Now, however, no one laughed, nor sang, and all the coffee-houses became deserted.

Ah, what a rapturous moment it was when one morning, about eight, Ura Paratinos, who had taken his stand at the top of the crag over the White Rocks, narrowed his eyes, bent forward, grappled the distance with his keen eyes, and suddenly sang out:

"There they are! They're coming!"

No one save Ura Paratinos could have made out that boat amid this black-blue stretch of the sea, heaving ponderously and slowly but still malevolently, quieting down after its recent wrath. But five minutes passed, then ten, and by now any urchin could see for himself that it was the *St. George the Conqueror* coming along under sail, tacking toward the cove. Great was the joy that now united all these men and women into one body and into one soul!

Before coming into the cove they lowered sail and came into the cove rowing, came into it as an arrow flying, gaily straining their last strength; they came into the cove as the fishermen come into it after an excellent haul of sturgeon. Mothers, wives, sweethearts, sisters, little brothers were weeping all around them for happiness. Do you think that even one fisherman from the crew of the *St. George the Conqueror* turned soft, burst into tears, went to kiss someone or to sob on someone's bosom? Not in the least! All the six of them, still sopping wet, grown hoarse and windburned, piled into Yuryich's coffee-house, called for wine, bawled songs at the top of their voices, ordered music and danced like madmen, leaving pools of sea-water on the floor. And only late at night did their comrades carry them, drunk and tuckered out, to their homes, and every man-jack of them slept for twenty hours without a break. And when they did awake, they regarded their sea-voyage no more seriously than, let us say, the short ride in the mail-wagon to Sebastopol, for half an hour or so, where they had a fling—oh, ever so mild and brief—after which they had come home. . . .

VIII. MAD WINE

The end of September is, in Balaklava, utterly enchanting. The water in the bay has become chillier; the days remain clear, calm, with a wondrous freshness and the strong smell of the sea of mornings, with a sky blue and cloudless, receding to God alone knows what height, with gold and purple upon the trees, with nights that are silent and black. The summer visitors who had come here for their health—noisy, ailing, egotistic, idle, and trivial—have scattered, each his or her own way, going north, to their homes. The grape-cure season is over.

And it is about this very time that the mad wine arrives.

Almost every Greek, a glorious captain and Læstrygone, owns a bit of a vineyard, even though it may be of the tiniest—there, above, up in the mountains, in the environs of the Italian cemetery, where the graves of several hundred unknown brave outlanders are crowned by an unassuming white monument. The vineyards are neglected, grown wild, over-luxuriant; the grapes have degenerated, become smaller. Five or six vineyard owners, it is true, produce and keep up the more expensive varieties, such as the *chaous, shashlia* and Napoleon, selling them as medicinal grapes to those who had come for their health (however, during the summer and fall seasons in the Crimea everything is medicinal: there are medicinal grapes, medicinal chicks, medicinal long veils on the native women, medicinal slippers—even the canes of boxthorn and the sea-shells peddled by wrinkled, crafty Tatars and pompous, bronzed, grimy Persians). The other proprietors visit their vineyards— or, as they call them here, their *gardens*—only twice a year: to gather the grapes at the beginning of autumn and, toward its end, to get cuttings from the vines, which they do in a most barbarous manner.

Times have changed now: morals are fallen low and folks have become poorer; the fish have gone off somewhere to Trebizond; nature has petered out. Now the descendants of the doughty Læstrygonians, those legendary freebooters and fishermen, row little children and their nurses about the bay for a five-kopeck copper and live by renting out their little houses to the first comer. The grapes used to grow *that* big, each grape the size of a baby's fist, and the clusters used to weigh five and thirty pounds each; but nowadays they're not even worth looking at: the grapes are just the least trifle bigger than currants, and their former potency isn't in 'em. Thus do the gaffers discourse among themselves as during the calm autumn dusk they sit near their whitewashed enclosures on stone benches which, through the centuries, had become rooted in the ground.

But the custom of old has still been observed down to our days. Everyone who is able to, either by himself or in partnership, crushes and presses the grapes by those primitive methods probably resorted to by our forefather Noah or by wily-minded Ulysses, who had contrived to make such a stalwart oaf as Polyphemus drunk. They press it right with their feet, and when the presser steps out of the vat his bare legs all the way up to the knees seem daubed and spattered with fresh blood. And the pressing is done under the open sky, in the mountains, in the midst of an ancient vineyard planted about with almond trees and tricentenarian walnuts.

I watch this spectacle often and an unusual, agitating fancy comes over my soul. There, on those very mountains, three, four—and, perhaps, even five—thousand years ago, under the very same azure sky and under the very same endearing, beautiful sun, the magnificent festival of Bacchus was being celebrated by all the people, and over there, where one now hears the wretched, snuffling tenor of some weak-chested vacationer, grating dismally:

> And bring chry-san-the-mmmums you may
> Unto my grave, e'en thrice a day—

there used to resound the madly-joyous, divinely-inebriated outcries:

> *Evoe! Evan! Evoe!*

Why, only a little over ten miles from Balaklava, there rise awesomely out of the sea the reddish-brown, jagged remains of the Cape of Phiolent, on which on a time there stood the temple of a goddess who demanded human sacrifices for herself. Ah, what a strange, deep, and delectable sway over our imaginations have these desolated, despoiled sites where on a time there lived so joyously and blithely people who were gay, joyous, free, and wise as the beasts!

However, the new wine is not merely given no chance to age—it isn't even allowed simply to settle.

And besides, there's so little of it produced that it isn't worth while going to any real bother about it. It hasn't been standing even a month in its cask when it is already being poured into bottles and carried off to town. It is still in ferment, it has still had no time *to come to its senses,* as the vintners so characteristically put it; it is turbid and rather muddy against the light, with a faintly roseate or apple-yellow tinge; but, just the same, it is easy and pleasant to drink. It is redolent of freshly crushed grapes, and sets the teeth on edge, leaving a tart, rather sourish taste.

But then, it is remarkable for its after effects. Drunk in any great amount the new wine refuses to come to its senses even in one's stomach and there goes on with the mysterious process of fermentation which it had begun as far back as its days in the cask. It compels men to dance, to leap, to chatter without cease, to roll about on the ground, to try their strength, to lift up enormous weights, to kiss, weep, go off into gales of laughter, tell monstrously tall tales. It has also another astonishing quality, which also appertains to *hanghin,* or Chinese whisky: if, on the morning after the night before, one drinks a glass of plain cold water, the new wine will start to ferment all over again, to bluster and play in the stomach and blood, while its harebrained effect is renewed with all its former force. That's the very reason they call this new wine the "mad wine."

The Balaklavians are a cunning folk, and besides they've been taught by the experience of thousands of years: therefore, on the morning after the night before, they skip the cold water and drink more of the same mad wine. And all the autochthonous male population of Balaklava goes about for two weeks at a stretch tipsy, unbridled, traipsing around, but benign and full of song. Who will condemn them, these fine fishermen, because of that? Behind them is the tedious summer with squabbling, supercilious, exacting vacationers; ahead of them lies harsh winter, raging nor'-easters, sturgeon fishing twenty, thirty miles from shore, now amid impenetrable fog, now in a storm, with death hanging over your head every second, and not a soul aboard the craft knowing where all of them are being borne by head-sea, current and wind!

There's but little visiting around—which has always been the case in conservative Balaklava. They meet one another in the coffee-houses, in eating-places and in the open air, on the outskirts of the town, where the luxuriant Baidar valley has its flat and richly colored start. Every man is happy to boast of his new wine, and even if it should run short, does it take long to send some shiftless brat home after a new supply? The wife will grumble a bit but, just the same, she'll send along two or three bottles, each one holding almost three quarts, of turbidly yellow or turbidly roseate, half-clear wine.

When the supply runs out, they set off wherever their legs lead them; to the nearest croft, to the country, to a lemonade stand three or six miles out on the Balaklava highway. They'll sit down in a circle amid the prickly stubble of maize; the proprietor will bring out the wine, right in a wide-topped enameled pail, with a loose wooden piece on the metal half-loop handle, and that pail is brimming over. They drink out of cups, with deferential decorum, wishing one another all sorts of good things—and it is a *must* for all to drink at the same time. One will lift up his cup and say: *"Stani-yasso!"* and all the others answer: *"Si-iva!"*

Then they'll launch into song. No one knows any Greek songs: it may be that they have been long since forgotten, it may be that the unassuming, taciturn cove of Balaklava had never disposed its folk to song. They sing the songs of the fishermen in the south of Russia; they sing in unison, with frightful, stony, wooden, metallic voices, each one trying to drown out the next. Their faces turn red, their mouths are wide open, the veins have swelled on their sweating brows.

> All the sea is boilin', foamin',
> There's a change of weather comin'—
>   Men, it's comin'!
> Head-sea upon head-sea follows,
> My old tub she floats but wallows—
>   Men, she wallows!
> On the bridge the old man stands,
> Tells the bosun: "Pipe all hands!"
>   Men, pipe all hands!

They think up ever new pretexts for a new drinking bout. Some one of them has recently bought himself a pair of those appalling fishermen's boots. How can one possibly do without asperging and baptizing such an acquisition? And again the blue-enameled pail appears on the scene, and again they sing their songs, that sound like the roaring of a winter hurricane out in the open sea.

And suddenly the possessor of those boots, his sentimentality all stirred up, calls out with tears in his voice:

"Lookit, pals! What do I need them boots for? The winter's still far off—plenty of time to get another pair. Let's drink 'em up!"

And after that they'll roll a pill of beeswax and tie it at the end of a tread and lower it into the opening (that looks as round as if it were turned on a lathe) of a tarantula nest, teasing the spider until it flies into a rage and sinks its paws into the wax, thus hopelessly entangling them. Then, with a quick and deft jerk, they draw the monster to the top, out on the grass. They will catch two tarantulas thus and pit them against each other, at the bottom of some broken bottle or other. There is nothing more terrifying and thrilling than the spectacle of the fight which begins between these venomous, many-legged, enormous spiders. The torn-off paws fly right and left; a thick, white liquid oozes out in drops from the pierced, soft, oviform trunks. Both spiders are standing up on their hind legs, their forelegs clasping each other, and each is trying to sink its mandibles into the eye or head of its adversary. And this fight is particularly weird because it inevitably ends with one foe putting the other to death and immediately sucking him dry, leaving only a pitiful, wrinkled casing on the ground.

As for the descendants of the blood-thirsty Læstrygonians, they form a star on the ground, lying on their bellies, their legs forming the periphery, their heads directed to the centre, their chins propped up on their palms, and are looking on in silence—that is, unless they are placing bets. My God! How many years does this horrifying diversion number—this most cruel of all of man's spectacles!

And in the evening we are again in a coffee-house. Rowing about the bay are boats with Tatar musicians: usually a tambourine and a clarinet. Wheezingly, monotonously, with infinite despondence, the far from intricate yet indescribable Asiatic motif keeps sniveling on and on. The tambourine beats and quavers as if it were in a frenzy. The boats cannot be seen in the darkness. These are the gaffers having their fling, true to the ways of yore. But then, it is light in our coffee-house because of the Lightning lamps, and two musicians—an

Italian with an accordeon and an Italian woman with a mandolin—are playing and singing in sweet though hoarse voices:

O! Nino, Nino, Marianino!

I sit there, mellowed by the fumes of tobacco smoke, by the singing, by the new wine I am regaled with on all sides. My head is hot and, so it seems, is puffing up and humming. But in my heart there is only gentle emotion. With pleasant tears in my eyes I keep repeating in my mind those words which one so often notices tattooed on the chests or even the hands of fishermen:

God keep the Mariner! [1]

---

[1] Apparently the equivalent of the cantrip of them that go down to the sea in American and British ships: HOLD FAST, tattooed on the backs of the fingers.—*Trans.-Ed.*

Post-Revolutionary

MAXIM GORKI [1]

About Tolstoy [2]

> More than once he [Chekhov] com-
> plained that there was no Eckermann
> close to Tolstoy, a man who would
> have painstakingly written down the
> keen, unexpected and frequently con-
> tradictory thoughts of the old sage.

II

HE HAS amazing hands—ugly, knotty with distended veins, yet for all that full of an especial ex-
pressiveness and creative power. Probably Leonardo da
Vinci had hands like that. With hands like that one can
do all things. At times, as he talks, he fidgets with his
fingers, gradually clenching them into a fist; then he will
suddenly open them and at the same time utter some
fine, full-weighted word. He resembles a god—but not
Sabaoth or an Olympian, but a kind of Russian god
who "sits on a throne of maplewood under a golden
linden" and, although he's not over-majestic, is more
cunning, perhaps, than all other gods.

---

[1] For Editor's Note on Gorki, see page 320.
[2] These selections, as well as those dealing with Chekhov, are from
Leo Tolstoy—A. P. Chekhov—V. G. Korolenko, published in 1928.

IV

Goldenweiser was playing Chopin, which called forth the following thoughts from Leo Nikolaievich:

"Some petty German kinglet said: 'Where one would have slaves, as much music as possible should be composed.' That's a true thought, a true observation: music dulls the mind. The Catholics understand this best of all—our priests, of course, would never reconcile themselves to Mendelssohn in church. One priest in Tula assured me that even Christ was not a Jew, although He was the son of a Jewish God and had a Jewess for a mother. He admitted all that. But nevertheless said: 'That could never be.' I asked him: 'But how then?' He shrugged his shoulders and said: 'That is a mystery to me.'

VI

"The minority stands in need of God because it has everything else, while the majority needs Him because it has nothing."

I would have put it differently: The majority believes in God through pusillanimity, and only a few do so through fullness of soul. . . .

VII

He advised me to read the Buddhistic catechism through. Of Buddhism and Christ he always speaks sentimentally; of Christ especially wretchedly—there is neither enthusiasm nor pathos in his words and not a single spark of that fire which comes from the heart. I think he considers Christ naïve, deserving of com-

miseration, and although—now and then—he eyes Him
admiringly, he nevertheless hardly loves Him. And
he seems, somehow, apprehensive: Were Christ ever to
come to a Russian village, the wenches would make un-
merciful fun of Him.

X

"Friedrich of Prussia put it very well: 'Every man
must save himself *à sa façon.*' It was he, too, who said:
'Reason as you like, but obey.' But, as he lay a-dying, he
confessed: 'I have wearied of ruling slaves.' The so-
called Great Men are always frightfully contradictory.
This is forgiven them along with every other folly.
Although contradictoriness isn't folly—a fool is stubborn, yet cannot be contradictory. Yes, Friedrich was a
strange man; he has earned the fame of being the best
sovereign among the Germans. Yet he could not stand
them—he wasn't fond even of Goethe and Wieland."

XIII

Had Tolstoy been a fish he would, of course, have
swum only in the ocean, never swimming into the mediterranean seas and, above all, not into the fresh waters
of the earth's rivers. Some sort of dace dart about him
here, making themselves at home; that which he utters
is neither of interest or need to them, and his silence
does not frighten them, touches them not. And when it
comes to being silent, he does it impressively, ably, like
a veritable anchorite withdrawn from this world. Even
though he does speak a great deal on his obligatory
themes, one senses that his silence is still greater. There
are some things one cannot say to anybody. He has,
probably, thoughts of which he is afraid.

XVII

In an exercise-book that he used as a diary, which he gave me to read, I was struck by an odd aphorism: "God is my desire."

Today, having returned the exercise-book, I asked him what that aphorism was.

"An unfinished thought," said he, regarding the page with puckered-up eyes. "I must have wanted to say: 'God is my desire to know Him. . . .' No, that's not it—" he began to laugh and, after rolling the exercise-book into a tube, thrust it into the roomy pocket of his blouse. With God he is on very indeterminate terms, but at times they remind me of those of "two bears in one lair."

XXI

He was sitting on a stone bench under the cypresses, a dried-up, small fellow, gray-hued, yet nonetheless looking like Sabaoth, Who had wearied somewhat and was now diverting Himself, by trying to chime in with the whistling of a chaffinch. The bird was singing in a thicket of dark greenery; he was looking in that direction, with his little eyes puckered up, and, having pursed his lips in a childlike way, was whistling far from skillfully.

"Look how lovestruck that dicky bird is! Trying to make love. What bird is that?"

I told him about the chaffinch, and of the emotion of jealousy so characteristic of this bird.

"All his life he can sing but the one song—yet he's jealous. Man has hundreds of songs in his soul, yet he is condemned for his jealousy—is there any justice in that?" he asked thoughtfully, and as if to himself. "There are certain moments when a man tells a woman more than she should know about him. He has told her and forgotten about it, but she remembers. Perhaps jealousy comes from fear of being humiliated and made to look ridiculous? Not that female is dangerous who has hold of your——, but the one that has hold of your soul."

When I told him that one could sense about this a contradiction to *The Kreutzer Sonata*, he let the glow of a smile spread all over his beard and answered:

"I am no chaffinch."

In the evening, while strolling, he uttered unexpectedly:

"Man lives through earthquakes, epidemics, the horrors of diseases and through all sorts of torments of the soul, but throughout all times the most excruciating tragedy for him has been, is, and shall be the tragedy of the bedroom."

As he said this he was smiling triumphantly—at times such a broad, calm smile will come to him, the smile of a man who has overcome something extremely difficult, or who has been long gnawn at by a keen pain—and suddenly it no longer is. Every thought bites into him like a tick; he either plucks it off at once, or else lets it drink its fill of blood and then, having thus swollen full, it imperceptibly falls off by itself.

Most frequently he spoke about the language of Dostoevsky:

"He wrote hideously and even with deliberate ugliness—I'm certain it was deliberate, out of coquetry. He was showing off—in *The Idiot* he wrote: 'In brazen importunity for and *affichevanië* of acquaintance.' I think he deliberately distorted the verb *afficherovat'* [to post bills, to flaunt] because it's of foreign origin, Western. But one can find other and unpardonable blunders of his: the Idiot says: 'The ass is a kindly and useful man,' yet nobody laughs, although these words are inevitably bound to call forth laughter or some remark or other. He says this before his three sisters, and they were fond of making fun of him. Especially Aglaia. This book is considered bad, but the worst thing about it is that Prince Myshkin is an epileptic. Were his health normal, his wholehearted naïveté, his purity would touch us very much. But Dostoevsky hadn't courage enough to depict him as a healthy man. And, besides, he had no love for healthy people. He felt certain that since he was sick himself, the whole universe was sick." [1]

XXII

Most of all he speaks of God, of the muzhik, and of woman. Of literature he speaks rarely and meagrely, as though literature were no business of his. His attitude toward woman is, as I see it, irreconcilably inimical, and he loves to punish her—if she isn't a Kitty or a Natasha Rostova—that is, a being insufficiently limited. Is this the inimicality of a man who has not contrived to drain as much happiness as he could have, or the inimicality of the spirit against the "debasing impulses of the flesh"? But inimicality it is, and a chill inimicality, as in *Anna Karenina*. . . .

XXIV

"With her body woman is more sincere than man, but her thoughts are false. When she lies, however, she doesn't believe herself, whereas Rousseau lied—and believed."

---

[1] The fact that Tolstoy is affectionately called the Magnificent Sloven by every Russian does not in the least militate against these criticisms of one master craftsman by another.—*Trans.-Ed.*

XXV

"Dostoevsky wrote of one of his insane characters that he lives wreaking vengeance upon himself and others because he had served that in which he did not believe. He wrote that about himself—that is, he might have said the same thing about himself."

XXVII

He loves to put difficult and treacherous questions:
"What do you think of yourself?"—"Do you love your wife?"—"In your opinion, is my son Leo talented?"—"Do you like Sophia Andreievna [his wife]?"

You can't lie when you're standing before him.

Once he asked me:

"Do you love me, Alexis Maximovich?"

This is the mischievousness of a *bogatyr*, a titan-knight: Vaska Buslaev, the giant mad wag of Novgorod, used to play games like that in his youth. He is *trying things out*, always testing something, as if getting set for a fight. That is interesting—however, it is not at all after my heart. He is a devil, while I am still an infant, and he ought not to start up with me.

XXXII

At times he is smug and intolerant, like some sectarian theologian from beyond the Volga, and this is horrible in him, so sonorous a bell in this world. Yesterday he said to me:

"I'm more of a muzhik than you and, when it comes to feeling like a muzhik, I do that better."

Oh, Lord! He ought not to boast of this—he ought not!

XXXVI

"I don't like men in drink, but I know people who, having taken a drop or two, become interesting, acquire wit, beauty of thought, dexterity in words, and a wealth of them—all of which things aren't theirs when they're sober. At such times I'm ready to bless wine."

XXXVII

Near the boundary of the estate of the Grand Duke A. M. Romanov, three Romanovs were standing on the road close to one another and talking: the master of Ai-Todor, another by the name of Georgii, and some other —I think it was Peter Nikolaievich, from Diulber—all of them soldierly, well-grown individuals. The road was blocked by a one-horse droshky; a saddle-horse was also standing across it; there was no room for Leo Niko-laievich, who was on horseback, to pass. He fixed the Romanovs with a stern, demanding gaze. But, even before this, they had turned away from him. The saddle-horse shifted in its place and then went off a little to one side, letting Tolstoy's horse pass by.

After riding a couple of minutes in silence he said:

"They recognized me, the fools."

And, a minute later:

"The horse understood that one ought to make way for Tolstoy."

XXXIX

"To know—what does that mean? There, I know that I am Tolstoy, a writer; I have a wife, children, gray hair, an ugly face, a beard—all those things are written down in passports. But about the soul they don't write in

passports; about the soul I know one thing: the soul desires nearness to God. And what is God? That, a particle
of which my soul is. And that's all there is to it. For him
who has learned to cogitate it is hard to have faith, yet
one can live in God only through faith. Tertullian said:
'Thought is an evil.' "

XL

Despite the sameness of his preaching this fabulous
man is illimitably diversified.

Today, in the park, conversing with the mullah of
Gaspri, he behaved like a trusting, simple little muzhik
soul, for whom the time had come to think of the end of
his days. Such a little man, and seeming somehow purposely still more shrunk into himself, he appeared alongside of the sturdy, stolid Tatar still more of a little ancient whose soul had for the first time begun to ponder
over the meaning of being and is afraid of the questions
that have arisen within it. He lifted up his shaggy eyebrows in wonder and, timorously blinking his keen little
eyes, extinguished their unbearable, piercing little flame.
His gaze, as if it were reading, was plunged immovably
into the mullah's broad face, and his pupils now lacked
that keenness which men found so confusing. He was
putting "childish" questions to the mullah about the
meaning of life, about the soul and God, substituting
with extraordinary dexterity verses from the Gospel and
the Prophets for verses from the Koran. In reality he
was play-acting, doing so with amazing art, within the
reach only of a great artist and sage.

Yet a few days before, talking about music with
Tanaëv and Suler, he had become as enraptured as a
child over its beauty, and one could see that he liked his
rapture—to put it more exactly, his ability to be enraptured. He said that Schopenhauer had written about

music better and more profoundly than all others, told, in passing, a funny story about Fet, and called music "the mute prayer of the soul".

"Come, how can it be mute?" asked Suler.

"Because it is without words. In sound there is more thought than in words. Thought—that's a purse, with coppers in it; whereas sound hasn't been sullied by anything—it is inwardly pure."

With obvious delight he spoke in charming, urchin words, having suddenly recalled the best, most caressing ones of these. And unexpectedly, smiling slightly into his beard, he uttered softly, as an endearment:

"All musicians are foolish people, and the more talented a musician, the more circumscribed he is. It's a strange thing—almost all of them are religious.

XLI

To Chekhov, on the telephone:

"Today is so fine a day for me, my soul is so joyous, that I want you to be joyous too. Especially you! You're a very fine person—very!"

XLIII

Sorting his mail:

"They're making a lot of noise, they write—but I'll die, and a year later they'll be asking: 'Tolstoy? Ah, that's the Count who tried his hand at cobbling boots and something happened to him—is that the fellow you mean?'"

XLIV

One never tires of being astounded at him, yet just the same it is wearing to see him often, and I would be unable to live in the same house with him—to say nothing of living in the same room. That would be as if in a desert, where everything has been scorched by the sun, while the sun itself is burning toward its end, threatening to bring on an endless dark night.

FROM A LETTER

At times it seemed that this old wizard was playing with death, coquetting with it and trying to deceive it somehow: "I'm not afraid of you; I love you; I'm awaiting you." Yet he himself was peeping with his keen little eyes: "Come, what are you like? And what's beyond you —there, further on? Will you annihilate me utterly, or will something remain and live?"

"Talent is love. Whoever loves is talented. Look at those in love—they're all talented!"

Suler, Chekhov, Sergei Lvovich, and somebody else were, as they sat in the park, discussing women; he listened a long time without uttering a word, and then suddenly spoke up:

"But I'll tell the truth about the females when I'll have one foot in the grave—I'll tell it, pop into my coffin, slam the lid down over me—and you just try to get me out of there!"

And the look in his eyes flared up with such eldritch mischievousness that for a minute all fell silent.

When he wanted to he would, somehow with an especial beauty about it, become delicate, sensitive and soft; his speech was enchantingly simple, exquisite; yet at times it was depressing to listen to him and unpleasant. I always disliked his judgments about women—in this he was "common-folk" to excess, and something assumed sounded in his words, something insincere and, at the same time, very personal. Just as though he had been affronted once, and he could neither forget nor forgive.

Then he began to talk about the girl in *Twenty-Six Men and a Girl,* uttering one after the other "indecent" words with a simplicity which struck me as cynicism and actually offended me somewhat. Subsequently I understood that he used the "banned" words only because he found them more exact and apt, but at that time it was unpleasant to me to listen to his speech.

When I said that Gogol had probably yielded to the influence of Hoffmann, Sterne and, perhaps, Dickens, he asked, after a look at me:

"Did you read that somewhere? No? That's not right. It's hardly likely that Gogol was familiar with Dickens. But you really have read a great deal; watch out—that's bad! Koltsov ruined himself that way."

About Chekhov, whom he tenderly loved:

"Medicine hinders him; if he weren't a physician, he'd write still better."

"The French have three writers: Stendhal, Balzac, Flaubert—well, yes, Maupassant also; but Chekhov is better than he."

He stands before me, this old sorcerer, a stranger to all, who had lonelily traversed all the deserts of thought in searchings after all-embracing truth and had failed to find it for himself; I look upon him and, although the sorrow for the loss is great, yet pride in that I have seen this man eases the pain and the grief.

And I, who do not believe in God, look upon him for some reason very cautiously, a trifle timorously—I look upon him and think:

"This man is godlike!"

About Chekhov

"SUCH an incongruous, unwieldy country—this Russia of ours."

This was a frequent occurrence with him: he would speak so warmly, seriously, sincerely—and suddenly smile slightly at himself and at what he was saying, and in this gentle, sad smile there was to be sensed the exquisite skepticism of a man who knew the value of words, the value of dreams. And also there could be glimpsed through this smile an endearing modesty, a sensitive delicacy.

Beautifully simple, he loved everything simple, real, sincere, and he had a way all his own of making people simpler.

He possessed the art of hitting upon and setting off vulgarity everywhere—an art which is accessible only to a man who makes high demands of life, which is created only through a fervent desire to see men simple, beautiful, harmonious. Vulgarity always found a harsh and stern judge in him.

One day some stout lady or other, hearty, handsome, handsomely dressed, came to him and began talking "the Chekhov way."

"Living is a bore, Anton Pavlovich! Everything's so gray—people, sky, sea—even flowers look gray to me. And there are no desires . . . the soul is filled with weariness. Just as if this were some sort of disease—"

"It is a disease!" said Anton Pavlovich with conviction. "It is. There's even a Latin name for it: *morbus pretendialis.*"

"Critics are like gadflies, which bother a horse as it ploughs," he said, smiling his intelligent, slight smile. "The horse is working away, all its muscles are as taut as the strings on a bull-fiddle, but no—a gadfly has to alight on its croup, and start tickling, and buzzing. The poor horse has to twitch its skin, to switch its tail. What's the gadfly buzzing about? It's hardly likely the gadfly itself understands that. It's simply of a restless disposition and wants to make its presence known—'There, now, I too live upon this earth! There, you hear?—I can even buzz; I can buzz about everything!' I've been reading criticisms of my stories for five and twenty years, yet can't remember a single hint of any value, haven't heard a single bit of sound advice. Only once was any impression made upon me—by Skabichevski: he wrote I would die under some fence, in a state of intoxication."

Yet, while disdaining, he felt sorry, and when on occasion one spoke harshly of somebody in his presence, Anton Pavlovich would immediately intercede:

"Come, what's that for? Why, he's an old man—he's seventy by now."

Or:

"Why, he's still a young man—it's all because of his foolishness."

And, when he spoke thus, I saw no squeamishness upon his face.

He was somehow chastely modest; he did not permit himself to say to people loudly and openly:

"Yea, be ye . . . more decent!"—hoping in vain that they themselves would surmise their urgent need for being decent. Hating that which was vulgar and foul, he described the abominations of life in the noble language of a poet, with the mocking smile of a humorist. . . .

Vulgarity was his foe; all his life did he strive against it; he mocked at it and depicted it with a dispassionate, barbed pen, being able to find the mildew of vulgarity even where, at first glance, everything seemed arranged very well, accommodatingly—even with eclat. And vulgarity avenged itself upon him for this by a vile little stunt, by placing his body—the body of a poet—in a freight-car for transporting *oysters*.[1]

The dirty-green blotch of this freight-car seems to me nothing else save the huge, triumphant grin of vulgarity over a wearied adversary. . . .

Had he not died ten years before the War [World War I], it would probably have killed him, after first poisoning him with hatred for people.

Of his literary labors he spoke but little, unwillingly—one wants to say "chastely" and, if you like, with the same discretion he used in speaking of Leo Tolstoy. Only infrequently, in a gay mood, smiling slightly, he would tell us the theme of some story—always a humorous one.

"Do you know, I'll write about a schoolmarm; she's an atheist, adores Darwin, is convinced of the need for combatting the superstitions of the common folk, but she herself, at the midnight hour, boils out a black tomcat in

---

[1] The title of one of Chekhov's most poignant stories.—*Trans.-Ed.*

a bathtub, to extract a certain arched bone which attracts a man, arousing love in him—there is a little bone like that—"

Of his plays he spoke as being "gay" and, apparently, was sincerely convinced that he was writing precisely "gay plays." Probably it was because of this that Sava Morozov stubbornly affirmed:

"Chekhov's plays ought to be staged as lyrical comedies." [1]

His eyes were fine when he laughed—somehow femininely kind and tenderly soft. And his laughter, almost soundless, was somehow especially fine. Laughing, he truly delighted in laughter, he exulted; I don't know who else could laugh so—so "spiritually," let me say.

Of Tolstoy he always spoke with some sort of especial, barely perceptible, tender and embarrassed little smile in his eyes; he lowered his voice, as if speaking of something spectral, mysterious, which demands cautious, gentle words.

It is good to recall such a man; at once vigor returns to your life; anew, a clear meaning enters into it.

---

[1] Both Chekhov and Morozov (the Mæcenas of the Moscow Art Theatre) were right; Andreiev was also of the same opinion: "Do not believe that *Three Sisters* is a pessimistic play. . . . It is a radiant, fine play." Stanislavsky, however, preferred in his superb productions of the Chekhov plays to stress certain tones which were minor to the author—and the author himself had once advised an actress: "Don't you be afraid of the author. The author is a free artist. You must create an image utterly different from the author's." At the same time Chekhov said of Stanislavsky that he played superbly in *The Sea Gull*—but not at all the character that he, Chekhov, had in mind. It is hardly likely, however, that any director would now have the courage to defy the mortmain of Stanislavsky, and Chekhov's comedies will probably be produced, to the end of time, as magnificent tear-jerkers.—*Trans.-Ed.*

ALEXIS NIKOLAIEVICH TOLSTOY

(1882–1945)

EDITOR'S NOTE

This popular author, one of the most prominent in the Soviets, was related to Count Leo Nikolaievich Tolstoy, as well as to that other great writing Tolstoy, Count Alexis Constantinovich (1817-1875), and was a Count in his own right before the Revolution; on his mother's side he was related to Ivan Sergheievich Turgenev.

He made his debut in 1908 with a volume of poems, curious and appealing; his first successful book, marking him as a master of characterization, was a series of studies of provincial "living fossils." His output was vast and varied. *Nikita's Childhood* is one of the best stories for children (which are a mother-lode in Russian); he is one of the first innovators in two fields of fiction which up to now have been but little cultivated by the Russians: fantastic-scientific fiction, where his stories are of the calibre of Jules Verne and the early Wells, and the novel of international intrigue—his *Death Box* (an American translation was published, unfortunately, only in England) is a combination of the two genres which makes Oppenheim and Buchan seem tame; he is a genuine humorist; his plays are excellent theatre; his *Peter the Great* (only the first part has been published in English, in an unspeakable translation) is veritably necromantic and demonstrates his greatness as a historical novelist (his preference is for turbulent, parlous times); his short stories are varied in theme and always absorbing—*The Ancient Way,* his greatest one, is the perfect antiphony to Bunin's *The Gentleman from San Francisco.*

In the Civil War he sided with the Whites, emigrated, and lived in Paris, but in 1921 went over to the Soviets and, in 1923, returned to Russia. Both in World War I, and the one now over, he served as correspondent.

His work has been translated into many languages; a number of his novels and stories have appeared even in English.

The Ancient Way

ALEXIS NIKOLAIEVICH TOLSTOY

ON a certain dark night in spring a tall man in a military cape mounted, by a steep trap-stair, to the forecastle of an ocean liner. Paul Taurain climbed slowly, surmounting each step with difficulty. A triple row of gold-braid gleamed on his képi in the light of the foremasthead lantern. He skirted the slime-covered anchor chain and halted at the very nose of the ship; he leaned his elbows on the rail and remained thus, without stirring—save that the hem of his cape bellied a little from the faint current of air that met the ship.

The ship was showing only its running-lights, red and green—these, and the two top-lights on the mast, lights lost far above, in the imperceptible veil of fog. The stars, too, were veiled over. The night was a dark one. Below, at a great depth, the iron nose of the ship was cutting through the water with low plashing.

Paul Taurain gazed at the water as he leaned against

the rail. Fever was searing his eyes. The breeze went through his whole body—and that wasn't at all bad. Of his cabin, of his stuffy berth, of the Sister of Mercy who had fallen asleep under a small electric bulb that made the eyes smart, it was painful to think. A white, tricornered coiff, a sanguine cross on her nurse's uniform, the parchment-like face of a dismal companion of those who suffer: such was the Sister who was accompanying Paul Taurain to the land of his birth, to France. It was when she had dozed off that he had left his cabin with the utmost caution.

Some sort of phosphorescent creature, shaped like a long, roseate hook, with the head of a sea-horse, swam by in the basalt-black water. As it lazily flipped its fins it seemed to be quizzically and casually eying the huge, advancing keel, until the currents that met the ship drew the sea-beast off to one side. The water was cool; its depth was a blessed thing. Let the Sister with her sanguine cross be angry! Existence (Paul felt this with sorrowful emotion) would soon be at an end for him, like a path breaking off into the abyss of night and, because of that, this nocturnal quiet wherein majestic recollections were adrift was immeasurably more important than all the medicinal mixtures, and the berth, and the tasteless food.

The route which the ship was following was one of mankind's ancient sea-paths; from the oak-groves of Attica to the Hyperborean lands of darkness. It was called the Hellespont, to commemorate hapless Helle who had tumbled into the sea off the back of the golden-fleeced ram whereon she and her brother were fleeing east from the wrath of their stepmother. Doubtlessly both the ram and the stepmother were inventions of the Pelasgi, the shepherds who roamed with their flocks through the gorges of Argolida. From craggy littorals they gazed out to sea and beheld sails and barques of strange outlines. Squat, fat, big-beaked men navigated these ships. Their cargoes consisted of copper weapons, ornaments of gold and woven stuffs gay and bright as flowers. Their copper-sheathed barques cast anchor near virgin shores, whereupon the Pelasgi, stalwart, white of skin and blue of eye, would come down to the sea, driving their flocks before them. Their grandsires still remembered glacier plains, reindeer running on moonlit nights, and caves adorned with wall-drawings of mammoths.

The Pelasgi bartered cattle, wool, cheese, and dried fish for the copper weapons. They marveled at the tall ships, adorned at prow and stern with cockscombs of copper. From what land had these squat, amply nosed merchants come sailing? The Pelasgi may, perhaps, have known on a time, but by now they had forgotten. Many ages afterward there was a legend current about certain shepherds who, apparently, had seen ships with wind-rent sails, driven along by a gale of fire, go racing past the shores of Hellas. And the men on those ships were lifting their hands up to heaven in despair. And (said legend) it must evidently have been in those times that the land of copper and gold had perished.

Had that really been the case? It must have: the memory of mankind does not lie. It had been handed down in songs that it was from that time that heroes girt in copper armor had begun to appear in desert Hellas. With sword and terror did they make helots of the Pelasgi; styling themselves Princes, they compelled them to build strongholds and great walls out of Cyclopaean monoliths. They taught agriculture, trade and war. They sowed the teeth of the Drakōn, and wars were engendered therefrom. They brought the spirit of unrest and covetousness into the hearts of the blue-eyed ones. The rosy-fingered Aurora of History was rising over Hellas. The copper sword, and the golden tripod whereon a heady incense smoked, were standing by the cradle of the European nations.

Paul Taurain, a descendant of the Pelasgi, had been, on the self-same shores of the Mediterranean, riddled by a bullet through the upper lobe of one of his lungs, had been poisoned by gas released from a plane and, dying from tuberculosis and malaria, was returning from the hecatombs of Hyperborea to Paris by that same ancient sea-road of the merchants and the conquerors, a sea-road joining two worlds: the West and the East; a road flowing between shores under whose knolls lie buried the shards of vanished kingdoms; a road, deep at the bottom of which, amid sea-growths, slumber the pinnaces of the Achaeans, the triremes of Mithridates, the ships-in-splendor of Byzantium; a road where, along the wayside-shoals under clayey cliffs, lie the rusted bottoms of steamships that had been torpedoed or driven ashore.

It seemed (thus it seemed to Paul) that he was at that moment consummating the cycle of the millennia. His mind, stirred up by fever and a sensation of his own imminent death, strove to embrace all the struggles, the flowering and perishing, of the multitude of nations that had traversed this sea-lane. Recollections rose up before him, as if the past had become resurgent. In a few days, perhaps, his brain would be extinguished; together with it would perish that which he was bearing within him: the universe would perish. What did it matter to him whether the universe would go on existing when there would be no Paul Taurain? The universe would perish in his consciousness: that was all. Hugging the dew-covered rail, gazing into the darkness, he was completing the cycle.

The bells struck. There was a change of watches. Above, over the captain's bridge, stood the unslumbering figure of the man at the wheel. Only his broad face was in the light as he bent over the binnacle whereon quivered the soul of the ship: the small black arrow of the compass. The darkness of the night was becoming denser. The water below was no longer visible. Now it seemed that the ship was flying through unembodied space. This was the murk preceding morning.

Paul's face and hands had become covered with dew. A shiver went through him. How many hands, flung over the ground in the last spasm of death, would on this night (on all these nights) be covered with just such dew. . . . Each of these dying men, sinking his teeth into earth mixed with blood, iron, and excrement, would bear off with him millennia of that which had been lived through; in every bullet-riddled brain would crash, with a dismal rumble, and vanish, millennia of culture. What absurdity! What despair!

Were one to show to one's primordial, blue-eyed forebear the book of life, turning all the leaves of that which is to come, showing all its pretty little colored pictures: "This," the lighthearted forebear would say, scratching himself under the ram's-fleece that clothes him, "is just a stupid and cruel book. There must be some mistake here. See how much good work has been put forth, how men and women have multiplied, how many splendid cities have been built—and yet, in this very last little picture, all this is ablaze wherever your eyes turn, and there are so many corpses that you could glut all the fish in the Aegean Sea with them for a whole week."

"There has been a mistake somewhere; somewhere a

false move has been allowed in this game of chess," Paul Taurain reflected. "History has swerved aside and is heading for an abyss. What a splendid world is perishing!"

He closed his eyes and with desperate pity recalled Paris: his window; a bluish morning; the light-blue shadows of the city; the *allée* of a boulevard, and half-rounded roofs losing themselves in a haze; the drops of rain, not yet dried, on his windowsill; below, the driver of a cart filled with carrots coaxing his nag to go on; the gay voices of those who were happy because they were alive on so lovely a morning. He recalled his desk, the books and manuscripts on it redolent of morning freshness. And his inebriating exaltation of happiness and of good will toward all men and all things. What a superb book he had been writing at that time about justice, goodness, and happiness! He was young, healthy, rich. He had wanted to proffer the promise of youth, health, and riches to all men. And it had seemed to him then that only ideas of kindheartedness, a new Social Contract enriched by the conquests of physics, chemistry, and technics, would hold these blessings out to all mankind.

What sentimental bosh! This had been in the spring, on the verge of the war. In the heat of the moment it had really seemed that the Boches were fiends, the offspring of the Devil, advancing to storm the divine citadels of humanism. In the heat of the moment it had seemed that the old banner of the National Convention had been unfurled over France, that the French battalions, mowed down by machine-guns, were perishing for the Rights of Man, for Liberty, Equality, and Fraternity.

How hard Paul longed to have faith anew in that morning when he, in an access of happiness, had flung his window open upon haze-covered Paris! "But if this happiness has been trampled into the earth by the boots of soldiers, shattered by projectiles, inundated with suppurating-gas—what is left, then? Wherefore had Hellas been, and Rome, and the Renaissance, and all the iron clangor of the nineteenth century? Or are all things fated to wind up as a midden-heap of shards and debris, grown over with the prickly grass of the desert? No, no! Somewhere there must be truth! "I do not want to, I cannot die on a night of such hopelessness!"

II

"M'sieu', you have again come out into the open air. M'sieu', you will feel worse again," the sleep-laden voice of the Sister of Mercy came from behind him.

Paul went back to his cabin and lay down without undressing. The Sister of Mercy made him take his medicine; she brought him something hot to drink. Somewhere, within the depths of the ship, its engines were clanking regularly and softly. The vials with the medicinal mixtures tinkled every now and then. This was, if you like, even pleasant—just as if it represented some sort of hope of being saved: the warm light of a shaded lamp; the soft berth into which his bony body, burning in a fever, plunged as if into a cloud. Paul dozed off, but it must have been for only a minute. And again, in a fevered procession, his thoughts came creeping. Insomnia was lying in wait for him: one must not sleep; only a few hours were left him; that which is passing through his brain is far too precious. . . .

One of his recollections remained longer than the others. Paul began to toss and turn; in his restlessness he interlaced his cold fingers and made them crackle.

Two months ago, in Odessa, he had received a long, familiar envelope. Lucie, his cousin and his bride, wrote him:

My dear and distant friend:

I feel infinitely lonely, infinitely sad. There is no news from you. You write to your mother and brother, but never to me. I know the depressed state you are in, and therefore am making one more attempt to write you. . . . Things are hard for you; things are hard for me. Four years of separation, four eternities, have flown over my poor life. Only the thought of you, the hope that, perhaps, the remnants of my youth, of my lacerated heart, and the whole of my tremendous love may yet prove necessary to you, compel me to live, to move about, to go through the same (*always* the same!) never varying round: the hospital; nights at the bedsides of the dying; the knitting of wristlets for the soldiers; reading, of mornings, the lists of those killed in battle. . . .

France is one great cemetery, wherein lies buried a whole generation of youth, of shattered hearts, of unfulfilled expectations. We—the women who are still alive—are keeners, nuns, forming the cortège for the dead. Paris is becoming an alien city. Paul, do you remember how fond we were, in our walks, of the old stones of the city? It was a majestic history they related to us. The stones of Paris have now fallen silent; they are being spurned by some species of new, unknown people. . . . And only the old men by the firesides still brandish their withered arms in soldierly fashion as they tell of the past glory of France. We, however, understand them but poorly. . . .

The text of the letter, which Paul had read a thousand times, broke off in his recollection. But he had not, after all, answered Lucie. He could not. What could he have written about to the young girl who was still trying to give him her melancholy love? What could he attempt to do with this love? What could a corpse attempt if a bouquet of roses were to be thrust into its contorted hands? Yet, for some reason, he was haunted by the memory of foolish little Lucie's lips, trembling like

those of a little child. A year ago he had been in Paris
(on one day's leave), and right then, torturing himself
and her, he had hurt Lucie. He had said:

"Have you ever seen a bourgeois, who had lost all his
means in the space of a single minute, coming down the
stairs of the Paris Bourse? Suppose you offer him a
nosegay of violets—by way of compensation. . . . There
you have it! It's horrible, Lucie. I am bankrupt; all that
is left me is to return to the dead embers of my paleo-
lithic cave, and there rummage among the rubbish until I find my good old stone ax—"

It was at precisely that point that the still innocent
lips of Lucie had begun to tremble. Yet to pity her was
nonsense—sheer nonsense. Pity was that same old nonsense out of that same old unfinished book which was
being written by blind luck—and it was the wind of
spring which was riffling its leaves. And besides, pity
had been cauterized by poison gas. . . .

Toward morning Paul again fell asleep for a short
while. It was the hoarse roar of the steamer's whistle
that awakened him. His nerves tautened. A beam of
light was falling through the porthole, and this made
the yellow creases on the Sister's face seem repulsive.
She picked up Paul's plaid and led him up on deck; she
seated him in a chaise longue and covered his feet.

With a full-throated roar the steamer was coming out
of the Dardanelles into the Aegean Sea. On the low,
clayey shores one could see the charred debris of
barracks and of shell-shattered fortresses. A rust-eaten
steamer was lying on a shoal, its stern underwater.
The war had been broken off for a time; the forces that
had called it forth were rebuilding themselves; the
nations had been granted permission to exult and make
merry. What could be better!

The morning was humid and warm. The ship (it was

the *Carcovado,* of six thousand tons, originally requisitioned from the Germans and now used by a South American line for transporting troops, refugees, and perishable cargoes), listing a little to port, was going farther and farther from land into the azure, watery desert. In its wake the tousled sun was climbing higher and higher into the fearful height of a cloudless sky. Ahead, the glistening-black back of a dolphin with its knifelike fin flew up, whirling like a wheel, out of the sun-shot water.

"Mamma, mamma—a dolphin!" a flaxen-fair child began shouting in Russian, standing near the rail and pointing out to sea with his thin little hand.

A school of dolphins was frolicking in the ship's path. And it became clear that it must have been on just such a morning, in the mirrorous Aegean, to the dance of the dolphins, that there had arisen out of the white foam, opening her radiant eyes, the beauty of life: Aphrodite.

"Ah, well, let's try to exult and make merry," reflected Paul.

The flaxen-fair child hung on the rail, delighting in the watery games of Aphrodite's outriders; he was held up by his mother whose small downy shawl was soiled, whose shoes were trodden down. Upon her tear-wasted face the horrors of the holocausts of Russia had by now become congealed. In one hand, which had long gone unwashed, she was clutching a piece of hardtack. What was it to her that in the blaze of the sun Paul's puckered eyes seemed to see the shadow of the *Argo,* with lateen sail, steep-sided, flashing with the copper of shields and sparkling with the drops trickling off the sweeps—*Argo,* the wondrous ship of the Argonauts, those sea-robbers and seekers after gold. . . . Over the same path as theirs had Paul sped out of pillaged Colchida.

An elderly woman in imitation sables atop a *capote* sewn out of a cretonne curtain passed over the broad deck. In face and movements she reminded one of a toad. Two exceedingly well-brought-up lap-dogs in pink bows were trotting behind her. This person, too, was traveling from Odessa, transporting in the steerage four prostitutes whom she had inveigled with tales of El Dorado: "Just you manage to get to Marseilles, my little chicks!"

There, she has quickened her steps, has inclined her head to one side and revealed both her lower and upper plates in greeting to an acquaintance: a tall, execrably dressed man with a foolish face and sporting a curled mustache. This individual had come aboard at Constantinople; he spoke Polish, sauntered about proudly, smoked a long pipe with spittle dribbling all over it, and was earnestly seeking aristocratic partners for a session with the pasteboards. As he went past Paul this fellow's very haunches began to wiggle with deference.

"Before a house falls, the bugs come crawling out of every crack," Paul reflected.

The ship was veering southwest. Pointed, lilac-hued summits were rising out of the sea to starboard. Clouds were swirling over them. An island that looked like a single ridge of gigantic mountains was coming up out of the water. All around the ship were the mirrorous sea and the sun-shot azure, yet the ridged island in the distance was all overcast with gloom. Thunder-laden clouds hung over it, a pall of rain was coming down upon it; as though the throne of Zeus were verily there, a flash of lightning zigzagged in a broken thread over the surface of the clouds. . . . A peal of thunder reached the vessel as a sigh.

"That's Imbros—a curious little island; there are always thunderstorms over it," remarked an unshaven, swarthy individual in a fez, who was standing behind Paul. Even yesterday, in port, he had offered Paul to change any sort of money for any other sort, or to arrange an acquaintance between Paul and the female toad who was transporting the four girlies and, incidentally, advised him not to sit down to cards with the mustachioed Pole.

Paul shut his eyes so that the bony face surmounted by the fez might not block visions of the glory of Zeus, the God of the gods. Nearing to port was the low shore of Asia Minor, where every knoll, every stone has been hymned in hexameters: Troada, the land of heroes. Beyond the littoral strip of sand stretched a tawny plain, furrowed by the beds of torrents that had dried up. In the distance, toward the east, the summits of Ida, still covered here and there with veins of snow, reared in a cloud-capped range.

Paul got up from his chaise longue and went toward the ship's side. Upon that plain fields of wheat and maize had rustled on a time; gardens had breathed forth their fragrance; countless flocks and herds had come to it from the mountains of Phrygia. Over there is the flinty estuary of the Scamander; its yellow stream, forming a streak, goes far out into the sea. To port are tumuli: the graves of Hector and Patroclos. Here had the black ships of the Achaeans been drawn up on the sands, and there, on that parched plain, where the earth is pitted everywhere, and the thin smoke of some lowly hovel is rising, the Cyclopaean walls of Troy had reared with their overhanging cornices, square towers, and the golden, many-breasted statue of the Asiatic Aphrodite.

From times immemorial had Aeolian Greeks come sailing to the shores of the Troad, had settled there and followed agriculture and cattle-raising. But they had soon put two and two together and realized that this was a good spot and a had begun building a fortress near the gates of the Hellespont, in order to seize upon the routes to the East. And Troy became a kingdom, strong and rich. On fair-days there came to the agora under the high walls of the town creaking carts laden with grain and fruit; there came perfidious Sclavs from the borders of Phracia, leading mad steeds celebrated for their speed; Hittites out of Byzacium, with wares made after the best Egyptian models; Phrygians and Lydians in leathern cowls, driving flocks of close-fleeced rams; Phoenician merchants in false beards, in garments of blue felt, urged on with lashes black slaves bearing bales and clay amphorae; dignified, elderly sea-robbers, armed with double-edged battle axes, brought handsome odalisques and tempting little boys; priests pitched their tents and put up their altars, ballyhooing with loud cries the names of the gods they had in stock, threatening and pulling in customers to make sacrificial offerings. The warriors on guard over the town gates looked down from the walls upon the bustle of the marketplace. Incomputable treasures were gathered within the town, and rumors thereof spread far and wide.

Hellas, in those times, was poor. The times-of-splendor of Mycenæ, of Tyrinthos and Thebæ, all builded of heroes, had long since passed. Their Cyclopaean walls had become overgrown with grass. The soil was not a fertile one; the population was scanty, consisting of shepherds, fishermen, and, to be sure, ever-hungry warriors. The Kings of Achaea, Argolida, Sparta dwelt in hovels, clay-daubed and straw-thatched. There was nary a thing to traffic in. There was nary a soul among themselves to rob. Trade was giving Hellas the go-by. All that remained to Hellas was the legendary glory of her past, the seething blood that rushed to the head, and an extraordinary spirit of enterprise. The goal was clear: to pillage and shatter Troy, to gain mastery of the Hellespont and to veer the ships of the merchants into the havens of Hellas. They began casting about for a pretext to war—and, as everyone knows, there's nothing in the world easier to find. Beauteous Helen was dragged in by the hair. A clamor was raised up throughout the peninsula. They summoned Achilles out of Thessaly with a pack of lies about letting him have half the booty. They questioned the Oracle of Dodona and then sailed off in their black ships to begin, in brazen-clangorous hexameters, the three-thousand-year history of European civilization.

From that time up to now there have never, evidently, been found any other means of repairing one's fortunes save sword, pillage, and chicanery. The heroes of the Trojan War were, at least, magnificent in their horse-maned helmets, with their mighty thighs and ox-hearts —nor were the latter corroded by any ideas of Good and Evil. They wrote no books about humanism, wool-gathering by an open window—not they!

The steamer veered west; the low shores began to recede. Paul sat down anew on his chaise longue.

"A surrogatum," he reflected, and repeated the word. "A lie in which no one wants to believe any longer. Ruin. . . . Ruin inevitable. History must be begun all over again. Or else—"

He smiled a wry smile and shrugged his shoulders feebly: this "Or else—" was followed by that which was preternatural: the world became turned inside out, as when the skin is peeled, like a glove, off some beast.

A knot of Russian émigrés appeared on deck. One, a young officer with brazen, frightening eyes, jerky and scratching himself, watched the frolicking of the dolphins.

"I can hit them. Want to bet?" he asked in a hoarse

little bass, and started pulling a rusty horse-pistol out
of his hip-pocket.

Another officer with him, pale, with a bifurcated little
beard, stopped his hand:

"Chuck it! You're not in Russia now. And, in general,
brother—chuck that shooting-iron into the sea."

"Oho—so you want me to chuck it away? Why, it has
sent a hundred and twenty souls to the Devil's dam. It
ought to be in some museum, by rights—"

The two broke into laughter that was not at all gay; a
third started hushing them, sibilantly:

"Stop your yelling! The Captain [indicating Paul] has
dozed off, I think—"

These Russian officers turned around to look at Paul
and, on tiptoes, walked some distance away. The sun
fell upon the deck, upon Paul's face: he dozed off. His
sleeping eyes saw, through their lids, a reddish light.
How odd (the thought came to him): wherever has the
sea gone to? What a pity—what a pity. . . . And he
saw a dismal, autumnal plain; telegraph poles, with
torn wires dangling. He felt a chilly little wind swoop-
ing down upon him. Yet his face feels hot. Below, at the
foot of a hillock, straw-thatched huts are blazing—without smoke, without crackling, like so many candles.
Without a crackle a battery is shelling the village: the
flames from the mouths of the cannon are blinding. The
artillery men have morose faces. They are all his own
people: all Parisians. They are fighting for the Rights
of Man. [Paul hears his own teeth gnashing.] "You must
fulfill your duty!" he shouts to the poilus—and feels his
horse foundering under him: it seems to be broken, to
have no bones. And right here, at the battery, is that
fellow with the brazen, frightening eyes and his horse-
pistol, weaving in-and-out among Paul's own men. He
fawns unbearably, scratching himself all the time, snick-

ering. And suddenly, with unbelievable quickness, he falls to digging the earth with his hands, the way dogs do with their paws. He drags out of the ground and starts worrying with his teeth two men in brimless sailor-hats; he comes trotting with them to the very muzzle of Paul's foundered horse: "Captain, sir, here are the Bolsheviks!" They have broad faces; their teeth are bared in a queer grin, while their eyes . . . ah, their eyes are mysteriously closed. "You shot them, you scoundrel!" Paul shouts at the brazen whirligig of a Russian and strives to get at him, to strike him with his riding-crop—but his hand and arm seem to be made of cotton-wool. His heart pounds frantically. If these sailors would but open their eyes he would fix them with his own— would unriddle everything, would understand. . . .

The dinner-bell awakened Paul. And, anew, the milky-blue sea was aglow. Mountainous islands were passing by in the distance. The rust-eaten, war-torn *Carcovado* seemed to be floating through the heavens, listing to port, as it plowed through this mirrorous abyss. The sun was inclining to its setting. At rare intervals a slender pillar of smoke would rise from beyond the rim of water and sky.

Toward evening his fever usually released Paul, and weakness would descend upon him like a mattress weighing three thousand pounds. His hands, his feet would turn cold. This was almost blissful.

III

Early next morning the *Carcovado* cast anchor near Salonika, in the dirty-yellow waters of a bay. The town, as visible between its tawny and chalky knolls as if it were lying on the palm of one's hand, had been burned down. The ruins of ancient walls confined in a quadrangle the dismal scene of the conflagration, with white minarets rising like needles. The sun was baking. The chalky knolls, it seemed, had been worn down to bedrock by the soles of the tribes that had passed this way in their seekings after happiness.

A barge filled with soldiers left the quay. A mite of a tugboat, puffing in the sun-suffused silence, brought the barge up to the *Carcovado*. A trap-ladder, creakingly protesting, was let down. And, two by two, Zouaves came up on the run in their short, red, baggy trousers, in grass-hued military jackets, in red, tasseled *chéchias* on their heads. Laughing, and tossing down their dufflebags and canteens, they lay down on the shady side of the top-deck. An odor of perspiration arose, and of dust; tobacco smoke swirled and crept through the air. The Zouaves didn't give one good hoot in hell for the Devil himself. There had been an attempt to throw them into Russia, on the Odessa front. At Salonika they had announced: "Head for home!"—and had elected a battalion council of soldier-deputies. It had thereupon been considered best to ship them back home.

"There, that's something like!" neighed the Zouaves, rolling about on deck from sheer excess of animal spirits. "To hell with the war! Head for home—and the wimmen!"

Until noon the ship took on coal. Bending under the weight of their baskets of coal ragamuffins, with their heads bound in rags, trudged up the unsteady gangplank: Greeks, Turks, Levantines, they were all equally black from coal-dust; the sweat trickled down their Attic noses in drops of shoe-blacking. The emptied baskets went spinning down into the barge. The first mate, up on the bridge, was cursing through a megaphone. The passengers lazed about, lolling halfway over the sides.

At last the *Carcovado* set up a roar; the dirty water in

its wake began to churn. The Zouaves started waving their *chéchias* to the people on shore. And, anew, there was the azure of the sky, the ancient tranquility.

In the distance, to starboard, Olympus floated by in its cap of snow veined with lilac. Gracious was Zeus this day: not a single cloudlet cast its shadow over the glittering summit. And now Olympus, too, was gone beyond the rim of the sea. The Zouaves were snoring in the shade under the suspended lifeboats. Some were playing dice, throwing them on deck out of a leather cup. One of the Zouaves, a broadshouldered fellow whose eyebrows and lashes were white by contrast with his tan, had seated the little Russian boy on his knees and, stroking the lad's hair with his paw, was gently questioning him about the essential actualities of life in an unfamiliar and wondrous tongue. The lad's mother was observing from a distance, with uneasiness and a joyous smile, her son's success among the Europeans. . . . No, no; not a man amongst these wanted to go crawling into the grave with Paul, to be winding up the history of mankind.

By now, near at hand, islands like rounded loaves of bread, covered with low-growing, sparse woods, with here and there a stony patch, were floating past, now to starboard, now to port. The sea at their bases was green; they were reflected in it as in a mirror. And there was no bottom: the sky only, inverted. The ship sailed so close by one of these islets that the passengers could see dark-headed children fossicking at the threshold of a hovel built of piled up stones and leaning against a cliff. A woman at work in a vineyard cupped her hands over her eyes as she watched the steamer. Vineyards, in terraced strips, took up the entire slope of a hill. From time out of mind the schist here had been gouged with pickaxes so that, out of the stone-dust saturated

with sunlight and dew, there might rise on the twisted
vine the golden-tinted cluster of the grape: the juice of
the sun.

The hilltop was bare. Rufous nannygoats meandered
about; a man stood leaning on his staff. He had on a felt
hat—one of those hats the Greeks of Homer were wont
to depict in brick-red pigment upon their black vases.
And the herdsman, and the woman in her striped skirt,
and the children at play with a puppy, and the white-
haired ancient in a boat below—all followed with indifferent glances the war-mutilated *Carcovado,* where
Paul Taurain was lying on his chaise longue, his teeth
chattering from fever and from the chill of his dying
thoughts.

When the *tra-ta-ta-taaaam* of a bugle pealed forth,
loud and clear, the Zouaves poured from the top-deck
to the stern like peas out of a pod. There, near an open
clapboard caboose, a tall Negro in a snowy chef's cap
was dipping up soup out of steaming caldrons, ladling
it into the soldiers' mess-kits.

"Fill it up—make it good and hot!" shouted the Zouaves, laughing and jostling. They sank their teeth into
the black bread; with brute savoring they supped their
bean pottage; throwing their heads far back they poured
the wine in a red stream out of their pannikins into their
mouths. Why not: on such a hot, azure day one could
devour a mountain of bread, drain a sea of bean pottage
and wine!

Behind the caboose, tied to the beam of a lift-crane,
stood an old, rust-colored bull, taken on at Salonika. He
turned his head glumly from time to time to look at the
soldiers. "They'll devour me," he was evidently thinking. "Tomorrow, without fail, they'll devour me!" A
Zouave, with a downy upper lip and elongated eyes,
called out to him loudly, with a flourish of his pannikin:

"Don't lose heart, my old—on the morrow we'll offer you up as a sacrifice to Zeus!"

The family of a sugar-refinery owner, in flight from Kiev, was looking down from the first-class deck upon the soldiers at dinner. Here were the sugar-refinery owner himself, resembling a baldheaded crab in a cutaway; his son, a lyrical poet, with a dainty little volume in his hand; *maman,* encased in a corset reaching down to her very heels and wearing sables, out of which the grayish top-knot of her coiffure was sticking up; the modishly dressed daughter-in-law, apprehensive of coarse impertinences; three children, and a nurse with a breast-baby. Papa Crab was grating in a low, hoarse voice, without taking the cigar out of his mouth:

"Those soldiers are but little to my liking; I can't see a single officer; they look as if they were but little to be trusted."

"They're simply ruffians," *maman* was saying. "They've already been eying our trunks."

The poetical son was gazing at the strip of the desolate shore of Euboea. "What a fine thing it would be to settle down there with one's wife and children; not to see all the things that surround a man nowadays; to walk about in a chiton—" such must have been the thoughts of the young man with the despondent nose.

The Zouaves below were letting off their witticisms:

"Look at that potbelly up there, with the cigar."

"Hey, Uncle Crab, throw us down a smoke!"

"Yes, and tell your daughter-in-law to come down here—we'll have a little fun with her!"

"He's angry! *O, la-la!* Never mind, Uncle Crab; just hold out a while, you won't be so badly off in Paree!"

"We'll write to the Bolsheviks to give you back your sugar-refineries!"

The Zouaves filled the whole day with noise, laughter,

skylarking. The hot deck crackled from their running about. Everything concerned them; they shoved their noses into everything, as though they had grappled the *Carcovado* and taken it by storm, first-class passengers and all. Papa Crab went off to the captain to complain; the latter merely threw up his hands: "Lodge a complaint against them in Marseilles, if you like."

The lady of the two lap-dogs, greatly alarmed over the fate of her four girls, had turned the key on them in a stoker's cabin. The Russian officers no longer showed themselves. The Pole, indignant over the preponderance of louts aboard, was seeking in vain for partners at cards. A Russian Man of Public Affairs crawled out of the hold, with a tousled beard wherein wisps of straw had caught, and started throwing everybody into a panic, asserting that there were disguised agents of the Cheka among the Zouaves, and that the intelligentsia on the *Carcovado* would never escape a pogrom.

At night the ship was skirting Peloponnesus—stern, stony Sparta. The great constellations shone over the dark mirror of the sea, as in the fairy-tale of Odysseus. A dry odor of wormwood was wafted from the land. Paul Taurain was recalling the names of the gods, recalling heroes and great events as he gazed at the stars, at their abysmal reflections. Again a night without sleep. He had been exhausted by the bustle of the day. A strange change had taken place in him, however. Every moment his eyes would become veiled over with tears. What majesty of worlds. . . . How little, how fleeting life was! How complex, deeply ensanguined its laws! How he pitied his heart: an ailing little clod, ticking off its seconds in a Creation a-glitter with stars. Wherefore had the desire to live returned? He was already reconciled, was already going off into nothingness, sadly and solemnly, like a discrowned king. And,

suddenly, this desperate regret. Wherefore? What spells
had compelled him to reach out anew for the wine of
life? Wherefore this piling-up of agonies?

He was trying to restore the web of his recent
thoughts anent the perishing of civilization, anent the
vicious circle of mankind, anent his bearing off with
him, when he departed, the universe, which exists only
insofar as he, Paul Taurain, thinks thereof and breathes
the breath of life into it. But the web had been rent
asunder: its tatters were vanishing like mist, while in
his memory the gay voices of the Zouaves were calling
to one another and their barbarous steps were tramping.
He recalled the herdsman on the summit of the island;
the woman cutting the grapes; the coal-blackened steve-
dores pitching their baskets down into the coal-barge.

"Be thou brave then, Paul Taurain! Thou hast nothing to lose. There are thy culture, thy truth, that
whereon thou hast grown up, that because of which
thou deemest every action of thine reasoned and necessary. But then there is the life of the millions. Hast
heard the tramping of their feet over the ship? And their
life does not coincide with thy truth. They, like those
blue-eyed Pelasgi, look on from the shore upon thy
foundering ship with its storm-riven sails. Call with up-
lifted arms upon thy gods. For answer from the heavens
there come only the fire and rumble of a cannon-
ade. . . ."

IV

This night Paul passed on deck. The morning glow
flowed and spread in a rosy, coral effulgence; a warm,
humid wind began to flutter the soldiers' linen hung on
the shrouds to dry; the rusty-red bull started to low, and
out of the water rose, like a miracle, the orb of the sun.
The wind died down. The bells struck. One could

hear the slightly hoarse voices of sleepers awaking. Another hot day had begun. The Zouaves, barefooted, hitching up their trousers, ran off to wash; howling like savages they doused one another at the pump. The clapboard caboose sent up a stream of smoke. The tall Negro in the chef's cap was baring his teeth in a grin.

Through the winding-sheet of his insomnia Paul Taurain saw a viscid bloody wake stretch out behind the stern of the ship, staining the foam. This meant that the bull had been offered up as a sacrifice to Zeus. The animal was lying on its side, its belly bloated; oozing out of its slit throat the blood ran through a scupper into the sea. Therein, too, were cast its livid entrails. The flayed carcass was drawn up on a mast. Brandishing his gargantuan ladle the cook was delivering a speech to the Zouaves, to the effect that on the Zambesi River (where he had been born) food was styled *cous-cous,* and that this carcass was Great *Cous-Cous,* and that it is a goodly thing when man has much *cous-cous,* and an evil thing when there is no *cous-cous.* . . .

"Bravo, Chocolate! Cook us some Great *Cous-Cous!*" shouted the Zouaves, stamping in delight.

The sun was blazing. A glittering pathway lay across the sea. Ethereal waves of heat shimmered to the south. It seemed that there, near Africa, one could see vagrant mirages.

At noon a short, piercing feminine scream rose out of the red-hot inwards of the ship. This was followed by a burst of laughter from several masculine throats. The female toad, with her eyes popping out and crossed, dashed across the deck, the lap-dogs with their pink bows trailing after her. It turned out that the Zouaves had smelt out where the four girlies were sitting in durance vile; the soldiers were now trying to break down the door of the stokers' cabin. Certain measures were taken. Everything quieted down. The first-class seemed to have died out. The Zouaves were lying on the red-hot deck in little else save their undershirts. Paul Taurain longed, excruciatingly, to warm himself, but the sun could not pierce his chill with its heat; his teeth chattered; the reddish light flooded his eyes.

"Feel bad, my old?" somebody's voice, low and stern, asked behind him.

Without curiosity, without turning around, Paul moved his parched lips:

"Yes—bad."

"Well, and why did you cook up this mess? Why are you still keeping it at a simmer? Now do you understand what sort of a thing your civilization is? Death—"

An icy little chill was running over Paul's dry skin; there was a whir in his ears, as if flywheels where whirring somewhere. It seemed to him that someone had walked away from his chaise longue. . . . Perhaps all this had been a prank of his imagination—because he had desired to hear human steps. But no: he had even caught the smell of army-cloth on the man who had dared to say such things to him. It must be true, then, that there were agents of the Cheka on board. What a pity that the conversation had been broken off. . . .

And at once the wavering picture of a recollection fell upon the screen of Paul's eyes. He saw:

. . . the clay walls of a stuffy hut; a large white stove therein, with birds and flowers daubed at its corners; a man in a sheepskin jacket lying on his side upon the earthen floor, his arms trussed up behind him. Blood has clotted on his curly hair. His face, pale with hatred and suffering, is turned toward Paul. He is speaking to Paul in French, with a rather uncouth accent:

"Go back where you came from. This isn't Africa: even though we are savage we still are no savages.

We're not going to sell our freedom: we'll fight to the last man. Russia is never fated to be a colony—do you hear? You are lying, brother—your beautiful words are just so much camouflage, screening the plantation owner."

"What nonsense!" Paul is dreadfully sincere. "What nonsense! It isn't colonies we're thinking of at all. We are out to save the greatest, most precious things in the world. There was, on a time, an invasion of the Huns. We overwhelmed them on the Rhine. Now we shall overwhelm them on the Dnieper."

The fellow on the floor grins impudently:

"Come, now—are you one of those idealists?"

"Silence!" Paul taps his ring on the deal table. "Talk respectfully to an officer of the French Army!"

"Why should I keep silent? You're going to turn me over to the firing squad anyway," says the trussed-up man. "And all for nothing. Oh, but you'll regret it! Better untie my arms, and I'll go away. As for you, you take yourself off to France, and on the way—don't forget—chuck your revolver into the sea. What's the odds —you fellows have lost the game anyway. There's half a billion of us. Your hands: they are we; your legs: they are we; your belly: it is we; your head—we, again. And what have *you* got? 'Most precious things'? Culture? It's ours. We'll place our guards over it—and it's ours. [The wounded man crept up to the table. His eyes—distended, wild, frightful—were obsessing Paul, were crushing him.] I can see you're an honest man; you are, it may be, one of the best. Why, then, are you on *their* side, and not on ours? They've poisoned you with gas, have infected you with malaria, have riddled your chest with bullets. They have made all the holy things to stink with corruption. Why, then, are you with them? If it's a matter of a piece of daily bread we, too, can offer you that much. Pass your hand over your eyes—sweep off the cobwebs of the ages. Awake! Awake, Paul!"

Paul Taurain opened his eyes with a moan. When would this inquisition end? Prickling, chaotic shards of recollections; the daily bustle before his eyes; the whir of glassy flywheels in his ears. . . . If darkness, silence, non-being but come as speedily as possible!

This day, too, became extinguished. Again, over the sea, appeared flaming worlds, torrents of black light, with nodules of primeval matter, arising out of quanta of energy, in the focuses of their intersections. And thus, driven by light, seeds of life go flying from one end of this lentil of a Creation to the other. Out of one such microbion had Paul Taurain arisen. And anew, some day, his body, his brain, his memory would be scattered abroad, as dust-of-atoms, through icy space.

On this night, even as on the one preceding, the Sister could not lead him off into his cabin. When, from vexation, she burst into tears, he lifted a trembling finger as withered as a twig, and pointed to the stars:

"All this is of greater need to me than all your medicines and mixtures."

v

Early next morning they were sailing past Calabria: a wild shore; jagged teeth of crags; great mounds of lilac-gray boulders. Scrubwood in the crevasses. Higher, the terraces of tawny plateaus. Here and there sheep, clustered. On a promontory a castle, of the same hue as the boulders: a tower, walls in ruins—an old robbers' roost, whence they were wont to issue for the looting of ships storm-driven upon this haunt of the Devil. To port, amid the murky, sun-shot mist, smoke was curling over the snowy summit of Aetna, and the shores of Sicily showed bluely.

The *Carcovado* raced over the choppy waves of the strait so dreaded of Odysseus. The family of the sugar-refinery owner came out on deck: all of them girt with life-belts. It turned out that there was danger hereabouts of running into some stray mine. The Zouaves were spitting at Scylla and Charybdis both. However, the whirlpool was passed safely. With its rusty nose the *Carcovado* was now cleaving the turquoise-blue waters of the Tyrrhenian Sea.

The Russian Man of Public Affairs, with wisps of straw caught in his beard, said loudly, addressing no one in particular:

"Gentlemen, the barometer is falling!"

The sultriness really was increasing. The sky had a metallic sheen. To the south the air was shimmering in murky waves, as though someone were boiling water there. From lack of anything to do, from the sultriness, from the unbearable light, something untoward began to brew aboard the steamer. It was bruited about that one of the toad's boarding-school misses had been carried off at night to the captain's cabin. The captain had not shown himself on the bridge since yesterday. It was also revealed that the female toad's remaining star boarders had likewise skipped out of the stokers' quarters. A searching party succeeded in finding one in the hold where, screaming and scratching, she was being ganged. She was locked up in the lazarette, under the guard of the doctor's assistant. The Zouaves were stirred up; they talked in whispers, gathering in small groups. Now one, now another would leap up from the red-hot deck and then vanish in the black inwards of the ship, where it smelt of rats and bilge, and the iron sides creaked from the sighs of the machinery.

The barometer was falling. The Russian lady was sitting in the shade of a lifeboat, in a woebegone mood.

Her little boy was asleep, his head, dripping with perspiration, pillowed on her knees. Even the clatter of cutlery in the caboose had died away. And suddenly, somewhere below, there was a short scuffle; there were sounds of blows and growling. Two men appeared on deck, bared to the waist, in soiled duck trousers. Their hair was standing up on end. They looked back over their shoulders and then started to run. The one ahead was showing his outstretched hand, all in blood:

"He bit my finger off! He bit my finger off!" he kept on repeating in a dull, breaking voice. He halted, frenziedly pulled off the sabot he still had on, and flung it into the sea. And, thus lightened, sped on:

"He bit my finger off!"

The other, who was taller, ran after him without a word. On his sinewy back, under one of the shoulder-blades, a bloody wen was visible, surrounded with tooth-marks. An odor of blood and pungent sweat spread over the deck. Immediately after these two a third jumped out of the ship's vitals—a hatchet-faced, black-haired fellow in a torn shirt of cheap cotton stuff. Spreading his legs wide he stopped, put two fingers in his mouth and emitted a piercing whistle, as though he were summoning his gang on a dark night on some deserted waste. The Zouaves leapt up. Their eyes were turning feral; their mustaches bristled. Quickly, closely, they surrounded the stokers. The stokers' coal-blackened chests were heaving; their breathing was hard. The one with the bloody wen on his back uttered in a soul-rending voice:

"He's got two of them tarts in his cabin!"

"Who has?"

"Chocolate!"

"He's got a knife!" the one with his finger bitten off screamed out. "He's got a big knife and a skewer. He bit my finger off. All of us here are going to have their throats slit! We'll never get to port alive."

Another piercing whistle. And thereupon all of them, both soldiers and stokers, started running down trap-ladders. A short while later an ominous hum of voices issued from the bowels of the ship. The female toad, hugging both her lap-dogs in her arms, jumped out on deck from the saloon: she began dashing about as if she were blind. In the first-class cabins Venetian blinds banged as they were pulled down. The first mate ran by with a scared face.

The Negro cook appeared at last in the midst of a milling crowd. He was stalwartly beating off the men with his long arms. His white jacket was in shreds and spotted with blood. He was backing toward a trap-ladder. Suddenly he snorted, hissed like a snake at his assailants, flew up on deck in two leaps and dashed off along it, his eyes, as white and big as hard-boiled eggs with the shells off, popping out of his head.

"Catch him! Catch him!" yelled the Zouaves, stream-ing after him. He scrambled still higher, up to the cap-tain's bridge, and from there his lacquered body flashed and, head down, plummeted into the water. His black, kinky head bobbed up, spluttering, far from the ship.

The *Carcovado's* engines stopped. Life-belts went fly-ing into the sea. The Negro swam up to the ship's side and seized a rope's end. With a gay grin he kept eying the heads hanging over the rails. It was plain the men would not beat him any further.

But the barometer still kept falling. The sky—molten lead—hung low. Gasping, the ship's engines throbbed; the blood throbbed in one's head. And again a whirl-wind sprang up on deck: the soldiers were whispering among themselves, darting from place to place; they got into a huddle. A high-pitched voice, panicky, canorously-distinct—evidently that of a Parisian—rang out:

"There's a storm heading this way. Everybody on deck will be washed off into the sea. They won't let us into the saloon, even. But in the first-class they have spring-beds for the profiteers. And silver spittoons for them to throw up in. Can it be that here, too, we will have to die for the bourgeoisie?"

"Into the hold with the profiteers!" voices began to shout. "The rich and the bourgeoisie—into the hold with them!"

The Zouaves, with throaty howls, dashed into the saloon through both its doors. But there was no one there. Dinner had been left unfinished on the tables. The cabin doors were locked. It was as stuffy in there as in one of those special stoves used for roasting geese. Some of the soldiers slumped on the settees, mopping the sweat that was coursing down their faces in streams. Those who really had their dander up took to hammering on the doors of the cabins:

"Hello, there! Hey, there, little ones, into the hold—into the hold with you!"

Out of one of the cabins, against the door of which a huge boot had crashed, Papa Crab thrust his head, with twitching, lilac-hued lips, and all in a sweat:

"Well? Just what *is* the matter? What are you making so much noise for?"

A swarthy hand had already raked in the collar of his cutaway; dozens of flaming faces, of distended eyes, had already drawn close to him. Things would have gone ill with Papa Crab, with his family, with his trunks. But at this point came the shrill whistling of the bo'sun, piping all hands on deck. And immediately the sky crashed and split over the ship; the thunder-peal was such that no one could remain standing. Lightning flashed through all the portholes. And the shrouds and rigging struck up a piteous song. The *Carcovado* listed hard to port. The storm swooped down. One could not make out the frightened faces—they were only so many blotches.

Tattered clouds scudded over the very water. The sea had become maned, leaden-somber, and the very waves beat ever more evilly, ever higher, against the *Carcovado's* rusty sides. The water was already lashing the deck. The lifeboats rocked on their davits. The wind caught up one of these boats, making its covering belly like a sail, tugged at it, tore it loose—and off the boat went, somersaulting in the raging foam. *Now* was the time to cast a cask filled with treasures to the Ruler of the Sea, or to slit the throat of an ox in order to incline that Ruler to mercy! What an oversight!

The *Carcovado* rattled, burrowed into the waves, wallowed therein, made its screws whir and spouted thick smoke. The hurricane was coming from the southeast, driving the ship to the shores the wind knew so well.

Paul Taurain, aroused, was sitting up in his berth surrounded with pillows. Neptune was knocking ferociously with his trident against the battened-down porthole. What a magnificent journey's end! Paul's eyes sparkled with tragic humor. *There*—that last blow against the ship's side was something like! The ship shuddered and began to fall, slowly. The medicine vials tumbled; all sorts of objects, big and little, started rolling and slipping toward the door of the cabin. The cabin was standing up on end, just as if Paul were on a swing at its ultimate upward soaring. The heart died away. The ship would never right itself.

"We're done for—done for!" the Sister began screaming, clutching at the upright of the berth.

But no: the old tub did right itself. The cabin began crawling upward. And regained its level. The Sister, having dropped on her knees, was, as she wept, picking up the broken medicine vials. And, anew, the trident of the Ruler of the Sea was knocking against the side of the ship.

"Sister," Paul was saying, smiling with a face as drawn as that of a corpse, "it is the hurricane of the times that has swept down upon us!"

VI

For more than a day and a night did the hurricane play pitch-and-toss with the *Carcovado*. The storm splintered to matchwood or washed away everything that had been on deck. It had swept two Zouaves off into the sea. It swept off both of the hapless she-toad's lap-dogs, as well as the leather-covered trunks, the bigger pieces of the Kiev sugar-refinery owner's mountain of baggage. Someone missed the Russian Man of Public Affairs with wisps of straw caught in his beard and, although they looked for him high and low, he was never found.

The last evening arrived.

"Ask the soldiers to bring me out on deck, please," Paul requested the Sister.

The Zouaves came, shook their heads in their red, tasseled *chéchias,* and clicked their tongues. They lifted Paul up on his small mattress and bore him off to a chaise longue on deck.

"I wish you happiness, *mes enfants,*" said he.

There, in the west (whither, rising and dipping, the heavy nose of the ship was eagerly heading) the sun, still wrathful after the tempest, was sinking into an orange waste. As it sank it passed behind the long streaks of gauzy cloudlets; bringing them to red-heat, it turned dark purple in its turn. Reddish shadows ran upward over its disk.

The sea was a somber lilac, filled with impenetrable horror. The sun-globe's reddish, sparkling reflections, as dense as though one were touching them with one's fingers, glided over the whitecaps. The mane of each wave had the sheen of blood.

This did not last for long, however. The sun set. The glint of the reflections faded, expired. And, in the glow of the sunset, miracles were being wrought. It was as though some planet unknown to man had drawn near to the darkened earth, and as though on that planet, spreading amid green, warm waters, were islands, bays, craggy sea-margents, all of such a joyously-scarlet, effulgent hue as never is or was: unless, perchance, one sees it in a dream. Certain cities were there, builded of fiery gold. Winged figures seemed to be hovering over a bay that was changing to green. . . .

Paul gripped the elbow-rests of his chair with fingers that were turning cold. His heart was throbbing in exaltation. Last on, last on, wondrous vision! But now its outlines were shadowed over, dimmed as if with ashes. The gold faded, became extinguished on the summits. The continents were crumbling into ruins. And there was nothing more. A sunset, dimming.

VII

Such was the last flare-up of Paul Taurain's life. Much later his indifferent gaze distinguished a white star, low over the sea: now bursting into glow, now vanishing. This was the Marseilles lighthouse. The ancient way had come to its end. The Zouaves were purring snatches of song, so pleased were they, and changing their footgear, slinging their dufflebags over their shoulders.

"Ah, there'll be someone to weep over this fellow," said one in a low voice as he passed by Paul.

Paul let his head drop. Then a chill mattress started sliding over him: upward, from his feet to his chest. It slid up to his face. But, one more time, it befell him to feel the breath of life. Someone bent over him; someone's cool, tremulous lips touched his, and a woman's voice—the voice of Lucie—was calling his name.

They lifted him up and started carrying him down unsteady steps, over creaking planks, to the noisy shore, redolent of dust and humanity, inundated with light.

ILF AND PETROV

ILYA ARNOLDOVICH ILF   (1897–1937)

AND

EUGENE PETROVICH KATAEV   (1907–1942)

EDITOR'S NOTE

ILF was born at Odessa, in a poor Jewish family. After graduation from a technical school he worked as an assembler in a machine shop, was a bookkeeper, and took charge of a stable; at eighteen he became a newspaperman in his native city (which as a literary center ranks next to Leningrad and Moscow). He is one of the comparatively few Russian humorists who began as one, starting to write for the funny papers in 1919, at the height of the Russian Civil War. Upon coming to Moscow he joined the staff of *Gudok* (*The Train-Whistle*), a railroading publication, where he formed his life-long partnership with Petrov, another staff-member. Later both joined the staff of the newspaper *Pravda* (*The Truth*), which gave them an audience of millions for their famous sketches, flaying bureaucrats and bureaucracy, philistines and philistinism. (It was at this period that they used the pseudonyms of Tolstoievski and The Chill Philosopher.)

Ilf's health was undermined by the two-month, 10,-000-mile automobile trip through the United States in 1936, which he and Petrov undertook to gather material for their *One-Story-High America*. According to the *New York Times* (July 6, 1942) he was drowned while swimming during this visit; actually he died of tuberculosis on April 13, 1937, at Moscow, where he was cremated.

From Petrov's poignant yet humorous article on how the famous partners worked one gathers that Ilf was very sensitive and shy, yet by no means a melancholic; from Ilf's own *Notebooks* (published posthumously) one perceives that, although he became famous as a humorist, he might have become a serious writer of the first rank.

Petrov edited several humorous periodicals, and also the exceedingly popular weekly, *Ogonë (Little Flame)*, which did so much to bring about a better understanding of the United States and England. He was also well known for his film-scenarios, such as those for *Musical Story* and *The Circus*—the latter written with his brother, the famous writer Valentin Kataev, and Ilf. Like most Soviet writers during World War II, Petrov served as a correspondent. He held the rank of Lieutenant-Colonel, working for the Soviet Information Bureau and the North American Newspaper Alliance, his despatches appearing in the *New York Times*. He was killed July 2, 1942, at Sebastopol, which he had covered for many months.

As a team, Ilf and Petrov wrote, among other things, *How Robinson Was Created* (a collection of their sketches), *A Radiant Personality,* and the famous picaresques, *Twelve Chairs* and *The Little Golden Calf,* both having Ostap Bender, the Great Manipulator, as their arch-rogue hero. (The last two have been translated into English, in abridgments, and have enjoyed a popularity abroad comparable to the Russian.) *The Little Golden Calf* was pronounced a work of genius by American critics—among others. However, some of their work has met the same curious fate as Zoshchenko's, and their satire has been turned into anti-Soviet propaganda.

Their work (especially the two Ostap Bender books) is marked by deft characterization, keen observation, engrossing narrative, extravagance and grotesquerie of situation, rollicking humor and pungent satire.

"Ellochka the Cannibal" is from *Twelve Chairs,* and was a favorite platform piece of the two great humorists.

Ellochka the Cannibal

ILF AND PETROV

THE vocabulary of William Shakespeare, as calculated by scholars, runs to 12,000 words. The vocabulary of an African of the cannibal tribe of Mumbo-Jumbo runs to 300 words.

Ellochka Shchukina got along easily and freely with thirty.

Here are the words, phrases, and interjections, captiously chosen by her out of the whole of a great, magniloquent, and mighty tongue:

1. "You're fresh."
2. Ho-ho! (*Expressing, in accordance with circumstances, Irony, Astonishment, Rapture, Hatred, Joy, Contempt, or Satisfaction.*)
3. Great.
4. Gloomy. (*In relation to everything. Examples:* "Gloomy Pete is here." "Gloomy weather." "A gloomy incident." "A gloomy cat," *and so forth.*)
5. "What gloom!"
6. Uncanniness, *or* Uncanny. (*Example: On meeting a very dear girl-friend:* "It's uncanny, the way we meet!")
7. Fellow. (*In relation to all male acquaintances, regardless of age or social standing.*)
8. "Don't you teach me how to live."
9. "Like a baby!" ("I trimmed him like a baby!"—*at cards.* "I shut him up like a baby!"—*evidently during a conversation with a lease-holder.*)
10. "Bee-utiful!" (*Beautiful.*)
11. Fat and handsome. (*Used to characterize both animate and inanimate objects.*)
12. "Let's take a horse-cab." (*Used to one's husband.*)
13. "Let's take a taxi." (*Used to male acquaintances.*)
14. "The back of your coat is all white!" (*Joke.*)
15. My, my!
16. —ulya. (*Affectionate name-ending. Examples:* Mishulya, Zinulya.)
17. Oho! (*Irony, Astonishment, Rapture, Hatred, Joy, Contempt, or Satisfaction.*)
13. "Oh, go on!" (*Conveying incredulity or warning.*)

The extremely insignificant quantity of words left over served as a transmission link between Ellochka and department store clerks.

If anyone were to scrutinize the photographs of Ellochka hung up over the bed of her husband, the engineer Ernest Pavlovich Shchukin (one *en face*, the other in profile), it would not be at all hard to notice a forehead of pleasing height and convexity, great humid eyes, the most charming little nose in all of Moscow

Province, and a chin with a tiny beauty-mark, that looked as if it had been done in India ink.

Men found Ellochka's height flattering. She was tiny, and even the scrawniest runts looked big and mighty he-men alongside of her.

As for any distinguishing characteristics, why, there just weren't any. And anyway, Ellochka had no need of them. She was pretty.

The two hundred rubles a month which her husband drew at the Electrolustre plant Ellochka considered an affront. They were of no help at all in that grandiose feud which Ellochka had been carrying on for four years by now, ever since she had assumed the social status of the mistress of a household, the wife of Shchukin. She carried on this feud with all her forces strained to the utmost. It swallowed up all resources. Ernest Pavlovich took extra work home, had refused to have any domestic, worked the kerosene stove himself, carried out the garbage, and even fried the cutlets.

But all this proved fruitless. The ominous foe was by now demolishing the household economy, more and more so with every year. Ellochka had, four years ago, perceived that she had a rival on the other side of the Atlantic. This calamity had come upon Ellochka on that joyous evening when she had been trying on the darlingest little blouse of crepe de Chine. In that outfit she looked practically a goddess.

"Ho-ho!" she had exclaimed, reducing to this cannibalistic outcry the overwhelmingly complex emotions that had gripped her soul.

In simplified form they might have been expressed and phrased somewhat as follows: "On beholding me thus the men will get all excited. They will quiver. They will follow me to the ends of the earth, stammering their love. But I am going to be frigid. For are they worthy of me? I am the most beautiful of women. Nobody on this terrestrial globe has a blouse as elegant as that!"

But there were only thirty words, and Ellochka chose the most expressive combination: "Ho-ho!"

It was at this auspicious hour that Phima Sòbak came to see her. She brought with her the frosty breath of January and a French fashion magazine. Ellochka came to a dead stop at its first page. The glossy photograph portrayed a daughter of the American billionaire Vanderbilt in an evening gown. It had furs and plumes, silk and pearls and a deft cut; the wearer's hair-do was extraordinary and deliriously stunning. This photograph settled everything.

"Oho!" said Ellochka to herself.

Which meant: "It's either she or I."

The morning of the next day found Ellochka in a beauty parlor. Here she lost her splendid black braid and henna'd what was left of her hair. Next she contrived to surmount one more step on the ladder which was to bring Ellochka nearer to that refulgent paradise wherein promenaded American billionaires' daughters, unfit to tie the shoelaces of Shchukina, that mistress of a household. Through an outlet that extended credit to workers a dog-skin, masquerading as muskrat, was purchased. It was used to trim an evening ensemble.

Mister Shchukin, who had long been nursing a dream of buying a new drawing-board, became somewhat despondent.

The gown, bordered with dog-muskrat, dealt the presumptious Vanderbilt woman the first telling blow. Next the haughty American was given the one-two-three. Ellochka acquired from Phimochka Sòbak's private furrier a chinchilla stole (Russian rabbit, put to death in the Province of Tula), took to wearing a dove-gray fedora of Argentine felt, and made the coat of her husband's new suit over into a stylish lady's jacket. The billionairess rocked on her heels but, evidently, the doting papa Vanderbilt came to her rescue.

The next number of the fashion magazine contained portraits of Ellochka's accursed rival in four poses: 1): Wearing black foxes; 2): With a diamond star on her forehead; 3): In flying-togs—high patent-leather boots, a green jacket of the finest cloth, and gauntlets, the slits of which were encrusted with medium-sized emeralds; and 4): In a ball gown—cascades of gems and a little silk.

Ellochka mobilized. Papa Shchukin took out a loan in a mutual-aid association. They wouldn't let him have more than thirty rubles. A new, mighty effort cut the domestic economy down at its roots. It was becoming necessary to carry on the good fight on all of life's battlefronts. Photographs had been recently received of the Miss in her new Florida castle. And Ellochka, too, had to get new furniture. She bought two upholstered chairs at an auction. (A lucky buy! You simply couldn't let the chance slip!) Without consulting her husband, Ellochka took the money budgeted for food. Until payday there remained ten days and four rubles. Ellochka and the chairs drove through Varsonofievsky Lane with great éclat. Her husband wasn't home. However, he put in his appearance shortly, lugging a brief-case as bulky and heavy as a trunk.

"The gloomy husband is here," said Ellochka distinctly.

All her words were pronounced distinctly, and popped out livelily, like peas out of a pod.

"Hello, Ellochka—but what's all this? Where did those chairs come from?"

"Ho-ho!"

"No, really?"

"Bee-utiful!"

"Yes, they're good chairs."

"Great!"

"Anybody make us a present of them?"

"Oho!"

"What! Surely, you didn't buy them? But what with? Not with the household money, surely? Why, I've told you a thousand times—"

"Ernestulya! You're fresh!"

"There, how could you do such a thing? Why, we won't have anything to eat!"

"My, my!"

"But that's outrageous! You're living beyond your means!"

"Oh, go on!"

"Yes, yes! You're living beyond your means—"

"Don't you teach me how to live!"

"No, really—let's talk this over seriously. I get two hundred a month—"

"What gloom!"

"I don't take bribes, I don't steal money and don't know how to counterfeit it—"

"It's uncanny!"

Ernest Pavlovich fell silent.

"Tell you what," said he at last, "we can't live like this."

"Ho-ho!" retorted Ellochka, sitting down on one of the new chairs.

"We'll have to separate."

"My, my!"

"We have incompatible characters. I—"

"You fat and handsome fellow—"

"How many times have I begged you not to call me a *fellow?*"

"Oh, go on!"

"Come, where do you get that idiotic jargon from?"

"Don't you teach me how to live!"

"Oh, hell!" the engineer shouted.

"You're fresh, Ernestulya."

"Let's separate peacefully."

"Oho!"

"You won't convince me of anything. This quarrel—"

"I'll trim you like a baby."

"No, this is downright unbearable. Your arguments can't keep me back from the step which I'm forced to take. I'm going after a moving van right now."

"Oh, go on!"

"We're dividing the furniture evenly."

"It's uncanny!"

"You'll get a hundred rubles a month. Even a hundred and twenty. You can keep the room. Lead whatever life you wish, but I can't go on like this—"

"Great," said Ellochka disdainfully.

"As for me, I'm moving to Ivan Alexeievich's place."

"Oho!"

"He's gone to the country and has left his whole apartment to me for the summer. Only it's unfurnished."

"Bee-utiful!"

Five minutes later Ernest Pavlovich came back with the janitor.

"There, I won't take the wardrobe—you need it more than I do; but as for the desk, if you'll be so kind. . . . And you can take out one of those chairs," he turned to the janitor. "I have a right to it, I think?"

Ernest Pavlovich tied his things in a big bundle, wrapped his boots in a newspaper, and turned to go.

"The back of your coat is all white," said Ellochka in a voice that sounded like a phonograph.

"Good-bye, Ellen."

He expected that his wife would, at least on this one occasion, refrain from her usual verbal small change. Ellochka in her turn sensed all the gravity of the moment. She strained with all her might and sought for words appropriate to the parting. She found them quickly enough:

"Are you taking a taxi? Bee-utiful!"

The engineer tumbled down the stairs like a landslide.

Ellochka passed that evening with Phima Sòbak. They discussed a situation of extraordinary importance, threatening to overturn the economics of the world.

"I think I'll go in for long and loose things," Phima was saying, drawing her head in between her shoulders like a hen.

"What gloom!"

And Ellochka glanced at Phima Sòbak with respect. Mlle. Sòbak had the reputation of a cultured girl: her vocabulary contained somewhere in the neighborhood of a hundred and eighty words. And not only that, but she knew one word of such a nature that Ellochka couldn't think of it even in her dreams. It was a rich word: *homosexuality*. Phima Sòbak was, beyond all doubt, a cultured girl.

The animated discussion lasted far beyond midnight.

ISAAC IMMANUELOVICH BABEL

(1894–)

EDITOR'S NOTE

BABEL, the son of a Jewish merchant, is a native of Odessa. He first appeared in print, with his *Odessa Stories*, in 1915, in Gorki's *Chronicle*. During the Russian Civil War he was attached to the Red Cavalry; the first of his unique *Horse Army* sketches appeared in 1924. His output can hardly be called vast: these two groups of stories, plus a play, *Sunset,* and *Benny Kriek,* a screen dramatization of the life of a gang-leader who is the hero of some of the *Odessa Stories,* comprise practically all his work, yet Babel has indisputably earned his place in the front ranks of the Soviet masters of the word.

When Benny Kriek promises to slit somebody's throat unless a certain sum is forthcoming, he does so in the politest yet the most exquisitely twisted Russian. Generally (with such exponents as Doroshevich or Averchenko) "Odessa stories" are a highly humorous genre; Yushkevich has struck deeper notes in it; in the hands of Babel it reaches the heights of purest literature. Poignant, poetic, sardonic, appealing, appalling in contrasts, a combination of exquisite lyricism and red-earth coarseness, Babel's *Odessa Stories* are an abiding masterpiece. Rabelais, Zola and Maupassant, combined, might well envy Babel his *Liubka the Cossack* alone. One can think of nothing written to compare these portscapes to —and of nothing to compare with them (not even Kuprin's *The Old City of Marseilles*).

Babel's exceedingly significant and equally famous *Horse Army* is utterly original in execution and to a large extent autobiographical. Grotesque, ironic, filled with wormwood poetry, delicate as a dandelion head at dusk, brutal as dark-red hacked horseflesh, it stands unsurpassed to this day as a series of goyaesques of the Revolution, of Russia's Civil War.

The book is available in an English version entitled *The Red Cavalry*.

Liubka the Cossack

ISAAC IMMANUELOVICH BABEL

OUT in Moldavanka, that notorious district, at the corner of Dalnitskaya and Balkovskaya streets, stands the house of Liubka Schneiweiss [Snow-White]. Her house accommodates a wine-cellar, an inn-yard, a feed store, and a dovecote holding a hundred pair pigeons of the Kriukov and Nikolaiev breeds. All these enterprises, and Section 6 in the Odessa stone quarries, belong to Liubka Schneiweiss, nicknamed the Cossack —all, that is, save for the dovecote, which is the property of Eusel the watchman, a veteran who had been decorated with a medal. Of Sundays Eusel comes out on the Ohotnitskaya and sells his pigeons to petty city officials and the local small fry.

Among the others living in Liubka's household, besides the watchman, is one Pessya Mindl, cook and go-between, and Tsudechkis, Liubka's general manager, a little bit of a Jew, whose short stature and shorter beard make him resemble our celebrated Moldavanka rabbi, Ben-Z'chary. Concerning this Tsudechkis I know a lot of stories. And the first of those stories has to do with how this Tsudechkis came to be the general manager of the inn-yard belonging to Liubka, nicknamed the Cossack.

Some ten years ago Tsudechkis had happened to act as a broker in getting a horse-drawn threshing-machine for a certain landowner, and that evening he had brought this landowner to Liubka's to celebrate the deal. This client of his had not only mustachios but chin-whiskers and sported patent-leather boots. Pessya Mindl gave him *gefülte fisch* for supper and, after supper, introduced him to a pretty young lady by the name of Nastya. The landowner stayed the night—and in the morning Eusel awoke Tsudechkis, who was lying curled up in a ball at the threshold of Liubka's room.

"There," said Eusel, "last evening you were bragging that that landowner had bought a threshing-machine through you, so you should know that, after spending the night here, he made tracks at daybreak, like the lowest of low-lives. Now shell out two rubles for the eats, and four for the young lady's time. Anybody can see you're an old man that's been through the mill."

But shell out Tsudechkis didn't. Whereupon Eusel shoved him inside Liubka's room and turned the key on him.

"There," said the watchman, "you stay here, and when Liubka gets back from the quarry she will, with God's help, drag your living soul out of you. Amen."

"You jailbird, you," Tsudechkis answered the veteran, "you don't know a thing, you jailbird, whereas, among other things, I believe in God, Who will bring me out of here, even as he brought all the Jews, first out of Egypt, and then out of the desert."

There was a great deal more which the little broker felt like telling Eusel, but the veteran took the key with

him and went off, his boots clattering. Thereupon Tsudechkis turned around and saw, near the window, Pessya
Mindl the go-between, who was reading a book, *The
Miracles and the Heart of Baal Shem Tov*. She was reading the gilt-edged Hassidic tome and at the same time
rocking with her foot an oaken cradle. Lying and bawling in this cradle was Liubka's son, little David.

"I can see how well things are run in this convict
colony," Tsudechkis remarked to Pessya Mindl. "The
child is lying there and crying fit to split his lungs all to
little pieces, so it's a pity just to look at him, but you,
you fat creature, just sit there like a bump on a log and
can't give him a bottle, even—"

"*You* give him a bottle," Pessya Mindl answered
him, without taking her eyes off the book. "He should
only take that bottle from an old faker like you—for
he's a big-grown oaf by now, yet the only thing he wants
is his mammy's milk. But his mammy is busy running
around her quarries, lapping tea with the Jews in the
Bear Tavern, buying up smuggled goods in the harbor,
and she gives just as much thought to her son as she does
to last year's snow."

"Yea," the little broker said to himself then, "thou
art delivered into the hands of Pharaoh, Tsudechkis,"
and, stepping over to the east wall, he mumbled not only
all the appropriate morning prayers but some additional
ones as well, and then took the crying infant in his
arms. Little David eyed him in perplexity and kicked
his little raspberry-hued legs, beaded all over with
infant-sweat, while the old man fell to pacing the room
and, swaying like a saintly sage at his prayers, began
singing an endless song for him.

"A-a-ah," he began his song, "all the children should
get fiddlesticks, but our Davy should get rolls, hot and

white, so's he'll sleep both day and night! A-a-ah, all children should get hard blows—"

Tsudechkis showed Liubka's son a fist all grown over with gray hair, and kept repeating about fiddlesticks and white rolls until the little boy fell asleep, and until the sun reached the zenith of the radiant sky. It reached the zenith, and there it began to quiver like a fly overcome with the heat. The wild muzhiks from Nerubaisk and Tatarka, who were stopping at Liubka's inn-yard, crawled under their carts and fell into savage, trillingly snoring slumber there; an artisan in his cups went toward the gates and there, flinging his plane and saw away from him, slumped to the earth, slumped to the earth and began snoring, began snoring in the midst of the universe, a universe all dotted with the golden flies and the azure lightnings of July. At no great distance from him, in a patch of cool shade, certain wrinkled German colonists settled themselves; they had brought wine from the Bessarabian border for Liubka's cellars. They lit their pipes, the stems of which were long and curved, and the smoke of those pipes tangled in the silvery stubble upon unshaven and senile cheeks. The sun was lolling out of the sky, like the rosy tongue of some thirsting hound; that Titan, the sea, was rolling in on the Peresip mole, and the masts of distant ships rocked over the emerald waters of the bay of Odessa. The day was aboard a gaily adorned galley; the day was nearing its mooring place of evening and, as if to greet the evening, Liubka came back from the city only when it was going on five o'clock.

She rode up on a little skewbald roan nag with its belly sucked full of wind and a mane that had been allowed to grow all by itself. A lad with stout legs and in a calico shirt swung the gates open for Liubka, Eusel

held her horse by the bridle, and it was then that Tsudechkis called out to her from his dungeon-keep:

"My respects to you, and a good day, Madam Schneiweiss. There, you went away on business for three years,
and have tossed a hungry child in my lap—"

"Quiet, scarecrow!" Liubka answered the old man,
and got down off the saddle. "Who's that there, opening
his yap in my window?"

"That's Tsudechkis, an old man who's been through
the mill," the old veteran with the medal informed his
mistress, and launched into an account of the whole
affair with the landowner, but he never did get to telling it to the end, inasmuch as the little broker set up a
squawk, interrupting him:

"What imperence!" he squawked at Liubka. "What
imperence, tossing a child in a stranger's lap, and then
getting lost for three years! There, go and give him your
teat!"

"I'm coming up to you right now, you little gangster,"
Liubka muttered, apostrophizing her son, and dashed
for the staircase. She came into the room and took her
breast out of her dusty blouse.

The boy stretched himself toward her; he kept biting
at her monstrous nipple but got never a drop of milk
out of it. A vein swelled up on the mother's brow, and
Tsudechkis chided her, shaking his skull-cap:

"You want to get everything into your clutches, greedy
Liubka; you tug the whole universe toward you, as
children tug at a tablecloth with bread crumbs; you
want the first wheat and the first grapes; you want to
bake white loaves in the baking sun—but your own
little one, a child like a little star, has to wilt away because he can't get milk—"

"Milk he's talking about yet!" yelled the woman, and
squeezed her breast. "When the *Plutarch* came into the

harbor today, and I had to cover ten miles in this heat! But as for you, you're singing a little too loud and a little too long, old Jew—better come across with that six rubles."

But again Tsudechkis wouldn't come across with the money. Instead, he loosened his sleeve, bared his arm, and thrust a gaunt and unwashed elbow into Liubka's mouth:

"There, choke on that, you female convict, you," said he, and spat in a corner.

Liubka took her time about releasing this strange elbow out of her mouth, then she turned the key in the lock and went out into the courtyard. There Mister Trottybury, who looked like a pillar of ruddy meat, was already awaiting her. Mister Trottybury was chief engineer on the *Plutarch*. He had brought two sailors with him to Liubka's. One of these sailors was a Briton, the other a Malayan. It took the three of them to drag into the yard the contraband they had brought from Port Saïd. The chest was heavy; they dropped it to the ground, and pouring out of the chest came cigars, tangled up in Japanese silk. A multitude of country-wives came flocking to that chest, while two chance-come Gypsy women, swaying and with their sequins tinkling, began sidling up to it.

"Git, you trash!" Liubka yelled at the women, and led the sailors off into the shade under an acacia, where they all seated themselves at a table. Eusel served them with wine, and Mister Trottybury spread out his wares. He took out of one bale cigars and fine silks, cocaine and files, tobacco from the State of Virginia, innocent of any revenue stamps, and black wine obtained on the Island of Chios. Each commodity had a price of its own, and each sum was wetted down with Bessarabian wine, redolent of sun and bedbugs. By this time twilight was rolling through the courtyard, like an evening billow over a broad river, and the tipsy Malayan, filled with wonder, touched Liubka's breast with his finger. He touched it with one finger, then with each of the others in turn.

His yellow and gentle eyes swung over the table, like paper lanterns over a Chinese lane; he struck up a song in a barely audible voice and toppled to the ground when Liubka brushed him off with her fist.

"Just see how a well-educated man behaves himself!" Liubka commented on the Malayan to Mister Trottybury. "My last milk is drying up because of this Malayan, yet that Jew up there ate me up alive because of that milk." And she indicated Tsudechkis who, standing by the window, was washing his socks. The little lamp in the room where Tsudechkis was imprisoned was smoking; the basin he was laundering in was foaming and burbling; having sensed that they were talking about him he leaned out of the window and began to shout desperately:

"Save me, good people!" he shouted, and waved his arms.

"Quiet, you scarecrow!" Liubka burst out laughing. "Quiet!"

She shied a stone at the old man, but at her first attempt missed him. Thereupon the woman grabbed an empty wine-bottle. But Mister Trottybury, the chief engineer, took the bottle from her, aimed, and sent it right through the open window.

"Miss Liubka," said the chief engineer, getting up and assembling his wine-logged legs under him, "many worthy people come to me, Miss Liubka, wanting goods, but I supply nobody—neither Mister Kuninzohn, nor Mister Batya, nor even Mister Kupchik; nobody except

you, because I find your talk to my liking, Miss
Liubka—"

And, having regained his shaky legs, he took his
sailors—one of them a Briton, the other a Malayan—
by their shoulders, and launched into a dance with them
through the yard, now grown cooler. Since they came
from a ship named *Plutarch,* they danced in a silence
fraught with deep meaning. An orange-hued star, having
rolled down to the very edge of the horizon, was staring
at them for all it was worth. Then they got their money,
linked their arms, and walked out into the street, swaying, the way a swinging ship's-lantern sways. From the
street they could behold the sea, the now black water of
the bay of Odessa, toy flags on sunken masts, and blinding lights in the spacious bowels of ships.

Liubka escorted her dancing guests to the crossing;
left alone on the deserted street she laughed at her
thoughts and went home. The sleepy lad in the calico
shirt locked the door after her. Eusel brought his mistress
the day's takings, and she went up to her room to sleep.
Pessya Mindl, that bawd, was already dozing there,
while Tsudechkis was rocking the oaken cradle with his
bare feet.

"How you have exhausted us, Liubka—you have no
conscience," said he, and took the child out of the cradle.
"There, learn from me, you abominable mother—"

He put a fine-toothed comb with its back against
Liubka's breast and laid her son down in her bed. The
child strained toward his mother, stuck himself against
the comb, and began to bawl. Thereupon the old man
shoved the baby-bottle at him, but little David turned
away from it.

"What kind of spell are you trying to work over me,
you old scoundrel?" muttered Liubka, falling off to sleep.

"Quiet, you abominable mother!" Tsudechkis told her. "Be quiet, and learn from me, may you perish—"

The little one again stuck himself against the comb; then he hesitatingly took the bottle—and fell to sucking thereon greedily.

"There!" said Tsudechkis, and began laughing. "I've weaned your child. Learn from me, may you perish—"

Little David lay in his cradle, sucking away at the bottle and dribbling beatified spittle. Liubka woke up, opened her eyes, and closed them again. She had seen her son, and the moon also, trying to break in at her window. The moon was leaping about among black clouds, like a strayed calf.

"Well, so be it," said Liubka then. "Open the door for Tsudechkis, Pessya Mindl, and let him come tomorrow for a pound of American tobacco—"

And the day following Tsudechkis came for his pound of tobacco, innocent of any revenue stamps, from the State of Virginia. He got it and, on top of that, a quarter of a pound of tea. And a week later, when I came to buy pigeons from Eusel, I beheld a new general manager in Liubka's inn-yard. He was as diminutive as Ben-Z'chary, our rabbi. Tsudechkis was this new manager. He spent fifteen years at this post of his, and during that time I learned a multitude of stories concerning him. And, if I can, I'll tell them all in orderly succession, inasmuch as they are ever so interesting.

VSEVOLOD VYACHESLAVOVICH IVANOV

(1895 or '96–)

EDITOR'S NOTE

HIS parentage is decidedly interesting: his father, a village schoolmaster, was the bastard of a Governor General of Turkestan; his mother was a mixture of Polish and Kirghiz. Ivanov was one of Gorki's innumerable protégés, and published his first short story in 1915 (or '16). After the October Revolution he served in the Red Army, defending Omsk against the Czechs. In 1920, again with the help of Gorki, he came to Leningrad, and joined the Serapion Brotherhood. The best thumbnail of Ivanov is by the author himself: "I was born at Lebiazhen, a steppe village on the Irtysh. . . . Received my education at the village school. . . . Began tramping at fourteen. Was by turns printer [typesetter, particularly: 1912-18], sailor, circus clown and fakir—billed as Ben Ali Bey the Dervish. I was sword-swallower, Human Pincushion, Torture Artist; I jumped through hoops of sharp-pointed knives and flaming torches. I tramped through Tomsk with a hurdy-gurdy, performed in show-booths at fairs, was a Speaking and Singing Clown in circuses, and was even featured as a Wrestling Champion; I entertained in third-rate cabarets. . . . I have written a number of books, and I don't think it's much fun to be a writer. Others fare better; their joys are simpler and more frequent. Still, a good many things make me happy, and whenever I ask myself what I have to complain about, I am stuck for an answer."

Besides contributing to the riches of Russian pica-
resque literature, Ivanov is concerned with certain aso-
cial, unregenerate petty-bourgeois tendencies. He has
by now escaped classification as a Siberian writer, and
is one of the leading Soviet authors.

The Oasis of Shehr-i-Sebeh[1]

VSEVOLOD VYACHESLAVOVICH IVANOV

DJALLANUM, wife of Ali-Akbyr, a dealer in
grapes from the *kishlak* of Shehr-i-Sebeh, contracted smallpox. Ali-Akbyr himself was a man well-
grown, handsome, with his nails tinted red after the
manner of the Persians. He had paid for his wife, five
years back, at a time of famine and wars, a great *kalym*
(or wedding ransom), and that not in Czar Nicky's
bogus money but in cattle, and that cattle, even unto
the days of the present, was enriching his father-in-law.
And so Ali-Akbyr felt sorry about losing his wife, and,
also, he felt sorry because during the time of wars many
handsome women had died out, or had been carried
off to Afghanistan. It was hard to find a good wife
nowadays—and the youthful element was growing up
flat-breasted and flat-buttocked. And so Ali-Akbyr at
once summoned to the sick woman the local saint, Hussein, and Hussein had hardly had time to gird his belly
and pick up his knobby staff when Ali-Akbyr had al-

[1] The Editor gratefully acknowledges his indebtedness to New
Directions, for permission to reproduce the Ivanov sketch from
Soviet Short Stories, and to the Vanguard Press, Inc., for permission
to quote from material used in connection with Ivanov's *The Adventures of a Fakir*.

ready saddled his own horse and sped off after the general practitioner. The general practitioner, a medico of the second-class, was a Russian, Gerassimov by name, yet he conducted himself as if he, too, were a saint: he got ready for the visit slowly, unwillingly; also, it may have been that he was afraid of smallpox. Upon his arrival the second-class medico demanded that Djallanum take off her coverings and, after Ali-Akbyr had promised him a ram, the medico felt her hand and said:

"The crisis is over; she'll live on!"

But, even before the physician, the sainted Hussein had said the same thing, and Ali-Akbyr had come to feel sorry for himself, and over the trouble he had gone to and the expenditures—and he chose his scrawniest ram for the medico and, when it came to entertaining him, the tea he brewed was of the weakest. However, after five days, Djallanum felt worse—and toward evening she died. She was quickly hauled off to the grave, seated therein, and covered over with sand. Ali-Akbyr was left all alone.

A road out into the desert went past the graveyard. A caravan was going by. At its head, seated upon a tiny ass, his bare feet dangling low, rode the leader of the caravan, a gray-headed Turkoman. Tied to his saddle by a lariat woven of hair was the first camel; a second camel was tied to the first; the camels ambled so quietly that one could hear the swish of the lariats, now slackening, now tautening. The Turkoman rode along in concentration, in quietude, and a long staff, mark of his authority, barely swayed in his hands. Slowly, treading one after the other, now clambering up on the sandy knolls, now disappearing in the hollows, now straightening out into a harp string, now forming a broken line over the winding road, the camels were going off into the desert. It was altogether windless; the caravan was leaving in its wake the tracks of camel-pads, but immediately this trail would be flooded over by the sand. A light haze showed blue upon the summits of the knolls: this was the sand, raised up by the breath of the desert. On beholding this sand Ali-Akbyr put his hand to his heart, which was oozing melancholy, and went home.

The grapes were maturing, and the peasant vintners came in the evening to chat about prices and to learn if Ali-Akbyr would be going to town soon. The lamp burned dully—after the wife's death there was no one to clean its chimney—and the room reeked of kerosene. They drank tea, each holding the cup around the rim of its bottom and, after each gulp, emitting a loud grunt. And then, for the first time (as he filled a third cup for each guest), Ali-Akbyr proclaimed that the holy Hussein was a thief and a swindler, notwithstanding that he knew all the laws of God so well. The peasants would not believe Ali-Akbyr, yet they would not enter into any dispute. Thereupon Ali-Akbyr solemnly raised a finger and said, drawing out his words:

"When you will have five more die among ye, and Hussein will have said of each one of the five that he was going to get well, you will not then be keeping silent, as you are keeping silent now!"

And lo, five new victims died of smallpox, even though Hussein had said that each one of them was going to get well, but just the same the peasants would not believe Ali-Akbyr.

The grapes were maturing, their leaves had taken on the color of blood—and the wine of desires matured in the veins of Ali-Akbyr. He had need of a sturdy wife and, although the laws of Moscow forbade any *kalym*, he must nevertheless give big money for a sturdy wife, and so Ali-Akbyr took to coming to town often. The water in the *arrik*-canal of Kochik was falling, and the passing pilgrims from beyond the mountains of Zarshan were saying that the snows were done with their melting, and that one could hardly expect spring-freshets in the fall. The grapes were ripening, but the water in the *arrik* kept decreasing and decreasing, just as though the grapes were drinking it dry. And thereupon the peasants, who still did not believe Ali-Akbyr, and who still listened in silence to his opprobrious speeches, hied them to the mosque and asked the saint to send up a prayer.

Hussein himself had been ailing of late: he had lived his life through honorably, in accordance with all the laws, and was proudly awaiting death and paradise, since he himself considered himself a saint. He felt hurt at seeing that the faith of the peasants in him had lessened, and that their offerings had diminished. No need had he of these offerings—much of that which was brought to him in offerings he distributed; it was the peasants, who were sinning before Allah, that he felt sorry for. He sternly told them that he would pray, and would hope that Allah might hearken to his prayer: there would be an increase of water, and the smallpox would cease. The smallpox, now, truth to tell, had long since gone, but the peasants did not contradict him. And Hussein did, actually, pray all night, as well as for half of a long and sultry day besides. He keeled over in exhaustion, and the mosque attendant, a young grandson of his, the rosy-cheeked Alimbai, reverently led him off to his skimpy couch. After resting Hussein again prayed a long time but, apparently, his prayers fell short of reaching Allah, so that the water continued to abate and the trees in the oasis of Shehr-i-Sebeh began to wilt.

During those days Ali-Akbyr had sought out for himself, in the nearby *kishlak* of Uchim, a bride by the name of Ydris, and one who in the matter of beauty could surpass the beauty of Djallanum. The *kalym* asked for her was great and, no matter how hard Ali-Akbyr haggled, his prospective father-in-law would not yield, but instead threatened to add to the sum. Money was hard to come by; there would be a great yield of grapes this year and the price for them had fallen. Ali-Akbyr had a notion that if Hussein wanted to he could go to the *kishlak* of Uchim to the kinsmen of Ydris, and cajole them into abating the *kalym*. But Hussein was a drone, a good-for-nought, a thief; all he was fit for was yowling from the summit of the hard-clay minaret prayers that were of no good either to Allah above or man below. Ali-Akbyr quickly learned to utter those words of blasphemy which one can now often hear in town, and it seemed to him that he knew no less of the Truth than Hussein and, were it not for the grapes and all the bother with getting a wife, it would be child's play for him to turn saint himself. However, Hussein himself evidently felt he was a drone; to the questions of the peasants he replied glumly and, gaunt and lanky, in his dirty, green turban [symbol of a completed pilgrimage to Mecca], he passed through the street not in the shade, as other men did, but in the sun, as though that vehement flame which was in his soul did not suffice him.

On the evening of a day when, in the vineyards not far from the *arrik*, three oxen had keeled over (and one of them Ali-Akbyr's own), Ali-Akbyr had announced that Hussein, that drone and swindler, ought to be carried off to town and tried in accordance with the laws of Moscow. The peasants, as always, tossed their beards, and one could not grasp whether they did so in assent

to the words of Ali-Akbyr or not. The veranda whereon
they were sitting had grapevines running all over it.
The sun was going down, and the shadows of the clusters glowed in dark blotches upon the beards of the old
men. In order to get at what these old men were thinking, Ali-Akbyr resorted to a lie:

"It would be better if we were to cart him to the
town ourselves, for otherwise five of the constabulary
will come riding and take the ancient one with them."

"That is so," answered the old men, "of a verity,"
and with melancholy they looked out at the dusty,
parched courtyard, and the tawny-brown clay of the
walls, which not even the sun could cover with gold.

And in the evening, when the peasants had congre-
gated for the *namaz* service, Hussein said, looking at the
heavens:

"Old am I by now; I have, evidently, committed
many sins, and Allah will not receive my prayers. I have
kinsmen in the near-by *kishlak* of Uchim; I am going
there to die."

The peasants let this pass in silence; but in the evening, after *namaz*, they came to Ali-Akbyr.

"What a dog and thief!" said Ali-Akbyr. "He is lying
from start to finish, as he hath lied all his life. At the
kishlak of Uchim he hath just as many kinsmen as I
now have wives. But doth not the *kishlak* of Uchim
already have the grave of the sainted Imiamin, called
Asalata-Budakchi, because of which grave fertility never
forsakes the fields of its people? But what graves of
saints have we? How many of them have we?"

And the old men looked with their vacant eyes at the
strong, darting hands of Ali-Akbyr. Out in the desert
the jackals were howling; an enormous moon was slowly
ascending heaven. The dying poplars were running with

crisp swishing along the *arrik*. The peasants walked over to the *arrik*, for a long while listened to the howling of a jackal, and then one of them spoke:

"He's howling at the moon—which means a death."

And, although there was no such omen, that did not stop them all from believing it.

After that Ali-Akbyr came to Hussein—and for a long while they kept salaaming to each other. As he salaamed, Ali-Akbyr recalled the eloquence he had acquired in town and asked, in flowery fashion: Was it true that the sainted Hussein desired to deprive the *kishlak* of Shehr-i-Sabeh of sanctity and divine fertility, and to leave for the *kishlak* of Uchim? And, if such was his desire, wherefore?

Everything about Ali-Akbyr was fraught with extraordinary kindliness, and even his darting hands were resting humbly on his belly but, having caught a look at the fixed and distraught eyes under the taut brows, the sainted Hussein put his hand to his heart and said that he had changed his mind and that he was remaining in his native region, and that his grave, Allah willing, would make the *kishlak* of Shehr-i-Sebeh celebrated throughout the ages.

"Blessed are thy hoary eyelashes, and a quietude that adorns the heart issueth therefrom," said Ali-Akbyr humbly, but through the sainted Hussein's voice, and through the way he was scrutinizing the length of the courtyard of the mosque, Ali-Akbyr grasped that that very night the sainted Hussein would make tracks out of the *kishlak* of Uchim, and would there, to the end of his days, keep cursing his impious and inhospitable fellow-villagers. And at this thought Ali-Akbyr became frightened, salaamed kindlily, and quickly left.

And at last Ali-Akbyr was enabled to hear from the lips of the peasants words that afforded him much joy;

and Ali-Akbyr, even as befits every sage, salaamed lower than ever to the peasants.

The crisp and rapid daybreak struck the poplars growing near the mosque. A wicket opened, and Ali-Akbyr began nudging the peasants with his elbow. The saint's attendant, the rosy-cheeked Alimbai, led out a saddled horse, and Hussein appeared next. His face was tired, dismal; he, apparently, had no wish to forsake either his couch or the mosque to which he had become so used. The attendant held the stirrup for Hussein, but at this point, from behind the poplars, Ali-Akbyr emerged and with a long, seasoned stick struck the back of Hussein's neck. So that there might be no blood the end of Ali-Akbyr's stick was wrapped in rags. The attendant, howling, ran into the mosque; one of the peasants went off to persuade him, and when this peasant came back Ali-Akbyr was already taking off Hussein's face the robe wherewith he had gagged the saint's mouth, until the old heart had stopped.

And lo, Hussein returned to his couch, dead. They laid him out in his best garments and called together keeners who most excelled in their profession. Toward evening folks began gathering from the neighboring hamlets for the funeral of the sainted Hussein, and many envied the *kishlak* of Shehr-i-Sebeh, which had acquired a holy grave, and the folks from the *kishlak* of Uchim were the only ones dubious of the saintliness of Hussein, but then nobody believed them. After that they earthed Hussein in the same graveyard where Ali-Akbyr had some time before buried his wife Djallanum.

The caravan, returning from the desert, halted by the graveyard, and the leader of the caravan, the gray-bearded Turkoman, got down off his burro and sent up a prayer.

The price of grapes rose unexpectedly in town; there

was need of many highwheeled carts; the snow upon the hills of Zarashan began to melt, and the water in the *arrik* of Kochik rose to the height necessary to ensure happiness.

Fertility and quietude descended upon the oasis of Shehr-i-Sebeh.

And, in due time, happiness visited Ali-Akbyr as well: he, having sold his grapes at a great profit, led into his house his new wife, Ydris, who in beauty and in the fullness of her breasts surpassed even the incomparable Djallanum. There was a feast in the compound of Ali-Akbyr; and, to feast the guests, four rams and a colt had their throats slit. A wandering singer sang songs of the happiness and loves of mighty knights, and Ali-Akbyr said in a whisper to his youthful wife:

"I shall adorn thy bosom with coins and happiness, even as the great and kindly knight in the song."

And a quiver ran through the bosom of Ydris, and her heart began to ache with untasted passions.

The next day, to ensure happiness and fertility, Ali-Akbyr led his wife to the grave of the sainted Hussein. There was a squat monument of clay upon that grave, with an unpretentious inscription calling upon men to think of quietude and resignation. Cloth torn into ribbons—offerings, these—were lying in the dust nearby. Ydris, having covered a corner of the clay marker with the silken *yashmak* that veiled like a thin cloud the moon of her face, was humbly praying for happiness and long life, while Ali-Akbyr stood by her side, tall, proud, and handsome, and his red-tinted nails rested upon his ruddy beard.

Again the caravan was going past the graveyard out into the desert. The camels left the tracks of their pads, but the sand immediately sucked down these tracks. The breath of the desert was rising over the distant knolls. And thereupon Ali-Akbyr knelt beside his wife Ydris, and with all the beautiful words that were at the disposal of his soul, thanked Allah and all His saints for that grace which had descended upon his house.

Then he arose, went into his house, and for three days and three nights reposed upon rugs, taking delight in his wife and his vigor. Having received from his wife rapture and tears of joy, he arose, performed ablution, combed his beard, and went forth into the sun, that he might carry out his usual labors.

ILYA GREGORIEVICH EHRENBURG

(1891–   )

EDITOR'S NOTE

EHRENBURG is, in this writer's unqualified opinion, the greatest living Soviet author. He is a most discerning critic, a master of paradox to whom no Shaw could hold a candle, a superjournalist, a satirist whose arsenal contains both the stiletto of irony and vialed sardonicism, triply distilled; he is a many-faceted writer, fantastic, vivid, unclassifiable.

Although his beginnings as a poet won him the labels of aesthete and mystic, he is anything but an ivory tower dweller. He was arrested (at fourteen) during the Revolution of 1905; in 1909 he emigrated to Paris, but in 1917 he came back to Russia in the throes of her Revolution. During the Second World War he was an outstanding correspondent in the front lines.

Publication of his *The Extraordinary Adventures of Julio Jurenito* (Moscow and Berlin, 1922; New York,

1929) created a sensation and made him an international figure. His *10 Horse Power: Chronicles of Our Time* (not available in English) is a savage and factual study of world monopolies in automobiles, motion pictures, matches, railways, grain, and so forth.

13 Pipes is characteristically Ehrenburgian: a devil's dozen of stories, each one revolving about a cherished pipe. The dedication is set in a mourning border, and concludes with a funereal cross: *A la memoria / del / Gran Maestro / Julio Jurenito / quien el 26 de Marzo / de mil novecientos trece me regalo / su / pipa / como garantia de la vericidad / de la existencia terrestre / dedico yo esas historias / de las trece pipas* (To the memory of the great Master Julio Jurenito, who on the twenty-sixth of March, 1913, presented me with his pipe as an assurance of the truth of earthly existence, I dedicate these stories of the *13 Pipes*).

Pipe II

ILYA GREGORIEVICH EHRENBURG

FOREWORD

ALTHOUGH the author of this book approves in every possible way of the *thingability* of art, and has even written a small work of 160 printed pages concerning the same, he himself in all his life never had any love for things, contenting himself wholly with the consciousness of the existence of things. Pipes constitute the sole exception, and then only because a pipe is not simply a thing, but a thing highly spiritualized. Tooth-marked, thoroughly broken in, it represents in itself the life of man, a chronicle of his variously visaged passions, inasmuch as in briar, in clay or in stone there lurks the trace of human breath.

Dykh. Dukh. Dusha. Breath. Spirit. Soul.

(Cordiality)

Thus this book manifests itself as a spiritual, and even a cordial, book. It is not a paean of profound wonder before its profound construction, but a history of a life of thirty-one years (thirteen of prime importance, eighteen supplementary, without taking into account minor personae). It is to be hoped that stern idealists will, on that account, forgive the versatile author the above-mentioned work on *thingability*.

Outside of affording satisfaction to the spiritual demands of exalted natures, the present book, according to the modest design of its author, must stand to the reader in lieu of:

1: The rudiments of Ethnography (how men live in this wide world)

2: A hand-book on the breaking-in of pipes of various makes

3. A motion-picture show (Emotional Drama, Knockout Comedy, Travelogue, and so forth)

If the reader, after reading the book through, should light his pipe and give himself up to meditations of how lofty and arduous love is, how swiftly the years pass by, how the smoke of hopes dissolves into thin air and how the ashes of recollections grow cold—if he, drawing evenly at his pipe, will yield to his soul at every draw, the assiduous labor of the author's June leisure will have been justified.

VII / 3 / 22

There are many splendidly beautiful cities; more splendidly beautiful than all others is Paris; insouciant

women laugh therein, under its clipped chestnut trees
dandies sip ruby-tinted liqueurs, and thousands of lights
swarm upon the flagstones of its squares.

Louis Roux, the stonemason, was born in Paris. He
remembered the July days of '48. He was seven then,
and he wanted to eat. Like a young raven he opened
his mouth without a sound and waited—and waited in
vain, inasmuch as his father, Jean Roux, had no bread.
He had nothing but a gun, and you can't eat a gun.
Louis remembered a morning in summer, when his father had been cleaning his gun, while his mother wept,
wiping her nose with her apron. Louis ran out at his
father's heels: he thought that his father would shoot
the baker with the gun he had cleaned, and take for
himself the baker's biggest loaf, a loaf bigger than
Louis—about the size of a house. But his father met
other downcast men, who also had guns. They began to
sing together and to shout "Bread!"

Louis expected, swooningly, that in answer to such
marvelous songs brioches, croissants and wafers would
come showering down from windows. But instead of
that a great din broke out, and there was a shower of
small bullets. One of the men who had been shouting
"Bread!" now shouted "I'm hurt!" and fell. Thereupon
Louis' father and the others began doing incomprehensible things: they overturned a couple of benches,
dragged a small keg out of a courtyard near by, and a
broken table, and even a small hen-coop. All these
things they piled up in the middle of the street, and
then laid down on the ground themselves. Louis understood that these despondent men were playing hide-
and-seek. Then they fired their guns and were fired at
in their turn. And then other men came. They, too, had
guns, but they were gay and smiling; great red cockades
flashed on their caps, and everybody called them the

Guards. These men seized his father and led him off along the Boulevard de St-Martin. Louis had an idea that the gay Guards would feed his father and he followed them, even though it was late. Women were laughing on this boulevard, under its clipped chestnut trees dandies were sipping ruby-tinted liqueurs, and thousands of lights were swarming upon the flagstones of its mirrorous trottoir. Near the St-Martin Gate one of the insouciant women, sitting in a café, called out to the Guards:

"Why do you take him so far? He can have his portion right here."

Louis ran up to the laughing woman and without a sound, like a young raven, opened his mouth. One of the Guards took his gun and fired anew. Louis' father let out a cry and fell; as for the woman, she was laughing. Louis ran up to his father, sank his nails into his legs, which were still jerking a little, as if his father wanted to walk while lying down, and set up a dreadful howl.

Thereupon the woman said:

"Shoot the puppy as well!"

But a dandy who was sipping a ruby-tinted liqueur at the next table raised an objection:

"Yes, but who will be left to work then?"

And Louis survived. After that awesome July came a tranquil August; no one sang and no one shot off guns any more. Louis grew up and justified the confidence of the goodnatured dandy. Jean Roux, the father, had been a stonemason, and it was a stonemason that Louis Roux became. In roomy corduroy trousers and blue canvas smock he built houses; he built them in summer and he built them in winter. Splendidly beautiful Paris wanted to become still more splendidly beautiful, and wherever new thoroughfares were being constructed

Louis would be there: the plaza of l'Etoile, the seven-rayed Star, the broad boulevards of Haussmann and Malesherbes, bordered with clipped chestnut trees, and the gala prospect of l'Opéra, with structures still sheathed in scaffoldings, yet into which the impatient traders were already carting their wondrous wares: furs, laces and precious stones. He built theaters and shops, cafés and banks; he built splendidly beautiful houses, so that insouciant women might smile as insouciantly as ever, even though the wind might be blowing from the La Manche and, in the mansards of the workers, the body became bone-stiff from the November fogs; he built bars, so that the dandies might not cease from sipping their ruby-tinted liqueurs on dark, starless nights. Lifting up heavy blocks of stone, he built the lightest of slate coverings for a city that was the most splendidly beautiful of all cities—Paris.

Among the thousands of smock-wearers there was one by the name of Louis Roux, in corduroy trousers powdered with lime, in a flat, broad-brimmed hat, with a clay pipe clenched between his teeth and, like thousands of others, he was honestly toiling over the splendor of the Second Empire.

He built wonderful houses, but his days he spent in standing on scaffoldings and his nights in lying in a malodorous cubbyhole in a tenement on the Street of the Black Widow, in the suburb of St-Antoine. The cubbyhole reeked of lime, human sweat, cheap black caporal; the tenement reeked of cat ordure and unwashed linen, while the Street of the Black Widow, even as all the streets in the suburb of St-Antoine reeked of tallow in braziers upon which hucksters were frying potatoes, of the fresh bloody smell of butcher-shops with lilac-hued horse-carcasses hanging in them, of herring, the refuse in the garbage-pits, and the smoke of wretched little stoves. But then, it is not for the Street of the Black Widow but for its broad boulevards, fragrant with lilies-of-the-valley, mandarin oranges, and the perfumery treasures of Rue de la Paix, for those boulevards and the seven-rayed l'Etoile, where the smock-wearers swayed on scaffoldings during the day, that Paris has been styled the most splendidly beautiful of all cities.

Louis Roux built cafés and bars; he lugged the stones for the Regency Café, beloved of chess players, for the Café Anglais, where foreign celebrities and the snobs who owned trotting racers used to congregate, for the Madrid Tavern, which collected within its walls the cabotins of more than a score different theaters, and for many other meritorious structures. But never had Louis, since the day of his father's death, come near any cafés once they were built, and not once had he tried any ruby-tinted liqueurs. Whenever he received a few small white coins from the contractor, it was the old pothouse keeper on the Street of the Black Widow who took these coins; in their stead he would give Louis several big black coins and pour a turbid liquid into his glass. Louis would drain the absinthe off at one breath and go off to his cubbyhole to sleep.

When there were neither white coins nor black, however, nor absinthe, nor bread, nor work, Louis, having scraped up a pinch of the tobacco that had spilt in his pocket, or having found a partly smoked cigarette in the street, would stuff his clay pipe and, puffing it, would glumly tramp the streets of the suburb of St Antoine. He did not sing any songs, nor did he shout "Bread!" as his father, Jean Roux, had once done, inasmuch as he had neither a gun to fire nor a son who opened his mouth wide to be fed, like a young raven.

Louis Roux had done his utmost so that the women

of Paris might laugh insouciantly, but whenever he caught their laughter he stepped aside in fright: that was the way a woman had once laughed on the Boulevard of St-Martin, when Jean Roux was lying on the pavement, still trying, although he was flat on his back, to walk. On the whole, Louis Roux had not seen any young woman close at hand until he was five and twenty. But when he had passed five and twenty and had moved from one mansard on the Street of the Black Widow to another, that befell him which sooner or later befalls all men. There was a young charwoman by the name of Juliette living in the mansard next to his. Louis met Juliette one evening on the narrow, winding staircase, dropped in on her to borrow matches, since his flint had worn out and no longer gave fire and, having dropped in, came out only toward morning. The next day Juliette transferred her two shifts, her one cup, and one brush, to Louis' mansard and became his wife, while a year later a new guest appeared in the cramped mansard, who was registered in the *mairie* as Polhème-Marie Roux.

Thus had Louis come to know woman but, in contradistinction to many others, of whom splendidly beautiful Paris is justly proud, Juliette never smiled insouciantly, even though Louis Roux loved her greatly, as only a stonemason who lifts heavy stones and builds splendidly beautiful structures can love. Probably she never laughed, inasmuch as she lived on the Street of the Black Widow, where the only one who had ever laughed insouciantly had been Marie, an old laundress, when she was being carted off to a hospital for the insane. Probably Juliette did not laugh also because she had but two shifts and Louis, who often had no coin, either white or black, glumly tramping the streets of the

suburb of St-Antoine with his pipe, was unable to give
her even a single yellow coin for a new dress.

In the spring of 1869, when Louis was twenty-eight,
and his son Paul two, Juliette took her two shifts, her
cup, and brush, and moved into the rooms of a butcher
dealing in horse-meat on the Street of the Black Widow.
She left Paul to her husband, since the butcher was a
nervous man and, while he loved young women very
much, had no love at all for children. Louis took his son,
rocked him a little to keep him from crying, and went
off to tramp the streets of the suburb of St-Antoine. He
loved Juliette greatly, but understood that she had acted
rightly: the butcher had a lot of yellow coins, he could
even move to another street, and with him Juliette
would begin to live insouciantly. He recalled that his
father, Jean, when he had been leaving that July morning with his gun, had said to his weeping wife, and
Louis' mother:

"It is my duty to go, and it is yours to keep me back.
A cock seeks a high perch, a ship the open sea, a
woman a tranquil life."

Having recalled his father's words, it occurred to
Louis once more that he had been right in trying to
keep Juliette back, but Juliette had been right, too, in
leaving him for the rich butcher.

After that Louis built houses anew and acted as nurse
to his son. But soon war came, and the evil Prussians
laid siege to Paris. No one wanted to build any houses
any more, and the scaffoldings of unfinished buildings
stood deserted. The projectiles from Prussian cannon
ruined, as they fell, many buildings of splendidly beautiful Paris, over which Louis Roux and other stonemasons had toiled. Louis had no work, yet the three-
year-old Paul could already open his mouth without a

sound, like a young raven. Then Louis was given a gun. Having taken it, he did not start singing and shouting "Bread!" but, like many thousands of stonemasons, carpenters, and blacksmiths, went to the defense of Paris, the most splendidly beautiful of all cities, against the evil Prussians. Mme. Moneau, a kindly woman who kept a vegetable store, gave shelter to little Paul. Louis Roux, together with the other smock-wearers, barefooted in the winter cold, was rolling projectiles up to a cannon at the Fort of St-Vincennes, and the cannon fired them at the evil Prussians. For long days at a stretch he had nothing to eat, inasmuch as hunger was king in Paris. His feet became frostbitten, inasmuch as during the siege unprecedented frosts prevailed in Paris. The Prussian projectiles fell upon the Fort of St-Vincennes, and the number of smock-wearers was ever decreasing, but Louis did not abandon his place at the small cannon, inasmuch as he was defending Paris. And the most splendidly beautiful of all cities merited such defense. Despite famine and frost the lights swarmed upon the Boulevards des Italiens and des Capucines, there was enough of ruby-tinted liqueurs for the dandies, and an insouciant smile never left the faces of the women.

Louis Roux knew that there was no longer any Emperor, and that now the République was dominant in Paris. As he rolled the projectiles to his cannon, he could not ponder over what this "République" was, but the smock-wearers who came to the Fort of St-Vincennes from the heart of Paris said that the cafés of Paris were just as full as ever of dandies and insouciant women. Louis Roux, as he listened to their angry muttering, conjectured that nothing had changed in Paris, that the "République" was not to be found on the Street of the Black Widow but on the broad perspectives of the seven-rayed Star, and that when the stonemasons

would succeed in driving off the evil Prussians little
Paul would be opening his mouth wide for bread once
more. Louis Roux was aware of this, but he did not
abandon his post at the cannon, and the Prussians could
not set foot in the city of Paris.

But one morning they ordered him to abandon the
cannon and to go back to the Street of the Black Widow.
The people who were called the République and who,
most probably, were the dandies and the insouciant
women, had let the evil Prussians into splendidly beautiful Paris. His pipe clenched between his teeth, glum
Louis Roux tramped the streets of the suburb of St-
Antoine.

The Prussians came and departed, but nobody built
any houses. Paul kept opening his mouth wide like a
young raven, and Louis Roux took to cleaning his gun.
Then an awesome decree was posted on the walls,
ordering all smock-wearers to give up their guns, inasmuch as the dandies and the insouciant women who
were called the République remembered the July Days
of the year '48.

Louis Roux did not want to give up his gun, and all
the smock-wearers of the suburb of St-Antoine and
many other suburbs felt much the same as he did. They
went out into the streets with their guns and shot them
off. This was on a warm evening, when spring was
barely beginning in Paris.

On the following day Louis Roux saw a long procession of dandified carriages, comfortable coaches, baggage wagons, and carts winding through the streets. All
sorts of goodly property lay in the carts, while lolling
in the carriages were the people whom Louis Roux had
become accustomed to see on the grand boulevards or
in the Bois de Boulogne. Here were diminutive generals
in raspberry-hued képis, their mustachios awesomely

drooping, young women in crinolines hemmed with laces, puffy abbés in violet soutanes, ancient dandies refulgent in raven-black, sand-colored and rust-hued opera hats, young officers who had never been either at the fort of St-Vincennes or any other, pompous and bald-pated flunkies, lap-dogs with small bows affixed to their smoothly groomed, silky coats, and even raucous parrots. All of these were hastening to the Versailles Gates. And when Louis Roux went that evening to the Place de l'Opéra he saw the depopulated cafés, where there were no more dandies sipping ruby-tinted liqueurs, and boarded-up shops near which there were no more women laughing insouciantly. The people from the districts of the Champs d'Elysées, Auteuil, and St-Germaine, thoroughly peeved at the smock-wearers who would not give up their guns, had abandoned splendidly beautiful Paris, and even the slate mirrors of its trottoirs, no longer reflecting the extinguished lights, were a melancholy black.

Louis Roux saw that the République had gone off in the coaches and baggage wagons. He asked other smock-wearers what had been left in its place; they answered him: "The Paris Commune," and Louis grasped that the Paris Commune lived somewhere not far from the Street of the Black Widow.

But the dandies and women who had abandoned Paris did not want to forget the most splendidly beautiful of all cities. They did not want to give it up to stonemasons, carpenters, and blacksmiths. And anew cannon-shot fell, demolishing the houses; these shots were no longer being despatched by evil Prussians but by the worthy habitués of the cafés—of the Café l'Anglais and the others. And Louis grasped that it behooved him to return to his old place at the Fort of St-Vincennes. But the proprietress of the vegetable store, Mme. Moneau, was not only a good woman but a good Catholic as well. She refused to keep under her roof the son of one of the godless who had killed the Bishop of Paris. Thereupon Louis put his pipe between his teeth and his son up on his shoulders and went off to the Fort of St-Vincennes. He kept rolling the projectiles up to the cannon, and Paul, alongside of him, played with empty cartridges. At night the boy slept in the house of the watchman at the water-station in the Fort of St-Vincennes. The watchman presented Paul with a brand-new pipe, every bit like the pipe Louis Roux smoked, and a small piece of soap. Now Paul, whenever he became bored with listening to the shots and watching the cannon spitting out projectiles, could also blow soap-bubbles. The bubbles were of various colors: pale-blue, rose-colored, and lilac. They resembled the little balloons which were bought for the well-dressed little boys who played in the Jardin des Tuilleries by dandies and insouciant women. True, the soap-bubbles of the smock-wearer's son had but an instant's life, whereas the little balloons of the children from the Champs d'Elysées lived through all of a day, yet both the balloons and the soap-bubbles were splendidly beautiful—and both the balloons and the soap-bubbles died quickly. As he blew soap-bubbles out of the clay pipe Paul would forget to open his mouth wide in expectation of a piece of bread. Whenever he approached the men whom all called Communards and of whom Louis Roux was one, he would gravely clench the empty pipe in his teeth, emulating his father. And the men, forgetting the cannon for a moment, would say kindlily to Paul:

"You're a real Communard."

The smock-wearers, however, had but few cannon, and the smock-wearers themselves were but few in number. But as for the people who had abandoned

Paris and who were now living in Versailles, the erstwhile residence of kings, they were with every day
bringing up ever-new soldiers—the sons of the peasants
of France, tight-fisted and slow-witted—and ever-new
cannon, presented to them by the evil Prussians. They
were coming closer and closer to the ramparts surrounding the city of Paris. By now many forts were in their
hands, and no one came any longer to replace the fallen
cannoneers who, together with Louis Roux, had been
defending the Fort of St-Vincennes. The stonemason
now had to roll up the projectiles himself, load the cannon himself, fire it himself, and was now helped only
by the two smock-wearers who had survived.

Gaiety reigned in the future residence of the kings of
France. Hastily opened cafés of clapboard could not contain all those who wanted ruby-tinted liqueurs. Abbés
in violet soutanes were celebrating solemn masses. Stroking their awesomely drooping mustachios the generals
were gaily chatting with the influx of Prussian officers.
And the bald-pated flunkies were now fussing with
the portmanteaux of their masters, in preparation for the
return to the most splendidly beautiful of all cities. The
magnificent park, built upon the bones of twenty thousand workers who had been digging the earth, chopping
clearings, draining swamps day and night so as not to
be late on the day set for its completion by the King of
the Sun, was now being decorated with flags in honor
of the victory. In the daytime the bronze trumpeters
puffed out their cheeks, the stone tritons of the nine
great fountains and the forty lesser ones shed crocodile
tears, while at night, when in a Paris drained of its
blood the dimmed lights no longer swarmed upon the
flagstones of its squares, exultingly triumphant initials,
formed of tallow fire-pots, blazed insolently amid the
verdure.

François d'Emognan, captain in the National Army of France, had brought his bride, Gabrielle de Bonnivet, a bouquet of tender lilies as witness to the nobility and innocency of his sentiments. The lilies were put in a golden porte-bouquet, ornamented with sapphires, and bought at Versailles from a jeweler of the Rue de la Paix who had managed to carry off his treasures during the first day of the insurrection. The bouquet had also been offered up to mark the victory: François d'Emognan had come for a day from the front at Paris. He informed Gabrielle that the insurgents had been smashed. On the morrow his soldiers would take the Fort of St-Vincennes and set foot in Paris.

"When will the season at the Opéra start?" asked Gabrielle.

After this they gave themselves up to billing and cooing, quite natural between a fiancé-hero who had arrived from the front and his bride, who was embroidering a tobacco-pouch for him. And, during a moment of especial tendresse, clasping the apricot-hued bodice of Gabrielle with the arm of a participant in an arduous campaign, François said:

"My dear, you don't know how cruel these Communards are. I myself saw, through my binoculars, a little boy firing the cannon in the Fort of St-Vincennes. And, just imagine!—this tiny Nero was already smoking a pipe!"

"But then, you will kill off all of them, together with the children," chirrupped Gabrielle, and her breast began to heave faster under the hand of a participant in the campaign.

François d'Emognan knew what he was talking about. On the next morning the soldiers of his regiment received the command to take the Fort of St-Vincennes. Louis Roux, together with the two surviving smock-

wearers, fired at the soldiers. Thereupon François d'Emognan ordered a flag of truce to be put out, and Louis
Roux, who had heard that a white flag signified peace,
ceased fire. It had occurred to him that the soldiers had
felt pity for the most splendid of cities and wanted, at
last, to make peace with the Paris Commune. The three
smock-wearers, smiling and puffing their pipes, awaited
the soldiers, while little Paul, who had no soap left, was
nevertheless holding his pipe in his mouth and was
likewise smiling. And when the soldiers had come right
up to the Fort of St-Vincennes, François d'Emognan
ordered three of them, the three best marksmen of
mountainous Savoy, to kill the three rebels. The little
Communard he wanted to take alive, in order to exhibit
him to his bride.

The Savoy mountaineers knew how to shoot and, entering the Fort of St-Vincennes at last, the soldiers beheld three men with pipes, sprawled out near the cannon. The soldiers had seen many slain men and were
not surprised. But, on seeing a little boy with a pipe
astride a cannon they were taken aback and some of
them invoked Jesus Christ, while others invoked a thousand devils.

"Where did you bob up from, you vile little bedbug?"
asked one of the Savoyards.

"I am a real Communard," Paul answered with a
smile.

The soldiers were about to finish him off by running
their bayonets through him, but their corporal said that
Captain François d'Emognan had given orders to have
the little Communard delivered at one of the eleven
points where all those taken prisoner were being herded
together.

"How many on our side he has killed, this little
angel!" grumbled the soldiers, urging Paul on with the

butts of their guns. As for little Paul, who had never killed anybody but had merely blown soap-bubbles out of his pipe, he could not understand why these men were scolding and abusing him.

The soldiers of the National Army of France led off the captured insurgent, Paul Roux, who was all of four, into vanquished Paris. The smock-wearers, perishing, were still firing back in the suburbs to the north, while in the streets of the Champs d'Elysées, around the Place de l'Opéra, and in the new quarters of the seven-rayed Star people were already having a gay time. It was the best month—May; the clipped chestnut trees of the broad boulevards were in blossom, while underneath them, around the little round tables of the cafés, dandies were sipping ruby-tinted liqueurs and women were laughing insouciantly. As the microscopic Communard was being led past them, they called out for him to be given up to them. But the corporal remembered the orders of his captain and safeguarded Paul. However, the soldiers did give up other prisoners—women as well as men. The spectators spat on them, beat them with their dainty canes, and as for those who were on their last legs, they finished them by running bayonets through them, borrowed for that purpose from one or another of the soldiers filing past.

Paul Roux was brought into the Jardin de Luxembourg. There, before the Palace, a large area had been fenced off, into which the captured insurgents were driven. Paul walked among them solemnly with his pipe and, wishing to console some of the women who were bitterly weeping, was saying to them:

"I know how to blow soap-bubbles. My father, Louis Roux, used to smoke a pipe and fire a cannon. I am a real Communard."

But the women, who were leaving their children behind, somewhere in the suburb of St-Antoine—even, perhaps, children who liked to blow soap-bubbles— wept still more bitterly as they listened to Paul.

So Paul sat down on the grass and began thinking of soap-bubbles: how beautiful they were, pale-blue, rose-colored, and lilac. But since he could not be thoughtful for long, and since the way from the Fort of St-Vincennes to the Garden of the Luxembourg had been a long and hard way, Paul soon fell asleep, without letting the pipe out of his hands.

While he was sleeping two trotters were drawing a light landeau over the Versailles highway. It held François d'Emognan, who was bringing his bride, Gabrielle de Bonnivet, into splendidly beautiful Paris. And never had Gabrielle de Bonnivet been as splendidly beautiful as on that day. The fine oval of her face reminded one of the portraits of the old Florentine masters. Her dress was of a lemon color, trimmed with lace woven at the Melcherin convent. A diminutive parasol safeguarded her lusterless skin, the tint of apple-blossom petals, from the direct rays of the May sun. Truly, she was the most splendidly beautiful woman of Paris and, aware of this, she was smiling insouciantly.

As soon as they entered the city François d'Emognan called over to him a chance-met soldier of his regiment and asked him where the prisoner from the Fort of St-Vincennes was to be found. And when the enamored couple came into the Garden of the Luxembourg and saw the old chestnut trees in bloom, the ivy over the Medici Fountain, and the blackbirds hopping over the garden walks, the heart of Gabrielle de Bonnivet over-flowed with tenderness and, pressing the arm of her fiancé, she whispered:

"My dear one, how splendidly beautiful it is to be alive!"

The prisoners, from among whom some were led off to the firing squad every hour, met the gold-braid of the captain with horror; each one thought that his turn to die had come. But François d'Emognan paid no attention to them; he was seeking the little Communard. Finding him asleep he awoke him with a light kick. The boy on awaking at first broke into tears, but then, catching sight of Gabrielle's gay face, so unlike the faces of the other women around him, he put his pipe in his mouth and said:

"I am a real Communard!"

"Really, he is so little!" uttered the pleased Gabrielle. "I think they are born murderers, and it is necessary to exterminate all of them now, even those just born."

"Now that you have had a look at him we can finish him off," said François, and called a soldier over.

But Gabrielle requested him to wait a little. She wanted to prolong the delectable sensation of this light and insouciant day. She had recalled that once, strolling at a fair in the Bois de Boulogne, she had seen a booth with suspended clay pipes: some of these were rapidly turning. Young people fired guns at these clay pipes. Although Gabrielle de Bonnivet came from a good, aristocratic family she was fond of the diversions of the common people, and for that reason, having recalled this amusement at the fair, she begged her fiancé:

"I want to learn to shoot. The wife of a fighting captain in the National Army must know how to handle a gun. Let me try to hit the clay pipe of this little hangman."

François d'Emognan never denied his bride anything. He had recently presented her with a necklace of pearls worth thirty thousand francs. Could he, then, refuse her this innocent rustic diversion? He took a gun from a soldier and handed it to her.

On seeing the girl with a gun the prisoners scattered and herded at the other end of the corral. Paul alone stood calmly with his pipe and smiled. Gabrielle wanted to hit the pipe in motion and so, taking aim, she said to the boy:

"Run, now! I'm going to shoot!"

But Paul had often seen men firing guns, and therefore kept right on standing calmly on the spot. Thereupon Gabrielle, growing impatient, fired—and, since she was using a gun for the first time, her miss was quite pardonable.

"My dear one," said François d'Emognan, "you are far better at transfixing hearts with arrows of love than clay pipes with bullets. See, you have killed this little vermin, but his pipe has remained undamaged."

Gabrielle de Bonnivet made no answer. As she looked at the small red blotch her breath quickened and, snuggling closer to François, she suggested that they go back home, feeling that now she could not do without the sultry caresses of her fiancé.

Paul Roux, who had lived four years on this earth, and who above all things in this world loved to blow soap-bubbles out of his clay pipe, was lying motionless.

Recently, in Brussels, I ran across Pierre Lautrec, an old Communard. I became friendly with him, and the lonely old man presented me with his sole possession: a clay pipe out of which, fifty years ago, little Paul Roux used to blow soap-bubbles. Pierre Lautrec, on that day when the four-year-old insurgent had been murdered by Gabrielle de Bonnivet, had been in the corral at the Garden of the Luxembourg. The people of Versailles had shot almost all of those who had been in it. Pierre Lautrec had survived because certain of the dandies had had sense enough to see that, after all, somebody has to work, and that splendidly beautiful Paris, which would want to become still more splendidly beautiful, would have need of stonemasons, carpenters, and blacksmiths. Pierre Lautrec was banished for five years; he escaped from Cayenne to Belgium, and through all his tribulations had carried this pipe, picked up near the little corpse of Paul Roux. He gave it to me, and told me all that I have written down here.

I often touch it with lips parched by rancor. Within it is the trace of the breath of one tender and innocent; also, it may be, a trace of the soap-bubbles that have burst long ago. But this toy of little Paul Roux, murdered by Gabrielle de Bonnivet, the most splendidly beautiful of the women in the most splendidly beautiful of cities, Paris, speaks to me of a great Hatred. As I put my lips to it, I pray for but one thing: on beholding a white flag not to lower one's gun, as poor Louis Roux had done, and for the sake of all the joy of life not to betray any Fort of St-Vincennes which is still the stronghold of three mad smock-wearers and an infant blowing soap-bubbles.

VALENTIN PETROVICH KATAEV

(1897–   )

EDITOR'S NOTE

A NATIVE of Odessa; the son of a teacher. In 1915, while still a student, Kataev volunteered; besides having been wounded twice, he suffered contusions and was gassed; between 1918 and 1920 he went through many adventures in the Ukraine. He began publishing before the Revolution, and worked on *Pravda* at the same time that Ilf and Petrov (the latter is his brother) were on the staff. Kataev called himself Alexander Dumas, *père*, and styled Ilf and Petrov his "plantation slaves," but the famous team acknowledged Kataev as the spiritual godfather of *The Twelve Chairs*. He also collaborated with them on several film scenarios.

His best-known novel is *The Embezzlers* (available in English); he has done many short stories, a number of them leaning toward grotesquerie and whimsicality; and most of his plays have enjoyed great success. His *Squaring the Circle* was (at least in its American production) turned into anti-Soviet propaganda; it would be highly curious to see just how funny its housing-shortage situations would be at present.

Life, to Kataev, is of direct and amazing beauty and its own justification. He is primarily humorist and satirist; some of his later works, however, show a serious trend: no unusual phenomenon among Russian writers who begin with humor.

Rodion Zhukov

VALENTIN PETROVICH KATAEV

THE small civilian cap is bound not to fit the capacious head with its crew-haircut, and the brim is bound to ride down off the forehead, somewhere as near as possible to the ear; the trousers, even though they be rolled up like a fisherman's, above the knees, buckle because of their good navy broadcloth, and the tapes of the drawers dangle about the calves, which are as rounded and hard as cobblestones; the calico shirt with its small buttons of cornflower-blue glass, the tails neatly tucked into the trousers, clings to the broad chest and blows up into a huge blister on the back. . . .

In a word, no matter what hand-me-downs a sailor of the Black Sea Squadron may throw over himself, no matter how he may pretend to be a civilian, no matter in what direction he may shift his hazel-hued eyes with their lashes singed by the stokehole—nothing will avail him. Every man-jack he comes across will perceive, in spite of everything, that he is no hired hand from any German colonist's farm; no fishing man gallivanting, because of a holiday, away from his lean-to of reeds in his native Cossack village and running after the wenches in the melon-patches; no vagabonding gypsy, so ready to help himself to the horses and cantaloupes that belong to others.

And the pockmarked constable, bouncing upon the leather cushions of a German brizka on springs, amid clouds of dust as white as flour, is bound, upon catching up with a fellow like that at a byroad, to thrust out from under a canvas hood his frightfully foolish face with its maize-colored mustachios, to adjust his saber under his duster, and, sneezing against the sun, reflect uneasily:

"Eh, but that fellow isn't at all to my liking! Oughtn't I to take this bosom pal of mine along, and turn back to the station-house?"

But the horses, their sweat-glistening tails beating off gadflies, are going at a lively out-in-the-fields trot—they've just rightly gotten into their stride! The quail scamper over the stubble; the air is lazily trickling over the horizon, and in its hot current float the grass-stalks, swaying like glassy whitecaps, the graves that have been islanded in the mowing, the ricks, and the wormwood growing along the boundaries of the fields. And over there, ahead, you look and catch sight, above the greenery, of the collodion-exuding tiled roofs of German farms, the masts of a cordon of ships, a harbor perched on the very edge of a precipice, and the gladsome sea, vivid as bluing. What's the sense, then, of stopping and turning back when you're halfway to your destination? This is the very time to take a dip, and you have an invitation for today from a landed proprietor to help him celebrate a holiday! It would be a pity not to attend.

Besides, the suspicious-looking fellow has been left far behind. Like as not, he isn't on the road at all by now. Like as not, he has turned off in among the corn, to do his business; has squatted over the earth, gray, split from its tautness, among the thick, jointed stalks, and is staring with craned neck at the nubbins, closely wrapped in tough, pointed husks; however, it's not silk, like the ruddy hair of young men, which escapes therefrom; instead, metallically green flies hover over them in ringing swarms. There, go and look for him! "Eh, to hell with him!" thinks the constable, hiding his face deeper in the hood. "There's not a few of them hanging about here, seeing how close it is to the frontier—all these navy-men, runaways of this kind and that. . . . Guess God will be kind to them. Let him roam around, until they hang him."

And the white dust wheels, rolls down the byroad; a faint breeze bears it off together with the ding-a-ling'ing of the little bells, off to one side, as if the dust were fine muslin and, as if sieved through silk, it settles through the air in the finest of powders on the wrinkles of the naval trousers (they turn velvety from the dust), upon the barley-colored eyebrows, and the up-curling lashes scorched in a famous fire, of a man who has walked out of the standing corn, with his belt over his neck.

II

Rodion Zhukov was one of the seven hundred sailors from the armorclad *Potëmkin* who had disembarked on a Rumanian shore. There was nothing to mark him off from the sailors who had mutinied on that ship. From the first moment of the uprising, that very moment when the commander of the armorclad had, in terror and despair, cast himself on his knees before the crew, when the first volleys of gunfire resounded and the corpses of certain officers had gone flying over the side, when Matiushenko, squat and well-built, just as if he had been poured out of bronze, had with a crash torn down the door of the commander's cabin—from that very moment on Rodion Zhukov had lived, thought, and acted in the very same way as the majority of the remaining sailors: in a slight fog, in rapture, in fervor— until such time as it became necessary to give in.

Never until then had Rodion set foot on a foreign land. And a foreign land, like useless freedom, is wide and bitter.

Unwontedly beautiful and white did the town of Constanza appear to Rodion Zhukov. A host of all sorts of interesting people came out on the quay to greet the Russian seamen as if they were heroes. There were boatmen in striped jerseys under their coats, and military officers in red trousers with black stripes running down their seams, and customs officials in capes, fastened at the breast with clasps in the form of lions' heads, and the masters of Turkish brigantines in fezes, and gentlemen with binoculars, and ladies in tight fitting jackets with puffed sleeves, and a multitude of other city-folks. Fancy parasols and straw hats bobbed

along against the green-blue of the deep, restless sea.
Longboats leapt up on the steep waves, their creaking
oarlocks rubbing against the rough stone of the quay,
and with a splash wooshed down into the murky water
redolent of catfish.

Police pushed back the crowd hemming in the sailors.
The military officers ceaselessly kept putting their
hands in lemon-colored gloves up to the brims of their
képis, embroidered with gold branches, and apologizing
to the ladies. The ladies were waving their postage-
stamp handkerchiefs. The crowd was hurrahing.

Amid the sympathy, noise, and general curiosity, embarrassed and trying to get the kinks out of their broad
shoulders weighed down with their sharp-cornered, tidy
sea-chests, the sailors passed over the quay and set foot
on the sidewalks of the city. And then, in a barracks-
yard, a photographer with horribly black side-whiskers
expanded the long accordion of his apparatus and, having thrust his pomaded head with its set curls under a
dark cloth and looking like some Cyclopaean monster
on five legs (two of them his own, three of wood), with
rattling, glinting brass screws, started creeping up,
creakingly, on the sailors. . . .

And twenty years and a bit over had passed since
those days.

Where hadn't that lilac-tinged, glossy group photograph, pasted upon stout cardboard decorated all over
with finicky seals and Medals from the Paris Exposition
—where in the world hadn't it been! For a long time it
was fading in the sun in the show-case of the Constanza
photographer, under the canvas marquee festooned with
pink; after that it was reproduced in a French illustrated
periodical and reprinted in an American one; bought
as a memento, it lay in more than one sea-chest under
the clean sailor-blouse, the spare blouse-collars, and the

razor in a cheap case, at the very bottom pasted over
with wallpaper; and in the dismal chancellery of the
Department of Secret Police at Odessa, on a table near
a semicircular window; there an emaciated functionary
with tobacco-ambered nails painstakingly stitched it
with thread to a report, after which a Colonel in a short
uniform jacket that diffused the odor of excellent broadcloth and eau de cologne, letting his overcooked-fish
eyes glide over it and using his pinky as a pointer, kept
questioning a stool-pigeon: "Know this fellow? And this
one, sitting without his cap—who may he be? Isn't it
Zhukov?"

Yes, not a few things had happened—

But twenty years had passed—twenty such years
that, if you like, they were as good as any hundred. The
gilt Imperial Eagles had been knocked off their perches
over the fronts of drug-stores; the people had burst
through the arch of the Chief Staff Headquarters into
the Winter Palace, had gone running through the highly
polished chambers of the Czar, had ripped the Czar's
portrait out of its frame, while the Czar himself the
sailors had whisked off upon troikas, into Siberia, into
the virgin wilderness, there where up to that time only
the howling of wolves had been heard and the clink of
the convicts' leg-irons. A blizzard had sprung up, the
forest had risen as a wall, had sent up a howl, had begun to crackle, to fire, making its branches sound like
gunfire—or it may have been something else—and that
was the last anyone saw of the Czar!

And now this photograph, scuffed and yellowed
with the years, hangs under glass in a place of honor on
the wall of a museum, housed in what was once a nobleman's beautiful mansion in Moscow. Excursionists, flaming from the frost, walk up to it: young girls, and youths
in patched, skimpy overcoats that had seen plenty of

wear; they stand there for a minute or so, look it over
with curiosity, and then hurry on through the exhibition
rooms, all their youthful poverty reflected in the plate-
glass of the showcases and the glistening parquets. Yes,
truth to tell, there is little to interest one in this still of a
group. Men, Russian sailors, ranged in four rows, standing, sitting, and half-lying on the ground, against the
background of a white wall with three grated windows.
Some of them are still in their battle dress; some have
already changed to civilian clothes. Off to one side you
can see Rumanian officers in tall képis and close-fitting
white jackets with unfamiliar medals. However, no
matter how hard you look for him, Rodion Zhukov is
not in that group-photograph. That's all there is to it.
It is a dead piece of cardboard, a calcined fossil of something that had at one time lived, a historical document.
Youth is avid and in a rush. You've got to hand to youth,
and be quick about it, proclamations, hand-grenades,
underground presses. Youth likes action, something concrete. . . . So that it may touch it, handle it, become
convinced. But a photograph, now—what does that
amount to!

And yet twenty years ago, in the Rumanian town of
Constanza, toward the end of June, after dinner, in the
barracks-yard, there had been black-eyed Susans and
Dutchman's-breeches growing. A summer breeze, strong
and salty, like brine for dill-pickled cucumbers, had
been blowing in gusts from the sea. The collars of the
sailors' blouses and their cap-ribbons fluttered in the
breeze, as if they were being rinsed. A filthy, supercilious goat was standing near the stable, up to his belly
in the burdocks. With his tether of rough rope tautened
and his camelish nostrils distended he was gazing fixedly
at the crowd being photographed and the man photo-
graphing it. And, as the photographer was clicking

with the wooden frame of the plate-holder and trying to get the focus, a young, old-looking Rumanian woman with her skirt tucked up passed through the yard with a waddle and threw slops out of a trough. The goat malevolently staggered to one side, gave a toss to his beard, and became petrified anew in amazement. The soapy water was blowing up into bubbles amid the earth-crushed blades of grass; it began to hiss with rainbow-hued soap-bubbles and immediately to dry, with a swishing sound. The photographer squatted a little and, lifting his left hand, quickly took the cover off the lens with his right. A throaty steamer whistle flowed out of the port. The sailors became unnaturally dead-still.

But at that very time Rodion Zhukov had been standing behind the stable and, his back propped up against its wall of rough gray stone, was gazing out to sea. The *Potëmkin* was riding at anchor altogether close to the quay. Amid the feluccas and freighters, surrounded by yawls, yachts, and cutters, alongside the gaunt Rumanian cruiser *Elizabeth*, it was uselessly huge, three-stacked, and gray. The white Flag of St Andrew, diagonally criss-crossed with blue and looking like an envelope, was still hanging high above the gun-turrets, the lifeboats, the yards. Deserted were the decks and bridges of the armorclad, save for the jutting rifle, stock up, of a Rumanian sentry here and there. But now the flag gave a shudder, sank a little, and in short leaps began its lowering. With both hands did Rodion take off his cap then, and bowed so low that the ends of his new *St George* ribbons fell in the dust, like orange-black Indian pinks growing in a field.

"What is it now, sailor—are you repenting?" a gay voice called out suddenly at Rodion's very shoulder.

Rodion lifted his head and saw a torpedoman he knew. The latter was standing with his stubby legs wide apart, his hot hands clutching the braided hem of his collar. His pockmarked, homely face with ursine eyes was all convulsed by a snub-nosed spasm. His Adam's apple was bobbing up and down with as much difficulty and as tightly as if he had just choked on an iron apple and, unable to swallow it, was strangling because of it.

"What is it, my countryman dear, are you saying farewell to your prison? Shedding bitter tears? Bowing to the precious flag of the Czar?"

"One feels sorry, after all, for a ship of the line, Stepan Andreich," Rodion Zhukov answered softly.

Whereupon the torpedoman smashed his cap with all his might against the ground and shouted:

"It was all for nothing, comrades, we went ashore— it was all for nothing we gave ourselves up!"

And, by now, several sailors had gathered about him.

"It's an out-and-out disgrace! Twelve-inch guns, ammunition past all counting, like muskmelons in a cellar, the gunners all first class. It was all in vain we didn't heed Koshuba! Koshuba was right when he told us: 'Take those mangy bastards of convoy officers and over the side with them; scuttle *St George the Conqueror;* go to Odessa and send a raiding party ashore!' We'd have raised up the whole garrison! The whole Black Sea! Eh, Koshuba, Koshuba—we ought to have heeded you. . . . But now look at the nonsense that's come of it all!"

And the sailors saw that which they had never seen up to then: the torpedoman was weeping.

"Farewell, Dorothei Koshuba, my shipmate," he got out, "farewell, *Count Potëmkin of Taurida,* a ship of the line; farewell, lost freedom—" here he bowed from the waist and, as if in answer to his bow, the colorful flag of Rumania unfurled over the ship.

Thereupon the torpedoman put on his crumpled,

dust-covered cap and the tears dried instantaneously upon his pockmarked cheeks. As though they had burst into a blaze. But his forehead paled.

"Well and good," he got out through clenched teeth. "Well and good! Well and good—Koshuba isn't the only one in this world. We won't let our chances slip. We'll raise up all of Russia. We'll burn all the land-owners to ashes. Am I telling the truth or no, Zhukov?"

He burst into dreadful oaths in which Christ, God, and maternal obscenities were involved, turned his back on the others and strode off, at a rolling walk, his arms, in their broad sleeves tightly buttoned at the very fists, held akimbo.

For the last time Rodion Zhukov bowed to his ship and, together with the other sailors, sadly returned to the barracks-yard.

III

Only two ensigns, all the convoying officers, and also thirty of the crew sold out their shipmates: they stayed on at Constanza, awaiting the arrival of a Russian squadron, to place themselves at the mercy of the Admiral. There is no use wasting breath on them.

The remaining sailors divvied up among themselves, in brotherly fashion, the cash in the ship's money-chest —it came to twenty rubles for each; sold the *St George* ribbons from their caps to the Rumanian dandies for neckties, got their documents from the prefect, bought themselves civilian clothes in the marketplace, and parted forever, scattering the wide world over, each man wherever he listed. They found their way into lands such as they had never even heard tell of before: into Canada, into America, into Switzerland. As for those who stayed on in Rumania, they got themselves jobs in factories, in mines, or went to work in the fields.

Together with Taras Popienko and Vanya Kovalev, two of his countrymen who also hailed from Nerubaisk, Rodion Zhukov hired himself out as a farmhand to a Russian settler, an Old Sectarian, in a big and dreary well-to-do hamlet not far from the town of Tulcza. During their two years' service in the fleet the backs and arms of the sailors had become rather unused to field-work. However, the season was now at its feverish height, and the way things are you just don't get to eat the bread of others for nothing.

So the three men of Nerubaisk threw off their shoes, rolled up their sleeves above the elbow, spat on their palms and sailed into the work until all you could see was the gold-glinting chaff rising up in pillars of dust from the earth right up to the burned-out sky of the steppe. For all of a month they used to get up long before dawn and ride off into the fields. All day they carted the grain and threshed it, and returned to the farmstead only after the sun had set, when the cookstove was already flaming brightly behind the cellar, in the dusk, under an overhang, the dried cornstalks crackling in the flames, while the cook, amid clouds of fiery steam, from time to time stirred the mess with a stick, turning away from the bitter smoke and wiping her eyes with the hem of her skirt.

Right after supper the sailors would bed down for the night in the middle of the yard and, under a sky warm and milky with stars, fall into sound sleep without dreams or thoughts.

Thus did the most feverish muzhik-month of July pass, and then one night at the beginning of August, when the grain had all been threshed and they had begun to cart the watermelons and cantaloupes from the melon patches, Rodion Zhukov happened to awake without any reason and, through the sleep that was still heavy on his eyelids, caught sight of Kovalev. He was standing stock-still in the middle of the yard. Rodion raised himself on one elbow. Kovalev still did not stir.

"What are you up to?" Zhukov asked him sleepily.

His bare feet treading the chilling earth gently and inaudibly, Kovalev walked up to Rodion, squatted on his heels close to Rodion's shoulder and peered into his face. Kovalev's elongated head, the head of a friend, at once blotted out half the sky of magnificent stars.

"Lie down, Vanya; go to sleep," whispered Zhukov. "Give over thinking."

But Kovalev was mysteriously beckoning to him and tugging ever so lightly at his sleeve. Rodion got up and followed him. They halted in the middle of the yard.

"Look," said Kovalev. "Look at the cellar—and look at the winnowing machine."

"Well, I'm looking."

"And those stars, those three stars, hanging so low over the very steppe—you see them?"

"I see them," Rodion got out, barely audibly.

"Why, they're those very same stars!" Kovalev cried out in rapture, slapping his legs. "Those very same stars you can see through our windows at home every summer!" And, baring his teeth, white as quicklime, under his dark little mustache, he went off into peals of soundless, happy, childlike laughter.

And sure enough: between the cellar and the winnowing machine, very far off, three stars were glowing, as though the expiring embers of a gypsy fire were lying scattered out in the steppe.

"Let's have a smoke, so's not to be longing for home."

Rodion grunted, took out of the bosom of his shirt a small sack of dry Rumanian flake-tobacco, rolled himself a cigarette, spattered red sparks out of his strike-a-light, and began puffing away.

It was on the very hour of midnight. The dogs had already stopped yapping, but the roosters had not yet begun their chanting. Throughout the big hamlet, amid the acacias, there was an even stream of warm, silvery air from the steppe, from those stars. On the roofs of the wattled sheds, upon the cellar-doors, upon the long clay ledge under the grated windows of the master-hut —wherever there was any elevation—were lying great round squashes, ponderously and solidly, as if they themselves were of clay.

"Listen, Rodion," Kovalev began to whisper anew, "there, don't you feel it? To the right of that thresher lies our own street, and farther on stands the church. And that church, upon the Feast of Our Saviour, is filled with sweet pinks and mint; there's folks standing in that church, and of all those there the most beautiful are the young girls; their sleeves are embroidered with rose-buds, their braids are rich with ribbons of all colors, there's necklaces and beads about their necks, and in their little hands they hold flowers that are beautiful beyond all telling. You feel it, Rodya? It makes your throat dry, actually."

Kovalev suddenly looked about him, thievishly and gaily, as though he wanted to say something important, but did not say it and, instead, started jigging. On enormous, noiseless feet he made a dash for the cellar, and a minute later was back, breathing hard.

"We'll get rid of our thirst right away, Rodion. Here, take the shell!"

Rodion held out his hands and the flying cantaloupe, cellar-chilled, smacked into his palms with all its ripe weight, like an elongated, ringing ordnance shell. The friends sat down on the clay ledge, and while Kovalev was trying to pry open with his thumbnail the tight blade of the knife he carried on a chain, Rodion Zhukov, having placed the cantaloupe on his knees and stroking it, was gazing unblinkingly into the darkness straight ahead of him. And now Rodion no longer saw either the familiar stars, nor his own hut at home, nor the blithe Feast of Our Saviour, when all around the church there is such an overpowering and joyous smell of axle-grease, poppies, and honey; he saw neither the embroidered sleeves of the young women, nor their ribbons, nor their hazel-hued eyes, nor the tapers within the church. As a black sea had the black alien earth surrounded Rodion; the stars had turned denser, had taken on a deeper glow and lowered before his eyes like the close-to-earth lights of a port city. Noisy became that city; the booms in the port burst into flame, people began running, becoming tangled amid the riotous fire; the metallic volleys of gunfire clanged forth like long steel rails; the barnyard swayed as if it were a ship's deck; a reflector, its seamed lens blinding, began to hiss overhead: a brazen cymbal; a circle of light was running, running over the undulating shore, flaring up, chalkily, wherever it struck and blanched the corners of houses, window-panes, darting soldiers, tatters of red, ammunition chests, guncarriages.

And next Rodion saw himself up in a gunturret, in the daytime. The gunner glued his eye to the rangefinder. The turret was turning automatically, bringing to bear upon the city the mouth of the gun, itself hollow from end to end, glittering within because of its mirrorlike rifling. Full stop! Right on the button, against the theater cupola that looked like a seashell. There, amid unbelievably luxurious surroundings, behind a table lined with green baize, a general of impressive mien was presiding over a council of war against the mutineers. A tenuous telephone bell droned boringly. An electric elevator, clanging leisurely, brought a projectile up out of the ammunition hold—a projectile swaying on chains—right into Rodion's hands. The projectile is heavy and chill, but strong are the sailor's hands.

"Gunturret, fire!"

At that instant his ears started to ring, just as if something had hit the outside of the turret's armor, as if that armor were no more than a tambourine. A flash of fire; a steamy stench, as if a comb had fallen into a fire. The roadstead shuddered through all its wide expanse. The boats out in the roadstead began to rock. A streak as of metal lay down between the armorclad and the city. Overshot. Rodion's hands were flaming. The 'phone again. And the second projectile was crawling of itself out of the elevator into his hands. We'll finish that general off—you wait and see!

"Gunturret, fire!"

And a second metal streak lay down across the bay. Overshot again. Never mind; guess we won't miss the third time. Never fear, there's no lack of projectiles. The hold is full of them. Lighter than a cantaloupe did the third one seem to Rodion. The only thing was to fire it as quickly as possible; the only thing was to have the smoke come billowing out of that cupola—but quick. And after that the party would really get lively! But, somehow, the 'phone wasn't ringing. Have all those damned bastards below decks died out, or what? The turret turns around as if of itself: "Cease firing!"—and the projectile, having slid out of Rodion's hands, sinks back into the hold, making the chains of the elevator rumble slowly and intermittently.

"Say, what's all this? Eh, they've sold us out, the devil's own tarts—they've sold out our freedom! They've let the ship drift! If you're going to fight, then fight to the end. So that there won't be one stone left standing upon another!"

Rodion came to: just as though a hundred years had passed, yet in reality it had been but one brief minute. Kovalev had managed to pry open the knife-blade and, having pulled the cantaloupe out of Rodion's numbed hands, deftly, at one curving sweep, cut it lengthways, split it open like a letter, and splashed out its inwards. The strong and fragrant odor of a ripe cantaloupe arose in the darkness. Kovalev held out a scoop of the melon to Rodion.

"A good muskmelon, that. We bought it off the grower himself, and did our own choosing. Eat hearty!"

His teeth gleamed faintly; he suddenly let his knife drop and, shyly as a bride, placed his head on Rodion's shoulder.

"I'm homesick, Rodion. So bad my soul aches. I want to go home."

"You're not lying, by any chance?"

"By God, I'm not. I'm homesick."

"The Danube is just a step away," Zhukov said then, softly smiling, "and it would take just two steps to cross it. Three to reach home. You coming with me, Vanya?"

Kovalev buried his face in his hands, shut his eyes hard, and quickly shook his head.

"No. . . . I'm not."

He patted Rodion's shoulder and got out in a shy whisper:

"I'm afraid, Rodya, of having to stand trial. The sentence would be hard labor in Siberia."

"Well and good, then," Zhukov said, his smile still softer. "Well and good, then. I know Taras. Taras wouldn't go. Taras has an old woman home that's worse than any witch."

He listened closely. Taras was wheezingly snoring in the middle of the barnyard, his face to the ground.

"I'm going alone."

IV

There's a head that's heavy, unstirring; it is drawn to sleep, to the dark earth, but what earth that is, one's own or an alien one, doesn't matter to it. A head like that you can't awaken. There's a head that's dear, a head merry, sly—but let it hear a song about freedom that has perished, let it see, glowing over an alien steppe, the stars it was born under—and it will suddenly turn pensive, will droop impotently upon a comrade's shoulder. In a word, it's no head but just a fine lad's headpiece. And then there's a head that's hard, knobby, with a crew-haircut; the brow is low but broad; the nape of the neck goes straight up and down; the neck is strong: there's no bending it. Once an idea gets into a head like that you won't knock it out with any wedge. A flame will flare up, will singe the tips of the lashes with a heat unbearable as that of stokeholes, a man's voice, grown hoarse, torn to tatters by sea winds, will send up a howl—and that's that. Write the man off as lost. For that, now, is no head but a steel projectile. And gunpowder is the sort of thing that will lie around and lie around but, just the same, will go off with a bang sooner or later: that's just what gunpowder was invented for. And there's no more rest for that head. The fuse smoulders unperceived. And then the head goes hurtling, consumed by fire, come what may.

A few days later Rodion made his way across the estuary of the Danube, near Vilkov, to the Russian side.

His plan was this: To go by way of the steppe, along the seashore, to Ackermann; then, by barge or steamer, to Odessa; all you had to do to reach the hamlet of Nerubaisk from there was to stretch out your hand. And then he would take things as they came. One thing only

did Rodion know for sure: that for him there was no
turning back to the past, that his former life, the sailor's
life of servitude on one of the Czar's ships, and the hard
life of a peasant back home, in a clay-daubed hut
painted light-blue and its small windows outlined in
indigo, amid the harsh pinks and yellows of the holly-
hocks, was cut off from him forever. Now it was either
Siberia for him or living underground, stirring up his
own people to rise up, burning the estates of the landowners, going to some city to join a revolutionary committee.

Rodion was expecting to learn from people, on his
way, what was going on in Russia: Whether there
would be peace soon with the Japanese; whether there
was an uprising anywhere; what word was there of the
Potëmkin; was the Czar, by any chance, granting freedom to the people?

But he had to go around the hamlets and big farms
by way of the steppe, and the people he came across out
in the steppe didn't know a thing. Time-blackened,
gray, age-deafened shepherds passed by amid the dust
raised by their flocks. Carts creaked by, filled with the
yellow cucumbers of the steppe; right on top of them,
stretched out at full length, belly down, snoozed the
yokels, bouncing. A huge barrel wallowed along on high
wheels, a bucket rattling under it. A freckled boy, in a
straw hat handed down to him by some German colonist, was bestriding it and lashing the sweating mare
with the sunwarmed leather reins; out of the spigot, for
all it was driven in so hard, the water seeped; large drops
fell on the road, curdled, and rolled along the dust, like
pills. Far off from the road, all bent over in a row, were
countrywives in pleated skirts, digging potatoes. Catching sight of Rodion they would drop their work and,
with their hands for sunshades, would follow him with

their eyes, long and apathetically. They didn't know a
thing.

At times the road would come up to the very shore
and stretch along some terrifically high, perpendicular
precipice. Thereupon Rodion would be swept by a wind
(while at the same time out in the steppe there was a
dead calm and the air was scorching), doused with the
chill roar of a storm, blinded by the snow and soda of
the raging spume, the blue greenishness of the horizon
cutting his eyes. Rodion would draw up to the very rim
of the precipice and, feeling vertigo, peer down. There
for many miles the glistening sand, inundated every
minute by the incoming tide, showed vividly white in
the sun. The ruffled waves were dragging and whirling
along the shore, over the gravel, the glistening black
body of a dead dolphin. Long tarred fishing smacks
were careened there, keel up, seines were drying on
poles, and a fisherman, getting the water all over him,
was drinking out of a squat keg, his head thrown back
and his knees slightly bent; he caught sight of Rodion,
started waving his arms and shouting something—it
may have been something of extreme importance. But
a fine watery haze hovered over the entire enormous
height of the precipice; the echo of a cannon rang as
bronze in the deafened air while the wind, gulping,
whistled in the ears, as if through a cannon hollow from
end to end. *Hai, hai, hai!* was all that floated up from
below to Rodion's ears.

And anew the road turned to the left into the unpeo-
pled steppe with its sheen, like that of the violet glaze
of immortelles—into the dead calm, into the sunbake.

And at night, when the stars were first coming out
and the crickets were first tuning up their crystal music,
a bonfire would spring up amid the darkness, and Rodion would head for it without any road, heels upon

cockleburs, straight on through the dark steppe, toward where there were people. They would be sitting silently around a clay-daubed firepot and supping. Rodion would loom up near the fire as a shadow so enormous that its head seemed to be propping up the stars. The men would not be in the least astonished and, without questioning him about anything, would offer him a spoon. Rodion sat down with them and, scalding his mouth, ate the smoke-bitter millet gruel and, after having eaten, he would wipe the spoon against the grass.

"Lie down here," the men would say. Rodion would lie down, with arms flung out, amid the strange, taciturn men, amid the strange, taciturn, ancient steppe.

"And what do you hear about freedom?" Rodion would suddenly ask, amid the night.

"Who knows? Men are shooting off their mouths about Kotovski having burned down another big farm close to Balabanovka. And maybe it weren't Kotovski. And maybe they're just plain lying. Who knows what's what? Us, all we do is wander up and down the steppe."

At dawn, awakened by the chill, Rodion would get up cautiously, so as not to awaken the others, and be off again, still bearing the freshness of the night upon his face.

And Rodion knew still less than he had known in Rumania about what was going on in Russia, and he went on, conjecturing his way, lonelily and uneasily, like one blind, without tiring, his only aim to get to the Dnestrovski estuary as quickly as possible.

Once, early in the morning, the road again turned off toward the cliffs, and Rodion caught sight in the distance of the mast of a cruiser, of tiled roofs, and an arbor overhanging the sea. The sun must have just risen but it could not be seen behind the morning clouds which let the light through chillily and softly, like seashells.

The sea had, after the storm, become silken. A dead swell, reflecting the dawn glow faintly and rolling it over its own sheen, lay in long wrinkles along the chill shore. The shoals raised by yesterday's storm were ruffling, distinctly and finically, barely underwater. Naked little boys, blue from the chill, were wading knee-deep over them; they kept bending over, their hands groping on the bottom, whacking the water with sticks and yelling. Suddenly one of them pulled out a broad, silvery-rosy fish. It gave a desperate tug and began to thresh about. Out of its gills, torn by tenacious fingers, blood purple as a cock's comb began to flow, spreading in turbid peonies upon the water.

"Here, ca-a-atch it!" yelled the boy and, swinging back, tossed the fish ashore. Two little girls with white-gold heads were standing bent over a willow basket, examining in terror and ecstasy fat, bloodied fish, writhing in powerful spasms and knocking off their large, transparent scales.

Then Rodion noticed that whole schools of these fish were in motion over these shoals. They bumped their heads against the little boys, passing between their legs, clumsily twisting and burying themselves in the sand. From above, exceedingly magnified by the convexity of the water, they resembled the dark shadows of torpedoes, moving slowly along the bottom.

"Blind fish! Blind fish!" several boys, with fancy designs upon their jerseys, screamed as they ran past Rodion. Pulling their sailor-jerseys off over their heads as they ran, they dashed as fast as their legs would carry them down the slope cut in the clay bank and, after tossing their clothing on the sand, belly-whopped into the water.

Blind fish. . . . Rodion had already happened to hear about them. Now and then, during great storms,

the wind drives into the sea from the estuary of the
Danube great schools of carp. The freshwater fish, finding themselves in salt water, become blinded and
stunned. The sea current hurries them, dazed by the
storm, ever farther and farther along the alien shore, for
many scores of miles from their calm native waters. The
storm quiets down and they, dying, weakened and unable to see anything in an inimical element they cannot understand, move about in their schools, bumping
against the shore, against the shoals and the legs of
those who had come to get them. A boatman-smuggler
had told Rodion about them while they had been sitting
among the dank reeds of the Danube waiting for the
patrolling cutter to steam past. Now Rodion saw them.

V

He went down to the shore, took off his clothes and
waded out into the sea. Up to his knees in the icy, glassy
water which made the legs ache naggingly, rocked by
the swell, Rodion got out to a shoal and peered into
the water. A great dark fish nudged his leg. Rodion
seized it around the body. It slipped out of his fingers,
darted off to one side and, with fins splashing, vanished
in the stirred-up sand. Rodion, lifted by a wave, missed
his footing and went in over his head. He was seared
with cold. Through the salt, so heavy that it floated before his eyes, he saw the fish which, with gills distended,
was swimming along, while its mouth, small and round
as a cipher, was thrust out of the water.

"No you don't!" said Rodion, gasping, and seized its
head. The fish started threshing, gave an extra hard flip
of its tail and dove down anew. Rodion smacked his
palm on the water. A naked boy galloped past him,
bringing his knees heavily out of the water, bent down,

pulled out the fish and flung it ashore. Rodion, becoming really irked, started running up and down the shoal, and kept up his running till he had cast two carp ashore. After which he came out on the sand and, his teeth chattering, began to dress.

In the meanwhile the shore was becoming crowded. The summer residents, men and women, were constantly appearing on the slope. Bearded men in black pongee shirts belted with tasseled silk cords flapped in canvas slippers over yielding dust, the color of dried cocoa. They were hugging thick books to their chests. Ladies in pince-nez were leading by the hand naked little children brown from the sun. Superb young ladies, their necks and arms considerably darker than their white dresses, swung their straw hats, which looked like flower-baskets on ribbons, as expertly as jugglers. Gay outcries and din hovered over the sea. That sea had turned a deeper blue. The sky had cleared. The sun flashed out vividly. Everything had become magnificently foreshortened.

Having dressed himself without drying off, all dripping under his clothes, Rodion picked up his fish and hurried to get up to the steppe.

"Sailor man, sailor man filled his pants 'stead of the can!" yelled a mischievous brat in a calico shirt and with his front teeth knocked out, as he rolled down head over heels past Rodion.

Rodion lengthened his stride. His lips had turned lilac, his knees were quivering, his fingers were bloodless; he kept shrinking into himself from the unaccustomed dampness of his long, icy dip. The wind doused him with cold for the last time at the top of the rise. He started off into the steppe, trying to skirt the summer villas. It was already hot out in the steppe but, despite this, Rodion kept on shivering. His eyes felt unpleas-

antly hot; the lashes tickled. "Damn those fish!" he got
out, his teeth barely hitting together. A villa appeared
before him. He skirted it, by way of its truck garden—
and ran into another villa. Behind a hedge of lilac and
evergreens one could glimpse a newly laid out garden.
Rodion's hands parted the resinous branches with their
tiny cones and he saw rows of fruit trees. A path lay
between them, strewn, as if with grits, by tiny green
marine shells. A checkered rubber ball was lying on this
path. Farther on he saw an awning bellying over a terrace, steps, a bed of yellow-white lilies that looked like
thin slices of hard-boiled eggs; among these were lacquered playthings and, lying in a hammock nearby, was
a man in a black blouse, with the collar buttoning at the
side.

"The whole point of the thing is, you see," he was
saying, waving his newspaper about, "that I agree with
you, in part. On the one hand we are face to face with
the indubitably encouraging fact of the masses awakening from their millennial sleep—of the masses having become conscious, at long last, of the yoke of autocracy
upon their necks and of the club-law over their heads;
we are face to face with the fact, so to say, of the movement for liberation on the part of the more advanced
elements among the proletariat and the peasantry, and
so forth. With that I am in complete agreement and, as
a revolutionary, I stand ready, from that point of view,
to greet the revolution which has come—which, I emphasize, *has come*. But—" he turned quickly with all
his corpulent body in the hammock, making it creak
and revealing a creamy cheek with a chocolate mole,
then, taking off his pince-nez with a stern gesture, fixed
his gaze on the man he was talking to. The latter was
standing on the terrace steps and, holding a glass of
iridescent milk, his eyes puckered, was eating a hunk

of fine wheaten bread smeared with honey, getting his lips all sticky and nearsightedly letting the crumbs fall on his untidy beard. "But, Doctor, on the other hand— I emphasize *on the other hand*—as a Marxist, I simply cannot agree that—"

A twig crackled under Rodion's foot. The gentleman in the hammock cut short his speech and caught sight of him. Rodion was standing by the hedge, not daring to stir from the spot. The gentleman, his speech cut short at its most important point by an extraneous sound, gave a stern cough, saw the fish in Rodion's hands and, pulling a wry face, started waving his arms:

"To the kitchen, dear fellow—bring them to the kitchen. There has been no getting away from those fish all morning. Go to the kitchen, brother. The cook will buy them from you. Go on! Well, sir—"

Rodion started going through the truck garden. Blotches like scraps of bright calico were floating before his eyes. His chill would not pass, even though his body had dried by now. The gentleman's voice kept annoyingly repeating in his head: *I simply cannot agree, I simply cannot agree, I simply cannot agree.* When he reached the end of the truck garden Rodion found himself confronted with the kitchen. It was off to one side, surrounded by burdocks. Smoke was pouring out of its chimney. The cook, all smeared with blood, was sitting on the threshold and cleaning fish. Making his way with difficulty through the burdocks, which powdered his trousers with the yellow pollen of their blossoms, Rodion approached the woman.

But she suddenly became alert, threw the carp half-cleaned into a blue-enameled basin, wiped her hands against her apron and, adjusting a metal comb in her hair, dashed off through the yard. In the middle of the yard, near the water-well, idlers had formed into a ring.

Well-dressed nurses, and children togged out in their best because it was Sunday, were hastening there from all directions. Certain sounds, odd in the highest degree, like nothing on earth yet remotely reminiscent now of a dog yapping, now of the hissing screech of a turning lathe, were borne from the center of the ring. Rodion approached the crowd and, over the backs and heads of the others, saw something unusual. A gaunt, clean-shaven fellow with a very long, non-Russian nose, clad in a dirty canvas duster and holding some sort of a crank, was standing on his knees, bent in concentration over some small contraption whose like Rodion had never yet seen. A thick, tubular roll, apparently of bone, was turning raspingly within it; a narrow brass tuba, of no great length, looking like a megaphone, was sticking out of the contraption. The hissing, squealing sounds were patiently, laboriously tearing themselves loose from it, spluttering and colliding with one another. Rodion shouldered his way to the front, cocked an ear —and suddenly was petrified. Beyond a doubt, these sounds were nothing else save a very small, squeaky, hoarse and hurried voice, inarticulately saying something through the hissing that issued from the mega-phone, as if through the sparks of a grindstone. Hardly had Rodion, by listening intently, made out a few words when the hissing intensified, changed to rumbling, and the man stopped the contraption. He rummaged in his bag and inserted another roll:

"*Homesickness,* a march," he announced, and wound up the crank.

Thereupon the diminutive roulades of a toy wind orchestra were heard, and Rodion clearly made out the tune of the gasping beats of a march:

> *Ta! Ta-tá!*
> *Ta-tá!   Ta-tá!   Ta-tá!*

" 'I'm going far away from here, I leave my wife and children dear!' " the cook hummed in astonishment, and stamped a bare foot lightly. They shushed her.

"It's the power of the Foul One himself!" said she, bewitched, and backed toward the kitchen, jigging and bending her knees.

Rodion went after her and offered his fish. The cook picked up the somnolent carp by their gills, hefted them, looked at Rodion suspiciously as he stood there against the sun, and asked:

"And where did you bob up from?"

Rodion waved his arm vaguely.

"Don't need them," said the cook malevolently, thrusting the fish back at him. "Traipse back to where you come from. It's the power of the Foul One, that thing. Go on, you gallowsbird!"

Rodion came out into the truck garden again. He threw the slimy carp in among the potatoes, upon the hot earth, and felt vertigo. It came floating in waves, it seemed to him, out of the yard, upon the barking sounds of the nauseating march; these sounds were constantly intensifying; by now they were thundering with cymbals and trombones in his very ears, which were growing deaf, so that the lobes of his brain were becoming painful from the nagging beat of these sounds; all the air around was ablaze with the tender and at the same time unbearable music at noonday. *I'm going far away from here, I leave my wife and children dear; I'm going far away from here, I leave my wife and children dear; I'm going far away from here, I leave my wife and children dear* a chorus was singing around him, its voices shifting. He passed a sharecropper's place and found himself in a field of stubble. Great, high stacks of straw practically hemmed in the summer villa. A brand new reaper shellacked in red, with a foreign trademark in gold, was standing on a patch of weatherbeaten granite, with hard-packed earth around it. Polished, gnawed clean by their work, the reaper's wooden rakes gleamed in the air, like the wings of a windmill. There was nobody out on the field of stubble. Rodion sat down on the metal seat of the reaper, which rocked under his weight, and threw up. He wiped his mouth with his sleeve, went off into a bit of shade, and lay down, propping his head against a prickly stack of straw. Somewhere on the grounds of the summer villa croquet balls were clicking crisply, echoing in his temples as pistol-shots. The white kerchiefs of curious country-wives bobbed up behind the share-cropper's place. Overcoming his sickness Rodion got up, went out into the steppe and struck on a road. Seeing nothing of what was around him Rodion started off along it and had covered about a mile, when suddenly he heard the ting-a-ling of small bells, and a cloud of dust white as flour sped past him. He stepped aside, and caught only the cracked leather wing of the britzka, the hood of a duster, maize-colored mustachios and a red nose. Wearily Rodion turned off the byroad, went deep into the standing corn and, disregarding any road, went off to one side. Reaching a grave, he lay down amid the worm-wood and, shivering, lay unconscious until nightfall.

VI

The earth was already covered with dew and the sky with stars when Rodion came to. His desire to drink was overwhelming. He plugged a sprig of wormwood and fell to sucking the gray, dew-filled cluster. But the dew was bitter and scalding in his mouth. It was then Rodion recalled the Danube: an enormous, dark mass of water, reflecting freshwater stars. He recalled the green smell of the reeds, acrid to nausea, the clicking speech of the frogs, as grating as small seashells, the marshy warmth of the river bottom, and suddenly grasped that he had sickened because he had drunk the Danube's water.

His head felt heavy and weak; as before, his belly was nagging away with a soft, sucking ache. Seized by the nausea of loneliness and thirst, not knowing how to come out on a road nor whither to follow it if he did come out on it, or how to disentangle himself from the wormwood and fever, Rodion stood up, overcoming with difficulty the ponderousness of his ailing body, and wandered off at haphazard across the steppe. In the calm and utterly clear air he could hear the sounds of string music. The notes of violin, flute, and double-bass floated blithely over the steppe. "Must be a wedding, for sure," reflected Rodion, submissively going in the direction of the music. He was stumbling and saw almost nothing around him, because of the swooning darkness in blotches before his eyes. The music was becoming ever more distinct. Rodion crashed his way through the corn and suddenly found himself confronted by the back wall of a sty. He caught the sour stench of pigs, the squelching of liquefied manure under their small hooves, and the heavy pressure of the animals as they scratched their sides against the wall. Somewhere horses were shifting from foot to foot upon a flooring of logs and turkeys were gobbling in their sleep. Rodion skirted the barnyard and saw at a distance, from an unfamiliar angle, a familiar garden. Paper lanterns, ready to burst lightly and warmly into an inward glow, hung between the trees of this newly laid out garden. Tall human shadows moved along the paths. Wild grapes glowed transparently green among the espaliers on terrace and in arbors.

Rodion made his way to the well and lifted up the

heavy, cold bucket. The water slopped heavily, the bucket tore loose out of the weakened hands and flew down, drawing the rattling chain after it and filling the concrete shaft of the well with the screeching rumble of the madly unwinding windlass. The iron crank hit Rodion a swinging blow on the shoulder and threw him to one side.

"Hey, there, who's that fooling around the well?" a man's voice shouted in the darkness. "Hey, there! I'll tear your ears off!"

Rodion dashed behind the kitchen, into the truck garden, and stopped to catch his breath. His heel trod on something cold and slippery. He bent down and saw the dead carp he had thrown away, gleaming dully white.

"Damn those fish," said he with disgust, and turned right to skirt the villa.

A precipice yawned before him. A great moon had just risen over the sea. A quarter of it was still concealed by the precipice. Long grasses showed with startling distinctness against its glowing red disk. Rodion walked up to the very edge, sat down on the grass, and let his legs hang over. He caught the broken surge of the incoming night tide, rolling along and shifting the tiny shells. The steppe, too, was naggingly aching, like a collar-bone after you hit it, and a dark-scarlet blotch was floating before the darkened eyes of the night.

Rodion let his head sink in despair—and suddenly, altogether near, he heard a noble, undulating voice, which had launched into:

> "The enemy's whirlwinds are howling overhead,
> The powers of darkness weigh and oppress—"

That was the very song to which the *Potëmkin*, like a phantom, used to loom up close to flame-enveloped shores and, like a phantom, pass thrice through the cordon of hostile ships, past the cannon directed against it. This was the song of Mitiushenko and Koshuba, the song of the mutinied ship's soviet, the song that fell like iron, like heavy iron, across roadsteads; the song that bent storm-clouds low to the sea and fluttered above the turret with its twelve-inch guns the flag with the words of glory: *Liberty, Equality, Fraternity.* It brought darkened consciousness to Rodion. The strong and pleasant tenor went on with its song:

> "To carnage glorious, holy, victorious,
> March, march ahead, ye who toil for your bread—"

Rodion clutched at the grass. Altogether near him, along the precipice, a couple was strolling, embraced: a tall student in a white jacket, his long hair thrown up and back, revealing a beautiful, bony forehead, and a girl in a light dress. A single cape covered their shoulders. They came alongside of Rodion.

> "To carnage glorious, holy, victorious—"

the woman's voice repeated.

Rodion drew himself up to his full height before them.

"Ah!" the girl cried out faintly and put her white hands up to her temples.

The student stopped and then retreated. The moon, risen quite high and more wan by now, lit up the sailor's face vividly. Tortured by typhus, it was dreadful. The girl quickly extricated herself from the cape and ran off toward the villa, her white dress flitting quickly.

"What the devil is all this?" muttered the student and, dragging the cape, started hurrying back, trying to overtake the girl with great strides. "Suspicious characters tramping around at night," he let drop from a

distance, by now threateningly. Two retreating white
blotches blended into one and disappeared, cloaked in
black. There came the sound of the girl's light laughter;
the man's wavering voice sang low:

> "I saw thee in my dream last night,
> And deeply drank of happiness—"

Rodion pulled a handful of grass out by the roots and
threw it underfoot. He took a deep gulp of the fresh
sea air and started off toward the villa.

Incredibly bright shrubbery and trees, lit through
and through by the arsenical smoke of green bengal
fire, were puffing up along the entire breadth of the
garden. Supper was going on in one of the arbors.
Rodion saw the glass chimneys of the candles, wine-
corks, leaden bottle-seals, pears, a caterpillar crawling
over the sleeve of a white jacket, an elbow, and a
creamy cheek.

"Gentlemen, the County Chairman isn't drinking a
thing," a loud bass boomed amid the clatter of china.
"Have a shot of vodka, County Chairman!"

Four rockets slithered, hissing, out of the thicket of
smoky bengal fire and, with difficulty, soared skyward.

"Children, children! Come to the croquet ground!" a
throaty feminine voice called out.

A long-legged little girl in a pink dress ran past
Rodion. His head catching at the Japanese lanterns, he
groped his way through the garden and saw the croquet
plot. A lady with a high bust was standing in the center
and clapping her palms:

"Get in line, two by two!"

"It's a Grand March! It's a Grand March!" the children, all amazingly gotten up, began to shout, hopping
about in the orange light of roman candles.

"Step out, Russia!" said the lady, leading out of the

crowd a big, red-cheeked girl in a peasant sleeveless
coat and a head-dress with a high front. A sheaf of rye
was nestling in her arms.

"Watch out you don't catch on fire, Verka!" squealed
a little boy in a yellow cap, who was dressed up as a
Japanese.

"Keep still, you little monkey, you miserable little
Jap!"

The paper feathers started swaying, and the silver
shield of a knight gleamed with incandescent lunar blue,
and with the same blue gleamed the dark water in a
tub under an apple tree, with a half-gnawed apple floating in it. The unseen orchestra struck up a march. Someone ran by with a lantern, catching Rodion with his
elbow.

"To the croquet ground, please, ladies and gentlemen!" the familiar bass called out, incredibly loud.
"Come, now, ladies and gentlemen! County Chairman,
let's go and look at the Grand March!"

Guests and servants surrounded the children. Rodion
escaped from the vivid fumes and, dazed, went off
swaying through the backlots and under trees, like one
of the blind fish amid underwater growths, constantly
finding himself within shoals of moonlight.

In the backyard, between stables and kitchen, the
hired hands who had come to congratulate the masters
on a good harvest, were having their fling. A keg of
beer, two square quart bottles of green vodka, a bowl
of fried fish and a wheaten twisted loaf were standing
on a table set out in the open. The cook, now drunk, in
a new pleated blouse of printed calico, was surlily serving portions of fish to the celebrating field-hands and
filling their mugs. The thoroughly tipsy accordion player,
his shirt unbuttoned, his legs spread out, was swaying
in his chair, fingering the bass keys of his gasping in-

strument. The lads, their faces apathetic and their torsos unbending, their arms around one another's ribs, were grinding their boot-heels, stomping through a polka. Several of the farm women, in new head kerchiefs, their coarse cheeks glossy with tomato juice, were languidly tapping their feet in uncomfortable shoes of goatskin. The landed proprietor himself, in a white-topped cap (symbolic of his nobility) and a pongee jacket crackling in small wrinkles about his by no means big body, stood smiling by the table. He was hefting a tumbler of vodka in his large hand. An utterly inebriated muzhik was stumblingly running around him and, winking to the cook, was saying with a badly twisting tongue:

"To our master, Andrew Andreievich, glory—to our master, to our own landowner, glory!"

Rodion walked all around the yard. In one of the garden paths, their paper costumes swishing and sending a wave of stifling wind over him, the children ran noisily past him. A gypsy was pounding her tambourine. A little Cossack, his cap on one side of his head, was lashing with his whip the Jap, who was grimacing like a monkey. The knight was gleaming with the blue silver of his cuirass; the little girl in the Russian head-dress was, amid peals of laughter, dragging the sheaf of rye after her. A dwarf with a tied-on beard was brandishing a bomb.

Beyond a rail-fence, up to his knees in burdocks, a frightfully drunk hired hand was meandering swayingly, his face wildly pale; he smashed his fist against a clay-daubed wall and yelled:

"Three rubles and fifty kopecks! May you choke, may you swell up and burst from my money. Three rubles and fifty kopecks!"

Rodion came out on a melon patch and stumbled against a muskmelon. He bent down and plucked it.

It was warm and heavy. Oh, to drink! The moon was high over the hay-stacks drily hemming in the big farm. A rocket slithered obliquely across the green sky. In the light of the moon Rodion saw all around him a great number of late muskmelons on the ground, ripening their last. The dark-purple smoke of bengal fires, the flashing and crackling fumes of catherine-wheels whirling and shooting over the villa, the human shadows striding as if on stilts—all this sprang up in a riot before Rodion's eyes. The heavy muskmelon was cradled in his hands like a projectile.

"Gunturret, fire!" thundered in Rodion's ears—and at that same instant a rocket flared up and detonated like a shot in the sky. He squeezed the muskmelon between his palms. His palms caught on fire. Oh, to drink! Rodion thrust his hand in his pocket to get out the knife —and his groping hand found matches. "Gunturret, fire! Gunturret, fire!" kept pounding in Rodion's ears, as if on a tambourine. "They've sold us out, the devil's own tarts—they've sold out our freedom! They wouldn't listen to Dorothei Koshuba!"

Rodion smashed the muskmelon to smithereens against the ground and pulled out the matchbox. An even breeze was drawing from the steppe, over the field of stubble, toward the villa. Leaping over the melons Rodion reached the first stack at a run and burrowed into the straw. A light, dry heat touched his face, and at that moment he recalled the unbearable heat of a stokehole, the firebars glowing at white heat, the engine with stinking, steaming water pouring down it, and the paint-striped billets of chopped-up lifeboats writhing in the furnace and scorching with their flames the tips of the eyelashes. . . .

And after that, going through the steppe but following no road, stumbling at field boundaries, scraping his legs against the stubble, swaying, and gasping from thirst, Rodion all night saw himself as in a dream sailing without end or limit, traversing a dark sea obliquely, passing unseen through squadrons, through cordons of hostile ships, chopping up lifeboats, firing the engines —and the rosy glow of the conflagration behind him seemed to be the glow of the conflagration of a city burned down by artillery.

He walked all night, and toward morning crawled into a vineyard and lay there unconscious until evening in the dry, drugging heat of an empty reed-shelter, amid downy clusters of grapes and oddly shaped leaves: turquoise and copperas. At evening he got up and went on again, seeing nothing before him and thinking nothing, and at midnight, sinking knee-deep in sand, he came to Ackermann. He made the circuit of the deserted streets, stumbled against a Cossack patrol, and hurriedly turned off toward the estuary beach.

On the dark shore, over the water green with moon-light, over the barges and scows, stood an ancient Turk-ish fortress. The moonlight lay obliquely within its nar-row embrasures. Nightbirds were noiselessly circling over its dentilated turrets. Rodion made his way across the rampart, a wilderness of thistles and weeds, with a battered cannon lying among them, its patinaed copper dully gleaming, and stepped into the fortress. In the middle of its courtyard stood a black, ancient, half-rotted gallows, with wormwood growing thickly under it. Rodion lay down in its magnificently chill dew and fell into unconsciousness.

And Rodion never knew that somewhere between Bucharest and Odessa a telegraph wire was humming low and whining over the steppe; that a tape like a white shaving was coiling, crawling out from under a brass wheel, to the tapping of the Morse code; that a Colonel, diffusing pleasant odors, was speaking over a 'phone; that the cook was standing before a desk in the chancellery of the County Chairman and making a deposition; that a man with a handlebar mustache in a black jacket and a canvas cap, who had arrived in Ackermann from Odessa on yesterday's steamer, was snoring on a bench, with his summer overcoat for a pillow, in the steamship line's cubbyhole of an office.

On awaking in the morning Rodion went to the marketplace and drank off a whole jug of milk. He threw it up right then and there. He walked off to the quay and lay down on some warm matting in the shade of some threshing machines nailed in their wooden crates and of round baskets of peaches and grapes, neatly sewn in canvas. Tormented by the nauseating glitter of the yellow water, flaming like lead in the sun all over the enormous breadth of the Dnestrovski estuary, deafened by the rumbling of small wagons, the silky swish of grain pouring down chutes, the squeal and clatter of steam winches on a loading steamer and the cursing of the draymen, stupefied by the stifling flour-dust hovering motionlessly in the heated air, by his thirst and sickness, Rodion did not see the man with the handlebar mustache who went past him twice, with his hands thrust apathetically into his pockets.

About three in the afternoon Rodion bought, for his last half-ruble, a third-class ticket to Odessa and went up the gangplank of the steamer.

VII

The steamer left Ackermann at four and arrived in Odessa at ten.

Fussily churning the coffee-colored water with the paddles of its wheels, it at first ran gaily past the dreary banks of the estuary, overtaking the sailships and barges. Then it turned Carolino-Bugass—a sandy, burning spit near which, riding low and ponderously in the water, was a leaden monitor ship. The boundary guards of the Bugass cordon, with green shoulder-stripes, were washing linen on the shore, their every detail lit up by the sun. Ahead, divided off sharply from the yellow water of the estuary, lay the black-blue streak of the shaggy sea. Hardly had the steamer, passing the small bobbing buoys and wherries, entered this streak when it was immediately caught up by the roll, was doused with waterdust by a strong sea wind. The somber swirls of soot, copiously billowing out of the snorting smokestacks in oblique brown streaks, fell upon the canvas awning of the poopdeck. The engine began to breathe more heavily. The hold started creaking with its heavy cargo of fruit-baskets.

Snow-white foam, churned up under the wheelboxes, streamed waveringly along the sides. A frocked waiter, grabbing at rails with his white cotton gloves, brought up on deck from the buffet a bottle of lemonade, smoking with froth. Four blind Jews in derbies and blue spectacles brought their bows down upon their fiddles. Someone's straw hat was floating away in the wake of the ship, rocking on a broad streak of foam. Some landowners from Bessarabia were playing cards in the salon of the second-class, now growing dark, now light, from the waves that flooded the closed portholes. The man with the handlebar mustache, the collar of his summer overcoat turned up and his canvas cap pulled down tight to his very ears, was bending over the side and spitting apathetically into the dark-green water running by in the light shadow of the steamer.

But nothing of this did Rodion see. He was lying below in deep delirium, among creaking baggage and

Jews tortured by the pitching of the boat, on the filthy floor, in a narrow passage between the galley and the engine-room out of which, through the air-vents, heated air issued, saturated with the odors of heated metal, scalding water, and oil.

When he came to it was already evening and the steamer was nearing the city. In a blue interstice between barrels and boxes Rodion saw the red, revolving eye of a lighthouse, the jagged stars of the port lamps over the goffered roofs of warehouses and offices, the fires of stokeholes, the green and raspberry-red riding-lights of scows.

Over his head, on the upper deck, sailors ran by thunderously. The quay piled up on the steamer. The passengers herded closely by the gangplank. Rodion wanted to get up, but could not manage it. The man in the summer overcoat walked up to him and took him under the elbows. Rodion got up with difficulty and, swaying, went toward the gangplank.

The nagging whine of horse-cars, the clatter of droshkies over the small cobbles of the roadways, the clacking of horse hooves striking fugitive sparks, the din of a crowd at night—all this vertiginous music lashed in a wave into Rodion's ears and deafened him. Swaying, he went down the gangplank to the quay, and at once two walked up to him.

"Zhukov?" asked one of them.

"The very same," the man in the summer overcoat answered gaily.

They pinioned Rodion's arms and seated him in a cab.

Feeling through his fever and delirium that something exceedingly untoward was befalling him, losing consciousness and slumping against the shoulders of the men with him, Rodion for the last time beheld the magnificent glitter of the city revolving like a catherine-wheel, heard music, playing a waltz on one of the boulevards. . . . For the last time there puffed up before him the dark-purple fumes of bengal fire, children ran past him in unbelievable costumes, a rocket detonated, white smoke billowed out of straw, people began scuttering about in the villa, enveloped in flames on three sides, the tocsin began its thunder peals. "Gunturret, fire!" struck at his ears, as if on a tambourine. Koshuba started running with a distorted face over a trap-stair that had been overlooked . . . and with that Rodion ceased to see.

"Get going," said the man with the handlebar mustache, with one foot on the step of the cab, and tenderly supporting Rodion's body, heavy and wilted in a faint and, at the same time, somehow empty. "You know where to go?"

The cabby silently nodded his head in its oilcloth tophat, lashed his horse and drove off with his fares past a charred and devastated boom, past booths in which Persians, under the unbearably bright glare of arc-lamps were shooing the flies off beautiful Crimean fruit with noisy paper sultans, past brothels, into the city. . . .

MIKHAIL MIKHAILOVICH ZOSHCHENKO
(1895–   )

EDITOR'S NOTE

SOVIET RUSSIA'S foremost humorist, and probably the best loved one since Chekhov, was born in the Ukraine. He studied law but did not graduate, volunteering in World War I and serving as an officer until he was gassed and wounded. After the Revolution he wandered all over Russia, following almost as many trades and professions as Gorki or Kuprin did: he was carpenter, trapper, apprentice shoemaker, telephone operator, policeman, detective, gambler, clerk, actor. In 1918 he volunteered again—for the Red Army. In 1921 he was one of the leading spirits in the famous Serapion Brotherhood and, in 1922, published his first story.

As a humorist, his understanding of human failings is as deep as Chekhov's, but without the older master's tenderness. His humor is that of incident, of situation, grotesque or homely, the humor of the faithful reporter, the keen observer whose eye is micro-, tele-, kaleidoscopic. The style he has worked for himself, motley, elliptical, clipped, coarse, broken—and pulsating—is so relished because the Russians, the most humorous people on earth, actually talk that way.

Zoshchenko has already paid the usual penalty of the writer who becomes known as a funnyman: although he had begun with "straight" stories (the tragicomedy of some of these being akin to that of Gogol), has made scholarly experiments, and has done (and is doing) serious work, all this is obscured by his hundreds of humorous stories, skits and parodies.

The Restless Little Ancient

MIKHAIL MIKHAILOVICH ZOSHCHENKO

WE HAD a case, right here in Leningrad, of a certain little old man who fell into a cataleptic sleep.

About a year before that, don't you know, he'd had a

spell of night-blindness. But he got over it, in due time. Why, he even used to go out into the communal kitchen to raise general hell about culture and things like that.

But the other day he ups and falls asleep—unexpected, like.

Well, then, he fell asleep in the night—but in a catalepsy. Comes morning, he wakes up and sees there's something wrong with him. That is, rightly speaking, his relatives see a body lying there, with no breath in it or showing any other signs of life. His pulse ain't beating, and his chest don't heave, and his breath don't leave no mist on a pocket mirror when they hold it close to his rosebud lips. Well, naturally, they all surmise at that point that the little old man has turned up his toes in his own quiet way and, naturally, they set about making various arrangements.

They're in a hurry about making those arrangements, seeing as how the whole family lives in that one room, and the room itself is none too large. And there's all those other communal rooms all around them. And there's no place to lay out that little old man anywheres, even, if you'll pardon me for mentioning it—that's how cramped the place was.

For it must be pointed out that this old timer who'd fallen into his long sleep had been living with his relatives. Meaning the head of the family, and his wife, and a baby, and a nurse. And besides he was the father, so to say, or, to put it more simply, the papa, of the wife of the head of the family—the woman's papa, that is. An erstwhile Toiler. He'd been living on a pension.

As for the nurse, she was a little wench of sixteen, taken on to help out in the family, seeing as how both of 'em, man and wife—that is, her papa's, or to put it more simply, her father's daughter—both of 'em, now, had to go out to do productive work.

So there they were, doing productive work and, you understand, toward morning they're faced with such a sad misunderstanding—papa had passed away.

Well, of course, they were grieved, their feelings were all upset—seeing as how that little room was none too large and, on top of that, there was this superfluous element.

So there was that superfluous element, lying there in the room. Such a clean little, dear little old man, an interesting little ancient, no longer able to think of housing problems, of over-crowding, of worldly frets and cares. He lay there, fresh as a wilted daisy, sound as a winesap that's been put through a dehydrator. He lay there, and recked nought, and wanted nought, and all he asked for was for the last respects to be paid him.

He asked only that he be clothed, somehow or another, as quickly as possible, that he be rendered the last "Forgive us in departing," and that he be buried, as quickly as possible, somewhere or another.

He asked that this be done as quickly as possible, seeing as how there is, after all, but the one room, and that one none too large and, in general, there's the inconvenience. And seeing how the baby is squawking its head off. And the nurse feels scary about living in the same room with dead folks. Well, she's a silly little wench, she feels like living all the time, and thinks that life never comes to an end. She feels scary looking at corpses. She's a fool.

The husband, the head of the family, that is, thereupon dashes off quick as he can to the burial bureau of the district. And comes back from there—but quick.

"Well," says he, "it's all set. Except for a slight hitch about the hosses. As for the hearse," he says, "they'll let us have one right off, but they ain't promising no hosses any earlier than four days from now."

"I just knew it!" says the little woman. "You," she tells him, "was always scrapping with my father whilst he was alive, and even now you can't do him a favor—you can't get no horses for him, even!"

"Aw, go to hell!" says her husband. "I ain't no horseman, and I ain't in charge of no livery stable. I myself," he says, "find no pleasure in having to wait so long. It's no end interesting," he says, "for me to be watching your old man all the time!"

That's when all those domestic scenes took place. The baby, not being used to seeing people no longer alive, gets frightened and bawls at the top of its lungs. And the nurse refuses to work for this family, in a room where there was a dead man living. But she was persuaded not to abandon her profession, and was promised that the death would be liquidated as soon as possible.

Thereupon the lady of the house, getting tired with all this business, hurried over to the bureau, but it weren't long before she comes back from there white as a sheet.

"The horses," she says, "are being promised in a week. If my husband—it's always the fools that live on and on!—if my husband had put down a reservation on them we could have had 'em in three days. But by now our turn is the sixteenth. But as for the hearse, they can give it to us right off, true enough."

And she wastes no time in dressing up her baby, grabs the bawling nurse by the hand and, just as she is, starts off for a near-by town, for a stay with some friends.

"My baby," says she, "is the dearest thing in the world to me. I can't be showing him any such horror-films during his childhood years. As for you," she turned to her husband, "you do whatever you like."

"I'm not going to remain with him either," says the

husband. "Do as you like. But he ain't *my* old man. I wasn't any too fond of him whilst he was alive," he says, "but right now," says he, "I find it particularly disgustful to live with him. Either I'll put him out in the hallway, or I'll move in on my brother. And as for him, let him bide here till the hosses come."

So the family goes off to the near-by town, whilst the husband, that head of the family, runs off to his brother, who's got only one room himself for living quarters.

Only it so happens that just then his brother's whole family is having a touch of diphtheria, and they won't let the welcome guest as much as set foot over the threshold—not for anything! So right then and there he came back, laid the slumbering little ancient on a dinky folding bridge-table, and put the whole business out in the hallway, next to the bathroom. And then he holed in in his room and never answered, no matter how they pounded on his door and yelled at him, for all of two days.

That's when all the stuff and nonsense, the bottlenecks and mixup, really started all through the communal quarters.

The tenants set up a squawk and raised a ruckus. The women and children just wouldn't *go*, saying they simply couldn't pass by without taking fright. Whereupon the men fell all over themselves to take the whole business and transfer it to the vestibule—where it threw all those who entered the house into panic and confusion.

The co-op manager, who lived in a corner room, announced that he had lady-friends coming to see him for one reason or another, and that he couldn't risk giving 'em nervous breakdowns. The house management committee was quickly summoned, but they didn't contribute to any extent to a rationalization of the matter. It was proposed that the whole business be placed out of doors, but the house manager put his foot down:

"That," he said, "might arouse an unwholesome confusion among those tenants who are still among the living and, most important of all, bring about a failure to pay rent, which, even without that, is held back half a year as a rule."

Thereupon shouts and threats arose, directed against the fellow to whom this little old man belonged; he had locked himself up in his room and was now burning sundry rags and other insignificant effects left behind by the late lamented.

It was decided to break down his door and put the whole business back in his room. They started yelling and moving the bridge-table—whereupon the little old man sighed, ever so gently, and began to stir.

There was just a trifling panic, and after that the tenants got used to the new situation. They made a dash for the son-in-law's room with renewed vigor and began pounding on his door, shouting that the little old man was alive and wanted to get in.

However, the besieged man wouldn't answer them for a long time. And it was only an hour later that he spoke up:

"Cut out them shenanigans. I'm on to you—you want to put one over on me."

After protracted parleys the fellow to whom the little old man belonged asked the latter to pipe up. Whereupon the old man, who wasn't gifted with any too much imagination, piped up in a falsetto: "Haw-haw!" Which the besieged man in the end refused to accept as the genuine article. Finally he took to peeping out through the keyhole, having first asked the others to place the old man so's he might see him. When they stood the old timer up, the head of the family for a long time refused to admit he was alive, claiming that the tenants were deliberately jiggling his legs and arms. The old man, losing all his patience at last, began rioting and swearing unmercifully, as he used to when he had been admittedly alive, whereupon the door opened and the ancient was solemnly re-established in the room. After squabbling with his son-in-law over this and that the resuscitated old man suddenly noticed that his belongings had vanished, while some of them were smouldering in the stove. And that the folding bed on which he had deigned to die was no longer around. So, with that brazenness which is common at his age, he took it upon himself to sprawl out on the family bed and issued orders to be served with food. He fell to drinking milk and eating, announcing that he wouldn't consider the fact of their being related but would institute suit for the misappropriation of his property.

It weren't long before the wife—the daughter of this deceased daddy, that is—arrived from the near-by town.

There were outcries of joy and fright. The little one, who didn't go into biological details any too deeply, regarded the resurrection rather tolerantly. But the nurse, that sixteen-year-old fool, began showing new signs of a disrelish for working in this family, where people were constantly either popping off or coming to life again.

On the ninth day a white hearse arrived, with torches and things, and drawn by a single black horse, with blinkers.

The husband, that head of the family, was the first to see its arrival as he was nervously looking out of the window.

"There, daddy," said he, "the hosses have come for you at last."

The old man took to spitting and said he wasn't going

anywheres now. He opened a ventilator and began spitting out of it, shouting in his feeble voice for the driver to get going, but fast, and stop being an eyesore to living folks.

The driver, in a long white coat and yellow tophat, having grown tired of waiting for the body to be carried out, came upstairs and began cursing, ever so rudely, demanding that they finally let him have that which he had come for, and not make him wait out in the cold.

"I can't understand the low level of the people living here," said he. "Everybody is aware what an acute shortage of hosses there is. And to be calling them out for no reason at all—why, it can bring about the final disruption and ruination of transportation. No," he said, "you don't catch me coming to this house again."

The tenants collected and, together with the little old man, shoved the driver out on the landing and then trickled him down the stairs, long coat, tophat and all. For a long time he wouldn't drive off, demanding that they at least sign some sort of a receipt he had. The reanimated old man kept spitting through the ventilator and shaking his fist at the driver, a very pointed altercation having broken out between them.

At last the driver, grown hoarse from yelling and all tuckered out, drove off in defeat, after which life again flowed on in its wonted course.

On the fourteenth day the little old man, having caught a cold at the time he had opened the ventilator, took sick and shortly died, but this time on the up and up.

At first no one would believe it, thinking the old man was horsing around, just as he had done before, but when they called in a doctor he reassured them all, telling them that this time there wasn't any trickery about it.

That's when perfect panic and confusion sprang up among those living in the communal quarters. Many tenants, having locked up their rooms, left for the time being, going wherever each could.

The wife—or, to put it more simply, her daddy's daughter—shying away from going to the funeral bureau, went off to the near-by town again with the baby and the bawling nurse.

The husband, that head of the family, managed to get into a sanatorium. And the little old man was left to the will of fate.

The little old man lay there in that room until such time as a policeman arrived on a dray and, having composed the little old man thereon, carted him off to the proper place.

After which they all began coming back, little by little, and in a short while life was again rolling along, as if on well-greased wheels.

❀

A Budget
of Letters

❀

DANIEL OF THE OUBLIETTE

(XIIIth Century [?])

EDITOR'S NOTE

OF ONE of her greatest poets, the bard of *The Lay of the Host of Igor,* Russia does not know even the name; of the author of the *Supplication,* one of the few surviving monuments of her early literature, she knows scarcely anything save his name—Danilo, or Daniel. According to one account he was a monk, imprisoned after *interrogation* (read *torture*) for the possession of a "sack of deadly herbs"; there are also Man-in-the-Iron-Mask undertones—he may have been a disgraced by-blow of a Prince; other scholars claim there was nothing noble about Daniel—he was just a low fellow trying to pull himself up in the world by the boot-straps of his learning, admittedly exceptional for his times (which may have been in the eleventh century, or the twelfth, or the thirteenth, or even the fourteenth). Some think it was a case of two other Daniels (one of them even Daniel the Palmer!); others maintain there wasn't any Daniel at all, actually—just an echo of the Prophet and the lions' den); a third group insists that, even if there ever was any such Daniel, he was never imprisoned—although, as late as 1378, there is mention in a chronicle of his imprisonment in a fortress on an island in Lake Lach, in Olonetz. And the *Supplication* (also variously titled *Missive* and *Recital*) might have been addressed to one of several Princes other than the turbulent Yaroslav, son of Vsevolod (1190-1246).

The literature on this Daniel is as inconclusive as it is vast; for this translation that redaction which is now usually considered the second has been followed, in the main, since it is of greater general interest. It differs from the conjectured first in that the writer does not grovel so much before the Prince his Lord, is not violent against petty nobles and black monks (evidently this version has undergone the doctoring usual at ecclesiastical hands) but gives still looser rein to his misogyny, does not parade so ostentatiously his lore of history and statecraft (his purpose having been to wheedle the Prince into an appointment as councillor), and does not quite as frequently quote, in his own fashion, the Bible.

Daniel is also heavily indebted to *The Physiologue* (a sort of bestiary), chronicles, hagiographies, *The Bee* (an old collection of proverbs and folk-sayings), and even adapts for his ending Herodotus' old, old story of the Ring of Polycrates; in his turn he became one of the main sources for a collection of folk-wisdom, *The Smaragd*. He has been called one of Russia's first *intelligents*—and his appellation, *of the Oubliette* (or the *Immured*) is decidedly symbolic of the lot of authors in old Russia.

DANIEL OF THE OUBLIETTE

His Supplication to Prince Yaroslav, son of Vsevolod, Prince of Novgorod, and of Vladimir also

Let us blare, brethren, upon trumpets of wrought gold, which are the reasoning of our minds; let us smite instruments of silver, let us proclaim our wisdom. . . .

Prince, my Lord! I am as blighted grass that groweth close to a wall, and no sunlight shineth on that grass, nor doth rain fall thereon. . . .

Prince, my Lord! Look not upon me as a wolf upon a lamb; *Lord, my Prince,* look upon me rather as a mother upon her babe. . . .

Alas, *Prince my Lord,* some men live a full life—I have but cruel grief; to some White Lake is white—to me 'tis black as pitch, and Lake Lach maketh me but to weep; to some Novgorod is a great city—to me 'tis a sink of iniquity. . . . Mine is no bed of roses, *Prince my Lord.*

Thou dost feast with boon companions—I eat stale crusts; thy drink is sweet—I hardly have tepid water; thou sleepest upon soft beds, under blankets of sable skins—I shiver under one thin, shroud-like garment. Winter is death unto me, and the rain-drops pierce through my heart like unto arrows. . . .

The dulcimer is played with the fingers; the body is moved by the sinews thereof; the oak is steadfast because of the multitude of its roots—thus is our city steadfast because of thy rule. . . .

The Prince that is generous is like a river without banks that floweth through a forest of green oaks, giving drink not only to man but to all cattle, and all beasts also. The Prince that is niggardly is like a river with steep, stony banks; man cannot drink from it, nor can one drench horses therefrom.

The generous noble is a well of sweet water; the niggardly noble is a well of brackish water.

Prince, my Lord! Look not upon my outward appearance—look within me. I am poor in garb, but rich in intelligence; young in years but old in reason; like an eagle upon air do I soar upon thought: shouldst thou send a sage anywhere, thou needst give no instructions;

send a man of little sense, and thou wilt have to go after him thy self.—Sow not wheat in brakes, sow not wisdom in the heart of a fool. For fools men neither plow nor sow—they are a crop that of itself doth grow. He that would teach a fool is pouring water into a skin full of holes. Dogs and swine have no need of gold and silver—fools have no need of the words of the wise. There is no making a dead man laugh; there is no teaching a fool. Children flee a freak, and the Lord flees a drunkard. When a tomtit will devour an eagle, when a swine will bark at a squirrel, then will a fool learn wisdom.

Prince, my Lord! 'Tis not the sea that sends a ship to the bottom but the winds; 'tis not fire that brings iron to white-heat but the blowing of the bellows; 'tis not the Prince that doth evil but the flatterers lead him thereto. With a good councillor a Prince can win a great throne; with a poor councillor he will lose a minor one.

No cattle among cattle is a she-goat; no beast among beasts is a hedgehog; no fish among fish is a crab; no bird among birds is a bat; no man among men is he who is under his wife's thumb; no wife among wives is she that sports away from her husband. Better bring an ox into the house than take a wicked woman to wife: an ox will say no evil, nor invent evil, but a wicked wife will rage like a very fiend if chastised, will be overweening if one tries to tame her; if she be rich, she boasteth; if she be poor, she condemneth others. What is a wicked wife? A guest that never sleepeth; one that liveth with fiends; a turbulence in this world; a blinding of the reason; an instigator of all rancor, an upholder of sin, an ambush to salvation. The husband that regardeth but the beauty of his wife, that listeneth to her fair words, without putting her deeds to the test

—the Lord will, by way of relief, send him an ague. . . . The worm gnaws a tree; the wicked wife will make her husband lose the roof over his head. Better sail in a leaky boat than trust any secrets to a wicked wife: a leaky boat will but wet one's netherclothes; a wicked wife will ruin her husband's whole life. Better chip away at a stone with an awl than teach a wicked wife. Better cook iron—it will be done to a turn before one teaches a wicked wife anything. . . . What is more ferocious than a lion among all the four-footed beasts? What is more cruel than a serpent among all the creatures that creep? Aye, but a wicked wife surpasseth in evil all living things.

Prince, my Lord! I have never been to sea; I studied not with the philosophers; but, even as a bee, by clinging to diverse flowers, mingles the honey that is sweet in a honeycomb, so have I gathered, out of many books, wisdom and the sweets of words, mingling them even as sea-water is mingled in a skin; not through my reason alone, however, but by the will of God.

I, Daniel, inscribed these words while immured upon White Lake, and, having sealed them up in wax, let them into the lake, and a fish did swallow them; a fisherman caught the fish and brought it to the Prince; when they began gutting the fish, lo, they found the writing. The Prince chanced to see the writing, and commanded that Daniel be freed from his durance bitter.

Lord God, send thou to our Prince the strength of Samson, the bravery of Alexander, the sharp wit of Joseph, the wisdom of Solomon, the fortitude of David. Multiply, O Lord, the people under his rule.

A Historic Correspondence

ANDREW MIKHAILOVICH KURBSKY

(1528–1583)

EDITOR'S NOTE

KURBSKY was descended from the Princes of Yaroslav, who in their turn traced their descent to Vladimir the Great, the Monomachos (or Single Combattant). At twenty he took part in the campaign against the Tatars of Crimea and some years later distinguished himself at the siege of Kazan and was honored by Ioann the Awesome. He led all the troops against Livonia and won eight victories, but in 1563, overwhelmed at Nevel and fearing Ioann's wrath, he fled to King Sigismund of Poland—the same who had begged Queen Elizabeth not to send any British craftsmen to Russia, lest the Russian giant awaken. From Volmar Kurbsky sent a letter to the Awesome Czar by the hand of his loyal retainer Shibanov. Upon learning whom the messenger was from Ioann transfixed his foot to the floor with the spiked tip of his staff and bade him read the letter, which Shibanov did with a stoicism worthy of Seneca, betraying no pain even though he was bleeding profusely (Alexei Constantinovich Tolstoy has done a magnificent ballad on Vassilii Shibanov).

Kurbsky was versed in the humanities and translated (by a method in which he anticipated Alexander Pope) Chrysostom, Eusebius, and Cicero, and wrote *The Narrations of Grand Duke Kurbsky,* a chronicle of the reign of Ioann the Awesome, the first work of Russian that may be justly described as genuinely historical.

The First Epistle of Prince Andrew Kurbsky, Writ to the Czar and Grand Duke of Muscovy, that hath been Most Cruel in the Persecution of Him.

TO THE CZAR, MADE GLORIOUS BY GOD, WHO ON A TIME WAS A LUMINARY OF ORTHODOXY, BUT NOW, FOR OUR SINS, HATH BECOME THE FOE BOTH OF GOD AND ORTHODOXY:

They that have understanding will understand how thy conscience hath become more corrupt than that of any even among the Paynim. . . . Never before have I let my tongue utter any such things, but I have borne the most grievous persecution from thee, and out of the bitterness of my heart I would tell thee somewhat.

Wherefore, O Czar, hast thou brought low the mighty in Israel? Wherefore hast thou put to death in sundry ways the Leaders-in-Battle placed in thy keeping by God, and wherefore hast thou shed the saintly blood of these victors in the temples of the Lord, and at thy royal feasts? Wherefore hast thou stained the thresholds of the churches with the blood of martyrs, and wherefore hast thou set on foot persecutions against them that have served thee with zeal and caused their deaths, bringing accusations against good Christians of treason and witchcraft and other unseemlinesses, and hast striven hard to turn light into darkness and to style as bitter that which is sweet?

What crimes were they guilty of, O Czar, and whereby had they aroused thy ire, O Vicar of Chris-

tians? Had they not, through their valor, brought proud
kingdoms low, and made those slaves to thee who on
a time had made our sires their slaves? Have not the
strongholds of the Dumb Ones [Germans], through their
foresight, been placed in thy hands by God? Is utter
ruin the destruction, the reward thou hast meted out to
us poor men? Dost deem thyself deathless, O Czar? Or
hast thou become possessed by some unheard-of heresy,
and dost think thou wilt not have to come before the
face of the Supreme Judge, the Divine Jesus, Who will
judge all the world, but cruel oppressors above all
others, and shall not fail to break in pieces the transgres-
sor, as it is told in Holy Writ? My Christ, Who sitteth
on the throne of the cherubim on high, at the right hand
of the Supreme Power, shall be the judge between thee
and me.

What evils and persecutions have I not suffered at
thy hands! What tribulations and torments hast thou not
brought upon me! So many are the tribulations that
have befallen me and so diverse that I can make no
reckoning of them this day, inasmuch as my heart is
still heavy because of them. Yet this much I shall say:
through thee I have been shorn of all things and have
been made an exile from God's own land. I pleaded not
with thee in soft words, I implored thee not with tears
and groans, I begged no boon of thee through the
clergy, and therefore hast thou repaid me with evil for
good, and hast requited my love with implacable hatred.

My blood, that has been shed for thee like unto
water, cries to my Lord against thee. God perceiveth
our hearts; diligently have I searched my mind, have
called upon my conscience to bear witness, have examined my heart and delved deeply, and have not
found myself at any fault before thee. Steadfastly have
I led thy war-hosts, nor have I brought any ignominy

upon thee; with the help of the Angel of the Lord have I gained illustrious victories that enhanced thy glory, and never did thy war-hosts [under me] turn their backs to any foe of thine, but it was ever the foe that was vanquished in glory, to do thee honor. And this I did not for one year, or for two years, but through a long course of years, and that with great travail and enduring much. Ever have I defended my land, and saw my parents but little and still less was I with my wife. Ever was I away on campaigns, in far-off cities, in the field against thy foes, and have suffered great privations and ill health, and Lord Jesus Christ is my witness thereunto. Oft, and in many a battle, have I been covered with wounds inflicted by the hands of barbarians, and all my body is covered with scars.

Yet all this, O Czar, is as if it had never been, and thou hast evinced against me thy unrelenting wrath and a bitter hatred that is more vehement than a fiery furnace.

I was fain to recount to thee, in due order, all the soldierly deeds I, with the aid of my Christ, have done to thy glory; yet have I not done so, since God hath better knowledge thereof than lies within the knowing of any man, for He rewardeth them all, even as He doth the giving of a cup of cold water; moreover, I know thou hast full knowledge of the said deeds. Know this likewise, O Czar: never again wilt thou behold my face in this world before the glorious Second Coming of my Christ. Neither think thou that I will forgive thee that which hath befallen me: I will unto the day of my death cry out in tears and without cease against thee to the ineffable Trinity that I believe in, and I summon to my succor the Mother of the Prince of the Cherubim, the Virgin Mary, my hope and my intercessor, and all the saints, the chosen ones of God, and my lordly forebear,

Prince Theodore, son of Rostislav, whose body remains incorrupt, preserved these many years, and which emits a sweet odor from its grave and worketh, by grace of the Holy Ghost, cures miraculous and many, as thou knowest full well, O Czar.

Think not, O Czar, in thy vainglory that all those have perished whom thou hast brought low in their innocency, who are in prison or in unjust banishment because of thee; rejoice not, and boast not of thy empty triumph. They whom thou hast slain stand before the throne of God, beseeching vengeance against thee, while they among us that are in prison or in unjust banishment from our land because of thee call upon God in the day and in the night. Though thou, in thy vanity, mayst boast of thy power in this temporal and passing world, and mayst invent new implements of torture against the generations of Christians, and mayst mock and trample underfoot the image of the Angel, to the yea-saying of thy sycophants and thy table-companions, and to the yea-saying of thy nobles, who are bringing thy body and soul to perdition, inasmuch as they incite thee to deeds that are Aphrodite's, and act against their children worse than the priests of Chronos did, I shall nonetheless command this my epistle, dank with my tears, to be placed in my sepulcher, that I may bring it with me when thou and I shall go up for judgment before the seat of my Lord, Jesus Christ. Amen. *Writ in Volmar, a City of My Lord King August Sigismund, from Whom, the Lord God Helping Me, I Hope for Favors and Assuagement of All My Sorrows, through His Royal Graciousness.* [No date.]

[The postscriptum, aimed against Theodore Alexeievich Basmanov, a favorite *boyar* of Ioann's, "a God-fight-

ing Antichrist," "begot of whoredom," although pictur-
esquely and Biblically virulent, really adds nothing to
the letter.]

IOANN IV, SON OF BASIL
STYLED THE AWESOME

(b. 1530; crowned 1547; d. 1584)

EDITOR'S NOTE

THIS CZAR, history's nearest approach to Torquemada,
has made at least partial payment for his sins by the
ignominy of not having either his name or his sobriquet
given correctly by most non-Russian historians. "In a
certain French chrestomathy for older children," Chekhov wrote in one of his squibs, "there is a section of
stories from Russian history. One biography, incidentally, bears the title: *Jean IV, nommé Wassiliewitch pour
sa cruauté* (*i.e.*, Ioann IV, styled Vassilevich because of
his cruelty)." He has fared but little better in English.
There have been eight specifically Russian royal Ioanns
[Johanns], six of them crowned, but Russian works of
reference usually have not even a cross-reference to any
royal *Ivan*—just as English ones haven't for any royal
Jack. Practically each Ioann had a sobriquet: The Bag,
The Benighted, The Meek; Ioann III, The Great, was
also styled The Sinister, which may (or may not) be the
reason for English historians choosing, by way of distinction, the sobriquet of The Terrible for the monster-
epistler we are dealing with, although The Awesome is
much nearer the Russian.

For almost a quarter of a century this tyrant (who,

even as Kurbsky, traced his descent from The Monomachos) made Russia a hell for the Russians, until they
not unnaturally came to consider him the reincarnation
(or double) of Vlad Tsepesh, the Wallachian Leader-in-
Battle, styled Dracula [The Devil]. Thus we find Collins
the Englishman, physician to the Awesome Czar, telling
the story of the hat nailed to the head of a not sufficiently deferential envoy—which is also the first epi-
sode in the Dracula cycle of drolleries. Ioann IV killed
"scores of thousands" of Russians—mostly commoners;
in the number of persons tortured he has been surpassed
only by the Inquisition, while in matrimonial ventures
he is one up on even Henry VIII, having been married
seven times. The only decent act of his whole life was
his killing his son (also an Ioann), who was something
more than a mere chip of the old headsman's block.

*Missive of Ioann, Son of Basil, Czar and Grand
Duke of All Russia, to Prince Andrew Kurbsky,
in Answer to the Epistle of the Said Prince,
Writ from the City of Volmar.*

Through Our God, the Trinity, Who hath been since
the start of time, but now, as Father, Son and Holy
Ghost, hath nor beginning nor end, through Him have
We Our life and motion; through Him do Czars reign
and the mighty ones write laws. The conquering stand-
ard of God's only Word and the Blessed Cross that has
never been overcome were given by Jesus Christ, Our
Lord, to Emperor Constantine, foremost in piety, and to
all the Czars, Orthodox and Champions of Orthodoxy,
and the word of God hath been fulfilled, in that they
have, like unto eagles in flight, come to all the pious
servants of the Word of God, and in that a spark of

piety hath fallen upon the realm of Russia. By the will
of God the Autocracy had its beginnings with the Grand
Duke Vladimir, who through baptism brought light to
all Russia, and with that great Czar, Vladimir the Monomachos, to whom the Greeks paid signal honors; also
with the great ruler, the Valiant Alexander Nevsky, who
gained so great a victory against the godless Germans,
and with the meritorious Czar Dimitri, who gained so
great a victory over the Hagarenes beyond the Don;
thereafter the rule passed to the great Czar Ioann, Our
ancestor, the righter of wrongs, who fashioned Russia
into a single whole from the domains of Our ancestors,
and then to the great Czar Basil of blessed memory, until it came down to Us, the humble scepter-bearer of
the Russian Empire.

And We glorify God for the great favor He hath
manifested Us, in not letting Our right hand to be
stained with the blood of Our line, inasmuch as We did
not usurp the realm from any but were born thereto,
through God's will and the blessings of Our ancestors
and parents; We were bred therein and therein ascended to the throne, accepting, through God's will and
the blessings of our ancestors, what appertained to Us,
and not usurping that which was not Ours.

Hereinafter is the decision of an Orthodox, truly
Christian Autocrat, Lord of many domains: Our humble, Christian reply to him who once was an Orthodox,
true Christian and a noble of our realm, a Councillor
and a Leader-in-Battle, but is now a felon before the
blessed, life-giving Cross of the Lord, an extirpator of
Christians, a servant of the adversaries of Christianity,
who hath strayed from the divine worship of holy images and has trampled underfoot all holy command-
ments, hath destroyed sacred edifices, hath calumniated
and spurned from him consecrated vessels and images,

who uniteth in himself Leo Flavius the Isaurian, Constantine Copronymos and Leo Flavius the Armenian—to Prince Andrew Kurbsky, son of Michael, who through perfidy would fain become the ruler of Yaroslav.

Wherefore, O Prince, if thou dost deem thyself pious, hast thou forfeited thy unigenital soul? What wilt thou render up in place thereof on Dread Judgment Day? Even shouldst thou gain all the world, death will have thee in the end. Wherefore hast thou sold thy soul for the sake of thy flesh? Is it that thou didst dread death because of the false tongues of thy familiar demons and thy powerful friends and advisers?

If thou art so righteous and devout, as thou sayest thou art, wherefore this craven dread of a blameless death, since it is not death but canonization? For thou art bound to die in the end, come what may! For it is the will of the Lord that one should suffer in doing good!

And if thou art righteous and devout, why wert thou unwilling to suffer because of me, a stiffnecked potentate, and thus inherit the crown of life?

Dost thou not blush before thy slave Vasska Shibanov, who was steadfast in his devotion and, having pledged loyalty to thee by kissing the Cross, would not abjure thee before the Czar and all the people, though at the door of death, but sang thy praises and was all too willing to die for thee? But thou didst not follow the ensample of his devotion; because of one wrathy word of mine thou didst lose not thy soul alone but the souls of all thy ancestors, since they had been given, through the will of God, for servants to Our grandsire, the great Czar, and did put their souls in his keeping, and did serve him to their very death, and did command all of you, their children, to serve the children and grandchildren of Our grandsire. Yet thou didst forget all

things and through perfidy, like a dog, hast turned
against the vow thou didst take by kissing the Cross and
hast gone over to the adversaries of Christianity and,
bereft of all reason by thy rancor, thou utterest folly,
hurling stones at the sky, as it were.

Well, now, thou dog! Dost thou write, and seekest
thou condolence, after having wrought such evil? To
what, then, may thy counsel be likened save to the stink
of a turd? . . .

Never have we shed blood in churches. As for the
saintly blood of victors—there has been none of that in
Our land, to Our knowledge. As for the *thresholds of
the churches*—insofar as Our wherewithal and intelligence permit, and Our subjects are zealous in their service to Us, the churches of the Lord are resplendent with
all sorts of adornments and because of the offerings We
have made since thou hast come under the sway of
Satan; not only the thresholds and pavements but even
the vestries glow with ornaments, so that even strangers
may behold them. We stain not the thresholds of the
churches with any blood whatsoever, and there are no
martyrs to the faith in Our midst—not any longer. . . .
Tortures, and persecutions, and deaths many and diverse, we have not devised against any. But, since thou
hast made mention of perfidies and witchcraft—such
dogs as practice these things are put to death everywhere. . . .

It hath pleased God to transport Our mother, the devout Czaritsa Helen, from the kingdom of this earth to
the Kingdom of Heaven. George, Our brother, who is
now at peace in Heaven, and I were left orphans, and
inasmuch as none looked after us we had to place our
trust in the Holy Virgin, and in the prayers of all the
Saints, and the blessings of Our parents. When We were
in Our eighth year, Our subjects behaved as they would,

for that they knew the Empire had no ruler, and did not deign of themselves to pay any heed to Us, their master but, even as they quarreled with one another, were bent upon acquiring riches and glory. And what harm did they not work! How many nobles, how many friends of Our sire and Leaders-in-Battle did they slay! And they seized the estates and the villages and demesnes of Our uncles, and set themselves up therein. The treasure that had been Our mother's they did trample upon and did pierce with sharp pikes or transfer to the general treasury, yet not without seizing somewhat for themselves— and it was thy grandsire, Mikhailo Tuchkov, who did that very thing. The Princes Basil and Ivan Shuisky had taken it upon themselves to have Us in their keeping, and they did release out of prison and make friends of them that had been chief traitors to Our father and mother.

Prince Basil Shuisky and his Judas horde did fall upon Our father-confessor, Theodore Mishurin, in the court of Our uncle, and mocked at him, and slew him; and they did immure Prince Ivan Belsky, son of Theodore, and numerous others, in sundry places, and did take up arms against the realm; the Metropolitan they ousted from his see and did banish him, and thus they bettered their chances and began their self-rule.

As for Us, my brother George of blessed memory and Ourself, they brought us up like outlanders and the children of the poorest folk. What have I not suffered, for lack of clothes and food! And all this was done contrary to Our will, and was no seemly thing to do to one of Our tender years. We shall cite but one instance: Once, when We were a child, and at play with Our brother, Prince Ivan Shuisky, son of Basil, as he sat on a bench leaned his elbow on Our father's bed and, as though that were not enough, even placed his foot thereon. Not as a father did he treat Us but as a master. . . . Who could endure such arrogance? How can We recount all the hardships which We underwent in Our youth? Oft, through no wish of Our own, We got nothing to eat until late. . . .

But when We had attained the age of fifteen We undertook, under the guidance of God, the rule of Our own realm and, by the will of Almighty God, it was at peace and undisturbed, as We would have it. But, for Our sins, it so fell out that a conflagration spread through Moscow and, by the will of God, the royal city of Moscow went up in flames. Our nobles, those traitors whom thou stylest martyrs, and whose very names We shall pass over, availed themselves of this favoring chance to further their base perfidy and whispered into the ears of the doltish commonalty that Our mother's mother, the Princess Anna Glinskaya, as well as her children and retainers, made a practice of cutting out men's hearts, and that through such witchcraft she had set Moscow on fire, and that We had knowledge of her deeds. Through the machinations of these our traitors a horde of senseless folk, crying out in the manner of the Jews, went to the Cathedral of the Holy Martyr Dimitri of Selun, hauled out therefrom one of Our nobles, Uriah Glinski, son of Basil, dragged him inhumanly into the Cathedral of the Assumption, and slew the innocent man within the church, before the Metropolitan's seat; with his blood did they stain the flagstones of the church, dragged his body out through the portals, and did expose him in the marketplace as a felon—all men knew of this slaying within the holy place. At that time We were residing at the hamlet of Vorobievo; the same traitors did stir up the commonalty to slay Us as well, using the pretext that We were hiding from them the mother of Prince Uriah, the Princess Anna, and his brother, Prince Michael—and thou, thou dog, dost repeat that lie after them. What can one do save laugh at such stupidity? Wherefore should We be the incendiaries of Our own realm? . . .

Then thou sayest that thy blood was shed in battles against the outlanders and, in thy vain madness, thou addest that it cries out to God against Us. That is downright laughable. It was shed by one—and it cries out against another. If it be true that thy blood was shed in opposing the enemy, then thou didst but thy duty to thy land; hadst thou not done so thou wouldst have been no Christian but an infidel. Howbeit, the matter concerneth Us not. How much more doth Our blood cry out to the Lord because of thee! Yet it was not because of mere wounds and trickling blood that we found thee a burden, needless and taxing our strength, but because of the great sweat and travail thou didst bring upon Us. And thy great malignancy and persecutions have caused Us to shed tears, many and bitter, and have wrung sighs and moans from Our heart. . . .

But if, as thou sayest, thou wouldst put thy epistle in thy sepulcher, it will be because thou hast put the last of thy Christianity from thee. For it is God's commandment not to resist evil, yet hast thou abjured that last pardon which is granted even to the ignorant. It is not meet, therefore, that any requiem be chanted over thee. . . .

And, thou writest, thou wilt not show thy face [to Us] until God's Dread Judgment Day. Thou dost put too high a value on that face of thine. Who would ever hanker to see such an Ethiopian visage? . . .

Thou namest the city of Volmar, which is in the land

of Liflandia, Our patrimony, as appertaining to Our foe, King Sigismund; thereby thou dost but carry out to the end the perfidy of a vicious dog. . . .

Given in Our Great Russia's Famed, Royal, Throne City of Moscow, on the Steps Leading to an Honorable Threshold, in the Year 7072 [1564 A.D.], in the Month of July, on the Fifth Day thereof.

EDITOR'S NOTE

WHETHER one wield pogniard or quill, the temptation to get at one's adversary's heel of Achilles is irresistible, and Kurbsky, with the practiced rhetorician's contempt for the tyro, made the unerring choice, in his *Brief Reply to the Much Too Ambagious Epistle*[1] *of the Grand Duke of Muscovy,* of beginning with a devastating attack on The Awesome as an author: "Thy stentorian and decidedly obstreperous screed I have received, and pondered thereon, and have even fathomed the same, albeit it was but belched forth by untamable wrath in words of venom, which would be unseemly not only in a Ruler so great and celebrated throughout Creation, but even in some simple, lowly warrior, and all the more so since it containeth so much that is snatched out of Holy Writ, and that with great frenzy and ferocity, not by lines and not by verses, after the wont of the skilled and the learned, as may fit the occasion and the person one may be writing to, putting much sense in words few and brief, but redundantly and shrilly beyond all measure, like a countrywife, in whole Books and Lessons and Epistles." He is amazed that The Awesome could ever

---

[1] It has been considerably—and considerately—abridged here.— *Trans.-Ed.*

send so disjointed a letter to an alien land, where there are men "versed not only in the grammatical and rhetorical sciences but the philosophical as well."

Whether Ioann IV took such literary criticism to heart or not, the facts remain that he did take his time about having his last word: a Devil's dozen of years, and that this *Missive,* sent by the hand of Prince Alexander Polubelinski, is shorter, simpler and clearer than his first, and almost colloquial in tone; in fact, he puns atrociously on Kurbsky's name, implying that the addressee is as barefooted as a hen. Shortly before inditing it The Awesome had captured the city of Volmar, in which Kurbsky had taken refuge, and the Czar does not miss the chance for a spot of gloating, actually waxing lyrical toward the end: "It would seem as if it were but to vex thyself that thou didst write of Our sending thee, for thy seeming disgrace, to towns to reach which a steed would have to go long and far, for now, by the will of God, We, despite Our gray hairs, have gone even beyond thy towns to reach which a steed would have to go long and far, and the hooves of Our steeds have traversed all the roads of thee and those who are thine, from Lithuania and into Lithuania, and likewise on foot did we fare, and drank water there, and now it cannot be said of Lithuania that the hooves of Our steed have not been everywhere. And if thou wert fain to find surcease from all thy travails in Volmar, why here, likewise, for the sake of thy tranquility, God hath brought Us; for by God's will we did get off Our steed, whereas thou didst have to get up on thine and fare further."

He concludes most piously: "And all this we have written not in pride, nor in vanity, God wot, but to admonish thee for thy correction, so that thou mightest meditate upon the salvation of thy soul.

"Writ in Our Own Hereditary Land of Liflandia, in the City of Volmar, in the Summer of the Year 7086 [1577 A.D.], the 43rd of Our Reign, and, of Our Reigns: of Russia, the 31st; of Kazan, the 25th; of Astorohan [Astrakhan], the 24th."

Kurbsky wrote once more (the letter is undated) this time addressing his Epistle to the "Czar of Muscovy," and styling himself the "lowly Andrew Kurbski, Prince of Kovel," but Ioann IV, The Awesome (probably savoring one of the most subtle forms of vengeance) never deigned to answer it.

The Retort Courteous

EDITOR'S NOTE

THE reader will perhaps recall *The Dniepr Cossacks* of I. E. Repin, a glorious picture which it took that genius thirteen years to finish. It shows the magnificent fighting men in Homeric, Rabelaisian laughter, garbed in vivid, motley costumes, sitting and standing around a scribe. An additional, descriptive title reads: "Ivan Dmitrievich Serco [Sirco], Chief Hetman, and his comrades, answering with mockeries the high-flown and threatening missive of Sultan Mahomet IV."

The date of Sirco's birth seems unknown; he was elected Koshevoi [Koshevyi], or Chief of all the Dniepr Hetmans, in 1663, and died in 1680. Mahomet IV was Sultan from 1648 to 1680.

The traditional text of the letter (here followed) is given in M. N. Pokrovsky's *Russian History from the Most Ancient Times;* it is undated.

The Cossacks of the Dniepr, to the Soldan of Turkey:

Thou Turkish Shaitan [Satan], brother and companion to the accursed Devil, and Secretary to Lucicer [Lucifer] himself, Greetings!

What the hell kind of noble knight art thou? The Devil voids, and thy army devours. Never wilt thou be fit to have the sons of Christ under thee; thy army we fear not, and by land and on sea will we do battle against thee.

Thou scullion of Babylon, thou wheelwright of Macedonia, thou beer-brewer of Jerusalem, thou goat-flayer of Alexandria, thou swineherd of Egypt, both the Greater and the Lesser, thou sow of Armenia, thou goat of Tatary, thou hangman of Kamenetz, thou evildoer of Podoliansk, thou grandson of the Basilisk [Devil] himself, thou great silly oaf of all the world and of the netherworld and, before our God, a blockhead, a swine's snout, a mare's —, a butcher's cur, an unbaptized brow, May the Devil take thee! That is what the Cossacks have to say to thee, thou basest-born of runts! Unfit art thou to lord it over true Christians!

The date we wot not, for no calendar have we got; the moon [month] is in the sky, the year is in a book, and the day is the same with us here as with ye over there, and thou canst kiss us thou knowest where!

KOSHEVYI HETMAN IVAN SIRCO,
and all the Dniepr Brotherhood with him

MIKHAIL VASSILIEVICH LOMONOSSOV

(b. between 1708–15; d. 1765)

EDITOR'S NOTE

THIS "muzhik of Archangel" (in Nekrassov's phrase),
is the Russian Benjamin Franklin *cum* Samuel Johnson,
with not a little of Leonardo's many-sidedness, taking
all Science for his province, and with something of
Lincoln's pertinacity in the acquisition of knowledge,
memorizing the books he walked miles to borrow. This
fisherman's son is the acknowledged founder of modern
Russian literature, and of modern Russian science and
culture. He fixed standards for Russian and formulated
a new prosody; as didactic poet he is equaled (but not
surpassed) only by Derzhavin, while his *Ode on a Beard*
makes him of kin to such satirists as Alexander Pope.
His experiments in electricity were as important as
Franklin's and very close in time to them. However,
even at the height of his powers he had very hard
sledding, forced to do drudgery far beneath his great
gifts and to spend his time in altercations with the Teutonic nonentities who had a Yorkshire stranglehold on
the Academy of Sciences (he had to sit seven months
in prison after one such brawl; his feud with Soumarokov is also famous).

Elizabeth II was not impressed by Lomonossov's scientific attainments, but was taken with his Odes; his affairs improved still further when the grandee I. I. Shuvalov, after attending one of his lectures, became his
patron. However, upon the accession of Catherine II,

Shuvalov fell out of grace, and Lomonossov had to leave
the Academy. But it took the Great Empress, with a
reputation as an Enlightened Sovereign to keep up, only
two or three weeks to come to her senses; the scientist-
poet was re-instated and even "honored" by a royal visit.
It is only now, however, that this superb genius has
come into his own. Present-day Russians have taken
Grandpa Lomonossov (so they affectionately call him)
to their hearts. His theories and discoveries are being
put to the test by Soviet scientists; Soviet exploring expeditions have found certain sea-routes suggested by him
practicable, and the Soviets have completed the monu-
mental edition of his works (many of them never published) which had been abandoned in 1901.

MIKHAIL VASSILIEVICH LOMONOSSOV

Letters to His Patron

On Poets in Garrets[1]

MY DEAR SIR, IVAN IVANOVICH!

Your Excellency's kindness in favoring me with your
last letter makes me feel assured, to my great rejoicing,
of your unaltered sentiments toward me, which I have
these many years considered among my blessings.

How could the royal generosity of our incomparable
Empress, which I enjoy through your paternal interest,
lead me away from my love for and zeal in the Sciences,
when that dire poverty which I had voluntarily borne

---

[1] In answer to a letter wherein Shuvalov had been apprehensive
that the Empress' gift of an estate to Lomonossov might make him
less ardent in his pursuit of Science.—Trans.-Ed.

for the sake of Learning could not divert me from pursuing it? Let Your Excellency not presume me self-laudatory if I venture to defend myself.

[An account of his early struggles follows: of the daily three kopecks he received as a scholar's stipend he "dared spend no more than half a kopeck for bread and half a kopeck for bread-cider; the rest had to provide writing paper, footwear and other necessities." Five years did he have to pass thus, "yet forsook not study." His father alternately threatened to disinherit him—or to marry him off to a wealthy girl—but Lomonossov preferred to stay at school, where little boys pointed their fingers at him, jeering: " 'Look at that yokel—coming to study Latin at twenty!' "]

I beg to assure Your Excellency, in all humility, that I shall do everything that within my power lies to allay the anxiety of those who wish me not to abate my zeal, and to shame those whose unjust opinion of me is due to envy and malice, as well as to teach them that they ought not to measure others with the yardstick they apply to themselves, as well as to remind them that the Muses are free to love whomsoever they like.

If there be any who adhere to the notion that a man of learning must dwell in poverty, I shall, as part of their argument, cite Diogenes, who shared an old tun with dogs and left a handful of epigrams to his compatriots, to make their vainglory wax greater; on the other hand I shall mention Newton, the wealthy Lord Boyle, who attained all his glory in the Sciences because he had great moneys at his disposal; Wolff,[1] who by his lectures and through gifts amassed more than five hundred thousand [rubles?], besides winning the title

---

[1] Christian Wolff (1679–1754); Lomonossov had studied mathematics, physics, and chemistry under him at Marburg (1736–39, and later).

of Freiherr; Sloane, in England, who left a library so rich that Parliament appropriated twenty thousand pounds for its acquisition, no private person being in a position to purchase it.

You will not find me remiss in carrying out your commands. Pray believe me, with profound esteem, Your Excellency's most humble Servant,

MIKHAILO LOMONOSSOV

St. Peterburg, May 10, 1753

Concerning Certain Experiments

MY DEAR SIR, IVAN IVANOVICH!

Your Excellency's favor of the 24th inst. to hand, and I see therein a token of your unchanged graciousness toward me, which is a source of great gratification to me, particularly since you were pleased to express your conviction that I would never forsake the Sciences.

The judgment of others is not at all a matter of surprise to me, inasmuch as they can point to certain instances of men who, having hardly found the road to their personal fortunes, have immediately struck out on other paths, seeking means for further advancement other than the Sciences, which they have forsaken utterly. But little is asked of them by their patrons, who are content with their mere repute—unlike Your Excellency, who asks to judge me by my works. All men can perceive in the case of the abovementioned men, who forsook Learning when good fortune came to them, that the sum of their knowledge consists only of what they learned in their tender years under the ministration of birchrods, and that they have added nothing new to that sum since becoming their own masters.

But my case has been quite different—if you will

allow me, my Dear Sir, to declare the truth, not out of any vainglory but merely to give my side. My father was a kindhearted man, yet one bred in utmost ignorance; my stepmother was an envious and malicious woman, who did her worst to set my father against me by claiming that I was forever idling my time away with books; hence I was oft forced to hide myself in isolated and deserted places to read and study anything that came my way, and to endure cold and hunger until I entered the school at the Monastery of the Saving Icon.

Now that, through your paternal interest, I have gained a competency from Her August Imperial Highness, and my labors have won the approbation of yourself and others who know and love the Sciences . . . how could I, in years of manhood, put my early life to shame?

However, instead of trying your patience with these matters, since I am aware of your fair opinion of me, I shall inform you as to what Your Excellency, in your meritorious zeal, wishes to know concerning the Sciences.

First, as to Electricity: Two experiments of importance have been recently performed here; one by Richmann, working with an apparatus, the other by myself, upon clouds. . . . The second experiment was performed on the 25th of April with my lightning apparatus, when, without any observable thunder or lightning, a cord was repelled from an iron rod and followed my hand; also, on the 28th of the same month, while a raincloud was passing, without any observable thunder or lightning, loud discharges issued from the lightning apparatus, accompanied by vivid sparks and a crackle that was audible at a great distance. Nothing of this sort had been observed heretofore, and it is in complete accord with my previous theory of Heat and my present one of Electric Force, and will be very useful to me at the next public lecture. I shall give it together with Professor Richmann; he will demonstrate his experiments, while I will explain the theory and the benefit to be derived from them; I am now getting ready for this lecture.

As for Part Two of the text-book on Rhetorick—it is coming along well, and I am in hopes of having it in print by the end of October. I shall endeavor to the utmost to issue it soon; I am not sending Your Excellency any of it in manuscript, since you have asked for printed sheets. As per my promise, I am likewise using my utmost endeavor in the matter of Volume One of the *History of Russia*, so as to have the manuscript thereof ready by the New Year.

From one who gives lectures in his special subject, who carries out new experiments, delivers public lectures and dissertations and, in addition, composes all sorts of verses and makes plans for triumphal celebrations and occasions of rejoicing, who formulates the rules of Rhetorick for his native tongue and writes a History of his native land—which, moreover, he has to hand in at a set date—from such a one I cannot demand anything additional, and I am inclined to have patience with him; that is, if something worth-while will come of it all.

Having repeatedly convinced myself that Your Excellency is fond of scientific converse, I eagerly look forward to the pleasure of a meeting with you, so that I may appraise you of my latest efforts to your satisfaction, for it is impossible to inform you as to all of them at this distance. When I shall be able to install the optical apparatus in Your Excellency's house, as per my promise, is something I cannot at present tell; for as yet there are no floors, or ceilings, or staircases, and when I recently made a tour of inspection through it it was not without considerable danger to my person. The electric globes, as per your wish, I shall send on to you with all despatch.[1]

I am bound to inform Your Excellency that mechanicians are very scarce here, so that I was unable to secure at any price, anywhere—not even upon your estate—a cabinetmaker to construct an electric apparatus for me, and consequently, up to the present, instead of using a terrestrial machine, I have been experimenting with the clouds, having had a pole put up on the roof for that purpose.

I beg of you to allow me to state in your name, at the Chancellery of the Academy, that orders should be issued to the mechanicians for whatever instruments Your Excellency may require—for otherwise the matter will drag on with never an end.

In conclusion, I remain, with expressions of profound esteem, Your most humble and devoted servant,

MIKHAILO LOMONOSSOV

St. Peterburg, May 31, 1753

NIKOLAI IVANOVICH NOVIKOV

(1744–1818)

EDITOR'S NOTE

NOVIKOV was of noble birth. He began as a publisher in 1766. 1769 was signalized by the appearance of a host of satirical sheets—the most remarkable of which was *The Drone*, edited and published by Novikov

---

[1] Leonardo, too, if the reader will recall, had to fix the plumbing in the bathroom of Beatrice, Duchess of Sforza.—*Trans.-Ed.*

(1769-70). In it, as well as his other early periodicals he strove to Canutize, with the broom of sharp satire, the ocean of slavocracy, bureaucracy, autocracy. He fared no better than Krylov; his publications were suppressed one after the other, some as fast as they appeared. He did a tremendous amount of other work as writer, publisher, promoter of literary, pedagogical, social, and political movements. In 1775 he joined the Freemasons, publishing the Masonic *Morning Glow* (1777-80), and became the "soul" of the Moscow Freemasonry organization—which Catherine fought tooth and nail. By the 1780's Novikov's publishing activities, both book and periodical, were "enormous." Finally the government got after him in real earnest. In 1792 (the same year that Krylov's tribulations began) Novikov, by Catherine's orders, was arrested and put (the vivid Russian verb is "planted") in Schlüsselburg (Key-Fastness) Fortress, which ranked with the equally notorious Fortress of SS. Peter and Paul as a forcing-bed for Russian genius. Not until Mad Paul succeeded Catherine in 1796 did he issue from his dungeon—"decrepit, old and broken."

The peculiar interest of the subjoined letter lies in that Novikov (like Fonvizin) tried polemics against someone who was something besides merely a rival writer-publisher. Catherine the Great had (in 1769) founded *Mish-Mash* which, since it was the very first of the funny sheets in Russia, was also nicknamed Great-Granny. Catherine, as satirist, belonged to the bear-and-fur-bear school—in our own day it still flourishes, with humor running almost entirely to Darktown Stories and Yiddish Dialect Pieces; her armory consisted of but two weapons: a fly-swatter for "human frailties" and a spike-studded shellelagh for those who disagreed with her. And it was not the fly-swatter she used on Novikov, although her letter on *The Drone* (published in *Mish-*

Mash and signed Athenogene Perochinov—Athens-born Quill-Mender) was a eulogy on the lighter weapon, as well as an attempt to teach Novikov the trade of funny-man. The letter here given is Novikov's second parry-and-thrust, unerringly penetrating the one chink in Catherine's auctorial armor—her weakness in Russian (she was much more at home in her native German and in French); the *Coup de* dis*grâce* was, probably, the reference to the lady's age: Catherine had edged into her forties.

NIKOLAI IVANOVICH NOVIKOV

Letter to the Publisher

DEAR SIR!

Madam Mish-Mash hath waxed wroth with you, and styled your morally edifying discourses as vilifications. But I now perceive that she is not as much at fault as I deemed her. All her fault lies in that she does not know how to explain herself in our tongue, and is unable to comprehend circumstantially the writings therein— which, by the by, is a fault appertaining to many of our writers.

From the words set forth by her . . . a Russian can come to no other conclusion save that her straw-man, Mr. A, is in the right, and that Madam Mish-Mash went all awry in criticizing him.

In the fifth issue of *The Drone* there is nought writ, as Madam Mish-Mash supposes, against either compassion or making allowances, and the Public, to whom I appeal, can discern that. If I have written that he who corrects vices hath greater love for his fellow-man than he who is a yea-sayer to those same vices, I truly know not how through such a declaration I could have impugned compassion. It is evident that Madam Mish-Mash hath been so spoiled by praises that now she considers it a crime even when someone doth not praise her.

I know not: Why doth she style my letter a vilification? Vilification is abuse expresst in vile terms; yet in my preceding letter, which went so much against the grain of this elderly dame's heart, there are neither *knouts,* nor *gallows,* nor other references that grate upon the ear and which are to be found in her publication.

Madam Mish-Mash has written that she *annihilates* the fifth issue of *The Drone.* Even that is said somehow not in our tongue. *Annihilation,* to wit, turning something into nothingness, is a word natural to absolute power, whereas power of any sort is not appropriate in any such kickshaws as her published broadsides; it is a superior power which *annihilates* some right belonging to others. But on Madam Mish-Mash's part it would have sufficed to have written that she *despises,* but does not *annihilate,* my criticism. For of those sheets containing that same criticism there is a multitude being circulated from hand to hand, and therefore annihilating them is beyond her.

She affirms I have an evil heart inasmuch as, in her opinion, I exclude through my discourses the making of allowances, and compassion. I wrote clearly, it would seem, that human frailties merit compassion, but that they call for correction and not yea-saying; and hence I am of the opinion that my declaration, to anyone conversant with our tongue and the truth, will not appear contrary either to justice or to compassion. As to her advice about medical treatment: I know not whether that advice is more applicable to me or to the lady herself. She, after saying that she had no wish to answer the fifth issue of *The Drone,* did put all her heart and mind into answering the same, and all her choler became apparent in her letter. And if she forgets herself and is so overcome with mucorrhea that she oft expectorates not where she should, it would appear that, for the sake of cleansing her thoughts and inwards, it might not be unbeneficial for her actually to undergo medical treatment.

This lady has styled my mind dull because I had not grasped her morally edifying discourses. To which I answer: That my eyes, as well as my mind, fail to perceive that which is non-existent. I am quite gratified that Madam Mish-Mash has given me over to the judgment of the Public. The Public will see, from our future letters, which one of us is in the right.

Your humble servant,
PRAVDOLIUBOV [*Lover-of-Truth*]

6th of June, A. D. 1769

IVAN SERGHEIEVICH TURGENEV

Turgenev's Last Letter[1]

Bougeval, June 27th or 28th, 1883

MY DEAR AND BELOVED LEO NIKOLAIEVICH:

I have not written you a long time for, to come right out with it, I was, and am, on my deathbed. There is no getting well for me, and there is no use in even thinking

---

[1] This letter to Tolstoy was written in pencil, and was unsigned. Postmarked Tula, July 3, 1883. Turgenev died September 3 of the same year.—*Trans.-Ed.* For Editor's Note on Turgenev, see page 100.

of it. But my real reason for writing you is to tell you how glad I am to have been a contemporary of yours, and to express my last, earnest request. My friend, resume your literary work! For this gift of yours comes from whence all else does. Ah, how happy I would be if I could think that my plea would prevail upon you! As for me, I am done for—the doctors don't know even what name to give my ailment—*névralgie stomacale goutteuse*. There is no walking, no eating, no sleeping for me. Oh, well! It's wearisome even to repeat all this. My friend, great writer of the land of Russia—heed my plea! Let me know if you receive this scrap of paper, and permit me once more to hold you, your wife, all of you, close—close!—to me. . . . I can write no more. . . . I am tired!

ANTON PAVLOVICH CHEKHOV[1]

Two Chekhov Letters

Wife and Mistress

[To A. S. SUVORIN:]

Moscow, Sept. 11th, 1888

. . . I'll undertake reading the proofs of your Moscow Aesculapian stuff for your almanac willingly, and will be glad if I make it come out right. They haven't been sent me yet. I'll fuss with the thing and do what I can, but I'm afraid that at my hands it will come out dissimilar to the Peterburg batch—that is, it'll be either fuller or slimmer. If you find this apprehension of mine

---

[1] For Editor's Note on Chekhov, see page 242.

not without basis, wire the printers to send me the Peterburg proofs as well, so that I may have something to guide me. It wouldn't be right if, in the one and the same section, Peterburg will represent a lean cow and Moscow a fat one, or the other way around; both capitals ought to be equally honored—or, at the worst, Moscow less so.

. . . Next year, if you permit, I will take the whole medical section of your almanac upon myself, but now I will only pour old wine into new bottles. . . .

You advise me not to run after two hares at the same time, and not to think of following medicine. I don't know—why shouldn't one run after two hares, even in the literal meaning of these words? As long as there are hounds one can go hunting. Of hunting hounds (speaking figuratively now) I may have none, but I feel spryer and more satisfied with myself when I realize I have two occupations and not one. Medicine is my lawful wife, while literature is my mistress. When I get fed up with the one I stay the night with the other. This may be irregular, but then it isn't so boring, and besides neither loses anything at all because of my infidelity. If I hadn't medicine, I would hardly be likely to devote my leisure and my spare thoughts to literature. There is no discipline in me. . . .

Yours,

A. CHEKHOV

Tolstoy, Electricity, Tobacco

[To A. S. SUVORIN:]

Yalta, March 27, 1894

Greetings! There, it's almost a month that I'm living in Yalta, in most drearisome Yalta, in the Hotel Russia, Room 39. . . . The weather is vernal; it is warm and bleak; the sea is as a sea should be, but the people are tedious, turbid, dull. I did a foolish thing in giving up all of March to the Crimea. I should have gone to Kiev and there gone in for contemplation of holy objects and of the Little Russian spring.

On the whole I am well; I am unwell only in certain particulars. After giving up smoking altogether, I am no longer subject to moods of moroseness and uneasiness. Perhaps because I am not smoking. Tolstoyan morals have ceased to move me; in the depth of my soul my attitude to them is inimical—and that, of course, is unjust. There is muzhik blood flowing in my veins, and you won't bowl me over with muzhik virtues. I had come to have faith in progress in my childhood, and could not but have that faith, since the difference between the time I was beaten and the time they ceased to beat me was a frightful one. I loved intelligent people, sensitiveness, courtesy, wit, and as to the fact that some people picked their corns, or that their foot-clouts emitted a stifling odor—I regarded that with the same indifference as the fact that young ladies walk about in curl-papers of mornings. But Tolstoy's philosophy moved me deeply, it possessed me for six or seven years, and it was not due so much to the basic theses, which were known to me even before, but to the Tolstoyan manner of expression, sagacity and, probably, a *sui generis* hypnotism. But now something within me protests; prudence and justice tell me that there is greater love for man in electricity and steam than in continence and abstention from meat. War is an evil and law is an evil, but it doesn't follow from that that I must needs wear bast sandals and sleep atop the oven with the hired hand and his wife, and so on, and so on. But the heart of the matter does not lie in that, nor in the *pro et contra,* but in the fact that, in one way or another,

Tolstoy is water over the dam as far as I am concerned, he is not within my soul, and he has departed from within me, after saying: I leave your house empty. I am exempted from having anyone billeted upon me. . . .

It seems as if everybody had been in love, has now fallen out of love, and is seeking some new enthusiasm. It is very likely, and seems very much so, that the Russian folk will again live through an enthusiasm for the natural sciences, and that the materialistic movement will again be in vogue. The natural sciences are working wonders now, and they may advance upon the public like Mamai,[1] and subdue it with their massiveness, their grandiosity. However, all things are in the hand of God. Once you launch into philosophizing, though, your head will start going 'round and 'round. . . .

Keep well and tranquil. How is your head? Does it ache more often or less than before? Mine has begun to ache less often—that's because I don't smoke.

Yours,

A. CHEKHOV

---

[1] A Mongol Prince of the Golden Horde (founded by Batyi, grandson of Genghis Khan, which held Russia in subjection for 237 years—1243–1480); in 1380 Mamai advanced against Dimitri Donskoy, Prince of Muscovy, and suffered a disastrous defeat.—Trans.-Ed.

A New Handful
of Old Proverbs

CATHERINE II

DAUGHTER OF ALEXIS; STYLED THE GREAT

(b. 1729; usurped throne 1762; d. 1796)

EDITOR'S NOTE

CATHERINE THE GREAT (who has also a recognized place in French literature) is freer from suspicions of ghostly collaboration than any other Royal Author—and her writings practically fill a five-foot shelf. She was decidedly a first-rate humorist and founded the first funny paper in Russia, although as satirist she definitely preferred not to aim her barbs any too near home; was a scholarly historian, an eminent and indefatigable letter-writer, author of charming fairy-tales and allegories, collaborator with other noble writers; and, as dramatist, almost all of Polonius's categorizing might apply to her versatility: she did tragedies, comedies, historical plays, masques, comic operas and humble adaptations, forthrightly acknowledged, of Shakespeare. It would be worth-while to master eighteenth century Russian just to read her delectable version of the *boyar* Falstaff's misadventures with the Merry Wives, and a certain dramatic fragment of hers could be staged in modern dress on Broadway, with hardly a word changed, and sound as of today. As author, her only weak point was a sprightly disregard of orthography. It must be admitted, however, that as proverbialist (or maximist) she was rather on the Guicciardini side, and had a predilection for rhyming. The following selections, nevertheless, do stand up.

Asterisks denote the exceedingly popular ones.

Choice Russian Proverbs

CATHERINE II

A kingdom by dissension made insecure will not very long endure.

The fugitive hath but one road; the pursuer hath an hundred.

Woe liveth next door to Folly.*

Profit and Loss are next door neighbors.*

Money can do much, yet Truth reigns supreme.

Green grapes gripe, and young men are not ripe.

He that says what he likes may hear that which he may not like.

He that cannot rule himself cannot instruct others in truth.

Fraternal love is stronger than stone walls.

Mercy is the guardian of good government.

Truth has no need of a large vocabulary.

Do not ask Age but Experience for Wisdom.

From fire, from flood, and from a mean wife, deliver us, O Lord!

God bless him that wines and dines another; bless him doubly, O Lord, that remembers hospitality.

There are as many different minds as there are heads in this world.

You cannot take towns by standing still.

He shot at a crane as it flew but 'twas a sparrow he slew.*

Firmness is brother to strength.

He that ploughs with zeal will always have luck and weal.

Do not play with what may slay.

The wise fear a word; the foolish not even a beating.

Stubbornness is a vice of the weak mind.

Morning is wiser than Evening.*

The jacket may be of sheepskin, but the soul is human.

Wonders in a sieve: the holes are many, yet there is no place to crawl through.*

KOSMA PETROVICH PRUTKOV
(1801 or 1803–1863)

EDITOR'S NOTE

KOSMA PETROVICH PRUTKOV, Poet and Director of the Assay Bureau, is the genial creation of the great poet, Count Alexis Constantinovich Tolstoy (1817-75), and the brothers Zhemchuzhnikov, Alexis Mikhailovich (1821-1908) and Vladimir M. (1830-84), talented poets both. Subsequently a third brother, Alexander M., poet, wit, and superb amateur actor, contributed a few pieces, while a fourth, Leo M. (1828-1912), well-known as an artist and folklorist, helped produce one of Prutkov's portraits. Tolstoy, the brothers Zhemchuzhnikov, and a few others formed a circle of wits who rocked St. Petersburg with pranks and hoaxes that Theodore Hook might have envied; their Prutkov became an effective means of ridicule during one of Russia's most abysmal periods of reaction and stagnation.

Prutkov's first comedy was produced, under the modest initials *Y and Z*, in January, 1851, at St. Petersburg; the public was bewildered, and all further performances were forbidden by one of the spectators, Nicholas I, who walked out on the play. Under his own name Prutkov first published in 1854.

This genuinely beloved author is best summed up in the memorabilia of Vladimir Zhemchuzhnikov: "When we were creating Prutkov . . . we were young and gay —and talented. . . . Prutkov, for the most part, energetically breaks down open doors. . . . His famous *Bdee!* [Be vigilant!] is reminiscent of the military command: *Plee!* [Fire!] . . . Being very limited, he gives counsels of wisdom. Without being a poet, he writes poems. . . . I loved Kosma Prutkov very much, and for that reason I state flatfootedly that he was a genius."

Prutkov's parodies have met the severest test: they remain excruciatingly funny, although most of the originals and genres parodied have been sloughed off by time. And many of his burlesque aphorisms have become genuine folk-sayings. Above all, Kosma Prutkov has attained to the status of a symbol. The fiftieth anniversary of his death was (more or less) solemnly marked throughout Russia: the fabulous *Satyricon* issued a Prutkov number that has in its turn become a classic; there were special performances at The Crooked Mirror Theatre, musical pieces written especially for the occasion were sung and played by stars, sculptors modeled new busts of the Poet, and so on.

Odd as it may sound, research fails to disclose anything of this classic author in English.

Fruits of Meditation

THOUGHTS AND APHORISMS
(Selected)

KOSMA PETROVICH PRUTKOV

> *Encouragement is just as necessary for a writer of genius as rosin is for the bow of a violin virtuoso.*

The wedding ring is the first link in the chains of marriage.

No one can encompass the unencompassable.

There is nothing so great that it may not be surpassed in magnitude by another; there is nothing so small that a still smaller may not find room therein!

Better say little, but say it well.

What will others say of thee, if thou canst say nought of thy own self?

The memory of man is a sheet of foolscap: sometimes that which is written thereon turns out well and, sometimes, bad.

The imagination of a poet weighed down with grief is like unto a foot confined in a new boot.

A married scamp is like unto a sparrow.

A diligent physician is like unto a pelican.

An egoist is like unto one that hath been sitting in a well for a long time.

If thou hast a fountain, stop it up: let even a fountain have a rest.

Many men are like unto sausages: whatever you stuff them with, that will they bear in them.

Undeserved wealth is like unto water-cress: it will grow anywhere.

If the shadows of objects depended not upon the objects themselves but had a growth of their own, then, mayhap, there would not be found in all the world a single light spot.

A rifle in the hands of the warrior is even as the apt word on the lips of the writer.

In a house without tenants you will not find certain insects.

.   .   .   .

Virtue serves as its own reward; man surpasses virtue when he serves but receives no reward.

Be vigilant!

A dog sitting on hay is harmful; a hen sitting on eggs is useful; because of sedentary life men put on flesh—thus, every money-changer is fat.

A barometer can be easily replaced by any case of rheumatism.

What we have we do not cherish, but we weep when it doth perish.

A specialist is like unto a gumboil: his fullness is one-sided.

A sensitive man is like unto an icicle; warm him a little, and he melts.

Spit in the eye of him that sayeth the unencompass-able can be encompassed!

If there were no colors, all would walk about in garments of the same hue!

Wind is the breath of Nature.

Should you read, upon an enclosure with an elephant, a sign saying *Buffalo,* believe not your eyes.

.   .   .   .   .

No one can encompass the unencompassable!

That is best for which one has an inclination: thus some prefer the croaking of frogs to the singing of nightingales.

The bureaucrat dies, but his decorations remain upon earth.

The publication of certain newspapers and periodicals must be profitable.

If you want to be handsome, join the hussars.[1]

Not every General is stout by nature.

Zeal overcometh all things!

There are occasions when zeal overcomes even reason.

While availing yourself of railroads, take care of your carriage also; such is the counsel of prudence.

A penknife in the hands of a skilled surgeon is far better than the sharpest lancet in the hands of another.

Who stops thee from inventing waterproof gunpowder?

---

[1] Kosma Petrovich Prutkov began his career as a junker in the Hussars.—*Trans.-Ed.*

Thou canst not hatch out the same egg twice!

When looking at objects at a considerable height, hold on to your hat.

A good cigar is like unto the terrestrial globe: it is rolled for the benefit of man.

A champagne cork, popping up and just as instantly tumbling: there you have a passable picture of love.

When gazing at the sun, pucker up your eyes—and you will fearlessly distinguish spots thereon.

Toil like an ant, if you would be likened to a bee.

What is cunning? Cunning is the weapon of the weak and the intelligence of the blind.

Seek not salvation in a separate treaty!

Wisdom, like unto turtle soup, is not within the reach of every man.

Know, reader, that wisdom decreases complaints but not sufferings!

No one will encompass the unencompassable!

A quite intelligent woman is like unto Semiramis.

Any fop is like unto a wagtail.

Any bureaucrat is like unto a quill.

Talents are verily mileposts of civilization, while their works are verily truthful telegrams sent to posterity.

The coefficient of luck is in reverse to the content of merit.

.   .   .   .   .

Why does the gray mare always envy the raven-black one?

Genius reasons and creates. The ordinary mortal carries the ideas out. The fool helps himself without a thank-you to anybody.

Why is a foreigner less eager to live among us than we are to live in his land? Because, even as it is, he is already abroad.

Before deciding on a business enterprise, make inquiries: Is a Jew or a German to be found in such a one? If so, go ahead: you will profit.

.   .   .   .   .

New boots always pinch.

All work is beneficial in that it kills time—which, however, is not in the least diminished thereby.

Man has his head set on top so that he may not walk with his feet in the air.

A Prussian [a cockroach] is one of the more pestiferous insects.

The star-strewn firmament I will always liken unto the breast of a long-serving General; the horizon, covered with close but gray clouds, I will boldly compare to the overcoat of a private.

Still, with all the zeal in the world, you will not hatch out the same egg twice.

Very many confirm my thought, that wind is the breath of Nature.

FOLK SAYINGS AND PROVERBS

EDITOR'S NOTE

PROVERBS are the salt of speech; Russian proverbs (to quote the skipping-rope rhyme) are pepper, salt, mustard, cider. "With a profound knowledge of the heart and a wise grasp of life will the word of the Englishman echo," wrote Gogol. "Like an airy dandy will the impermanent word of the Frenchman flash and then burst into smithereens; finically, intricately, will the German fashion his intellectually gaunt word, which is not within the easy reach of all men. But there is never a word which can be so sweeping, so boisterous, which would burst out so, from out the very heart, which would seethe so, and quiver and throb so much like a living thing, as an aptly uttered Russian word!"

The following despairing handful is from many sources: the pioneering collection of the gentle Dahl, whose vast and classical Dictionary is as absorbing as anything he wrote under the pseudonym of The Cossack Luganski; from Knyazev; from a compilation by an authentic hermit; from Trachtenberg's *Blatnaya* (*Underworld*) *Music,* from regional collections and many others.

There is no more comprehensiveness about the following than about a drop in an ocean, but there should be some variety. The reader will find a few proverbs from White-Russia (with the charm of homespun), a few from Little-Russia (the more robust and rollicking ones), a group about thieves; there are even nonsense proverbs—about thirty topics in all.

PROVERBS ON PROVERBS

> *This proverb is about Peter Petrovich Petrov, who doesn't live here but in Pskov.*

The muzhik went afoot to Moscow, just to hear a proverb.

For every sin there is a proverb.

No proverb is uttered in vain.

An old proverb is uttered to the winds.

ANIMAL SAWS

A snipe is small game, but it's a bird just the same.

Don't change a cuckoo for a hawk.

His cage may be of gold, but that doesn't make the nightingale any happier.

When an old crow croaks, heed.

A scared crow will shy at a bush.

Even the crow got in the soup.[1]

The early bird that sings may wake a hungry cat.

In a cat-and-mouse game the stakes are not the same.

Two cats in one bag [or two bears in one lair] won't be over-friendly.

---

[1] A sly dig at the French, who literally had to eat crow during the Great Retreat of 1812. Another proverb, however, runs: When a Frenchman cooks a crow, it tastes like pheasant.—*Trans.-Ed.*

The fox's paw, the wolf's jaw, the priest's maw—there's no satisfying them.

CHARACTERIZATIONS

Some men are like billy-goats: they give nor milk nor wool.

Wanton as a cat; timid as a hare.

The mouth of a wolf, the tail of a fox.

Smart as a jackass, pious as a priest, honest as a Pole.

She wants a hound puppy—only he mustn't be a son of a bitch.

You can't beg ice from a miser even at Christmas time.

He can get a bushel out of a peck.

THE DEVIL

Nobody ever saw the devil, but all curse (or blame) him.

"The devil tempted me," says the monk. "First I hear tell of it," says the devil.

The devil is no match for a monk.

The devil found a cowl, but it wouldn't go over his horns.

Don't you go teaching a priest—that's the devil's business.

FOOD, DRINK AND TOBACCO

If the belly weren't such a nagger, we'd all get corns on our cans. (*Ukrainian.*)

If the belly didn't prod, we'd all die of bedsores. (*White-Russian.*)

He eats most porridge who's nearest the pot.

He that hath a priest for kin will have flour in his bin.

We eat out of a trough but get enough; you eat off a platter, but your food's no great matter.

Better know a fool than the way to the pothouse.

FOOLS—

> *Against a proverb, a fool, and the truth there is no appeal.*

The world stands on fools.

Fools are the glory of the world.

If there were no fools, there'd be no sages either.

One can't give over wondering at a fool.

God loves fools.

Even God forgives a fool.[1]

Make a fool pray to God and he'll smash his forehead.

There's a difference even amongst fools.

He's a clever fellow, only there's no sense to him.

---

[1] An ignoramus angers even God.—*Catherine II.*

You'll get nor milk nor cheese from a fool—only whey.

With a fool you can neither weep nor laugh.

One fool can work mischief that ten wise men cannot mend.

Better to be with a sage in hell than with a fool in heaven.

A drunkard will sleep off his drink; a fool won't sleep off his folly, not if he was to sleep till Judgment Day.

Even tipsiness will not make a fool more foolish.

A fool has no fear of going crazy.

—AND PLUMB FOOLISHNESS

Only a fool would believe a Pole.

Even our fool can shoe a cat.

You can't brew beer if a fool stands near.

He lifted the load high but forgot to prop it up.

He eats treacle with an awl.

He's cutting hay for dogs.

FRIENDSHIP

One old friend is better than two new ones.

An old friend is better than a new enemy.

You've got to eat five-and-thirty pounds of salt with a man to learn what he's like.

There's no pattern for liking somebody.

For a friend that is dear, pawn the ring from your ear.

A friend is not dear because he is good, but good because he is dear.

Iron kettle and clay pot had best keep apart.

Fear not a clever enemy but the foolish friend.

IF ONLY—

If only our gray gelding had a black tail, and something else didn't fail, he'd be a raven-black stallion.

If only horns and hoofs had been given our sow, she'd be our cow.

If only we could harness a lark to a plough and a flea to a harrow!

If only the muzhik weren't so very thick, he'd be the squire.

If only a Gypsy's foresight were as good as a muzhik's hindsight, he'd put all the world out of sight.

LAW

You don't know what grief is till you go to law.

The law is a spider's web: the bumble-bee will tear it to shreds, the midge will get stuck.

Denim is always guilty when it comes up against velvet. (*Noted by Gogol.*)

Don't fear the law—fear lawyers.

LEARNING

Live long, learn long.

The greater the sage, the quicker he'll age.

He that knowledge would keep will have little sleep.

Even the fool may ride, and even the sage may walk.

He is wisest whose pocket is fullest.

LIFE AND DEATH

Life is only a long week.

Today honor is thine; tomorrow thou mayst herd swine.

Royal purple today; the dark grave tomorrow.

Between life and death is less than a flea's hop.

Build your house and sing your song, but remember the house of seven boards lasts ever so long.

Life may be hard, but death is harder.

There are many terrors; there is but one death.

GOOD LUCK—

Luck is better than wealth.

Luck is no horse—you can't bridle it.

He that's lucky can milk a bull.

If you're lucky, you can shave with an awl.

Two mushrooms in the spoon—and a third clinging to the handle.

Keep a stiff upper lip, Cossack—you'll be a hetman yet!

From your lips to God's ears!

—AND BAD

Ermak gained three boils on his back.

His face was bad enough, so he lost his nose.

He had only a crust, so he choked on that.

My only hope was in a fool—so he got wise.

The Tatar dreamt of cranberry sauce but had no spoon; he lay down to sleep with a spoon, but didn't dream of cranberry sauce.

He that knew no ill will not treasure weal.

MAN

Lots of people; few men.

The world is wonderful and dear; it's only man that is queer.

As in the cradle, so in the coffin.

A man's soul is the fire in a flint.

MASTERS

The squire is all right till his own lice start to bite.

If the poor did not feed the rich with bread, they would have to eat gold instead.

The rich would feel straitened even in Paradise.

The horny hand opens easily; the lily-white is tight-fisted.

The rich do as they like; the poor as best they can.

The poor sing; the rich listen.

The threats of the rich do not heed, but the tears of the man in need.

"MAYBE" AND "NEVER MIND"

Maybe is a thief that brings grief.

Maybe weaves a rope, and *Never Mind* ties it into a noose.

Maybe hung on to *Never Mind,* and both drowned.

MONEY AND TRADE

> *The belly may be sated; the eyes, never.*

When gold speaks, you can hear a pin drop.

You can do a lot with love, but still more with money.

When a cudgel fails, try what a ruble will do.

Grunt, and clink a coin or two, and all things will come to you.

Money will get you friends.

Time is money, but money is not time.

Money is like a stone; it lies heavy on the soul.

> *When your pocket is empty, death has no terrors.*

A lot of money may be a fall from grace; too little money is a disgrace; but no money at all is worst of all.

Poverty is no sin, but it's twice as bad.

Poverty is no disgrace, but you won't get any medals for it, either.

MOSCOW

It took ages to build Moscow.

It took only a spark to destroy Moscow.

Moscow is fair because of its women's hair.

The brave are no rare sight in Moscow.

You can find everything in Moscow except birds' milk —maybe.

Petersburg is the breadwinner; Moscow is bread.

Petersburg is the head; Moscow is the heart.

Vast is the land of Russia, but the dear sun shines on every bit of it.

NONSENSE[1]

"Hey, lookit! I drive the front wheels, and the hind ones go of themselves!"

See how clever the Germans are—they even invented monkeys! [2]

"Come, Theodule, why so down in the mouth?"—"I burned a hole in my coat."—"You could mend it."—"But I have no needle."—"Is it a big hole?"—"There's only the collar left."

"What are you doing now?"—"Nothing?"—"Who's that with you?"—"That's my helper."

RELIGION

> *It is a sin to accuse the Russian folk of intolerance and fanaticism; it is rather to be praised for its exemplary indifference to this faith business.*
> —*Belinski*, Letter to Gogol

Nobody has a contract with God. (*Ukrainian.*)

God waits long, but his blow is strong.

The Czar is not nigh, and God is too high.

Even God can't please everybody.

---

[1] The entire group is Ukrainian—not that each section of Russia could not have produced a representation as large and *almost* as good-natured.—*Trans.-Ed.*

[2] "Only they [the monkeys] couldn't squat but kept jumping all the while; until a Moscow furrier sewed tails on them—and they had to squat." Variant noted by Leskov.—*Trans.-Ed.*

God is with him who is deft and bold.

Trust in God but don't let your breeches slip.

Even Adam didn't escape sin.

Even a saint sins seven times a day.

There's no prophet without vice.

God alone is without sin.

Like God, like candle.

If you want to find the devil, look behind a cross.

You can make a cross, or a shovel, or a poker for the devil, out of the same piece of wood.

Not icons but meat-pies grace a house.

SLUGGARDS

Sloth came into the world before we did.

If you want to live long, send a sluggard to fetch Death.

When a Cossack isn't drinking vodka he's killing lice—but you'll never catch *him* loafing. (*Ukrainian.*)

Sluggard's Week: Holy Sunday; Blue Monday; Tuesday's a No-Use day; Wednesday is a past day; Thursday is the worst day; Friday is a Fast Day; and Saturday's a Rest Day. (*White-Russian.*)

One chops; seven grunt.

Last in the field; first at the feast.[1]

---

[1] To the latter end of a fray and the beginning of a feast
Fits a dull fighter and a keen guest.—*King Henry IV, Part I,* IV 2.

THIEVES

Falstaff: There lives not three good men unhanged . . . and one of them is fat, and grows old.—*King Henry IV, Part I,* II 4

All men live by thievery, saving only thee and me.

There is grief for every thief.

Whenever there's a fair, the thieves are right there.

Tears come easy to the thief; piety comes easy to the knave.

A kopeck thief is hanged; the ruble thief is honored.

The rich thief pays with money; the poor thief with his head.

Nothing is as guilty as guilt.

Only the grave can straighten out the crooked.

THE TONGUE

Your tongue will lead you to Kiev.

Your tongue will bring you either to palace or prison.

You can get to the ends of the earth by lying, but you'll never get back. (*Noted by Gogol.*)

Hear all; believe half.

There's no eyesore like truth.

Keep your tongue in your head and you'll eat wheaten bread.

WOMEN AND MARRIAGE

> *Cities with too many women soon*
> *fall—but without women they will not*
> *stand at all.*

A woman has a trick in stock for every tick of the clock. (*Ukrainian.*)

Women and drunkards cry easily.

Let a woman into heaven, and she'll want to drag her cow in.

All maids are pretty, all girls are witty—but where the devil do all the mean wives come from?

Smart are the women of Kazan, but still smarter the women of Astrakhan.

Never buy a horse from a Gypsy, and never marry a priest's daughter.

Never buy a horse from a priest, and never marry a widow's daughter.

Your death and your wife are both sent by God.

WORK

> *Toil is bitter, but bread is sweet.*

Toil soils, but money buys honey.

If there be bread, even earth is a bed.

Fairy-tales aren't the best fare for nightingales.

He that wins bread with a shovel will die in a hovel.

The plough-horse eats straw; the circus-horse eats oats.

Fawning drinks mead; freedom means need.

Cats, doctors, and priests live on the fat of the land. (*Ukrainian.*)

A knacker flays the dead; a priest the quick and the dead.

Up with the dawn, but not much work done.

Lose an hour, and you won't make it up in a year.

WORLDLY WISDOM

The heart hears.

The fleetest steed will not fate's noose outspeed.

Don't brag of the day before nightfall.

Ill weeds grow apace and are hard to displace.

He whose bread you eat can make you dance to his tune.

Seven nurses make for a one-eyed child.

Love, fire, and coughing can't be hid.

If you don't know the ford, don't wade in.

If you're stingy with water you won't cook any porridge.

If you sow rapes you will not garner grapes.

If you can't leap over, try crawling through.

Mead takes a long time to ferment, but when it does, it bursts the bottle.

Drive too fast and you won't last.